THE
OXFORD BOOK OF
TWENTIETH-CENTURY
GHOST STORIES

THE
OXFORD BOOK OF
TWENTIETH-CENTURY
GHOST STORIES

Edited by

Michael Cox

Oxford   New York

OXFORD UNIVERSITY PRESS

1996

Oxford University Press, Walton Street, Oxford OX2 6DP
Oxford New York
Athens Auckland Bangkok Bogota Bombay
Buenos Aires Calcutta Cape Town Dar es Salaam
Delhi Florence Hong Kong Istanbul Karachi
Kuala Lumpur Madras Madrid Melbourne
Mexico City Nairobi Paris Singapore
Taipei Tokyo Toronto
and associated companies in
Berlin Ibadan

Oxford is a trade mark of Oxford University Press

British Library Cataloguing in Publication Data
Data available

Library of Congress Cataloging in Publication Data
The Oxford book of twentieth-century ghost stories / edited by Michael Cox.
p.   cm.
1. Ghost stories, English.   2. Ghost stories, American.   I. Cox, Michael, 1948–   .
PR1309.G50945   1996   823'.0873308091—dc20   96-4913
ISBN 0-19-214260-7

1 3 5 7 9 10 8 6 4 2

Typeset by Best-set Typesetter Ltd., Hong Kong
Printed in Great Britain
on acid-free paper by
Mackays Ltd
Chatham, Kent

For My Parents

CONTENTS

INTRODUCTION

In 1944 the critic Edmund Wilson expressed surprise that the ghost story was still alive and well in the age of the electric light. But why should he have been surprised? Though ghost stories, as a literary genre, are deeply imbued with their own past, and though innovation has come more through ingenious reinterpretation than radical reinvention, they have always maintained an adaptable relationship with the contemporary world. And, of course, a belief in ghosts—even the literary pretence of a belief—is a peculiarly resilient one, culturally speaking, and provides a potent fictional dynamic that seems continually attractive to both writers and readers.

Ghosts themselves have an ancient cultural lineage. But literary ghost stories—those deliberate fictional constructs that are designed to make their readers feel pleasurably afraid—are of relatively recent origin. Their main characteristics were developed during the first half of the nineteenth century, and from the earliest stages of their evolution they reflected the ordinary landscapes and circumstances of contemporary life. This, indeed, was what distinguished them from their immediate literary antecedents, most notably the Gothic romances of the late eighteenth century. Where Gothic fiction had been romantically remote in its settings and often flamboyantly atemporal, ghost stories anchored themselves firmly in the contemporary, or near contemporary, here and now. Domestication, of both settings and incidents, was the crucial distinction between the Victorian ghost story and its Gothic relations, and this has continued to be a defining characteristic of the whole genre. Ghost stories generally (though not exclusively) concern themselves, in some way, with the returning human dead, but they must be set in a recognizable actuality. This provides a clear distinction with works of supernatural fantasy set in worlds that are completely imaginary and inherently impossible. Ghost stories operate in familiar environments in which ordinary human beings are engaged in ordinary activities. We need to know that the fictional world is *our* world; that the characters are, in a sense, our representatives. The trick of a good ghost story, in other words, is to make us feel that such things may happen to *us*. For it to work, in literary terms, the supernatural requires firm grounding in the natural—the more banal the setting, the greater the impact of its violation of the normal.

Thus the ghost stories of Victorian England typically reflected the times in which they were written. The increasing pace of material change did not extinguish supernatural fiction: it was, on the contrary, a prerequisite for its development. To the ascendancy of secularism and science, supernatural fiction offered a counterbalancing viewpoint. This might appear in the aspect of a dark and terrible theology, as when J. S. le Fanu (Victorian supernaturalist *par excellence*) postulated 'a system whose workings are generally in mercy hidden from us' in which 'retribution follows guilt, in ways the most mysterious and stupendous—by agencies the most inexplicable and terrible' ('The Watcher', 1851). Or it might simply take the shape of a more general warning against trusting merely to reason. 'Some people do not believe in ghosts,' says the narrator of Charlotte Riddell's 'The Open Door' (1882) pointedly. 'For that matter, some people do not believe in anything.' The comment is equally applicable a hundred years on, except that one would now probably substitute 'most' for 'some'. Ghost stories have continued to flourish in the technological culture of the twentieth century: conservative in style and form, but perpetually adaptive to the mood of the times, and still providing alternative readings of reality. The ghosts of fiction were not killed off by the advent of the electric light, the invention of the telephone, the coming of the motor car, or even by the once unthinkable horrors of technological warfare. Instead they took over the trappings, landscapes, and cultural assumptions of the twentieth century for their ancient purposes, as they had done in the nineteenth, and so continued—against all the odds—to thrive. As Elizabeth Bowen put it in 1952:

The universal battiness of our century looks like providing [ghosts] with a propitious climate—hitherto confined to antique manors, castles, graveyards, crossroads, yew walks, cloisters, cliff-edges, moors or city backwaters, they may now roam at will. They do well in flats, and are villa-dwellers. They know how to curdle electric light, chill off heating, or de-condition air. Long ago, they captured railway trains and installed themselves in liners' luxury cabins; now telephones, motors, planes and radio wave-lengths offer them self-expression. The advance of psychology has gone their way; the guilt-complex is their especial friend.[1]

Yet the traditional ghost-story form appears to have been eclipsed by horror, science fiction, and fantasy fiction. Its triumphs are many, but have largely gone unrecognized, except amongst *aficionados*. One reason

[1] Elizabeth Bowen, introduction to *The Second Ghost Book*, ed. Cynthia Asquith (1952), vii.

may be that writers of ghost stories are far more ubiquitous, far less susceptible to categorization, than those in related genres. There is, of course, a well-defined canon and a corresponding body of genrist authors who either wrote ghost fiction exclusively, or whose reputation now rests on that part of their literary output. In the twentieth century such figures include M. R. James, Algernon Blackwood, R. H. Malden, E. G. Swain, H. Russell Wakefield, W. F. Harvey, and Robert Aickman. But unlike science or horror fiction, the ghost story enjoys a vigorous life beyond the confines of its genre; indeed, it might be argued that some of the best stories have been written by mainstream authors who have only occasionally accommodated the supernatural in their fiction. Examples from the present collection include Graham Greene, Marghanita Laski, F. Scott Fitzgerald, and Jane Gardam—none of whom could strictly be classified as ghost-story writers in the genrist sense.

In addition to this dispersal of activity and achievement, not a few twentieth-century ghost stories have deliberately cultivated a retrospective ambience that, on the face of it at least, has far less contemporary appeal than the visceral impact of horror fiction, or the escapist possibilities of fantasy. The highly influential strand of antiquarianism which began with M. R. James in the early years of the century, and which still has its purveyors and eager devotees, has tended to produce a static, self-referential style in which the contemporary world is only distantly felt as a shaping force (James felt that actuality was necessary in a ghost story, but not a very insistent one): the pulse of the action, and the source of supernatural intrusion, in stories of this type is the historical past, typically accessed through scholarly research, or channelled through ancient artefacts and objects. In the hands of M. R. James, the antiquarian ghost story achieved a classic blend of narrative detachment, plausible detail, and a sure instinct for manipulating primal sources of fear. The malevolence, palpability, and sheer variety of his supernatural entities were entirely new and gained in fearsomeness by being generally unleashed by apparently trivial triggers. The relatively late story selected here, 'The Diary of Mr Poynter', is built on the most banal of circumstances: the refurnishing of a new house, involving 'particulars of carpets, of chairs, of wardrobes, and of bedroom china'. Only gradually is the trigger revealed—a piece of fabric contained in a set of early eighteenth-century diaries, purchased by Mr Denton for £12 10s. Here we are in 1919, or thereabouts, in a comfortable middle-class world of tennis parties and house guests; and yet the seemingly innocuous circumstance of commissioning some new curtains to be made from a fragment of old fabric provides a gateway for an enraged supernatural pursuer from the seventeenth century. As always with James, there seems to be an admonitory, though unspoken, subtext to which the surface narrative is anchored, signalled by the incomplete Shakespearian quotation with which the story ends—'There are more things . . .'

Though few of James's many followers hit the authentic note of his first landmark collection, *Ghost Stories of an Antiquary* (1904), and though James himself did not always write at the same impressive level, within the genre he remains a powerful and much-imitated presence. The antiquarian mode is a satisfying one for both writers and readers, bringing with it a well-established repertoire of conventions and expectations; but it would be possible to argue that James's influence has been a constricting one. The Jamesian style requires skills that few possess to bring it off successfully, and in many imitative hands it has become a sanctuary for cosy nostalgia. As 'The Diary of Mr Poynter' illustrates, the wider realities of the post-war world of 1919 are wholly absent, but at least the world of the story partially reflects the life of its creator in the figure of the bachelor scholar Denton. It is this alignment of the text with James's own environment and experiences—anachronistic though they may have been, even in 1919—that makes it so difficult for his imitators to succeed.

The history of the ghost story in the twentieth century, however, is more than a succession of variations on the Jamesian theme. The universalism of the supernatural in literature has ensured that many contemporary ghost stories have avoided the kind of narrow generic typing of some other genres—science fiction, for example, which demands specialism and dedication to the form in both producers and consumers. This is not to say that conventions and traditions have been rejected: the twentieth century has continued to produce its own versions of the haunted-house story, the tale of supernatural vengeance, and other hallowed scenarios. But it is remarkable how the dead hand of formula and custom has been circumvented by a large number of writers who, at the same time, draw back from openly defying or radically subverting their literary precedents.

One inescapable fact of supernatural fiction in the twentieth century, as in the nineteenth, has been the dominance of women. It has been claimed, by the writer Jessica Amanda Salmonson, that 'supernatural fiction written in English in the last two hundred years has been *predominantly* women's literature, and much of it is clearly feminist'.[2]

---

[2] Jessica Amanda Salmonson (ed.), *What Did Miss Darrington See? An Anthology of Feminist Supernatural Fiction* (1989), preface, ix.

Perhaps the second part of the claim is slightly overstated; but in terms of the number and quality of stories produced, it remains incontestable that women have helped shape supernatural fiction to a degree that can only be matched in the related genre of crime fiction. A mere select tally of names confirms the point: Mary Elizabeth Braddon, Charlotte Riddell, Margaret Oliphant, Amelia Edwards, Rhoda Broughton, Rosa Mulholland, Mrs Molesworth in the nineteenth century; Violet Hunt, Edith Wharton, May Sinclair, Cynthia Asquith, Marjorie Bowen, D. K. Broster, Joan Aiken, Elizabeth Walter, Elizabeth Bowen, Margaret Irwin, Rosemary Timperley, Mary Williams, Lisa Tuttle, and Alison Lurie (amongst many others) in the twentieth. In the oral story-telling tradition women had always played an important, perhaps even the leading, role. (It is entirely appropriate that one of the best early Victorian ghost stories, published in 1852, is Elizabeth Gaskell's 'The Old Nurse's Story'.) When supernaturalism attained literary form in the mid-eighteenth century, Gothic fiction, written for a largely female audience, was employed by women writers to articulate themes—for instance, of alienation and persecution—that can be seen as having an especial relevance to female experience. The potent line of the female Gothic, running from Ann Radcliffe and Mary Shelley to Margaret Atwood and Angela Carter, is paralleled by the still unfolding tradition of ghost-story writing by women. From a feminist perspective, the embracing of the irrational by women, in narratives that subvert the dominant tradition of realistic fiction, can be interpreted as offering a direct challenge to established forms of representational literature that are seen as being inherently 'patriarchal'. Supernatural fiction by women, in the words of one critic, 'explores and thereby threatens to dissolve many of the structures upon which social definitions of reality depend, those rigid boundaries between life and death, waking and dream states, self and not-self, bodily and non-bodily existence, past and future, reason and madness . . .'.[3] It is, from this point of view, a response to social and political disempowerment, a strategy for extending 'our sense of the human, the real, beyond the blinkered limits of male science, language, and rationalism'.[4]

Valid though this critique may be in some cases, it is equally clear that many women have written ghost stories with no higher purpose than to excite in readers what Edith Wharton called 'the fun of the shudder'. As

[3] Rosemary Jackson, introduction to *What Did Miss Darrington See?*, preface, xviii.

[4] Ibid.

[5] Robert Aickman, introduction to *The Fontana Book of Great Ghost Stories* (1964), 7.

M. R. James himself pointed out, the ghost story is merely a particular sort of short story. This is not quite as obvious as it sounds. It suggests that replicating formulaic components is not enough; that the literary qualities discernible in a good short story in general should also be present in a ghost story. Dozens of ghost-story writers have failed to observe this fundamental truth, but then the challenge of writing an effective short story that is also an effective ghost story is a peculiarly formidable one—so formidable that Robert Aickman once declared categorically that 'There are only about thirty or forty first-class ghost stories in the whole of western literature'.[5] It requires a kind of bravery to tackle the form, for even the slightest lapse—especially in the execution of the crisis—can instantaneously arouse disengagement, even perhaps inappropriate laughter, in the reader. For we know (do we not?) that these things cannot be; and so whilst we comply with the need to suspend our reason we become impatient with an author who assumes our indulgence has no limits. Ghost stories become ineffectual when they completely disregard the established limitations of the genre. With those writers who are most at ease with the form, restraint co-exists with an instinct for manipulating our responses. In any genre there are rules to be obeyed, yet those same rules also need to be broken. The best writers are happy to accept preconditions and expectations; but they also recognize the need to flaunt both. In the twentieth century, writers of ghost stories have been liberated from the need for their ghosts to conform to a narrow range of types, but this new latitude has only increased the difficulty of the task. L. P. Hartley observed in 1955 that 'a stylized ghost is much easier to handle, so to speak, than one whose limitations are uncertain. If he can only squeak or clank a chain, we know where we are with him. If he can only appear as a smell or a current of cold air, we also know . . . But if the ghost can be so like an ordinary human being that we can scarcely tell the difference, what is that difference to be? Where is the line to be drawn?'[6] Hartley's words could almost be a commentary on his own story 'Night-Fears', reprinted here. The stranger who inhabits the blind alley opposite the night-watchman's compound, and who induces in the watchman such a depression of spirits that he commits suicide, is a strange kind of ghost indeed, quite unlike the brash spooks of Gothicism. Human in form (though we are given no physical description) and speech, and unremarkable in every way, he is revealed for what he is only by the lowest

---

[6] L. P. Hartley, introduction to *The Third Ghost Book*, ed. Cynthia Asquith (1955), viii-ix.

of low-key pay-off lines: 'Then he climbed back and, crossing the street, entered a blind alley opposite, leaving a track of dark, irregular foot-prints; and since he did not return it is probable that he lived there.'

Hartley's story succeeds because of what it does not tell us. Literalness is fatal to the ghost story. There must be gaps left in the narrative fabric for the individual imagination of each reader to fill up. If the twentieth-century ghost story has a leading characteristic it is the exploitation of this principle of obliquity. Ambiguity, and an acceptance of the incon-clusive, characterize the work of two major figures, Walter de la Mare and Robert Aickman, both of whom were adept at implying the pres-ence of supernatural menace lurking on the margins of normality—'the icy summons of some dreadful nothing, when all around us had seemed commonplace and safe', as de la Mare expressed it.[7] All de la Mare's stories convey a sense that the human characters are somehow impli-cated, as part of an active but ultimately unknowable metaphysic, in the supernatural manifestations that confront them: the exterior 'unknown' and the great internal mystery of human consciousness appear to be somehow linked by an unbreakable chain of causality. One of his characters, the verger in 'Strangers and Pilgrims', asks in respect of the returning dead: ' "What purpose could call so small a sprinkling of them back—a few grains of sand out of the wilderness, unless, it may be, some festering grievance; or hunger for the living, sir; or duty left undone? In which case, mark you, which of any of us is safe?" ' But this marks the limit of speculation in de la Mare; and explanation there is none. Even the presence of the supernatural itself is rarely asserted outright; more typically it is left hovering just this side of denial: 'The evidence on the one side and on the other is softly falling like imperceptible dust into the scale pans. But finally, surely, that on the preternatural side should waver gently downwards.'[8]

In Aickman, too, a direct connection is made between the ghost story and the unconscious mind, and with the eternally unknowable. The essential quality of the ghost story, according to Aickman, is that it gives 'satisfying form to the unanswerable', dealing, as it does, 'with the experience behind experience': 'ghost stories should be stories con-cerned not with appearance and consistency, but with the spirit behind appearance, the void behind the face of order. Ghost stories inquire and hint, waver and dissemble, startle and astonish. They are a last refuge

---

[7] Walter de la Mare, introduction to *They Walk Again: An Anthology of Ghost Stories*, chosen by Colin de la Mare (1931), 29.

[8] Ibid. 17.

from the universal, affirmative shout.'⁹ Here, though the working out in
fictional terms is very different, a direct link is forged with the impulses
that encouraged that rise of the literary ghost story in the nineteenth
century. During an age of rapid material expansion and scientific
progress there was a corresponding erosion of uncertainty and mystery.
So too in the atomic age, the need to submit to the unknown has been
culturally denied. Aickman saw the ghost story as providing a necessary
corrective to affirmation and certainty:

The successful ghost story does not close a door and leave inside it still another
definition, a still further solution. On the contrary, it must open a door,
preferably where no one had previously noticed a door to exist; and, at the end,
leave it open, or, possibly, ajar . . . We think we want certainty and security, but
the steadily increasing popularity of ghost stories [in the mid 1960s] is only one
of many contemporary indications that, in our 'hearts', or our unconscious
minds (ten times wider than our conscious, say the experts), we want no such
stuff.¹⁰

Much the same point had been made by Edith Wharton thirty years
earlier, though she shifted the weight of her argument towards the
changed physical conditions of the modern world:

What drives ghosts away is not the aspidistra or the electric cooker; I can
imagine them more wistfully haunting a mean house in a dull street than the
battlemented castle with its boring stage properties. What the ghost really needs
is not echoing passages and hidden doors behind tapestry, but only continuity
and silence. For where a ghost has once appeared it seems to hanker to appear
again; and it obviously prefers the silent hours, when at last the wireless has
ceased to jazz. These hours, prophetically called 'small', are in fact continually
growing smaller; and even if a few diviners keep their wands, the ghost may
after all succumb first to the impossibility of finding standing room in a roaring
and discontinuous universe.¹¹

All the writers brought together in this anthology display an aware-
ness of what has been called 'the world next door'.¹² They all observe the
proprieties of the genre; but, equally, they are united by an ability to
refute or refashion the merely conventional. A few stories, such as Ellen

⁹ Aickman, introduction to *The Fourth Fontana Book of Great Ghost Stories*
(1967), 8, 10.
¹⁰ Aickman, introduction to *The Third Fontana Book of Great Ghost Stories*
(1966), 7.
¹¹ Edith Wharton, preface to *Ghosts* (1937).
¹² Elizabeth Walter, *In the Mist and Other Uncanny Encounters* (1979), preface,
vii.

Glasgow's 'The Shadowy Third' or Aickman's 'Ringing the Changes', have attained something like classic status. Many will be familiar to enthusiasts; one or two may be less so. Inevitably, lack of space has prevented me including a number of authors who, ideally, ought to be represented. But a line had to be drawn somewhere. The selection has been based on examples of the form that seem to me effective both as ghost stories *and* as self-contained short stories. Above all, I have tried to include only stories that are, in some essential way, distinctive of the century in which they were written. In some cases this may be simply a matter of the story's setting; in others it is located in narrative style or language, in characterization or social context. In Fritz Leiber's 'Smoke Ghost', for instance, it takes the form of an overt alignment of the supernatural with the anxieties of the contemporary industrial world:

'Have you ever thought what a ghost of our times would look like, Miss Millick? Just picture it. A smoky composite face with the hungry anxiety of the unemployed, the neurotic restlessness of the person without purpose, the jerky tension of the high-pressure metropolitan worker, the uneasy resentment of the striker, the callous opportunism of the scab, the aggressive whine of the panhandler, the inhibited terror of the bombed civilian, and a thousand other twisted emotional patterns. Each one overlying and yet blending with the other, like a pile of semi-transparent masks?'

If the ghost story is less obviously popular in the last decade of the twentieth century—for many reasons, including the disappearance of former vehicles such as the monthly magazine and the serial anthology—the roots of its appeal remain perennially embedded in all of us. It may be that detective fiction speaks more naturally to a notionally rationalistic age, for the successful resolution of a crime satisfies our belief in the human power to explain. The ghost story, on the other hand, has always cautioned against putting too great a faith in explication. It did so in the Victorian age; it does so still. In its stubborn refusal to consign itself to the footnotes of literary history, the ghost story continues to define a role for itself as a needful means of shedding a little darkness on our lives.

MICHAEL COX

In the Dark

E. Nesbit

It may have been a form of madness. Or it may be that he really was what is called haunted. Or it may—though I don't pretend to understand how—have been the development, through intense suffering, of a sixth sense in a very nervous, highly strung nature. Something certainly led him where They were. And to him They were all one.

He told me the first part of the story, and the last part of it I saw with my own eyes.

I

Haldane and I were friends even in our school-days. What first brought us together was our common hatred of Visger, who came from our part of the country. His people knew our people at home, so he was put on to us when he came. He was the most intolerable person, boy and man, that I have ever known. He would not tell a lie. And that was all right. But he didn't stop at that. If he were asked whether any other chap had done anything—been out of bounds, or up to any sort of lark—he would always say, 'I don't know, sir, but I believe so.' He never did know—we took care of that. But what he believed was always right. I remember Haldane twisting his arm to say how he knew about that cherry-tree business, and he only said, 'I don't know—I just feel sure. And I was right, you see.' What can you do with a boy like that?

We grew up to be men. At least Haldane and I did. Visger grew up to be a prig. He was a vegetarian and a teetotaller, and an all-wooler and a Christian Scientist, and all the things that prigs are—but he wasn't a common prig. He knew all sorts of things that he oughtn't to have known, that he *couldn't* have known in any ordinary decent way. It wasn't that he found things out. He just knew them. Once, when I was very unhappy, he came into my rooms—we were all in our last year at Oxford—and talked about things I hardly knew myself. That was really why I went to India that winter. It was bad enough to be unhappy, without having that beast knowing all about it.

I was away over a year. Coming back, I thought a lot about how jolly it would be to see old Haldane again. If I thought about Visger at all, I wished he was dead. But I didn't think about him much.

I did want to see Haldane. He was always such a jolly chap—gay, and kindly, and simple, honourable, upright, and full of practical sympathies. I longed to see him, to see the smile in his jolly blue eyes, looking out from the net of wrinkles that laughing had made round them, to hear his jolly laugh, and feel the good grip of his big hand. I went straight from the docks to his chambers in Gray's Inn, and I found him cold, pale, anaemic, with dull eyes and a limp hand, and pale lips that smiled without mirth, and uttered a welcome without gladness.

He was surrounded by a litter of disordered furniture and personal effects half packed. Some big boxes stood corded, and there were cases of books, filled and waiting for the enclosing boards to be nailed on.

'Yes, I'm moving,' he said. 'I can't stand these rooms. There's something rum about them—something devilish rum. I clear out tomorrow.'

The autumn dusk was filling the corners with shadows. 'You got the furs,' I said, just for something to say, for I saw the big case that held them lying corded among the others.

'Furs?' he said. 'Oh yes. Thanks awfully. Yes. I forgot about the furs.' He laughed, out of politeness, I suppose, for there was no joke about the furs. They were many and fine—the best I could get for money, and I had seen them packed and sent off when my heart was very sore. He stood looking at me, and saying nothing.

'Come out and have a bit of dinner,' I said as cheerfully as I could.

'Too busy,' he answered, after the slightest possible pause, and a glance round the room—'look here—I'm awfully glad to see you—If you'd just slip over and order in dinner—I'd go myself—only—Well, you see how it is.'

I went. And when I came back, he had cleared a space near the fire, and moved his big gate-table into it. We dined there by candle light. I tried to be amusing. He, I am sure, tried to be amused. We did not succeed, either of us. And his haggard eyes watched me all the time, save in those fleeting moments when, without turning his head, he glanced back over his shoulder into the shadows that crowded round the little lighted place where we sat.

When we had dined and the man had come and taken away the dishes, I looked at Haldane very steadily, so that he stopped in a pointless anecdote, and looked interrogatively at me.

'Well?' I said.

'You're not listening,' he said petulantly. 'What's the matter?'

'That's what you'd better tell me,' I said.

He was silent, gave one of those furtive glances at the shadows, and stooped to stir the fire to—I knew it—a blaze that must light every corner of the room.

'You're all to pieces,' I said cheerfully. 'What have you been up to? Wine? Cards? Speculation? A woman? If you won't tell me, you'll have to tell your doctor. Why, my dear chap, you're a wreck.'

'You're a comfortable friend to have about the place,' he said, and smiled a mechanical smile not at all pleasant to see.

'I'm the friend you want, I think,' said I. 'Do you suppose I'm blind? Something's gone wrong and you've taken to something. Morphia, perhaps? And you've brooded over the thing till you've lost all sense of proportion. Out with it, old chap. I bet you a dollar it's not so bad as you think it.'

'If I could tell you—or tell anyone,' he said slowly, 'it wouldn't be so bad as it is. If I could tell anyone, I'd tell you. And even as it is, I've told you more than I've told anyone else.'

I could get nothing more out of him. But he pressed me to stay—would have given me his bed and made himself a shake-down, he said. But I had engaged my room at the Victoria, and I was expecting letters. So I left him, quite late—and he stood on the stairs, holding a candle over the bannisters to light me down.

When I went back next morning, he was gone. Men were moving his furniture into a big van with Somebody's Pantechnicon painted on it in big letters.

He had left no address with the porter, and had driven off in a hansom with two portmanteaux—to Waterloo, the porter thought.

Well, a man has a right to the monopoly of his own troubles, if he chooses to have it. And I had troubles of my own that kept me busy.

II

It was more than a year later that I saw Haldane again. I had got rooms in the Albany by this time, and he turned up there one morning, very early indeed—before breakfast in fact. And if he looked ghastly before, he now looked almost ghostly. His face looked as though it had worn thin, like an oyster shell that has for years been cast up twice a day by the sea on a shore all pebbly. His hands were thin as bird's claws, and they trembled like caught butterflies.

I welcomed him with enthusiastic cordiality and pressed breakfast on him. This time, I decided, I would ask no questions. For I saw that none were needed. He would tell me. He intended to tell me. He had come here to tell me, and for nothing else.

I lit the spirit lamp—I made coffee and small talk for him, and I ate and drank, and waited for him to begin. And it was like this that he began:

'I am going,' he said, 'to kill myself—oh, don't be alarmed,'—I suppose I had said or looked something—'I shan't do it here, or now. I shall do it when I have to—when I can't bear it any longer. And I want someone to know why. I don't want to feel that I'm the only living creature who does know. And I can trust you, can't I?'

I murmured something reassuring.

'I should like you, if you don't mind, to give me your word, that you won't tell a soul what I'm going to tell you, as long as I'm alive. Afterwards . . . you can tell whom you please.'

I gave him my word.

He sat silent looking at the fire. Then he shrugged his shoulders.

'It's extraordinary how difficult it is to say it,' he said, and smiled. 'The fact is—you know that beast, George Visger.'

'Yes,' I said. 'I haven't seen him since I came back. Some one told me he'd gone to some island or other to preach vegetarianism to the cannibals. Anyhow, he's out of the way, bad luck to him.'

'Yes,' said Haldane, 'he's out of the way. But he's not preaching anything. In point of fact, he's dead.'

'Dead?' was all I could think of to say.

'Yes,' said he; 'it's not generally known, but he is.'

'What did he die of?' I asked, not that I cared. The bare fact was good enough for me.

'You know what an interfering chap he always was. Always knew everything. Heart to heart talks—and have everything open and above board. Well, he interfered between me and some one else—told her a pack of lies.'

'Lies?'

'Well, the *things* were true, but he made lies of them the way he told them—*you* know.' I did. I nodded. 'And she threw me over. And she died. And we weren't even friends. And I couldn't see her—before—I couldn't even . . . Oh, my God . . . But I went to the funeral. He was there. They'd asked *him*. And then I came back to my rooms. And I was sitting there, thinking. And he came up.'

'He would do. It's just what he would do. The beast! I hope you kicked him out.'

'No, I didn't. I listened to what he'd got to say. He came to say, No doubt it was all for the best. And he hadn't known the things he told her. He'd only guessed. He'd guessed right, damn him. What right had he to guess right? And he said it was all for the best, because, besides that, there was madness in my family. He'd found that out too—'

'And is there?'

'If there is, I didn't know it. And that was why it was all for the best. So then I said, "There wasn't any madness in my family before, but there is now," and I got hold of his throat. I am not sure whether I meant to kill him; I ought to have meant to kill him. Anyhow, I did kill him. What did you say?'

I had said nothing. It is not easy to think at once of the tactful and suitable thing to say, when your oldest friend tells you that he is a murderer.

'When I could get my hands out of his throat—it was as difficult as it is to drop the handles of a galvanic battery—he fell in a lump on the hearth-rug. And I saw what I'd done. How is it that murderers ever get found out?'

'They're careless, I suppose,' I found myself saying, 'they lose their nerve.'

'I didn't,' he said. 'I never was calmer, I sat down in the big chair and looked at him, and thought it all out. He was just off to that island—I knew that. He'd said goodbye to everyone. He'd told me that. There was no blood to get rid of—or only a touch at the corner of his slack mouth. He wasn't going to travel in his own name because of interviewers. Mr Somebody Something's luggage would be unclaimed and his cabin empty. No one would guess that Mr Somebody Something was Sir George Visger, FRS. It was all as plain as plain. There was nothing to get rid of, but the man. No weapon, no blood—and I got rid of him all right.'

'How?'

He smiled cunningly.

'No, no,' he said; 'that's where I draw the line. It's not that I doubt your word, but if you talked in your sleep, or had a fever or anything. No, no. As long as you don't know where the body is, don't you see, I'm all right. Even if you could prove that I've said all this—which you can't—it's only the wanderings of my poor unhinged brain. See?'

I saw. And I was sorry for him. And I did not believe that he had killed Visger. He was not the sort of man who kills people. So I said:

'Yes, old chap, I see. Now look here. Let's go away together, you and I—travel a bit and see the world, and forget all about that beastly chap.'

His eyes lighted up at that.

'Why,' he said, 'you understand. You don't hate me and shrink from me. I wish I'd told you before—you know—when you came and I was packing all my sticks. But it's too late now.'

'Too late? Not a bit of it,' I said. 'Come, we'll pack our traps and be off tonight—out into the unknown, don't you know.'

'That's where *I'm* going,' he said. 'You wait. When you've heard what's been happening to me, you won't be so keen to go travelling about with me.'

'But you've told me what's been happening to you,' I said, and the more I thought about what he had told me, the less I believed it.

'No,' he said, slowly, 'no—I've told you what happened to *him*. What happened to me is quite different. Did I tell you what his last words were? Just when I was coming at him. Before I'd got his throat, you know. He said, "Look out. You'll never to able to get rid of the body—Besides, anger's sinful." You know that way he had, like a tract on its hind legs. So afterwards I got thinking of that. But I didn't think of it for a year. Because I did get rid of his body all right. And then I was sitting in that comfortable chair, and I thought, "Hullo, it must be about a year now, since that—" and I pulled out my pocket-book and went to the window to look at a little almanac I carry about—it was getting dusk—and sure enough it was a year, to the day. And then I remembered what he'd said. And I said to myself, "Not much trouble about getting rid of *your* body, you brute." And then I looked at the hearth-rug and—Ah!' he screamed suddenly and very loud—'I can't tell you—no, I can't.'

My man opened the door—he wore a smooth face over his wriggling curiosity. 'Did you call, sir?'

'Yes,' I lied. 'I want you to take a note to the bank, and wait for an answer.'

When he was got rid of, Haldane said: 'Where was I?—'

'You were just telling me what happened after you looked at the almanac. What was it?'

'Nothing much,' he said, laughing softly, 'oh, nothing much—only that I glanced at the hearthrug—and there *he* was—the man I'd killed a year before. Don't try to explain, or I shall lose my temper. The door was shut. The windows were shut. He hadn't been there a minute before. And he was there then. That's all.'

Hallucination was one of the words I stumbled among.

'Exactly what I thought,' he said triumphantly, 'but—I touched it. It was quite real. Heavy, you know, and harder than live people are somehow, to the touch—more like a stone thing covered with kid the hands were, and the arms like a marble statue in a blue serge suit. Don't you hate men who wear blue serge suits?'

'There are hallucinations of touch too,' I found myself saying.

'Exactly what I thought,' said Haldane more triumphant than ever, 'but there are limits, you know—limits. So then I thought someone had got him out—the real him—and stuck him there to frighten me—while my back was turned, and I went to the place where I'd hidden him, and he was there—ah!—just as I'd left him. Only . . . it was a year ago. There are two of him there now.'

'My dear chap,' I said 'this is simply comic.'

'Yes,' he said, 'It is amusing. I find it so myself. Especially in the night when I wake up and think of it. I hope I shan't die in the dark, Winston: That's one of the reasons why I think I shall have to kill myself. I could be sure then of not dying in the dark.'

'Is *that* all?' I asked, feeling sure that it must be.

'No,' said Haldane at once. 'That's *not* all. He's come back to me again. In a railway carriage it was. I'd been asleep. When I woke up, there he was lying on the seat opposite me. Looked just the same. I pitched him out on the line in Red Hill Tunnel. And if I see him again, I'm going out myself. I can't stand it. It's too much. I'd sooner go. Whatever the next world's like, there aren't things in it like that. We leave them here, in graves and boxes and . . . You think I'm mad. But I'm not. You can't help me—no one can help me. He *knew*, you see. He said I shouldn't be able to get rid of the body. And I can't get rid of it. I can't. I can't. He knew. He always did know things that he *couldn't* know. But I'll cut his game short. After all, I've got the ace of trumps, and I'll play it on his next trick. I give you my word of honour, Winston, that I'm not mad.'

'My dear old man,' I said, 'I don't think you're mad. But I do think your nerves are very much upset. Mine are a bit, too. Do you know why I went to India? It was because of you and her. I couldn't stay and see it, though I wished for your happiness and all that; you know I did. And when I came back, she . . . and you . . . Let's see it out together,' I said. 'You won't keep fancying things if you've got me to talk to. And I always said you weren't half a bad old duffer.'

'She liked you,' he said.

'Oh, yes,' I said, 'she liked me.'

III

That was how we came to go abroad together. I was full of hope for him. He'd always been such a splendid chap—so sane and strong. I couldn't believe that he was gone mad, gone for ever, I mean, so that he'd never come right again. Perhaps may own trouble made it easy for me to see things not quite straight. Anyway, I took him away to recover his mind's health, exactly as I should have taken him away to get strong after a fever. And the madness seemed to pass away, and in a month or two we were perfectly jolly, and I thought I had cured him. And I was very glad because of that old friendship of ours, and because she had loved him and liked me.

We never spoke of Visger. I thought he had forgotten all about him. I thought I understood how his mind, over-strained by sorrow and anger, had fixed on the man he hated, and woven a nightmare web of horror round that detestable personality. And I had got the whip hand of my own trouble. And we were as jolly as sandboys together all those months.

And we came to Bruges at last in our travels, and Bruges was very full, because of the Exhibition. We could only get one room and one bed. So we tossed for the bed, and the one who lost the toss was to make the best of the night in the armchair. And the bedclothes we were to share equitably.

We spent the evening at a *café chantant* and finished at a beer hall, and it was late and sleepy when we got back to the Grande Vigne. I took our key from its nail in the concierge's room, and we went up. We talked awhile, I remember, of the town, and the belfry, and the Venetian aspect of the canals by moonlight, and then Haldane got into bed, and I made a chrysalis of myself with my share of the blankets and fitted the tight roll into the armchair. I was not at all comfortable, but I was compensatingly tired, and I was nearly asleep when Haldane roused me up to tell me about his will.

'I've left everything to you, old man,' he said. 'I know I can trust you to see to everything.'

'Quite so,' said I, 'and if you don't mind, we'll talk about it in the morning.'

He tried to go on about it, and about what a friend I'd been, and all that, but I shut him up and told him to go to sleep. But no. He wasn't comfortable, he said. And he'd got a thirst like a lime kiln. And he'd noticed that there was no water-bottle in the room. 'And the water in the jug's like pale soup,' he said.

'Oh, all right,' said I. 'Light your candle and go and get some water, then, in Heaven's name, and let me get to sleep.'

But he said, 'No—you light it. I don't want to get out of bed in the dark. I might—I might step on something, mightn't I—or walk into something that wasn't there when I got into bed.'

'Rot,' I said, 'walk into your grandmother.' But I lit the candle all the same. He sat up in bed and looked at me—very pale—with his hair all tumbled from the pillow, and his eyes blinking and shining.

'That's better,' he said. And then, 'I say—look here. Oh—yes—I see. It's all right. Queer how they mark the sheets here. Blest if I didn't think it was blood, just for the minute.'

The sheet was marked, not at the corner, as sheets are marked at home, but right in the middle where it turns down, with big, red, cross-stitching.

'Yes, I see,' I said, 'it is a queer place to mark it.'

'It's queer letters to have on it,' he said. 'G.V.'

'Grande Vigne,' I said. 'What letters do you expect them to mark things with? Hurry up.'

'You come too,' he said. 'Yes, it does stand for Grande Vigne, of course. I wish you'd come down too, Winston.'

'I'll *go* down,' I said and turned with the candle in my hand.

He was out of bed and close to me in a flash.

'No,' said he, 'I don't want to stay alone in the dark.'

He said it just as a frightened child might have done.

'All right then, come along,' I said. And we went. I tried to make some joke, I remember, about the length of his hair, and the cut of his pyjamas—but I was sick with disappointment. For it was almost quite plain to me, even then, that all my time and trouble had been thrown away, and that he wasn't cured after all. We went down as quietly as we could, and got a carafe of water from the long bare dining table in the *salle à manger*. He got hold of my arm at first, and then he got the candle away from me, and went very slowly, shading the light with his hand, and looking very carefully all about, as though he expected to see something that he wanted very desperately not to see. And of course, I knew what that something was. I didn't like the way he was going on. I can't at all express how deeply I didn't like it. And he looked over his shoulder every now and then, just as he did that first evening after I came back from India.

The thing got on my nerves so that I could hardly find the way back to our room. And when we got there, I give you my word, I more than half expected to see what *he* had expected to see—that, or something like that, on the hearth-rug. But of course there was nothing.

I blew out the light and tightened my blankets round me—I'd been trailing them after me in our expedition. And I was settled in my chair when Haldane spoke.

'You've got all the blankets,' he said.

'No, I haven't,' said I, 'only what I've always had.'

'I can't find mine then,' he said and I could hear his teeth chattering. 'And I'm cold. I'm . . . For God's sake, light the candle. Light it. Light it. Something horrible . . .'

And I couldn't find the matches.

'Light the candle, light the candle,' he said, and his voice broke, as a boy's does sometimes in chapel. 'If you don't he'll come to me. It is so easy to come at any one in the dark. Oh Winston, light the candle, for the love of God! I can't die in the dark.'

'I am lighting it,' I said savagely, and I was feeling for the matches on the marble-topped chest of drawers, on the mantelpiece—everywhere but on the round centre table where I'd put them. 'You're not going to die. Don't be a fool,' I said. 'It's all right. I'll get a light in a second.'

He said, 'It's cold. It's cold. It's cold,' like that, three times. And then he screamed aloud, like a woman—like a child—like a hare when the dogs have got it. I had heard him scream like that once before.

'What is it?' I cried, hardly less loud. 'For God's sake, hold your noise. What is it?'

There was an empty silence. Then, very slowly:

'It's Visger,' he said. And he spoke thickly, as through some stifling veil.

'Nonsense. Where?' I asked, and my hand closed on the matches as he spoke.

'Here,' he screamed sharply, as though he had torn the veil away, 'here, beside me. In the bed.'

I got the candle alight. I got across to him.

He was crushed in a heap at the edge of the bed. Stretched on the bed beyond him was a dead man, white and very cold.

Haldane had died in the dark.

It was all so simple.

We had come to the wrong room. The man the room belonged to was there, on the bed he had engaged and paid for before he died of heart disease, earlier in the day. A French *commis-voyageur* representing soap and perfumery; his name, Felix Leblanc.

Later, in England, I made cautious enquiries. The body of a man had been found in the Red Hill tunnel—a haberdasher man named

Simmons, who had drunk spirits of salts, owing to the depression of trade. The bottle was clutched in his dead hand.

For reasons that I had, I took care to have a police inspector with me when I opened the boxes that came to me by Haldane's will. One of them was the big box, metal lined, in which I had sent him the skins from India—for a wedding present, God help us all!

It was closely soldered.

Inside were the skins of beasts? No. The bodies of two men. One was identified, after some trouble, as that of a hawker of pens in city offices—subject to fits. He had died in one, it seemed. The other body was Visger's, right enough.

Explain it as you like. I offered you, if you remember, a choice of explanations before I began the story. I have not yet found the explanation that can satisfy me.

ROOUM

Oliver Onions

For all I ever knew to the contrary, it was his own name; and something about him, name or man or both, always put me in mind, I can't tell you how, of negroes. As regards the name, I dare say it was something hugger-mugger in the mere sound—something that I classed, for no particular reason, with the dark and ignorant sort of words, such as 'Obi' and 'Hoodoo'. I only know that after I learned that his name was Rooum, I couldn't for the life of me have thought of him as being called anything else.

The first impression that you got of his head was that it was a patchwork of black and white—black bushy hair and short white beard, or else the other way about. As a matter of fact, both hair and beard were piebald, so that if you saw him in the gloom a dim patch of white showed down one side of his head, and dark tufts cropped up here and there in his beard. His eyebrows alone were entirely black, with a little sprouting of hair almost joining them. And perhaps his skin helped to make me think of negroes, for it was very dark, of the dark brown that always seems to have more than a hint of green behind it. His forehead was low, and scored across with deep horizontal furrows.

We never knew when he was going to turn up on a job. We might not have seen him for weeks, but his face was always as likely as not to appear over the edge of a crane-platform just when that marvellous mechanical intuition of his was badly needed. He wasn't certificated. He wasn't even trained, as the rest of us understood training; and he scoffed at the drawing-office, and laughed outright at logarithms and our laborious methods of getting out quantities. But he could set sheers and tackle in a way that made the rest of us look silly. I remember once how, through the parting of a chain, a sixty-foot girder had come down and lay under a ruck of other stuff, as the bottom chip lies under a pile of spellikins—a hopeless-looking smash. Myself, I'm certificated twice or three times over; but I can only assure you that I wanted to kick myself when, after I'd spent a day and a sleepless night over the job, I saw the game of tit-tat-toe that Rooum made of it in an hour or two. Certificated or not, a man isn't a fool who can do that sort of thing. And he was one of these fellows, too, who can 'find water'—tell you where water is and what amount of getting it is likely to take, by just walking over the place. We aren't certificated up to that yet.

He was offered good money to stick to us—to stick to our firm—but he always shook his black-and-white piebald head. He'd never be able to keep the bargain if he were to make it, he told us quite fairly. I know there are these chaps who can't endure to be clocked to their work with a patent time-clock in the morning and released of an evening with a whistle—and it's one of the things no master can ever understand. So Rooum came and went erratically, showing up maybe in Leeds or Liverpool, perhaps next on Plymouth Breakwater, and once he turned up in an out-of-the-way place in Glamorganshire just when I was wondering what had become of him.

The way I got to know him (got to know him, I mean, more than just to nod) was that he tacked himself on to me one night down Vauxhall way, where we were setting up some small plant or other. We had knocked off for the day, and I was walking in the direction of the bridge when he came up. We walked along together; and we had not gone far before it appeared that his reason for joining me was that he wanted to know 'what a molecule was'.

I stared at him a bit.

'What do you want to know that for?' I said. 'What does a chap like you, who can do it all backwards, want with molecules?'

Oh, he just wanted to know, he said.

So, on the way across the bridge, I gave it him more or less from the book—molecular theory and all the rest of it. But, from the childish questions he put, it was plain that he hadn't got the hang of it all. 'Did the molecular theory allow things to pass through one another?' he wanted to know; '*Could* things pass through one another?' and a lot of ridiculous things like that. I gave it up.

'You're a genius in your own way, Rooum,' I said finally; 'you know these things without the books we plodders have to depend on. If I'd luck like that, I think I should be content with it.'

But he didn't seem satisfied, though he dropped the matter for that time. But I had his acquaintance, which was more than most of us had. He asked me, rather timidly, if I'd lend him a book or two. I did so, but they didn't seem to contain what he wanted to know, and he soon returned them, without remark.

Now you'd expect a fellow to be specially sensitive, one way or another, who can tell when there's water a hundred feet beneath him; and as you know, the big men are squabbling yet about this water-

finding business. But, somehow, the water-finding puzzled me less than
it did that Rooum should be extraordinarily sensitive to something
far commoner and easier to understand—ordinary echoes. He couldn't
stand echoes. He'd go a mile round rather than pass a place that he knew
had an echo; and if he came on one by chance, sometimes he'd
hurry through as quick as he could, and sometimes he'd loiter and
listen very intently. I rather joked about this at first, till I found it
really distressed him; then, of course, I pretended not to notice. We're
all cranky somewhere, and for that matter, I can't touch a spider
myself.

For the remarkable thing that overtook Rooum—(that, by the way,
is an odd way to put it, as you'll see presently; but the words came that
way into my head, so let them stand)—for the remarkable thing that
overtook Rooum, I don't think I can begin better than with the first
time, or very soon after the first time, that I noticed this peculiarity
about the echoes.

It was early on a particularly dismal November evening, and this time
we were somewhere out south-east London way, just beyond what they
are pleased to call the building-line—you know these districts of
wretched trees and grimy fields and market-gardens that are about the
same to real country that a slum is to a town. It rained that night; rain
was the most appropriate weather for the brickfields and sewage-farms
and yards of old carts and railway-sleepers we were passing. The rain
shone on the black handbag that Rooum always carried; and I sucked at
the dottle of a pipe that it was too much trouble to fill and light again.
We were walking in the direction of Lewisham (I think it would be),
and were still a little way from that eruption of red-brick houses
that . . . but you've doubtless seen them.

You know how, when they're laying out new roads, they lay down the
narrow strip of kerb first, with neither setts on the one hand nor
flagstones on the other? We had come upon one of these. (I had noticed
how, as we had come a few minutes before under a tall hollow-ringing
railway arch, Rooum had all at once stopped talking—it was the echo,
of course, that bothered him.) The unmade road to which we had come
had headless lamp-standards at intervals, and ramparts of grey road-
metal ready for use; and save for the strip of kerb, it was a broth of mud
and stiff clay. A red light or two showed where the road-barriers were—
they were laying the mains; a green railway light showed on an embank-
ment; and the Lewisham lamps made a rusty glare through the rain.
Rooum went first, walking along the narrow strip of kerb.

The lamp-standards were a little difficult to see, and when I heard

Rooum stop suddenly and draw in his breath sharply, I thought he had walked into one of them.

'Hurt yourself?' I said.

He walked on without replying; but half a dozen yards further on he stopped again. He was listening again. He waited for me to come up.

'I say,' he said, in an odd sort of voice, 'go a yard or two ahead, will you?'

'What's the matter?' I asked, as I passed ahead. He didn't answer.

Well, I hadn't been leading for more than a minute before he wanted to change again. He was breathing very quick and short.

'Why, what ails you?' I demanded, stopping.

'It's all right. . . . You're not playing any tricks, are you? . . .'

I saw him pass his hand over his brow.

'Come, get on,' I said shortly; and we didn't speak again till we struck the pavement with the lighted lamps. Then I happened to glance at him.

'Here,' I said brusquely, taking him by the sleeve, 'you're not well. We'll call somewhere and get a drink.'

'Yes,' he said, again wiping his brow. 'I say . . . did you hear?'

'Hear what?'

'Ah, you didn't . . . and, of course, you didn't feel anything. . . .'

'Come, you're shaking.'

When presently we came to a brightly lighted public-house or hotel, I saw that he was shaking even worse than I had thought. The shirt-sleeved barman noticed it too, and watched us curiously. I made Rooum sit down, and got him some brandy.

'What was the matter?' I asked, as I held the glass to his lips.

But I could get nothing out of him except that it was 'All right—all right,' with his head twitching over his shoulder almost as if he had touch of the dance. He began to come round a little. He wasn't the kind of man you'd press for explanations, and presently we set out again. He walked with me as far as my lodgings, refused to come in, but for all that lingered at the gate as if loath to leave. I watched him turn the corner in the rain.

We came home together again the next evening, but by a different way, quite half a mile longer. He had waited for me a little pertinaciously. It seemed he wanted to talk about molecules again.

Well, when a man of his age—he'd be near fifty—begins to ask questions, he's rather worse than a child who wants to know where Heaven is or some such thing—for you can't put him off as you can the child. Somewhere or other he'd picked up the word 'osmosis', and seemed to have some glimmering of its meaning. He dropped the molecules, and began to ask me about osmosis.

'It means, doesn't it,' he demanded, 'that liquids will work their way into one another—through a bladder or something? Say a thick fluid and a thin: you'll find some of the thick in the thin, and the thin in the thick?'

'Yes. The thick into the thin is ex-osmosis, and the other end-osmosis. That takes place more quickly. But I don't know a deal about it.'

'Does it ever take place with solids?' he next asked.

What was he driving at? I thought; but replied: 'I believe that what is commonly called "adhesion" is something of the sort, under another name.'

'A good deal of this bookwork seems to be finding a dozen names for the same thing,' he grunted; and continued to ask his questions.

But what it was he really wanted to know I couldn't for the life of me make out.

Well, he was due any time now to disappear again, having worked quite six weeks in one place; and he disappeared. He disappeared for a good many weeks. I think it would be about February before I saw or heard of him again.

It was February weather, anyway, and in an echoing enough place that I found him—the subway of one of the Metropolitan stations. He'd probably forgotten the echoes when he'd taken the train; but, of course, the railway folk won't let a man who happens to dislike echoes go wandering across the metals where he likes.

He was twenty yards ahead when I saw him. I recognized him by his patched head and black handbag. I ran along the subway after him.

It was very curious. He'd been walking close to the white-tiled wall, and I saw him suddenly stop; but he didn't turn. He didn't even turn when I pulled up, close behind him; he put out one hand to the wall, as if to steady himself. But, the moment I touched his shoulder, he just dropped—just dropped, half on his knees against the white tiling. The face he turned round and up to me was transfixed with fright.

There were half a hundred people about—a train was just in—and it isn't a difficult matter in London to get a crowd for much less than a man crouching terrified against a wall, looking over his shoulder as Rooum looked, at another man almost as terrified. I felt somebody's hand on my own arm. Evidently somebody thought I'd knocked Rooum down.

The terror went slowly from his face. He stumbled to his feet. I shook myself free of the man who held me and stepped up to Rooum.

'What the devil's all this about?' I demanded, roughly enough.

'It's all right . . . it's all right, . . .' he stammered.

'Heavens, man, you shouldn't play tricks like that!'

'No . . . no . . . but for the love of God don't do it again! . . .'

'We'll not explain here,' I said, still in a good deal of a huff; and the small crowd melted away—disappointed, I dare say, that it wasn't a fight.

'Now,' I said, when we were outside in the crowded street, 'you might let me know what all this is about, and what it is that for the love of God I'm not to do again.'

He was half apologetic, but at the same time half blustering, as if I had committed some sort of an outrage.

'A senseless thing like that!' he mumbled to himself. 'But there: you didn't know. . . . You *don't* know, do you? . . . I tell you, d'you hear, *you're not to run at all when I'm about!* You're a nice fellow and all that, and get your quantities somewhere near right, if you do go a long way round to do it—but I'll not answer for myself if you run, d'you hear? . . . Putting your hand on a man's shoulder like that, just when . . .'

'Certainly I might have spoken,' I agreed, a little stiffly.

'Of course you ought to have spoken! Just you see you don't do it again. It's monstrous!'

I put a curt question.

'Are you sure you're quite right in your head, Rooum?'

'Ah,' he cried, 'don't you think I just fancy it, my lad! Nothing so easy! I thought you guessed that other time, on the new road . . . it's as plain as a pikestaff . . . no, no, no! *I* shall be telling *you* something about molecules one of these days!'

We walked for a time in silence.

Suddenly he asked: 'What are you doing now?'

'I myself, do you mean? Oh, the firm. A railway job, past Pinner. But we've a big contract coming on in the West End soon they might want you for. They call it "alterations", but it's one of these big shop-rebuildings.'

'I'll come along.'

'Oh, it isn't for a month or two yet.'

'I don't mean that. I mean I'll come along to Pinner with you now, tonight, or whenever you go.'

'Oh!' I said.

I don't know that I specially wanted him. It's a little wearing, the company of a chap like that. You never know what he's going to let you in for next. But, as this didn't seem to occur to him, I didn't say anything. If he really liked catching the last train down, a three-mile walk, and then sharing a double-bedded room at a poor sort of alehouse (which was my own programme), he was welcome. We walked a little further; then I told him the time of the train and left him.

He turned up at Euston, a little after twelve. We went down together. It was getting on for one when we left the station at the other end, and then we began the tramp across the Weald to the inn. A little to my surprise (for I had begun to expect unaccountable behaviour from him) we reached the inn without Rooum having dodged about changing places with me, or having fallen cowering under a gorse-bush, or anything of that kind. Our talk, too, was about work, not molecules and osmosis.

The inn was only a roadside beerhouse—I have forgotten its name—and all its sleeping accommodation was the one double-bedded room. Over the head of my own bed the ceiling was cut away, following the roof-line; and the wall paper was perfectly shocking—faded bouquets that made V's and A's, interlacing everywhere. The other bed was made up, and lay across the room.

I think I only spoke once while we were making ready for bed, and that was when Rooum took from his black handbag a brush and a torn nightgown.

'That's what you always carry about, is it?' I remarked; and Rooum grunted something: 'Yes . . . never knew where you'd be next . . . no harm, was it?' We tumbled into bed.

But, for all the lateness of the hour, I wasn't sleepy; so from my own bag I took a book, set the candle on the end of the mantel, and began to read. Mark you, I don't say I was much better informed for the reading I did, for I was watching the V's on the wallpaper mostly—that, and wondering what was wrong with the man in the other bed who had fallen down at a touch in the subway. He was already asleep.

Now I don't know whether I can make the next clear to you. I'm quite certain he was sound asleep, so that it wasn't just the fact that he spoke. Even that is a little unpleasant, I always think, any sort of sleep-talking; but it's a very queer sort of sensation when a man actually answers a question that's put to him, knowing nothing whatever about it in the morning. Perhaps I ought not to have put that question; having put it, I did the next best thing afterwards, as you'll see in a moment . . . but let me tell you.

He'd been asleep perhaps an hour, and I wool-gathering about the wallpaper, when suddenly, in a far more clear and loud voice than he ever used when awake, he said:

'*What the devil is it prevents me seeing him, then?*'

That startled me, rather, for the second time that evening; and I really think I had spoken before I had fully realized what was happening.

'From seeing whom?' I said, sitting up in bed.

'Whom? . . . You're not attending. The fellow I'm telling you about, who runs after me,' he answered—answered perfectly plainly.

I could see his head there on the pillow, black and white, and his eyes were closed. He made a slight movement with his arm, but that did not wake him. Then it came to me, with a sort of start, what was happening. I slipped half out of bed. Would he—would he?—answer another question? . . . I risked it, breathlessly.

'Have you any idea who he is?'

Well, that too he answered.

'Who he is? The Runner? . . . Don't be silly. *Who else should it be?*'

With every nerve in me tingling, I tried again.

'What happens, then, when he catches you?'

This time, I really don't know whether his words were an answer or not; they were these:

'To hear him catching you up . . . and then padding away ahead again! All right, all right . . . but I guess it's weakening *him* a bit, too. . . .'

Without noticing it, I had got out of bed, and had advanced quite to the middle of the floor.

'What did you say his name was?' I breathed.

But that was a dead failure. He muttered brokenly for a moment, gave a deep troubled sigh, and then began to snore loudly and regularly.

I made my way back to bed; but I assure you that before I did so I filled my basin with water, dipped my face into it, and then set the candlestick afloat in it, leaving the candle burning. I thought I'd like to have a light. . . . It had burned down by morning, Rooum, I remember, remarked on the silly practice of reading in bed.

Well, it was a pretty kind of obsession for a man to have, wasn't it? Somebody running after him all the time, and then . . . running on ahead? And, of course, on a broad pavement there would be plenty of room for this running gentleman to run round; but on an eight- or nine-inch kerb, such as that of the new road out Lewisham way . . . but perhaps he was a jumping gentleman too, and could jump over a man's head. You'd think he'd have to get past some way, wouldn't you? . . . I remember vaguely wondering whether the name of that Runner was not Conscience; but Conscience isn't a matter of molecules and osmosis. . . .

One thing, however, was clear; I'd got to tell Rooum what I'd learned: for you can't get hold of a fellow's secrets in ways like that. I lost no time about it. I told him, in fact, soon after we'd left the inn the next morning—told him how he'd answered in his sleep.

And—what do you think of this?—he seemed to think I ought to have guessed it! *Guessed* a monstrous thing like that!

'You're less clever than I thought, with your books and that, if you didn't,' he grunted.

'But . . . Good God, man!'

'Queer, isn't it? But you don't know the queerest . . .'

He pondered for a moment, and then suddenly put his lips to my ear.

'I'll tell you,' he whispered. '*It gets harder every time!* . . . At first, he just slipped through: a bit of a catch at my heart, like when you nod off to sleep in a chair and jerk up awake again; and away he went. But now it's getting grinding, sluggish; and the pain. . . . You'd notice, that night on the road, the little check it gave me; that's past long since; and last night, when I'd just braced myself up stiff to meet it, and you tapped me on the shoulder . . .' He passed the back of his hand over his brow.

'I tell you,' he continued, 'it's an agony each time. I could scream at the thought of it. It's oftener, too, now, and he's getting stronger. The end-osmosis is getting to be ex-osmosis—is that right? Just let me tell you one more thing——'

But I'd had enough. I'd asked questions the night before, but now—well, I knew quite as much as, and more than, I wanted.

'Stop, please,' I said. 'You're either off your head, or worse. Let's call it the first. Don't tell me any more, please.'

'Frightened, what? Well, I don't blame you. But what would *you* do?'

'I should see a doctor; I'm only an engineer,' I replied.

'Doctors? . . . Bah!' he said, and spat.

I hope you see how the matter stood with Rooum. What do you make of it? Could you have believed it—*do* you believe it? . . . He'd made a nearish guess when he'd said that much of our knowledge is giving names to things we know nothing about; only rule-of-thumb Physics thinks everything's explained in the Manual; and you've always got to remember one thing: You can call it Force or what you like, but it's a certainty that things, solid things of wood and iron and stone, would explode, just go off in a puff into space, if it wasn't for something just as inexplicable as that that Rooum said he felt in his own person. And if you can swallow that, it's a relatively small matter whether Rooum's light-footed Familiar slipped through him unperceived, or had to struggle through obstinately. You see now why I said that 'a queer thing overtook Rooum'.

More: I saw it. This thing, that outrages reason—I saw it happen. That is to say, I saw its effects, and it was in broad daylight, on an ordinary afternoon, in the middle of Oxford Street, of all places. There wasn't a shadow of doubt about it. People were pressing and jostling about him, and suddenly I saw him turn his head and listen, as I'd seen him before. I tell you, an icy creeping ran all over my skin I fancied *I* felt it approaching too, nearer and nearer. . . . The next moment he had made a sort of gathering of himself, as if against a gust. He stumbled and thrust—thrust with his body. He swayed, physically, as a tree sways in a wind; he clutched my arm and gave a loud scream. Then, after seconds—minutes—I don't know how long—he was free again.

And for the colour of his face when by and by I glanced at it . . . well, I once saw a swarthy Italian fall under a sunstroke, and *his* face was much the same colour that Rooum's negro face had gone; a cloudy, whitish green.

'Well—you've seen it—what do you think of it?' he gasped presently, turning a ghastly grin on me.

But it was night before the full horror of it had soaked into me.

Soon after that he disappeared again. I wasn't sorry.

Our big contract in the West End came on. It was a time-contract, with all manner of penalty clauses if we didn't get through; and I assure you that we were busy. I myself was far too busy to think of Rooum.

It's a shop now, the place we were working at, or rather one of these huge weldings of fifty shops where you can buy anything; and if you'd seen us there . . . but perhaps you did see us, for people stood up on the tops of omnibuses as they passed, to look over the mud-splashed hoarding into the great excavation we'd made. It was a sight. Staging rose on staging, tier on tier, with interminable ladders all over the steel structure. Three or four squat Otis lifts crouched like iron turtles on top, and a lattice-crane on a towering three-cornered platform rose a hundred and twenty feet into the air. At one end of the vast quarry was a demolished house, showing flues and fireplaces and a score of thicknesses of old wallpaper; and at night—they might well have stood up on the tops of the buses! A dozen great spluttering violet arc-lights half-blinded you; down below were the watchmen's fires; overhead, the

riveters had their fire-baskets; and in odd corners naphtha-lights gut-
tered and flared. And the steel rang with the riveters' hammers, and the
crane-chains rattled and clashed. . . . There's not much doubt in *my*
mind, it's the engineers who are the architects nowadays. The chaps
who think they're the architects are only a sort of paperhangers, who
hang brick and terracotta on our work and clap a pinnacle or two on
top—but never mind that. There we were, sweating and clanging and
navvying, till the day shift came to relieve us.

And I ought to say that fifty feet above our great gap, and from end
to end across it, there ran a travelling crane on a skeleton line, with
platform, engine, and wooden cab all compact in one.

It happened that they had pitched in as one of the foremen some
fellow or other, a friend of the firm's, a rank duffer, who pestered me
incessantly with his questions. I did half his work and all my own, and
it hadn't improved my temper much. On this night that I'm telling
about, he'd been playing the fool with his questions as if a time-contract
was a sort of summer holiday; and he'd filled me up to that point that
I really can't say just when it was that Rooum put in an appearance
again. I think I *had* heard somebody mention his name, but I'd paid no
attention.

Well, our Johnnie Fresh came up to me for the twentieth time that
night, this time wanting to know something about the overhead crane.
At that I fairly lost my temper.

'What ails the crane?' I cried. 'It's doing its work, isn't it? Isn't
everybody doing their work except you? Why can't you ask Hopkins?
Isn't Hopkins there?'

'I don't know,' he said.

'Then,' I snapped, 'in that particular I'm as ignorant as you, and I
hope it's the only one.'

But he grabbed my arm.

'Look at it now!' he cried, pointing; and I looked up.

Either Hopkins or somebody was dangerously exceeding the speed-
limit. The thing was flying along its thirty yards of rail as fast as a tram,
and the heavy fall-blocks swung like a ponderous kite-tail, thirty feet
below. As I watched, the engine brought up within a yard of the end of
the way, the blocks crashed like a ram into the broken house end,
fetching down plaster and brick, and then the mechanism was reversed.
The crane set off at a tear back.

'Who in Hell . . .' I began; but it wasn't a time to talk. '*Hi!*' I yelled,
and made a spring for a ladder.

The others had noticed it, too, for there were shouts all over the place. By that time I was halfway up the second stage. Again the crane tore past, with the massive tackle sweeping behind it, and again I heard the crash at the other end. Whoever had the handling of it was managing it skilfully, for there was barely a foot to spare when it turned again.

On the fourth platform, at the end of the way, I found Hopkins. He was white, and seemed to be counting on his fingers.

'What's the matter here?' I cried.

'It's Rooum,' he answered. 'I hadn't stepped out of the cab, not a minute, when I heard the lever go. He's running somebody down, he says; he'll run the whole shoot down in a minute—look! . . .'

The crane was coming back again. Half out of the cab I could see Rooum's mottled hair and beard. His brow was ribbed like a gridiron, and as he ripped past one of the arcs his face shone like porcelain with the sweat that bathed it.

'Now . . . you! . . . *Now*, damn you! . . .' he was shouting.

'Get ready to board him when he reverses!' I shouted to Hopkins.

Just how we scrambled on I don't know. I got one arm over the lifting-gear (which, of course, wasn't going), and heard Hopkins on the other footplate. Rooum put the brakes down and reversed; again came the thud of the fall-blocks; and we were speeding back again over the gulf of misty orange light. The stagings were thronged with gaping men.

'Ready? Now!' I cried to Hopkins; and we sprang into the cab.

Hopkins hit Rooum's wrist with a spanner. Then he seized the lever, jammed the brake down and tripped Rooum, all, as it seemed, in one movement. I fell on top of Rooum. The crane came to a standstill half-way down the line. I held Rooum panting.

But either Rooum was stronger than I, or else he took me very much unawares. All at once he twisted clear from my grasp and stumbled on his knees to the rear door of the cab. He threw up one elbow, and staggered to his feet as I made another clutch at him.

'Keep still, you fool!' I bawled. 'Hit him over the head, Hopkins!'

Rooum screamed in a high voice.

'Run him down—cut him up with the wheels—down, you!—down, I say!—Oh, my God! . . . *Ha!*'

He sprang clear out from the crane door, wellnigh taking me with him.

I told you it was a skeleton line, two rails and a tie or two. He'd actually jumped to the right-hand rail. And he was running along it—running along that iron tightrope, out over that well of light and watching men. Hopkins had started the travelling-gear, as if with some insane idea of catching him; but there was only one possible end to it. He'd gone fully a dozen yards, while I watched, horribly fascinated; and then I saw the turn of his head. . . .

He didn't meet it this time; he sprang to the other rail, as if to evade it. . . .

Even at the take-off he missed. As far as I could see, he made no attempt to save himself with his hands. He just went down out of the field of my vision. There was an awful silence; then, from far below . . .

They weren't the men on the lower stages who moved first. The men above went a little way down, and then they too stopped. Presently two of them descended, but by a distant way. They returned, with two bottles of brandy, and there was a hasty consultation. Two men drank the brandy off there and then—getting on for a pint of brandy apiece; then they went down, drunk.

I, Hopkins tells me, had got down on my knees in the crane cab, and was jabbering away cheerfully to myself. When I asked him what I said, he hesitated, and then said: 'Oh, you don't want to know that, sir,' and I haven't asked him since.

What do *you* make of it?

THE SHADOWY THIRD

Ellen Glasgow

When the call came I remember that I turned from the telephone in a romantic flutter. Though I had spoken only once to the great surgeon, Roland Maradick, I felt on that December afternoon that to speak to him only once—to watch him in the operating-room for a single hour—was an adventure which drained the colour and the excitement from the rest of life. After all these years of work on typhoid and pneumonia cases, I can still feel the delicious tremor of my young pulses; I can still see the winter sunshine slanting through the hospital windows over the white uniforms of the nurses.

'He didn't mention me by name. Can there by a mistake?' I stood, incredulous yet ecstatic, before the superintendent of the hospital.

'No, there isn't a mistake. I was talking to him before you came down.' Miss Hemphill's strong face softened while she looked at me. She was a big, resolute woman, a distant Canadian relative of my mother's, and the kind of nurse I had discovered in the month since I had come up from Richmond, that Northern hospital boards, if not Northern patients, appear instinctively to select. From the first, in spite of her hardness, she had taken a liking—I hesitate to use the word 'fancy' for a preference so impersonal—to her Virginia cousin. After all, it isn't every Southern nurse, just out of training, who can boast a kinswoman in the superintendent of a New York hospital.

'And he made you understand positively that he meant me?' The thing was so wonderful that I simply couldn't believe it.

'He asked particularly for the nurse who was with Miss Hudson last week when he operated. I think he didn't even remember that you had a name. When I asked if he meant Miss Randolph, he repeated that he wanted the nurse who had been with Miss Hudson. She was small, he said, and cheerful-looking. This, of course, might apply to one or two of the others, but none of these was with Miss Hudson.'

'Then I suppose it is really true?' My pulses were tingling. 'And I am to be there at six o'clock?'

'Not a minute later. The day nurse goes off duty at that hour, and Mrs Maradick is never left by herself for an instant.'

'It is her mind, isn't it? And that makes it all the stranger that he should select me, for I have had so few mental cases.'

'So few cases of any kind,' Miss Hemphill was smiling, and when she smiled I wondered if the other nurses would know her. 'By the time you have gone through the treadmill in New York, Margaret, you will have lost a good many things besides your inexperience. I wonder how long you will keep your sympathy and your imagination? After all, wouldn't you have made a better novelist than a nurse?'

'I can't help putting myself into my cases. I suppose one ought not to?'

'It isn't a question of what one ought to do, but of what one must. When you are drained of every bit of sympathy and enthusiasm, and have got nothing in return for it, not even thanks, you will understand why I try to keep you from wasting yourself.'

'But surely in a case like this—for Doctor Maradick?'

'Oh, well, of course—for Doctor Maradick.' She must have seen that I implored her confidence, for, after a minute, she let fall carelessly a gleam of light on the situation: 'It is a very sad case when you think what a charming man and a great surgeon Doctor Maradick is.'

Above the starched collar of my uniform I felt the blood leap in bounds to my cheeks. 'I have spoken to him only once,' I murmured, 'but he is charming, and so kind and handsome, isn't he?'

'His patients adore him.'

'Oh, yes, I've seen that. Everyone hangs on his visits.' Like the patients and the other nurses, I also had come by delightful, if imperceptible, degrees to hang on the daily visits of Doctor Maradick. He was, I suppose, born to be a hero to women. From my first day in his hospital, from the moment when I watched, through closed shutters, while he stepped out of his car, I have never doubted that he was assigned to the great part in the play. If I had been ignorant of his spell—of the charm he exercised over his hospital—I should have felt it in the waiting hush, like a dawn breath, which followed his ring at the door and preceded his imperious footstep on the stairs. My first impression of him, even after the terrible events of the next year, records a memory that is both careless and splendid. At that moment, when, gazing through the chinks in the shutters, I watched him, in his coat of dark fur, cross the pavement over the pale streaks of sunshine, I knew beyond any doubt— I knew with a sort of infallible prescience—that my fate was irretrievably bound up with his in the future. I knew this, I repeat, though Miss Hemphill would still insist that my foreknowledge was merely a sentimental gleaning from indiscriminate novels. But it wasn't only first love, impressionable as my kinswoman believed me to be. It wasn't only the way he looked. Even more than his appearance—more than the shining dark of his eyes, the silvery brown of his hair, the dusky glow in his face—even more than his charm and his magnificence, I think, the beauty and sympathy in his voice won my heart. It was a voice, I heard someone say afterwards, that ought always to speak poetry.

So you will see why—if you do not understand at the beginning, I can never hope to make you believe impossible things!—so you will see why I accepted the call when it came as an imperative summons. I couldn't have stayed away after he sent for me. However much I may have tried not to go, I know that in the end I must have gone. In those days, while I was still hoping to write novels, I used to talk a great deal about 'destiny' (I have learned since then how silly all such talk is), and I suppose it was my 'destiny' to be caught in the web of Roland Maradick's personality. But I am not the first nurse to grow lovesick about a doctor who never gave her a thought.

'I am glad you got the call, Margaret. It may mean a great deal to you. Only try not to be too emotional.' I remember that Miss Hemphill was holding a bit of rose-geranium in her hand while she spoke—one of the patients had given it to her from a pot she kept in her room, and the scent of the flower is still in my nostrils—or my memory. Since then— oh, long since then—I have wondered if she also had been caught in the web.

'I wish I knew more about the case.' I was pressing for light. 'Have you ever seen Mrs Maradick?'

'Oh, dear, yes. They have been married only a little over a year, and in the beginning she used to come sometimes to the hospital and wait outside while the doctor made his visits. She was a very sweet-looking woman then—not exactly pretty, but fair and slight, with the loveliest smile, I think, I have ever seen. In those first months she was so much in love that we used to laugh about it among ourselves. To see her face light up when the doctor came out of the hospital and crossed the pavement to his car, was as good as a play. We never tired of watching her—I wasn't superintendent then, so I had more time to look out of the window while I was on day duty. Once or twice she brought her little girl in to see one of the patients. The child was so much like her that you would have known them anywhere for mother and daughter.'

I had heard that Mrs Maradick was a widow, with one child, when she first met the doctor, and I asked now, still seeking an illumination I had not found, 'There was a great deal of money, wasn't there?'

'A great fortune. If she hadn't been so attractive, people would have said, I suppose, that Doctor Maradick married her for her money. Only,' she appeared to make an effort of memory, 'I believe I've heard somehow that it was all left in trust away from Mrs Maradick if she married again. I can't, to save my life, remember just how it was; but it was a queer will, I know, and Mrs Maradick wasn't to come into the money unless the child didn't live to grow up. The pity of it——'

A young nurse came into the office to ask for something—the keys, I think, of the operating-room, and Miss Hemphill broke off inconclusively as she hurried out of the door. I was sorry that she left off just when she did. Poor Mrs Maradick! Perhaps I was too emotional, but even before I saw her I had begun to feel her pathos and her strangeness.

My preparations took only a few minutes. In those days I always kept a suitcase packed and ready for sudden calls; and it was not yet six o'clock when I turned from Tenth Street into Fifth Avenue, and stopped for a minute, before ascending the steps, to look at the house in which Doctor Maradick lived. A fine rain was falling, and I remember thinking, as I turned the corner, how depressing the weather must be for Mrs Maradick. It was an old house, with damp-looking walls (though that may have been because of the rain) and a spindle-shaped iron railing which ran up the stone steps to the black door, where I noticed a dim flicker through the old-fashioned fanlight. Afterwards I discovered that Mrs Maradick had been born in the house—her maiden name was Calloran—and that she had never wanted to live anywhere else. She was a woman—this I found out when I knew her better—of strong attachments to both persons and places; and though Doctor Maradick had tried to persuade her to move uptown after her marriage, she had clung, against his wishes, to the old house in lower Fifth Avenue. I dare say she was obstinate about it in spite of her gentleness and her passion for the doctor. Those sweet, soft women, especially when they have always been rich, are sometimes amazingly obstinate. I have nursed so many of them since—women with strong affections and weak intellects—that I have come to recognize the type as soon as I set eyes upon it.

My ring at the bell was answered after a little delay, and when I entered the house I saw that the hall was quite dark except for the waning glow from an open fire which burned in the library. When I gave my name, and added that I was the night nurse, the servant appeared to think my humble presence unworthy of illumination. He was an old negro butler, inherited perhaps from Mrs Maradick's mother, who, I learned afterwards, was from South Carolina; and while he passed me on his way up the staircase, I heard him vaguely muttering that he 'wa'n't gwinter tu'n on dem lights twel de chile had done playin'.

To the right of the hall, the soft glow drew me into the library, and crossing the threshold timidly, I stooped to dry my wet coat by the fire. As I bent there, meaning to start up at the first sound of a footstep, I thought how cosy the room was after the damp walls outside to which some bared creepers were clinging; and I was watching the strange shapes and patterns the firelight made on the old Persian rug, when the lamps of a slowly turning motor flashed on me through the white shades at the window. Still dazzled by the glare, I looked round in the dimness and saw a child's ball of red and blue rubber roll towards me out of the gloom of the adjoining room. A moment later, while I made a vain attempt to capture the toy as it spun past me, a little girl darted airily, with peculiar lightness and grace, through the doorway, and stopped quickly, as if in surprise at the sight of a stranger. She was a small child—so small and slight that her footsteps made no sound on the polished floor of the threshold; and I remember thinking while I looked at her that she had the gravest and sweetest face I had ever seen. She couldn't—I decided this afterwards—have been more than six or seven years old, yet she stood there with a curious prim dignity, like the dignity of an elderly person, and gazed up at me with enigmatical eyes. She was dressed in Scotch plaid, with a bit of red ribbon in her hair, which was cut in a fringe over her forehead and hung very straight to her shoulders. Charming as she was, from her uncurled brown hair to the white socks and black slippers on her little feet, I recall most vividly the singular look in her eyes, which appeared in the shifting light to be of an indeterminate colour. For the odd thing about this look was that it was not the look of childhood at all. It was the look of profound experience, of bitter knowledge.

'Have you come for your ball?' I asked; but while the friendly question was still on my lips, I heard the servant returning. In my confusion I made a second ineffectual grasp at the plaything, which had rolled away from me into the dusk of the drawing-room. Then, as I raised my head, I saw that the child also had slipped from the room; and without looking after her I followed the old negro into the pleasant study above, where the great surgeon awaited me.

Ten years ago, before hard nursing had taken so much out of me, I blushed very easily, and I was aware at the moment when I crossed Doctor Maradick's study that my cheeks were the colour of peonies. Of course, I was a fool—no one knows this better than I do—but I had never been alone, even for an instant, with him before, and the man was more than a hero to me, he was—there isn't any reason now why I should blush over the confession—almost a god. At that age I was mad about the wonders of surgery, and Roland Maradick in the operating-room was magician enough to have turned an older and more sensible head than mine. Added to his great reputation and his marvelous skill, he was, I am sure of this, the most splendid-looking man, even at forty-five, that one could imagine. Had he been ungracious—had he been positively rude to me, I should still have adored him; but when he held out his hand, and greeted me in the charming way he had with women, I felt that I would have died for him. It is no wonder that a saying went about the hospital that every woman he operated on fell in love with him. As for the nurses—well, there wasn't a single one of them who had escaped his spell—not even Miss Hemphill, who could have been scarcely a day under fifty.

'I am glad you could come, Miss Randolph. You were with Miss Hudson last week when I operated?'

I bowed. To save my life I couldn't have spoken without blushing the redder.

'I noticed your bright face at the time. Brightness, I think, is what Mrs Maradick needs. She finds her day nurse depressing.' His eyes rested so kindly upon me that I have suspected since that he was not entirely unaware of my worship. It was a small thing, heaven knows, to flatter his vanity—a nurse just out of a training-school—but to some men no tribute is too insignificant to give pleasure.

'You will do your best, I am sure.' He hesitated an instant—just long enough for me to perceive the anxiety beneath the genial smile on his face—and then added gravely, 'We wish to avoid, if possible, having to send her away.'

I could only murmur in response, and after a few carefully chosen words about his wife's illness, he rang the bell and directed the maid to take me upstairs to my room. Not until I was ascending the stairs to the third storey did it occur to me that he had really told me nothing. I was as perplexed about the nature of Mrs Maradick's malady as I had been when I entered the house.

I found my room pleasant enough. It had been arranged—at Doctor Maradick's request, I think—that I was to sleep in the house, and after my austere little bed at the hospital, I was agreeably surprised by the cheerful look at the apartment into which the maid led me. The walls were papered in roses, and there were curtains of flowered chintz at the window, which looked down on a small formal garden at the rear of the house. This the maid told me, for it was too dark for me to distinguish more than a marble fountain and a fir tree, which looked old, though I afterwards learned that it was replanted almost every season.

In ten minutes I had slipped into my uniform and was ready to go to my patient; but for some reason—to this day I have never found out what it was that turned her against me at the start—Mrs Maradick refused to receive me. While I stood outside her door I heard the day nurse trying to persuade her to let me come in. It wasn't any use, however, and in the end I was obliged to go back to my room and wait until the poor lady got over her whim and consented to see me. That was long after dinner—it must have been nearer eleven than ten o'clock— and Miss Peterson was quite worn out by the time she came for me.

'I'm afraid you'll have a bad night,' she said as we went downstairs together. That was her way, I soon saw, to expect the worst of everything and everybody.

'Does she often keep you up like this?'

'Oh, no, she is usually very considerate. I never knew a sweeter character. But she still has this hallucination——'

Here again, as in the scene with Doctor Maradick, I felt that the explanation had only deepened the mystery. Mrs Maradick's hallucination, whatever form it assumed, was evidently a subject for evasion and subterfuge in the household. It was on the tip of my tongue to ask, 'What is her hallucination?'—but before I could get the words past my lips we had reached Mrs Maradick's door, and Miss Peterson motioned me to be silent. As the door opened a little way to admit me, I saw that Mrs Maradick was already in bed, and that the lights were out except for a night-lamp burning on a candle-stand beside a book and a carafe of water.

'I won't go in with you,' said Miss Peterson in a whisper; and I was on the point of stepping over the threshold when I saw the little girl, in the dress of Scotch plaid, slip by me from the dusk of the room into the electric light of the hall. She held a doll in her arms, and as she went by she dropped a doll's work-basket in the doorway. Miss Peterson must have picked up the toy, for when I turned in a minute to look for it I found that it was gone. I remember thinking that it was late for a child to be up—she looked delicate, too—but, after all, it was no business of mine, and four years in a hospital had taught me never to meddle in things that do not concern me. There is nothing a nurse learns quicker than not to try to put the world to rights in a day.

When I crossed the floor to the chair by Mrs Maradick's bed, she turned over on her side and looked at me with the sweetest and saddest smile.

'You are the night nurse,' she said in a gentle voice; and from the moment she spoke I knew that there was nothing hysterical or violent about her mania—or hallucination, as they called it. 'They told me your name, but I have forgotten it.'

'Randolph—Margaret Randolph.' I liked her from the start, and I think she must have seen it.

'You look very young, Miss Randolph.'

'I am twenty-two, but I suppose I don't look quite my age. People usually think I am younger.'

For a minute she was silent, and while I settled myself in the chair by the bed, I thought how strikingly she resembled the little girl I had seen first in the afternoon, and then leaving her room a few moments before. They had the same small, heart-shaped faces, coloured ever so faintly; the same straight, soft hair, between brown and flaxen; and the same large, grave eyes, set very far apart under arched eyebrows. What surprised me most, however, was that they both looked at me with that enigmatical and vaguely wondering expression—only in Mrs Maradick's face the vagueness seemed to change now and then to a definite fear—a flash, I had almost said, of startled horror.

I sat quite still in my chair, and until the time came for Mrs Maradick to take her medicine not a word passed between us. Then, when I bent over her with the glass in my hand, she raised her head from the pillow and said in a whisper of suppressed intensity:

'You look kind. I wonder if you could have seen my little girl?'

As I slipped my arm under the pillow I tried to smile cheerfully down on her. 'Yes, I've seen her twice. I'd know her anywhere by her likeness to you.'

A glow shone in her eyes, and I thought how pretty she must have been before illness took the life and animation out of her features. 'Then I know you're good.' Her voice was so strained and low that I could barely hear it. 'If you weren't good you couldn't have seen her.'

I thought this queer enough, but all I answered was, 'She looked delicate to be sitting up so late.'

A quiver passed over her thin features, and for a minute I thought she was going to burst into tears. As she had taken the medicine, I put the glass back on the candle-stand, and bending over the bed, smoothed the straight brown hair, which was as fine and soft as spun silk, back from her forehead. There was something about her—I don't know what it was—that made you love her as soon as she looked at you.

'She always had that light and airy way, though she was never sick a day in her life,' she answered calmly after a pause. Then, groping for my hand, she whispered passionately, 'You must not tell him—you must not tell anyone that you have seen her!'

'I must not tell anyone?' Again I had the impression that had come to me first in Doctor Maradick's study, and afterwards with Miss Peterson on the staircase, that I was seeking a gleam of light in the midst of obscurity.

'Are you sure there isn't any one listening—that there isn't any one at the door?' she asked, pushing aside my arm and raising herself on the pillows.

'Quite, quite sure. They have put out the lights in the hall.'

'And you will not tell him? Promise me that you will not tell him.' The startled horror flashed from the vague wonder of her expression. 'He doesn't like her to come back, because he killed her.'

'Because he killed her!' Then it was that light burst on me in a blaze. So this was Mrs Maradick's hallucination! She believed that her child was dead—the little girl I had seen with my own eyes leaving her room; and she believed that her husband—the great surgeon we worshipped in the hospital—had murdered her. No wonder they veiled the dreadful obsession in mystery! No wonder that even Miss Peterson had not dared to drag the horrid thing out into the light! It was the kind of hallucination one simply couldn't stand having to face.

'There is no use telling people things that nobody believes,' she resumed slowly, still holding my hand in a grasp that would have hurt me if her fingers had not been so fragile. 'Nobody believes that he killed her. Nobody believes that she comes back every day to the house. Nobody believes—and yet you saw her——'

'Yes, I saw her—but why should your husband have killed her?' I spoke soothingly, as one would speak to a person who was quite mad. Yet she was not mad, I could have sworn this while I looked at her.

For a moment she moaned inarticulately, as if the horror of her thoughts were too great to pass into speech. Then she flung out her thin, bare arm with a wild gesture.

'Because he never loved me!' she said. 'He never loved me!'

'But he married you,' I urged gently while I stroked her hair. 'If he hadn't loved you, why should he have married you?'

'He wanted the money—my little girl's money. It all goes to him when I die.'

'But he is rich himself. He must make a fortune from his profession.'

'It isn't enough. He wanted millions.' She had grown stern and tragic. 'No, he never loved me. He loved someone else from the beginning—before I knew him.'

It was quite useless, I saw, to reason with her. If she wasn't mad, she was in a state of terror and despondency so black that it had almost crossed the borderline into madness. I though once that I would go upstairs and bring the child down from her nursery; but, after a moment's hesitation, I realized that Miss Peterson and Doctor Maradick must have long ago tried all these measures. Clearly, there was nothing to do except soothe and quiet her as much as I could; and this I did until she dropped into a light sleep which lasted well into the morning.

By seven o'clock I was worn out—not from work but from the strain on my sympathy—and I was glad, indeed, when one of the maids came in to bring me an early cup of coffee. Mrs Maradick was still sleeping— it was a mixture of bromide and chloral I had given her—and she did not wake until Miss Peterson came on duty an hour or two later. Then, when I went downstairs, I found the dining-room deserted except for the old housekeeper, who was looking over the silver. Doctor Maradick, she explained to me presently, had his breakfast served in the morning-room on the other side of the house.

'And the little girl? Does she take her meals in the nursery?'

She threw me a startled glance. Was it, I questioned afterwards, one of distrust or apprehension?

'There isn't any little girl. Haven't you heard?'

'Heard? No. Why, I saw her only yesterday.'

The look she gave me—I was sure of it now—was full of alarm.

'The little girl—she was the sweetest child I ever saw—died just two months ago of pneumonia.'

'But she couldn't have died.' I was a fool to let this out, but the shock had completely unnerved me. 'I tell you I saw her yesterday.'

The alarm in her face deepened. 'That is Mrs Maradick's trouble. She believes that she still sees her.'

'But don't you see her?' I drove the question home bluntly.

'No.' She set her lips tightly. 'I never see anything.'

So I had been wrong, after all, and the explanation, when it came, only accentuated the terror. The child was dead—she had died of pneumonia two months ago—and yet I had seen her, with my own eyes, playing ball in the library; I had seen her slipping out of her mother's room, with her doll in her arms.

'Is there another child in the house? Could there be a child belonging to one of the servants?' A gleam had shot through the fog in which I was groping.

'No, there isn't any other. The doctors tried bringing one once, but it threw the poor lady into such a state she almost died of it. Besides, there wouldn't be any other child as quiet and sweet-looking as Dorothea. To see her skipping along in her dress of Scotch plaid used to make me think of a fairy, though they say that fairies wear nothing but white or green.'

'Has anyone else seen her—the child, I mean—any of the servants?'

'Only old Gabriel, the coloured butler, who came with Mrs Maradick's mother from South Carolina. I've heard that negroes often have a kind of second sight—though I don't know that that is just what you would call it. But they seem to believe in the supernatural by instinct, and Gabriel is so old and dotty—he does no work except answer the doorbell and clean the silver—that nobody pays much attention to anything that he sees——'

'Is the child's nursery kept as it used to be?'

'Oh, no. The doctor had all the toys sent to the children's hospital. That was a great grief to Mrs Maradick; but Doctor Brandon thought, and all the nurses agreed with him, that is was best for her not to be allowed to keep the room as it was when Dorothea was living.'

'Dorothea? Was that the child's name?'

'Yes, it means the gift of God, doesn't it? She was named after the mother of Mrs Maradick's first husband, Mr Ballard. He was the grave, quiet kind—not the least like the doctor.'

I wondered if the other dreadful obsession of Mrs Maradick's had drifted down through the nurses or the servants to the housekeeper; but she said nothing about it, and since she was, I suspected, a garrulous person, I thought it wiser to assume that the gossip had not reached her.

A little later, when breakfast was over and I had not yet gone upstairs to my room, I had my first interview with Doctor Brandon, the famous alienist who was in charge of the case. I had never seen him before, but from the first moment that I looked at him I took his measure almost by intuition. He was, I suppose, honest enough—I have always granted him that, bitterly as I have felt towards him. It wasn't his fault that he lacked red blood in his brain, or that he had formed the habit, from long association with abnormal phenomena, of regarding all life as a disease. He was the sort of physician—every nurse will understand what I mean—who deals instinctively with groups instead of with individuals. He was long and solemn and very round in the face; and I hadn't talked to him ten minutes before I knew he had been educated in Germany, and that he had learned over there to treat every emotion as a pathological manifestation. I used to wonder what he got out of life—what any one got out of life who had analyzed away everything except the bare structure.

When I reached my room at last, I was so tired that I could barely remember either the questions Doctor Brandon had asked or the directions he had given me. I fell asleep, I know, almost as soon as my head touched the pillow; and the maid who came to enquire if I wanted luncheon decided to let me finish my nap. In the afternoon, when she returned with a cup of tea, she found me still heavy and drowsy. Though I was used to night nursing, I felt as if I had danced from sunset to daybreak. It was fortunate, I reflected, while I drank my tea, that every case didn't wear on one's sympathies as acutely as Mrs Maradick's hallucination had worn on mine.

Through the day I did not see Doctor Maradick; but at seven o'clock when I came up from my early dinner on my way to take the place of Miss Peterson, who had kept on duty an hour later than usual, he met me in the hall and asked me to come into his study. I thought him handsomer than ever in his evening clothes, with a white flower in his buttonhole. He was going to some public dinner, the housekeeper told me, but, then, he was always going somewhere. I believe he didn't dine at home a single evening that winter.

'Did Mrs Maradick have a good night?' He had closed the door after us, and turning now with the question, he smiled kindly, as if he wished to put me at ease in the beginning.

'She slept very well after she took the medicine. I gave her that at eleven o'clock.'

For a minute he regarded me silently, and I was aware that his personality—his charm—was focused upon me. It was almost as if I stood in the centre of converging rays of light, so vivid was my impression of him.

'Did she allude in any way to her—to her hallucination?' he asked.

How the warning reached me—what invisible waves of sense-perception transmitted the message—I have never known; but while I stood there, facing the splendour of the doctor's presence, every intuition cautioned me that the time had come when I must take sides in the household. While I stayed there I must stand either with Mrs Maradick or against her.

'She talked quite rationally,' I replied after a moment.

'What did she say?'

'She told me how she was feeling, that she missed her child, and that she walked a little every day about her room.'

His face changed—how I could not at first determine.

'Have you seen Doctor Brandon?'

'He came this morning to give me his directions.'

'He thought her less well today. He has advised me to send her to Rosedale.'

I have never, even in secret, tried to account for Doctor Maradick. He may have been sincere. I tell you only what I know—not what I believe or imagine—and the human is sometimes as inscrutable, as inexplicable, as the supernatural.

While he watched me I was conscious of an inner struggle, as if opposing angels warred somewhere in the depths of my being. When at last I made my decision, I was acting less from reason, I knew, than in obedience to the pressure of some secret current of thought. Heaven knows, even then, the man held me captive while I defied him.

'Doctor Maradick,' I lifted my eyes for the first time frankly to his, 'I believe that your wife is as sane as I am—or as you are.'

He started. 'Then she did not talk freely to you?'

'She may be mistaken, unstrung, piteously distressed in mind'—I brought this out with emphasis—'but she is not—I am willing to stake my future on it—a fit subject for an asylum. It would be foolish—it would be cruel to send her to Rosedale.'

'Cruel, you say?' A troubled look crossed his face, and his voice grew very gentle. 'You do not imagine that I could be cruel to her?'

'No, I do not think that.' My voice also had softened.

'We will let things go on as they are. Perhaps Doctor Brandon may have some other suggestion to make.' He drew out his watch and compared it with the clock—nervously, I observed, as if his action were a screen for his discomfiture or perplexity. 'I must be going now. We will speak of this again in the morning.'

But in the morning we did not speak of it, and during the month that I nursed Mrs Maradick I was not called again into her husband's study. When I met him in the hall or on the staircase, which was seldom, he was as charming as ever; yet, in spite of his courtesy, I had a persistent feeling that he had taken my measure on that evening, and that he had no further use for me.

As the days went by Mrs Maradick seemed to grow stronger. Never, after our first night together, had she mentioned the child to me; never had she alluded by so much as a word to her dreadful charge against her husband. She was like any woman recovering from a great sorrow, except that she was sweeter and gentler. It is no wonder that everyone who came near her loved her; for there was a mysterious loveliness about her like the mystery of light, not of darkness. She was, I have always thought, as much of an angel as it is possible for a woman to be on this earth. And yet, angelic as she was, there were times when it seemed to

me that she both hated and feared her husband. Though he never
entered her room while I was there, and I never heard his name on her
lips until an hour before the end, still I could tell by the look of terror
in her face whenever his step passed down the hall that her very soul
shivered at his approach.

During the whole month I did not see the child again, though one
night, when I came suddenly into Mrs Maradick's room, I found a little
garden, such as children make out of pebbles and bits of box, on the
window-sill. I did not mention it to Mrs Maradick, and a little later,
as the maid lowered the shades, I noticed that the garden had vanished.
Since then I have often wondered if the child were invisible only to
the rest of us, and if her mother still saw her. But there was no way
of finding out except by questioning, and Mrs Maradick was so well
and patient that I hadn't the heart to question. Things couldn't have
been better with her than they were, and I was beginning to tell myself
that she might soon go out for an airing, when the end came so
suddenly.

It was a mild January day—the kind of day that brings the foretaste
of spring in the middle of winter, and when I came downstairs in the
afternoon, I stopped a minute by the window at the end of the hall to
look down on the box maze in the garden. There was an old fountain,
bearing two laughing boys in marble, in the centre of the gravelled walk,
and the water, which had been turned on that morning for Mrs
Maradick's pleasure, sparkled now like silver as the sunlight splashed
over it. I had never before felt the air quite so soft and springlike in
January; and I thought, as I gazed down on the garden, that it would be
a good idea for Mrs Maradick to go out and bask for an hour or so in
the sunshine. It seemed strange to me that she was never allowed to get
any fresh air except the air that came through her windows.

When I went into her room, however, I found that she had no wish
to go out. She was sitting, wrapped in shawls, by the open window,
which looked down on the fountain; and as I entered she glanced up
from a little book she was reading. A pot of daffodils stood on the
window-sill—she was very fond of flowers and we tried always to keep
some growing in her room.

'Do you know what I am reading, Miss Randolph?' she asked in her
soft voice; and she read aloud a verse while I went over to the candle-
stand to measure out a dose of medicine.

'"If thou hast two loaves of bread, sell one and buy daffodils, for
bread nourisheth the body, but daffodils delight the soul." That is very
beautiful, don't you think so?'

I said 'Yes,' that it was beautiful; and then I asked her if she wouldn't go downstairs and walk about in the garden.

'He wouldn't like it,' she answered; and it was the first time she had mentioned her husband to me since the night I came to her. 'He doesn't want me to go out.'

I tried to laugh her out of the idea; but it was no use, and after a few minutes I gave up and began talking of other things. Even then it did not occur to me that her fear of Doctor Maradick was anything but a fancy. I could see, of course, that she wasn't out of her head; but sane persons, I knew, sometimes have unaccountable prejudices, and I accepted her dislike as a mere whim or aversion. I did not understand then and—I may as well confess this before the end comes—I do not understand any better today. I am writing down the things I actually saw, and I repeat that I have never had the slightest twist in the direction of the miraculous.

The afternoon slipped away while we talked—she talked brightly when any subject came up that interested her—and it was the last hour of day—that grave, still hour when the movement of life seems to droop and falter for a few precious minutes—that brought us the thing I had dreaded silently since my first night in the house. I remember that I had risen to close the window, and was leaning out for a breath of the mild air, when there was the sound of steps, consciously softened, in the hall outside, and Doctor Brandon's usual knock fell on my ears. Then, before I could cross the room, the door opened, and the doctor entered with Miss Peterson. The day nurse, I knew, was a stupid woman; but she had never appeared to me so stupid, so armoured and encased in her professional manner, as she did at that moment.

'I am glad to see that you are taking the air.' As Doctor Brandon came over to the window, I wondered maliciously what devil of contradictions had made him a distinguished specialist in nervous diseases.

'Who was the other doctor you brought this morning?' asked Mrs Maradick gravely; and that was all I ever heard about the visit of the second alienist.

'Someone who is anxious to cure you.' He dropped into a chair beside her and patted her hand with his long, pale fingers. 'We are so anxious to cure you that we want to send you away to the country for a fortnight or so. Miss Peterson has come to help you to get ready, and I've kept my car waiting for you. There couldn't be a nicer day for a trip, could there?'

The moment had come at last. I knew at once what he meant, and so did Mrs Maradick. A wave of colour flowed and ebbed in her thin cheeks, and I felt her body quiver when I moved from the window and put my arms on her shoulders. I was aware again, as I had been aware that evening in Doctor Maradick's study, of a current of thought that beat from the air around into my brain. Though it cost me my career as a nurse and my reputation for sanity, I knew that I must obey that invisible warning.

'You are going to take me to an asylum,' said Mrs Maradick.

He made some foolish denial or evasion; but before he had finished I turned from Mrs Maradick and faced him impulsively. In a nurse this was flagrant rebellion, and I realized that the act wrecked my professional future. Yet I did not care—I did not hesitate. Something stronger than I was driving me on.

'Doctor Brandon,' I said, 'I beg you—I implore you to wait until tomorrow. There are things I must tell you.'

A queer look came into his face, and I understood, even in my excitement, that he was mentally deciding in which group he should place me—to which class of morbid manifestations I must belong.

'Very well, very well, we will hear everything,' he replied soothingly; but I saw him glance at Miss Peterson, and she went over to the wardrobe for Mrs Maradick's fur coat and hat.

Suddenly, without warning, Mrs Maradick threw the shawls away from her, and stood up. 'If you send me away,' she said, 'I shall never come back. I shall never live to come back.'

The grey of twilight was just beginning, and while she stood there, in the dusk of the room, her face shone out as pale and flower-like as the daffodils on the window-sill. 'I cannot go away!' she cried in a sharper voice. 'I cannot go away from my child!'

I saw her face clearly; I heard her voice; and then—the horror of the scene sweeps back over me!—I saw the door open slowly and the little girl run across the room to her mother. I saw the child lift her little arms, and I saw the mother stoop and gather her to her bosom. So closely locked were they in that passionate embrace that their forms seemed to mingle in the gloom that enveloped them.

'After this can you doubt?' I threw out the words almost savagely—and then, when I turned from the mother and child to Doctor Brandon and Miss Peterson, I knew breathlessly—oh, there was a shock in the discovery!—that they were blind to the child. Their blank faces revealed the consternation of ignorance, not of conviction. They had seen nothing except the vacant arms of the mother and the swift, erratic gesture with which she stooped to embrace some invisible presence. Only my vision—and I have asked myself since if the power of sympathy enabled me to penetrate the web of material fact and see the spiritual form of the child—only my vision was not blinded by the clay through which I looked.

'After this can you doubt?' Doctor Brandon had flung my words back to me. Was it his fault, poor man, if life had granted him only the eyes of flesh? Was it his fault if he could see only half of the thing there before him?

But they couldn't see, and since they couldn't see I realized that it was useless to tell them. Within an hour they took Mrs Maradick to the asylum; and she went quietly, though when the time came for parting from me she showed some faint trace of feeling. I remember that at the last, while we stood on the pavement, she lifted her black veil, which she wore for the child, and said: 'Stay with her, Miss Randolph, as long as you can. I shall never come back.'

Then she got into the car and was driven off, while I stood looking after her with a sob in my throat. Dreadful as I felt it to be, I didn't, of course, realize the full horror of it, or I couldn't have stood there quietly on the pavement. I didn't realize it, indeed, until several months afterwards when word came that she had died in the asylum. I never knew what her illness was, though I vaguely recall that something was said about 'heart failure'—a loose enough term. My own belief is that she died simply of the terror of life.

To my surprise Doctor Maradick asked me to stay on as his office nurse after his wife went to Rosedale; and when the news of her death came there was no suggestion of my leaving. I don't know to this day why he wanted me in the house. Perhaps he thought I should have less opportunity to gossip if I stayed under his roof; perhaps he still wished to test the power of his charm over me. His vanity was incredible in so great a man. I have seen him flush with pleasure when people turned to look at him in the street, and I know that he was not above playing on the sentimental weakness of his patients. But he was magnificent, heaven knows! Few men, I imagine, have been the objects of so many foolish infatuations.

The next summer Doctor Maradick went abroad for two months, and while he was away I took my vacation in Virginia. When we came back the work was heavier than ever—his reputation by this time was tremendous—and my days were so crowded with appointments, and hurried flittings to emergency cases, that I had scarcely a minute left in which to remember poor Mrs Maradick. Since the afternoon when she went to the asylum the child had not been in the house; and at last I was beginning to persuade myself that the little figure had been an optical

illusion—the effect of shifting lights in the gloom of the old rooms—
not the apparition I had once believed it to be. It does not take long for
a phantom to fade from the memory—especially when one leads the
active and methodical life I was forced into that winter. Perhaps—who
knows?—(I remember telling myself) the doctors may have been right,
after all, and the poor lady may have actually been out of her mind.
With this view of the past, my judgement of Doctor Maradick insen-
sibly altered. It ended, I think, in my acquitting him altogether. And
then, just as he stood clear and splendid in my verdict of him, the
reversal came so precipitately that I grow breathless now whenever I try
to live it over again. The violence of the next turn in affairs left me, I
often fancy, with a perpetual dizziness of the imagination.

It was in May that we heard of Mrs Maradick's death, and exactly a
year later, on a mild and fragrant afternoon, when the daffodils were
blooming in patches around the old fountain in the garden, the housekeeper came into the office, where I lingered over some accounts, to
bring me news of the doctor's approaching marriage.

'It is no more than we might have expected,' she concluded rationally. 'The house must be lonely for him—he is such a sociable man. But
I can't help feeling,' she brought out slowly after a pause in which I felt
a shiver pass over me, 'I can't help feeling that it is hard for that other
woman to have all the money poor Mrs Maradick's first husband left
her.'

'There is a great deal of money, then?' I asked curiously.

'A great deal.' She waved her hand, as if words were futile to express
the sum. 'Millions and millions!'

'They will give up this house, of course?'

'That's done already, my dear. There won't be a brick left of it by this
time next year. It's to be pulled down and an apartment-house built on
the ground.'

Again the shiver passed over me. I couldn't bear to think of Mrs
Maradick's old home falling to pieces.

'You didn't tell me the name of the bride,' I said. 'Is she someone he
met while he was in Europe?'

'Dear me, no! She is the very lady he was engaged to before he
married Mrs Maradick, only she threw him over, so people said, because
he wasn't rich enough. Then she married some lord or prince from over
the water; but there was a divorce, and now she has turned again to her
old lover. He is rich enough now, I guess, even for her!'

It was all perfectly true, I suppose; it sounded as plausible as a story
out of a newspaper; and yet while she told me I felt, or dreamed that I

felt, a sinister, an impalpable hush in the air. I was nervous, no doubt; I was shaken by the suddenness with which the housekeeper had sprung her news on me; but as I sat there I had quite vividly an impression that the old house was listening—that there was a real, if invisible, presence somewhere in the room or the garden. Yet, when an instant afterwards I glanced through the long window which opened down to the brick terrace, I saw only the faint sunshine over the deserted garden, with its maze of box, its marble fountain, and its patches of daffodils.

The housekeeper had gone—one of the servants, I think, came for her—and I was sitting at my desk when the works of Mrs Maradick on that last evening floated into my mind. The daffodils brought her back to me; for I thought, as I watched them growing, so still and golden in the sunshine, how she would have enjoyed them. Almost unconsciously I repeated the verse she had read to me:

'If thou hast two loaves of bread, sell one and buy daffodils'—and it was at this very instant, while the words were still on my lips, that I turned my eyes to the box maze, and saw the child skipping rope along the gravelled path to the fountain. Quite distinctly, as clear as day, I saw her come, with what children call the dancing step, between the low box borders to the place where the daffodils bloomed by the fountain. From her straight brown hair to her frock of Scotch plaid and her little feet, which twinkled in white socks and black slippers over the turning rope, she was as real to me as the ground on which she trod or the laughing marble boys under the splashing water. Starting up from my chair, I made a single step to the terrace. If I could only reach her—only speak to her—I felt that I might at last solve the mystery. But with the first flutter of my dress on the terrace, the airy little form melted into the quiet dusk of the maze. Not a breath stirred the daffodils, not a shadow passed over the sparkling flow of the water; yet, weak and shaken in every nerve, I sat down on the brick step of the terrace and burst into tears. I must have known that something terrible would happen before they pulled down Mrs Maradick's home.

The doctor dined out that night. He was with the lady he was going to marry, the housekeeper told me; and it must have been almost midnight when I heard him come in and go upstairs to his room. I was downstairs because I had been unable to sleep, and the book I wanted to finish I had left that afternoon in the office. The book—I can't remember what it was—had seemed to me very exciting when I began it in the morning; but after the visit of the child I found the romantic novel as dull as a treatise on nursing. It was impossible for me to follow the lines, and I was on the point of giving up and going to bed, when

Doctor Maradick opened the front door with his latchkey and went up the staircase. 'There can't be a bit of truth in it.' I thought over and over again as I listened to his even step ascending the stairs. 'There can't be a bit of truth in it.' And yet, though I assured myself that 'there couldn't be a bit of truth in it,' I shrank, with a creepy sensation, from going through the house to my room in the third storey. I was tired out after a hard day, and my nerves must have reacted morbidly to the silence and the darkness. For the first time in my life I knew what it was to be afraid of the unknown, of the unseen; and while I bent over my book, in the glare of the electric light, I became conscious presently that I was straining my senses for some sound in the spacious emptiness of the rooms overhead. The noise of a passing motor-car in the street jerked me back from the intense hush of expectancy; and I can recall the wave of relief that swept over me as I turned to my book again and tried to fix my distracted mind on its pages.

I was still sitting there when the telephone on my desk rang, with what seemed to my overwrought nerves a startling abruptness, and the voice of the superintendent told me hurriedly that Doctor Maradick was needed at the hospital. I had become so accustomed to these emergency calls in the night that I felt reassured when I had rung up the doctor in his room and had heard the hearty sound of his response. He had not yet undressed, he said, and would come down immediately while I ordered back his car, which must just have reached the garage.

'I'll be with you in five minutes!' he called as cheerfully as if I had summoned him to his wedding.

I heard him cross the floor of his room; and before he could reach the head of the staircase, I opened the door and went out into the hall in order that I might turn on the light and have his hat and coat waiting. The electric button was at the end of the hall, and as I moved towards it, guided by the glimmer that fell from the landing above, I lifted my eyes to the staircase, which climbed dimly, with its slender mahogany balustrade, as far as the third storey. Then it was, at the very moment when the doctor, humming gaily, began his quick descent of the steps, that I distinctly saw—I will swear to this on my deathbed—a child's skipping rope lying loosely coiled, as if it had dropped from a careless little hand, in the bend of the staircase. With a spring I had reached the electric button, flooding the hall with light; but as I did so, while my arm was still outstretched behind me, I heard the humming voice change to a cry of surprise or terror, and the figure on the staircase tripped heavily and stumbled with groping hands into emptiness. The scream of warning died in my throat while I watched him pitch forward down the long flight of stairs to the floor at my feet. Even before I bent over him, before I wiped the blood from his brow and felt for his silent heart, I knew that he was dead.

Something—it may have been, as the world believes, a misstep in the dimness, or it may have been, as I am ready to bear witness, an invisible judgement—something had killed him at the very moment when he most wanted to live.

THE DIARY OF MR POYNTER

M. R. James

The sale-room of an old and famous firm of book auctioneers in London is, of course, a great meeting-place for collectors, librarians, and dealers: not only when an auction is in progress, but perhaps even more notably when books that are coming on for sale are upon view. It was in such a sale-room that the remarkable series of events began which were detailed to me not many months ago by the person whom they principally affected—namely, Mr James Denton, MA, FSA, etc., etc., sometime of Trinity Hall, now, or lately, of Rendcomb Manor in the county of Warwick.

He, on a certain spring day in a recent year, was in London for a few days upon business connected principally with the furnishing of the house which he had just finished building at Rendcomb. It may be a disappointment to you to learn that Rendcomb Manor was new; that I cannot help. There had, no doubt, been an old house; but it was not remarkable for beauty or interest. Even had it been, neither beauty nor interest would have enabled it to resist the disastrous fire which about a couple of years before the date of my story had razed it to the ground. I am glad to say that all that was most valuable in it had been saved, and that it was fully insured. So that it was with a comparatively light heart that Mr Denton was able to face the task of building a new and considerably more convenient dwelling for himself and his aunt who constituted his whole *ménage*.

Being in London, with time on his hands, and not far from the sale-room at which I have obscurely hinted, Mr Denton thought that he would spend an hour there upon the chance of finding, among that portion of the famous Thomas collection of manuscripts, which he knew to be then on view, something bearing upon the history or topography of his part of Warwickshire.

He turned in accordingly, purchased a catalogue and ascended to the sale-room, where, as usual, the books were disposed in cases and some laid out upon the long tables. At the shelves, or sitting about at the tables, were figures, many of whom were familiar to him. He exchanged nods and greetings with several, and then settled down to examine his catalogue and note likely items. He had made good progress through about two hundred of the five hundred lots—every now and then rising to take a volume from the shelf and give it a cursory glance—when a hand was laid on his shoulder, and he looked up. His interrupter was one of those intelligent men with a pointed beard and a flannel shirt, of whom the last quarter of the nineteenth century was, it seems to me, very prolific.

It is no part of my plan to repeat the whole conversation which ensued between the two. I must content myself with stating that it largely referred to common acquaintances, e.g., to the nephew of Mr Denton's friend who had recently married and settled in Chelsea, to the sister-in-law of Mr Denton's friend who had been seriously indisposed, but was now better, and to a piece of china which Mr Denton's friend had purchased some months before at a price much below its true value. From which you will rightly infer that the conversation was rather in the nature of a monologue. In due time, however, the friend bethought himself that Mr Denton was there for a purpose, and said he, 'What are you looking out for in particular? I don't think there's much in this lot.' 'Why, I thought there might be some Warwickshire collections, but I don't see anything under Warwick in the catalogue.' 'No, apparently not,' said the friend. 'All the same, I believe I noticed something like a Warwickshire diary. What was the name again? Drayton? Potter? Painter—either a P or a D, I feel sure.' He turned over the leaves quickly. 'Yes, here it is. Poynter. Lot 486. That might interest you. There are the books, I think: out on the table. Someone has been looking at them. Well, I must be getting on. Goodbye—you'll look us up, won't you? Couldn't you come this afternoon? we've got a little music about four, Well, then, when you're next in town.' He went off. Mr Denton looked at his watch and found to his confusion that he could spare no more than a moment before retrieving his luggage and going for the train. The moment was just enough to show him that there were four largish volumes of the diary—that it concerned the years about 1710, and that there seemed to be a good many insertions in it of various kinds. It seemed quite worth while to leave a commission of five and twenty pounds for it, and this he was able to do, for his usual agent entered the room as he was on the point of leaving it.

That evening he rejoined his aunt at their temporary abode, which was a small dower-house not many hundred yards from the Manor. On the following morning the two resumed a discussion that had now lasted for some weeks as to the equipment of the new house. Mr Denton laid before his relative a statement of the results of his visit to town—

particulars of carpets, of chairs, of wardrobes, and of bedroom china. 'Yes, dear,' said his aunt, 'but I don't see any chintzes here. Did you go to ——?' Mr Denton stamped on the floor (where else, indeed, could he have stamped?). 'Oh dear, oh dear,' he said, 'the one thing I missed. I *am* sorry. The fact is I was on my way there and I happened to be passing Robins's. His aunt threw up her hands. 'Robins's! Then the next thing will be another parcel of horrible old books at some outrageous price. I do think, James, when I am taking all this trouble for you, you might contrive to remember the one or two things which I specially begged you to see after. It's not as if I was asking it for myself. I don't know whether you think I get any pleasure out of it, but if so I can assure you it's very much the reverse. The thought and worry and trouble I have over it you have no idea of, and *you* have simply to go to the shops and order the things.' Mr Denton interposed a moan of penitence. 'Oh, aunt——' 'Yes that's all very well, dear, and I don't want to speak sharply, but you *must* know how very annoying it is: particularly as it delays the whole of our business for I can't tell how long: here is Wednesday—the Simpsons come tomorrow, and you can't leave them. Then on Saturday we have friends, as you know, coming for tennis. Yes, indeed, you spoke of asking them yourself, but, of course, I had to write the notes, and it is ridiculous, James, to look like that. We must occasionally be civil to our neighbours: you wouldn't like to have it said we were perfect bears. What was I saying? Well, anyhow it comes to this, that it must be Thursday in next week at least, before you can go to town again, and until we have decided upon the chintzes it is impossible to settle upon one single other thing.'

Mr Denton ventured to suggest that as the paint and wallpapers had been dealt with, this was too severe a view: but this his aunt was not prepared to admit at the moment. Nor, indeed, was there any proposition he could have advanced which she would have found herself able to accept. However, as the day went on, she receded a little from this position: examined with lessening disfavour the samples and price lists submitted by her nephew, and even in some cases gave a qualified approval to his choice.

As for him, he was naturally somewhat dashed by the consciousness of duty unfulfilled, but more so by the prospect of a lawn-tennis party, which, though an inevitable evil in August, he had thought there was no occasion to fear in May. But he was to some extent cheered by the arrival on the Friday morning of an intimation that he had secured at the price of £12 10s. the four volumes of Poynter's manuscript diary, and still more by the arrival on the next morning of the diary itself.

THE DIARY OF MR POYNTER 49

The necessity of taking Mr and Mrs Simpson for a drive in the car on Saturday morning and of attending to his neighbours and guests that afternoon prevented him from doing more than open the parcel until the party had retired to bed on the Saturday night. It was then that he made certain of the fact, which he had before only suspected, that he had indeed acquired the diary of Mr William Poynter, Squire of Acrington (about four miles from his own parish)—that same Poynter who was for a time a member of the circle of Oxford antiquaries, the center of which was Thomas Hearne, and with whom Hearne seems ultimately to have quarrelled—a not uncommon episode in the career of that excellent man. As is the case with Hearne's own collections, the diary of Poynter contained a good many notes from printed books, descriptions of coins and other antiquities that had been brought to his notice, and drafts of letters on these subjects, besides the chronicle of everyday events. The description in the sale catalogue had given Mr Denton no idea of the amount of interest which seemed to lie in the book, and he sat up reading in the first of the four volumes until a reprehensibly late hour.

On the Sunday morning, after church, his aunt came into the study and was diverted from what she had been going to say to him by the sight of the four brown leather quartos on the table. 'What are these?' she said suspiciously. 'New, aren't they? Oh! are these the things that made you forget my chintzes? I thought so. Disgusting. What did you give for them, I should like to know? Over Ten Pounds: James, it is really sinful. Well, if you have money to throw away on this kind of thing, there *can* be no reason why you should not subscribe—and subscribe handsomely—to my anti-Vivisection League. There is not, indeed, James, and I shall be very seriously annoyed if——. Who did you say wrote them? Old Mr Poynter, of Acrington? Well, of course, there is some interest in getting together old papers about this neighbourhood. But Ten Pounds!' She picked up one of the volumes— not that which her nephew had been reading—and opened it at random, dashing it to the floor the next instant with a cry of disgust as an earwig fell from between the pages. Mr Denton picked it up with a smothered expletive and said, 'Poor book! I think you're rather hard on Mr Poynter.' 'Was I, my dear? I beg his pardon, but you know I cannot abide those horrid creatures. Let me see if I've done any mischief.' 'No, I think all's well: but look here what you've opened him on.' 'Dear me, yes, to be sure! how very interesting. Do unpin it, James, and let me look at it.'

It was a piece of patterned stuff about the size of the quarto page, to which it was fastened by an old-fashioned pin. James detached it and handed it to his aunt, carefully replacing the pin in the paper.

Now, I do not know exactly what the fabric was; but it had a design printed upon it, which completely fascinated Miss Denton. She went into raptures over it, held it against the wall, made James do the same, that she might retire to contemplate it from a distance: then pored over it at close quarters, and ended her examination by expressing in the warmest terms her appreciation of the taste of the ancient Mr Poynter who had had the happy idea of preserving this sample in his diary. 'It is a most charming pattern,' she said, 'and remarkable too. Look, James, how delightfully the lines ripple. It reminds one of hair, very much, doesn't it? And then these knots of ribbon at intervals. They give just the relief of colour that is wanted. I wonder——' 'I was going to say,' said James with deference, 'I wonder if it would cost much to have it copied for our curtains.' 'Copied? how could you have it copied, James?' 'Well, I don't know the details, but I suppose that is a printed pattern, and that you could have a block cut from it in wood or metal.' 'Now, really, that is a capital idea, James. I am almost inclined to be glad that you were so—that you forgot the chintzes on Wednesday. At any rate, I'll promise to forgive and forget if you get this *lovely* old thing copied. No one will have anything in the least like it, and mind, James, we won't allow it to be sold. Now I *must* go, and I've totally forgotten what it was I came in to say: never mind, it'll keep.'

After his aunt had gone James Denton devoted a few minutes to examining the pattern more closely than he had yet had a chance of doing. He was puzzled to think why it should have struck Miss Denton so forcibly. It seemed to him not specially remarkable or pretty. No doubt it was suitable enough for a curtain pattern: it ran in vertical bands, and there was some indication that these were intended to converge at the top. She was right, too, in thinking that these main bands resembled rippling—almost curling—tresses of hair. Well, the main thing was to find out by means of trade directories, or otherwise, what firm would undertake the reproduction of an old pattern of this kind. Not to delay the reader over this portion of the story, a list of likely names was made out, and Mr Denton fixed a day for calling on them, or some of them, with his sample.

The first two visits which he paid were unsuccessful: but there is luck in odd numbers. The firm in Bermondsey which was third on his list was accustomed to handling this line. The evidence they were able to produce justified their being entrusted with the job. 'Our Mr Cattell' took a fervent personal interest in it. 'It's' eartrending, isn't it, sir,' he said, 'to picture the quantity of reelly lovely medeevial stuff of this kind that lays wellnigh unnoticed in many of our residential country 'ouses: much of it in peril, I take it, of being cast aside as so much rubbish. What is it Shakespeare says—unconsidered trifles. Ah, I often say he 'as a word for us all, sir. I say Shakespeare, but I'm well aware all don't 'old with me there—I 'ad something of an upset the other day when a gentleman came in—a titled man, too, he was, and I think he told me he'd wrote on the topic, and I 'appened to cite out something about 'Ercules and the painted cloth. Dear me, you never see such a pother. But as to this, what you've kindly confided to us, it's a piece of work we shall take a reel enthusiasm in achieving it out to the very best of our ability. What man 'as done, as I was observing only a few weeks back to another esteemed client, man can do, and in three to four weeks' time, all being well, we shall 'ope to lay before you evidence to that effect, sir. Take the address, Mr 'Iggins, if you please.'

Such was the general drift of Mr Cattell's observations on the occasion of his first interview with Mr Denton. About a month later, being advised that some samples were ready for his inspection, Mr Denton met him again, and had, it seems, reason to be satisfied with the faithfulness of the reproduction of the design. It had been finished off at the top in accordance with the indication I mentioned, so that the vertical bands joined. But something still needed to be done in the way of matching the colour of the original. Mr Cattell had suggestions of a technical kind to offer, with which I need not trouble you. He had also views as to the general desirability of the pattern which were vaguely adverse. 'You say you don't wish this to be supplied excepting to personal friends equipped with a authorization from yourself, sir. It shall be done. I quite understand your wish to keep it exclusive: lends a catchit, does it not, to the suite? What's every man's, it's been said, is no man's.'

'Do you think it would be popular if it were generally obtainable?' asked Mr Denton.

'I 'ardly think it, sir,' said Cattell, pensively clasping his beard. 'I 'ardly think it. Not popular: it wasn't popular with the man that cut the block, was it, Mr 'Iggins?'

'Did he find it a difficult job?'

'He'd no call to do so, sir; but the fact is that the artistic temperament—and our men are artists, sir, every one of them—true artists as much as many that the world styles by that term—it's apt to take some strange 'ardly accountable likes or dislikes, and here was an example. The twice or thrice that I went to inspect his progress: language I could understand, for that's 'abitual to him, but reel distaste for what I should call a dainty enough thing, I did not, nor am I now able to fathom. It seemed,' said Mr Cattell, looking narrowly upon Mr Denton, 'as if the man scented something almost Hevil in the design.'

'Indeed? did he tell you so? I can't say I see anything sinister in it myself.'

'Neether can I, sir. In fact I said as much. "Come, Gatwick," I said, "what's to do here? What's the reason of your prejudice—for I can call it no more than that?" But, no! no explanation was forthcoming. And I was merely reduced, as I am now, to a shrug of the shoulders, and a *cui bono*. However, here it is,' and with that the technical side of the question came to the front again.

The matching of the colours for the background, the hem, and the knots of ribbon was by far the longest part of the business, and necessitated many sendings to and fro of the original pattern and of new samples. During part of August and September, too, the Dentons were away from the Manor. So that it was not until October was well in that a sufficient quantity of the stuff had been manufactured to furnish curtains for the three or four bedrooms which were to be fitted up with it.

On the feast of Simon and Jude the aunt and nephew returned from a short visit to find all completed, and their satisfaction at the general effect was great. The new curtains, in particular, agreed to admiration with their surroundings. When Mr Denton was dressing for dinner, and took stock of his room, in which there was a large amount of the chintz displayed, he congratulated himself over and over again on the luck which had first made him forget his aunt's commission and had then put into his hands this extremely effective means of remedying his mistake. The pattern was, as he said at dinner, so restful and yet so far from being dull. And Miss Denton—who, by the way, had none of the stuff in her own room—was much disposed to agree with him.

At breakfast next morning he was induced to qualify his satisfaction to some extent—but very slightly. 'There is one thing I rather regret,' he said, 'that we allowed them to join up the vertical bands of the pattern at the top. I think it would have been better to leave that alone.'

'Oh?' said his aunt interrogatively.

'Yes: as I was reading in bed last night they kept catching my eye rather. That is, I found myself looking across at them every now and then. There was an effect as if someone kept peeping out between the curtains in one place or another, where there was no edge, and I think that was due to the joining up of the bands at the top. The only other thing that troubled me was the wind.'

'Why, I thought it was a perfectly still night.'

'Perhaps it was only on my side of the house, but there was enough to sway my curtains and rustle them more than I wanted.'

That night a bachelor friend of James Denton's came to stay, and was lodged in a room on the same floor as his host, but at the end of a long passage, half-way down which was a red baize door, put there to cut off the draught and intercept noise.

The party of three had separated. Miss Denton a good first, the two men at about eleven. James Denton, not yet inclined for bed, sat him down in an armchair and read for a time. Then he dozed, and then he woke, and bethought himself that his brown spaniel, which ordinarily slept in his room, had not come upstairs with him. Then he thought he was mistaken: for happening to move his hand which hung down over the arm of the chair within a few inches of the floor, he felt on the back of it just the slightest touch of a surface of hair, and stretching it out in that direction he stroked and patted a rounded something. But the feel of it, and still more the fact that instead of a responsive movement, absolute stillness greeted his touch, made him look over the arm. What he had been touching rose to meet him. It was in the attitude of one that had crept along the floor on its belly, and it was, so far as could be recollected, a human figure. But of the face which was now rising to within a few inches of his own no feature was discernible, only hair. Shapeless as it was, there was about it so horrible an air of menace that as he bounded from his chair and rushed from the room he heard himself moaning with fear: and doubtless he did right to fly. As he dashed into the baize door that cut the passage in two, and—forgetting that it opened towards him—beat against it with all the force in him, he felt a soft ineffectual tearing at his back which, all the same, seemed to be growing in power, as if the hand, or whatever worse than a hand was there, were becoming more material as the pursuer's rage was more concentrated. Then he remembered the trick of the door—he got it open—he shut it behind him—he gained his friend's room, and that is all we need know.

It seems curious that, during all the time that had elapsed since the purchase of Poynter's diary, James Denton should not have sought an explanation of the presence of the pattern that had been pinned into it. Well, he had read the diary through without finding it mentioned, and had concluded that there was nothing to be said. But, on leaving Rendcomb Manor (he did not know whether for good), as he naturally insisted upon doing on the day after experiencing the horror I have tried to put into words, he took the diary with him. And at his seaside lodgings he examined more narrowly the portion whence the pattern had been taken. What he remembered having suspected about it turned out to be correct. Two or three leaves were pasted together, but written upon, as was patent when they were held up to the light. They yielded easily to steaming, for the paste had lost much of its strength and they contained something relevant to the pattern.

The entry was made in 1707.

Old Mr Casbury, of Acrington, told me this day much of young Sir Everard Charlett, whom he remember'd Commoner of University College, and thought was of the same family as Dr Arthur Charlett, now master of yᵉ Coll. This Charlett was a personable young gent., but a loose atheistical companion, and a great lifter, as they then call'd the hard drinkers, and for what I know do so now. He was noted, and subject to severall censures at different times for his extravagancies: and if the full history of his debaucheries had bin known, no doubt would have been expell'd yᵉ Coll., supposing that no interest had been imploy'd on his behalf, of which Mr Casbury had some suspicion. He was a very beautiful person, and constantly wore his own Hair, which was very abundant, from which, and his loose way of living, the cant name for him was Absalom, and he was accustom'd to say that indeed he believ'd he had short-ened old David's days, meaning his father, Sir Job Charlett, an old worthy cavalier.

Note that Mr Casbury said that he remembers not the year of Sir Everard Charlett's death, but it was 1692 or 3. He died suddenly in October. [Several lines describing his unpleasant habits and reputed delinquencies are omitted.] Having seen him in such topping spirits the night before, Mr Casbury was amaz'd when he learn'd the death. He was found in the town ditch, the hair as was said pluck'd clean off his head. Most bells in Oxford rung out for him, being a nobleman, and he was buried next night in St Peter's in the East. But two years after, being to be moved to his country estate by his successor, it was said the coffin, breaking by mischance, proved quite full of Hair: which sounds fabulous, but yet I believe precedents are upon record, as in Dr Plot's *History of Staffordshire.*

His chambers being afterwards stripp'd Mr Casbury came by part of the hangings of it, which 'twas said this Charlett had design'd expressly for a memoriall of his Hair, giving the Fellow that drew it a lock to work by, and the piece which I have fasten'd in here was parcel of the same, which Mr Casbury gave to me. He said he believ'd there was a subtlety in the drawing, but had never discover'd it himself, nor much liked to pore upon it.

The money spent upon the curtains might as well have been thrown into the fire, as they were. Mr Cattell's comment upon what he heard of the story took the form of a quotation from Shakespeare. You may guess it without difficulty. It began with the words 'There are more things'.

MRS PORTER AND MISS ALLEN

Hugh Walpole

O ne of the largest flats on the fourth floor of Hortons was taken in March 1919 by a Mrs Porter, a widow. The flat was seen, and all business in connection with it was done, by a Miss Allen, her lady companion. Mr Nix, who considered himself a sound and trenchant judge of human nature, liked Miss Allen from the first; and then when he saw Mrs Porter he liked her too. These were just the tenants for Hortons—modest, gentle ladies with ample means and no extravagant demands on human nature. Mrs Porter was one of those old ladies, now, alas, in our turbulent times, less and less easy to discover—'something straight out of a book,' Mr Nix called her. She was little and fragile, dressed in silver grey, forehead puckered a little with a sort of anticipation of being a trial to others, her voice cultured, soft, a little remote like the chime of a distant clock. She moved with gestures a little deprecatory, a little resigned, extremely modest—she would not disturb anyone for the world. . . .

Miss Allen was, of course, another type—a woman of perhaps forty years of age, refined, quiet, efficient, her dark hair, turning now a little grey, waved decorously from her high white forehead, pince-nez, eyes of a grave, considering brown, a woman resigned, after, it might be, abandoning young ambitions for a place of modest and decent labour in the world—one might still see, in the rather humorous smile that she bestowed once and again upon men and things, the hint of defiance at the necessity that forced abnegation.

Miss Allen had not been in Mrs Porter's service for very long. Wearied with the exactions of a family of children whose idle and uninspiring intelligences she was attempting to governess, she answered, at the end of 1918, an advertisement in the 'Agony' column of *The Times*, that led her to Mrs Porter. She loved Mrs Porter at first sight.

'Why, she's a dear old lady,' she exclaimed to her ironic spirit—'dear old ladies' being in those days as rare as crinolines. She was of the kind for which Miss Allen had unconsciously been looking: generous, gentle, refined, and intelligent. Moreover, she had, within the last six months, been left quite alone in the world—Mr Porter had died of apoplexy in

August 1918. He had left her very wealthy, and Miss Allen discovered quickly in the old lady a rather surprising desire to see and enjoy life— surprising, because old ladies of seventy-one years of age and of Mrs Porter's gentle appearance do not, as a rule, care for noise and bustle and the buzz of youthful energy.

'I want to be in the very middle of things, dear Miss Allen,' said Mrs Porter, 'right in the very middle. We lived at Wimbledon long enough, Henry and I—it wasn't good for either of us. Find me somewhere within two minutes of all the best theatres.'

Miss Allen found Hortons, which is, as everyone knows, in Duke Street, just behind Piccadilly and Fortnum and Mason's, and Hatchard's and the Hammam Turkish Baths and the Royal Academy and Scott's hat-shop and Jackson's Jams—how could you be more perfectly in the centre of London?

Then Miss Allen discovered a curious thing—namely, that Mrs Porter did not wish to keep a single piece, fragment, or vestige of her Wimbledon effects. She insisted on an auction—everything was sold. Miss Allen attempted a remonstrance—some of the things in the Wimbledon house were very fine, handsome, solid mid-Victorian sideboards and cupboards, and chairs and tables.

'You really have no idea, Mrs Porter,' said Miss Allen, 'of the cost of furniture these days. It is quite terrible; you will naturally get a wonderful price for your things, but the difficulty of buying——'

Mrs Porter was determined. She nodded her bright bird-like head, tapped with her delicate fingers on the table and smiled at Miss Allen.

'If you don't mind, dear. I know it's tiresome for you, but I have my reasons.' It was not tiresome at all for Miss Allen; she loved to buy pretty new things at someone else's expense, but it was now, for the first time, that she began to wonder how dearly Mrs Porter had loved her husband.

Through the following weeks this became her principal preoccupation—Mr Henry Porter. She could not have explained to herself why this was. She was not, by nature, an inquisitive and scandal-loving woman, nor was she unusually imaginative. People did not, as a rule, occur to her as existing unless she saw them physically there in front of her. Nevertheless she spent a good deal of her time in considering Mr Porter.

She was able to make the Horton flat very agreeable. Mrs Porter wanted 'life and colour', so the sitting-room had curtains with pink roses and a bright yellow cage with two canaries, and several pretty water-colours, and a handsome fire-screen with golden peacocks, and a deep Turkish carpet, soft and luxurious to the feet. Not one thing from the Wimbledon house was there, not any single picture of Mr Porter. The next thing that Miss Allen discovered was that Mrs Porter was nervous.

Although Hortons sheltered many human beings within its boundaries, it was, owing to the thickness of its walls and the beautiful training of Mr Nix's servants, a very quiet place. It had been even called in its day 'cloistral'. It simply shared with London that amazing and never-to-be-overlauded gift of being able to offer, in the very centre of the traffic of the world, little green spots of quiet and tranquillity. It seemed, after a week or two, that it was almost too quiet for Mrs Porter.

'Open a window, Lucy dear, won't you,' she said. 'I like to hear the omnibuses.'

It was a chill evening in early April, but Miss Allen threw up the window. They sat there listening. There was no sound, only suddenly, as though to accentuate the silence, St James's Church clock struck the quarter. Then an omnibus rumbled, rattled, and was gone. The room was more silent than before.

'Shall I read to you?' said Miss Allen.

'Yes, dear, do.' And they settled down to *Martin Chuzzlewit*.

Mrs Porter's apprehensiveness became more and more evident. She was so dear an old lady, and had won so completely Miss Allen's heart, that that kindly woman could not bear to see her suffer. For the first time in her life she wanted to ask questions. It seemed to her that there must be some very strange reason for Mrs Porter's silences. She was not by nature a silent old lady; she talked continually, seemed, indeed, positively to detest the urgency of silence. She especially loved to tell Miss Allen about her early days. She had grown up as a girl in Plymouth, and she could remember all the events of that time—the balls, the walks on the Hoe, the shops, the summer visits into Glebeshire, the old dark house with the high garden walls, the cuckoo clock and the pictures of the strange old ships in which her father, who was a retired sea-captain, had sailed. She could not tell Miss Allen enough about these things, but so soon as she arrived at her engagement to Mr Porter there was silence. London shrouded her married life with its thick, grey pall. She hated that Miss Allen should leave her. She was very generous about Miss Allen's freedom, always begging her to take an afternoon or evening and amuse herself with her own friends; but Miss Allen had very few friends, and on her return from an expedition she always found the old lady miserable, frightened, and bewildered. She found that she loved her, that she cared for her as she had cared for no human being for many years, so she stayed with her and read to her and talked to her, and saw less and less of the outside world.

The two ladies made occasionally an expedition to a theatre or a concert, but these adventures, although they were anticipated with eagerness and pleasure, were always in the event disappointing. Mrs Porter loved the theatre; especially did she adore plays of sentiment—plays where young people were happily united, where old people sat cosily together reminiscing over a blazing fire, where surly guardians where suddenly generous, and poor orphan girls were unexpectedly given fortunes.

Mrs Porter started her evening with eager excitement. She dressed for the occasion, putting on her best lace cap, her cameo brooch, her smartest shoes. A taxi came for them, and they always had the best stalls, near the front, so that the old lady should not miss a word. Miss Allen noticed, however, that very quickly Mrs Porter began to be disturbed. She would glance around the theatre and soon her colour would fade, her hands begin to tremble; then, perhaps at the end of the first act, perhaps later, a little hand would press Miss Allen's arm:

'I think, dear, if you don't mind—I'm tired—shall we not go?'

After a little while Miss Allen suggested the cinema. Mrs Porter received the idea with eagerness. They went to the West-End house, and the first occasion was a triumphant success. How Mrs Porter loved it! Just the kind of story for her—Mary Pickford in *Daddy Long Legs*. To tell the truth, Mrs Porter cried her eyes out. She swore that she had never in her life enjoyed anything so much. And the music! How beautiful! How restful! They would go every week. . . .

The second occasion was, unfortunately, disastrous. The story was one of modern life, a woman persecuted by her husband, driven by his brutality into the arms of her lover. The husband was the customary cinema villain—broad, stout, sneering, and over-dressed. Mrs Porter fainted and had to be carried out by two attendants. A doctor came to see her, said that she was suffering from nervous exhaustion and must be protected from all excitement. . . . The two ladies sat now every evening in their pretty sitting-room, and Miss Allen read aloud the novels of Dickens one after the other.

More and more persistently, in spite of herself, did curiosity about the late Mr Porter drive itself in upon Miss Allen. She told herself that curiosity was vulgar and unworthy of the philosophy that she had created for herself out of life. Nevertheless it persisted. Soon she felt that, after all, it was justified. Were she to help this poor old lady to whom she was now most deeply attached, she must know more. She

could not give her any real help unless she might gauge more accurately
her trouble—but she was a shy woman, shy, especially, of forcing
personal confidences. She hesitated; then she was aware that a barrier
was being created between them. The evening had many silences, and
Miss Allen detected many strange, surreptitious glances thrown at her
by the old lady. The situation was impossible. One night she asked her
a question.

'Dear Mrs Porter,' she said, her heart beating strangely as she spoke,
'I do hope that you will not think me impertinent, but you have been
so good to me that you have made me love you. You are suffering, and
I cannot bear to see you unhappy. I want, oh, so eagerly, to help you! Is
there nothing I can do?'

Mrs Porter said nothing. Her hands quivered; then a tear stole down
her cheek. Miss Allen went over to her, sat down beside her and took her
hand.

'You must let me help you,' she said. 'Dismiss me if I am asking you
questions that I should not. But I would rather leave you altogether,
happy though I am with you, than see you so miserable. Tell me what
I can do.'

'You can do nothing, Lucy dear,' said the old lady.

'But I must be able to do something. You are keeping from me some
secret——'

Mrs Porter shook her head. . . .

It was one evening in early May that Miss Allen was suddenly
conscious that there was something wrong with the pretty little sitting-
room, and it was shortly after her first consciousness of this that poor
old Mrs Porter revealed her secret. Miss Allen, looking up for a moment, fancied that the little white marble clock on the mantelpiece had
ceased to tick.

She looked across the room, and for a strange moment fancied that
she could see neither the clock nor the mantelpiece—a grey dimness
filled her sight. She shook herself, glanced down at her hands, looked up
for reassurance, and found Mrs Porter, with wide, terrified eyes, staring
at her, her hands trembling against the wood of the table.

'What is it, Lucy?'

'Nothing, Mrs Porter.'

'Did you see something?'

'No, dear.'

'Oh, I thought . . . I thought . . .' Suddenly the old lady, with a
fierce impetuous movement, pushed the table away from her. She
got up, staggered for a moment on her feet, then tumbled to the pink

sofa, cowering there, huddled, her sharp fingers pressing against her face.

'Oh, I can't bear it. . . . I can't bear it. . . . I can't bear it any more! He's coming. He's coming. Oh, what shall I do? What shall I do?'

Miss Allen, feeling nothing but love and affection for her friend, but realizing strangely too the dim and muted attention of the room, knelt down beside the sofa and put her strong arms around the trembling, fragile body.

'What is it? Dear, dear Mrs Porter. What is it? Who is coming? Of whom are you afraid?'

'Henry's coming! Henry, who hated me. He's coming to carry me away!'

'But Mr Porter's dead!'

'Yes. . . .' The little voice was now the merest whisper. 'But he'll come all the same. . . . He always does what he says!'

The two women waited, listening. Miss Allen could hear the old lady's heart thumping and leaping close to her own. Through the opened windows came the sibilant rumble of the motor-buses. Then Mrs Porter gently pushed Miss Allen away. 'Sit on a chair, Lucy dear. I must tell you everything. I must share this with someone.'

She seemed to have regained some of her calmness. She sat straight up upon the sofa, patting her lace cap with her hands, feeling for the cameo brooch at her breast. Miss Allen drew a chair close to the sofa; turning again towards the mantelpiece, she saw that it stood out boldly and clearly; the tick of the clock came across to her with almost startling urgency.

'Now, dear Mrs Porter, what is it that is alarming you?' she said.

Mrs Porter cleared her throat. 'You know, Lucy, that I was married a great many years ago. I was only a very young girl at the time, very ignorant of course, and you can understand, my dear, that my father and mother influenced me very deeply. They liked Mr Porter. They thought that he would make me a good husband and that I should be very happy. . . . I was not happy, Lucy dear, never from the very first moment!'

Here Mrs Porter put out her hand and took Miss Allen's strong one. 'I am very willing to believe that much of the unhappiness was due to myself. I was a young, foolish girl; I was disturbed from the very first by the stories that Mr Porter told me, and the pictures he showed me. I was foolish about those things. He saw that they shocked me, and I think that that amused him. From the first it delighted him to tease me. Then—soon—he tired of me. He had mistresses. He brought them to our house. He insulted me in every way possible. I had years of that misery. God only knows how I lived through it. It became a habit with him to frighten and shock me. It was a game that he loved to play. I think he wanted to see how far I would go. But I was patient through all those many years. Oh! so patient! It was weak, perhaps, but there seemed nothing else for me to be.

'The last twenty years of our married life he hated me most bitterly. He said that I had scorned him, that I had not given him children, that I had wasted his money—a thousand different things! He tortured me, frightened me, disgusted me, but it never seemed to be enough for him, for the vengeance he felt I deserved. Then one day he discovered that he had a weak heart—a doctor frightened him. He saw perhaps for a moment in my eyes my consciousness of my possible freedom. He took my arm and shook me, bent his face close to mine, and said: "Ah, you think that after I'm dead you will be free. You are wrong. I will leave you everything that I possess, and then—just as you begin to enjoy it—I will come and fetch you!" What a thing to say, Lucy dear! He was mad, and so was I to listen to him. All those years of married life together had perhaps turned both our brains. Six months later he fell down in the street dead. They brought him home, and all that summer afternoon, my dear, I sat beside him in the bedroom, he all dressed in his best clothes and his patent leather shoes, and the band playing in the Square outside. Oh! he was dead, Lucy dear, he was indeed. For a week or two I thought that he was gone altogether. I was happy and free. Then—oh, I don't know—I began to imagine . . . to fancy. . . . I moved from Wimbledon. I advertised for someone, and you came. We moved here. . . . It ought to be . . . it is . . . it *must* be all right, Lucy dear; hold me, hold me tight! Don't let me go! He *can't* come back! He can't, he can't!'

She broke into passionate sobbing, cowering back on to the sofa as she had done before. The two women sat there, comforting one another. Miss Allen gathered the frail, trembling little body into her arms, and like a mother with her child, soothed it.

But, as she sat there, she realized with a chill shudder of alarm that moment, a quarter of an hour before, when the room had been dimmed and the clock stilled. Had that been fancy? Had some of Mrs Porter's terror seized her in sympathy? Were they simply two lonely women whose nerves were jagged by the quiet monotony and seclusion of their lives? Why was it that from the first she, so unimaginative and definite, should have been disturbed by the thought of Mr Porter? Why was it that even now she longed to know more surely about him, his face, his clothes, his height . . . everything.

'You must go to bed, dear. You are tired out. Your nerves have never recovered from the time of Mr Porter's death. That's what it is. . . . You must go to bed, dear.'

Mrs Porter went. She seemed to be relieved by her outburst. She felt perhaps now less lonely. It seemed, too, that she had less to fear now that she had betrayed her ghost into sunlight. She slept better that night than she had done for a long time past. Miss Allen sat beside the bed staring into the darkness, thinking. . . .

For a week after this they were happy. Mrs Porter was in high spirits. They went to the Coliseum and heard Miss Florence Smithson sing 'Roses of Picardy', and in the cinema they were delighted with the charm and simplicity of Alma Taylor. Mrs Porter lost her heart to Alma Taylor. 'That's a *sweet* girl,' she said. 'I would like to meet her. I'm sure she's *good.*' 'I'm sure she is,' said Miss Allen. Mrs Porter made friends in the flat. Mr Nix met them one day at the bottom of the lift and talked to them so pleasantly. '*What* a gentleman!' said Mrs Porter afterwards as she took off her bonnet.

Then one evening Miss Allen came into the sitting-room and stopped dead, frozen rigid on the threshold. Someone was in the room. She did not at first think of Mr Porter. She was only sure that someone was there. Mrs Porter was in her bedroom changing her dress.

Miss Allen said, 'Who's there?' She walked forward. The dim evening saffron light powdered the walls with trembling colour. The canaries twittered, the clock ticked; no one was there. After that instant of horror she was to know no relief. It was as though that spoken 'Who's there?' had admitted her into the open acceptance of a fact that she ought for ever to have denied.

She was a woman of common sense, of rational thought, scornful of superstition and sentiment. She realized now that there was something quite definite for her to fight, something as definite as disease, as pain, as poverty and hunger. She realized too that she was there to protect Mrs Porter from everything—yes, from everything and everybody!

Her first thought was to escape from the flat, and especially from everything in the flat—from the pink sofa, the gate-legged table, the birdcage, and the clock. She saw then that, if she yielded to this desire, they would be driven, the two of them, into perpetual flight, and that the very necessity of escaping would only admit the more the conviction of defeat. No, they must stay where they were; that place was their battleground.

She determined, too, that Mr Porter's name should not be mentioned between them again. Mrs Porter must be assured that she had forgotten his very existence.

Soon she arrived at an exact knowledge of the arrival of these 'attacks' as she called them. That month of May gave them wonderful weather. The evenings were so beautiful that they sat always with the windows open behind them, and the dim colour of the night-glow softened the lamplight and brought with it scents and breezes and a happy murmurous undertone. She received again and again in these May evenings that earlier impression of someone's entrance into the room. It came to her, as she sat with her back to the fireplace, with the conviction that a pair of eyes were staring at her. Those eyes willed her to him, and she would not; but soon she seemed to know them, cold, hard, and separated from her, she fancied, by glasses. They seemed, too, to bend down upon her from a height. She was desperately conscious at these moments of Mrs Porter. Was the old lady also aware? She could not tell. Mrs Porter still cast at her those odd, furtive glances, as though to see whether she suspected anything, but she never looked at the fireplace nor started as though the door was suddenly opened.

There were times when Miss Allen, relaxing her self-control, admitted without hesitation that someone was in the room. He was tall, wore spectacles behind which he scornfully peered. She challenged him to pass her guard and even felt the stiff pride of a victorious battle. They were fighting for the old lady, and she was winning. . . .

At all other moments she scorned herself for this weakness. Mrs Porter's nerves had affected her own. She had not believed that she could be so weak. Then, suddenly, one evening Mrs Porter dropped her cards, crumpled down into her chair, screamed, 'No, no . . . Lucy! . . . Lucy! He's here! . . .'

She was strangely, at the moment of that cry, aware of no presence in the room. It was only when she had gathered her friend into her arms, persuading her that there was nothing, loving her, petting her, that she was conscious of the dimming of the light, the stealthy withdrawal of sound. She was facing the fireplace; before the mantelpiece there seemed to her to hover a shadow, something so tenuous that it resembled a film of dust against the glow of electric light. She faced it with steady eyes and a fearless heart.

But against her will her soul admitted that confrontation. From that moment Mrs Porter abandoned disguise. Her terror was now so persistent that soon, of itself, it would kill her. There was no remedy; doctors could not help, nor change of scene. Only if Miss Allen still saw and felt nothing could the old lady still hope. Miss Allen lied and lied again and again.

'You saw nothing, Lucy?'

'Nothing.'

'Not there by the fireplace?'

'Nothing, dear. . . . Of course, nothing!'

Events from then moved quickly, and they moved for Miss Allen quite definitely in the hardening of the sinister shadow. She led now a triple existence: one life was Mrs Porter's, devoted to her, delivered over to her, helping her, protecting her; the second life was her own, her rational, practical self, scornful of shadow and of the terror of death; the third was the struggle with Henry Porter, a struggle now as definite and concrete as though he were a blackmailer confining her liberty.

She could never tell when he would come, and with every visit that he paid he seemed to advance in her realization of him. It appeared that he was always behind her, staring at her through those glasses that had, she was convinced, large gold rims and thin gold wires. She fancied that she had before her a dim outline of his face—pale, the chin sharp and pointed, the ears large and protuberant, the head dome shaped and bald. It was now that, with all her life and soul in the struggle for her friend, she realized that she did not love her enough. The intense love of her life had been already in earlier years given. Mrs Porter was a sweet old lady, and Miss Allen would give her life for her—but her soul was atrophied a little, tired a little, exhausted perhaps in the struggle so sharp and persistent for her own existence.

'Oh, if I were younger I could drive him away!' came back to her again and again. She found too that her own fear impeded her own self-sacrifice. She hated this shadow as something strong, evil, like mildew on stone, chilling breath. 'I'm not brave enough. . . . I'm not good enough. . . . I'm not young enough! Incessantly she tried to determine how real her sensations were. Was she simply influenced by Mrs Porter's fear? Was it the blindest imagination? Was it bred simply of the close, confined life that they were leading?

She could not tell. They had resumed their conspiracy of silence, of false animation and ease of mind. They led their daily lives as though there was nothing between them. But with every day Mrs Porter's strength was failing; the look of horrified anticipation in her eyes was now permanent. At night they slept together, and the little frail body trembled like a leaf in Miss Allen's arms.

The appearances were now regularized. Always when they were in the middle of their second game of 'Patience' Miss Allen felt that impulse to turn, that singing in her ears, the force of his ironical gaze. He was now almost complete to her, standing in front of the Japanese screen, his thin legs apart, his hostile, conceited face bent towards them, his pale, thin hands extended as though to catch a warmth that was not there.

A Sunday evening came. Earlier than usual they sat down to their cards. Through the open window shivered the jangled chimes of the bells of St James's.

'Well, he won't come yet . . .' was Miss Allen's thought. Then with that her nightly resolve: 'When he comes I must not turn—I must not look. She must not know that I know.'

Suddenly he was with them, and with a dominant force, a cruelty, a determination that was beyond anything that had been before.

'Four, five, six. . . .' The cards trembled in Mrs Porter's hand. 'And there's the spade, Lucy dear.'

He came closer. He was nearer to her than he had ever been. She summoned all that she had—her loyalty, her love, her honesty, her self-discipline. It was not enough.

She turned. He was there as she had always known that she would see him, his cruel, evil, supercilious face, conscious of its triumph, bent toward them, his grey clothes hanging loosely about his thin body, his hands spread out. He was like an animal about to spring.

'God help me! God help me!' she cried. With those words she knew that she had failed. She stood as though she would protect with her body her friend. She was too late.

Mrs Porter's agonized cry, 'You see him, Lucy! . . . You see him, Lucy!' warned her.

'No, no,' she answered. She felt something like a cold breath of stagnant water pass her. She turned back to see the old woman tumble across the table, scattering the little cards.

The room was emptied. They two were alone; she knew, without moving, horror and self-shame holding her there, that her poor friend was dead.

THE NATURE OF THE EVIDENCE

May Sinclair

This is the story Marston told me. He didn't want to tell it. I had to tear it from him bit by bit. I've pieced the bits together in their time order, and explained things here and there, but the facts are the facts he gave me. There's nothing that I didn't get out of him somehow.

Out of *him*—you'll admit my source is unimpeachable. Edward Marston, the great KC, and the author of an admirable work on 'The Logic of Evidence'. You should have read the chapters on 'What Evidence Is and What It Is Not'. You may say he lied; but if you knew Marston you'd know he wouldn't lie, for the simple reason that he's incapable of inventing anything. So that, if you ask me whether I believe this tale, all I can say is, I believe the things happened, because he said they happened and because they happened to him. As for what they *were*—well, I don't pretend to explain it, neither would he.

You know he was married twice. He adored his first wife, Rosamund, and Rosamund adored him. I suppose they were completely happy. She was fifteen years younger than he, and beautiful. I wish I could make you see how beautiful. Her eyes and mouth had the same sort of bow, full and wide-sweeping, and they stared out of her face with the same grave, contemplative innocence. Her mouth was finished off at each corner with the loveliest little moulding, rounded like the pistil of a flower. She wore her hair in a solid gold fringe over her forehead, like a child's, and a big coil at the back. When it was let down it hung in a heavy cable to her waist. Marston used to tease her about it. She had a trick of tossing back the rope in the night when it was hot under her, and it would fall smack across his face and hurt him.

There was a pathos about her that I can't describe—a curious, pure, sweet beauty, like a child's; perfect, and perfectly immature; so immature that you couldn't conceive its lasting—like that—any more than childhood lasts. Marston used to say it made him nervous. He was afraid of waking up in the morning and finding that it had changed in the night. And her beauty was so much a part of herself that you couldn't think of her without it. Somehow you felt that if it went she must go too.

Well, she went first.

For a year afterwards Marston existed dangerously, always on the edge of a breakdown. If he didn't go over altogether it was because his work saved him. He had no consoling theories. He was one of those bigoted materialists of the nineteenth-century type who believe that consciousness is a purely physiological function, and that when your body's dead, *you're* dead. He saw no reason to suppose the contrary. 'When you consider,' he used to say, 'the nature of the evidence!'

It's as well to bear this in mind, so as to realize that he hadn't any bias or anticipation. Rosamund survived for him only in his memory. And in his memory he was still in love with her. At the same time he used to discuss quite cynically the chances of his marrying again.

It seems that on their honeymoon they had gone into that. Rosamund said she hated to think of his being lonely and miserable, supposing she died before he did. She would like him to marry again. If, she stipulated, he married the right woman.

He had put it to her: 'And if I marry the wrong one?'

And she had said, That would be different. She couldn't bear that.

He remembered all this afterwards; but there was nothing in it to make him suppose, at the time, that she would take action.

We talked it over, he and I, one night.

'I suppose,' he said, 'I shall have to marry again. It's a physical necessity. But it won't be anything more. I shan't marry the sort of woman who'll expect anything more. I won't put another woman in Rosamund's place. There'll be no unfaithfulness about it.'

And there wasn't. Soon after that first year he married Pauline Silver.

She was a daughter of old Justice Parker, who was a friend of Marston's people. He hadn't seen the girl till she came home from India after her divorce.

Yes, there'd been a divorce. Silver had behaved very decently. He'd let her bring it against *him*, to save her. But there were some queer stories going about. They didn't get round to Marston, because he was so mixed up with her people; and if they had he wouldn't have believed them. He'd made up his mind he'd marry Pauline the first minute he'd seen her. She was handsome; the hard, black, white, and vermilion kind, with a little aristocratic nose and a lascivious mouth.

It was, as he had meant it to be, nothing but physical infatuation on both sides. No question of Pauline's taking Rosamund's place.

Marston had a big case on at the time.

They were in such a hurry that they couldn't wait till it was over; and as it kept him in London they agreed to put off their honeymoon till the autumn, and he took her straight to his own house in Curzon Street.

This, he admitted afterwards, was the part he hated. The Curzon Street house was associated with Rosamund; especially their bedroom—Rosamund's bedroom—and his library. The library was the room Rosamund liked best, because it was his room. She had her place in the corner by the hearth, and they were always alone there together in the evenings when his work was done, and when it wasn't done she would still sit with him, keeping quiet in her corner with a book.

Luckily for Marston, at the first sight of the library Pauline took a dislike to it.

I can hear her. 'Br-rr-rh! There's something beastly about this room, Edward. I can't think how you can sit in it.'

And Edward, a little caustic:

'*You* needn't, if you don't like it.'

'I certainly shan't.'

She stood there—I can see her—on the hearthrug by Rosamund's chair, looking uncommonly handsome and lascivious. He was going to take her in his arms and kiss her vermilion mouth, when, he said, something stopped him. Stopped him clean, as if it had risen up and stepped between them. He supposed it was the memory of Rosamund, vivid in the place that had been hers.

You see it was just that place, of silent, intimate communion, that Pauline would never take. And the rich, coarse, contented creature didn't even want to take it. He saw that he would be left alone there, all right, with his memory.

But the bedroom was another matter. That, Pauline had made it understood from the beginning, she would have to have. Indeed, there was no other he could well have offered her. The drawing-room covered the whole of the first floor. The bedrooms above were cramped, and this one had been formed by throwing the two front rooms into one. It looked south, and the bathroom opened out of it at the back. Marston's small northern room had a door on the narrow landing at right angles to his wife's door. He could hardly expect her to sleep there, still less in any of the tight boxes on the top floor. He said he wished he had sold the Curzon Street house.

But Pauline was enchanted with the wide, three-windowed piece that was to be hers. It had been exquisitely furnished for poor little Rosamund; all seventeenth-century walnut wood, Bokhara rugs, thick silk curtains, deep blue with purple linings, and a big, rich bed covered with a purple counterpane embroidered in blue.

One thing Marston insisted on: that *he* should sleep on Rosamund's side of the bed, and Pauline in his own old place. He didn't want to see Pauline's body where Rosamund's had been. Of course he had to lie about it and pretend he had always slept on the side next the window.

I can see Pauline going about in that room, looking at everything; looking at herself, her black, white, and vermilion, in the glass that had held Rosamund's pure rose and gold; opening the wardrobe where Rosamund's dresses used to hang, sniffing up the delicate, flower scent of Rosamund, not caring, covering it with her own thick trail.

And Marston (who cared abominably)—I can see him getting more miserable and at the same time more excited as the wedding evening went on. He took her to the play to fill up the time, or perhaps to get her out of Rosamund's rooms; God knows. I can see them sitting in the stalls, bored and restless, starting up and going out before the thing was half over, and coming back to that house in Curzon Street before eleven o'clock.

It wasn't much past eleven when he went to her room.

I told you her door was at right angles to his, and the landing was narrow, so that anybody standing by Pauline's door must have been seen the minute he opened his. He hadn't even to cross the landing to get to her.

Well, Marston swears that there was nothing there when he opened his own door; but when he came to Pauline's he saw Rosamund standing up before it; and, he said, '*She wouldn't let me in.*'

Her arms were stretched out, barring the passage. Oh yes, he saw her face, Rosamund's face; I gathered that it was utterly sweet, and utterly inexorable. He couldn't pass her.

So he turned into his own room, backing, he says, so that he could keep looking at her. And when he stood on the threshold of his own door she wasn't there.

No, he wasn't frightened. He couldn't tell me what he felt; but he left his door open all night because he couldn't bear to shut it on her. And he made no other attempt to go in to Pauline; he was so convinced that the phantasm of Rosamund would come again and stop him.

I don't know what sort of excuse he made to Pauline the next morning. He said she was very stiff and sulky all day; and no wonder. He was still infatuated with her, and I don't think that the phantasm of Rosamund had put him off Pauline in the least. In fact, he persuaded himself that the thing was nothing but a hallucination, due, no doubt, to his excitement.

Anyhow, he didn't expect to see it at the door again the next night.

Yes. It was there. Only, this time, he said, it drew aside to let him pass. It smiled at him, as if it were saying, 'Go in, if you must; you'll see what'll happen.'

He had no sense that it had followed him into the room; he felt certain that, this time, it would let him be.

It was when he approached Pauline's bed, which had been Rosamund's bed, that she appeared again, standing between it and him, and stretching out her arms to keep him back.

All that Pauline could see was her bridegroom backing and backing, then standing there, fixed, and the look on his face. That in itself was enough to frighten her.

She said, 'What's the matter with you, Edward?'

He didn't move.

'What are you standing there for? Why don't you come to bed?'

Then Marston seems to have lost his head and blurted it out:

'I can't. I can't.'

'Can't what?' said Pauline from the bed.

'Can't sleep with you. She won't let me.'

'She?'

'Rosamund. My wife. She's there.'

'What on earth are you talking about?'

'She's there, I tell you. She won't let me. She's pushing me back.'

He says Pauline must have thought he was drunk or something. Remember, she *saw* nothing but Edward, his face, and his mysterious attitude. He must have looked very drunk.

She sat up in bed, with her hard, black eyes blazing away at him, and told him to leave the room that minute. Which he did.

The next day she had it out with him. I gathered that he kept on talking about the 'state' he was in.

'You came to my room, Edward, in a *disgraceful* state.'

I suppose Marston said he was sorry; but he couldn't help it; he wasn't drunk. He stuck to it that Rosamund was there. He had seen her. And Pauline said, if he wasn't drunk then he must be mad, and he said meekly, 'Perhaps I *am* mad.'

That set her off, and she broke out in a fury. He was no more mad than she was; but he didn't care for her; he was making ridiculous excuses; shamming, to put her off. There was some other woman.

Marston asked her what on earth she supposed he'd married her for. Then she burst out crying and said she didn't know.

Then he seems to have made it up with Pauline. He managed to make her believe he wasn't lying, that he really had seen something, and between them they arrived at a rational explanation of the appearance. He had been overworking. Rosamund's phantasm was nothing but a hallucination of his exhausted brain.

This theory carried him on till bedtime. Then, he says, he began to wonder what would happen, what Rosamund's phantasm would do next. Each morning his passion for Pauline had come back again, increased by frustration, and it worked itself up crescendo, towards night. Supposing he *had* seen Rosamund. He might see her again. He had become suddenly subject to hallucinations. But as long as you *knew* you were hallucinated you were all right.

So what they agreed to do that night was by way of precaution, in case the thing came again. It might even be sufficient in itself to prevent his seeing anything.

Instead of going in to Pauline he was to get into the room before she did, and she was to come to him there. That, they said, would break the spell. To make him feel even safer he meant to be in bed before Pauline came.

Well, he got into the room all right.

It was when he tried to get into bed that—he saw her (I mean Rosamund).

She was lying there, in his place next the window, her own place, lying in her immature child-like beauty and sleeping, the firm full bow of her mouth softened by sleep. She was perfect in every detail, the lashes of her shut eyelids golden on her white cheeks, the solid gold of her square fringe shining, and the great braided golden rope of her hair flung back on the pillow.

He knelt down by the bed and pressed his forehead into the bed-clothes, close to her side. He declared he could feel her breathe.

He stayed there for the twenty minutes Pauline took to undress and come to him. He says the minutes stretched out like hours. Pauline found him still kneeling with his face pressed into the bedclothes. When he got up he staggered.

She asked him what he was doing and why he wasn't in bed. And he said, 'It's no use. I can't. I can't.'

But somehow he couldn't tell her that Rosamund was there. Rosamund was too sacred; he couldn't talk about her. He only said:

'You'd better sleep in my room tonight.'

He was staring down at the place in the bed where he still saw Rosamund. Pauline couldn't have seen anything but the bedclothes, the sheet smoothed above an invisible breast, and the hollow in the pillow.

She said she'd do nothing of the sort. She wasn't going to be frightened out of her own room. He could do as he liked.

He couldn't leave them there; he couldn't leave Pauline with Rosamund, and he couldn't leave Rosamund with Pauline. So he sat up in a chair with his back turned to the bed. No. He didn't make any attempt to go back. He says he knew she was still lying there, guarding his place, which was her place. The odd thing is that he wasn't in the least disturbed or frightened or surprised. He took the whole thing as a matter of course. And presently he dozed off into a sleep.

A scream woke him and the sound of a violent body leaping out of the bed and thudding on to its feet. He switched on the light and saw the bedclothes flung back and Pauline standing on the floor with her mouth open.

He went to her and held her. She was cold to the touch and shaking with terror, and her jaws dropped as if she was palsied.

She said, 'Edward, there's something in the bed.'

He glanced again at the bed. It was empty.

'There isn't,' he said. 'Look.'

He stripped the bed to the foot-rail, so that she could see.

'There *was* something.'

'Do you see it.'

'No, I felt it.'

She told him. First something had come swinging, smack across her face. A thick, heavy rope of woman's hair. It had waked her. Then she had put out her hands and felt the body. A woman's body, soft and horrible; her fingers had sunk in the shallow breasts. Then she had screamed and jumped.

And she couldn't stay in the room. The room, she said, was 'beastly'.

She slept in Marston's room, in his small single bed, and he sat up with her all night, on a chair.

She believed now that he had really seen something, and she remembered that the library was beastly, too. Haunted by something. She supposed that was what she had felt. Very well. Two rooms in the house were haunted; their bedroom and the library. They would just have to avoid those two rooms. She had made up her mind, you see, that it was nothing but a case of an ordinary haunted house; the sort of thing you're always hearing about and never believe in till it happens to yourself. Marston didn't like to point out to her that the house hadn't been haunted till she came into it.

The following night, the fourth night, she was to sleep in the spare room on the top floor, next to the servants, and Marston in his own room.

But Marston didn't sleep. He kept on wondering whether he would or would not go up to Pauline's room. That made him horribly restless, and instead of undressing and going to bed, he sat up on a chair with a book. He wasn't nervous; but he had a queer feeling that something was going to happen, and that he must be ready for it, and that he'd better be dressed.

It must have been soon after midnight when he heard the door knob turning very slowly and softly.

The door opened behind him and Pauline came in, moving without a sound, and stood before him. It gave him a shock; for he had been thinking of Rosamund, and when he heard the door knob turn it was the phantasm of Rosamund that he expected to see coming in. He says, for the first minute, it was this appearance of Pauline that struck him as the uncanny and unnatural thing.

She had nothing, absolutely nothing on but a transparent white chiffony sort of dressing-gown. She was trying to undo it. He could see her hands shaking as her fingers fumbled with the fastenings.

He got up suddenly, and they just stood there before each other, saying nothing, staring at each other. He was fascinated by her, by the sheer glamour of her body, gleaming white through the thin stuff, and by the movement of her fingers. I think I've said she was a beautiful woman, and her beauty at that moment was overpowering.

And still he stared at her without saying anything. It sounds as if their silence lasted quite a long time, but in reality it couldn't have been more than some fraction of a second.

Then she began. 'Oh, Edward, for God's sake *say* something. Oughtn't I to have come?'

And she went on without waiting for an answer. 'Are you thinking of *her*? Because, if—if you are, I'm not going to let her drive you away from me. . . . I'm not going to. . . . She'll keep on coming as long as we don't——Can't you see that this is the way to stop it . . . ? When you take me in your arms.'

She slipped off the loose sleeves of the chiffon thing and it fell to her feet. Marston says he heard a queer sound, something between a groan and a grunt, and was amazed to find that it came from himself.

He hadn't touched her yet—mind you, it went quicker than it takes to tell, it was still an affair of the fraction of a second—they were holding out their arms to each other, when the door opened again without a sound, and, without visible passage, the phantasm was there.

It came incredibly fast, and thin at first, like a shaft of light sliding between them. It didn't do anything; there was no beating of hands, only, as it took on its full form, its perfect likeness of flesh and blood, it made its presence felt like a push, a force, driving them asunder.

Pauline hadn't seen it yet. She thought it was Marston who was beating her back. She cried out: 'Oh, don't, don't push me away!' She stooped below the phantasm's guard and clung to his knees, writhing and crying. For a moment it was a struggle between her moving flesh and that still, supernatural being.

And in that moment Marston realized that he hated Pauline. She was fighting Rosamund with her gross flesh and blood, taking a mean advantage of her embodied state to beat down the heavenly, discarnate thing.

He called to her to let go.

'It's not I,' he shouted. 'Can't you *see* her?'

Then, suddenly, she saw, and let go, and dropped, crouching on the floor and trying to cover herself. This time she had given no cry.

The phantasm gave way; it moved slowly towards the door, and as it went it looked back over its shoulder at Marston, it trailed a hand, signalling to him to come.

He went out after it, hardly aware of Pauline's naked body that still writhed there, clutching at his feet as they passed, and drew itself after him, like a worm, like a beast, along the floor.

She must have got up at once and followed them out on to the landing; for, as he went down the stairs behind the phantasm, he could see Pauline's face, distorted with lust and terror, peering at them above the stairhead. She saw them descend the last flight, and cross the hall at the bottom and go into the library. The door shut behind them.

Something happened in there. Marston never told me precisely what it was, and I didn't ask him. Anyhow, that finished it.

The next day Pauline ran away to her own people. She couldn't stay in Marston's house because it was haunted by Rosamund, and he wouldn't leave it for the same reason.

And she never came back; for she was not only afraid of Rosamund, she was afraid of Marston. And if she *had* come it wouldn't have been any good. Marston was convinced that, as often as he attempted to get to Pauline, something would stop him. Pauline certainly felt that, if Rosamund were pushed to it, she might show herself in some still more sinister and terrifying form. She knew when she was beaten.

And there was more in it than that. I believe he tried to explain it to her; said he had married her on the assumption that Rosamund was dead, but that now he knew she was alive; she was, as he put it, 'there'. He tried to make her see that if he had Rosamund he couldn't have *her*. Rosamund's presence in the world annulled their contract.

You see I'm convinced that something *did* happen that night in the library. I say, he never told me precisely what it was, but he once let something out. We were discussing one of Pauline's love-affairs (after the separation she gave him endless grounds for divorce).

'Poor Pauline,' he said, 'she thinks she's so passionate.'

'Well,' I said, 'wasn't she?'

Then he burst out. 'No. She doesn't know what passion is. None of you know. You haven't the faintest conception. You'd have to get rid of your bodies first. *I* didn't know until——'

He stopped himself. I think he was going to say, 'until Rosamund came back and showed me.' For he leaned forward and whispered: 'It isn't a localized affair at all. . . . If you only knew——'

So I don't think it was just faithfulness to a revived memory. I take it there had been, behind that shut door, some experience, some terrible and exquisite contact. More penetrating than sight or touch. More— more extensive: passion at all points of being.

Perhaps the supreme moment of it, the ecstasy, only came when her phantasm had disappeared.

He couldn't go back to Pauline after *that*.

Night-Fears

L. P. Hartley

The coke-brazier was elegant enough but the night-watchman was not, consciously at any rate, sensitive to beauty of form. No; he valued the brazier primarily for its warmth. He could not make up his mind whether he liked its light. Two days ago, when he first took on the job, he was inclined to suspect the light; it dazzled him, made a target of him, increased his helplessness; it emphasized the darkness. But tonight he was feeling reconciled to it; and aided by its dark, clear rays, he explored his domain—a long narrow rectangle, fenced off from the road by poles round and thick as flag-posts and lashed loosely at the ends. By day they seemed simply an obstacle to be straddled over; but at night they were boundaries, defences almost. At their junctions, where the warning red lanterns dully gleamed, they bristled like a barricade. The night-watchman felt himself in charge of a fortress.

He took a turn up and down, musing. Now that the strangeness of the position had worn off he could think with less effort. The first night he had vaguely wished that the 'No Thoroughfare' board had faced him instead of staring uselessly up the street: it would have given his thoughts a rallying-point. Now he scarcely noticed its blankness. His thoughts were few but pleasant to dwell on, and in the solitude they had the intensity of sensations. He arranged them in cycles, the rotation coming at the end of ten paces or so when he turned to go back over his tracks. He enjoyed the thought that held his mind for the moment, but always with some agreeable impatience for the next. If he surmised there would be a fresh development in it, he would deliberately refrain from calling it up, leave it fermenting and ripening, as it were, in a luxury of expectation.

The night-watchman was a domesticated man with a wife and two children, both babies. One was beginning to talk. Since he took on his job wages had risen, and everything at home seemed gilt-edged. It made a difference to his wife. When he got home she would say, as she had done on the preceding mornings, 'Well, you do look a wreck. This night work doesn't suit you, I'm sure.' The night-watchman liked being addressed in that way and hearing his job described as night work; it showed an easy competent familiarity with a man's occupation. He would tell her, with the air of one who had seen much, about the incidents of his vigil, and what he hadn't seen he would invent, just for the pleasure of hearing her say: 'Well, I never! You do have some experiences, and no mistake.' He was very fond of his wife. Why, hadn't she promised to patch up the old blue-paper blinds, used once for the air-raids, but somewhat out of repair as a consequence of their being employed as a quarry for paper to wrap up parcels? He hadn't slept well, couldn't get accustomed to sleeping by day, the room was so light; but these blinds would be just the thing, and it would be nice to see them and feel that the war was over and there was no need for them, really.

The night-watchman yawned as for the twentieth time perhaps he came up sharp against the boundary of his walk. Loss of sleep, no doubt. He would sit in his shelter and rest a bit. As he turned and saw the narrowing gleams that transformed the separating poles into thin lines of fire, he noticed that nearly at the end, just opposite the brazier in fact and only a foot or two from the door of his hut, the left line was broken. Someone was sitting on the barrier, his back turned on the night-watchman's little compound. 'Strange I never heard him come,' thought the man, brought back with a jerk from his world of thoughts to the real world of darkness and the deserted street—well, no, not exactly deserted, for here was someone who might be inclined to talk for half an hour or so. The stranger paid no attention to the watchman's slowly advancing tread. A little disconcerting. He stopped. Drunk, I expect, he thought. This would be a real adventure to tell his wife. 'I told him I wasn't going to stand any rot from him. "Now, my fine fellow, you go home to bed; that's the best place for you," I said.' He had heard drunk men addressed in that way, and wondered doubtfully whether he would be able to catch the tone; it was more important than the words, he reflected. At last, pulling himself together, he walked up to the brazier and coughed loudly, and feeling ill-at-ease, set about warming his hands with such energy he nearly burned them.

As the stranger took no notice, but continued to sit wrapped in thought, the night-watchman hazarded a remark to his bent back. 'A fine night,' he said rather loudly, though it was ridiculous to raise one's voice in an empty street. The stranger did not turn round.

'Yes,' he replied, 'but cold; it will be colder before morning.' The night-watchman looked at his brazier, and it struck him that the coke was not lasting so well as on the previous nights. I'll put some more on, he thought, picking up a shovel; but instead of the little heap he had expected to see, there was nothing but dust and a few bits of grit—his night's supply had been somehow overlooked. 'Won't you turn round and warm your hands?' he said to the person sitting on the barrier. 'The fire isn't very good, but I can't make it up, for they forgot to give me any extra, unless somebody pinched it when my back was turned.' The night-watchman was talking for effect; he did not really believe that anyone had taken the coke. The stranger might have made a movement somewhere about the shoulders.

'Thank you,' he said, 'but I prefer to warm my back.'

Funny idea that, thought the watchman.

'Have you noticed,' proceeded the stranger, 'how easily men forget? This coke of yours, I mean; it looks as if they didn't care about you very much, leaving you in the cold like this.' It had certainly grown colder, but the man replied cheerfully: 'Oh, it wasn't that. They forgot it. Hurrying to get home, you know.' Still, they might have remembered, he thought. It was Bill Jackson's turn to fetch it—Old Bill, as the fellows call him. He doesn't like me very much. The chaps are a bit stand-offish. They'll be all right when I know them better.

His visitor had not stirred. How I would like to push him off, the night-watchman thought, irritated and somehow troubled. The stranger's voice broke in upon his reflections.

'Don't you like this job?'

'Oh, not so bad,' said the man carelessly; 'good money, you know.'

'Good money,' repeated the stranger scornfully. 'How much do you get?'

The night-watchman named the sum.

'Are you married, and have you got any children?' the stranger persisted.

The night-watchman said 'Yes,' without enthusiasm.

'Well, that won't go very far when the children are a bit older,' declared the stranger. 'Have you any prospect of a rise?' The man said no, he had just had one.

'Prices going up, too,' the stranger commented.

A change came over the night-watchman's outlook. The feeling of hostility and unrest increased. He couldn't deny all this. He longed to say, 'What do you think you're getting at?' and rehearsed the phrase under his breath, but couldn't get himself to utter it aloud; his visitor had created his present state of mind and was lord of it. Another picture floated before him, less rosy than the first: an existence drab-coloured with the dust of conflict, but relieved by the faithful support of his wife and children at home. After all, that's the life for a man, he thought; but he did not cherish the idea, did not walk up and down hugging it, as he cherished and hugged the other.

'Do you find it easy to sleep in the daytime?' asked the stranger presently.

'Not very,' the night-watchman admitted.

'Ah,' said the stranger, 'dreadful thing, insomnia.'

'When you can't go to sleep, you mean,' interpreted the night-watchman, not without a secret pride.

'Yes,' came the answer. 'Makes a man ill, mad sometimes. People have done themselves in sooner than stand the torture.'

It was on the tip of the night-watchman's tongue to mention that panacea, the blue blinds. But he thought it would sound foolish, and wondered whether they would prove such a sovereign remedy after all.

'What about your children? You won't see much of them,' remarked the stranger, 'while you are on this job. Why, they'll grow up without knowing you! Up when their papa's in bed, and in bed when he's up! Not that you miss them much, I dare say. Still, if children don't get fond of their father while they're young, they never will.'

Why didn't the night-watchman take him up warmly, assuring him they were splendid kids; the eldest called him daddy, and the younger, his wife declared, already recognized him. She knew by its smile, she said. He couldn't have forgotten all that; half an hour ago it had been one of his chief thoughts. He was silent.

'I should try and find another job if I were you,' observed the stranger. 'Otherwise you won't be able to make both ends meet. What will your wife say then?'

The man considered; at least he thought he was facing the question, but his mind was somehow too deeply disturbed, and circled wearily and blindly in its misery. 'I was never brought up to a trade,' he said hesitatingly; 'father's fault.' It struck him that he had never confessed that before; had sworn not to give his father away. What am I coming to? he thought. Then he made an effort. 'My wife's all right, she'll stick to me.' He waited, positively dreading the stranger's next attack. Though the fire was burning low, almost obscured under the coke ashes that always seem more lifeless than any others, he felt drops of perspiration on his forehead, and his clothes, he knew, were soaked. I shall get a chill, that'll be the next thing, he thought; but it was involuntary: such an idea hadn't occurred to him since he was a child, supposedly delicate.

'Yes, your wife,' said the stranger at last, in tones so cold and clear that they seemed to fill the universe; to admit of no contradiction; to be graven with a fine unerring instrument out of the hard rock of truth itself. 'You won't see much of her either. You leave her pretty much to herself, don't you? Now with these women, you know, that's a *risk*.' The last word rang like a challenge; but the night-watchman had taken the offensive, shot his one little bolt, and the effort had left him more helpless than ever.

'When the eye doth not see,' continued the stranger, 'the heart doth not grieve; on the contrary, it makes merry.' He laughed, as the night-watchman could see from the movement of his shoulders. 'I've known cases very similar to yours. When the cat's away, you know! It's a pity you're under contract to finish this job' (the night-watchman had not mentioned a contract), 'but as you are, take my advice and get a friend to keep an eye on your house. Of course, he won't be able to stay the night—of course not; but tell him to keep his eyes open.'

The stranger seemed to have said his say, his head drooped a little more; he might even be dropping off to sleep. Apparently he did not feel the cold. But the night-watchman was breathing hard and could scarcely stand. He tottered a little way down his territory, wondering absurdly why the place looked so tidy; but what a travesty of his former progress. And what a confusion in his thoughts, and what a thumping in his temples. Slowly from the writhing, tearing mass in his mind a resolve shaped itself; like a cuckoo it displaced all others. He loosened the red handkerchief that was knotted round his neck, without remembering whose fingers had tied it a few hours before, or that it had been promoted (not without washing) to the status of a garment from the menial function of carrying his lunch. It had been an extravagance, that tin carrier, much debated over, and justified finally by the rise in the night-watchman's wages. He let the handkerchief drop as he fumbled for the knife in his pocket, but the blade, which was stiff, he got out with little difficulty. Wondering vaguely if he would be able to do it, whether the right movement would come to him, why he hadn't practised it, he took a step towards the brazier. It was the one friendly object in the street. . . .

Later in the night the stranger, without putting his hands on the pole to steady himself, turned round for the first time and regarded the body of the night-watchman. He even stepped over into the little compound and, remembering perhaps the dead man's invitation, stretched out his hands over the still warm ashes in the brazier. Then he climbed back and, crossing the street, entered a blind alley opposite, leaving a track of dark, irregular footprints; and since he did not return it is probable that he lived there.

BEWITCHED

Edith Wharton

The snow was still falling thickly when Orrin Bosworth, who farmed the land south of Lonetop, drove up in his cutter to Saul Rutledge's gate. He was surprised to see two other cutters ahead of him. From them descended two muffled figures. Bosworth, with increasing surprise, recognized Deacon Hibben, from North Ashmore, and Sylvester Brand, the widower, from the old Bearcliff farm on the way to Lonetop.

It was not often that anybody in Hemlock County entered Saul Rutledge's gate; least of all in the dead of winter, and summoned (as Bosworth, at any rate, had been) by Mrs Rutledge, who passed, even in that unsocial region, for a woman of cold manners and solitary character. The situation was enough to excite the curiosity of a less imaginative man than Orrin Bosworth.

As he drove in between the broken-down white gateposts topped by fluted urns the two men ahead of him were leading their horses to the adjoining shed. Bosworth followed, and hitched his horse to a post. Then the three tossed off the snow from their shoulders, clapped their numb hands together, and greeted each other.

'Hallo, Deacon.'

'Well, well, Orrin—' They shook hands.

''Day, Bosworth,' said Sylvester Brand, with a brief nod. He seldom put any cordiality into his manner, and on this occasion he was still busy about his horse's bridle and blanket.

Orrin Bosworth, the youngest and most communicative of the three, turned back to Deacon Hibben, whose long face, queerly blotched and moldy-looking, with blinking peering eyes, was yet less forbidding than Brand's heavily-hewn countenance.

'Queer, our all meeting here this way. Mrs Rutledge sent me a message to come,' Bosworth volunteered.

The Deacon nodded. 'I got a word from her too—Andy Pond come with it yesterday noon. I hope there's no trouble here—'

He glanced through the thickening fall of snow at the desolate front of the Rutledge house, the more melancholy in its present neglected state because, like the gateposts, it kept traces of former elegance. Bosworth had often wondered how such a house had come to be built in that lonely stretch between North Ashmore and Cold Corners. People said there had once been other houses like it, forming a little township called Ashmore, a sort of mountain colony created by the caprice of an English Royalist officer, one Colonel Ashmore, who had been murdered by the Indians, with all his family, long before the Revolution. This tale was confirmed by the fact that the ruined cellars of several smaller houses were still to be discovered under the wild growth of the adjoining slopes, and that the Communion plate of the moribund Episcopal church of Cold Corners was engraved with the name of Colonel Ashmore, who had given it to the church of Ashmore in the year 1723. Of the church itself no traces remained. Doubtless it had been a modest wooden edifice, built on piles, and the conflagration which had burnt the other houses to the ground's edge had reduced it utterly to ashes. The whole place, even in summer, wore a mournful solitary air, and people wondered why Saul Rutledge's father had gone there to settle.

'I never knew a place,' Deacon Hibben said, 'as seemed as far away from humanity. And yet it ain't so in miles.'

'Miles ain't the only distance,' Orrin Bosworth answered; and the two men, followed by Sylvester Brand, walked across the drive to the front door. People in Hemlock County did not usually come and go by their front doors, but all three men seemed to feel that, on an occasion which appeared to be so exceptional, the usual and more familiar approach by the kitchen would not be suitable.

They had judged rightly; the Deacon had hardly lifted the knocker when the door opened and Mrs Rutledge stood before them.

'Walk right in,' she said in her usual dead-level tone; and Bosworth, as he followed the others, thought to himself: 'Whatever's happened, she's not going to let it show in her face.'

It was doubtful, indeed, if anything unwonted could be made to show in Prudence Rutledge's face, so limited was its scope, so fixed were its features. She was dressed for the occasion in a black calico with white spots, a collar or crochet lace fastened by a gold brooch, and a gray woolen shawl, crossed under her arms and tied at the back. In her small narrow head the only marked prominence was that of the brow projecting roundly over pale spectacled eyes. Her dark hair, parted above this prominence, passed tight and flat over the tips of her ears into a small braided coil at the nape; and her contracted head looked still narrower from being perched on a long hollow neck with cord-like throat muscles. Her eyes were of a pale cold gray, her complexion was an even white. Her age might have been anywhere from thirty-five to sixty.

The room into which she led the three men had probably been the dining room of the Ashmore house. It was now used as a front parlor, and a black stove planted on a sheet of zinc stuck out from the delicately fluted panels of an old wooden mantel. A newly-lit fire smoldered reluctantly, and the room was at once close and bitterly cold.

'Andy Pond,' Mrs Rutledge cried out to someone at the back of the house, 'Step out and call Mr Rutledge. You'll likely find him in the woodshed, or round the barn somewheres.' She rejoined her visitors. 'Please suit yourselves to seats,' she said.

The three men, with an increasing air of constraint, took the chairs she pointed out, and Mrs Rutledge sat stiffly down upon a fourth, behind a rickety beadwork table. She glanced from one to the other of her visitors.

'I presume you folks are wondering what it is I asked you to come here for,' she said in her dead-level voice. Orrin Bosworth and Deacon Hibben murmured an assent; Sylvester Brand sat silent, his eyes, under their great thicket of eyebrows, fixed on the huge boot tip swinging before him.

'Well, I allow you didn't expect it was for a party,' continued Mrs Rutledge.

No one ventured to respond to this chill pleasantry, and she continued: 'We're in trouble here, and that's the fact. And we need advice—Mr Rutledge and myself do.' She cleared her throat, and added in a lower tone, her pitilessly clear eyes looking straight before her: 'There's a spell been cast over Mr Rutledge.'

The Deacon looked up sharply, an incredulous smile pinching his thin lips. 'A spell?'

'That's what I said: he's bewitched.'

Again the three visitors were silent; then Bosworth, more at ease or less tongue-tied than the others, asked with an attempt at humor: 'Do you use the word in the strict Scripture sense, Mrs Rutledge?'

She glanced at him before replying: 'That's how *he* uses it.'

The Deacon coughed and cleared his long rattling throat. 'Do you care to give us more particulars before your husband joins us?'

Mrs Rutledge looked down at her clasped hands, as if considering the question. Bosworth noticed that the inner fold of her lids was of the same uniform white as the rest of her skin, so that when she drooped them her rather prominent eyes looked like the sightless orbs of a marble statue. The impression was unpleasing, and he glanced away at the text over the mantelpiece, which read:

The Soul That Sinneth It Shall Die.

'No,' she said at length, 'I'll wait.'

At this moment Sylvester Brand suddenly stoop up and pushed back his chair. 'I don't know,' he said, in his rough bass voice, 'as I've got any particular lights on Bible mysteries; and this happens to be the day I was to go down to Starkfield to close a deal with a man.'

Mrs Rutledge lifted one of her long thin hands. Withered and wrinkled by hard work and cold, it was nevertheless of the same leaden white as her face. 'You won't be kept long,' she said. 'Won't you be seated?'

Farmer Brand stood irresolute, his purplish underlip twitching. 'The Deacon here—such things is more in his line   '

'I want you should stay,' said Mrs Rutledge quietly; and Brand sat down again.

A silence fell, during which the four persons present seemed all to be listening for the sound of a step; but none was heard, and after a minute or two Mrs Rutledge began to speak again.

'It's down by that old shack on Lamer's pond; that's where they meet,' she said suddenly.

Bosworth, whose eyes were on Sylvester Brand's face, fancied he saw a sort of inner flush darken the farmer's heavy leathern skin. Deacon Hibben leaned forward, a glitter of curiosity in his eyes.

'They—*who*, Mrs Rutledge?'

'My husband, Saul Rutledge . . . and her. . . .'

Sylvester Brand again stirred in his seat. 'Who do you mean by *her?*' he asked abruptly, as if roused out of some far-off musing.

Mrs Rutledge's body did not move; she simply revolved her head on her long neck and looked at him.

'Your daughter, Sylvester Brand.'

The man staggered to his feet with an explosion of inarticulate sounds. 'My—my daughter? What the hell are you talking about? My daughter? It's a damned lie . . . it's . . . it's. . . .'

'Your daughter *Ora*, Mr Brand,' said Mrs Rutledge slowly.

Bosworth felt an icy chill down his spine. Instinctively he turned his eyes away from Brand, and they rested on the mildewed countenance of Deacon Hibben. Between the blotches it had become as white as Mrs Rutledge's, and the Deacon's eyes burned in the whiteness like live embers among ashes.

Brand gave a laugh: the rusty creaking laugh of one whose springs of mirth are never moved by gaiety. 'My daughter *Ora?*' he repeated.

'Yes.'

'My *dead* daughter?'

'That's what he says.'

'Your husband?'

'That's what Mr Rutledge says.'

Orrin Bosworth listened with a sense of suffocation; he felt as if he were wrestling with long-armed horrors in a dream. He could no longer resist letting his eyes turn to Sylvester Brand's face. To his surprise it had resumed a natural imperturbable expression. Brand rose to his feet. 'Is that all?' he queried contemptuously.

'All? Ain't it enough? How long is it since you folks seen Saul Rutledge, any of you?' Mrs Rutledge flew out at them.

Bosworth, it appeared, had not seen him for nearly a year; the Deacon had only run across him once, for a minute, at the North Ashmore post office, the previous autumn, and acknowledged that he wasn't looking any too good then. Brand said nothing, but stood irresolute.

'Well, if you wait a minute you'll see with your own eyes; and he'll tell you with his own words. That's what I've got you here for—to see for yourselves what's come over him. Then you'll talk different,' she added, twisting her head abruptly toward Sylvester Brand.

The Deacon raised a lean hand of interrogation.

'Does your husband know we've been sent for on this business, Mrs Rutledge?'

Mrs Rutledge signed assent.

'It was with his consent, then—?'

She looked coldly at her questioner. 'I guess it had to be,' she said. Again Bosworth felt the chill down his spine. He tried to dissipate the sensation by speaking with an affectation of energy.

'Can you tell us, Mrs Rutledge, how this trouble you speak of shows itself . . . what makes you think . . . ?'

She looked at him for a moment; then she leaned forward across the rickety beadwork table. A thin smile of disdain narrowed her colorless lips. 'I don't think—I know.'

'Well—but how?'

She leaned closer, both elbows on the table, her voice dropping. 'I seen 'em.'

In the ashen light from the veiling of snow beyond the windows the

Deacon's little screwed-up eyes seemed to give out red sparks. 'Him and the dead?'

'Him and the dead.'

'Saul Rutledge and—and Ora Brand?'

'That's so.'

Sylvester Brand's chair fell backward with a crash. He was on his feet again, crimson and cursing. 'It's a God-damned fiend-begotten lie. . . .'

'Friend Brand . . . friend Brand . . .' the Deacon protested.

'Here, let me get out of this. I want to see Saul Rutledge himself, and tell him—'

'Well, here he is,' said Mrs Rutledge.

The outer door had opened; they heard the familiar stamping and shaking of a man who rids his garments of their last snowflakes before penetrating to the sacred precincts of the best parlor. Then Saul Rutledge entered.

II

As he came in he faced the light from the north window, and Bosworth's first thought was that he looked like a drowned man fished out from under the ice—'self-drowned', he added. But the snow light plays cruel tricks with a man's color, and even with the shape of his features; it must have been partly that, Bosworth reflected, which transformed Saul Rutledge from the straight muscular fellow he had been a year before into the haggard wretch now before them.

The Deacon sought for a word to ease the horror. 'Well, now, Saul—you look's if you'd ought to set right up to the stove. Had a touch of ague, maybe?'

The feeble attempt was unavailing. Rutledge neither moved nor answered. He stood among them silent, incommunicable, like one risen from the dead.

Brand grasped him roughly by the shoulder. 'See here, Saul Rutledge, what's this dirty lie your wife tells us you've been putting about?'

Still Rutledge did not move. 'It's no lie,' he said.

Brand's hand dropped from his shoulder. In spite of the man's rough bullying power he seemed to be undefinably awed by Rutledge's look and tone.

'No lie? You've gone plumb crazy, then, have you?'

Mrs Rutledge spoke. 'My husband's not lying, nor he ain't gone crazy. Don't I tell you I seen 'em?'

Brand laughed again. 'Him and the dead?'

'Yes.'

'Down by the Lamer pond, you say?'

'Yes.'

'And when was that, if I might ask?'

'Day before yesterday.'

A silence fell on the strangely assembled group. The Deacon at length broke it to say to Mr Brand: 'Brand, in my opinion we've got to see this thing through.'

Brand stood for a moment in speechless contemplation: there was something animal and primitive about him, Bosworth thought, as he hung thus, lowering and dumb, a little foam beading the corners of that heavy purplish underlip. He let himself slowly down into his chair. 'I'll see it through.'

The two other men and Mrs Rutledge had remained seated. Saul Rutledge stood before them, like a prisoner at the bar, or rather like a sick man before the physicians who were to heal him. As Bosworth scrutinized that hollow face, so wan under the dark sunburn, so sucked inward and consumed by some hidden fever, there stole over the sound healthy man the thought that perhaps, after all, husband and wife spoke the truth, and that they were all at that moment really standing on the edge of some forbidden mystery. Things that the rational mind would reject without a thought seemed no longer so easy to dispose of as one looked at the actual Saul Rutledge and remembered the man he had been a year before. Yes; as the Deacon said, they would have to see it through. . . .

'Sit down then, Saul; draw up to us, won't you?' the Deacon suggested, trying again for a natural tone.

Mrs Rutledge pushed a chair forward, and her husband sat down on it. He stretched out his arms and grasped his knees in his brown bony fingers; in that attitude he remained, turning neither his head nor his eyes.

'Well, Saul,' the Deacon continued, 'your wife says you thought mebbe we could do something to help you through this trouble, whatever it is.'

Rutledge's gray eyes widened a little. 'No; I didn't think that. It was her idea to try what could be done.'

'I presume, though, since you've agreed to our coming, that you don't object to our putting a few questions?'

Rutledge was silent for a moment; then he said with a visible effort: 'No; I don't object.'

'Well—you've heard what your wife says?'

Rutledge made a slight motion of assent.

'And—what have you got to answer? How do you explain . . . ?'

Mrs Rutledge intervened. 'How can he explain? I seen 'em.'

There was a silence; then Bosworth, trying to speak in an easy reassuring tone, queried: 'That so, Saul?'

'That's so.'

Brand lifted up his brooding head. 'You mean to say you . . . you sit here before us all and say. . . .'

The Deacon's hand again checked him. 'Hold on, friend Brand. We're all of us trying for the facts, ain't we?' He turned to Rutledge. 'We've heard what Mrs Rutledge says. What's your answer?'

'I don't know as there's any answer. She found us.'

'And you mean to tell me the person with you was . . . was what you took to be . . .' the Deacon's thin voice grew thinner, 'Ora Brand?'

Saul Rutledge nodded.

'You knew . . . or thought you knew . . . you were meeting with the dead?'

Rutledge bent his head again. The snow continued to fall in a steady unwavering sheet against the window, and Bosworth felt as if a winding sheet were descending from the sky to envelop them all in a common grave.

'Think what you're saying! It's against our religion! Ora . . . poor child! . . . died over a year ago. I saw you at her funeral, Saul. How can you make such a statement?'

'What else can he do?' thrust in Mrs Rutledge.

There was another pause. Bosworth's resources had failed him, and Brand once more sat plunged in dark meditation. The Deacon laid his quivering finger tips together, and moistened his lips.

'Was the day before yesterday the first time?' he asked.

The movement of Rutledge's head was negative.

'Not the first? Then when . . . ?'

'Nigh on a year ago, I reckon.'

'God! And you mean to tell us that ever since—?'

'Well . . . look at him,' said his wife. The three men lowered their eyes.

After a moment Bosworth, trying to collect himself, glanced at the Deacon. 'Why not ask Saul to make his own statement, if that's what we're here for?'

'That's so,' the Deacon assented. He turned to Rutledge. 'Will you try and give us your idea . . . of . . . of how it began?'

There was another silence. Then Rutledge tightened his grasp on his gaunt knees, and still looking straight ahead, with his curiously clear, unseeing gaze: 'Well,' he said, 'I guess it begun away back, afore even I was married to Mrs Rutledge. . . .' He spoke in a low automatic tone, as if some invisible agent were dictating his words, or even uttering them for him. 'You know,' he added, 'Ora and me was to have been married.'

Sylvester Brand lifted his head. 'Straighten that statement out first, please,' he interjected.

'What I mean is, we kept company. But Ora she was very young. Mr Brand here he sent her away. She was gone nigh to three years, I guess. When she come back I was married.'

'That's right,' Brand said, relapsing once more into his sunken attitude.

'And after she came back did you meet her again?' the Deacon continued.

'Alive?' Rutledge questioned.

A perceptible shudder ran through the room.

'Well—of course,' said the Deacon nervously.

Rutledge seemed to consider. 'Once I did—only once. There was a lot of other people round. At Cold Corners Fair it was.'

'Did you talk with her then?'

'Only a minute.'

'What did she say?'

His voice dropped. 'She said she was sick and knew she was going to die, and when she was dead she'd come back to me.'

'And what did you answer?'

'Nothing.'

'Did you think anything of it at the time?'

'Well, no. Not till I heard she was dead I didn't. After that I thought of it—and I guess she drew me.' He moistened his lips.

'Drew you down to that abandoned house by the pond?'

Rutledge made a faint motion of assent, and the Deacon added: 'How did you know it was there she wanted you to come?'

'She . . . just drew me. . . .'

There was a long pause. Bosworth felt, on himself and the other two men, the oppressive weight of the next question to be asked. Mrs Rutledge opened and closed her narrow lips once or twice, like some beached shellfish gasping for the tide. Rutledge waited.

'Well, now, Saul, won't you go on with what you was telling us?' the Deacon at length suggested.

'That's all. There's nothing else.'

The Deacon lowered his voice. 'She just draws you?'

'Yes.'

'Often?'

'That's as it happens. . . .'

'But if it's always there she draws you, man, haven't you the strength to keep away from the place?'

For the first time, Rutledge wearily turned his head toward his questioner. A spectral smile narrowed his colorless lips. 'Ain't any use. She follers after me. . . .'

There was another silence. What more could they ask, then and there? Mrs Rutledge's presence checked the next question. The Deacon seemed hopelessly to revolve the matter. At length he spoke in a more authoritative tone. 'These are forbidden things. You know that, Saul. Have you tried prayer?'

Rutledge shook his head.

'Will you pray with us now?'

Rutledge cast a glance of freezing indifference on his spiritual adviser. 'If you folks want to pray, I'm agreeable,' he said. But Mrs Rutledge intervened.

'Prayer ain't any good. In this kind of thing it ain't no manner of use; you know it ain't. I called you here, Deacon, because you remember the last case in this parish. Thirty years ago it was, I guess; but you remember. Lefferts Nash—did praying help *him?* I was a little girl then, but I used to hear my folks talk of it winter nights. Lefferts Nash and Hannah Cory. They drove a stake through her breast. That's what cured him.'

'Oh—' Orrin Bosworth exclaimed.

Sylvester Brand raised his head. 'You've speaking of that old story as if this was the same sort of thing?'

'Ain't it? Ain't my husband pining away the same as Lefferts Nash did? The Deacon here knows—'

The Deacon stirred anxiously in his chair. 'These are forbidden things,' he repeated. 'Supposing your husband is quite sincere in thinking himself haunted, as you might say. Well, even then, what proof have we that the . . . the dead woman . . . is the specter of that poor girl?'

'Proof? Don't he say so? Didn't she tell him? Ain't I seen 'em?' Mrs Rutledge almost screamed.

The three men sat silent, and suddenly the wife burst out: 'A stake through the breast! That's the old way; and it's the only way. The Deacon knows it!'

'It's against our religion to disturb the dead.'

'Ain't it against your religion to let the living perish as my husband is perishing?' She sprang up with one of her abrupt movements and took the family Bible from the whatnot in a corner of the parlor. Putting the book on the table, and moistening a livid fingertip, she turned the pages rapidly, till she came to one on which she laid her hand like a stony paperweight. 'See here,' she said, and read out in her level chanting voice:

'"*Thou shalt not suffer a witch to live.*"

'That's in Exodus, that's where it is,' she added, leaving the book open as if to confirm the statement.

Bosworth continued to glance anxiously from one to the other of the four people about the table. He was younger than any of them, and had had more contact with the modern world; down in Starkfield, in the bar of the Fielding House, he could hear himself laughing with the rest of the men at such old wives' tales. But it was not for nothing that he had been born under the icy shadow of Lonetop, and had shivered and hungered as a lad through the bitter Hemlock County winters. After his parents died, and he had taken hold of the farm himself, he had got more out of it by using improved methods, and by supplying the increasing throng of summer boarders over Stotesbury way with milk and vegetables. He had been made a Selectman of North Ashmore; for so young a man he had a standing in the county. But the roots of the old life were still in him. He could remember, as a little boy, going twice a year with his mother to that bleak hill farm out beyond Sylvester Brand's, where Mrs Bosworth's aunt, Cressidora Cheney, had been shut up for years in a cold clean room with iron bars to the windows. When little Orrin first saw Aunt Cressidora she was a small white old woman, whom her sisters used to 'make decent' for visitors the day that Orrin and his mother were expected. The child wondered why there were bars on the window. 'Like a canary bird,' he said to his mother. The phrase made Mrs Bosworth reflect. 'I do believe they keep Aunt Cressidora too lonesome,' she said; and the next time she went up the mountain with the little boy he carried to his great-aunt a canary in a little wooden cage. It was a great excitement; he knew it would make her happy.

The old woman's motionless face lit up when she saw the bird, and her eyes began to glitter. 'It belongs to me,' she said instantly, stretching her soft bony hand over the cage.

'Of course it does, Aunt Cressy,' said Mrs Bosworth, her eyes filling.

But the bird, startled by the shadow of the old woman's hand, began to flutter and beat its wings distractedly. At the sight, Aunt Cressidora's calm face suddenly became a coil of twitching features. 'You she-devil, you!' she cried in a high squealing voice; and thrusting her hand into the cage she dragged out the terrified bird and wrung its neck. She was plucking the hot body, and squealing 'she-devil, she-devil!' as they drew little Orrin from the room. On the way down the mountain his mother wept a great deal, and said: 'You must never tell anybody that poor Auntie's crazy, or the men would come and take her down to the asylum at Starkfield, and the shame of it would kill us all. Now promise.' The child promised.

He remembered the scene now, with its deep fringe of mystery, secrecy and rumor. It seemed related to a great many other things below the surface of his thoughts, things which stole up anew, making him feel that all the old people he had known, and who 'believed in these thing', might after all be right. Hadn't a witch been burned at North Ashmore? Didn't the summer folk still drive over in jolly buckboard loads to see the meetinghouse where the trial had been held, the pond where they had ducked her and she had floated? . . Deacon Hibben believed; Bosworth was sure of it. If he didn't, why did people from all over the place come to him when their animals had queer sicknesses, or when there was a child in the family that had to be kept shut up because it fell down flat and foamed? Yes, in spite of his religion, Deacon Hibben *knew*. . . .

And Brand? Well, it came to Bosworth in a flash: that North Ashmore woman who was burned had the name of Brand. The same stock, no doubt; there had been Brands in Hemlock County ever since the white men had come there. And Orrin, when he was a child, remembered hearing his parents say that Sylvester Brand hadn't ever oughter married his own cousin, because of the blood. Yet the couple had had two healthy girls, and when Mrs Brand pined away and died nobody suggested that anything had been wrong with her mind. And Vanessa and Ora were the handsomest girls anywhere round. Brand knew it, and scrimped and saved all he could to send Ora, the eldest, down to Starkfield to learn bookkeeping. 'When she's married I'll send you,' he used to say to little Venny, who was his favorite. But Ora never married. She was away three years, during which Venny ran wild on the slopes of Lonetop; and when Ora came back she sickened and died— poor girl! Since then Brand had grown more savage and morose. He was a hard-working farmer, but there wasn't much to be got out of those barren Bearcliff acres. He was said to have taken to drink since his wife's death; now and then men ran across him in the 'dives' of Stotesbury. But not often. And between times he labored hard on his stony acres and did his best for his daughters. In the neglected graveyard of Cold Corners there was a slanting headstone marked with his wife's name;

near it, a year since, he had laid his eldest daughter. And sometimes, at dusk, in the autumn, the village people saw him walk slowly by, turn in between the graves, and stand looking down on the two stones. But he never brought a flower there, or planted a bush; nor Venny either. She was too wild and ignorant. . . .

Mrs Rutledge repeated: 'That's in Exodus.'

The three visitors remained silent, turning about their hats in reluctant hands. Rutledge faced them, still with that empty pellucid gaze which frightened Bosworth. What was he seeing?

'Ain't any of you folks got the grit—?' his wife burst out again, half hysterically.

Deacon Hibben held up his hand. 'That's no way, Mrs Rutledge. This ain't a question of having grit. What we want first of all is . . . proof . . .'

'That's so,' said Bosworth, with an explosion of relief, as if the words had lifted something black and crouching from his breast. Involuntarily the eyes of both men had turned to Brand. He stood there smiling grimly, but did not speak.

'Ain't it so, Brand?' the Deacon prompted him.

'Proof that spooks walk?' the other sneered.

'Well—I presume you want this business settled too?'

The old farmer squared his shoulders. 'Yes—I do. But I ain't a sperritualist. How the hell are you going to settle it?'

Deacon Hibben hesitated; then he said, in a low incisive tone: 'I don't see but one way—Mrs Rutledge's.'

There was a silence.

'What?' Brand sneered again. 'Spying?'

The Deacon's voice sank lower. 'If the poor girl *does* walk . . . her that's your child . . . wouldn't you be the first to want her laid quiet? We all know there've been such cases . . . mysterious visitations. . . . Can any one of us here deny it?'

'I seen 'em,' Mrs Rutledge interjected.

There was another heavy pause. Suddenly Brand fixed his gaze on Rutledge. 'See here, Saul Rutledge, you've got to clear up this damned calumny, or I'll know why. You say my dead girl comes to you.' He labored with his breath, and then jerked out: 'When? You tell me that, and I'll be there.'

Rutledge's head drooped a little, and his eyes wandered to the window. 'Round about sunset, mostly.'

'You know beforehand?'

Rutledge made a sign of assent.

'Well, then—tomorrow, will it be?'

Rutledge made the same sign.

Brand turned to the door. 'I'll be there.' That was all he said. He strode out between them without another glance or word. Deacon Hibben looked at Mrs Rutledge. 'We'll be there too,' he said, as if she had asked him; but she had not spoken, and Bosworth saw that her thin body was trembling all over. He was glad when he and Hibben were out again in the snow.

III

They thought that Brand wanted to be left to himself, and to give him time to unhitch his horse they made a pretense of hanging about in the doorway while Bosworth searched his pockets for a pipe he had no mind to light.

But Brand turned back to them as they lingered. 'You'll meet me down by Lamer's pond tomorrow?' he suggested. 'I want witnesses. Round about sunset.'

They nodded their acquiescence, and he got into his sleigh, gave the horse a cut across the flanks, and drove off under the snow-smothered hemlocks. The other two men went to the shed.

'What do you make of this business, Deacon?' Bosworth asked, to break the silence.

The Deacon shook his head. 'The man's a sick man—that's sure. Something's sucking the life clean out of him.'

But already, in the biting outer air, Bosworth was getting himself under better control. 'Looks to me like a bad case of the ague, as you said.'

'Well—ague of the mind, then. It's his brain that's sick.'

Bosworth shrugged. 'He ain't the first in Hemlock County.'

'That's so,' the Deacon agreed. 'It's a worm in the brain, solitude is.'

'Well, we'll know this time tomorrow, maybe,' said Bosworth. He scrambled into his sleigh, and was driving off in his turn when he heard his companion calling after him. The Deacon explained that his horse had cast a shoe; would Bosworth drive him down to the forge near North Ashmore, if it wasn't too much out of his way? He didn't want the mare slipping about on the freezing snow, and he could probably get the blacksmith to drive him back and shoe her in Rutledge's shed. Bosworth made room for him under the bearskin, and the two men drove off, pursued by a puzzled whinny from the Deacon's old mare.

The road they took was not the one that Bosworth would have followed to reach his own home. But he did not mind that. The shortest way to the forge passed close by Lamer's pond, and Bosworth, since he was in for the business, was not sorry to look the ground over. They drove on in silence.

The snow had ceased, and a green sunset was spreading upward into the crystal sky. A stinging wind barbed with ice flakes caught them in the face on the open ridges, but when they dropped down into the hollow by Lamer's pond the air was as soundless and empty as an unswung bell. They jogged along slowly, each thinking his own thoughts.

'That's the house . . . that tumble-down shack over there, I suppose?' the Deacon said, as the road drew near the edge of the frozen pond.

'Yes: that's the house. A queer hermit fellow built it years ago, my father used to tell me. Since then I don't believe it's ever been used but by the gypsies.'

Bosworth had reined in his horse, and sat looking through pine trunks purpled by the sunset at the crumbling structure. Twilight already lay under the trees, though day lingered in the open. Between two sharply-patterned pine boughs he saw the evening star, like a white boat in a sea of green.

His gaze dropped from that fathomless sky and followed the blue-white undulations of the snow. It gave him a curious agitated feeling to think that here, in this icy solitude, in the tumbledown house he had so often passed without heeding it, a dark mystery, too deep for thought, was being enacted. Down that very slope, coming from the graveyard at Cold Corners, the being they called 'Ora' must pass toward the pond. His heart began to beat stiflingly. Suddenly he gave an exclamation: 'Look!'

He had jumped out of the cutter and was stumbling up the bank toward the slope of snow. On it, turned in the direction of the house by the pond, he had detected a woman's footprints; two; then three; then more. The Deacon scrambled out after him, and they stood and stared.

'God—barefoot!' Hibben gasped. 'Then it is . . . the dead. . . .'

Bosworth said nothing. But he knew that no live woman would travel with naked feet across that freezing wilderness. Here, then, was the proof the Deacon had asked for—they held it. What should they do with it?

'Supposing we was to drive up nearer—round the turn of the pond, till we get close to the house,' the Deacon proposed in a colorless voice. 'Mebbe then. . . .'

Postponement was a relief. They got into the sleigh and drove on. Two or three hundred yards further the road, a mere lane under steep bushy banks, turned sharply to the right, following the bend of the pond. As they rounded the turn they saw Brand's cutter ahead of them. It was empty, the horse tied to a treetrunk. The two men looked at each other again. This was not Brand's nearest way home.

Evidently he had been actuated by the same impulse which had made them rein in their horse by the pondside, and then hasten on to the deserted hovel. Had he too discovered those spectral footprints? Perhaps it was for that very reason that he had left his cutter and vanished in the direction of the house. Bosworth found himself shivering all over under his bearskin. 'I wish to God the dark wasn't coming on,' he muttered. He tethered his own horse near Brand's, and without a word he and the Deacon ploughed through the snow, in the track of Brand's huge feet. They had only a few yards to walk to overtake him. He did not hear them following him, and when Bosworth spoke his name, and he stopped short and turned, his heavy face was dim and confused, like a darker blot on the dusk. He looked at them dully, but without surprise.

'I wanted to see the place,' he merely said.

The Deacon cleared his throat. 'Just take a look . . . yes . . . we thought so. . . . But I guess there won't be anything to *see*. . . .' He attempted a chuckle.

The other did not seem to hear him, but labored on ahead through the pines. The three men came out together in the cleared space before the house. As they emerged from beneath the trees they seemed to have left night behind. The evening star shed a luster on the speckless snow, and Brand, in that lucid circle, stopped with a jerk, and pointed to the same light footprints turned toward the house—the track of a woman in the snow. He stood still, his face working. 'Bare feet. . . .' he said.

The Deacon piped up in a quavering voice: 'The feet of the dead.'

Brand remained motionless. 'The feet of the dead,' he echoed.

Deacon Hibben laid a frightened hand on his arm. 'Come away now, Brand; for the love of God come away.'

The father hung there, gazing down at those light tracks on the snow—light as fox or squirrel trails they seemed, on the white immensity. Bosworth thought to himself: 'The living couldn't walk so light— not even Ora Brand couldn't have, when she lived. . . .' The cold seemed to have entered into his very marrow. His teeth were chattering.

Brand swung about on them abruptly. '*Now!*' he said, moving on as if to an assault, his head bowed forward on his bull neck.

'Now—now? Not in there?' gasped the Deacon. 'What's the use? It was tomorrow he said—' He shook like a leaf.

'It's now,' said Brand. He went up to the door of the crazy house, pushed it inward, and meeting with an unexpected resistance, thrust his heavy shoulder against the panel. The door collapsed like a playing card, and Brand stumbled after it into the darkness of the hut. The others, after a moment's hesitation, followed.

Bosworth was never quite sure in what order the events that succeeded took place. Coming in out of the snow dazzle, he seemed to be plunging into total blackness. He groped his way across the threshold, caught a sharp splinter of the fallen door in his palm, seemed to see something white and wraithlike surge up out of the darkest corner of the hut, and then heard a revolver shot at his elbow, and a cry—

Brand had turned back, and was staggering past him out into the lingering daylight. The sunset, suddenly flushing through the trees, crimsoned his face like blood. He held a revolver in his hand and looked about him in his stupid way.

'They *do* walk, then,' he said and began to laugh. He bent his head to examine his weapon. 'Better here than in the churchyard. They shan't dig her up *now*,' he shouted out. The two men caught him by the arms, and Bosworth got the revolver away from him.

IV

The next day Bosworth's sister Loretta, who kept house for him, asked him, when he came in for his midday dinner, if he had heard the news.

Bosworth had been sawing wood all the morning, and in spite of the cold and the driving snow, which had begun again in the night, he was covered with an icy sweat, like a man getting over a fever.

'What news?'

'Venny Brand's down sick with pneumonia. The Deacon's been there. I guess she's dying.'

Bosworth looked at her with listless eyes. She seemed far off from him, miles away. 'Venny Brand?' he echoed.

'You never liked her, Orrin.'

'She's a child. I never knew much about her.'

'Well,' repeated his sister, with the guileless relish of the unimaginative for bad news, 'I guess she's dying.' After a pause she added: 'It'll kill Sylvester Brand, all alone up there.'

Bosworth got up and said: 'I've got to see to poulticing the gray's fetlock.' He walked out into the steadily falling snow.

Venny Brand was buried three days later. The Deacon read the service; Bosworth was one of the pallbearers. The whole countryside turned out, for the snow had stopped falling, and at any season a funeral offered an opportunity for an outing that was not to be missed. Besides, Venny Brand was young and handsome—at least some people thought her handsome, though she was so swarthy—and her dying like that, so suddenly, had the fascination of tragedy.

'They say her lungs filled right up. . . . Seems she'd had bronchial troubles before . . . I always said both them girls was frail. . . . Look at Ora, how she took and wasted away! And it's colder'n all outdoors up there to Brand's. . . . Their mother, too, *she* pined away just the same. They don't ever make old bones on the mother's side of the family. . . . There's that young Bedlow over there; they say Venny was engaged to him. . . . Oh, Mrs Rutledge, excuse *me*. . . . Step right into the pew; there's a seat for you alongside of grandma. . . .'

Mrs Rutledge was advancing with deliberate step down the narrow aisle of the bleak wooden church. She had on her best bonnet, a monumental structure which no one had seen out of her trunk since old Mrs Silsee's funeral, three years before. All the women remembered it. Under its perpendicular pile her narrow face, swaying on the long thin neck, seemed whiter than ever; but her air of fretfulness had been composed into a suitable expression of mournful immobility.

'Looks as if the stonemason had carved her to put atop of Venny's grave,' Bosworth thought as she glided past him; and then shivered at his own sepulchral fancy. When she bent over her hymn book her lowered lids reminded him again of marble eyeballs; the bony hands clasping the book were bloodless. Bosworth had never seen such hands since he had seen old Aunt Cressidora Cheney strangle the canary bird because it fluttered.

The service was over, the coffin of Venny Brand had been lowered into her sister's grave, and the neighbors were slowly dispersing. Bosworth, as pallbearer, felt obliged to linger and say a word to the stricken father. He waited till Brand had turned from the grave with the Deacon at his side. The three men stood together for a moment; but not one of them spoke. Brand's face was the closed door of a vault, barred with wrinkles like bands of iron.

Finally the Deacon took his hand and said: 'The Lord gave—'

Brand nodded and turned away toward the shed where the horses were hitched. Bosworth followed him. 'Let me drive along home with you,' he suggested.

Brand did not so much as turn his head. 'Home? What home?' he said; and the other fell back.

Loretta Bosworth was talking with the other women while the men unblanketed their horses and backed the cutters out into the heavy snow. As Bosworth waited for her, a few feet off, he saw Mrs Rutledge's tall bonnet lording it above the group. Andy Pond, the Rutledge farm-hand, was backing out the sleigh.

'Saul ain't here today, Mrs Rutledge, is he?' one of the village elders piped, turning a benevolent old tortoise head about on a loose neck, and blinking up into Mrs Rutledge's marble face.

Bosworth heard her measure out her answer in slow incisive words. 'No. Mr Rutledge he ain't here. He would'a' come for certain, but his aunt Minorca Cummins is being buried down to Stotesbury this very day and he had to go down there. Don't it sometimes seem zif we was all walking right in the Shadow of Death?'

As she walked toward the cutter, in which Andy Pond was already seated, the Deacon went up to her with visible hesitation. Involuntarily Bosworth also moved nearer. He heard the Deacon say: 'I'm glad to hear that Saul is able to be up and around.'

She turned her small head on her rigid neck, and lifted the lids of marble.

'Yes, I guess he'll sleep quieter now. And *her* too, maybe, now she don't lay there alone any longer,' she added in a low voice, with a suddent twist of her chin toward the fresh black stain in the graveyard snow. She got into the cutter, and said in a clear tone to Andy Pond: ''S long as we're down here I don't know but what I'll just call round and get a box of soap at Hiram Pringle's.'

A SHORT TRIP HOME

F. Scott Fitzgerald

I was near her, for I had lingered behind in order to get the short walk with her from the living-room to the front door. That was a lot, for she had flowered suddenly and I, being a man and only a year older, hadn't flowered at all, had scarcely dared to come near her in the week we'd been home. Nor was I going to say anything in that walk of ten feet, or touch her; but I had a vague hope she'd do something, give a gay little performance of some sort, personal only in so far as we were alone together.

She had bewitchment suddenly in the twinkle of short hairs on her neck, in the sure, clear confidence that at about eighteen begins to deepen and sing in attractive American girls. The lamplight shopped in the yellow strands of her hair.

Already she was sliding into another world—the world of Joe Jelke and Jim Cathcart waiting for us now in the car. In another year she would pass beyond me forever.

As I waited, feeling the others outside in the snowy night, feeling the excitement of Christmas week and the excitement of Ellen here, blooming away, filling the room with 'sex appeal'—a wretched phrase to express a quality that isn't like that at all—a maid came in from the dining-room, spoke to Ellen quietly and handed her a note. Ellen read it and her eyes faded down, as when the current grows weak on rural circuits, and smouldered off into space. Then she gave me an odd look—in which I probably didn't show—and without a word, followed the maid into the dining-room and beyond. I sat turning over the pages of a magazine for a quarter of an hour.

Joe Jelke came in, red-faced from the cold, his white silk muffler gleaming at the neck of his fur coat. He was a senior at New Haven, I was a sophomore. He was prominent, a member of Scroll and Keys, and, in my eyes, very distinguished and handsome.

'Isn't Ellen coming?'

'I don't know,' I answered discreetly. 'She was all ready.'

'Ellen!' he called. 'Ellen!'

He had left the front door open behind him and a great cloud of frosty air rolled in from outside. He went half-way up the stairs—he was a familiar in the house—and called again, till Mrs Baker came to the banister and said that Ellen was below. Then the maid, a little excited, appeared in the dining-room door.

'Mr Jelke,' she called in a low voice.

Joe's face fell as he turned towards her, sensing bad news.

'Miss Ellen says for you to go to the party. She'll come later.'

'What's the matter?'

'She can't come now. She'll come later.'

He hesitated, confused. It was the last big dance of vacation, and he was mad about Ellen. He had tried to give her a ring for Christmas, and failing that, got her to accept a gold mesh bag that must have cost two hundred dollars. He wasn't the only one—there were three or four in the same wild condition, and all in the ten days she'd been home—but his chance came first, for he was rich and gracious and at that moment the 'desirable' boy of St Paul. To me it seemed impossible that she could prefer another, but the rumour was she'd described Joe as much too perfect. I suppose he lacked mystery for her, and when a man is up against that with a young girl who isn't thinking of the practical side of marriage yet—well—.

'She's in the kitchen,' Joe said angrily.

'No, she's not.' The maid was defiant and a little scared.

'She is.'

'She went out the back way, Mr Jelke.'

'I'm going to see.'

I followed him. The Swedish servants washing dishes looked up sideways at our approach and an interested crashing of pans marked our passage through. The storm door, unbolted, was flapping in the wind, and as we walked out into the snowy yard we saw the tail light of a car turn the corner at the end of the back alley.

'I'm going after her,' Joe said slowly. 'I don't understand this at all.'

I was too awed by the calamity to argue. We hurried to his car and drove in a fruitless, despairing zigzag all over the residence section, peering into every machine on the streets. It was half an hour before the futility of the affair began to dawn upon him—St Paul is a city of almost three hundred thousand people—and Jim Cathcart reminded him that we had another girl to stop for. Like a wounded animal he sank into a melancholy mass of fur in the corner, from which position he jerked upright every few minutes and waved himself backward and forward a little in protest and despair.

Jim's girl was ready and impatient, but after what had happened her impatience didn't seem important. She looked lovely though. That's one thing about Christmas vacation—the excitement of growth and change and adventure in foreign parts transforming the people you've known all your life. Joe Jelke was polite to her in a daze—he indulged in one burst of short, loud, harsh laughter by way of conversation—and we drove to the hotel.

The chauffeur approached it on the wrong side—the side on which the line of cars was not putting forth guests—and because of that we came suddenly upon Ellen Baker just getting out of a small coupé. Even before we came to a stop, Joe Jelke had jumped excitedly from the car.

Ellen turned towards us, a faintly distracted look—perhaps of surprise, but certainly not of alarm—in her face; in fact, she didn't seem very aware of us. Joe approached her with a stern, dignified, injured and, I thought, just exactly correct reproof in his expression. I followed.

Seated in the coupé—he had not dismounted to help Ellen out—was a hard thin-faced man of about thirty-five with an air of being scarred, and a slight sinister smile. His eyes were a sort of taunt to the whole human family—they were the eyes of an animal, sleepy and quiescent in the presence of another species. They were helpless yet brutal, unhopeful yet confident. It was as if they felt themselves powerless to originate activity, but infinitely capable of profiting by a single gesture of weakness in another.

Vaguely I placed him as one of the sort of men whom I had been conscious of from my earliest youth as 'hanging around'—leaning with one elbow on the counters of tobacco stores, watching, through heaven knows what small chink of the mind, the people who hurried in and out. Intimate to garages, where he had vague business conducted in undertones, to barber shops and to the lobbies of theatres—in such places, anyhow, I placed the type, if type it was, that he reminded me of. Sometimes his face bobbed up in one of Tad's more savage cartoons, and I had always from earliest boyhood thrown a nervous glance towards the dim borderland where he stood, and seen him watching me and despising me. Once, in a dream, he had taken a few steps towards me, jerking his head back and muttering 'Say, kid' in what was intended to be a reassuring voice, and I had broken for the door in terror. This was that sort of man.

Joe and Ellen faced each other silently; she seemed, as I have said, to be in a daze. It was cold, but she didn't notice that her coat had blown open; Joe reached out and pulled it together, and automatically she clutched it with her hand.

Suddenly the man in the coupé, who had been watching them

silently, laughed. It was a bare laugh, done with the breath—just a noisy jerk of the head—but it was an insult if I had ever heard one; definite and not to be passed over. I wasn't surprised when Joe, who was quick tempered, turned to him angrily and said:

'What's your trouble?'

The man waited a moment, his eyes shifting and yet staring, and always seeing. Then he laughed again in the same way. Ellen stirred uneasily.

'Who is this—this—' Joe's voice trembled with annoyance.

'Look out now,' said the man slowly.

Joe turned to me.

'Eddie, take Ellen and Catherine in, will you?' he said quickly. . . . 'Ellen, go with Eddie.'

'Look out now,' the man repeated.

Ellen made a little sound with her tongue and teeth, but she didn't resist when I took her arm and moved her towards the side door of the hotel. It struck me as odd that she should be so helpless, even to the point of acquiescing by her silence in this imminent trouble.

'Let it go, Joe!' I called back over my shoulder. 'Come inside!'

Ellen, pulling against my arm, hurried us on. As we were caught up into the swinging doors I had the impression that the man was getting out of his coupé.

Ten minutes later, as I waited for the girls outside the women's dressing-room, Joe Jelke and Jim Cathcart stepped out of the elevator. Joe was very white, his eyes were heavy and glazed, there was a trickle of dark blood on his forehead and on his white muffler. Jim had both their hats in his hand.

'He hit Joe with brass knuckles,' Jim said in a low voice. 'Joe was out cold for a minute or so. I wish you'd send a bell boy for some witch-hazel and court-plaster.'

It was late and the hall was deserted; brassy fragments of the dance below reached us as if heavy curtains were being blown aside and dropping back into place. When Ellen came out I took her directly downstairs. We avoided the receiving line and went into a dim room set with scraggly hotel palms where couples sometimes sat out during the dance; there I told her what had happened.

'It was Joe's own fault,' she said, surprisingly. 'I told him not to interfere.'

This wasn't true. She had said nothing, only uttered one curious little click of impatience.

'You ran out the back door and disappeared for almost an hour,' I protested. 'Then you turned up with a hard-looking customer who laughed in Joe's face.'

'A hard-looking customer,' she repeated, as if tasting the sound of the words.

'Well, wasn't he? Where on earth did you get hold of him, Ellen?'

'On the train,' she answered. Immediately she seemed to regret this admission. 'You'd better stay out of things that aren't your business, Eddie. You see what happened to Joe.'

Literally I gasped. To watch her, seated beside me, immaculately glowing, her body giving off wave after wave of freshness and delicacy— and to hear her talk like that.

'But that man's a thug!' I cried. 'No girl could be safe with him. He used brass knuckles on Joe—brass knuckles!'

'Is that pretty bad?'

She asked this as she might have asked such a question a few years ago. She looked at me at last and really wanted an answer; for a moment it was as if she were trying to recapture an attitude that had almost departed; then she hardened again. I say 'hardened', for I began to notice that when she was concerned with this man her eyelids fell a little, shutting other things—everything else—out of view.

That was a moment I might have said something, I suppose, but in spite of everything, I couldn't light into her. I was too much under the spell of her beauty and its success. I even began to find excuses for her— perhaps that man wasn't what he appeared to be; or perhaps—more romantically—she was involved with him against her will to shield someone else. At this point people began to drift into the room and come up to speak to us. We couldn't talk any more, so we went in and bowed to the chaperones. Then I gave her up to the bright restless sea of the dance, where she moved in an eddy of her own among the pleasant islands of coloured favours set out on tables and the south winds from the brasses moaning across the hall. After a while I saw Joe Jelke sitting in a corner with a strip of court-plaster on his forehead watching Ellen as if she herself had struck him down, but I didn't go up to him. I felt queer myself—like I feel when I wake up after sleeping through an afternoon, strange and portentous, as if something had gone on in the interval that changed the values of everything and that I didn't see.

The night slipped on through successive phases of cardboard horns, amateur tableaux and flashlights for the morning papers. Then was the grand march and supper, and about two o'clock some of the committee dressed up as revenue agents pinched the party, and a facetious newspaper was distributed, burlesquing the events of the evening. And all the time out of the corner of my eye I watched the shining orchid on Ellen's shoulder as it moved like Stuart's plume about the room. I watched it with a definite foreboding until the last sleepy groups had crowded into the elevators, and then, bundled to the eyes in great shapeless fur coats, drifted out into the clear dry Minnesota night.

II

There is a sloping mid-section of our city which lies between the residence quarter on the hill and the business district on the level of the river. It is a vague part of town, broken by its climb into triangles and odd shapes—there are names like Seven Corners—and I don't believe a dozen people could draw an accurate map of it, though every one traversed it by trolley, auto or shoe leather twice a day. And though it was a busy section, it would be hard for me to name the business that comprised its activity. There were always long lines of trolley cars waiting to start somewhere; there was a big movie theatre and many small ones with posters of Hoot Gibson and Wonder Dogs and Wonder Horses outside; there were small stores with 'Old King Brady' and 'The Liberty Boys of '76' in the windows, and marbles, cigarettes, and candy inside; and—one definite place at least—a fancy costumer whom we all visited at least once a year. Some time during boyhood I became aware that on one side of a certain obscure street there were bawdy houses, and all through the district were pawnshops, cheap jewellers, small athletic clubs and gymnasiums and somewhat too blatantly run-down saloons.

The morning after the Cotillion Club party, I woke up late and lazy, with the happy feeling that for a day or two more there was no chapel, no classes—nothing to do but wait for another party tonight. It was crisp and bright—one of those days when you forget how cold it is until your cheek freezes—and the events of the evening before seemed dim and far away. After luncheon I started down-town on foot through a light, pleasant snow of small flakes that would probably fall all after-noon, and I was about half through that halfway section of town—so far as I know, there's no inclusive name for it—when suddenly whatever idle thought was in my mind blew away like a hat and I began thinking hard of Ellen Baker. I began worrying about her as I'd never worried about anything outside myself before. I began to loiter, with an instinct to go up on the hill again and find her and talk to her; then I remem-bered that she was at a tea, and I went on again, but still thinking of her, and harder than ever. Right then the affair opened up again.

It was snowing, I said, and it was four o'clock on a December afternoon, when there is a promise of darkness in the air and the street lamps are just going on. I passed a combination pool parlour and restaurant, with a stove loaded with hot-dogs in the window, and a few loungers hanging around the door. The lights were on inside—not bright lights but just a few pale yellow high up on the ceiling—and the glow they threw out into the frosty dusk wasn't bright enough to tempt you to stare inside. As I went past, thinking hard of Ellen all this time, I took in the quartet of loafers out of the corner of my eye. I hadn't gone half a dozen steps down the street when one of them called to me, not by name but in a way clearly intended for my ear. I thought it was a tribute to my raccoon coat and paid no attention, but a moment later whoever it was called to me again in a peremptory voice. I was annoyed and turned around. There, standing in the group not ten feet away and looking at me with the half-sneer on his face with which he'd looked at Joe Jelke, was the scarred, thin-faced man of the night before.

He had on a black fancy-cut coat, buttoned up to his neck as if he were cold. His hands were deep in his pockets and he wore a derby and high button shoes. I was startled, and for a moment I hesitated, but I was most of all angry, and knowing that I was quicker with my hands than Joe Jelke, I took a tentative step back towards him. The other men weren't looking at me—I don't think they saw me at all—but I knew that this one recognized me; there was nothing casual about his look, no mistake.

'Here I am. What are you going to do about it?' his eyes seemed to say.

I took another step towards him and he laughed soundlessly, but with active contempt, and drew back into the group. I followed. I was going to speak to him—I wasn't sure what I was going to say—but when I came up he had either changed his mind and backed off, or else he wanted me to follow him inside, for he had slipped off and the three men watched my intent approach without curiosity. They were the same kind—sporty, but, unlike him, smooth rather than truculent; I didn't find any personal malice in their collective glance.

'Did he go inside?' I asked.

They looked at one another in that cagey way; a wink passed between them, and after a perceptible pause, one said:

'Who go inside?'

'I don't know his name.'

There was another wink. Annoyed and determined, I walked past them and into the pool room. There were a few people at a lunch counter along one side and a few more playing billiards, but he was not among them.

Again I hesitated. If his idea was to lead me into any blind part of the establishment—there were some half-open doors further back—I wanted more support. I went up to the man at the desk.

'What became of the fellow who just walked in here?'

Was he on his guard immediately, or was that my imagination?

'What fellow?'

'Thin face—derby hat.'

'How long ago?'

'Oh—a minute.'

He shook his head again. 'Didn't see him,' he said.

I waited. The three men from outside had come in and were lined up beside me at the counter. I felt that all of them were looking at me in a peculiar way. Feeling helpless and increasingly uneasy, I turned suddenly and went out. A little way down the street I turned again and took a good look at the place, so I'd know it and could find it again. On the next corner I broke impulsively into a run, found a taxicab in front of the hotel and drove back up the hill.

Ellen wasn't home. Mrs Baker came downstairs and talked to me. She seemed entirely cheerful and proud of Ellen's beauty, and ignorant of anything amiss or of anything unusual having taken place the night before. She was glad that vacation was almost over—it was a strain and Ellen wasn't very strong. Then she said something that relieved my mind enormously. She was glad that I had come in, for of course Ellen would want to see me, and the time was so short. She was going back at half past eight tonight.

'Tonight!' I exclaimed. 'I thought it was the day after tomorrow.'

'She's going to visit the Brokaws in Chicago,' Mrs Baker said. 'They want her for some party. We just decided it today. She's leaving with the Ingersoll girls tonight.'

I was so glad I could barely restrain myself from shaking her hand. Ellen was safe. It had been nothing all along but a moment of the most casual adventure. I felt like an idiot, but I realized how much I cared about Ellen and how little I could endure anything terrible happening to her.

'She'll be in soon?'

'Any minute now. She just phoned from the University Club.'

I said I'd be over later—I lived almost next door and I wanted to be alone. Outside I remembered I didn't have a key, so I started up the Bakers' driveway to take the old cut we used in childhood through the intervening yard. It was still snowing, but the flakes were bigger now against the darkness, and trying to locate the buried walk I noticed that the Bakers' back door was ajar.

I scarcely know why I turned and walked into that kitchen. There was a time when I would have known the Bakers' servants by name. That wasn't true now, but they knew me, and I was aware of a sudden suspension as I came in—not only a suspension of talk but of some mood of expectation that had filled them. They began to go to work too quickly; they made unnecessary movements and clamour—those three. The parlour maid looked at me in a frightened way and I suddenly guessed she was waiting to deliver another message. I beckoned her into the pantry.

'I know all about this,' I said. 'It's a very serious business. Shall I go to Mrs Baker now, or will you shut and lock that back door?'

'Don't tell Mrs Baker, Mr Stinson!'

'Then I don't want Miss Ellen disturbed. If she is—and if she is I'll know of it—' I delivered some outrageous threat about going to all the employment agencies and seeing she never got another job in the city. She was thoroughly intimidated when I went out; it wasn't a minute before the back door was locked and bolted behind me.

Simultaneously I heard a big car drive up in front, chains crunching on the soft snow; it was bringing Ellen home, and I went in to say goodbye.

Joe Jelke and two other boys were along, and none of the three could manage to take his eyes off her, even to say hello to me. She had one of those exquisite rose skins frequent in our part of the country, and beautiful until the little veins begin to break at about forty; now, flushed with the cold, it was a riot of lovely delicate pinks like many carnations. She and Joe had reached some sort of reconciliation, or at least he was too far gone in love to remember last night; but I saw that though she laughed a lot she wasn't really paying any attention to him or any of them. She wanted them to go, so that there'd be a message from the kitchen, but I knew that the message wasn't coming—that she was safe. There was talk of the Pump and Slipper dance at New Haven and of the Princeton Prom, and then, in various moods, we four left and separated quickly outside. I walked home with a certain depression of spirit and lay for an hour in a hot bath thinking that vacation was all over for me now that she was gone; feeling, even more deeply than I had yesterday, that she was out of my life.

And something eluded me, some one more thing to do, something that I had lost amid the events of the afternoon, promising myself to go back and pick it up, only to find that it had escaped me. I associated it vaguely with Mrs Baker, and now I seemed to recall that it had poked up its head somewhere in the stream of conversation with her. In my relief about Ellen I had forgotten to ask her a question regarding something she had said.

The Brokaws—that was it—where Ellen was to visit. I knew Bill Brokaw well; he was in my class at Yale. Then I remembered and sat bolt upright in the tub—the Brokaws weren't in Chicago this Christmas, they were at Palm Beach!

Dripping I sprang out of the tub, threw an insufficient union suit around my shoulders and sprang for the phone in my room. I got the connection quick, but Miss Ellen had already started for the train.

Luckily our car was in, and while I squirmed, still damp, into my clothes, the chauffeur brought it around to the door. The night was cold and dry, and we made good time to the station through the hard, crusty snow. I felt queer and insecure starting out this way, but somehow more confident as the station loomed up bright and new against the dark, cold air. For fifty years my family had owned the land on which it was built and that made my temerity seem all right somehow. There was always a possibility that I was rushing in where angels feared to tread, but that sense of having a solid foothold in the past made me willing to make a fool of myself. This business was all wrong—terribly wrong. Any idea I had entertained that it was harmless dropped away now; between Ellen and some vague overwhelming catastrophe there stood me, or else the police and a scandal. I'm no moralist—there was another element here, dark and frightening, and I didn't want Ellen to go through it alone.

There are three competing trains from St Paul to Chicago that all leave within a few minutes of half past eight. Hers was the Burlington, and as I ran across the station I saw the grating being pulled over and the light above it go out. I knew, though, that she had a drawing-room with the Ingersoll girls, because her mother had mentioned buying the ticket, so she was, literally speaking, tucked in until tomorrow.

The C., M., & St P. gate was down at the other end and I raced for it and made it. I had forgotten one thing, though, and that was enough to keep me awake and worried half the night. This train got into Chicago ten minutes after the other. Ellen had that much time to disappear into one of the largest cities in the world.

I gave the porter a wire to my family to send from Milwaukee, and at eight o'clock next morning I pushed violently by a whole line of passengers, clamouring over their bags parked in the vestibule, and shot out of the door with a sort of scramble over the porter's back. For a moment the confusion of a great station, the voluminous sounds and echoes and cross-currents of bells and smoke struck me helpless. Then I dashed for the exit and towards the only chance I knew of finding her.

I had guessed right. She was standing at the telegraph counter, sending off heaven knows what black lie to her mother, and her expression when she saw me had a sort of terror mixed up with its surprise. There was cunning in it too. She was thinking quickly—she would have liked to walk away from me as if I weren't there, and go about her own business, but she couldn't. I was too matter-of-fact a thing in her life. So we stood silently watching each other and each thinking hard.

'The Brokaws are in Florida,' I said after a minute.

'It was nice of you to take such a long trip to tell me that.'

'Since you've found it out, don't you think you'd better go on to school?'

'Please let me alone, Eddie,' she said.

'I'll go as far as New York with you. I've decided to go back early myself.'

'You'd better let me alone.' Her lovely eyes narrowed and her face took on a look of dumb-animal resistance. She made a visible effort, the cunning flickered back into it, then both were gone, and in their stead was a cheerful reassuring smile that all but convinced me.

'Eddie, you silly child, don't you think I'm old enough to take care of myself?' I didn't answer. 'I'm going to meet a man, you understand. I just want to see him today. I've got my ticket East on the five o'clock train. If you don't believe it, here it is in my bag.'

'I believe you.'

'The man isn't anybody that you know and—frankly, I think you're being awfully fresh and impossible.'

'I know who the man is.'

Again she lost control of her face. The terrible expression came back into it and she spoke with almost a snarl:

'You'd better let me alone.'

I took the blank out of her hand and wrote out an explanatory telegram to her mother. Then I turned to Ellen and said a little roughly:

'We'll take the five o'clock train East together. Meanwhile you're going to spend the day with me.'

The mere sound of my own voice saying this so emphatically encouraged me, and I think it impressed her too; at any rate, she submitted—

at least temporarily—and came along without protest while I bought my ticket.

When I start to piece together the fragments of that day a sort of confusion begins, as if my memory didn't want to yield up any of it, or my consciousness let any of it pass through. There was a bright, fierce morning during which we rode about in a taxicab and went to a department store where Ellen said she wanted to buy something and then tried to slip away from me by a back way. I had the feeling, for an hour, that someone was following us along Lake Shore Drive in a taxicab, and I would try to catch them by turning quickly or looking suddenly into the chauffeur's mirror; but I could find no one, and when I turned back I could see that Ellen's face was contorted with mirthless, unnatural laughter.

All morning there was a raw, bleak wind off the lake, but when we went to the Blackstone for lunch a light snow came down past the windows and we talked almost naturally about our friends, and about casual things. Suddenly her tone changed; she grew serious and looked me in the eye, straight and sincere.

'Eddie, you're the oldest friend I have,' she said, 'and you oughtn't to find it too hard to trust me. If I promise you faithfully on my word of honour to catch that five o'clock train, will you let me alone a few hours this afternoon?'

'Why?'

'Well'—she hesitated and hung her head a little—'I guess everybody has a right to say—goodbye.'

'You want to say goodbye to that—'

'Yes, yes,' she said hastily; 'just a few hours, Eddie, and I promise faithfully that I'll be on that train.'

'Well, I suppose no great harm could be done in two hours. If you really want to say goodbye—'

I looked up suddenly, and surprised a look of such tense cunning in her face that I winced before it. Her lip was curled up and her eyes were slits again; there wasn't the faintest touch of fairness and sincerity in her whole face.

We argued. The argument was vague on her part and somewhat hard and reticent on mine. I wasn't going to be cajoled again into any weakness or be infected with any—and there was a contagion of evil in the air. She kept trying to imply, without any convincing evidence to bring forward, that everything was all right. Yet she was too full of the thing itself—whatever it was—to build up a real story, and she wanted to catch at any credulous and acquiescent train of thought that might start in my head, and work that for all it was worth. After every reassuring suggestion she threw out, she stared at me eagerly, as if she hoped I'd launch into a comfortable moral lecture with the customary sweet at the end—which in this case would be her liberty. But I was wearing her away a little. Two or three times it needed just a touch of pressure to bring her to the point of tears—which, of course, was what I wanted—but I couldn't seem to manage it. Almost I had her—almost possessed her interior attention—then she would slip away.

I bullied her remorselessly into a taxi about four o'clock and started for the station. The wind was raw again, with a sting of snow in it, and the people in the streets, waiting for buses and street cars too small to take them all in, looked cold and disturbed and unhappy. I tried to think how lucky we were to be comfortably off and taken care of, but all the warm, respectable world I had been part of yesterday had dropped away from me. There was something we carried with us now that was the enemy and the opposite of all that; it was in the cabs beside us, the streets we passed through. With a touch of panic, I wondered if I wasn't slipping almost imperceptibly into Ellen's attitude of mind. The column of passengers waiting to go aboard the train were as remote from me as people from another world, but it was I that was drifting away and leaving them behind.

My lower was in the same car with her compartment. It was an old fashioned car, its lights somewhat dim, its carpets and upholstery full of the dust of another generation. There were half a dozen other travellers, but they made no special impression on me, except that they shared the unreality that I was beginning to feel everywhere around me. We went into Ellen's compartment, shut the door and sat down.

Suddenly I put my arms around her and drew her over to me, just as tenderly as I knew how—as if she were a little girl—as she was. She resisted a little, but after a moment she submitted and lay tense and rigid in my arms.

'Ellen,' I said helplessly, 'you asked me to trust you. You have much more reason to trust me. Wouldn't it help to get rid of all this, if you told me a little?'

'I can't,' she said, very low—'I mean, there's nothing to tell.'

'You met this man on the train coming home and you fell in love with him, isn't that true?'

'I don't know.'

'Tell me, Ellen. You fell in love with him?'

'I don't know. Please let me alone.'

'Call it anything you want,' I went on, 'he has some sort of hold over you. He's trying to use you; he's trying to get something from you. He's not in love with you.'

'What does that matter?' she said in a weak voice.

'It does matter. Instead of trying to fight this—this thing—you're trying to fight me. And I love you, Ellen. Do you hear? I'm telling you all of a sudden, but it isn't new with me. I love you.'

She looked at me with a sneer on her gentle face; it was an expression I had seen on men who were tight and didn't want to be taken home. But it was human. I was reaching her, faintly and from far away, but more than before.

'Ellen, I want you to answer me one question. Is he going to be on this train?'

She hesitated; then, an instant too late, she shook her head.

'Be careful, Ellen. Now I'm going to ask you one thing more, and I wish you'd try very hard to answer. Coming West, when did this man get on the train?'

'I don't know,' she said with an effort.

Just at that moment I became aware, with the unquestionable knowledge reserved for facts, that he was just outside the door. She knew it, too; the blood left her face and that expression of low-animal perspicacity came creeping back. I lowered my face into my hands and tried to think.

We must have sat there, with scarcely a word, for well over an hour. I was conscious that the lights of Chicago, then of Englewood and of endless suburbs, were moving by, and then there were no more lights and we were out on the dark flatness of Illinois. The train seemed to draw in upon itself; it took on the air of being alone. The porter knocked at the door and asked if he could make up the berth, but I said no and he went away.

After a while I convinced myself that the struggle inevitably coming wasn't beyond what remained of my sanity, my faith in the essential all-rightness of things and people. That this person's purpose was what we call 'criminal' I took for granted, but there was no need of ascribing to him an intelligence that belonged to a higher plane of human, or inhuman endeavour. It was still as a man that I considered him, and tried to get at his essence, his self-interest—what took the place in him of a comprehensible heart—but I suppose I more than half knew what I would find when I opened the door.

When I stood up Ellen didn't seem to see me at all. She was hunched into a corner staring straight ahead with a sort of film over her eyes, as if she were in a state of suspended animation of body and mind. I lifted her and put two pillows under her head and threw my fur coat over her knees. Then I knelt beside her and kissed her two hands, opened the door and went out into the hall.

I closed the door behind me and stood with my back against it for a minute. The car was dark save for the corridor lights at each end. There was no sound except the groaning of the couplers, the even click-a-click of the rails and someone's loud sleeping breath further down the car. I became aware after a moment that the figure of a man was standing by the water cooler just outside the men's smoking-room, his derby hat on his head, his coat collar turned up around his neck as if he were cold, his hands in his coat pockets. When I saw him, he turned and went into the smoking-room, and I followed. He was sitting in the far corner of the long leather bench; I took the single armchair beside the door.

As I went in I nodded to him and he acknowledged my presence with one of those terrible soundless laughs of his. But this time it was prolonged, it seemed to go on forever, and mostly to cut it short, I asked: 'Where are you from?' in a voice I tried to make casual.

He stopped laughing and looked at me narrowly, wondering what my game was. When he decided to answer, his voice was muffled as though he were speaking through a silk scarf, and it seemed to come from a long way off.

'I'm from St Paul, Jack.'

'Been making a trip home?'

He nodded. Then he took a long breath and spoke in a hard, menacing voice:

'You better get off at Fort Wayne, Jack.'

He was dead. He was dead as hell—he had been dead all along, but what force had flowed through him, like blood in his veins, out to St Paul and back, was leaving him now. A new outline—the outline of him dead—was coming through the palpable figure that had knocked down Joe Jelke.

He spoke again, with a sort of jerking effort:

'You get off at Fort Wayne, Jack, or I'm going to wipe you out.' He moved his hand in his coat pocket and showed me the outline of a revolver.

I shook my head. 'You can't touch me,' I answered. 'You see, I know.' His terrible eyes shifted over me quickly, trying to determine whether or not I did know. Then he gave a snarl and made as though he were going to jump to his feet.

'You climb off here or else I'm going to get you, Jack!' he cried hoarsely. The train was slowing up for Fort Wayne and his voice rang loud in the comparative quiet, but he didn't move from his chair—he was too weak, I think—and we sat staring at each other while workmen passed up and down outside the window banging the brakes and wheels, and the engine gave out loud mournful pants up ahead. No one got into our car. After a while the porter closed the vestibule door and passed back along the corridor, and we slid out of the murky yellow station light and into the long darkness.

What I remember next must have extended over a space of five or six hours, though it comes back to me as something without any existence in time—something that might have taken five minutes or a year. There began a slow, calculated assault on me, wordless and terrible. I felt what I can only call a strangeness stealing over me—akin to the strangeness I had felt all afternoon, but deeper and more intensified. It was like nothing so much as the sensation of drifting away, and I gripped the arms of the chair convulsively, as if to hang onto a piece in the living world. Sometimes I felt myself going out with a rush. There would be almost a warm relief about it, a sense of not caring; then, with a violent wrench of the will, I'd pull myself back into the room.

Suddenly I realized that from a while back I had stopped hating him, stopped feeling violently alien to him, and with the realization, I went cold and sweat broke out all over my head. He was getting around my abhorrence, as he had got around Ellen coming West on the train; and it was just that strength he drew from preying on people that had brought him up to the point of concrete violence in St Paul, and that, fading and flickering out, still kept him fighting now.

He must have seen that faltering in my heart, for he spoke at once, in a low, even, almost gentle voice: 'You better go now.'

'Oh, I'm not going,' I forced myself to say.

'Suit yourself, Jack.'

He was my friend, he implied. He knew how it was with me and he wanted to help. He pitied me. I'd better go away before it was too late. The rhythm of his attack was soothing as a song: I'd better go away— *and let him get at Ellen.* With a little cry I sat bolt upright.

'What do you want of this girl?' I said, my voice shaking. 'To make a sort of walking hell of her.'

His glance held a quality of dumb surprise, as if I were punishing an animal for a fault of which he was not conscious. For an instant I faltered; then I went on blindly:

'You've lost her; she's put her trust in me.'

His countenance went suddenly black with evil, and he cried: 'You're a liar!' in a voice that was like cold hands.

'She trusts me,' I said. 'You can't touch her. She's safe!'

He controlled himself. His face grew bland, and I felt that curious weakness and indifference begin again inside me. What was the use of all this? What was the use?

'You haven't got much time left,' I forced myself to say, and then, in a flash of intuition, I jumped at the truth. 'You died, or you were killed, not far from here!'—Then I saw what I had not seen before—that his forehead was drilled with a small round hole like a larger picture nail leaves when it's pulled from a plaster wall. 'And now you're sinking. You've only got a few hours. The trip home is over!'

His face contorted, lost all semblance of humanity, living or dead. Simultaneously the room was full of cold air and with a noise that was something between a paroxysm of coughing and a burst of horrible laughter, he was on his feet, reeking of shame and blasphemy.

'Come and look!' he cried. 'I'll show you—'

He took a step towards me, then another and it was exactly as if a door stood open behind him, a door yawning out to an inconceivable abyss of darkness and corruption. There was a scream of mortal agony, from him or from somewhere behind, and abruptly the strength went out of him in a long husky sigh and he wilted to the floor. . . .

How long I sat there, dazed with terror and exhaustion, I don't know. The next thing I remember is the sleepy porter shining shoes across the room from me, and outside the window the steel fires of Pittsburgh breaking the flat perspective of the night. There was something extended on the bench also—something too faint for a man, too heavy for a shadow. Even as I perceived it it faded off and away.

Some minutes later I opened the door of Ellen's compartment. She was asleep where I had left her. Her lovely cheeks were white and wan, but she lay naturally—her hands relaxed and her breathing regular and clear. What had possessed her had gone out of her, leaving her exhausted but her own dear self again.

I made her a little more comfortable, tucked a blanket around her, extinguished the light and went out.

III

When I came home for Easter vacation, almost my first act was to go down to the billiard parlour near Seven Corners. The man at the cash register quite naturally didn't remember my hurried visit of three months before.

'I'm trying to locate a certain party who, I think, came here a lot some time ago.'

I described the man rather accurately, and when I had finished, the cashier called to a little jockeylike fellow who was sitting near with an air of having something very important to do that he couldn't quite remember.

'Hey, Shorty, talk to this guy, will you? I think he's looking for Joe Varland.'

The little man gave me a tribal look of suspicion. I went and sat near him.

'Joe Varland's dead, fella,' he said grudgingly. 'He died last winter.'

I described him again—his overcoat, his laugh, the habitual expression of his eyes.

'That's Joe Varland you're looking for all right, but he's dead.'

'I want to find out something about him.'

'What you want to find out?'

'What did he do, for instance?'

'How should I know?'

'Look here! I'm not a policeman. I just want some kind of information about his habits. He's dead now and it can't hurt him. And it won't go beyond me.'

'Well'—he hesitated, looking me over—'he was a great one for travelling. He got in a row in the station in Pittsburgh and a dick got him.'

I nodded. Broken pieces of the puzzle began to assemble in my head.

'Why was he a lot on trains?'

'How should I know, fella?'

'If you can use ten dollars, I'd like to know anything you may have heard on the subject.'

'Well,' said Shorty reluctantly, 'all I know is they used to say he worked the trains.'

'Worked the trains?'

'He had some racket of his own he'd never loosen up about. He used to work the girls travelling alone on the trains. Nobody ever knew much about it—he was a pretty smooth guy—but sometimes he'd turn up here with a lot of dough and he let 'em know it was the janes he got it off of.'

I thanked him and gave him the ten dollars and went out, very thoughtful, without mentioning that part of Joe Varland had made a last trip home.

Ellen wasn't West for Easter, and even if she had been I wouldn't have gone to her with the information, either—at least I've seen her almost every day this summer and we've managed to talk about everything else. Sometimes, though, she gets silent about nothing and wants to be very close to me, and I know what's in her mind.

Of course she's coming out this fall, and I have two more years at New Haven; still, things don't look so impossible as they did a few months ago. She belongs to me in a way—even if I lose her she belongs to me. Who knows? Anyhow, I'll always be there.

BLIND MAN'S BUFF

H. Russell Wakefield

'Well, thank heavens that yokel seemed to know the place,' said Mr Cort to himself. '"First to the right, second to the left, black gates." I hope the oaf in Wendover who sent me six miles out of my way will freeze to death. It's not often like this in England—cold as the penny in a dead man's eye.' He'd barely reach the place before dusk. He let the car out over the rasping, frozen roads. 'First to the right'— must be this—second to the left, must be this—and there were the black gates. He got out, swung them open, and drove cautiously up a narrow, twisting drive, his headlights peering suspiciously round the bends. Those hedges wanted clipping, he thought, and this lane would have to be remetalled—full of holes. Nasty drive up on a bad night; would cost some money, though.

The car began to climb steeply and swing to the right, and presently the high hedges ended abruptly, and Mr Cort pulled up in front of Lorn Manor. He got out of the car, rubbed his hands, stamped his feet, and looked about him.

Lorn Manor was embedded half-way up a Chiltern spur and, as the agent had observed, 'commanded extensive vistas'. The place looked its age, Mr Cort decided, or rather ages, for the double Georgian brick chimneys warred with the Queen Anne left front. He could just make out the date, 1703, at the base of the nearest chimney. All that wing must have been added later. 'Big place, marvellous bargain at seven thousand; can't understand it. How those windows with their little curved eye-brows seem to frown down on one!' And then he turned and examined the 'vistas'. The trees were tinted exquisitely to an uncertain glory as the great red sinking sun flashed its rays on their crystal mantle. The Vale of Aylesbury was drowsing beneath a slowly deepening shroud of mist. Above it the hills, their crests rounded and shaded by silver and rose coppices, seemed to have set in them great smoky eyes of flame where the last rays burned in them.

'It is like some dream world,' thought Mr Cort. 'It is curious how, wherever the sun strikes it seems to make an eye, and each one fixed on me; those hills, even those windows. But, judging from that mist, I shall have a slow journey home; I'd better have a quick look inside, though I have already taken a prejudice against the place—I hardly know why. Too lonely and isolated, perhaps.' And then the eyes blinked and closed, and it was dark. He took a key from his pocket and went up three steps and thrust it into the keyhole of the massive oak door. The next moment he looked forward into absolute blackness, and the door swung to and closed behind him. This, of course, must be the 'palatial panelled hall' which the agent described. He must strike a match and find the light-switch. He fumbled in his pockets without success, and then he went through them again. He thought for a moment. 'I must have left them on the seat in the car,' he decided; 'I'll go and fetch them. The door must be just behind me here.'

He turned and groped his way back, and then drew himself up sharply, for it had seemed that something had slipped past him, and then he put out his hands—to touch the back of a chair, brocaded, he judged. He moved to the left of it and walked into a wall, changed his direction, went back past the chair, and found the wall again. He went back to the chair, sat down, and went through his pockets again, more thoroughly and carefully this time. Well, there was nothing to get fussed about; he was bound to find the door sooner or later. Now, let him think. When he came in he had gone straight forward, three yards perhaps; but he couldn't have gone straight back, because he'd stumbled into this chair. The door must be a little to the left or right of it. He'd try each in turn. He turned to the left first, and found himself going down a little narrow passage; he could feel its sides when he stretched out his hands. Well, then, he'd try the right. He did so, and walked into a wall. He groped his way along it, and again it seemed as if something slipped past him. 'I wonder if there's a bat in here?' he asked himself, and then found himself back at the chair.

How Rachel would laugh if she could see him now. Surely he had a stray match somewhere. He took off his overcoat and ran his hands round the seam of every pocket, and then he did the same to the coat and waistcoat of his suit. And then he put them on again. Well, he'd try again. He'd follow the wall along. He did so, and found himself in a narrow passage. Suddenly he shot out his right hand, for he had the impression that something had brushed his face very lightly. 'I'm beginning to get a little bored with that bat, and with this blasted room generally,' he said to himself. 'I could imagine a more nervous person than myself getting a little fussed and panicky; but that's the one thing not to do.' Ah, here was that chair again. 'Now, I'll try the wall the other side.' Well, that seemed to go on for ever, so he retraced his steps till he found the chair, and sat down again. He whistled a little snatch resignedly. What an echo! The little tune had been flung back at him so fiercely, almost menacingly. Menacingly: that was just the feeble, panicky word a nervous person would use. Well, he'd go to the left again this time.

As he got up, a quick spurt of cold air fanned his face. 'Is anyone there?' he said. He had purposely not raised his voice—there was no need to shout. Of course, no one answered. Who could there have been to answer, since the caretaker was away? Now let him think it out. When he came in he must have gone straight forward and then swerved slightly on the way back; therefore—no, he was getting confused. At that moment he heard he whistle of a train, and felt reassured. The line from Wendover to Aylesbury ran half-left from the front door, so it should be about there—he pointed with his finger, got up, groped his way forward, and found himself in a little narrow passage. Well, he must turn back and go to the right this time. He did so, and something seemed to slip just past him, and then he scratched his finger slightly on the brocade of the chair. 'Talk about a maze,' he thought to himself; 'it's nothing to this.' And then he said to himself, under his breath: 'Curse this vile, Godforsaken place!' A silly, panicky thing to do he realized— almost as bad as shouting aloud. Well, it was obviously no use trying to find the door, he *couldn't* find it—*couldn't*. He'd sit in the chair till the light came. He sat down.

How very silent it was; his hands began searching in his pockets once more. Except for that sort of whispering sound over on the left somewhere—except for that, it was absolutely silent—except for that. What could it be? The caretaker was away. He turned his head slightly and listened intently. It was almost as if there were several people whispering together. One got curious sounds in old houses. How absurd it was! The chair couldn't be more than three or four yards from the door. There was no doubt about that. I must be slightly to one side or the other. He'd try the left once more. He got up, and something lightly brushed his face. 'Is anyone there?' he said, and this time he knew he had shouted. 'Who touched me? Who's whispering? Where's the door?' What a nervous fool he was to shout like that; yet someone outside might have heard him. He went groping forward again, and touched a wall. He followed along it, touching it with his finger-tips, and there was an opening.

The door, the door, it must be! And he found himself going down a little narrow passage. He turned and ran back. And then he remembered! He had put a match-booklet in his note-case! What a fool to have forgotten it, and made such an exhibition of himself. Yes, there it was; but his hands were trembling, and the booklet slipped through his fingers. He fell to his knees, and began searching about on the floor. 'It must be just here, it can't be far'—and then something icy-cold and damp was pressed against his forehead. He flung himself forward to seize it, but there was nothing there. And then he leapt to his feet, and with tears streaming down his face cried: 'Who is there? Save me! Save me!' And then he began to run round and round, his arms outstretched. At last he stumbled against something, the chair—and something touched him as it slipped past. And then he ran screaming round the room; and suddenly his screams slashed back at him, for he was in a little narrow passage.

'Now, Mr Runt,' said the coroner, 'you say you heard screaming coming from the direction of the Manor. Why didn't you go to find out what was the matter?'

'None of us chaps goes to Manor after sundown,' said Mr Runt.

'Oh, I know there's some absurd superstition about the house; but you haven't answered the question. There were screams, obviously coming from someone who wanted help. Why didn't you go to see what was the matter, instead of running away?'

'None of us chaps goes to Manor after sundown,' said Mr Runt.

'Don't fence with the question. Let me remind you that the doctor said Mr Cort must have had a seizure of some kind, but that had help been quickly forthcoming, his life might have been saved. Do you mean to tell me that, even if you had known this, you would still have acted in so cowardly a way?'

Mr Runt fixed his eyes on the ground and fingered his cap.

'None of us chaps goes to Manor after sundown,' he repeated.

THE BLACKMAILERS

Algernon Blackwood

Alexander's experience with the blackmailer was unique—it happened once only.

He had been happily married for some years, with two children, and was doing well enough in his insurance business. Life, indeed, was quite rosy, when one day a stranger called at the office and asked to see him alone. This stranger was an elderly man of perhaps rather shabby appearance, but his face and manner were quite engaging, and he had a really pleasant smile. His voice was cultured. He was obviously a gentleman, a university man probably. At the same time, there was something about him that hesitated; he seemed shy, a trifle nervous even. In spite of the worn, cheap clothing, however, he made the best impression, and Alexander believed that a bit of good business was coming his way.

They went into the inner private room. The interview began in the bluntest possible way. Something very determined had come into the stranger's manner, almost as though he had screwed himself to say what he came to say and meant to see it through.

'My name is Lawson,' he announced, 'and I need money badly.'

He spoke rapidly, yet with a curious reluctance, as though he said something he had learned by heart, and rather hated saying. 'Some letters of yours,' he went on—'it doesn't matter how—have come into my possession. If you will give me £20, they're yours,' And he drew from his pocket a small packet, fluttering them before the other's eyes so that the handwriting was plainly visible. The hand that held the letters shook.

The shock to Alexander, instead of the pleasant surprise he had rather expected, was overwhelming. With one look he had recognized the paper and the handwriting. He blenched. A cold sweat broke out on him. He was not naturally a man of much nerve and he realized that a bluff of any sort was useless. He *had* written those letters. He was frightened to the bone. All he could do in that first instant was to stagger to a chair, for his legs were too weak to support him. He just sat down. The other man remained standing, keeping a certain distance.

'T-twenty pounds,' stammered Alexander, half to himself, trying vainly to collect his thoughts. He was shivering visibly. Hot and cold he was. He knew he was quite helpless. This was blackmail.

'And I'll hand them over,' Lawson was saying. Then he added, as though relieved to say it: 'And you'll never set eyes on me again.'

'But—I—I haven't got it,' went on Alexander in a panic, his mind flooding with pictures of his wife, his children, his happy home. 'It's impossible—utterly impossible.'

'But you can get it,' suggested Lawson quietly. And though his voice sounded determined, merciless even, there was that odd touch of reluctance again in his manner, as though he was ashamed to say the words. He stood there on the office carpet, watching his victim's face, giving him time apparently. Putting the letters back into his pocket, he waited in silence. A hint of contempt, it may be, lay in this silence, contempt for the other's craven attitude and lack of fight. And Alexander somehow was aware of this, even while he tried frantically to think out ways and means. He would have paid £1,000, let alone £20, to have those letters back and see them burn. But where could he find £20 at a moment's notice? Though recovering a little from the first awful shock, his mind worked badly. He *did* think once of the Law which allowed a plaintiff in a blackmail case to conceal his name. He also thought of threatening to go to the police at once. Only the pluck to carry the bluff through failed him—and he knew it. He was so terrified, so painfully anxious to get those letters back that he kept his mind chiefly on the £20 and where in the devil he could find it. The name of a pal who might lend it crossed his bewildered mind at last.

'If you will come back in an hour, in half an hour even,' he said at last in a low, stammering voice, 'I—I think I can have it for you.' Without knowing exactly why, he suddenly added then: 'You're a—gentleman, I see.' The words came on their own accord. Lawson lowered his eyes. He didn't answer. 'If you go out,' he said then quietly, 'I'm afraid I must come with you. I'm sorry—but—you understand.'

'Oh, yes, I understand—of course,' said the other.

In the end this is what happened. They went out together. Alexander, greatly to his surprise, got his £20. They came back together, always side by side. Alexander handed over the money and took the letters in his hand. He counted them. He was shaking so violently that he had to count them a second time. One, two, three! The cold sweat broke out on him afresh.

'Three,' he whispered. 'Is that *all* you've got?'

Lawson, he saw, actually blushed. He was already at the door on his way out. 'I think so,' he replied, forcing the pleasant smile on to his face as he told the deliberate lie. 'I'll look again when I get home, and if there is another you shall have it.'

The expression on the face startled Alexander, for behind the forced smile, behind the sudden blush, was misery—abject misery. The hideous shame was clear to see, but the grim determination too.

'Another . . . ?' repeated Alexander. 'But you've got a lot more—a dozen at least . . .' he cried.

But Lawson was gone.

Alexander sat motionless for some minutes, clutching the letters feverishly as though they might be snatched away. He had gone to pieces badly. How the man had come into possession of the horrible letters puzzled him utterly. But that did not matter: he *had* got them, and he, Alexander, *had* written them—oh, a dozen at least, perhaps two dozen. Twenty pounds for three! With more to follow! He thought of his wife, his children, his happy home. . . . He thought of Lawson—his voice, his manner, his whole attitude. A gentleman, yes, a man of education and refinement. That sudden blush, the nervous, deprecating air, the reluctance, the look of shame. A man ashamed of yielding to the temptation chance has put in his way, eager to get away the moment the hideous deal was over and the money in his pocket. Yet a man, Alexander now began too late to realize, he might have bargained and pleaded with. The fellow's better nature was plain to see—underneath.

Alexander cursed himself for his collapse and lack of pluck. A bold front, a threat of the police, and Lawson in his turn would have weakened, possibly collapsed himself. A good bluff and Alexander might have got those letters—all of them, not merely three for nothing.

The telephone rang. He realized he still sat clutching his three letters, and that it was office hours and he had much to do. But the instant he was free again, he quickly locked the door and lit a match. He burnt the letters—without reading them—and smudged the black ashes into dust in his waste-paper basket.

Still trembling with the shock and horror of it all, he could not work. He took the afternoon off, walking feverishly round and round the parks, thinking feverishly, but without result. The night at home was the most miserable he had ever known, the children on his knee, the wife he loved beside him. If he slept at all, he hardly knew it. He had come, however, to a decision—to two in fact. And next day he went to a solicitor, putting a hypothetical case before him. But the strong advice to go straight to the police was beyond his powers. Even as 'Mr X', he could not face a trial. His second decision was to plead with Lawson, plead for time at any rate. The man had a better nature he felt he could appeal to. He would do this—the next time. For he knew, or course, there would be a next time. Lawson before long would call again.

But Lawson did not call again. After weeks of unspeakable terror and anguish, a letter came, to his home address this time. It was very brief, the handwriting rather suggesting the scholar.

I *have* come across another letter. Perhaps you would prefer to call for it yourself. A fiver would meet the case. I do not wish to cause unnecessary pain. It is, apparently, the only one.

The address was in Kilburn, and Alexander took five Treasury notes and went, one thing comforting him a little—the obvious fact, namely that Lawson was not a thoroughgoing and experienced blackmailer, or he would never have taken risks and laid himself open to such an easy trap. In his mind he had already rehearsed what he meant to say. His plea would be as moving as only truth could make it. But he planned a threat as well, a bluff of course, but a bluff that would sound genuine—that if driven to kill himself, he would leave the evidence behind him and Lawson would be at once arrested.

He could be firm this time, with the firmness of a desperate man. Desperate indeed he was, but firmness did not belong to his weak, impulsive, rather nerveless type.

Expecting a block of cheap flats, or a single room in a mean lodging-house, he found instead a small detached building, quite a decent little place, and a deaf old woman admitted him, announcing him by name, into a room that looked half study, half library. For it held numerous books, and a writing table was covered with papers. Lawson, at the far end of it, stood to receive him. But the interview hardly went according to plan, for as Alexander handed over the Treasury notes and received the letter in exchange, the other again took the cash as with a kind of shrinking, horrible reluctance. He was trembling, his face was very white, his voice, as he said 'Thank you,' trembled too. And before Alexander could recover from his moment's surprise and bring out either his plea or his threat, Lawson was speaking.

'I'm in a terrible position myself,' He said in a very low voice, '*Terrible.*' His face expressed real anguish. 'With any luck,' he went on in a whisper, his eyes on the floor, 'I would repay you—one day.'

He placed the notes in a drawer of his desk, while Alexander's eye, watching the movement, read the titles of some books above: a volume of Matthew Arnold's poems, a Greek lexicon, Gibbon's *Decline and*

Fall. But it was Lawson's sign of weakness that then helped the other to find some, at least, of the words he had meant to use. It was the bluff that rose first to the surface of his bewildered mind.

'You know—that I can go to the police,' he heard himself saying.

The other looked sideways towards the window, so that Alexander caught the face at a new angle. He noticed the ravaged expression. Lawson was suffering intensely.

'I know,' came the reply calmly, without turning the head. 'But you wouldn't—any more than *I* would.'

The conviction in the words, their truth as well, confused and bewildered the wretched victim still more. His thoughts scattered hopelessly. He said the first thing that came into his head. All idea of a plea for mercy had vanished.

'If you drive me to kill myself—and I'm near it now—you'd be arrested at once. I could leave the proofs.'

It was the way Lawson shrugged his shoulders that completed his feeling of utter hopelessness. It had dawned upon him suddenly that Lawson's position was somehow similar to his own, his desperation as dreadful. Lawson himself was at the last gasp.

'You've got a lot more, of course?' he heard himself asking in a faint voice.

Lawson now turned and faced him. His expression was awful, if pitiful at the same time.

'I'm afraid so,' he whispered, and his manner again showed that deep reluctance, with a sort of shame and horror against himself. 'One or two—I'm afraid,' he repeated. He drew a heavy sigh and put up his hand to hide his eyes. 'I'm . . . frightfully sorry,' he muttered, half to himself. He was trembling from head to foot.

The interview was over. Alexander left the house an utterly hopeless man. The situation was now clear to him, of course. Lawson, normally a decent fellow probably, was being blackmailed himself. Alexander understood, he even sympathized, but with this understanding vanished the last vestige also of any hope. He realized now *precisely* how desperate Lawson was.

The ghastly suffering and anguish of the weeks and months that followed need no description—his sleeplessness, his frantic resorts to finding cash, the moneylenders, his wife's discovery that something very serious was wrong, the way he fobbed her off with a story of bad business. The visits to Kilburn were repeated and repeated, though the interview usually took place in silence now. Money was paid, letters were handed over—without a word, both men, indeed, seemed approaching the last gasp. As for Alexander, he found it difficult to believe that he had written so many letters. But he had.

The cumulative effect at last broke his life to pieces. His health was gone, his mind became queer. Turning frantically to one desperate plan after another, all of them useless, he was driven finally into that dreadful, final corner where an Emergency Exit seemed inevitable. And this was not nerve, it was merely the ultimate decision of an utterly ruined, ordinary man. He bought a pistol. In his mind came the mad suggestion that it was as easy to end two lives as one. He went to the little Kilburn house for the last time. This was definitely to be his last visit. He took no money with him, but in his hip-pocket lay the Browning with three cartridges in the chamber—the third in case of mischance.

Exactly how he intended to act was far from clear to him. He had rehearsed no plan. That time was past. The loaded pistol lay in his pocket. He left the rest to impulse.

It was an evening in late October, summertime now over, and dusk spread over the dreary Kilburn streets. He came straight from the office by Tube. After leaving the train he walked very rapidly. Then he broke into a run, with the feeling that the faster he went the sooner the awful thing would be over. He arrived panting, reaching the house almost before he knew it. He was utterly distraught, his mind, even his senses, behaving wildly, inaccurately.

There was no answer to the violent pull he gave the bell, the deaf old woman did not appear, and then he noticed for the first time that the front door stood ajar. And he just walked in. The tiny hall was empty too. He closed the door behind him and walked across to the library. Only too well he knew it. There was no need to be shown in. He was expected. And he was punctual. Six was striking.

The house, it then occurred to him, was exceptionally quiet. There was an extraordinary stillness about it—a stillness he didn't like. There was also—though he only recalled this afterwards—a faint odour of a peculiar kind. Giving a loud knock without waiting for an answer, he opened it the same instant and walked straight in without further ado.

He saw Lawson at once. He was not standing as usual, but sitting facing him in the leather armchair with its patches of untidy horsehair sticking out. And he declares that the moment his eyes rested on him a disagreeable shudder ran down his spine. It was not the shudder of loathsome anxiety he knew so well, but something he had never felt before. Distracted, half crazy though his mind undoubtedly was at the time, it took in one thing at least quite clearly. Lawson looked different. He had changed. Wherein this alteration lay exactly Alexander could not say. He only knew that it frightened him in a new way and that his back had goose-flesh. An awful fear crawled over him.

Lawson not only looked different—he behaved differently. He did not get up, but sat in the chair staring into his visitor's face. There was something wrong, not merely different. And Alexander stopped dead just inside the door, forgetting even to close it behind him. He stood there spellbound, returning the stare. His first instinct was to turn tail and run, only his legs felt suddenly weak, his control of the muscles gone. He held his breath. What amazed him more than anything else was the expression on his enemy's face. For it wore a happy, kindly smile; the ravaged, suffering look had left it, there lay a curious soft pity on it. Unaccountably, he felt his heart beginning to swell. He could not take his eyes from that happy, pitiful face, that motionless figure in the chair. It was perhaps two minutes, perhaps only two seconds, before he heard the voice.

For Lawson spoke—in a scarcely audible whisper. There was obviously a tremendous strain and effort behind the whisper, as though he could only just manage it: yet Alexander heard every syllable distinctly.

'You won't need that pistol, either for me or for yourself. I have posted the others to you—with what—money I had. . . .' and the whisper died away into silence. The lips still moved, but no sound came from them. Lawson himself had not moved at all—he had not made even the smallest movement—once.

There was a sound in the hall, and Alexander involuntarily turned his head an instant. He recognized the deaf woman's shuffling tread. Turning back to the room again almost the same moment, Lawson the blackmailer was no longer staring at him from the leather chair. He was not in the chair at all. He was not even in the room. The room was empty. The only visible living person in it was himself, Alexander.

It flashed across him, as the deaf servant came stumbling through the door behind him, that he had gone crazy, that his mind was gone. There was icy perspiration all over him. He was shaking violently. He heard the old woman's words in a confused jumble only, but their meaning was plain enough. Lawson, she was trying to tell him, had shot himself several hours ago . . . but had not killed himself . . . the police . . . doctors had come . . . there had been an anaesthetic . . . he had been taken away . . . but had died in the ambulance.

Alexander does not remember how he got out of the house. All he remembers is walking the streets furiously, for hours even, and somewhere or other telephoning to his wife that he was detained and would not be home till after dinner. He knows he did that. He knows also that on reaching the house very late, he talked incoherently to his frightened wife, that the children were long since in bed and asleep, and that his wife put a registered packet into his trembling hands in due course. He knows too that it contained several letters he had written years before to another woman—dreadful, damaging letters—that a couple of twenty-pound notes fell at his feet, and that the postmark on the label was 11.30 Kilburn that very morning.

YESTERDAY STREET

Thomas Burke

Dominic left the taxi at the foot of the High Street, and settled himself to look up the length of the street from the station to the Park. Its features met his eye so familiarly that, though forty years had passed since he last walked along it, he felt that he had left it but a month ago. There had been little rebuilding. He saw motors and taxis in place of carriages and cabs, and motor-buses and electric trams in place of the old horse-vehicles, and a movie-theatre where the Gospel Hall had been.

But there, unchanged, was the draper's whose Christmas windows had been his delight. There, too, were the little side-streets, changed only in the direction of creeping shabbiness; and there was the very sweet-stuff shop which had once had his halfpennies and pennies, its window arranged precisely as in the past. There was the Diamond Jubilee Clock Tower. There was the Italian restaurant. And there was the confectioner's, whose window, occupied each December by a Christmas cake of twelve huge tiers, had been one of the Christmas sights of North London.

Nothing these points, he thought, as all men think on Going Back—Had he really been away forty years? Or did he only fancy it? Had all those things—what he called his Life—really happened to him, or had he only invented them as something he would like to happen? Had he really lived in a dozen countries, and was he really rich and living in a suite at the Palermo? Funny thing, growth.

Often, in the past, he had thought of the place, and of the boy who used to live in it, but the thought had been merely abstract and perfunctory; he hadn't been interested. Now, with his feet on its stones, he found how easily he could recapture it all, and how thickly long-buried memories perked up. The confectioner's, bearing the same name and the same fascia front as in his day, reminded him that he used to buy there, from a table in the doorway, assortments of yesterday's cakes—two or three for a penny. And with that came memory of a crime, when once, in buying a pennyworth, he had, by sleight of hand, gone off with five instead of three. He looked away from the shop; he had an idea that the back of his neck was blushing. Two shops into which he could see had, in his day, been kept by erect, slightly-grey men, with beards. It had been the custom, he remembered, to slip into the doorways of those shops and shout 'Kruger!' and run. They were now kept, he noted, by bald, withered men; but in the movements of those men he recognized the terrifying seniors of his own day. He felt that if they looked at him he would run.

He turned and went slowly up the street, noting on right and left many a familiar name. He tried to discover the effect upon him of seeing again a crude kind of life with which for years he had had nothing to do, and at first he could not locate or name it, definite though it was. Then, as he went further into the street, he found that he felt, of all things, just a little frightened. Yes; it *was* a little frightening to re-cross the threshold of the past, and to see again so much of the furniture of his early life in the position in which he had left it. There it stood, as though in a locked room, just as when he had said farewell to it (as he thought, for ever) and had left his boyhood there, and entered youth and manhood elsewhere. Walking among it now, unlocking it, as it were, he caught all the stored odours of that boyhood, and half-wished that the street had been pulled down and rebuilt. For of these buildings almost every one had known him and had received something of him. Through forty years he had been moving, changing, widening his interests, seeing and hearing new things, and living six different kinds of life. While here, static and scarcely touched by the forty years which had given him forty outlooks and a million emotions, here were the relics and fixtures of the beginning of it all—a beginning he had until now forgotten.

Strolling up to the Clock Tower, the thought came to him that with the High Street almost as it was, the little fountain still there, the Park just as it was, and those two old men still there, it was possible that his own street was still there—Levant Street, wasn't it? And just possible that his very home was still there—the little cottage with the tiny front garden. And even possible that the garden had the same flowers— London Pride, he thought they were. In coming here he had had no thought of seeking out his home; he had assumed that it would long ago have been swept away. He had come merely to look at the old suburb, though he couldn't have said why he wanted to look at it; why the fancy, or rather imperative desire, should suddenly have possessed him on this particular morning to go and look at it. For the past ten years he had made extended visits to London three times a year, and never once had he even thought of coming here. Yet this morning the fancy to see the place had been so strong that he had meekly followed it. Now that he was here, and so little change had happened, he decided to look for Levant Street. With all the other old stuff and old people still here, it was quite likely that the street and the old cottage were still here. Where forty years had left no mark, anything was possible. Everything about the place, he thought, was so set and solid, that it even wouldn't surprise him to find the boys still there—just as he had left them—Jimmy Gregory, his special friend, and—who was it?—yes, Victor Jones—and—ah, yes—Jenny Wrenn. The High Street and the shops hadn't grown up, so perhaps. . . .

He shook his shoulders. Stop it. You're getting morbid. You're a bit depressed at Coming Back, and finding it all as it was. One ought to be able to look at it coldly—as a cast-off skin. But one can't. Funny. . . . Street looks bright enough, and yet it's all—somehow—melancholy. Aching. As though there were a shadow behind it, pressing on me. Pulling me and claiming me.

He stopped by the brown granite pillars of the familiar grocery store, and here his mind began to waver between the man he was, with his affairs centred in a suite at the Palermo, and the boy he had been. For a while he could not fix himself in either. Then, staring about the street, he found that his visual memory had called up the faces of those boys and their clothes, and his ear had called up their voices, not vaguely, as in reverie, but vividly. And Jenny Wrenn. Little Jenny Wrenn, the fourth party of the quartet. It was the thought of her, on this spot, and the clear image of her, that for a space blurred the fact of his Palermo life, and took him right back. The forty years, the travel, the experience, and the money, now slid out of his mind and left it empty, save for three boys and a girl in these streets.

Memories fell upon him as sharply and as separately as raindrops. How many times he had come with her, or she with him, to this very store, each pretending to assist the other in 'errands' for their mothers? And how many times they had gone laggingly home in the winter twilight, hand in hand, and silent. Jenny Wrenn in her blue-and-white pinafore and darned stockings and red tam o'shanter. Jenny Wrenn with the brown hair and the solemn eyes and the trick of standing on one leg and nursing the ankle of the other in her hand. How often they had stood together at dark corners, thrilling to the music of a street-organ. How often she had brought him buttonholes of marigolds from her front garden. How often they had waited for each other after school and gone on forbidden walks in the Park. How often they had 'joined' things—the Band of Hope, the Sunday School—so that they might be more together.

He was letting these memories come to him on the pavement outside the store, when, in one special moment, there came with the memories the odour and flavour of strawberries and cream—and so potently that the dish might have been in his hands. He recalled then that their last meeting had been over a feast of strawberries and cream provided for them by the childless and 'comfortable' widow, Mrs Johnson, in honour of his leaving school and going away.

Following this came a sharp memory of a long-distant summer. Had the memory come when he had left his taxi, it would have been of something from a remote world and of another creature; but outside this store it came to him as intimately as last week. It was a summer when he and Jenny Wrenn had been sent together for a fortnight at a farm in Surrey. He recalled fourteen days and evenings of bliss. Of climbing trees, and lying in the sapphire dusk of the wood, and knocking each other about, and getting bad-tempered, and calling each other nasty names, and 'making it up'. He recalled the afternoon when he had buried her too deeply in the hay, and she had struggled out and fought him with real hatred. And he recalled those quiet half-hours in the coppice before bedtime, when they had sat on a low branch of a tree and stared at the country, and held hands, and didn't know why.

Fourteen days and evenings of bliss; two hundred and twenty-four hours of active being, every ten minutes of which had been *lived*. Since those days he had given much of his leisure to poetry, and had even played at the practice of it. But though today his mind was stored with it, and though as a boy he had known nothing about it, he realized now that he had known something better. He had known poetry itself, and had lived it. He wondered again whether he had ever really had any life than that; and then he was irritated with himself for wondering such nonsense. He moved away from the store and jerked himself back to his everyday, and wished he hadn't come to this dilapidated suburb.

He decided that he wouldn't stay long. He had a lunch appointment at the Palermo with some friends who had never seen this London suburb, and could not have said where it was; friends who had never played marbles in a side-street. He would just go along and see if Levant Street was still there, and then he would find a taxi and get out of this place which, much against his expectation, was so depressing and disarranging him. He had thought to look at it with superior eyes—success kindly glancing at its early beginning; but it wasn't following the rules. It was gripping him and reclaiming him. If he had guessed that it would be doing this to him he wouldn't have obeyed that sudden wish and wasted a morning on it. However, now he was here, he would just take a look at the old street, if it was still there, and then get back to civilization.

He strolled along the High Street to the point where he remembered his street had stood, and with not much surprise he found it still there. Where, in his day, the corner shops had been a cheap greengrocer's and a cheap butcher's, they were now a tobacconist's and a cheap draper's; but generally the silhouette of the street was the same. At the top end was a new row of flats, but beyond them still stood the school and the little houses with their tiny front gardens.

He stood for a moment looking into it, and again the Palermo and the rest of his life was swept out of his mind, and again, as he entered the street, a troop of things-past entered and took possession of him, and changed him from the serious figure known to many serious people into just Don, a boy of thirteen. He entered it with timid, hesitating steps, and the 'frightened' feeling was a little stronger here than it had been in the High Street. From the school downward, the rest of its length held all the points it had held forty years ago. The little front gardens, some trim, some neglected; the Chapel; the little shops; the tiny public-house; and the one house which belonged to a century ago, set back behind a carriage-sweep, empty in his day and empty now.

Before each of these points he paused, his mind dazzled by a confetti of memories which the sight of each showered upon him. Then very slowly, he moved on to look for number 64, and point by point—each clearly remembered—he came to it. There it was—almost as he had left it. Number 64, the little house which had been his first home. And sure enough, its garden was still bright with London Pride. He crossed the street and stood before it. Smaller, of course, than when he was a boy. He had expected that. Windows which look large to children, and knockers which only an effort can lift, become minute when seen again through the eyes of manhood. But, though smaller, it was still itself. The wooden palings, the fanlight, and the cobblestone edging to the bed of London Pride were just as he had left them. In imagination he looked beyond its door and saw the little rooms which had known him so intimately; which had known his first breath and his first dreams, and which held, as it were, the spiritual fingerprints of the creature he had been and now was not, and yet was. In that little house were preserved, as in acid or in amber, all the little moments, the particles of himself, which he had given it.

And as he stood before it, it seemed to him that all those particles came rushing out to greet him, bringing with them excitement, amusement, sadness, and here and there a touch of shame. Here, even more

clearly than in the High Street, he could see himself; and it was disconcerting thus to see himself. Between the two, that self and this self, he
was aware of reproach, regret, disappointment, weariness.

He did not look long. He stayed only for an aching minute; then
turned away. But in turning away he sent a glance down the street
towards other of the little houses where he had been a guest of school-
friends.

And then, with head half-turned, he stumbled off the kerb, and was
only half-aware that he had stumbled. He did not step back to the kerb.
He stood where he was and kept his glance where it was. His glance was
held by the little house numbered 82, and he gave it even more attention
than he had given to his own house. His mind spoke the number,
'Eighty-two'. Yes; that was right. That had been her house.

He stepped back to the pavement and continued to gaze at number
82. He could not take his eyes from number 82, because, outside
number 82, leaning against the wooden gate of the little garden, filled,
as in the past, with marigolds, was a slim figure in red tammy and blue-
and-white pinafore, standing on one leg.

Manhood had taught him to control all outward expression of emotion,
and the two people who were then passing saw only a middle-aged man
stepping on to the pavement and looking idly at the the houses opposite. They saw no staring eyes or pursed lips or rutted frown, but his
mental state was that which some people express in this way. His face
and eyes were calm; it was the spasm that went across his chest and
down his spine which was the private equivalent of staring eyes and
pursed lips. The resemblance of the scene to the scenes of forty years ago
was so acute that for a few moments he could only pace up and down.
The very house—and outside it a child matching in every detail, so far
as he could see, the Jenny Wrenn who had lived there and had been his
sweetheart. It was so striking a likeness that in default of any other
explanation he wondered whether his Jenny Wrenn could still be there
and this child her granddaughter. If she were there, he wondered
whether he could face her, and decided that he couldn't, and again
wished he hadn't come.

But, being here, he wanted to know; so, under pretence of examining
the numbers of the houses, he began to cross the street. He did not wish
to embarrass or scare the child by looking closely at her, but he wanted
a nearer view. He proposed to pass her, and pause, and ask if she knew
a Mrs—he would invent a name. But he had scarcely reached the
middle of the road when he stopped. From that point he could see

something which made the likeness frighteningly exact. There, on the brown stocking of the left leg, was the self-same darn in black wool which he remembered, had so distressed his Jenny's sense of fitness. At sight of that, the 'frightened' feeling which this coming-back had inspired reached its crisis and became panic. He felt that he must get out of that street—and quickly.

But he was not allowed to get out. Even as he turned she removed any scruple he had had of embarrassing or scaring her, and offered him every chance of looking closely at her. She came forward from the gate, and stepped into the road, and stood in front of him. Then as she stood there, swinging one leg backward and forward in the familiar way, a hotter spasm went across his chest. Jenny Wrenn looked at him and smiled and said: 'Hullo, Don. Where you been? Jimmy Gregory's looking for you.'

Standing in the middle of the road, he stared deep into the young face; stared for some seconds. Then, forgetting his panic, forgetting himself and all rule and all law, he said, without thinking and very softly: 'O-oh . . . It's really *you*. You're still here?' The screwed-up black eyes gave him a mischievous smile. Through the smile she said: 'Why, of course. Look—Jimmy Gregory wants you.'

He turned; and there, in the school playground, was Jimmy Gregory, waving to him and running. And down the street he saw Victor Jones coming towards them with his usual weary slouch. And, as both boys approached them, Jenny sidled up to him and leaned upon him, as she always did; and in that moment he was no more depressed or frightened or amazed. The common air of that little street became in that moment a great and gentle wave of peace and well-being which poured upon him and through him. Lacing the air, was the faint odour of strawberries and cream.

One little spot of everyday remained with him to tell him that the oddest thing about all this was that none of them seemed to recognize that he was grown-up, or to pay any attention to his gold-headed cane and his slim, brilliant boots. They treated him as they always had treated him. He looked up the street to the point where it entered the High Street, and he saw that everything of the High Street was as it was five minutes ago—taxis, motor-buses, electric trams—and that the little houses among which they stood were showing wireless aerials. Yet there they were, the four of them, making a casual cluster in the roadway, as usual, giggling and talking of this and of that—of what their teacher had said or done that morning; of the magic-lantern show at the Chapel last night; of the coming Band of Hope Treat. They were all going that evening—all four of them—to get their tickets for the Treat, and he found himself telling them that he had heard that part of the Treat would be a nigger entertainment. From somewhere unseen came the pathetic music of a street-organ. It was playing a popular song of their time—a song he had once thought 'lovely'—*Little Dolly Daydream*. Jenny began twinkling her feet to its time.

The last remnants of his today self slipped from him. He found it impossible to think, and, having tried, found that he didn't want to. He was caught in some silver-silken net, and he was content to be caught. He couldn't bother to make out what had gone wrong (or perhaps right) with Space and Time; he accepted as a fact that the modern world was all about him, and that here he was with his gold-headed cane and the children he had known long ago. And they were real; visible and touchable. He tested this by giving a gentle tug at one of Jenny's curls, as he had often done. She replied by jerking her head and butting his arm—hard enough to hurt. After that, he was conscious of nothing save that he was Don among his old friends, with a faint memory of having been other things.

Jimmy Gregory nudged him. 'Got your marbles?' He said: 'No. Left 'em indoors.' 'All right—lend you some of mine. You can pay what you lose after dinner.'

Then he and Jimmy Gregory were crouched in the roadway playing marbles, and Jenny was stooping over them, with brown curls hanging, bubbling rude remarks about his bad play; and he was very happy. He found, while playing, that his gold cane *had* been noticed, and that, most oddly, they did not question it or appear to regard it as unusual. Jenny took it from him—'I'll hold that stick while you're playing—or trying to.'

At the end of the game he had lost heavily. He had borrowed ten of Jimmy Gregory's marbles, and, despite a few fluking wins, which at one time gave him sixteen, had lost the lot. 'That's ten,' Jimmy said; and Dominic said: 'That's right. I'll bring 'em out after dinner. See you before class.' 'That's all right.'

Jenny wanted to know what he was going to have for dinner, but he had no information. He never had known until he got home. Jenny reported that she had seen her mother preparing a large steak pie. Gregory and Jones looked wistful. Then, with the sudden transitions of boys, Jones caught him by the shoulder. 'Look here, Don—know why you're always losing?'

'No.' He listened with respect to Jones. Jones always knew things—

except the kind of things you learn in school, which he never could learn.

'Well, you haven't got the knack. You put your thumb too far back on the finger. Look here—this is how.'

They stooped over the little hole in the roadway, and Jones took Dominic's large hand in his small hand, without appearing to notice its size, and bent the large thumb to the right position on the large finger. 'Now try.' He tried, and found that the marble had better direction. 'I see. I see, Vic. Thanks for the tip.'

For some few more minutes they stood talking, arms on each other's shoulders. Then, abruptly as they had met, they parted; and the episode was ended. Jenny was just asking what they should do now, and Gregory and Jones were suggesting a game of egg-cap, when a factory-hooter sent out its melancholy howl. In chorus they said 'Hooter. One o'clock,' and turned to break up. Dominic too turned; he knew that one o'clock was dinner-time in their homes and his. Gregory and Jones sauntered down the street, looking back to cry 'See you after'. Jenny slipped into her garden and pulled a marigold, and came to him and stuck it in his coat, with gurgles of laughter. Under the laughing, with her face close to his, she whispered 'After school?' He nodded. 'Go over the Park—round the Fern Pond?' He nodded and she nodded. They parted in a ballet of conspiratory nods. He saw her slip into her house, and saw the door close on her waving hand. Then, save for three commonplace women, he was alone in that little by-street. Alone, but with dusty trouser-knees, and with a marigold in his coat.

He did not remember getting out of the street. The next thing he knew was that he had reached the High Street, and was moving a little unsteadily, and blinking at the speeding traffic. The glowing peace that had enveloped him and filled him while with the children was gone, and he was now aware, not of his earlier depression and fright, but of disturbance; a shake-up of his inner being and of his relations with daily life. He knew that he had in his nature a dark streak of the dreamer, and was sometimes apt to let imagination and fancy play a little wantonly. But he also knew that what had happened had been no prank of imagination or fancy; no trance or dream-state. What had happened had happened as definitely and as really as the passing of those motor-buses and taxis. The children had been there, and they had been real; and they were there now. He could see them, he was sure, again. Though perhaps nobody else could.

He realized that he had been visited by an Experience; something that had never before visited his sober life. But that was all he did know. Neither imagination nor fancy could suggest why he should have had this particular Experience just now. He had met none of the other people he had known in those days—not his mother, or Jenny's mother, or Mrs Johnson, or the schoolteachers. Only those three. But he had had the Experience. There was the marigold in his coat, and he could still feel the bump on the arm which Jenny's head had given him.

They had all gone in to their dinner, but he did not go to his dinner, or to his lunch. He forgot the Palermo appointment; forgot everything save his mental chaos. He was just able to retain enough control to recognize that it was chaos.

He lifted his stick to an empty taxi, and ordered the driver to Westminster. At a Westminster garage he hired a car. 'Drive into the country. What? Oh, anywhere you like, so long as it's the country.'

Once out of London, with the car open, and trees and fields and hills and sky about him, his mind cooled. He did not try to think out his adventure; he lay back in the car and brooded upon it. Underneath the disturbance he was aware of a little thrill of delight. The figure of Jenny, and her chatter, remained close to him and held an aroma of—of what? Violets? Daffodils? Hawthorn? The image of London, and of the Palermo and its dining room and grill-room, and of the solid, adult people who lived there or lunched there, came to him distastefully. Thrusting themselves into his mind, also distastefully, came the people he would have to see tomorrow—City people, who took him seriously as a business-man. He half-wished that they could have seen him playing marbles.

Brooding upon Jenny and the boys, he began to see that the ache of which for many years he had been conscious, and of which many middle-aged men are conscious, was simply an unappeased desire to return to the point where the thread of childhood's other-world had been snapped. By some grace he had been allowed, just for an hour, to return.

He did not notice where the car was going or in what county they were. He noticed only green-hedged lanes and high downs and skies and rushing air, and it was not until he realized that these things had been around him for some long time that he looked at his watch. Five o'clock. By force of habit, the sight of five o'clock on his watch told him that he needed tea, and he took up the speaking-tube and directed the chauffeur to stop at the next decent-looking inn.

After passing two or three at which the chauffeur shook his head, they stopped at a trim little place on a river-bank. 'You'll find this all right, sir.' He entered the inn's little lounge, gave an order to the landlord for tea, and for the chauffeur's tea, and sat down by the window. The landlord bustled out and within a few seconds bustled back.

'Seen today's paper, sir?'

'No. . . . Thanks very much.' It was not true. He had, in fact, seen six papers but had scarcely looked at them. He had seen them in bed, with his early tea, and had glanced at the political article and the foreign page of one of them, and had then decided on his visit to his old suburb, and had tossed the rest aside. He took the paper from the landlord listlessly, and went on staring through the window. But the view from the window was not attractive, and he began idly to look through the paper. It was necessary, before tomorrow, that he should re-adjust himself to the man he was. It was for this reason that he had taken the car trip. The paper might be an additional help.

Drinking his tea, he ran his eye down column after column. The paper was one of the popular sort, with all the popular features. Without absorbing what he was reading he read the facetious column; read the Social Gossip column; read the Special Article; and wondered whether anybody else ever read these things. He turned to the secondary news page and the provincial reports. For a few seconds he glanced at this as he had glanced at the other pages, and was about to drop the paper when his glancing changed to positive attention. His eye, as though under guidance, fell upon three paragraphs in different columns of the page. It ignored all the rest of the page and went one—two—three—to the different points. They brought him from his slack, lounging attitude, and made him sit upright. His casual interest became eager. His tea became cold.

He read them one by one, and when he had read them he sat back again and stared at the flowered wallpaper. He stared motionless for some twenty minutes, and at the end of that time his disturbance had gone, and he was himself.

He got up, put the paper gently aside, and strolled out to the passage to settle his bill. The landlord, in taking his money, noted his quiet smile, and spoke about it in the kitchen. It was the smile of a man who appeared to like the place and to find it good. The chauffeur, too, noted it, and returned it.

'Back to the shadows now.'

'Beg pardon, sir?'

'Back to the old Palermo.'

'Very good, sir.'

The paragraphs which had caught his attention were three small news items. There had been a motor smash in Devon, in which two people were killed. One of them was a James Gregory, director of a chemical works. There had been a fatal fire-damp disaster at a northern colliery. The chief engineer, Victor Jones, in attempting a rescue, had himself perished. There had been a climbing disaster in the Alps, which had resulted in the death of three tourists; among them an Englishwoman, a Miss Jane Wrenn, schoolteacher, of London.

Smoke Ghost

Fritz Leiber Jun.

Miss Millick wondered just what had happened to Mr Wran. He kept making the strangest remarks when she took dictation. Just this morning he had quickly turned around and asked, 'Have you ever seen a ghost, Miss Millick?' And she had tittered nervously and replied, 'When I was a girl there was a thing in white that used to come out of the closet in the attic bedroom when I slept there, and moan. Of course it was just my imagination. I was frightened of lots of things.' And he had said, 'I don't mean that kind of ghost. I mean a ghost from the world today, with the soot of the factories on its face and the pounding of machinery in its soul. The kind that would haunt coal-yards and slip around at night through deserted office buildings like this one. A real ghost. Not something out of books.' And she hadn't known what to say.

He'd never been like this before. Of course he might be joking, but it didn't sound that way. Vaguely Miss Millick wondered whether he mightn't be seeking some sort of sympathy from her. Of course, Mr Wran was married and had a little child, but that didn't prevent her from having daydreams. The daydreams were not very exciting, still they helped fill up her mind. But now he was asking her another of those unprecedented questions.

'Have you ever thought what a ghost of our times would look like, Miss Millick? Just picture it. A smoky composite face with the hungry anxiety of the unemployed, the neurotic restlessness of the person without purpose, the jerky tension of the high-pressure metropolitan worker, the uneasy resentment of the striker, the callous opportunism of the scab, the aggressive whine of the panhandler, the inhibited terror of the bombed civilian, and a thousand other twisted emotional patterns. Each one overlying and yet blending with the other, like a pile of semi-transparent masks?'

Miss Millick gave a little self-conscious shiver and said, 'That would be terrible. What an awful thing to think of.'

She peered furtively across the desk. She remembered having heard that there had been something impressively abnormal about Mr Wran's childhood, but she couldn't recall what it was. If only she could do something—laugh at his mood or ask him what was really wrong. She shifted the extra pencils in her left hand and mechanically traced over some of the shorthand curlicues in her notebook.

'Yet, that's just what such a ghost or vitalized projection would look like, Miss Millick,' he continued, smiling in a tight way. 'It would grow out of the real world. It would reflect the tangled, sordid, vicious things. All the loose ends. And it would be very grimy. I don't think it would seem white or wispy, or favor graveyards. It wouldn't moan. But it would mutter unintelligibly, and twitch at your sleeve. Like a sick, surly ape. What would such a thing want from a person, Miss Millick? Sacrifice? Worship? Or just fear? What could you do to stop it from troubling you?'

Miss Millick giggled nervously. There was an expression beyond her powers of definition in Mr Wran's ordinary, flat-cheeked, thirtyish face, silhouetted against the dusty window. He turned away and stared out into the gray downtown atmosphere that rolled in from the railroad yards and the mills. When he spoke again his voice sounded far away.

'Of course, being immaterial, it couldn't hurt you physically—at first. You'd have to be peculiarly sensitive to see it, or be aware of it at all. But it would begin to influence your actions. Make you do this. Stop you from doing that. Although only a projection, it would gradually get its hooks into the world of things as they are. Might even get control of suitably vacuous minds. Then it could hurt whomever it wanted.'

Miss Millick squirmed and read back her shorthand, like the books said you should do when there was a pause. She became aware of the failing light and wished Mr Wran would ask her to turn on the over-head. She felt scratchy, as if soot were sifting down on to her skin.

'It's a rotten world, Miss Millick,' said Mr Wran, talking at the window. 'Fit for another morbid growth of superstition. It's time the ghosts, or whatever you call them, took over and began a rule of fear. They'd be no worse than men.'

'But'—Miss Millick's diaphragm jerked, making her titter inanely—'of course, there aren't any such things as ghosts.'

Mr Wran turned around.

'Of course there aren't, Miss Millick,' he said in a loud, patronizing voice, as if she had been doing the talking rather than he. 'Science and common sense and psychiatry all go to prove it.'

She hung her head and might even have blushed if she hadn't felt so all at sea. Her leg muscles twitched, making her stand up, although she hadn't intended to. She aimlessly rubbed her hand along the edge of the desk.

'Why, Mr Wran, look what I got off your desk,' she said, showing him a heavy smudge. There was a note of clumsily playful reproof in her voice. 'No wonder the copy I bring you always gets so black. Somebody ought to talk to those scrubwomen. They're skimping on your room.'

She wished he would make some normal joking reply. But instead he drew back and his face hardened.

'Well, to get back,' he rapped out harshly, and began to dictate.

When she was gone, he jumped up, dabbed his finger experimentally at the smudged part of the desk, frowned worriedly at the almost inky smears. He jerked open a drawer, snatched out a rag, hastily swabbed off the desk, crumpled the rag into a ball and tossed it back. There were three or four other rags in the drawer, each impregnated with soot.

Then he went over to the window and peered out anxiously through the dusk, his eyes searching the panorama of roofs, fixing on each chimney and water tank.

'It's a neurosis. Must be. Compulsions. Hallucinations,' he muttered to himself in a tired, distraught voice that would have made Miss Millick gasp. 'It's that damned mental abnormality cropping up in a new form. Can't be any other explanation. But it's so damned real. Even the soot. Good thing I'm seeing the psychiatrist. I don't think I could force myself to get on the elevated tonight.' His voice trailed off, he rubbed his eyes, and his memory automatically started to grind.

It had all begun on the elevated. There was a particular little sea of roofs he had grown into the habit of glancing at just as the packed car carrying him homeward lurched around a turn. A dingy, melancholy little world of tar-paper, tarred gravel, and smoky brick. Rusty tin chimneys with odd conical hats suggested abandoned listening posts. There was a washed-out advertisement of some ancient patent medicine on the nearest wall. Superficially it was like ten thousand other drab city roofs. But he always saw it around dusk, either in the smoky half-light, or tinged with red by the flat rays of a dirty sunset, or covered by ghostly windblown white sheets of rain-splash, or patched with blackish snow; and it seemed unusually bleak and suggestive; almost beautifully ugly though in no sense picturesque; dreary, but meaningful. Unconsciously it came to symbolize for Catesby Wran certain disagreeable aspects of the frustrated, frightened century in which he lived, the jangled century of hate and heavy industry and total wars. The quick daily glance into the half darkness became an integral part of his life. Oddly, he never saw it in the morning, for it was then his habit to sit on the other side of the car, his head buried in the paper.

One evening toward winter he noticed what seemed to be a shapeless black sack lying on the third roof from the tracks. He did not think about it. It merely registered as an addition to the well-known scene and his memory stored away the impression for further reference. Next evening, however, he decided he had been mistaken in one detail. The object was a roof nearer than he had thought. Its color and texture, and the grimy stains around it, suggested that it was filled with coal dust, which was hardly reasonable. Then, too, the following evening it seemed to have been blown against a rusty ventilator by the wind— which could hardly have happened if it were at all heavy. Perhaps it was filled with leaves. Catesby was surprised to find himself anticipating his next daily glance with a minor note of apprehension. There was something unwholesome in the posture of the thing that stuck in his mind— a bulge in the sacking that suggested a misshaped head peering around the ventilator. And his apprehension was justified, for that evening the thing was on the nearest roof, though on the further side, looking as if it had just flopped down over the low brick parapet.

Next evening the sack was gone. Catesby was annoyed at the momentary feeling of relief that went through him, because the whole matter seemed too unimportant to warrant feelings of any sort. What difference did it make if his imagination had played tricks on him, and he'd fancied that the object was slowly crawling and hitching itself closer across the roofs? That was the way any normal imagination worked. He deliberately chose to disregard the fact that there were reasons for thinking his imagination was by no means a normal one. As he walked home from the elevated, however, he found himself wondering whether the sack was really gone. He seemed to recall a vague, smudgy trail leading across the gravel to the nearer side of the roof, which was masked by a parapet. For an instant an unpleasant picture formed in his mind— that of an inky, humped creature crouched behind the parapet, waiting.

The next time he felt the familiar grating lurch of the car, he caught himself trying not to look out. That angered him. He turned his head quickly. When he turned it back, his compact face was definitely pale. There had been only time for a fleeting rearward glance at the escaping roof. Had he actually seen in silhouette the upper part of a head of some sort peering over the parapet? Nonsense, he told himself. And even if he had seen something, there were a thousand explanations which did not involve the supernatural or even true hallucination. Tomorrow he would take a good look and clear up the whole matter. If necessary, he would visit the roof personally, though he hardly knew where to find it and disliked in any case the idea of pampering a silly fear.

He did not relish the walk home from the elevated that evening, and visions of the thing disturbed his dreams, and were in and out of his mind all next day at the office. It was then that he first began to relieve his nerves by making jokingly serious remarks about the supernatural to Miss Millick, who seemed properly mystified. It was on the same day, too, that he became aware of a growing antipathy to grime and soot. Everything he touched seemed gritty, and he found himself mopping and wiping at his desk like an old lady with a morbid fear of germs. He reasoned that there was no real change in his office, and that he'd just now become sensitive to the dirt that had always been there, but there was no denying an increasing nervousness. Long before the car reached the curve, he was straining his eyes through the murky twilight, determined to take in every detail.

Afterward he realized he must have given a muffled cry of some sort, for the man beside him looked at him curiously, and the woman ahead gave him an unfavorable stare. Conscious of his own pallor and uncontrollable trembling, he stared back at them hungrily, trying to regain the feeling of security he had completely lost. They were the usual reassuringly wooden-faced people everyone rides home with on the elevated. But suppose he had pointed out to one of them what he had seen—that sodden, distorted face of sacking and coal dust, that boneless paw which waved back and forth, unmistakably in his direction, as if reminding him of a future appointment—he involuntarily shut his eyes tight. His thoughts were racing ahead to tomorrow evening. He pictured this same windowed oblong of light and packed humanity surging around the curve—then an opaque monstrous form leaping out from the roof in a parabolic swoop—an unmentionable face pressed close against the window, smearing it with wet coal dust—huge paws fumbling sloppily at the glass—

Somehow he managed to turn off his wife's anxious enquiries. Next morning he reached a decision and made an appointment for that evening with a psychiatrist a friend had told him about. It cost him a considerable effort, for Catesby had a well-grounded distaste for anything dealing with psychological abnormality. Visiting a psychiatrist meant raking up an episode in his past which he had never fully described even to his wife. Once he had made the decision, however, he felt considerably relieved. The psychiatrist, he told himself, would clear everything up. He could almost fancy him saying, 'Merely a bad case of nerves. However, you must consult the oculist whose name I'm writing down for you, and you must take two of these pills in water every four hours,' and so on. It was almost comforting, and made the coming revelation he would have to make seem less painful.

But as the smoky dusk rolled in, his nervousness had returned and he had let his joking mystification of Miss Millick run away with him until he had realized he wasn't frightening anyone but himself.

He would have to keep his imagination under better control, he told himself, as he continued to peer out restlessly at the massive, murky shapes of the downtown office buildings. Why, he had spent the whole afternoon building up a kind of neo-medieval cosmology of superstition. It wouldn't do. He realized then that he had been standing at the window much longer than he'd thought, for the glass panel in the door was dark and there was no noise coming from the outer office. Miss Millick and the rest must have gone home.

It was then he made the discovery that there would have been no special reason for dreading the swing around the curve that night. It was, as it happened, a horrible discovery. For, on the shadowed roof across the street and four stories below, he saw the thing huddle and roll across the gravel and, after one upward look of recognition, merge into the blackness beneath the water tank.

As he hurriedly collected his things and made for the elevator, fighting the panicky impulse to run, he began to think of hallucination and mild psychosis as very desirable conditions. For better or for worse, he pinned all his hopes on the psychiatrist.

'So you find yourself growing nervous and . . . er . . . jumpy, as you put it,' said Dr Trevethick, smiling with dignified geniality. 'Do you notice any more definite physical symptoms? Pain? Headache? Indigestion?'

Catesby shook his head and wet his lips. 'I'm especially nervous while riding in the elevated,' he murmured swiftly.

'I see. We'll discuss that more fully. But I'd like you first to tell me about something you mentioned earlier. You said there was something about your childhood that might predispose you to nervous ailments. As you know, the early years are critical ones in the development of an individual's behavior pattern.'

Catesby studied the yellow reflections of frosted globes in the dark surface of the desk. The palm of his left hand aimlessly rubbed the thick nap of the armchair. After a while he raised his head and looked straight into the doctor's small brown eyes.

'From perhaps my third to my ninth year,' he began, choosing the words with care, 'I was what you might call a sensory prodigy.'

The doctor's expression did not change. 'Yes?' he enquired politely.

'What I mean is that I was supposed to be able to see through walls, read letters through envelopes and books through their covers, fence and play ping-pong blindfolded, find things that were buried, read thoughts.' The words tumbled out.

'And could you?' The doctor's voice was toneless.

'I don't know. I don't suppose so,' answered Catesby, long-lost emotions flooding back into his voice. 'It's all confused now. I thought I could, but then they were always encouraging me. My mother . . . was . . . well . . . interested in psychic phenomena. I was . . . exhibited. I seem to remember seeing things other people couldn't. As if most opaque objects were transparent. But I was very young. I didn't have any scientific criteria for judgement.'

He was reliving it now. The darkened rooms. The earnest assemblages of gawking, prying adults. Himself alone on a little platform, lost in a straight-backed wooden chair. The black silk handkerchief over his eyes. His mother's coaxing, insistent questions. The whispers. The gasps. His own hate of the whole business, mixed with hunger for the adulation of adults. Then the scientists from the university, the experiments, the big test. The reality of those memories engulfed him and momentarily made him forget the reason why he was disclosing them to a stranger.

'Do I understand that your mother tried to make use of you as a medium for communicating with the . . . er . . . other world?'

Catesby nodded eagerly.

'She tried to, but she couldn't. When it came to getting in touch with the dead, I was a complete failure. All I could do—or thought I could do—was see real, existing, three-dimensional objects beyond the vision of normal people. Objects anyone could have seen except for distance, obstruction, or darkness. It was always a disappointment to mother.'

He could hear her sweetish, patient voice saying. 'Try again, dear, just this once. Katie was your aunt. She loved you. Try to hear what she's saying.' And he had answered, 'I can see a woman in a blue dress standing on the other side of Dick's house.' And she had replied, 'Yes, I know, dear. But that's not Katie. Katie's a spirit. Try again. Just this once, dear.' The doctor's voice gently jarred him back into the softly gleaming office.

'You mentioned scientific criteria for judgement, Mr Wran. As far as you know, did anyone ever try to apply them to you?'

Catesby's nod was emphatic.

'They did. When I was eight, two young psychologists from the university got interested in me. I guess they did it for a joke at first, and I remember being very determined to show them I amounted to something. Even now I seem to recall how the note of polite superiority and amused sarcasm drained out of their voices. I suppose they decided at first that it was very clever trickery, but somehow they persuaded mother to let them try me out under controlled conditions. There were lots of tests that seemed very businesslike after mother's slipshod little exhibitions. They found I was clairvoyant—or so they thought. I got worked up and on edge. They were going to demonstrate my supernormal sensory powers to the university psychology faculty. For the first time I began to worry about whether I'd come through. Perhaps they kept me going at too hard a pace, I don't know. At any rate, when the test came, I couldn't do a thing. Everything became opaque. I got desperate and made things up out of my imagination. I lied. In the end I failed utterly, and I believe the two young psychologists got into a lot of hot water as a result.'

He could hear the brusque, bearded man saying, 'You've been taken in by a child, Flaxman, a mere child. I'm greatly disturbed. You've put yourself on the same plane as common charlatans. Gentlemen, I ask you to banish from your minds this whole sorry episode. It must never be referred to.' He winced at the recollection of his feeling of guilt. But at the same time he was beginning to feel exhilarated and almost light-hearted. Unburdening his long-repressed memories had altered his whole viewpoint. The episodes on the elevated began to take on what seemed their proper proportions as merely the bizarre workings of overwrought nerves and an overly suggestible mind. The doctor, he anticipated confidently, would disentangle the obscure subconscious causes, whatever they might be. And the whole business would be finished off quickly, just as his childhood experience—which was beginning to seem a little ridiculous now—had been finished off.

'From that day on,' he continued, 'I never exhibited a trace of my supposed powers. My mother was frantic and tried to sue the university. I had something like a nervous breakdown. Then the divorce was granted, and my father got custody of me. He did his best to make me forget it. We went on long outdoor vacations and did a lot of athletics, associated with normal matter-of-fact people. I went to business college eventually. I'm in advertising now. But,' Catesby paused, 'now that I'm having nervous symptoms, I've wondered if there mightn't be a connection. It's not a question of whether I was really clairvoyant or not. Very likely my mother taught me a lot of unconscious deceptions, good enough to fool even young psychology instructors. But don't you think it may have some important bearing on my present condition?'

For several moments the doctor regarded him with a professional frown. Then he said quietly, 'And is there some . . . er . . . more specific connection between your experiences then and now? Do you by any chance find that you are once again beginning to . . . er . . . see things?'

Catesby swallowed. He had felt an increasing eagerness to unburden himself of his fears, but it was not easy to make a beginning, and the doctor's shrewd question rattled him. He forced himself to concentrate. The thing he thought he had seen on the roof loomed up before his inner eye with unexpected vividness. Yet it did not frighten him. He groped for words.

Then he saw that the doctor was not looking at him but over his shoulder. Color was draining out of the doctor's face and his eyes did not seem so small. Then the doctor sprang to his feet, walked past Catesby, threw up the window and peered into the darkness.

As Catesby rose, the doctor slammed down the window and said in a voice whose smoothness was marred by a slight, persistent gasping, 'I hope I haven't alarmed you. I saw the face of . . . er . . . a Negro prowler on the fire escape. I must have frightened him, for he seems to have gotten out of sight in a hurry. Don't give it another thought. Doctors are frequently bothered by *voyeurs* . . . er . . . Peeping Toms.'

'A Negro?' asked Catesby, moistening his lips.

The doctor laughed nervously. 'I imagine so, though my first odd impression was that it was a white man in blackface. You see, the color didn't seem to have any brown in it. It was dead-black.'

Catesby moved toward the window. There were smudges on the glass. 'It's quite all right, Mr Wran.' The doctor's voice had acquired a sharp note of impatience, as if he were trying hard to reassume his professional authority. 'Let's continue our conversation. I was asking you if you were'—he made a face—'seeing things.'

Catesby's whirling thoughts slowed down and locked into place. 'No. I'm not seeing anything that other people don't see, too. And I think I'd better go now. I've been keeping you too long.' He disregarded the doctor's half-hearted gesture of denial. 'I'll phone you about the physical examination. In a way you've already taken a big load off my mind.' He smiled woodenly. 'Goodnight, Dr Trevethick.'

Catesby Wran's mental state was a peculiar one. His eyes searched every angular shadow, he glanced sideways down each chasm-like alley and barren basement passageway, and kept stealing looks at the irregular line of the roofs, yet he was hardly conscious of where he was going. He pushed away the thoughts that came into his mind, and kept moving. He became aware of a slight sense of security as he turned into a lighted street where there were people and high buildings and blinking signs.

After a while he found himself in the dim lobby of the structure that housed his office. Then he realized why he couldn't go home, why he daren't go home—after what had happened at the office of Dr Trevethick.

'Hello, Mr Wran,' said the night elevator man, a burly figure in overalls, sliding open the grille-work door to the old-fashioned cage. 'I didn't know you were working nights now, too.'

Catesby stepped in automatically. 'Sudden rush of orders,' he murmured inanely. 'Some stuff that has to be gotten out.'

The cage creaked to a stop at the top floor. 'Be working very late, Mr Wran?'

He nodded vaguely, watched the car slide out of sight, found his keys, swiftly crossed the outer office, and entered his own. His hand went out to the light switch, but then the thought occurred to him that the two lighted windows, standing out against the dark bulk of the building, would indicate his whereabouts and serve as a goal toward which something could crawl and climb. He moved his chair so that the back was against the wall and sat down in the semidarkness. He did not remove his overcoat.

For a long time he sat there motionless, listening to his own breathing and the faraway sounds from the streets below: the thin metallic surge of the crosstown streetcar, the further one of the elevated, faint lonely cries and honkings, indistinct rumblings. Words he had spoken to Miss Millick in nervous jest came back to him with the bitter taste of truth. He found himself unable to reason critically or connectedly, but by their own volition thoughts rose up into his mind and gyrated slowly and rearranged themselves with the inevitable movement of planets.

Gradually his mental picture of the world was transformed. No longer a world of material atoms and empty space, but a world in which the bodiless existed and moved according to its own obscure laws or unpredictable impulses. The new picture illuminated with dreadful clarity certain general facts which had always bewildered and troubled him and from which he had tried to hide: the inevitability of hate and war, the diabolically timed mischances which wreck the best of human intentions, the walls of willful misunderstanding that divide one man from another, the eternal vitality of cruelty and ignorance and greed. They seemed appropriate now, necessary parts of the picture. And superstition only a kind of wisdom.

Then his thoughts returned to himself and the question he had asked Miss Millick, 'What would such a thing want from a person? Sacrifices?

Worship, Or just fear? What could you do to stop it from troubling you?' It had become a practical question.

With an explosive jangle, the phone began to ring. 'Cate, I've been trying everywhere to get you,' said his wife. 'I never thought you'd be at the office. What are you doing? I've been worried.'

He said something about work.

'You'll be home right away?' came the faint anxious question. 'I'm a little frightened. Ronny just had a scare. It woke him up. He kept pointing to the window saying. "Black man, black man." Of course it's something he dreamed. But I'm frightened. You will be home? What's that, dear? Can't you hear me?'

'I will. Right away,' he said. Then he was out of the office, buzzing the night bell and peering down the shaft.

He saw it peering up the shaft at him from the deep shadows three floors below, the sacking face pressed against the iron grille-work. It started up the stair at a shockingly swift, shambling gait, vanishing temporarily from sight as it swung into the second corridor below.

Catesby clawed at the door to the office, realized he had not locked it, pushed it in, slammed and locked it behind him, retreated to the other side of the room, cowered between the filing cases and the wall. His teeth were clicking. He heard the groan of the rising cage. A silhouette darkened the frosted glass of the door, blotting out part of the grotesque reverse of the company name. After a little the door opened.

The big-globed overhead light flared on and, standing inside the door, her hand on the switch, was Miss Millick.

'Why, Mr Wran,' she stammered vacuously, 'I didn't know you were here. I'd just come in to do some extra typing after the movie. I didn't . . . but the lights weren't on. What were you—'

He stared at her. He wanted to shout in relief, grab hold of her, talk rapidly. He realized he was grinning hysterically.

'Why, Mr Wran, what's happened to you?' she asked embarrassedly, ending with a stupid titter. 'Are you feeling sick? Isn't there something I can do for you?'

He shook his head jerkily and managed to say, 'No, I'm just leaving. I was doing some extra work myself.'

'But you *look* sick,' she insisted, and walked over toward him. He inconsequentially realized she must have stepped in mud, for her high-heeled shoes left neat black prints.

'Yes, I'm sure you must be sick. You're so terribly pale.' She sounded like an enthusiastic, incompetent nurse. Her face brightened with a sudden inspiration. 'I've got something in my bag, that'll fix you up right away,' she said. 'It's for indigestion.'

She fumbled at her stuffed oblong purse. He noticed that she was absent-mindedly holding it shut with one hand while she tried to open it with the other. Then, under his very eyes, he saw her bend back the thick prongs of metal locking the purse as if they were tinfoil, or as if her fingers had become a pair of steel pliers.

Instantly his memory recited the words he had spoken to Miss Millick that afternoon. 'It couldn't hurt you physically—at first . . . gradually get its hooks into the world . . . might even get control of suitably vacuous minds. Then it could hurt whomever it wanted.' A sickish, cold feeling grew inside him. He began to edge toward the door.

But Miss Millick hurried ahead of him.

'You don't have to wait, Fred,' she called. 'Mr Wran's decided to stay a while longer.'

The door to the cage shut with a mechanical rattle. The cage creaked. Then she turned around in the door.

'Why, Mr Wran,' she gurgled reproachfully, 'I just couldn't think of letting you go home now. I'm sure you're terribly unwell. Why, you might collapse in the street. You've just got to stay here until you feel different.'

The creaking died away. He stood in the center of the office, motionless. His eyes traced the coal-black course of Miss Millick's footprints to where she stood blocking the door. Then a sound that was almost a scream was wrenched out of him, for it seemed to him that the blackness was creeping up her legs under the thin stockings.

'Why, Mr Wran,' she said, 'you're acting as if you were crazy. You must lie down for a while. Here, I'll help you off with your coat.'

The nauseously idiotic and rasping note was the same; only it had been intensified. As she came toward him he turned and ran through the storeroom, clattered a key desperately at the lock of the second door to the corridor.

'Why, Mr Wran,' he heard her call, 'are you having some kind of a fit? You must let me help you.'

The door came open and he plunged out into the corridor and up the stairs immediately ahead. It was only when he reached the top that he realized the heavy steel door in front of him led to the roof. He jerked up the catch.

'Why, Mr Wran, you mustn't run away. I'm coming after you.'

Then he was out on the gritty gravel of the roof. The night sky was clouded and murky, with a faint pinkish glow from the neon signs. From the distant mills rose a ghostly spurt of flame. He ran to the edge. The street lights glared dizzily upward. Two men were tiny round blobs of hat and shoulders. He swung around.

The thing was in the doorway. The voice was no longer solicitous but moronically playful, each sentence ending in a titter.

'Why, Mr Wran, why have you come up here? We're all alone. Just think, I might push you off.'

The thing came slowly toward him. He moved backward until his heels touched the low parapet. Without knowing why, or what he was going to do, he dropped to his knees. He dared not look at the face as it came nearer, a focus for the worst in the world, a gathering point for poisons from everywhere. Then the lucidity of terror took possession of his mind, and words formed on his lips.

'I will obey you. You are my god,' he said. 'You have supreme power over man and his animals and his machines. You rule this city and all others. I recognize that.'

Again the titter, closer. 'Why, Mr Wran, you never talked like this before. Do you mean it?'

'The world is yours to do with as you will, save or tear to pieces,' he answered fawningly, the words automatically fitting themselves together in vaguely liturgical patterns. 'I recognize that. I will praise, I will sacrifice. In smoke and soot I will worship you for ever.'

The voice did not answer. He looked up. There was only Miss Millick, deathly pale and swaying drunkenly. Her eyes were closed. He caught her as she wobbled toward him. His knees gave way under the added weight and they sank down together on the edge of the roof.

After a while she began to twitch. Small noises came from her throat and her eyelids edged open.

'Come on, we'll go downstairs,' he murmured jerkily, trying to draw her up. 'You're feeling bad.'

'I'm terribly dizzy,' she whispered. 'I must have fainted, I didn't eat enough. And then I'm so nervous lately, about the war and everything, I guess. Why, we're on the roof! Did you bring me up here to get some air? Or did I come up without knowing it? I'm awfully foolish. I used to walk in my sleep, my mother said.'

As he helped her down the stairs, she turned and looked at him. 'Why, Mr Wran,' she said, faintly, 'you've got a big black smudge on your forehead. Here, let me get it off for you.' Weakly she rubbed at it with her handkerchief. She started to sway again and he steadied her.

'No, I'll be all right,' she said, 'Only I feel cold. What happened, Mr Wran? Did I have some sort of fainting spell?'

He told her it was something like that.

Later, riding home in the empty elevated car, he wondered how long he would be safe from the thing. It was a purely practical problem. He had no way of knowing, but instinct told him he had satisfied the brute for some time. Would it want more when it came again? Time enough to answer that question when it arose. It might be hard, he realized, to keep out of an insane asylum. With Helen and Ronny to protect, as well as himself, he would have to be careful and tight-lipped. He began to speculate as to how many other men and women had seen the thing or things like it.

The elevated slowed and lurched in a familiar fashion. He looked at the roofs near the curve. They seemed very ordinary, as if what made them impressive had gone away for a while.

THE CHEERY SOUL

Elizabeth Bowen

On arriving, I first met the aunt of whom they had told me, the aunt who had not yet got over being turned out of Italy. She sat resentfully by the fire, or rather the fireplace, and did not look up when I came in. The acrid smell that curled through the drawing-room could be traced to a grate full of sizzling fir cones that must have been brought in damp. From the mantelpiece one lamp, with its shade tilted, shed light on the parting of the aunt's hair. It could not be said that the room was cheerful: the high, curtained bow windows made draughty caves; the armchairs and sofas, pushed back against the wall, wore the air of being renounced for ever. Only a row of discreet greeting-cards (few with pictures) along the top of a bureau betrayed the presence of Christmas. There was no holly, and no pieces of string.

I coughed and said: 'I feel I should introduce myself,' and followed this up by giving the aunt my name, which she received with apathy. When she did stir, it was to look at the parcel that I coquettishly twirled from its loop of string. 'They're not giving presents, this year,' she said in alarm. 'If I were you, I should put that back in my room.'

'It's just—my rations.'

'In that case,' she remarked, 'I really don't know what you had better do.' Turning away from me she picked up a small bent poker, and with this began to interfere with the fir cones, of which several, steaming, bounced from the grate. 'A good wood stove,' she said, 'would make all the difference. At Sienna, though they say it is cold in winter, we never had troubles of this kind.'

'How would it be,' I said, 'if I sat down?' I pulled a chair a little on to the hearthrug, if only for the idea of the thing. 'I gather our hosts are out. I wonder where they have gone to?'

'Really, I couldn't tell you.'

'My behaviour,' I said, 'has been shockingly free-and-easy. Having pulled the bell three times, waited, had a go at the knocker . . .'

'. . . I heard,' she said, slightly bowing her head.

'I gave *that* up, tried the door, found it unlocked, so just marched in.'

'Have you come about something?' she said with renewed alarm.

'Well, actually, I fear that I've come to stay. They have been so very kind as to . . .'

'. . . Oh, I remember—someone *was* coming.' She looked at me rather closely. 'Have you been here before?'

'Never. So this is delightful,' I said firmly. 'I am billeted where I work' (I named the industrial town, twelve miles off, that was these days in a ferment of war production), 'my landlady craves my room for these next two days for her daughter, who is on leave, and, on top of this, to be frank, I'm a bit old-fashioned: Christmas alone in a strange town didn't appeal to me. So you can see how I sprang at . . .'

'Yes, I can see,' she said. With the tongs, she replaced the cones that had fallen out of the fire. 'At Orvieto,' she said, 'the stoves were so satisfactory that one felt no ill effects from the tiled floors.'

As I could think of nothing to add to this, I joined her in listening attentively to the hall clock. My entry into the drawing-room having been tentative, I had not made so bold as to close the door behind me, so a further coldness now seeped through from the hall. Except for the clock—whose loud tick was reluctant—there was not another sound to be heard: the very silence seemed to produce echoes. The Rangerton-Karneys' absence from their own house was becoming, virtually, ostentatious. 'I understand,' I said, 'that they are tremendously busy. Practically never not on the go.'

'They expect to have a finger in every pie.'

Their aunt's ingratitude shocked me. She must be (as they had hinted) in a difficult state. They had always spoken with the most marked forbearance of her enforced return to them out of Italy. In England, they said, she had no other roof but theirs, and they were constantly wounded (their friends told me) by her saying she would have preferred internment in Italy.

In common with all my fellow-workers at ——, I had a high regard for the Rangerton-Karneys, an admiration tempered, perhaps, with awe. Their energy in the promotion of every war effort was only matched by the austerity of their personal lives. They appeared to have given up almost everything. That they never sat down could be seen from their drawing-room chairs. As 'local people' of the most solid kind they were on terms with the bigwigs of every department, the key minds of our small but now rather important town. Completely discreet, they were palpably 'in the know'.

Their house in the Midlands, in which I now so incredibly found myself, was largish, built of the local stone, *circa* 1860 I should say from its style. It was not very far from a railway junction, and at a still less distance from a canal. I had evaded the strictures on Christmas travel by making the twelve-mile journey by bicycle—indeed, the suggestion that I should do this played a prominent part in their invitation. So I bicycled over. My little things for the two nights were contained in one of those useful American-cloth suitcases, strapped to my back-wheel carrier, while my parcel of rations could be slung, I found, from my handlebar. The bumping of this parcel on my right knee as I pedalled was a major embarrassment. To cap this, the misty damp of the after-noon had caused me to set off in a mackintosh. At the best of times I am not an expert cyclist. The grateful absence of hills (all this country is very flat) was cancelled out by the greasiness of the roads, and army traffic often made me dismount—it is always well to be on the safe side. Now and then, cows or horses looked up abruptly to peer at me over the reeking hedgerows. The few anonymous villages I passed through all appeared, in the falling dusk, to be very much the same: their inhabit-ants wore an air of wartime discretion, so I did not dare risk snubs by asking how far I had come. My pocket map, however, proved less unhelpful when I found that I had been reading it upside down. When, about half-way, I turned on my lamp, I watched mist curdle under its wobbling ray. My spectacles dimmed steadily; my hands numbed inside my knitted gloves (the only Christmas present I had received so far) and the mist condensed on my muffler in fine drops.

I own that I had sustained myself through this journey on thoughts of the cheery welcome ahead. The Rangerton-Karneys' invitation, deliv-ered by word of mouth only three days ago, had been totally unex-pected, as well as gratifying. I had had no reason to think they had taken notice of me. We had met rarely, when I reported to the committees on which they sat. That the brother and two sisters (so much alike that people took them for triplets) had attracted *my* wistful notice, I need not say. But not only was my position a quite obscure one; I am not generally sought out; I make few new friends. None of my colleagues had been to the Rangerton-Karneys' house: there was an idea that they had given up guests. As the news of their invitation to me spread (and I cannot say I did much to stop it spreading) I rose rapidly in everyone's estimation.

In fact, their thought had been remarkably kind. Can you wonder that I felt myself favoured? I was soon, now, to see their erstwhile committee faces wreathed with seasonable and genial smiles. I never was one to doubt that people unbend at home. Perhaps a little feverish from my cycling, I pictured blazing hearths through holly-garlanded doors.

Owing to this indulgence in foolish fancy, my real arrival rather deflated me.

'I suppose they went out after tea?' I said to the aunt.

'After lunch, I think,' she replied. 'There was no tea.' She picked up her book, which was about Mantegna, and went on reading, pitched rather tensely forward to catch the light of the dim-bulbed lamp. I hesitated, then rose up saying that perhaps I had better deliver my rations to the cook. 'If you can,' she said, turning over a page.

The whirr of the clock preparing to strike seven made me jump. The hall had funny acoustics—so much so that I strode across the wide breaches from rug to rug rather than hear my step on the stone flags. Draught and dark coming down a shaft announced the presence of stairs. I saw what little I saw by the flame of a night-light, palpitating under a blue glass inverted shade. The hall and the staircase windows were not blacked out yet. (Back in the drawing-room, I could only imagine, the aunt must have so far bestirred herself as to draw the curtains.)

The kitchen was my objective—as I had said to the aunt. I pushed at a promising baize door: it immediately opened upon a vibration of heat and rich, heartening smells. At these, the complexion of everything changed once more. If my spirits, just lately, had not been very high, this was no doubt due to the fact that I had lunched on a sandwich, then had not dared leave my bicycle to look for a cup of tea. I was in no mood to reproach the Rangerton-Karneys for this Christmas break in their well-known austere routine.

But, in view of this, the kitchen was a surprise. Warm, and spiced with excellent smells, it was in the dark completely but for the crimson glow from between the bars of the range. A good deal puzzled, I switched the light on—the black out, here, had been punctiliously done.

The glare made me jump. The cook must have found, for her own use, a quadruple-power electric bulb. This now fairly blazed down on the vast scrubbed white wood table, scored and scarred by decades of the violent chopping of meat. I looked about—to be staggered by what I did not see. Neither on range, table, nor outsize dresser were there signs of the preparation of any meal. Not a plate, not a spoon, not a canister showed any signs of action. The heat-vibrating top of the range was bare; all the pots and pans were up above, clean and cold, in their places along the rack. I went so far as to open the oven door—a roasting smell came out, but there was nothing inside. A tap drip-drop-dripped on an upturned bowl in the sink—but nobody had been peeling potatoes there.

I put my rations down on the table and was, dumbfounded, preparing to turn away, when a white paper on the white wood caught my eye. This paper, in an inexpert line of block-printing, bore the somewhat unnecessary statement: I AM NOT HERE. To this was added, in brackets: 'Look in the fish kettle.' Though this be no affair of mine, could I fail to follow it up? Was this some new demonstration of haybox cookery; was I to find our dinner snugly concealed? I identified the fish kettle, a large tin object (about the size, I should say, of an infant's bath) that stood on a stool half-way between the sink and range. It wore a tight-fitting lid, which came off with a sort of plop: the sound in itself had an ominous hollowness. Inside, I found, again, only a piece of paper. This said: 'Mr & the 2 Misses Rangerton-Karney can boil their heads. This holds 3.'

I felt the least I could do for my hosts the Rangerton-Karneys was to suppress this unkind joke, so badly out of accord with the Christmas spirit. I *could* have dropped the paper straight into the kitchen fire, but on second thoughts I went back to consult the aunt. I found her so very deep in Mantegna as to be oblivious of the passage of time. She clearly did not like being interrupted. I said: 'Can you tell me if your nephew and nieces had any kind of contretemps with their cook today?'

She replied: 'I make a point of not asking questions.'

'Oh, so do I,' I replied, 'in the normal way. But I fear . . .'

'You fear what?'

'She's gone,' I said. 'Leaving this. . . .'

The aunt looked at the paper, then said: 'How curious.' She added: 'Of course, she has gone: that happened a year ago. She must have left several messages, I suppose. I remember that Etta found one in the mincing machine, saying to tell them to mince their gizzards. Etta seemed very much put out. That was *last* Christmas Eve, I remember— dear me, what a coincidence . . . So you found this, did you?' she said, re-reading the paper with less repugnance than I should have wished to see. 'I expect, if you went on poking about the kitchen . . .'

Annoyed, I said tartly: 'A reprehensible cook!'

'No worse than other English cooks,' she replied. 'They all declare they have never heard of a *pasta*, and that oil in cookery makes one repeat. But I always found her cheerful and kind. And of course I miss her—Etta's been cooking since.' (This was the elder Miss Rangerton-Karney.)

'But look,' I said, 'I was led to *this* dreadful message, by another one, on the table. *That* can't have been there a year.'

'I suppose not,' the aunt said, showing indifference. She picked up her book and inclined again to the lamp.

I said: 'You don't think some other servant . . .'

She looked at me like a fish.

'They *have* no other servants. Oh no: not since the cook . . .'

Her voice trailed away. 'Well, it's all very odd, I'm sure.'

'It's worse than odd, my dear lady: there won't be any dinner.'

She shocked me by emitting a kind of giggle. She said: 'Unless they *do* boil their heads.'

The idea that the Rangerton-Karneys might be out on a cook-hunt rationalized this perplexing evening for me. I am always more comfortable when I can tell myself that people are, after all, behaving accountably. The Rangerton-Karneys always acted in trio. The idea that one of them should stay at home to receive me while the other two went ploughing round the dark country would, at this crisis, never present itself. The Rangerton-Karneys' three sets of thoughts and feelings always appeared to join at the one root: one might say that they had a composite character. One thing, I could reflect, about misadventures is that they make for talk and often end in a laugh. I tried in vain to picture the Rangerton-Karneys laughing—for that was a thing I had never seen.

But if Etta is now resigned to doing the cooking . . . ? I thought better not to puzzle the thing out.

Screening my electric torch with my fingers past the uncurtained windows, I went upstairs to look for what might be my room. In my other hand I carried my little case—to tell the truth, I was anxious to change my socks. Embarking on a long passage, with doors ajar, I discreetly projected my torch into a number of rooms. All were cold; some were palpably slept in, others dismantled. I located the resting-places of Etta, Max, and Paulina by the odour of tar soap, shoe-leather, and boiled woollen underclothes that announced their presences in so many committee rooms. At an unintimate distance along the passage, the glint of my torch on Florentine bric-à-brac suggested the headquarters of the aunt. I did at last succeed, by elimination, in finding the spare room prepared for me. They had put me just across the way from their aunt. My torch and my touch revealed a made-up bed, draped in a glacial white starched quilt, two fringed towels straddling the water-jug, and virgin white mats to receive my brushes and comb. I successively bumped my knee (the knee still sore from the parcel) on two upright chairs. Yes, this must be the room for me. Oddly enough, it was much less cold than the others—but I did not think of that at the time. Having done what was necessary to the window, I lit up, to consider my new domain.

Somebody had been lying on my bed. When I rest during the day, I always remove the quilt, but whoever it was had neglected to do this. A deep trough, with a map of creases, appeared. The creases, however, did not extend far. Whoever it was had lain here in a contented stupor.

I worried—Etta might blame me. To distract my thoughts, I opened my little case and went to put my things on the dressing-table. The mirror was tilted upwards under the light, and something was written on it in soap: DEARIE, DON'T MIND ME. I at once went to the washstand, where the soap could be verified—it was a used cake, one corner blunted by writing. On my way back, I kicked over a black bottle, which, so placed on the floor as to be in easy reach from the bed, now gaily and noisily bowled away. It was empty—I had to admit that its contents, breathed out again, gave that decided character to my room.

The aunt was to be heard, pattering up the stairs. Was this belated hostess-ship on her part? She came into view of my door, carrying the night-light from the hall table. Giving me a modest, affronted look she said: 'I thought I'd tidy my hair.'

'The cook has been lying on my bed.'

'That would have been very possible, I'm afraid. She was often a little—if you know what I mean. But, she left last Christmas.'

'She's written something.'

'I don't see what one can do,' the aunt said, turning into her room. For my part, I dipped a towel into the jug and reluctantly tried to rub out the cook's message, but this only left a blur all over the glass. I applied to this the drier end of the towel. Oddly enough (perhaps) I felt fortified: this occult good feeling was, somehow, warming. The cook was supplying that touch of nature I had missed since crossing the Rangerton-Karneys' threshold. Thus, when I stepped back for another look at the mirror, I was barely surprised to find that a sprig of mistletoe had been twisted around the cord of the hanging electric light.

My disreputable psychic pleasure was to be interrupted. Downstairs, in the caves of the house, the front door bell jangled, then jangled again. This was followed by an interlude with the knocker: an imperious rat-a-tat-tat. I called across to the aunt: 'Ought one of us to go down? It might be a telegram.'

'I don't think so—why?'

We heard the glass door of the porch (the door through which I had made my so different entry) being rattled open; we heard the hall traversed by footsteps with the weight of authority. In response to a mighty '*Anyone there?*' I defied the aunt's judgement and went hurrying down. Coming on a policeman outlined in the drawing-room door, my first thought was that this must be about the blackout. I edged in, silent, just behind the policeman: he looked about him suspiciously, then saw me. 'And who might you be?' he said. The bringing out of his notebook gave me stage fright during my first and other replies. I explained that the Rangerton-Karneys had asked me to come and stay.

'Oh, they did?' he said. 'Well, that is a laugh. Seen much of them?' 'Not so far.'

'Well, you won't.' I asked why: he ignored my question, asked for all my particulars, quizzed my identity card. 'I shall check up on all this,' he said heavily. 'So they asked you for Christmas, did they? And just *when*, may I ask, was this invitation issued?'

'Well, er—three days ago.'

This made me quite popular. He said: 'Much as I thought. Attempt to cover their tracks and divert suspicion. I dare say you blew off all round about them having asked you here?'

'I may have mentioned it to one or two friends.'

He looked pleased again and said: 'Just what they reckoned on. Not a soul was to guess they had planned to bolt. As for you—*you're* a cool hand, I must say. Just walked in, found the place empty and dossed down. Never once strike you there was anything fishy?'

'A good deal struck me,' I replied austerely. 'I took it, however, that my host and his sisters had been unexpectedly called out—perhaps to look for a cook.'

'Ah, cook,' he said. 'Now what brought that to your mind?'

'Her whereabouts seemed uncertain, if you know what I mean.'

Whereupon, he whipped over several leaves of his notebook. 'The last cook employed here,' he said, 'was in residence here four days, departing last Christmas Eve, 24 December, 194–. We have evidence that she stated locally that she was unable to tolerate certain goings-on. She specified interference in her department, undue advantage taken of the rationing system, mental cruelty to an elderly female refugee . . .'

I interposed: 'That would certainly be the aunt.'

'. . . and failure to observe Christmas in the appropriate manner. On this last point she expressed herself violently. She further adduced (though with less violence of feeling) that her three employers were "dirty spies with their noses in everything". Subsequently, she withdrew this last remark; her words were, "I do not wish to make trouble, as I know how to make trouble in a way of my own." However, certain remarks she had let drop have been since followed up, and proved useful in our inquiries. Unhappily, we cannot check up on them, as the deceased met her end shortly after leaving this house.'

'The *deceased*?' I cried, with a sinking heart.

'Proceeding through the hall door and down the approach or avenue, in an almost total state of intoxication, she was heard singing "God rest you merry, gentlemen, let nothing you dismay". She also shouted: "Me for an English Christmas!" Accosting several pedestrians, she informed them that in her opinion times were not what they were. She spoke with emotion (being intoxicated) of turkey, mince pies, ham, plum pudding, etc. She was last seen hurrying in the direction of the canal, saying she must get brandy to make her sauce. She was recovered from the canal on Boxing Day, 26 December, 194-.'

'But what,' I said, 'has happened to the Rangerton-Karneys?'

'Now, now!' said the policeman, shaking his finger sternly. 'You *may* hear as much as is good for you, one day—or you may not. Did you ever hear of the Safety of the Realm? I don't mind telling you one thing— you're lucky. You might have landed yourself in a nasty mess.'

'But, good heavens—the *Rangerton-Karneys*! They know everyone.'

'Ah!' he said, 'but it's that kind you have to watch.' Heavy with this reflection, his eye travelled over the hearthrug. He stooped with a creak and picked up the aunt's book. 'Wop name,' he said, 'propaganda: sticks out a mile. Now, don't you cut off anywhere, while I am now proceeding to search the house.'

'Cut off?' I nearly said, 'What do you take me for?' Alone, I sat down in the aunt's chair and dropped a few more fir cones into the extinct fire.

ALL BUT EMPTY

Graham Greene

It is not often that one finds an empty cinema, but this one I used to frequent In the early 1930s because of its almost invariable, almost total emptiness. I speak only of the afternoons, the heavy grey after-noons of late winter; in the evenings, when the lights went up in the Edgware Road and the naphtha flares, and the peep-shows were crowded, this cinema may have known prosperity. But I doubt it.

It had so little to offer. There was no talkie apparatus, and the silent films it showed did not appeal to the crowd by their excitement or to the connoisseur by their unconscious humour. They were merely banal, drawing-room drama of 1925.

I suspect that the cinema kept open only because the owner could not sell or let the building and he could not afford to close it. I went to it because it was silent, because it was all but empty, and because the girl who sold the tickets had a bright, common, venal prettiness.

One passed out of the Edgware Road and found it in a side street. It was built of boards like a saloon in an American western, and there were no posters. Probably no posters existed of the kind of films it showed. One paid one's money to the girl of whom I spoke, taking an unneces-sarily expensive seat in the drab emptiness on the other side of the red velvet curtains, and she would smile, charming and venal, and address one by a name of her own; it was not difficult for her to remember her patrons. She may be there still, but I haven't visited the cinema for a long time now.

I remember I went in one afternoon and found myself quite alone. There was not even a pianist; blurred metallic music was relayed from a gramophone in the pay-box. I hoped the girl would soon leave her job and come in. I sat almost at the end of a row with one seat free as an indication that I felt like company, but she never came. An elderly man got entangled in the curtain and billowed his way through it and lost himself in the dark. He tried to get past me, though he had the whole cinema to choose from, and brushed my face with a damp beard. Then he sat down in the seat I had left, and there we were, close together in the wide dusty darkness.

The flat figures passed and repassed, their six-year-old gestures as antique as designs on a Greek coin. They were emotional in great white flickering letters, but their emotions were not comic nor to me moving. I was surprised when I heard the old man next me crying to himself— so much to himself and not to me, not a trace of histrionics in those slow, carefully stifled sobs that I felt sorry for him and did not grudge him the seat. I said:

'Can I do anything?'

He may not have heard me, but he spoke: 'I can't hear what they are saying.'

The loneliness of the old man was extreme; no one had warned him that he would find only silent pictures here. I tried to explain, but he did not listen, whispering gently, 'I can't see them.'

I thought that he was blind and asked him where he lived, and when he gave an address in Seymour Terrace, I felt such pity for him that I offered to show him the way to another cinema and then to take him home. It was because we shared a desolation, sitting in the dark and stale air, when all around us people were lighting lamps and making tea and gas fires glowed. But no! He wouldn't move. He said that he always came to this cinema of an evening, and when I said that it was only afternoon, he remarked that afternoon and evening were now to him 'much of a muchness'. I still didn't realize what he was enduring, what worse thing than blindness and age he might be keeping to himself.

Only a hint of it came to me a moment after, when he turned suddenly towards me, brushing my lips with his damp beard, and whispered.

No one could expect me to see, not after I've seen what I've seen,' and then in a lower voice, talking to himself, 'From ear to ear.'

That startled me because there were only two things he could mean, and I did not believe that he referred to a smile.

'Leave them to it,' he said, 'at the bottom of the stairs. The black-beetles always came out of that crack. Oh, the anger,' and his voice had a long weary *frisson*.

It was extraordinary how he seemed to read my thoughts, because I had already begun to comfort myself with the fact of his age and that he must be recalling something very far away, when he spoke again: 'Not a minute later than this morning. The clock had just struck two and I came down the stairs, and there he was. Oh, I was angry. He was smiling.'

'From ear to ear,' I said lightly, with relief.

'That was later,' he corrected me, and then he startled me by reading out suddenly from the screen the words, 'I love you. I will not let you go.' He laughed and said, 'I can see a little now. But it fades, it fades.'

I was quite sure then that the man was mad, but I did not go. For one thing, I thought that at any moment the girl might come and two people could deal with him more easily than one; for another, stillness seemed safest. So I sat very quietly, staring at the screen and knew that he was weeping again beside me, shivering and weeping and shivering. Among all the obscurities one thing was certain, something had upset him early that morning.

After a while he spoke again so low that his words were lost in the tin blare of the relayed record, but I caught the words 'serpent's tooth' and guessed that he must have been quoting scripture. He did not leave me much longer in doubt, however, of what had happened at the bottom of the stairs, for he said quite casually, his tears forgotten in curiosity:

'I never thought the knife was so sharp. I had forgotten I had had it reground.'

Then he went on speaking, his voice gaining strength and calmness: 'I had just put down the borax for the black-beetles that morning. How could I have guessed? I must have been very angry coming downstairs. The clock struck two, and there he was, smiling at me. I must have sent it to be reground when I had the joint of pork for Sunday dinner. Oh, I was angry when he laughed: the knife trembled. And there the poor body lay with the throat cut from ear to ear,' and hunching up his shoulders and dropping his bearded chin towards his hands, the old man began again to cry.

Then I saw my duty quite plainly. He might be mad and to be pitied, but he was dangerous.

It needed courage to stand up and press by him into the gangway, and then turn the back and be lost in the blind velvet folds of the curtains which would not part, knowing that he might have the knife still with him. I got out into the grey afternoon light at last, and startled the girl in the box with my white face. I opened the door of the kiosk and shut it again behind me with immeasurable relief. He couldn't get at me now.

'The police station,' I called softly into the telephone, afraid that he might hear me where he sat alone in the cinema, and when a voice answered, I said hurriedly, 'That murder in Seymour Terrace this morning.'

The voice at the other end became brisk and interested, telling me to hold the line, and then the seconds drummed away.

All the while I held the receiver I watched the curtain, and presently it began to shake and billow, as if somebody was fumbling for the way out. 'Hurry, hurry,' I called down the telephone, and then as the voice spoke I saw the old man wavering in the gap of the curtain. 'Hurry. The murderer's here,' I called, stumbling over the name of the cinema and so intent on the message I had to convey that I could not take in for a moment the puzzled and puzzling reply: 'We've got the murderer. It's the body that's disappeared.'

THREE MILES UP

Elizabeth Jane Howard

There was absolutely nothing like it.

An unoriginal conclusion, and one that he had drawn a hundred times during the last fortnight. Clifford would make some subtle and intelligent comparison, but he, John, could only continue to repeat that it was quite unlike anything else. It had been Clifford's idea, which, considering Clifford, was surprising. When you looked at him, you would not suppose him capable of it. However, John reflected, he had been ill, some sort of breakdown these clever people went in for, and that might account for his uncharacteristic idea of hiring a boat and travelling on canals. On the whole, John had to admit, it was a good idea. He had never been on a canal in his life, although he had been in almost every kind of boat, and thought he knew a good deal about them; so much indeed, that he had embarked on the venture in a light-hearted, almost a patronizing manner. But it was not nearly as simple as he had imagined. Clifford, of course, knew nothing about boats; but he had admitted that almost everything had gone wrong with a kind of devilish versatility which had almost frightened him. However, that was all over, and John, who had learned painfully all about the boat and her engine, felt that the former at least had run her gamut of disaster. They had run out of food, out of petrol, and out of water; had dropped their windlass into the deepest lock, and, more humiliating, their boat-hook into a side-pond. The head had come off the hammer. They had been disturbed for one whole night by a curious rustling in the cabin, like a rat in a paper bag, when there was no paper, and, so far as they knew, no rat. The battery had failed and had had to be recharged. Clifford had put his elbow through an already cracked window in the cabin. A large piece of rope had wound itself round the propeller with a malignant intensity which required three men and half a morning to unravel. And so on, until now there was really nothing left to go wrong, unless one of them drowned, and surely it was impossible to drown in a canal.

'I suppose one might easily drown in a lock?' he asked aloud.

'We must be careful not to fall into one,' Clifford replied.

'What?' John steered with fierce concentration, and never heard anything people said to him for the first time, almost on principle.

'I said we must be careful not to fall *into* a lock.'

'Oh. Well there aren't any more now until after the Junction. Anyway, we haven't yet, so there's really no reason why we should start now. I only wanted to know whether we'd drown if we did.'

'Sharon might.'

'What?'

'Sharon might.'

'Better warn her then. She seems agile enough.' His concentrated frown returned, and he settled down again to the wheel. John didn't mind where they went, or what happened, so long as he handled the boat, and all things considered, he handled her remarkably well. Clifford planned and John steered: and until two days ago they had both quarrelled and argued over a smoking and unusually temperamental primus. Which reminded Clifford of Sharon. Her advent and the weather were really their two unadulterated strokes of good fortune. There had been no rain, and Sharon had, as it were, dropped from the blue on to the boat, where she speedily restored domestic order, stimulated evening conversation, and touched the whole venture with her attractive being: the requisite number of miles each day were achieved, the boat behaved herself, and admirable meals were steadily and regularly prepared. She had, in fact, identified herself with the journey, without making the slightest effort to control it: a talent which many women were supposed in theory to possess, when, in fact, Clifford reflected gloomily, most of them were bored with the whole thing, or tried to dominate it.

Her advent was a remarkable, almost a miraculous piece of luck. He had, after a particularly ill-fed day, and their failure to dine at a small hotel, desperately telephoned all the women he knew who seemed in the least suitable (and they were surprisingly few), with no success. They had spent a miserable evening, John determined to argue about everything, and he, Clifford, refusing to speak; until, both in a fine state of emotional tension, they had turned in for the night. While John snored, Clifford had lain distraught, his resentment and despair circling round John and then touching his own smallest and most random thoughts: until his mind found no refuge and he was left, divided from it, hostile and afraid, watching it in terror racing on in the dark like some malignant machine utterly out of his control.

The next day things had proved no better between them, and they had continued throughout the morning in a silence which was only occasionally and elaborately broken. They had tied up for lunch beside a wood, which hung heavy and magnificent over the canal. There was a small clearing beside which John then proposed to moor, but Clifford failed to achieve the considerable leap necessary to stop the boat; and they had drifted helplessly past it. John flung him a line, but it was not until the boat was secured, and they were safely in the cabin, that the storm had broken. John, in attempting to light the primus, spilt a quantity of paraffin on Clifford's bunk. Instantly all his despair of the previous evening had contracted. He hated John so much that he could have murdered him. They both lost their tempers, and for the ensuing hour and a half had conducted a blazing quarrel, which, even at the time, secretly horrified them both in its intensity.

It had finally ended with John striding out of the cabin, there being no more to say. He had returned almost at once, however.

'I say, Clifford. Come and look at this.'

'At what?'

'Outside, on the bank.'

For some unknown reason Clifford did get up and did look. Lying face downwards quite still on the ground, with her arms clasping the trunk of a large tree, was a girl.

'How long has she been there?'

'She's asleep.'

'She can't have been asleep all the time. She must have heard some of what we said.'

'Anyway, who is she? What is she doing here?'

Clifford looked at her again. She was wearing a dark twill shirt and dark trousers, and her hair hung over her face, so that it was almost invisible. 'I don't know. I suppose she's alive?'

John jumped cautiously ashore. 'Yes, she's alive all right. Funny way to lie.'

'Well, it's none of our business anyway. Anyone can lie on a bank if they want to.'

'Yes, but she must have come in the middle of our row, and it does seem queer to stay, and then go to sleep.'

'Extraordinary,' said Clifford wearily. Nothing was really extraordinary, he felt, nothing. 'Are we moving on?'

'Let's eat first. I'll do it.'

'Oh, I'll do it.'

The girl stirred, unclasped her arms, and sat up. They had all stared at each other for a moment, the girl slowly pushing the hair from her forehead. Then she had said: 'If you will give me a meal, I'll cook it.'

Afterwards they had left her to wash up, and walked about the wood, while Clifford suggested to John that they ask the girl to join them. 'I'm sure she'd come,' he said. 'She didn't seem at all clear about what she was doing.'

'We can't just pick somebody up out of a wood,' said John, scandalized.

'Where do you suggest we pick them up? If we don't have someone, this holiday will be a failure.'

'We don't know anything about her.'

'I can't see that that matters very much. She seems to cook well. We can at least ask her.'

'All right. Ask her then. She won't come.'

When they returned to the boat, she had finished the washing up, and was sitting on the floor of the cockpit, with her arms stretched behind her head. Clifford asked her; and she accepted as though she had known them a long time and they were simply inviting her to tea.

'Well, but look here,' said John, thoroughly taken aback. 'What about your things?'

'My things?' she looked enquiringly and a little defensively from one to the other.

'Clothes and so on. Or haven't you got any? Are you a gipsy or something? Where do you come from?'

'I am not a gipsy,' she began patiently; when Clifford, thoroughly embarrassed and ashamed, interrupted her.

'Really, it's none of our business who you are, and there is absolutely no need for us to ask you anything. I'm very glad you will come with us, although I feel we should warn you that we are new to this life, and anything might happen.'

'No need to warn me,' she said and smiled gratefully at him.

After that, they both felt bound to ask her nothing; John because he was afraid of being made to look foolish by Clifford, and Clifford because he had stopped John.

'Good Lord, we shall never get rid of her; and she'll fuss about condensation,' John had muttered aggressively as he started the engine. But she was very young, and did not fuss about anything. She had told them her name, and settled down, immediately and easily: gentle, assured and unselfconscious to a degree remarkable in one so young. They were never sure how much she had overheard them, for she gave no sign of having heard anything. A friendly but uncommunicative creature.

The map on the engine box started to flap, and immediately John asked, 'Where are we?'

'I haven't been watching, I'm afraid. Wait a minute.'

'We just passed under a railway bridge,' John said helpfully.

'Right. Yes. About four miles from the Junction, I think. What is the time?'

'Five-thirty.'

'Which way are we going when we get to the Junction?'

'We haven't time for the big loop. I must be back in London by the 15th.'

'The alternative is to go up as far as the basin, and then simply turn round and come back, and who wants to do that?'

'Well, we'll know the route then. It'll be much easier coming back.'

Clifford did not reply. He was not attracted by the route being easier, and he wanted to complete his original plan

'Let us wait till we get there.' Sharon appeared with tea and marmalade sandwiches.

'All right, let's wait.' Clifford was relieved.

'It will be almost dark by six-thirty. I think we ought to have a plan,' John said. 'Thank you, Sharon.'

'Have tea first.' She curled herself on the floor with her back to the cabin doors and a mug in her hands.

They were passing rows of little houses with gardens that backed on to the canal. They were long narrow strips, streaked with cinder paths, and crowded with vegetables and chicken huts, fruit trees and perambulators; sometimes ending with fat white ducks, and sometimes in a tiny patch of grass with a bench on it.

'Would you rather keep ducks or sit on a bench?' asked Clifford.

'Keep ducks,' said John promptly. 'More useful. Sharon wouldn't mind which she did. Would you, Sharon?' He liked saying her name, Clifford noticed. 'You could be happy anywhere, couldn't you?' He seemed to be presenting her with the widest possible choice.

'I might *be* anywhere,' she answered after a moment's thought.

'Well you happen to be on a canal, and very nice for us.'

'In a wood, and then on a canal,' she replied contentedly, bending her smooth dark head over her mug.

'Going to be fine tomorrow,' said John. He was always a little embarrassed at any mention of how they found her and his subsequent rudeness.

'Yes. I like it when the whole sky is so red and burning and it begins to be cold.'

'*Are* you cold?' said John, wanting to worry about it: but she tucked her dark shirt into her trousers and answered composedly:

'Oh no. I am never cold.'

They drank their tea in a comfortable silence. Clifford started to read his map, and then said they were almost on to another sheet. 'New country,' he said with satisfaction. 'I've never been here before.'

'You make it sound like an exploration; doesn't he, Sharon?' said John.

'Is that a bad thing?' She collected the mugs. 'I am going to put these away. You will can me if I am wanted for anything.' And she went into the cabin again.

There was a second's pause, a minute tribute to her departure; and, lighting cigarettes, they settled down to stare at the long silent stretch of water ahead.

John thought about Sharon. He thought rather desperately that really they still knew nothing about her, and that when they went back to London, they would, in all probability, never see her again. Perhaps Clifford would fall in love with her, and she would naturally reciprocate, because she was so young and Clifford was reputed to be so fascinating and intelligent, and because women were always foolish and loved the wrong man. He thought all these things with equal intensity, glanced cautiously at Clifford, and supposed he was thinking about her; then wondered what she would be like in London, clad in anything else but her dark trousers and shirt. The engine coughed; and he turned to it in relief.

Clifford was making frantic calculations of time and distance; stretching their time, and diminishing the distance, and groaning that with the utmost optimism they could not be made to fit. He was interrupted by John swearing at the engine, and then for no particular reason he remembered Sharon, and reflected with pleasure how easily she left the mind when she was not present, how she neither obsessed nor possessed one in her absence, but was charming to see.

The sun had almost set when they reached the Junction, and John slowed down to neutral while they made up their minds. To the left was the straight cut which involved the longer journey originally planned; and curving away to the right was the short arm which John advocated. The canal was fringed with rushes, and there was one small cottage with no light in it. Clifford went into the cabin to tell Sharon where they were, and then, as they drifted slowly in the middle of the Junction, John suddenly shouted: 'Clifford! What's the third turning?'

'There are only two.' Clifford reappeared. 'Sharon is busy with dinner.'

'No, look. Surely that is another cut.'

Clifford stared ahead. 'Can't see it.'

'Just to the right of the cottage. Look. It's not so dark as all that.'

Then Clifford saw it very plainly. It seemed to wind away from the cottage on a fairly steep curve, and the rushes shrouding it from anything but the closest view were taller than the rest.

'Have another look at the map. I'll reverse for a bit.'

'Found it. It's just another arm. Probably been abandoned,' said Clifford eventually.

The boat had swung round; and now they could see the continuance of the curve dully gleaming ahead, and banked by reeds.

'Well, what shall we do?'

'Getting dark. Let's go up a little way, and moor. Nice quiet mooring.'

'With some nice quiet mudbanks,' said John grimly. 'Nobody uses that.'

'How do you know?'

'Well, look at it. All those rushes, and it's sure to be thick with weed.'

'Don't go up it then. But we shall go aground if we drift about like this.'

'*I* don't mind going up it,' said John doggedly. 'What about Sharon?'

'What about her?'

'Tell her about it.'

'We've found a third turning,' Clifford called above the noise of the primus through the cabin door.

'One you had not expected?'

'Yes. It looks very wild. We were thinking of going up it.'

'Didn't you say you wanted to explore?' she smiled at him.

'You are quite ready to try it? I warn you we shall probably run hard aground. Look out for bumps with the primus.'

'I am quite ready, and I am quite sure we shan't run aground,' she answered with charming confidence in their skill.

They moved slowly forward in the dusk. Why they did not run aground, Clifford could not imagine: John really was damned good at it. The canal wound and wound, and the reeds grew not only thick on each bank, but in clumps across the canal. The light drained out of the sky into the water and slowly drowned there; the trees and the banks became heavy and black.

Clifford began to clear things away from the heavy dew which had begun to rise. After two journeys he remained in the cabin, while John crawled on, alone. Once, on a bend, John thought he saw a range of hills ahead with lights on them, but when he was round the curve, and had time to look again he could see no hills: only a dark indeterminate waste of country stretched ahead.

He was beginning to consider the necessity of moorning, when they came to a bridge; and shortly after, he saw a dark mass which he took to be houses. When the boat had crawled for another fifty yards or so, he stopped the engine, and drifted in absolute silence to the bank. The houses, about half a dozen of them, were much nearer than he had at first imagined, but there were no lights to be seen. Distance is always deceptive in the dark, he thought, and jumped ashore with a bow line. When, a few minutes later, he took a sounding with the boathook, the water proved unexpectedly deep; and he concluded that they had by incredible good fortune moored at the village wharf. He made everything fast, and joined the others in the cabin with mixed feelings of pride and resentment; that he should have achieved so much under such difficult conditions, and that they (by 'they' he meant Clifford), should have contributed so little towards the achievement. He found Clifford reading Bradshaw's *Guide to the Canals and Navigable Rivers* in one corner, and Sharon, with her hair pushed back behind her ears, bending over the primus with a knife. Her ears are pale, exactly the colour of her face, he thought; wanted to touch them; then felt horribly ashamed, and hated Clifford.

'Let's have a look at Bradshaw,' he said, as though he had not noticed Clifford reading it.

But Clifford handed him the book in the most friendly manner, remarking that he couldn't see where they were. 'In fact you have surpassed yourself with your brilliant navigation. We seem to be miles from anywhere.'

'What about your famous ordnance?'

'It's not on any sheet I have. The new one I thought we should use only covers the loop we planned. There is precisely three quarters of a mile of this canal shown on the present sheet and then we run off the map. I suppose there must once have been trade here, but I cannot imagine what, or where.'

'I expect things change,' said Sharon. 'Here is the meal.'

'How can you see to cook?' asked John, eyeing his plate ravenously.

'There is a candle.'

'Yes, but we've selfishly appropriated that.'

'Should I need more light?' she asked, and looked troubled.

'There's no should about it. I just don't know how you do it, that's all. Chips exactly the right colour, and you never drop anything. It's marvellous.'

She smiled a little uncertainly at him and lit another candle. 'Luck, probably,' she said, and set it on the table.

They ate their meal, and John told them about the mooring. 'Some sort of village. I think we're moored at the wharf. I couldn't find any rings without the torch, so I've used the anchor.' This small shaft was intended for Clifford, who had dropped the spare torch-battery in the washing-up bowl, and forgotten to buy another. But it was only a small shaft, and immediately afterwards John felt much better. His aggression slowly left him, and he felt nothing but a peaceful and well-fed affection for the other two.

'Extraordinary cut off this is,' he remarked over coffee.

'It is very pleasant in here. Warm, and extremely full of us.'

'Yes. I know. A quiet village, though, you must admit.'

'I shall believe in your village when I see it.'

'Then you would believe it?'

'No he wouldn't, Sharon. Not if he didn't want to, and couldn't find it on the map. That map!'

The conversation turned again to their remoteness, and to how cut off one liked to be and at what point it ceased to be desirable; to boats, telephones, and, finally, canals: which, Clifford maintained, possessed the perfect proportions of urbanity and solitude.

Hours later, when they had turned in for the night, Clifford reviewed the conversation, together with others they had had, and remembered with surprise how little Sharon had actually said. She listened to everything and occasionally, when they appealed to her, made some small composed remark which was oddly at variance with their passionate interest. 'She has an elusive quality of freshness about her,' he thought, 'which is neither naïve nor stupid nor dull, and she invokes no responsibility. She does not want us to know what she was, or why we found her as we did, and curiously, I, at least, do not want to know. She is what women ought to be,' he concluded with sudden pleasure; and slept.

He woke the next morning to find it very late, and stretched out his hand to wake John.

'We've all overslept. Look at the time.'

'Good Lord! Better wake Sharon.'

Sharon lay between them on the floor, which they had ceded her because, oddly enough, it was the widest and most comfortable bed. She seemed profoundly asleep, but at the mention of her name sat up immediately, and rose, almost as though she had not been asleep at all.

The morning routine which, involving the clothing of three people and shaving of two of them, was necessarily a long and complicated business, began. Sharon boiled water, and Clifford, grumbling gently, hoisted himself out of his bunk and repaired with a steaming jug to the cockpit. He put the jug on a seat, lifted the canvas awning, and leaned out. It was absolutely grey and still; a little white mist hung over the canal, and the country stretched out desolate and unkempt on every side with no sign of a living creature. The village, he thought suddenly: John's village: and was possessed of a perilous uncertainty and fear. I am getting worse, he thought, this holiday is doing me no good. I am mad. I imagined that he said we moored by a village wharf. For several seconds he stood gripping the gunwale, and searching desperately for anything, huts, a clump of trees, which could in the darkness have been mistaken for a village. But there was nothing near the boat except tall rank rushes which did not move at all. Then, when his suspense was becoming unbearable, John joined him with another steaming jug of water.

'We shan't get anywhere at this rate,' he began; and then . . . 'Hullo! Where's my village?'

'I was wondering that,' said Clifford. He could almost have wept with relief, and quickly began to shave, deeply ashamed of his private panic.

'Can't understand it,' John was saying. It was no joke, Clifford decided, as he listened to his hearty puzzled ruminations.

At breakfast John continued to speculate upon what he had or had not seen, and Sharon listened intently while she filled the coffee pot and cut bread. Once or twice she met Clifford's eye with a glance of discreet amusement.

'I must be mad, or else the whole place is haunted,' finished John comfortably. These two possibilities seemed to relieve him of any further anxiety in the matter, as he ate a huge breakfast and set about greasing the engine.

'Well,' said Clifford, when he was alone with Sharon. 'What do you make of that?'

'It is easy to be deceived in such matters,' she answered perfunctorily.

'Evidently. Still, John is an unlikely candidate you must admit. Here, I'll help you dry.'

'Oh no. It is what I am here for.'

'Not entirely, I hope.'

'Not entirely.' She smiled and relinquished the cloth.

John eventually announced that they were ready to start. Clifford, who had assumed that they were to recover their journey, was surprised, and a little alarmed, to find John intent upon continuing it. He seemed undeterred by the state of the canal, which, as Clifford immediately pointed out, rendered navigation both arduous and unrewarding. He announced that the harder it was, the more he liked it, adding very firmly that 'anyway we must see what happens'.

'We shan't have time to do anything else.'

'Thought you wanted to explore.'

'I do, but . . . what do you think, Sharon?'

'I think John will have to be a very good navigator to manage that.' She indicated the rush and weed-ridden reach before them. 'Do you think it's possible?'

'Of course it's possible. I'll probably need some help though.'

'I'll help you,' she said.

So on they went.

They made incredibly slow progress. John enjoys showing off his powers to her, thought Clifford, half amused, half exasperated, as he struggled for the fourth time in an hour to scrape weeds off the propeller.

Sharon eventually retired to cook lunch.

'Surprising amount of water here,' John said suddenly.

'Oh?'

'Well, I mean, with all this weed and stuff, you'd expect the canal to have silted up. I'm sure nobody uses it.'

'The whole thing is extraordinary.'

'Is it too late in the year for birds?' asked Clifford later.

'No, I don't think so. Why?'

'I haven't heard one, have you?'

'Haven't noticed, I'm afraid. There's someone anyway. First sign of life.'

An old man stood near the bank watching them. He was dressed in corduroy and wore a straw hat.

'Good morning,' shouted John, as they drew nearer.

He made no reply, but inclined his head slightly. He seemed very old. He was leaning on a scythe, and as they drew almost level with him, he turned away and began slowly cutting rushes. A pile of them lay neatly stacked beside him.

'Where does this canal go? Is there a village further on?' Clifford and

John asked simultaneously. He seemed not to hear, and as they chugged steadily past, Clifford was about to suggest that they stop and ask again, when he called after them: 'Three miles up you'll find the village. Three miles up that is,' and turned away to his rushes again.

'Well, now we know something, anyway,' said John.

'We don't even know what the village is called.'

'Soon find out. Only three miles.'

'Three miles!' said Clifford darkly. 'That might mean anything.'

'Do you want to turn back?'

'Oh no, not now. I want to see this village now. My curiosity is thoroughly aroused.'

'Shouldn't think there'll be anything to see. Never been in such a wild spot. Look at it.'

Clifford looked at it. Half wilderness, half marsh, dank and grey and still, with single trees bare of their leaves; clumps of hawthorn that might once have been hedge, sparse and sharp with berries; and, in the distance, hills and an occasional wood: these were all one could see, beyond the lines of rushes which edged the canal winding ahead.

They stopped for a lengthy meal, which Sharon described as lunch and tea together, it being so late; and then, appalled at how little daylight was left, continued.

'We've hardly been any distance at all,' said John forlornly. 'Good thing there were no locks. I shouldn't think they'd have worked if there were.'

'*Much* more than three miles,' he said, about two hours later. Darkness was descending and it was becoming very cold.

'Better stop,' said Clifford.

'Not yet. I'm determined to reach that village.'

'Dinner is ready,' said Sharon sadly. 'It will be cold.'

'Let's stop.'

'You have your meal. I'll call if I want you.'

Sharon looked at them, and Clifford shrugged his shoulders. 'Come on. I will. I'm tired of this.'

They shut the cabin doors. John could hear the pleasant clatter of their meal, and just as he was coming to the end of the decent interval which he felt must elapse before he gave in, they passed under a bridge, the first of the day, and, clutching at any straw, he immediately assumed that it prefaced the village. 'I think we're nearly there,' he called.

Clifford opened the door. 'The village?'

'No, a bridge. Can't be far now.'

'You're mad, John. It's pitch dark.'

'You can see the bridge though.'

'Yes. Why not moor under it?'

'Too late. Can't turn round in this light, and she's not good at reversing. Must be nearly there. You go back, I don't need you.'

Clifford shut the door again. He was beginning to feel irritated with John behaving in this childish manner and showing off to impress Sharon. It was amusing in the morning, but really he was carrying it a bit far. Let him manage the thing himself then. When, a few minutes later, John shouted that they had reached the sought after village, Clifford merely pulled back the little curtain over a cabin window, rubbed the condensation, and remarked that he could see nothing. 'No light at least.'

'He is happy anyhow,' said Sharon peaceably.

'Going to have a look round,' said John, slamming the cabin doors and blowing his nose.

'Surely you'll eat first?'

'If you've left anything. My God it's cold! It's *unnaturally* cold.'

'We won't be held responsible if he dies of exposure will we?' said Clifford.

She looked at him, hesitated a moment, but did not reply, and placed a steaming plate in front of John. She doesn't want us to quarrel, Clifford thought, and with an effect of friendliness he asked: 'What does tonight's village look like?'

'Much the same. Only one or two houses you know. But the old man called it a village.' He seemed uncommunicative; Clifford thought he was sulking. But after eating the meal, he suddenly announced, almost apologetically, 'I don't think I shall walk round. I'm absolutely worn out. You go if you like. I shall start turning in.'

'All right. I'll have a look. You've had a hard day.'

Clifford pulled on a coat and went outside. It was, as John said, incredibly cold and almost overwhelmingly silent. The clouds hung very low over the boat, and mist was rising everywhere from the ground, but he could dimly discern the black huddle of cottages lying on a little slope above the bank against which the boat was moored. He did actually set foot on shore, but his shoe sank immediately into a marshy hole. He withdrew it, and changed his mind. The prospect of groping round those dark and silent houses became suddenly distasteful, and he joined the others with the excuse that it was too cold and that he also was tired.

A little later, he lay half conscious in a kind of restless trance, with John sleeping heavily opposite him. His mind seemed full of foreboding, fear of something unknown and intangible: he thought of them lying in warmth on the cold secret canal with desolate miles of water behind and probably beyond; the old man and the silent houses; John, cut off and asleep, and Sharon, who lay on the floor beside him. Immediately he was filled with a sudden and most violent desire for her, even to touch her, for her to know that he was awake.

'Sharon,' he whispered; 'Sharon, Sharon,' and stretched down his fingers to her in the dark.

Instantly her hand was in his, each smooth and separate finger warmly clasped. She did not move or speak, but his relief was indescribable and for a long while he lay in an ecstasy of delight and peace, until his mind slipped imperceptibly with her fingers into oblivion.

When he woke he found John absent and Sharon standing over the primus. 'He's outside,' she said.

'Have I overslept again?'

'It is late. I am boiling water for you now.'

'We'd better try and get some supplies this morning.'

'There is no village,' she said, in a matter of fact tone.

'What?'

'John says not. But we have enough food, if you don't mind this queer milk from a tin.'

'No, I don't mind,' he replied, watching her affectionately. 'It doesn't really surprise me,' he added after a moment.

'The village?'

'No village. Yesterday I should have minded awfully. Is that you, do you think?'

'Perhaps.'

'It doesn't surprise you about the village at all, does it? Do you love me?'

She glanced at him quickly, a little shocked, and said quietly: 'Don't you know?' then added: 'It doesn't surprise me.'

John seemed very disturbed. 'I don't like it,' he kept saying as they shaved. 'Can't understand it at all. I could have sworn there were houses last night. You saw them didn't you?'

'Yes.'

'Well, don't you think it's very odd?'

'I do.'

'Everything looks the same as yesterday morning. I don't like it.'

'It's an adventure you must admit.'

'Yes, but I've had enough of it. I suggest we turn back.'

Sharon suddenly appeared, and, seeing her, Clifford knew that he did not want to go back. He remembered her saying: 'Didn't you say you wanted to explore?' She would think him weak-hearted if they turned back all those dreary miles with nothing to show for it. At breakfast, he exerted himself in persuading John to the same opinion. John finally agreed to one more day, but, in turn, extracted a promise that they would then go back whatever happened. Clifford agreed to this, and Sharon for some inexplicable reason laughed at them both. So that eventually they prepared to set off in an atmosphere of general good humour.

Sharon began to fill the water tank with their four-gallon can. It seemed too heavy for her, and John dropped the starter and leapt to her assistance.

She let him take the can and held the funnel for him. Together they watched the rich even stream of water disappear.

'You shouldn't try to do that,' he said. 'You'll hurt yourself.'

'Gipsies do it,' she said.

'I'm awfully sorry about that. You know I am.'

'I should not have minded if you had thought I was a gipsy.'

'I do like you,' he said, not looking at her. 'I do like you. You won't disappear altogether when this is over, will you?'

'You probably won't find I'll disappear for good,' she replied comfortingly.

'Come on,' shouted Clifford.

It's all right for *him* to talk to her, John thought, as he struggled to swing the starter. He just doesn't like me doing it; and he wished, as he had begun often to do, that Clifford was not there.

They had spasmodic engine trouble in the morning, which slowed them down; and the consequent halts, with the difficulty they experienced of mooring anywhere (the banks seemed nothing but marsh), were depressing and cold. Their good spirits evaporated: by lunch-time John was plainly irritable and frightened, and Clifford had begun to hate the grey silent land on either side, with the woods and hills which remained so consistently distant. They both wanted to give it up by then, but John felt bound to stick to his promise, and Clifford was secretly sure that Sharon wished to continue.

While she was preparing another late lunch, they saw a small boy who stood on what once had been the towpath watching them. He was bareheaded, wore corduroy, and had no shoes. He held a long reed, the end of which he chewed as he stared at them.

'Ask him where we are,' said John; and Clifford asked.

He took the reed out of his mouth, but did not reply.

'Where do you live then?' asked Clifford as they drew almost level with him.

'I told you. Three miles up,' he said; and then he gave a sudden little shriek of fear, dropped the reed, and turned to run down the bank the way they had come. Once he looked back, stumbled and fell, picked himself up sobbing, and ran faster. Sharon had appeared with lunch a moment before, and together they listened to his gasping cries growing fainter and fainter, until he had run himself out of their sight.

'What on earth frightened him?' said Clifford.

'I don't know. Unless it was Sharon popping out of the cabin like that.'

'Nonsense. But he was a very frightened little boy. And, I say, do you realize . . .'

'He was a very foolish little boy,' Sharon interrupted. She was angry, Clifford noticed with surprise, really angry, white and trembling, and with a curious expression which he did not like.

'We might have got something out of him,' said John sadly.

'Too late now,' Sharon said. She had quite recovered herself.

They saw no one else. They journeyed on throughout the afternoon; it grew colder, and at the same time more and more airless and still. When the light began to fail, Sharon disappeared as usual to the cabin. The canal became more tortuous, and John asked Clifford to help him with the turns. Clifford complied unwillingly: he did not want to leave Sharon, but as it had been he who had insisted on their continuing, he could hardly refuse. The turns were nerve wracking, as the canal was very narrow and the light grew worse and worse.

'All right if we stop soon?' asked John eventually.

'Stop now if you like.'

'Well, we'll try and find a tree to tie up to. This swamp is awful. Can't think how that child ran.'

'That child . . .' began Clifford anxiously; but John, who had been equally unnerved by the incident, and did not want to think about it, interrupted. 'Is there a tree ahead anywhere?'

'Can't see one. There's a hell of a bend coming though. Almost back on itself. Better slow a bit more.'

'Can't. We're right down as it is.'

They crawled round, clinging to the outside bank, which seemed always to approach them, its rushes to rub against their bows, although the wheel was hard over. John grunted with relief, and they both stared ahead for the next turn.

They were presented with the most terrible spectacle. The canal immediately broadened, until no longer a canal but a sheet, an infinity, of water stretched ahead; oily, silent, and still, as far as the eye could see, with no country edging it, nothing but water to the low grey sky above it. John had almost immediately cut out the engine, and now he tried desperately to start it again, in order to turn round. Clifford instinctively glanced behind them. He saw no canal at all, no inlet, but grasping and close to the stern of the boat, the reeds and rushes of a marshy waste closing in behind them. He stumbled to the cabin doors and pulled them open. It was very neat and tidy in there, but empty. Only one stern door of the cabin was free of its catch, and it flapped irregularly backwards and forwards with their movements in the boat.

There was no sign of Sharon at all.

CLOSE BEHIND HIM

John Wyndham

'You didn't ought to of croaked him,' Smudger said resentfully. 'What in hell did you want to do a fool thing like that for?'

Spotty turned to look at the house, a black spectre against the night sky. He shuddered.

'It was him or me,' he muttered. 'I wouldn't of done it if he hadn't come for me—and I wouldn't even then, not if he'd come ordinary . . .'

'What do you mean ordinary?'

'Like anybody else. But he was queer . . . He wasn't—well, I guess he was crazy—dangerous crazy . . .'

'All he needed was a tap to keep him quiet,' Smudger persisted. 'There's was no call to bash his loaf in.'

'You didn't see him. I tell you, he didn't act human.' Spotty shuddered again at the recollection, and bent down to rub the calf of his right leg tenderly.

The man had come into the room while Spotty was sifting rapidly through the contents of a desk. He'd made no sound. It had been just a feeling, a natural alertness, that had brought Spotty round to see him standing there. In that very first glimpse Spotty had felt there was something queer about him. The expression on his face—his attitude—they were wrong. In his biscuit-coloured pyjamas, he should have looked just an ordinary citizen awakened from sleep, too anxious to have delayed with dressing-gown and slippers. But some way he didn't. An ordinary citizen would have shown nervousness, at least wariness; he would most likely have picked up something to use as a weapon. This man stood crouching, arms a little raised, as though he were about to spring.

Moreover, any citizen whose lips curled back as this man's did to show his tongue licking hungrily between his teeth, should have been considered sufficiently unordinary to be locked away safely. In the course of his profession Spotty had developed reliable nerves, but the look of this man rocked them. Nobody should be pleased by the discovery of a burglar at large in his house. Yet, there could be no doubt that this victim was looking at Spotty with satisfaction. An unpleasant gloating kind of satisfaction, like that which might appear on a fox's face at the sight of a plump chicken. Spotty hadn't liked the look of him at all, so he had pulled out the convenient piece of pipe that he carried for emergencies.

Far from showing alarm, the man took a step closer. He poised, sprung on his toes like a wrestler.

'You keep off me, mate,' said Spotty, holding up his nine inches of lead pipe as a warning.

Either the man did not hear—or the words held no interest for him. His long, bony face snarled. He shifted a little closer. Spotty backed up against the edge of the desk. 'I don't want no trouble. You just keep off me,' he said again.

The man crouched a little lower. Spotty watched him through narrowed eyes. An extra tensing of the man's muscles gave him a fractional warning before the attack.

The man came without feinting or rushing: he simply sprang, like an animal.

In mid-leap he encountered Spotty's boot suddenly erected like a stanchion in his way. It took him in the middle and felled him. He sprawled on the floor doubled up, with one arm hugging his belly. The other hand threatened, with fingers bent into hooks. His head turned in jerks, his jaws with their curiously sharp teeth were apart, like a dog's about to snap.

Spotty knew just as well as Smudger that what was required was a quietening tap. He had been about to deliver it with professional skill and quality when the man, by an extraordinary wriggle, had succeeded in fastening his teeth into Spotty's leg. It was unexpected, excruciating enough to ruin Spotty's aim and make the blow ineffectual. So he had hit again; harder this time. Too hard. And even then he had more or less had to pry the man's teeth out of his leg . . .

But it was not so much his aching leg—nor even the fact that he had killed the man—that was the chief cause of Spotty's concern. It was the kind of man he had killed.

'Like an animal he was,' he said, and the recollection made him sweat. 'Like a bloody wild animal. And the way he looked! His eyes! Christ, they wasn't human.'

That aspect of the affair held little interest for Smudger. He'd not seen the man until he was already dead and looking like any other corpse. His present concern was that a mere matter of burglary had been abruptly transferred to the murder category—a class of work he had always kept clear of until now.

The job had looked easy enough. There shouldn't have been any trouble. A man living alone in a large house—a pretty queer customer with a pretty queer temper. On Fridays, Sundays, and sometimes on Wednesdays, there were meetings at which about twenty people came to the house and did not leave until the small hours of the following morning. All this information was according to Smudger's sister, who learned it third hand from the woman who cleaned the house. The woman was darkly speculative, but unspecific, about what went on at these gatherings. But from Smudger's point of view the important thing was that on other nights the man was alone in the house.

He seemed to be a dealer of some kind. People brought odd curios to the house to sell him. Smudger had been greatly interested to hear that they were paid for—and paid for well—in cash. That was a solid, practical consideration. Beside it, the vaguely ill reputation of the place, the queerness of its furnishings, and the rumours of strange goings-on at the gatherings, were unimportant. The only thing worthy of any attention were the facts that the man lived alone and had items of value in his possession.

Smudger had thought of it as a one-man job at first, and with a little more information he might have tackled it on his own. He discovered that there was a telephone, but no dog. He was fairly sure of the room in which the money must be kept, but unfortunately his sister's source of information had its limitations. He did not know whether there were burglar alarms or similar precautions, and he was too uncertain of the cleaning woman to attempt to get into the house by a subterfuge for a preliminary investigation. So he had taken Spotty in with him on a fifty-fifty basis.

The reluctance with which he had taken that step had now become an active regret—not only because Spotty had been foolish enough to kill the man, but because the way things had been he could easily have made a hundred per cent haul on his own—and not be fool enough to kill the man had he been detected.

The attaché case which he carried now was well-filled with bundles of notes, along with an assortment of precious-looking objects in gold and silver, probably eminently traceable, but useful if melted down. It was irritating to think that the whole load, instead of merely half of it, might have been his.

The two men stood quietly in the bushes for some minutes and listened. Satisfied, they pushed through a hole in the hedge, then moved cautiously down the length of the neighbouring field in its shadow.

Spotty's chief sensation was relief at being out of the house. He hadn't liked the place from the moment they had entered. For one thing, the furnishings weren't like those he was used to. Unpleasant idols or carved figures of some kind stood about in unexpected places, looming suddenly out of the darkness into his flashlight's beam with hideous expressions on their faces. There were pictures and pieces of tapestry that were macabre and shocking to a simple burglar. Spotty was not particularly sensitive, but these seemed to him highly unsuitable to have about the home.

The same quality extended to more practical objects. The legs of a large oak table had been carved into mythical miscegenates of repulsive appearance. The two bowls which stood upon the table were either genuine or extremely good representations of polished human skulls. Spotty could not imagine why, in one room, anybody should want to mount a crucifix on the wall upside down and place on a shelf beneath it a row of sconces holding nine black candles—then flank the whole with two pictures of an indecency so revolting it almost took his breath away. All these things had somehow combined to rattle his usual hard-headedness.

But even though he was out of the place now, he didn't feel quite free of its influence. He decided he wouldn't feel properly himself again until they were in the car and several miles away.

After working around two fields they came to the dusty white lane off which they had parked the car. They prospected carefully. By now the sky had cleared of clouds and the moonlight showed the road empty in both directions. Spotty scrambled through the hedge, across the ditch, and stood on the road in a quietness broken only by Smudger's progress through the hedge. Then he started to walk towards the car.

He had gone about a dozen paces when Smudger's voice stopped him: 'Hey. Spotty. What've you got on your feet?'

Spotty stooped and looked down. There was nothing remarkable about his feet; his boots looked just as they had always looked.

'What?' he began.

'No! Behind you!'

Spotty looked back. From the point where he had stepped on to the road to another some five feet behind where he now stood was a series of footprints, dark in the white dust. He lifted his foot and examined the sole of his boot; the dust was clinging to it. He turned his eyes back to the footmarks once more. They looked black, and seemed to glisten.

Smudger bent down to peer more closely. When he looked up again there was a bewildered expression on his face. He gazed at Spotty's boots, and then back to the glistening marks. The prints of bare feet . . .

'There's something funny going on here,' he said inadequately.

Spotty, looking back over his shoulder, took another step forward. Five feet behind him a new mark of a bare foot appeared from nowhere.

A watery feeling swept over Spotty. He took another experimental step. As mysteriously as before, another footmark appeared. He turned widened eyes on Smudger. Smudger looked back at him. Neither said anything for a moment. Then Smudger bent down, touched one of the marks with his finger, then shone his flashlight on the finger.

'Red,' he said. 'Like blood . . .'

The words broke the trance that had settled on Spotty. Panic seized him. He stared around wildly, then began to run. After him followed the footprints. Smudger ran too. He noticed that the marks were no longer the prints of a full foot but only its forepart, as if whatever made them were also running.

Spotty was frightened, but not badly enough to forget the turn where they had parked the car beneath some trees. He made for it, and clambered in. Smudger, breathing heavily, got in on the other side and dropped the attaché case in the back.

'Going to get out of this lot quick,' Spotty said, pressing the starter.

'Take it easy,' advised Smudger. 'We got to think.'

But Spotty was in no thinking mood. He got into gear, jolted out of hiding, and turned down the lane.

A mile or so further on Smudger turned back from craning out of the window.

'Not a sign,' he said relieved. 'Reckon we've ditched it—whatever it was.' He thought for some moments, then he said: 'Look here, if those marks were behind us all the way from the house, they'll be able to follow them by daylight to where we parked the car.'

'They'd've found the car marks anyway,' Spotty replied.

'But what if they're *still* following?' Smudger suggested.

'You just said they weren't.'

'Maybe they couldn't keep up with us. But suppose they're coming along somewhere behind us, leaving a trail?'

Spotty had greatly recovered, he was almost his old practical self again. He stopped the car. 'All right. We'll see,' he said grimly. 'And if they are—what then?'

He lit a cigarette with a hand that was almost steady. Then he leaned out of the car, studying the road behind them. The moonlight was strong enough to show up any dark marks.

'What do you reckon it was?' he said, over his shoulder. 'We can't both've been seeing things.'

'They were real enough.' Smudger looked at the stain still on his finger.

On a sudden idea, Spotty pulled up his right trouser leg. The marks of the teeth were there, and there was a little blood, too, soaked into his sock, but he couldn't make that account for anything.

The minutes passed. Still there was no manifestation of footprints. Smudger got out and walked a few yards back along the road to make sure. After a moment's hesitation Spotty followed him.

'Not a sign,' Smudger said. 'I reckon—hey!' He broke off, looking beyond Spotty.

Spotty turned around. Behind him was a trail of dark, naked foot-prints leading *from* the car.

Spotty stared. He walked back to the car; the footprints followed. It was a chastened Spotty who sat down in the car.

'Well?'

Smudger had nothing to offer. Smudger, in fact, was considerably confused. Several aspects of the situation were competing for his attention. The footsteps were not following *him*, so he found himself less afraid of them than of their possible consequences. They were laying a noticeable trail for anyone to follow to Spotty, and the trouble was that the trail would lead to him, too, if he and Spotty kept together.

The immediate solution that occurred to him was that they split up, and Spotty take care of his own troubles. The best way would be to divide the haul right here and now. If Spotty could succeed in shaking off the footprints, good for him. After all, the killing was none of Smudger's affair.

He was about to make the suggestion when another aspect occurred to him. If Spotty were picked up with part of the stuff on him, the case would be clinched. It was also possible that Spotty, in a bad jam with nothing to lose, might spill. A far safer way would be for him to hold the stuff. Then Spotty could come for his share when, and if, he succeeded in losing the telltale prints.

It was obviously the only safe and reasonable course. The trouble was that Spotty, when it was suggested to him, did not see it that way.

They drove a few more miles, each occupied with his own thoughts. In a quiet lane they stopped once more. Again Spotty got out of the car and walked a few yards away from it. The moon was lower, but it still gave enough light to show the footprints following him. He came back looking more worried than frightened. Smudger decided to cut a possible loss and go back to his former plan.

'Look here,' he suggested, 'what say we share out the takings now, and you drop me off a bit up the road?'

Spotty looked doubtful, but Smudger pressed: 'If you can shake that trail off, well and good. If you can't—well, there's no sense in us both getting pinched, is there? Anyway, it was you who croaked him. And one has a better chance of getting away than two.'

Spotty was still not keen, but he had no alternative to offer.

Smudger pulled the attaché case out of the back and opened it between them. Spotty began to separate the bundles of notes into two piles. It had been a good haul. As Smudger watched, he felt a great sadness that half of it was going to benefit nobody when Spotty was picked up. Sheer waste, it seemed to him.

Spotty, with his head bent over his work, did not notice Smudger draw the piece of lead pipe out of his pocket. Smudger brought it down on the back of his head with such force and neatness that it is doubtful whether Spotty ever knew anything about it.

Smudger stopped the car at the next bridge and pushed Spotty's body over the low wall. He watched as the ripples widened out across the canal below. Then he drove on.

It was three days later that Smudger got home. He arrived in the kitchen soaked to the skin, and clutching his attaché case. He was looking worn, white, and ready to drop. He dragged a chair away from the table and slumped into it.

'Bill!' his wife whispered. 'What is it? Are they after you?'

'No, Liz—at least, it ain't the cops. But something is.'

He pointed to a mark close inside the door. At first she thought it was his own wet footprint.

'Get a wet cloth, Liz, and clean up the front step and the passage before anyone sees it,' he said.

She hesitated, puzzled.

'For God's sake, do it quick, Liz,' he urged her.

Still half bewildered, she went through the dark passage and opened the door. The rain was pelting down, seeming to bounce up from the road as it hit. The gutters were running like torrents. Everything streamed with wetness save the doorstep protected by the small jutting porch. And on the step was the blood-red print of a naked foot . . .

In a kind of trance she went down on her knees and swabbed it clean with the wet cloth. Closing the door, she switched on the lights and saw the prints leading towards the kitchen. When she had cleaned them up, she went back to her husband.

'You been hit, Bill?'

He looked at her, elbows on the table, his head supported between his hands.

'No,' he said. 'It ain't me what's making them marks, Liz—it's what's followin' me.'

'Following you? You mean they been following you all the way from the job?' she said incredulously. 'How did you get back?'

Smudger explained. His immediate anxiety, after pitching Spotty into the canal, had been to rid himself of the car. It had been a pinch for the job, and the number and description would have been circulated. He had parked it in a quiet spot and got out to walk, maybe pick up a life. When he had gone a few yards he had looked back and seen the line of prints behind him. They had frightened him a good deal more than he now admitted. Until that moment he had assumed that since they had been following Spotty they would have followed him into the canal. Now, it seemed, they had transferred their attentions to himself. He tried a few more steps: they followed. With a great effort he got a grip on himself, and refrained from running. He perceived that unless he wanted to leave a clear trail he must go back to the car. He did.

Further on he tried again, and with a sinking, hopeless feeling observed the same result. Back in the car, he lit a cigarette and considered plans with as much calmness as he could collect.

The thing to do was to find something that would not show tracks—or would not hold them. A flash of inspiration came to him, and he headed the car towards the river.

The sky was barely grey yet. He fancied that he managed to get the car down to the towpath without being seen. At any rate, no one had hailed him as he cut through the long grass to the water's edge. From there he had made his way downstream, plodding along through a few inches of water until he found a rowboat. It was a venerable and decrepit affair, but it served his purpose.

From then on his journey had been unexciting, but also uncomfortable. During the day he had become extremely hungry, but he did not dare to leave the boat until after dark, and then he moved only in the darkest streets where the marks might not be seen. Both that day and the next two he had spent hoping for rain. This morning, in a drenching downpour that looked like it might continue for hours, he had sunk the boat and made his way home, trusting that the trail would be washed away. As far as he knew, it had been.

Liz was less impressed than she ought to have been.

'I reckon it must be something on your boots,' she said practically. 'Why didn't you buy some new ones?'

He looked at her with a dull resentment. 'It ain't nothing on my boots,' he said. 'Didn't I tell you it was following me? You seen the marks. How could they come off my boots? Use your head.'

'But it don't make sense. Not the way you say it. *What's* following you?'

'How do I know,' he said bitterly. 'All I know is that it makes them marks—and they're getting closer, too.'

'How do you mean closer?'

'Just what I say. The first day they was about five feet behind me. Now they're between three and four.'

It was not the kind of thing that Liz could take in too easily.

'It don't make sense,' she repeated.

It made no sense during the days that followed, but she ceased to doubt. Smudger stayed in the house; whatever was following stayed with him. The marks of it were everywhere: on the stairs, upstairs, downstairs. Half Liz's time was spent in cleaning them up lest someone should come in and see them. They got on her nerves. But not as badly as they got on Smudger's.

Even Liz could not deny that the feet were stepping a little more closely behind him—a little more closely each day.

'And what happens when they catch up?' Smudger demanded fearfully. 'Tell me what. What can I do? What the hell can I do?'

But Liz had no suggestions. Nor was there anyone else they dared ask about it.

Smudger began to dream nights. He'd whimper and she'd wake him up asking what was the matter. The first time he could not remember, but the dream was repeated, growing a little clearer with each recurrence. A black shape appeared to hang over him as he lay. It was vaguely manlike in form, but it hovered in the air as if suspended. Gradually it sank lower and lower until it rested upon him—but weightlessly, like a pattern of fog. It seemed to flow up towards his head, and he was in panic lest it should cover his face and smother him, but at his throat it stopped. There was a prickling at the side of his neck. He felt strangely weak, as though tiredness suddenly invaded him. At the same time, the shadow appeared to grow denser. He could feel, too, that there began to be some weight in it as it lay upon them. Then, mercifully, Liz would wake him.

So real was the sensation that he inspected his neck carefully in the mirror when he shaved. But there was no mark there.

Gradually the glistening red prints closed in behind him. A foot behind his heels, six inches, three inches . . .

Then came a morning when he awoke tired and listless. He had to force himself to get up, and when he looked in the mirror, there *was* a mark on his throat. He called Liz, in a panic. But it was only a very small mark, and she made nothing of it.

But the next morning his lassitude was greater. It needed all his will-power to drag himself up. The pallor of his face shocked Liz—and himself, too, when he saw it in the shaving mirror. The red mark on his neck stood out more vividly . . .

The next day he did not get up.

Two days later Liz became frightened enough to call in the doctor. It was a confession of desperation. Neither of them cared for the doctor, who knew or guessed uncomfortably much about the occupations of his patients. One called a doctor for remedies, not for homilies on one's way of life.

He came, he hummed, he ha'ed. He prescribed a tonic, and had a talk with Liz.

'He's seriously anaemic,' he said. 'But there's more to it than that. Something on his mind.' He looked at her. 'Have you any idea what it is?'

Liz's denial was unconvincing. He did not even pretend to believe it.

'I'm no magician,' he said. 'If you don't help me, I can't help him. Some kinds of worry can go on pressing and nagging like an abscess.'

Liz continued to deny. For a moment she had been tempted to tell about the footmarks, but caution warned her that once she began she would likely be trapped into saying more than was healthy.

'Think it over,' the doctor advised. 'And let me know tomorrow how he is.'

The next morning there was no doubt that Smudger was doing very badly. The tonic had done him no good at all. He lay in bed with his eyes, when they were open, looking unnaturally large in a drawn white face. He was so weak that she had to feed him with a spoon. He was frightened, too, that he was going to die. So was Liz. The alarm in her voice when she telephoned the doctor was unmistakably genuine.

'All right, I'll be around within an hour,' he told her. 'Have you found out what's on his mind yet?' he added.

'N-no,' Liz told him.

When he came he told her to stay downstairs while he went up to see the patient. It seemed to her that an intolerably long time passed before she heard his feet on the stairs and she went out to meet him in the hall. She looked up into his face with mute anxiety. His expression was serious, and puzzled, so that she was afraid to hear him speak.

But at last she asked: 'Is—is he going to die, Doctor?'

'He's very weak—very weak indeed,' the doctor said. After a pause, he added: 'Why didn't you tell me about those footprints he thought were following him?'

She looked up at him in alarm.

'It's all right. He's told me all about it now. I knew there was something on his mind. It's not very surprising, either.'

Liz stared at him. 'Not—?'

'In the circumstances, no,' the doctor said. 'A mind oppressed by a sense of sin can play a lot of nasty tricks. Nowadays they talk of guilt complexes and inhibitions. Names change. When I was a boy the same sort of thing was known as a bad conscience.

'When one has the main facts, these things become obvious to anyone of experience. Your husband was engaged in—well, to put it bluntly, burgling the house of a man whose interests were mystic and occult. Something that happened there gave him a shock and unbalanced his judgement.

'As a result, he has difficulty in distinguishing between the real things he sees and the imaginary ones his uneasy conscience shows him. It isn't very complicated. He feels he is being dogged. Somewhere in his subconscious lie the lines from 'The Ancient Mariner':

> *Because he knows, a frightful fiend*
> *Doth close behind him tread*

and the two come together. And, in addition to that, he appears to have developed a primitive, vampiric type of phobia.

'Now, once we are able to help him dispel this obsession, he——' he broke off, suddenly aware of the look on his listener's face, 'What is it?' he asked.

'But, Doctor,' Liz said. 'Those footmarks, I——' She was cut short abruptly by a sound from above that was half groan and half scream.

The doctor was up the stairs before she could move. When she followed him, it was with a heavy certainty in her heart.

She stood in the doorway watching as he bent over the bed. In a moment he turned, grave-eyed, and gave her a slight shake of his head. He put his hand on her shoulder, then went quietly past her out of the room.

For some seconds Liz stood without moving. Then her eyes dropped from the bed to the floor. She trembled. Laughter, a high-pitched, frightening laughter shook her as she looked at the red naked footprints which led away from the bedside, across the floor and down the stairs, after the doctor . . .

THE QUINCUNX

Walter de la Mare

On opening the door and in no good humour at so late and apparently timid a summons I fancied at first glance that the figure standing at the foot of the four garden steps was my old and precious friend Henry Beverley—unexpectedly back in England again. At the moment there was only obscured moonlight to see him by and he stood rather hummocked up and partly in shadow. If it hadn't been Henry one might have supposed *this* visitor was the least bit apprehensive.

'Bless my heart!' I began—delight mingled with astonishment—then paused. For at that moment a thin straight shaft of moonlight had penetrated between the chimney stacks and shone clear into the face of a far less welcome visitor—Henry's brother, Walter.

I knew he was living rather dangerously near, but had kept this knowledge to myself. And now in his miniature car, which even by moonlight I noticed would have been none the worse off for a dusting, he had not only routed me out, but was also almost supplicating me to spend the night with him—in a house which had, I heard with surprise, been left to him by an eccentric aunt, recently deceased—about two miles away.

Seldom can moonshine have flattered a more haggard face. Had he no sedatives? Sedatives or not, how could I refuse him? Besides, he was Henry's brother. So having slowly climbed the stairs again, with a lingering glance of regret at the book I had been reading, I extinguished my green glass-shaded lamp (the reflex effects of which may have given poor Walter an additional pallor) pushed myself into a greatcoat, and jammed a hat on my head, and in a moment or so we were on our way, with a din resembling that of a van-load of empty biscuit-tins. I am something of a snob about cars, though I prefer them borrowed. It was monstrous to be shattering the silence of night with so fiendish a noise, all the blinds down and every house asleep. 'On such a night . . .' And as for poor Walter's gear-changing—heaven help the hardiest of Army lorries!

'Of course,' he repeated, 'it would be as easy as chalk to dismiss the whole affair as pure fancy. But that being so, how could it possibly have

stood up to repeated rational experiment? Don't think I really care a
hoot concerning the "ghostly" side of this business. Not in the least. I
am out for the definite, I am dog-tired, and I am all but beaten.'

Beaten, I thought to myself not without some little satisfaction. But
beaten by what, by whom?

'Beaten?' I shouted through the din. We were turning a corner.

'You see—for very good reasons I don't doubt—my late old aunt
could not away with me. She found precious little indeed to please her
in my complete side of the family—not even the saintly Henry. My own
idea is that all along she had been in love with my father. And I, thank
heaven, don't take after *him*. There is a limit to imbecile unpracticality,
and—' he dragged at his handbrake, having failed to notice earlier a
crossroad immediately in front of us under a lamp-post.

'She never intended me to inherit so much as a copper bed-warmer,
or the leg of a chair. Irony was not her strong point   otherwise I think
she might have bequeathed me her wheezy old harmonium. I always
had Salvation Army leanings. But Fate was too quick for her, and the
house came to *me*—to me, the least beloved of us all. At first merely out
of curiosity, I decided to live in the place, but there's living and living,
and there's deucedly little cash.'

'But she must have . . .' I began.

'Of course she must have,' he broke in. 'Even an old misbegotten
aunt-by marriage can't have lived on air. She *had* money; it was meant,
I believe—she mistrusted lawyers—for my cousin Arthur and the rest.
And'—he accelerated—'I am as certain as instinct and common sense
can make me, that there are stocks, shares, documents, all sorts of riff-
raff, and *possibly* private papers, hidden away somewhere in her own old
house. Where she lived for donkeys' years. Where I am trying to exist
now.' He shot me a rapid glance rather like an animal looking round.

'In short, I am treasure-hunting; and there's interference. That's the
situation, naked and a bit ashamed of it. But the really odd thing is—
she knows it.'

'Knows what?'

'She knows I am after the loot,' he answered, 'and cannot rest in her
grave. Wait till you have seen her face my dear feller, then scoff, if you
can. She was a secretive old cat and she hated bipeds. Soured, I suppose.
And she never stirred out of her frowsy seclusion for nearly twenty years.
And *now*—her poor Arthur left gasping—she is fully aware of what her
old enemy is at. Of every move I make. It's a fight to—well, past "the
death between us". And *she* is winning.'

'But my dear Beverley . . .' I began.

'My dear Rubbish,' he said, squeezing my arm. 'I am as sane as you are—only a little jarred and piqued. Besides I am not dragging you out at this time of night on evidence as vague as all that. I'll give you positive proof. *Perhaps* you shall have some pickings!'

We came at length to a standstill before his antiquated inheritance. An ugly awkward house, it abutted sheer on to the pavement. A lamp shone palely on its walls, its few beautifully-proportioned windows; and it seemed, if possible, a little quieter behind its two bay-trees—more resigned to night—than even its darkened neighbours were. We went in, and Beverley with a candle led the way down a long corridor.

'The front room', he said, pointing back, 'is the dining-room. There's nothing there—simply the odour of fifty years of lavendered cocoon; fifty years of seed-cake and sherry. But even to sit on, there alone, munching one's plebeian bread-and-cheese, is to become conscious— well, is to become *conscious*. In *here*, though, is the mystery.'

We stood together in the doorway, peering beneath our candle into a low-pitched, silent, strangely-attractive and old-fashioned parlour. Everything within it, from its tarnished cornice to its little old parrot-green beaded footstool, was the accumulated record of one mind, one curious, solitary human individuality. And it was as silent and unresponsive as a clam.

'What a fascinating old lady!' I said.

'Yes,' he answered in a low voice. 'There she is!'

I turned in some confusion, but only to survey the oval painted portrait of Miss Lemieux herself. She was little, narrow, black-mittened, straight-nosed, becurled; and she encountered my eyes so keenly, darkly, tenaciously, that I began to sympathize with both antagonists.

'Now this is the problem,' he said, making a long nose at it, and turning his back on the picture. 'I searched the house last week from garret to cellar and intend to begin again. The doubloons, the diamonds, the documents are here somewhere, and as R.L.S. said in another connection, If she's *Hide*, then I'm Seek. On Sunday I came in here to have a think. I sat there, in that little chair, by the window staring vacantly in front of me, when presently in some indescribable fashion I became aware that I was being stared *at*.' He touched the picture hanging up on its nail behind him with the back of his head. 'So we sat, she and I, for about ten solid minutes, I should think. Then I tired of it. I turned the old Sphinx to the wall again, and went out. A little after nine I came back. There wasn't a whisper in the house. I had my supper, sat thinking again, and fell asleep. When I awoke, I was shivering cold.

I got up immediately, went out, shut the dining-room door with my
face towards this one, went up a few stairs, my hand on the banister and
then vaguely distinguished by the shadow that the door I had shut was
ajar. I was certain I had shut it. I came back to investigate. And saw—
her.' He nodded towards the picture again. 'I had left her as I supposed
in disgrace, face to the wall: she had, it seemed, righted herself. But this
may have been a mistake. So I deliberately took the old lady down from
her ancestral nail and hid her peculiarly intent physiognomy in that
cushion:

> Dare not, wild heart, grow fonder!
> Lie there, my love, lie yonder!

Then I locked windows, shutters and door and went to bed.'

He paused and glanced at me out of the corner of his eye. 'I dare say
it sounds absurd,' he said, 'but next morning when I came down I
dawdled about for at least half an hour before I felt impelled to open this
door. The chair was empty. She was "up"!'

'Any charwoman?' I ventured.

'On Tuesdays, Fridays, and at the weekends,' he said.

'You are *sure* of it?' He looked vaguely at me, tired and protesting.
'Oh, yes,' he said, 'last night's was my fifth experiment.'

'And you want me . . . ?'

'Just to stay here and keep awake. *I can't.* That's all. Theorizing is
charming—and easy. But the nights are short. You don't appear to have
a vestige of nerves. Tell me who is playing this odd trick on me! Mind
you, I *know* already. *Some*how it's this old She's who is responsible, who
is manœuvring. But how?'

I exchanged a long look with him—with the cold blue gaze in the
tired pallid face; then glanced back at the portrait. Into those small,
feminine, dauntless, ink-black eyes.

He turned away with a vague shrug of his shoulders. 'Of course,' he
said coldly, 'if you'd rather *not.*'

'Go to bed, Beverley,' I answered, 'I'll watch till morning. . . . We
are, you say, absolutely alone in this house?'

'Physically, yes; absolutely alone. Apart from *that* old cat there is not
so much as a mouse stirring.'

'No rival heirs? No positive claimants?'

'None,' he said. 'Though, of course. . . . It's only—my aunt.' We
stood in silence.

'Well, good night, then; but honestly I am rather sceptical.'

He raised his eyebrows, faintly smiled—something between derision and relief, lifted the portrait from the wall, carried it across the room, leaned it against the armchair in the corner. 'There!' he muttered. 'Check! you old witch! . . . It's very good of you. I'm sick of it. It has relieved me immensely. Good night!' He went out quickly, leaving the door ajar. I heard him go up the stairs, and presently another door, above, slammed.

I thought at first how few candles stood between me and darkness. It was now too late to look for more. Not, of course, that I felt any real alarm. Only a kind of curiosity—that might perhaps leap into something a little different when off its guard! I sat down and began meditating on Beverley, his nerves, his pretences, his venomous hatred of . . . well, what? Of a dozen things. But beneath all this I was gazing in imagination straight into the pictured eyes of a little old lady, already months in her grave.

The hours passed slowly. I changed from chair to chair—'t.e.g.' giftbooks, albums of fading photographs, old picture magazines. I pored over some marvellously fine needlework, and a few enchanting little water-colours. My candle languished; its successor was kindled. I was already become cold, dull, sleepy, and depressed, when in the extreme silence I heard the rustling of silk. Screening my candle with my hand, I sat far back into my old yellow damask sofa. Slow, shuffling footsteps were quietly drawing near. I fixed my eyes on the door. A pale light beyond it began stealing inwards, mingling with mine. Faint shadows zigzagged across the low ceiling. The door opened wider, stealthily, and a most extraordinary figure discovered itself, and paused on the threshold.

For an instant I hesitated, my heart thumping at my ribs; and then I recognized, beneath a fantastic disguise, no less tangible an interloper than Beverley himself. He was in his pyjamas; his feet were bare; but thrown over his shoulders was an immense old cashmere shawl that might have once graced Prince Albert's Exhibition in the Crystal Palace. And his head was swathed in what seemed to be some preposterous eighteenth-century night-gear. The other hand outstretched, he was carrying his candlestick a few inches from his face, so that I could see his every feature with exquisite distinctness beneath his voluminous head-dress.

It was Beverley right enough—I noticed even a very faint likeness to his brother, Henry, unperceived till then. His pale eyes were wide and glassily open. But behind this face, as from out of a mask—keen, wizened, immensely absorbed—peered his little old enemy's unmistakable visage, Miss Lemieux's! He was in a profound sleep, there could be no doubt of that. So closely burned the flame to his entranced face I feared he would presently be setting himself on fire. He moved past me slowly with an odd jerky constricted gait, something like that of a very old lady. He was muttering, too, in an aggrieved queer far-away voice. Stooping with a sigh, he picked up the picture; returned across the room; drew up and mounted the parrot-green footstool, and groped for the nail in the wall not six inches above his head. At length he succeeded in finding it; sighed again and turned meditatively; his voice rising a little shrill, as if in altercation. Once more he passed me by unheeded and came to a standstill; for a moment, peering through curtains a few inches withdrawn, into the starry garden. Whether the odd consciousness within him was aware of *me*, I cannot say. Those unspeculating, window-like eyes turned themselves full on me crouched there in the yellow sofa. The voice fell to a whisper; I think that he hastened a little. He went out and closed the door, and I'd swear my candle solemnly ducked when his was gone!

I huddled myself up again, pulled up a rug and woke to find the candle-stub still alight in the dusk of dawn—battling faintly together to illuminate the little vivid painted face leaning from the wall. And that, on my soul—showing not a symptom of fatigue—in this delicate Spring daybreak, indeed appeared more redoubtable than ever!

I sat for a time undecided what to be doing, what even to be thinking. And then, as if impelled by an inspiration, I got up, took down again the trophy from its nail, and with my penknife gently prised open the back of its gilded frame. Surely, it had occurred to me, it could not be mere vanity, mere caprice or rancour that could take such posthumous pains as this! Perhaps, ever dimly aware of it as he was in his waking moments, merely the pressing subconscious thought of the portrait had lured Beverly out of his sleep. Perhaps . . .

I levered up the thin dusty wood; there was nothing beneath. I drew it out from the frame. And then was revealed, lightly pasted on the back, a scrap of yellowed paper, scrawled with five crosses in the form of a quincunx. In one corner of this was a large, capital Italianate 'P'. And beneath a central cross was drawn a small square. Here was the veritable answer before my eyes. How very like old age to doubt its memory even on such a crucial matter as this. Or was it only doubt?

For whose guidance had this odd quincunx been intended? Not for Walter Beverley's—that was certain. Standing even where I was I could see between the curtains the orchard behind the house pale in the dawn with its fast-fading fruit-blossom. There, then, lay concealed the old lady's secret 'hoard'. We had but to exercise a little thought, a little dexterity and precaution; and Beverley had won.

And then suddenly, impetuously, rose up in my mind an obstinate distaste of meddling in the matter. Surely, if there is any such thing as desecration, *this* would be desecration.

I glanced at the old attentive face looking up at me, the face of one who had, it seemed, so easily betrayed her most intimate secret, and in some unaccountable fashion there now appeared to be something quite other than mere malice in its concentration—a hint even of the apprehension and entreaty of a heart too proud to let them break through the veil of the small black fearless eyes.

I determined to say nothing to Beverley; watch yet again. And—if I could find a chance—dig by myself, and make sure of the actual contents of Miss Lemieux's treasury before surrendering it to her greedy, insensitive heir. So once more the portrait was re-hung on its rusty nail.

He was prepared for my scepticism; but he did not believe, I think, that I had kept unceasing watch.

'I am sure,' he said repeatedly, 'absolutely sure that what I told you last night has recurred repeatedly. How can you disprove my positive personal evidence by this one failure—by a million negatives? It is you who are to blame—that tough, bigoted *common* sense of yours.'

I willingly accepted his verdict and offered to watch once more. He seemed content. And yet by his incessant restlessness and the curious questioning dismay that haunted his face I felt that his nocturnal guest was troubling and fretting him more than ever.

It was a charming old house, intensely still, intensely self-centred, as it were. One could imagine how unwelcome the summons of death would be in such a familiar home on earth as this. I wandered, and brooded, and searched in the garden: and found at length without much difficulty my 'quincunx'. The orchard was full of fruit trees, cherry, plum, apple: but the five towering pear trees, their rusty crusted bloom not yet all shed, might become at once unmistakably conspicuous to anyone in possession of the clue; though not till then. But how hopeless a contest had my friend set himself with no guidance, and one spade, against such an aunt, against such an orchard!

Evening began to narrow in the skies. My host and I sat together over a bottle of wine. Much as he seemed to cling to my company, I knew he longed for solitude. Twice he rose, as if urged by some sudden caprice to leave me, and twice he sat down again in even deeper constraint.

But soon after midnight I was left once more to my vigil. This time I forestalled his uneasy errand and replaced the portrait myself. I rested awhile; then, when it was still very early morning, I ventured out into the mists of the garden to find a spade. But I had foolishly forgotten on which side of the mid-most tree Miss Lemieux had set her tell-tale square. So back again I was compelled to go, and this time I took the flimsy, precious scrap of paper with me. Somewhere a waning moon was shedding light, for the mists of the garden were white as milk and the trees stood phantom-like above the drenched grasses.

I pinned the paper to the mid-most pear tree, measured out with my eye a rough narrow oblong a foot or two from the trunk and drove the rusty spade into the soil.

At that instant I heard a cautious minute sound behind me. I turned and once more confronted the pathetic bedizened figure of the night before. It was fumbling with the handle of the window, holding aloft a candle. The window opened at length and Beverley stood peering out into the garden. I fancied even a shrill voice called. And then without hesitation, with the same odd, shuffling gait Beverley stepped out on to the dew-damped gravel path and came groping towards me. He stood then, quietly watching me, not two paces distant; and so utterly still was the twilight that his candle flame burned slim and unwavering in the mist, shedding its small, pale light on leaf-sprouting flowerless bough and dewdrop, and upon that strange set haunted face.

I could not gaze very long into the grey unseeing eyes. His lips moved. His fingers, oddly bent, twitched. And then he turned from me. The large pale eyes wandered to my spade, to the untrampled grasses, and finally, suddenly fixed their gaze on the tiny square of fading paper. He uttered a little cry, shrill and desperate, and stretched out his hand to snatch it. But I was too quick for him. Doubling it up, I thrust it into my pocket and stepped back beneath the trees. Then, intensely anxious not to awaken the sleep-walker, I drew back with extreme caution. None the less, I soon perceived that, however gradual my retreat, he was no less patiently driving me into a little shrubbery where there would be no chance of eluding him, and we should stand confronting one another face to face.

I could not risk a struggle in such circumstances. A wave of heat spread over me; I tripped, and then ran as fast as I could back to the house, hastened into the room and threw myself down in my old yellow sleeping-place—closing my eyes as if I were lost to the world. Presently followed the same faint footfall near at hand. Then, hearing no sound at all, and supposing he had passed, I cautiously opened my eyes—only to gaze once more unfathomably deep into his, stooping in the light of his candle, searching my face insanely, entreatingly—I cannot describe with how profound a disquietude.

I did not stir, until, with a deep sigh, like that of a tired-out child, he turned from me and left the room.

I waited awhile, my thoughts like a disturbed nest of ants. What should I do? To whom was my duty obligatory?—to Beverley, feverishly hunting for wealth not his (even if it existed) by else than earthly right; or to this unquiet spirit—that I could not but believe had taken possession of him—struggling, only *I* knew how bravely, piteously, and desperately, to keep secret—what? Not mere money or valuables or private papers or personal secrets which might lie hidden beneath the shadow of the pear tree. Surely never had eyes pleaded more patiently and intensely and less covetously for a stranger's chivalry, nor from a wilder ambush than these that had but just now gazed into mine. What was the secret; what lure was detaining on earth a shade so much in need of rest?

I took the paper from my pocket. Light was swiftly flowing into the awakening garden. A distant thrush broke faintly into song. Undecided—battling between curiosity and pity, between loyalty to my friend and loyalty to even *more* than a friend—to this friendless old woman's solitary perturbed spirit, I stood with vacant eyes upon the brightening orchard—my back turned on portrait and room.

A hand (no *man's* asleep, or awake) touched mine. I turned—debated no more. The poor jaded face was grey and drawn. He seemed himself to be inwardly wrestling—possessed against possessor. And still the old bygone eyes within his own, across how deep an abyss, argued, pleaded with mine. They seemed to snare me, to persuade me beyond denial. I held out the flimsy paper between finger and thumb.

Like the limb of an automaton, Beverley's arm slowly raised his guttering candle. The flame flowed soft and blue. I held the paper till its heat scorched my thumb. Something changed; something but just now there was suddenly gone. The old, drawn face melted, as it were, into another. And Beverley's voice broke out inarticulate and feverish. I sat him down and let him slowly awaken. He stared incredulously to and fro, from the window to me, to the portrait, and at last his eye fell on his extraordinary attire.

'I say,' he said, 'what's this?'

'Seemingly,' I said, 'they are the weeds of the malevolent aunt who has been giving you troubled nights.'

'Me?' he said, not yet quite free from sleep.

'Yes,' I said.

He yawned. 'Then—I have been fooled?' he said. I nodded. I think that even tears came into his eyes. The May-morning choragium of the wild birds had begun, every singer seemingly a soloist in the enraptured medley of voices.

'Well, look here!' he said, nodding a stupid sleep-drowsed head at me, 'look here! What . . . you think of an aunt who hates a fellow as much as that, eh? What you think?'

'I don't know what to think,' I said.

THE TOWER

Marghanita Laski

The road begins to rise in a series of gentle curves, passing through pleasing groves of olives and vines. 5 km. on the left is the fork for Florence. To the right may be seen the Tower of Sacrifice (470 steps) built in 1535 by Niccolo di Ferramano; superstitious fear left the tower intact when, in 1549, the surrounding village was completely destroyed.

Triumphantly Caroline lifted her finger from the fine italic type. There was nothing to mar the success of this afternoon. Not only had she taken the car out alone for the first time, driving unerringly on the right-hand side of the road, but what she had achieved was not a simple drive but a cultural excursion. She had taken the Italian guidebook Neville was always urging on her and hesitantly, haltingly, she had managed to piece out enough of the language to choose a route that took in four well-thought-of frescos, two universally-admired campaniles, and one wooden crucifix in a village church quite a long way from the main road. It was not, after all, such a bad thing that a British Council meeting had kept Neville in Florence. True, he was certain to know all about the campaniles and the frescos, but there was just a chance that he hadn't discovered the crucifix, and how gratifying if she could, at last, have something of her own to contribute to his constantly accumulating hoard of culture.

But could she add still more? There was at least another hour of daylight, and it wouldn't take more than thirty-five minutes to get back to the flat in Florence. Perhaps there would just be time to add this tower to her dutiful collection? What was it called? She bent to the guidebook again carefully tracing the text with her finger to be sure she was translating it correctly, word by word.

But this time her moving finger stopped abruptly at the name of Niccolo di Ferramano. There had risen in her mind a picture—no, not a picture, a portrait—of a thin white face with deep-set black eyes that stared intently into hers. Why a portrait? she asked, and then she remembered.

It had been about three months ago, just after they were married, when Neville had first brought her to Florence. He himself had already lived there for two years, and during that time had been at least as concerned to accumulate Tuscan culture for himself as to disseminate English culture to the Italians. What more natural than that he should wish to share—perhaps even to show off—his discoveries to his young wife?

Caroline had come out to Italy with the idea that when she had worked through one or two galleries and made a few trips—say to Assisi and Siena—she would have done her duty as a British Council wife, and could then settle down to examining the Florentine shops, which everyone had told her were too marvellous for words. But Neville had been contemptuous of her programme. 'You can see the stuff in the galleries at any time,' he had said. 'but I'd like you to start with the pieces that the ordinary tourist doesn't see,' and of course Caroline couldn't possibly let herself be classed as an ordinary tourist. She had been proud to accompany Neville to castles and palaces privately owned to which his work gave him entry, and there to gaze with what she hoped was pleasure on the undiscovered Raphael, the Titian that had hung on the same wall ever since it was painted, the Giotto fresco under which the family that had originally commissioned it still said their prayers.

It had been on one of these pilgrimages that she had seen the face of the young man with the black eyes. They had made a long slow drive over narrow ill-made roads and at last had come to a castle on the top of a hill. The family was, to Neville's disappointment, away, but the housekeeper remembered him and led them to a long gallery lined with five centuries of family portraits.

Though she could not have admitted it even to herself, Caroline had become almost anaesthetized to Italian art. Dutifully she had followed Neville along the gallery, listening politely while in his light well-bred voice he had told her intimate anecdotes of history, and involuntarily she had let her eyes wander round the room, glancing anywhere but at the particular portrait of Neville's immediate dissertation.

It was thus that her eye was caught by a face on the other side of the room, and forgetting what was due to politeness she caught her husband's arm and demanded, 'Neville, who's that girl over there?'

But he was pleased with her. He said, 'Ah, I'm glad you picked that one out. It's generally thought to be the best thing in the collection—a Bronzino, of course,' and they went over to look at it.

The picture was painted in rich pale colours, a green curtain, a blue dress, a young face with calm brown eyes under plaits of honey-gold hair. Caroline read out the name under the picture—*Giovanna di Ferramano, 1531–1549.* That was the year the village was destroyed, she remembered now, sitting in the car by the roadside, but then she had exclaimed, 'Neville, she was only eighteen when she died.'

'They married young in those days,' Neville commented, and Caroline said in surprise, 'Oh, was she married?' It had been the radiantly virginal character of the face that had caught at her inattention.

'Yes, she was married,' Neville answered, and added, 'Look at the portrait beside her. It's Bronzino again. What do you think of it?'

And this was when Caroline had seen the pale young man. There were no clear light colours in this picture. There was only the whiteness of the face, the blackness of the eyes, the hair, the clothes, and the glint of gold letters on the pile of books on which the young man rested his hand. Underneath this picture was written *Portrait of an Unknown Gentleman.*

'Do you mean he's her husband?' Caroline asked. 'Surely they'd know if he was, instead of calling him an Unknown Gentleman?'

'He's Niccolo di Ferramano all right,' said Neville. 'I've seen another portrait of him somewhere, and it's not a face one would forget, but—' he added reluctantly, because he hated to admit ignorance, 'there's apparently some queer scandal about him, and though they don't turn his picture out, they won't even mention his name. Last time I was here, the old Count himself took me through the gallery. I asked him about little Giovanna and her husband.' He laughed uneasily. 'Mind you, my Italian was far from perfect at that time, but it was horribly clear that I shouldn't have asked.' 'But what did he *say?*' Caroline demanded. 'I've tried to remember,' said Neville. 'For some reason it stuck in my mind. He said either "She was lost" or "She was damned" but which word it was I can never be sure. The portrait of Niccolo he just ignored altogether.'

'What was wrong with Niccolo, I wonder?' mused Caroline, and Neville answered. 'I don't know but I can guess. Do you notice the lettering on those books up there, under his hand? It's all in Hebrew or Arabic. Undoubtedly the unmentionable Niccolo dabbled in Black Magic.'

Caroline shivered. 'I don't like him,' she said. 'Let's look at Giovanna again,' and they had moved back to the first portrait, and Neville had said casually, 'Do you know, she's rather like you.'

'I've just got time to look at the tower,' Caroline now said aloud, and she put the guidebook back in the pigeon-hole under the dashboard, and drove carefully along the gentle curves until she came to the fork for Florence on the left.

On the top of a little hill to the right stood a tall round tower. There was no other building in sight. In a land where every available piece of ground is cultivated, there was no cultivated ground around this tower. On the left was the fork for Florence: on the right a rough track led up to the top of the hill.

Caroline knew that she wanted to take the fork to the left, to Florence and home and Neville and—said an urgent voice inside her—for safety. This voice so much shocked her that she got out of the car and began to trudge up the dusty track towards the tower.

After all, I may not come this way again, she argued; it seems silly to miss the chance of seeing it when I've already got a reason for being interested. I'm only just going to have a quick look—and she glanced at the setting sun, telling herself that she would indeed have to be quick if she were to get back to Florence before dark.

And now she had climbed the hill and was standing in front of the tower. It was built of narrow red bricks, and only thin slits pierced its surface right up to the top where Caroline could see some kind of narrow platform encircling it. Before her was an arched doorway. I'm just going to have a quick look, she assured herself again, and then she walked in.

She was in an empty room with a low arched ceiling. A narrow stone staircase clung to the wall and circled round the room to disappear through a hole in the ceiling.

'There ought to be a wonderful view at the top,' said Caroline firmly to herself, and she laid her hand on the rusty rail and started to climb, and as she climbed, she counted.

'—thirty-nine, forty, forty-one,' she said, and with the forty-first step she came through the ceiling and saw over her head, far far above, the deep blue evening sky, a small circle of blue framed in a narrowing shaft round which the narrow staircase spiralled. There was no inner wall; only the rusty railing protected the climber on the inside.

'—eighty-three, eighty-four—' counted Caroline. The sky above her was losing its colour and she wondered why the narrow slit windows in the wall had all been so placed that they spiralled round the staircase too high for anyone climbing it to see through them.

'It's getting dark very quickly,' said Caroline at the hundred-and-fiftieth step. 'I know what the tower is like now. It would be much more sensible to give up and go home.

At the two-hundred-and-sixty-ninth step, her hand, moving forward on the railing, met only empty space. For an interminable second she shivered, pressing back to the hard brick on the other side. Then hesitantly she groped forward, upwards, and at last her fingers met the rusty rail again, and again she climbed.

But now the breaks in the rail became more and more frequent.

Sometimes she had to climb several steps with her left shoulder pressed tightly to the brick wall before her searching hand could find the tenuous rusty comfort again.

At the three-hundred-and seventy-fifth step the rail, as her moving hand clutched it, crumpled away under her fingers. 'I'd better just go by the wall,' she told herself, and now her left hand traced the rough brick as she climbed up and up.

'Four-hundred-and-twenty-two,   four-hundred-and-twenty-three,' counted Caroline with part of her brain. 'I really ought to go down now,' said another part, 'I wish—oh, I want to go down now—' but she could not. 'It would be so silly to give up,' she told herself, desperately trying to rationalise what drove her on. 'Just because one's afraid—' and then she had to stifle that thought too, and there was nothing left in her brain but the steadily mounting tally of the steps.

'—four-hundred-and-seventy!' said Caroline aloud with explosive relief, and then she stopped abruptly because the steps had stopped too. There was nothing ahead but a piece of broken railing barring her way, and the sky, drained now of all its colour, was still some twenty feet above her head.

'But how idiotic,' she said to the air. 'The whole thing's absolutely pointless,' and then the fingers of her left hand, exploring the wall beside her, met not brick but wood.

She turned to see what it was, and there in the wall, level with the top step, was a small wooden door. 'So it does go somewhere after all,' she said, and she fumbled with the rusty handle. The door pushed open and she stepped through.

She was on a narrow stone platform about a yard wide. It seemed to encircle the tower. The platform sloped downwards away from the tower and its stones were smooth and very shiny—and this was all she noticed before she looked beyond the stones and down.

She was immeasurably, unbelievably high and alone and the ground below was a world away. It was not credible, not possible that she should be so far from the ground. All her being was suddenly absorbed in the single impulse to hurl herself from the sloping platform. 'I cannot go down any other way,' she said, and then she heard what she said and stepped back, frenziedly clutching the soft rotten wood of the doorway with hands sodden with sweat. There is no other way, said the voice in her brain, there is no other way.

'This is vertigo,' said Caroline, 'I've only got to close my eyes and keep still for a minute and it will pass off. It's bound to pass off. I've never had it before but I know what it is and it's vertigo,' She closed her eyes and kept very still and felt the cold sweat running down her body.

'I should be all right now,' she said at last, and carefully she stepped back through the doorway on to the four-hundred-and-seventieth step and pulled the door shut before her. She looked up at the sky, swiftly darkening with night. Then, for the first time, she looked down into the shaft of the tower, down to the narrow unprotected staircase spiralling round and round and round, and disappearing into the dark. She said— she screamed—'I can't go down.'

She stood still on the top step, staring downwards, and slowly the last light faded from the tower. She could not move. It was not possible that she should dare to go down, step by step down the unprotected stairs into the dark below. It would be much easier to fall, said the voice in her head, to take one step to the left and fall and it would all be over. You cannot climb down.

She began to cry, shuddering with the pain of her sobs. It could not be true that she had brought herself to this peril, that there could be no safety for her unless she could climb down the menacing stairs. The reality *must* be that she was safe at home with Neville—but this was the reality and here were the stairs; at last she stopped crying and said 'Now I shall go down.'

'One!' she counted and, her right hand tearing at the brick wall, she moved first one and then the other foot down to the second step. 'Two!' she counted, and then she thought of the depth below her and stood still, stupefied with terror. The stone beneath her feet, the brick against her hand were too frail protections for her exposed body. They could not save her from the voice that repeated that it would be easier to fall. Abruptly she sat down on the step.

'Two,' she counted again, and spreading both her hands tightly against the step on each side of her, she swung her body off the second step, down on to the third. 'Three,' she counted, then 'four' then 'five,' pressing closer and closer into the wall, away from the empty drop on the other side.

At the twenty-first step she said, 'I think I can do it now.' She slid her right hand up the rough wall and slowly stood upright. Then with the other hand she reached for the railing it was now too dark to see, but it was not there.

For timeless time she stood there, knowing nothing but fear. 'Twenty-one,' she said, 'twenty-one' over and over again, but she could not step on to the twenty-second stair.

Something brushed her face. She knew it was a bat not a hand that touched her but still it was horror beyond conceivable horror, and it was this horror, without any sense of moving from dread to safety, that at last impelled her down the stairs.

'Twenty-three, twenty-four, twenty-five—' she counted, and around her the air was full of whispering skin-stretched wings. If one of them should touch her again, she must fall. 'Twenty-six, twenty-seven, twenty-eight—' The skin of her right hand was torn and hot with blood, for she would never lift it from the wall, only press it slowly down and force her rigid legs to move from the knowledge of each step to the peril of the next.

So Caroline came down the dark tower. She could not think. She could know nothing but fear. Only her brain remorselessly recorded the tally. 'Five-hundred-and-one,' it counted, 'five-hundred-and-two—and three—and four—.'

POOR GIRL

Elizabeth Taylor

Miss Chasty's first pupil was a flirtatious little boy. At seven years, he was alarmingly precocious and sometimes she thought that he despised his childhood, regarding it as a waiting time which he used only as a rehearsal for adult life. He was already more sophisticated than his young governess and disturbed her with his air of dalliance, the mockery with which he set about his lessons, the preposterous conversations he led her into, guiding her skilfully away from work, confusing her with bizarre conjectures and irreverent ideas, so that she would clasp her hands tightly under the plush tablecloth and pray that his father would not choose such a moment to observe her teaching, coming in abruptly as he sometimes did and signalling to her to continue her lesson.

At those times, his son's eyes were especially lively, fixed cruelly upon his governess as he listened, smiling faintly, to her faltering voice, measuring her timidity. He would answer her questions correctly, but significantly, as if he knew that by his aptitude he rescued her from dismissal. There were many governesses waiting employment, he implied—and this was so at the beginning of the century. He underlined her good fortune at having a pupil who could so easily learn, could display the results of her teaching to such advantage for the benefit of the rather sombre, pompous figure seated at the window. When his father, apparently satisfied, had left them without a word, the boy's manner changed. He seemed fatigued and too absent-minded to reply to any more questions.

'Hilary!' she would say sharply. 'Are you attending to me?' Her sharpness and her foolishness amused him, coming as he knew they did from the tension of the last ten minutes.

'Why, my dear girl, of course.'

'You must address me by my name.'

'Certainly, dear Florence.'

'Miss Chasty.'

His lips might shape the words, which he was too weary to say.

Sometimes, when she was correcting his sums, he would come round the table to stand beside her, leaning against her heavily, looking closely at her face, not at his book, breathing steadily down his nose so that tendrils of hair wavered on her neck and against her cheeks. His still-ness, his concentration on her and his too heavy leaning, worried her. She felt something experimental in his attitude, as if he were not leaning against her at all, but against someone in the future. 'He is only a baby,' she reminded herself, but she would try to shift from him, feeling a vague distaste. She would blush, as if he were a grown man, and her heart could be heard beating quickly. He was aware of this and would take up the corrected book and move back to his place.

Once he proposed to her and she had the feeling that it was a proposal-rehearsal and that he was making use of her, as an actor might ask her to hear his lines.

'You must go on with your work,' she said.

'I can shade in a map and talk as well.'

'Then talk sensibly.'

'You think I am too young, I daresay; but you could wait for me to grow up. I can do that quickly enough.'

'You are far from grown-up at the moment.'

'You only say these things because you think that governesses ought to. I suppose you don't known *how* governesses go on, because you have never been one until now, and you were too poor to have one of your own when you were young.'

'That is impertinent, Hilary.'

'You once told me that your father couldn't afford one.'

'Which is a different way of putting it.'

'I shouldn't have thought they cost much.' He had a way of just making a remark, of breathing it so gently that it was scarcely said, and might conveniently be ignored.

He was a dandified little boy. His smooth hair was like a silk cap, combed straight from the crown to a level line above his topaz eyes. His sailor-suits were spotless. The usual boldness changed to an agonized fussiness if his serge sleeve brushed against chalk or if he should slip on the grassy terrace and stain his clothes with green. On their afternoon walks he took no risks and Florence, who had younger brothers, urged him in vain to climb a tree or jump across puddles. At first, she thought him intimidated by his mother or nurse; but soon she realized that his mother entirely indulged him and the nurse had her thoughts all bent upon the new baby: his fussiness was just another part of his grown-upness come too soon.

The house was comfortable, although to Florence rather too sealed-up and overheated after her own damp and draughty home. Her work was not hard and her loneliness only what she had expected. Cut off from the kitchen by her education, she lacked the feuds and camaraderie, gossip and cups of tea, which made life more interesting for the domestic staff. None of the maids—coming to light the lamp at dusk or laying the schoolroom-table for tea—ever presumed beyond a remark or two about the weather.

One late afternoon, she and Hilary returned from their walk and found the lamps already lit. Florence went to her room to tidy herself before tea. When she came down to the schoolroom, Hilary was already there, sitting on the window-seat and staring out over the park as his father did. The room was bright and warm and a maid had put a white cloth over the plush one and was beginning to lay the table.

The air was full of a heavy scent, dry and musky. To Florence, it smelt quite unlike the Eau de Cologne she sometimes sprinkled on her handkerchief, when she had a headache and she disapproved so much that she returned the maid's greeting coldly and bade Hilary open the window.

'Open the window, dear girl?' he said. 'We shall catch our very deaths.'

'You will do as I ask and remember in future how to address me.'

She was angry with the maid—who now seemed to her an immoral creature—and angry to be humiliated before her.

'But why?' asked Hilary.

'I don't approve of my schoolroom being turned into a scented bower.' She kept her back to the room and was trembling, for she had never rebuked a servant before.

'I approve of it,' Hilary said, sniffing loudly.

'I think it's lovely,' the maid said. 'I noticed it as soon as I opened the door.'

'Is this some joke, Hilary?' Florence asked when the maid had gone.

'No. What?'

'This smell in the room?'

'No. You smell of it most, anyhow.' He put his nose to her sleeve and breathed deeply.

It seemed to Florence that this was so, that her clothes had caught the perfume among their folds. She lifted her palms to her face, then went to the window and leant out into the air as far as she could.

'Shall I pour out the tea, dear girl?'

'Yes, please.'

She took her place at the table abstractedly, and as she drank her tea she stared about the room, frowning. When Hilary's mother looked in, as she often did at this time, Florence stood up in a startled way.

'Good-evening, Mrs Wilson. Hilary, put a chair for your mamma.'

'Don't let me disturb you.'

Mrs Wilson sank into the rocking-chair by the fire and gently tipped to and fro.

'Have you finished your tea, darling boy?' she asked. 'Are you going to read me a story from your book? Oh, there is Lady scratching at the door. Let her in for mamma.'

Hilary opened the door and a balding old pug-dog with bloodshot eyes waddled in.

'Come Lady! Beautiful one. Come to mistress! What is wrong with her, poor pet lamb?'

The bitch had stopped just inside the room and lifted her head and howled. 'What has frightened her, then? Come, beauty! Coax her with a sponge-cake, Hilary.'

She reached forward to the table to take the dish and doing so noticed Florence's empty teacup. On the rim was a crimson smear, like the imprint of a lip. She gave a sponge-finger to Hilary, who tried to quieten the pug, then she leaned back in her chair and studied Florence again as she had studied her when she had engaged her a few weeks earlier. The girl's looks were appropriate enough, appropriate to a clergyman's daughter and a governess. Her square chin looked resolute, her green eyes innocent, her dress was modest and unbecoming. Yet Mrs Wilson could detect an excitability, even feverishness, which she had not noticed before and she wondered if she had mistaken guardedness for innocence and deceit for modesty.

She was reaching this conclusion—rocking back and forth when she saw Florence's hand stretch out and turn the cup round in its saucer so that the red stain was out of sight.

'What is wrong with Lady?' Hilary asked, for the dog would not be pacified with sponge-fingers, but kept making barking advances further into the room, then growling in retreat.

'Perhaps she is crying at the new moon,' said Florence and she went to the window and drew back the curtain. As she moved, her skirts rustled. 'If she has silk underwear as well!' Mrs Wilson thought. She had clearly heard the sound of taffetas and she imagined the drab, shiny alpaca dress concealing frivolity and wantonness.

'Open the door Hilary!' she said. 'I will take Lady away. Vernon shall give her a run in the park. I think a quiet read for Hilary and then an early bedtime, Miss Chasty. He looks pale this evening.'

'Yes, Mrs Wilson.' Florence stood respectfully by the table, hiding the cup.

'The hypocrisy!' Mrs Wilson thought and she trembled as she crossed the landing and went downstairs.

She hesitated to tell her husband of her uneasiness, knowing his susceptibilities to women whom his conscience taught him to deplore. Hidden below the apparent urbanity of their married life were old unhappinesses—little acts of treachery and disloyalty which pained her to remember, bruises upon her peace of mind and her pride: letters found, a pretty maid dismissed, an actress who had blackmailed him. As he read the Lesson in Church, looking so perfectly upright and honourable a man, she sometimes thought of his escapades; but not with bitterness or cynicism, only with pain at her memories and a whisper of fear about the future. For some time she had been spared those whispers and had hoped that their marriage had at last achieved its calm. To speak of Florence as she must might both arouse his curiosity and revive the past. Nevertheless, she had her duty to her son to fulfil and her own anger to appease and she opened the Library door very determinedly.

'Oliver, I am sorry to interrupt your work, but I must speak to you.'

He put down the *Strand* magazine quite happily, aware that she was not a sarcastic woman.

Oliver and his son were extraordinarily alike. 'As soon as Hilary has grown a moustache we shall not know them apart,' Mrs Wilson often said, and her husband liked this little joke which made him feel more youthful. He did not know that she added a silent prayer—'O God, please do not let him *be* like him, though.'

'You seem troubled, Louise.' His voice was rich and authoritative. He enjoyed setting to rights her little domestic flurries and waited indulgently to hear of some tradesman's misdemeanour or servant's laziness.

'Yes, I am troubled about Miss Chasty.'

'Little Miss Mouse? I was rather troubled myself. I noticed two spelling-faults in Hilary's botany essay, which she claimed to have corrected. I said nothing before the boy; but I shall acquaint her with it when the opportunity arises.

'Do you often go to the schoolroom, then?'

'From time to time. I like to be sure that our choice was wise.'

'It was not. It was misguided *and* unwise.'

'All young people seem slipshod nowadays.'

'She is more than slipshod. I believe she should go. I think she is quite brazen. Oh, yes, I should have laughed at that myself if it had been said to me an hour ago, but I have just come from the schoolroom and it occurs to me that now she has settled down and feels more secure—since you pass over her mistakes—she is beginning to take advantage of your leniency and to show herself in her true colours. I felt a sinister atmosphere up there and I am quite upset and exhausted by it. I went up to hear Hilary's reading. They were finishing tea and the room was full of the most overpowering scent—*her* scent. It was disgusting.'

'Unpleasant?'

'No, not at all. But upsetting.'

'Disturbing?'

She would not look at him or reply, hearing no more indulgence or condescension in his voice, but the quality of warming interest.

'And then I saw her teacup and there was a mark on it—a red smear where her lips had touched it. She did not know I saw it and as soon as she noticed it herself she turned it round, away from me. She is an immoral woman and she has come into our house to teach our son.'

'I have never noticed a trace of artificiality in her looks. It seemed to me that she was rather colourless.'

'She has been sly. This evening she looked quite different, quite flushed and excitable. I know that she had rouged her lips or painted them, or whatever those women do.' Her eyes filled with tears.

'I shall observe her for a day or two,' Oliver said, trying to keep anticipation from his voice.

'I should like her to go at once.'

'Never act rashly. She is entitled to a quarter's notice unless there is definite blame. We could make ourselves very foolish if you have been mistaken. Oh, I know that you are sure; but it has been known for you to misjudge others. I shall take stock of her and decide if she is suitable. She is still Miss Mouse to me and I cannot think otherwise until I see the evidence with my own eyes.'

'There was something else as well,' Mrs Wilson said wretchedly.

'And what was that?'

'I should rather not say.' She had changed her mind about further accusations. Silk underwear would prove, she guessed, too inflammatory.

'I shall go up ostensibly to mention Hilary's spelling-faults.' He could not go fast enough and stood up at once.

'But Hilary will be in bed.'

'I could not mention the spelling-faults if he were not.'

'Shall I come with you?'

'My dear Louise, why should you? It would look very strange—a deputation about two spelling-faults.'

'Then don't be long, will you? I hope you won't be long.'

He went to the schoolroom, but there was no one there. Hilary's story-book lay closed upon the table and Miss Chasty's sewing was folded neatly. As he was standing there looking about him and sniffing hard, a maid came in with a tray of crockery.

'Has Master Hilary gone to bed?' he asked, feeling rather foolish and confused.

The only scent in the air was a distinct smell—even a haze—of cigarette smoke.

'Yes, sir.'

'And Miss Chasty—where is she?'

'She went to bed, too, sir.'

'Is she unwell?'

'She spoke of a chronic head, sir.'

The maid stacked the cups and saucers in the cupboard and went out. Nothing was wrong with the room apart from the smell of smoke and Mr Wilson went downstairs. His wife was waiting in the hall. She looked up expectantly, in some relief at seeing him so soon.

'Nothing,' he said dramatically. 'She has gone to bed with a head-ache. No wonder she looked feverish.'

'You noticed the scent.'

'There was none,' he said. 'No trace. Nothing. Just imagination, dear Louise. I thought that it must be so.'

He went to the library and took up his magazine again, but he was too disturbed to read and thought with impatience of the following day.

Florence could not sleep. She had gone to her room, not with a headache but to escape conversations until she had faced her predica-ment alone. This she was doing, lying on the honeycomb quilt which, since maids do not wait on governesses, had not been turned down.

The schoolroom this evening seemed to have been wreathed about with a strange miasma; the innocent nature of the place polluted in a way which she could not understand or have explained. Something new it seemed, had entered the room which had not belonged to her or became a part of her—the scent had clung about her clothes; the stained cup was her cup and her handkerchief with which she had rubbed it clean was still reddened; and, finally, as she had stared in the mirror, trying to re-establish her personality, the affected little laugh which startled her had come from herself. It had driven her from the room.

'I cannot explain the inexplicable,' she thought wearily and began to prepare herself for bed. Home-sickness hit her like a blow on the head. 'Whatever they do to me, I have always my home,' she promised herself. But she could not think who 'they' might be; for no one in this house had threatened her. Mrs Wilson had done no more than irritate her with her commonplace fussing over Hilary and her dog, and Florence was prepared to overcome much more than irritations. Mr Wilson's pomposity, his constant watch on her work, intimidated her, but she knew that all who must earn their living must have fears lest their work should not seem worth the payment. Hilary was easy to manage; she had quickly seen that she could always deflect him from rebelliousness by opening a new subject for conversation; any idea would be a counter-attraction to naughtiness; he wanted her to sharpen his wits upon. 'And is that all that teaching is, or should be?' she had wondered. The servants had been good to her realizing that she would demand nothing of them. She had suffered great loneliness, but had foreseen it as part of her position. Now she felt fear nudging it away. 'I am not lonely any more,' she thought. 'I am not alone any more. And I have lost something.' She said her prayers; then sitting up in bed, kept the candle alight while she brushed her hair and read the Bible.

'Perhaps I have lost my reason,' she suddenly thought, resting her finger on her place in the Psalms. She lifted her head and saw her shadow stretch up the powdery, rose-sprinkled wall. 'Now can I keep *that* secret?' she wondered. 'When there is no one to help me to do it? Only those who are watching to see it happen.'

She was not afraid in her bedroom as she had been in the schoolroom, but her perplexed mind found no replies to its questions. She blew out the candle and tried to fall asleep but lay and cried for a long time, and yearned to be at home again and comforted in her mother's arms.

In the morning she met kind enquiries. Nurse was so full of solicitude that Florence felt guilty. 'I came up with a warm drink and put my head round the door but you were in the land of Nod so I drank it myself. I should take a grey powder; or I could mix you a gargle. There are a lot of throats about.'

'I am quite better this morning,' said Florence and she felt calmer as she sat down at the schoolroom-table with Hilary. 'Yet it was all true' her reason whispered. 'The morning hasn't altered that.'

'You have been crying,' said Hilary. 'Your eyes are red.'

'Sometimes people's eyes are red from other causes—headaches and colds.' She smiled brightly.

'And sometimes from crying, as I said. I should think *usually* from crying.'

'Page fifty-one,' she said, locking her hands together in her lap.

'Very well.' He opened the book, pressed down the pages and lowered his nose to them, breathing the smell of print. 'He is utterly sensuous,' she thought. 'He extracts every pleasure, every sensation, down to the most trivial.'

They seemed imprisoned in the schoolroom, by the silence of the rest of the house and by the rain outside. Her calm began to break up into frustration and she put her hands behind her chair and pressed them against the hot mesh of the fireguard to steady herself. As she did so, she felt a curious derangement of both mind and body; of desire unsettling her once sluggish, peaceful nature, desire horribly defined, though without direction.

'I have soon finished those,' said Hilary, bringing his sums and placing them before her. She glanced at her palms which were criss-crossed deep with crimson where she had pressed them against the fire-guard, then she took up her pen and dipped it into the red ink.

'Don't lean against me, Hilary,' she said.

'I love the scent so much.'

It had returned, musky, enveloping, varying as she moved. She ticked the sums quickly, thinking that she would set Hilary more work and escape for a moment to calm herself—change her clothes or cleanse herself in the rain. Hearing Mr Wilson's footsteps along the passage, she knew that her escape was cut off and raised wild-looking eyes as he came in. He mistook panic for passion, thought that by opening the door suddenly he had caught her out and laid bare her secret, her pathetic adoration.

'Good-morning,' he said musically and made his way to the window-seat. 'Don't let me disturb you.' He said this without irony, although he thought: 'So it is that way the wind blows! Poor creature!' He had never found it difficult to imagine that women were in love with him.

'I will hear your verbs,' Florence told Hilary, and opened the French Grammar as if she did not know them herself. Her eyes—from so much crying—were a pale and brilliant green and as the scent drifted in Oliver's direction and he turned to her, she looked fully at him.

'Ah, the still waters!' he thought and stood up suddenly. '*Ils vont*,' he corrected Hilary and touched his shoulder as he passed. 'Are you attending to Miss Chasty?'

'Is she attending to me?' Hilary murmured. The risk was worth taking, for neither heard. His father appeared to be sleep-walking and Florence deliberately closed her eyes, as if looking down were not enough to blur the outlines of her desire.

'I find it difficult,' Oliver said to his wife, 'to reconcile your remarks about Miss Chasty with the young woman herself. I have just come from the schoolroom and she was engaged in nothing more immoral than teaching French verbs—that not very well, incidentally.'

'But can you *explain* what I have told you?'

'I can't do that,' he said gaily. For who can explain a jealous woman's fancies? he implied.

He began to spend more time in the schoolroom; for surveillance, he said. Miss Chasty, though not outwardly of an amorous nature, was still not what he had at first supposed. A suppressed wantonness hovered beneath her primness. She was the ideal governess in his eyes—irreproachable, yet not unapproachable. As she was so conveniently installed, he could take his time in divining the extent of her willingness; especially as he was growing older and the game was beginning to be worth more than the triumph of winning it. To his wife, he upheld Florence, saw nothing wrong save in her scholarship, which needed to be looked into—the explanation for his more frequent visits to the schoolroom. He laughed teasingly at Louise's fancies.

The schoolroom indeed became a focal point of the house—the stronghold of Mr Wilson's desire and his wife's jealousy.

'We are never alone,' said Hilary. 'Either Papa or Mamma is here. Perhaps they wonder if you are good enough for me.'

'Hilary!' His father had heard the last sentence as he opened the door and the first as he hovered outside listening. 'I doubt if my ears deceived me. You will go to your room while you think of a suitable apology and I think of an ample punishment.'

'Shall I take my history book with me or shall I just waste time?'

'I have indicated how to spend your time.'

'That won't take long enough,' said Hilary beneath his breath as he closed the door.

'Meanwhile, I apologize for him,' said his father. He did not go to his customary place by the window, but came to the hearth-rug where Florence stood behind her chair. 'We have indulged him too much and he has been too much with adults. Have there been other occasions?'

'No, indeed, sir.'

'You find him tractable?'

'Oh, yes.'

'And you are happy in your position?'

'Yes.'

As the dreaded, the now so familiar scent began to wreathe about the room, she stepped back from him and began to speak rapidly, as urgently as if she were dying and must make some explanation while she could. 'Perhaps, after all, Hilary is right, and you do wonder about my competence—and if I can give him all he should have. Perhaps a man would teach him more. . . .'

She began to feel a curious infraction of the room and of her person-ality, seemed to lose the true Florence, and the room lightened as if the season had been changed.

'You are mistaken,' he was saying. 'Have I ever given you any hint that we were not satisfied?'

Her timidity had quite dissolved and he was shocked by the sudden boldness of her glance.

'No, no hint,' she said, smiling. As she moved, he heard the silken swish of her clothes.

'I should rather give you a hint of how well pleased I am.'

'Then why don't you?' she asked.

She leaned back against the chimney-piece and looped about her fingers a long necklace of glittering green beads. 'Where did these come from?' she wondered. She could not remember ever having seen them before, but she could not pursue her bewilderment, for the necklace felt familiar to her hands, much more familiar than the rest of the room.

'*When* shall I?' he was insisting. 'This evening, perhaps? when Hilary is in bed?'

'Then who is *he*, if Hilary is to be in bed?' she wondered. She glanced at him and smiled again. 'You are extraordinarily alike,' she said. 'You and Hilary.' 'But Hilary is a little boy,' she reminded herself. 'It is silly to confuse the two.'

'We must discuss Hilary's progress,' he said, his voice so burdened with meaning that she began to laugh at him.

'Indeed we must,' she agreed.

'Your necklace is the colour of your eyes.' He took it from her fingers and leaned forward, as if to kiss her. Hearing footsteps in the passage she moved sharply aside, the necklace broke and the beads were scattered over the floor.

'Why is Hilary in the garden at this hour?' Mrs Wilson asked. Her husband and the governess were on their knees, gathering up the beads.

'Miss Chasty's necklace broke,' her husband said. She had heard that submissive tone before: his voice lacked authority only when he was caught out in some infidelity.

'I was asking about Hilary. I have just seen him running in the shrubbery without a coat.'

'He was sent to his room for being impertinent to Miss Chasty.'

'Please fetch him at once,' Mrs Wilson told Florence. Her voice always gained in authority what her husband's lacked.

Florence hurried from the room, still holding a handful of beads. She felt badly shaken—as if she had been brought to the edge of some experience which had then retreated beyond her grasp.

'He was told to stay in his room,' Mr Wilson said feebly.

'Why did her beads break?'

'She was fidgeting with them. I think she was nervous. I was making it rather apparent to her that I regarded Hilary's insubordination as proof of too much leniency on her part.'

'I didn't know that she had such a necklace. It is the showiest trash that I have ever seen.'

'We cannot blame her for the cheapness of her trinkets. It is rather pathetic.'

'There is nothing pathetic about her. We will continue this in the morning-room and *they* can continue their lessons, which are, after all, her reason for being here.'

'Oh, they are gone,' said Hilary. His cheeks were pink from the cold outside.

'Why did you not stay in your bedroom as you were told?'

'I had nothing to do. I thought of my apology before I got there. It was: "I am sorry, dear girl, that I spoke too near the point".'

'You could have spent longer and thought of a real apology.'

'Look how long papa spent and he did not even think of a punishment, which is a much easier thing.'

Several times during the evening, Mr Wilson said: 'But you cannot dismiss a girl because her beads break.'

'There have been other things and will be more,' his wife replied.

So that there should not be more that evening, he did not move from the drawing-room where he sat watching her doing her wool-work. For the same reason, Florence left the schoolroom empty. She went out and walked rather nervously in the park, feeling remorseful, astonished and upset.

'Did you mend your necklace?' Hilary asked her in the morning.

'I lost the beads.'

'But, my poor girl, they must be somewhere.'

She thought: 'There is no reason to suppose that I shall get back what I never had in the first place.'

'Have you got a headache?'

'Yes. Go on with your work Hilary.'

'Is it from losing the beads?'

'No.'

'Have you a great deal of jewellery I have not seen yet?'

She did not answer and he went on: 'You still have your brooch with your grandmother's plaited hair in it. Was it cut off her head when she was dead?'

'Your *work*, Hilary.'

'I shudder to think of chopping it off a corpse. You could have some of my hair, now, while I am living.' He fingered it with admiration, regarded a sum aloofly and jotted down its answer. 'Could I cut some of yours?' he asked, bringing his book to be corrected. He whistled softly, close to her, and the tendrils of hair round her ears were gently blown about.

'It is ungentlemanly to whistle,' she said.

'My sums are always right. It shows how I can chatter and subtract at the same time. Any governess would be annoyed by that. I suppose your brothers never whistle.'

'Never.'

'Are they to be clergymen like your father?'

'It is what we hope for one of them.'

'I am to be a famous judge. When you read about me, will you say: "And to think I might have been his wife if I had not been so self-willed"?'

'No, but I hope that I shall feel proud that once I taught you.'

'You sound doubtful.'

He took his book back to the table. 'We are having a quiet morning,' he remarked. 'No one has visited us. Poor Miss Chasty, it is a pity about the necklace,' he murmured, as he took up his pencil again.

Evenings were dangerous to her. 'He said he would come,' she told herself, 'and I allowed him to say so. On what compulsion did I?'

Fearfully, she spent her lonely hours out in the dark garden or in her cold and candlelit bedroom. He was under his wife's vigilance and Florence did not know that he dared not leave the drawing-room. But the vigilance relaxed, as it does: his carelessness returned and steady rain and bitter cold drove Florence to warm her chilblains at the schoolroom fire.

Her relationship with Mrs Wilson had changed. A wary hostility took the place of meekness and when Mrs Wilson came to the schoolroom at tea-times, Florence stood up defiantly and cast a look round the room as if to say: 'Find what you can. There is nothing here.' Mrs Wilson's suspicious ways increased her rebelliousness. 'I have done nothing wrong,' she told herself. But in her bedroom at night: '*I* have done nothing wrong,' she would think.

'They have quite deserted us,' Hilary said from time to time. 'They have realized you are worth your weight in gold, dear girl; or perhaps I made it clear to my father that in this room he is an interloper.'

'Hilary!'

'You want to put yourself in the right in case that door opens suddenly as it has been doing lately. There, you see! Good-evening, mamma. I was just saying that I have scarcely seen you all day.' He drew forward her chair and held the cushion behind her until she leaned back.

'I have been resting.'

'Are you ill, mamma?'

'I have a headache.'

'I will stroke it for you, dear lady.'

He stood behind her chair and began to smooth her forehead. 'Or shall I read to you?' he asked, soon tiring of his task. 'Or play the musical-box?'

'No, nothing more, thank you.'

Mrs Wilson looked about her, at the teacups, then at Florence. Sometimes it seemed to her that her husband was right and that she was growing fanciful. The innocent appearance of the room lulled her and she closed her eyes for a while, rocking gently in her chair.

'I dozed off,' she said when she awoke. The table was cleared and Florence and Hilary sat playing chess, whispering so that they should not disturb her.

'It made a domestic scene for us,' said Hilary. 'Often Miss Chasty and I feel that we are left too much in solitary bliss.'

The two women smiled and Mrs Wilson shook her head. 'You have too old a head on your shoulders,' she said. 'What will they say of you when you go to school?'

'What shall I say of *them*?' he asked bravely, but he lowered his eyes and kept them lowered. When his mother had gone, he asked Florence: 'Did you go to school?'

'Yes.'

'Were you unhappy there?'

'No. I was homesick at first.'

'If I don't like it, there will be no point in my staying,' he said hurriedly. 'I can learn anywhere and I don't particularly want the corners knocked off, as my father once spoke of it. I shouldn't like to play cricket and all those childish games. Only to do boxing and draw blood,' he added, with sudden bravado. He laughed excitedly and clenched his fists.

'You would never be good at boxing if you lost your temper.'

'I suppose your brothers told you that. They don't sound very manly to me. They would be afraid of a good fight and the sight of blood, I daresay.'

'Yes, I daresay. It is bedtime.'

He was whipped up by the excitement he had created from his fears.

'Chess is a woman's game,' he said and upset the board. He took the cushion from the rocking-chair and kicked it inexpertly across the room. 'I should have thought the door would have opened then,' he said. 'But as my father doesn't appear to send me to my room, I will go there of my own accord. It wouldn't have been a punishment at bedtime in any case. When I am a judge I shall be better at punishments than he is.'

When he had gone, Florence picked up the cushion and the chess-board. 'I am no good at punishments either,' she thought. She tidied the room, made up the fire, then sat down in the rocking-chair, thinking of all the lonely schoolroom evenings of her future. She bent her head over her needlework—the beaded sachet for her mother's birthday present. When she looked up she thought the lamp was smoking and she went to the table and turned down the wick. Then she noticed that the smoke was wreathing upwards from near the fireplace, forming rings which drifted towards the ceiling and were lost in a haze. She could hear a woman's voice humming softly and the floorboards creaked as if someone were treading up and down the room impatiently.

She felt in herself a sense of burning impatience and anticipation and watching the door opening found herself thinking: 'If it is not he, I cannot bear it.'

He closed the door quietly. 'She has gone to bed,' he said in a lowered voice. 'For days I dared not come. She has watched me at every moment. At last, this evening, she gave way to a headache. Were you expecting me?'

'Yes.'

'And once I called you Miss Mouse! And you are still Miss Mouse when I see you about the garden, or at luncheon.'

'In this room I can be myself. It belongs to us.'

'And not to Hilary as well—ever?' he asked her in amusement.

She gave him a quick and puzzled glance.

'Let no one intrude,' he said hastily. 'It is our room, just as you say.'

She had turned the lamp too low and it began to splutter. 'Firelight is good enough for us,' he said, putting the light out altogether.

When he kissed her, she felt an enormous sense of disappointment, almost as if he were the wrong person embracing her in the dark. His arch masterfulness merely bored her. 'A long wait for so little,' she thought.

He, however, found her entirely seductive. She responded with a sensuous languor, unruffled and at ease like the most perfect hostess.

'Where did you practise this, Miss Mouse?' he asked her. But he did not wait for the reply, fancying that he heard a step on the landing. When his wife opened the door, he was trying desperately to light a taper at the fire. His hand was trembling and when at last, in the terribly silent room, the flame crept up the spill it simply served to show up Florence's disarray which, like a sleep-walker, she had not noticed or put right.

She did not see Hilary again, except as a blurred little figure at the schoolroom window—blurred because of her tear-swollen eyes.

She was driven away in the carriage, although Mrs Wilson had suggested the station fly. 'Let us keep her disgrace and her tearfulness to ourselves,' he begged, although he was exhausted by the repetitious burden of his wife's grief.

'*Her* disgrace!'

'My mistake, I have said, was in not taking your accusations about her seriously. I see now that I was in some way bewitched—yes, bewitched is what it was—acting against my judgement; nay, my very nature. I am astonished that anyone so seemingly meek could have cast such a spell upon me.'

Poor Florence turned her head aside as Williams, the coachman, came to fetch her little trunk and the basket-work holdall. Then she put on her cloak and prepared herself to go downstairs, fearful lest she should meet anyone on the way. Yet her thoughts were even more on her journey's end; for what, she wondered, could she tell her father and how expect him to understand what she could not understand herself?

Her head was bent as she crossed the landing and she hurried past the schoolroom door. At the turn of the staircase she pressed back against the wall to allow someone to pass. She heard laughter and then up the stairs came a young woman and a little girl. The child was clinging to the woman's arm and coaxing her, as sometimes Hilary had tried to coax Florence. 'After lessons,' the woman said firmly, but gaily. She looked ahead, smiling to herself. Her clothes were unlike anything that Florence had ever seen. Later, when she tried to describe them to her mother, she could only remember the shortness of a tunic which scarcely covered the knees, a hat like a helmet drawn down over eyes intensely green and matching the long necklace of glass beads which swung on her flat bosom. As she came up the stairs and drew near to Florence, she was humming softly against the child's pleading; silk rustled against her silken legs and all of the staircase, as Florence quickly descended, was full of fragrance.

In the darkness of the hall a man was watching the two go round the bend of the stairs. The woman must have looked back, for Florence saw him lift his hand in a secretive gesture of understanding.

'It is Hilary, not his father!' she thought. But the figure turned before she could be sure and went into the library.

Outside on the drive Williams was waiting with her luggage stowed away in the carriage. When she had settled herself, she looked up at the schoolroom window and saw Hilary standing there rather forlornly and she could almost imagine him saying: 'My poor dear girl; so you were not good enough for me, after all?'

'When does the new governess arrive?' she asked Williams in a casual voice, which hoped to conceal both pride and grief.

'There's nothing fixed as far as I have heard,' he said.

They drove out into the lane.

'When will it be *her* time?' Florence wondered. 'I am glad that I saw her before I left.'

'We are sorry to see you going, Miss.' He had heard that the maids were sorry, for she had given them no trouble.

'Thank you, Williams.'

As they went on towards the station, she leaned back and looked at the familiar places where she had walked with Hilary. 'I know what I shall tell my father now,' she thought, and she felt peaceful and meek as though beginning to be convalescent after a long illness.

I Kiss Your Shadow—

Robert Bloch

J oe Elliot sat down in my favorite chair, helped himself to a drink of
my best whiskey, and lighted one of my special cigarettes.

I didn't object.

But when he said, 'I saw your sister last night,' I was ready to protest.
After all, a man can only take so much.

So I opened my mouth and then realized there was nothing to say.
What *could* I say to a statement like that? I'd heard it from his lips a
hundred times before, during their engagement, and it sounded perfectly natural then.

It would sound perfectly natural now, except for one thing—my
sister had been dead for three weeks.

Joe Elliot smiled, not too successfully. 'I suppose it sounds crazy,' he
said. 'But it's the truth. I saw Donna last night. Or, at least, her shadow.'

He still wasn't giving me the opportunity for a sensible answer; the
only sensible thing I could do was remain silent and listen.

'She came into the bedroom and leaned over me. I've had trouble
getting to sleep nights, ever since the accident, but I guess you know
that. Anyway, I was lying there looking up at the ceiling and trying to
decide if I should get up and pull down the shade, because the moonlight was so bright. Then I turned on my side and got ready to swing my
legs out of bed, and there she was. Just standing there, bending over me
and holding her arms out.'

Elliot leaned forward. 'Sure, I know what you're thinking. The
moonlight was deflected by something in the room and made a shadow,
and I made the rest of it myself. Or I really was asleep and didn't know
it. But I know what I saw. It was Donna, all right—I'd recognize her
anywhere, just from the silhouette.'

I found my voice, or a reasonable facsimile. 'What did she do?' I
asked.

'*Do?* She didn't do anything. Just stood there, holding her arms out
as if she were waiting for something.'

'What was she waiting for?'

Elliot stared at the floor. 'This is really the hard part,' he murmured.

'It sounds so—well, the hell with how it sounds. When Donna and I were engaged, she had this trick of hers. We'd be talking, or perhaps getting ready to do the dishes when I ate over at her place, some ordinary thing like that. And then, all at once she'd hold out her arms. I got so I recognized the gesture. It meant she wanted to be kissed. So I'd kiss her. And—go ahead, laugh?—that's what I did last night. I got up out of bed and kissed her shadow.'

I didn't laugh. I didn't do anything. I just sat there and waited for him to continue. When he showed no signs of saying anything further, I had to fill the gap. 'You kissed her. And then what happened?'

'Why, nothing. She just went away.'

'Disappeared?'

'No. She went away. The shadow released me and then turned around and walked through the door.'

'The shadow *released* you,' I said. 'Does this mean you—?'

He nodded. I'm not a nod-interpreter, but it was obvious that there was no defiance in his movement; only a sort of resignation. 'That's right. When I kissed her she put her arms around me. I—I saw it. And I *felt* it. I felt her kiss, too. Funny sensation, kissing a shadow. Real, and yet not all there.' He glanced down at the glass in his hand. 'Like a watered drink.'

There was something wrong with his comparison, but then there was something wrong with the whole story. I suppose the main trouble lay in mere chronology—he'd come to me with it just about fifty years too late.

Fifty years ago, it might not have sounded quite so odd. Not in the days when people still believed in ghosts, by and large; the days when even so eminent and hardheaded a psychologist as William James was active in the Society for Psychical Research. There was a certain receptivity then to the sentimental approach—undying love, capable of reaching beyond the grave, and all that sort of thing. But to hear it *now* was wrong.

The only thing that kept me from coming right out and saying so was the realization that there was another aspect to the business even more wrong than the rest. Joe Elliot himself. *He* was the professional skeptic, the confirmed scoffer.

Of course, maybe the shock of Donna's death—

'Don't say it,' he sighed. 'I know how cockeyed and corny it all sounds, and I know what you're thinking. I won't argue with you. The accident did hit me pretty hard, you understand that. And I admit I was in some kind of shock-state when they pulled me out of the car down there in the ravine. But I snapped out of it before the funeral. You know that, too. And if you don't believe it, just check with Doc Foster.'

My turn to nod.

'I was all right at the funeral and after,' he continued. 'You've seen me almost every day since then. Have you noticed anything—off-beat?'

'No.'

'So it wasn't just imagination. It couldn't be.'

'Then what's your answer?'

He stood up. 'I have no answer. I just wanted to tell you what happened. Because it's one of those things where you must tell some-one, and you're the logical person. I can trust you not to go around repeating it. Besides, you're her brother, and there's a chance that she might—come to you.'

Joe Elliot moved to the door.

'Leaving so soon?' I asked.

'Tired,' he said. 'I didn't sleep very much last night, afterwards.'

'Look,' I said. 'How about a sedative? I've got some stuff here that—'

'Thanks, but I'd rather not.' He opened the door. 'I'll call you in a day or so. We can have lunch together.'

'You're sure you're—'

'Yes, I'm all right.' He smiled and went out.

I frowned and stayed in. I was still frowning as I got ready for bed. Something was definitely wrong with Elliot's story and that meant something was definitely wrong with Elliot. I wished I knew the answer.

'*There's a chance that she might—come to you.*'

I crawled between the sheets and noted that the moonlight was bright on my ceiling tonight, too. But I didn't look at the moonlight very long. I closed my eyes and contemplated the chance. It seemed to be a very slim one, as chances go.

My sister Donna was dead and in her grave. I hadn't seen her die, but I was the first one summoned right after the accident, as soon as the police arrived on the scene. I saw them lift her out of the crumpled car, and she was dead, no doubt about it. I didn't like to think about seeing her. I didn't like to think about seeing Joe Elliot, either, shaking in shock; unconscious of my presence, unconscious of the gash in his forehead, unconscious even of the fact that Donna was dead. He'd kept talking to her while they carried her to the ambulance, trying to make her understand that it was an accident, there was oil-slick on the road, the car had skidded. But Donna never heard him because she was already dead. She had died when her head went through the windshield.

That's what they thought at the inquest, too. Verdict of accidental death. And surely the morticians who embalmed her had no doubts, nor did the minister who preached the sermon over her casket, the workmen who lowered her body into the grave out there at Forest Hills. Donna was dead.

And now, three weeks later, Joe Elliot came to me and said, 'I saw your sister. Or at least, her shadow.' Hardheaded Joe, a rewrite man on the desk and cynical as they come, kissing a shadow. He had said she stood there with her arms extended and he recognized her.

Well, I hadn't seen fit to mention it, but I recognized that particular gesture from his description. Because it so happens I'd seen it myself, long before Joe Elliot came into the picture. Way back when Donna was engaged to Frankie Hankins, she used to pull the same trick with him. I wondered if Frankie had heard the news yet, over there in Japan. He'd enlisted and that broke the affair up.

Come to remember, there was another time Donna used the open-arms technique. With Gil Turner. Of course, that hadn't lasted, it was obvious from the start: Turner was just a namby-pamby. Surprised everybody to see a wishy-washy character like him pull up stakes and leave town in such a hurry.

It must have surprised Donna, too, but not for long. Because just about that time I introduced her to Joe Elliot and the heat was on.

There was no question about this being the big thing for both of them. They were engaged inside of a month, and planning to be married before the summer was out. Donna just took over, lock, stock and barrel.

Of course I'd always known my sister was a determined woman (let's face it, she made a habit of getting her own way, and she was a hellcat if you crossed her) but it was interesting to watch how she worked on Joe Elliot. Talk about Pygmalion—here was one case where Galatea reversed the play. Before anyone knew it, Joe Elliot was out of his sloppy sports-jacket and into gray tweeds, out of smelly cigars and into briar pipes, out of cuppa-cawfee-'n-a-hamburger and into Donna's comfortable little apartment for regular evening meals.

Oh, she made a lot of changes in that boy! Got so that he was shaving twice a day, and he trotted around the corner to the bank with his paycheck instead of over to Smitty's Tap.

I had to give Donna credit. She knew what she wanted, and she knew just how to get it. Maybe she was ruthless, but she was feminine-ruthless. She remade Joe Elliot, but she also made him like it. He certainly didn't seem to object. I got so used to the new Elliot that I

virtually forgot about the old one—the old one who used to sit in
Smitty's and swear a mighty oath that the girl didn't breathe who could
ensnare him into unholy dreadlock.

By the time the wedding drew near, Donna was already openly
talking about their plans for buying a house—'You can't raise a family
in an apartment'—and Elliot would listen and actually grin.

('And another thing,' he used to say, shaking his finger at Smitty in
solemn warning, 'I may be a poor downtrodden wage-slave, but you'll
never catch me being a house-slave. Or turning into that typical figure
of fun—the American Father. Dear Old Dad, the butt of every family
radio and TV show in the country! Not for me. I believe in the old
saying: children should be seen and not had.')

But this was *before* Donna. Before, I suppose, he found out how nice
it is to have a woman around who lights your pipe, and straightens your
tie, and fixes the fried potatoes at just the right time so they won't get
soggy when the steak is served. Before he found out what it is to have
somebody who holds out her arms and doesn't say anything, except
with her eyes.

This much I was sure of: Donna wasn't playing any trick. She loved
the guy. She died loving him, the night they were driving back from my
party. That part was real.

Everything was real, up to now. Now, and Joe Elliot's story of the
shadow.

I looked up at the shimmering ceiling. Somehow, here in the dark,
with its mingling of moonlight, I could almost begin to believe.

Maybe we're not quite as sophisticated as we like to think we are;
ghosts happen to be unfashionable, and the concept of love conquering
the grave went out with *Outward Bound.* But set a sophisticate down in
the pitch-black bowels of a haunted house, bar the exit, and leave him
there for the night. Maybe his hair won't turn white by morning; still,
there'll be some reaction. Intellectually, we reject. Emotionally, we're
not so sure. Not when the chips are down and the lights are low.

Well, the lights were low and I kept waiting for Donna to come. I
waited and waited, and finally I guess I just fell asleep.

I told Joe Elliot about it at lunch two days later. 'She never showed,'
I said.

He cocked his head at me. 'Of course not,' he answered. 'She
couldn't. She was at my place.'

I finally managed to speak. 'Again?'

'Two nights ago, and last night.'

'Same thing?'

'Same thing.' He hesitated. 'Only—she stayed longer.'

'How much longer?'

More than hesitation now; a lasting silence. Until he brushed his napkin from his lap, stooped down to pick it up, and barely whispered, 'All night.'

I didn't ask the next question. I didn't have to. One look at his face was enough.

'She's real,' Elliot said. 'Donna. The shadow. You remember what I said the first time? About the watered whiskey?' He leaned forward. 'It's not like that now. Maybe they get stronger once they break through. Do you think that's it? They learn the way, and then they get stronger.'

He was close enough so that I could smell his breath, and he hadn't been drinking—any more than he'd been drinking the night of the accident. I'd testified to that, and it helped seal the verdict.

No, Elliot wasn't drunk. I wished to heaven he was, so I wouldn't have to say what I was going to say. But I had to.

'Why don't you take a run up to see Doc Foster?' I asked him.

Joe Elliot spread his palms on the table. 'I knew you'd say that,' he grinned. 'So I already called him this morning, for an appointment.'

I managed to withhold the sigh of relief, but it was there, and I could feel it. For a minute I'd been afraid of an argument—not because I dreaded arguments, but because of what it would imply about Elliot, I was glad to see he hadn't gone completely overboard.

'You needn't worry,' he assured me. 'I know what Doc will tell me. Sedatives, relaxation, and if that doesn't work, see a head-shrinker. And if he does, I'll follow orders.'

'Promise?'

'Sure.' He gave me the grin again, but this time it was a little twisted. 'Want to know something funny? I'm beginning to be a bit scared of that sister of yours—even if she is only a shadow.'

I put a large *No Comment* sign on my face and we went out together in silence. We separated in the street—I went back to the office and Elliot went over to Doc Foster's

I didn't learn about his visit for several days. Because when I got back to the office they had a surprise for me.

The same newspaper employing Joe Elliot on the rewrite desk sees fit to retain me in the capacity of roving correspondent. And the ME was waiting for me with a suggestion that I rove in the direction of Indo-China. As of two days from now, with all watches synchronized.

I got busy. So busy that I never managed to call Joe Elliot. So busy that if he called me, I wasn't around to get the message.

He finally caught me at the airport, actually, just before I took off for the west coast and the first leg of the flight.

'Sorry I couldn't be on hand,' he said. '*Bon voyage* and all that.'

'You sound pretty happy.'

'Why not?'

'Doc's sedatives do the trick?'

He chuckled. 'Not exactly. When I told him, he didn't even bother with the first part of the routine. Sent me packing right away to the you-know-who. Name of Partridge. Heard of him?'

I had. 'Good man,' I said.

'The best.' He paused. 'Well, I mustn't keep you—'

'You're all right?' My voice was insistent.

'Sure. I'm fine. I sailed for the works. Some of the things the guy told me make sense. I guess I'm more tangled up than I thought—oh, not just what I told you about, but there are other angles. Anyway, I'm going in to him twice a week for I don't know how long. And it's not as phoney as I thought it might be, either. None of this couch business. He really gets results.' Another pause. 'I mean, I've been there just twice, and she's gone.'

'The shadow, you mean?'

'The guilt-fantasy.' He chuckled again. 'See, I'm picking up the lingo already. Time you come back, I'll be ready to hand out my shingle. Well, lots of luck, kid. And keep in touch.'

'Will do,' I said. And hung up, listening to them announce my flight. And took the flight, and made my transfer in Frisco, and went to Manila, and went from there to Singapore, and from there to hell.

It was hot as hell in hell, and although I managed to get enough dispatches back to satisfy my ME, I had no opportunity to keep in touch.

You know what happened in Indo-China, and when they opened a branch hell in Formosa, my ME sent me over there, and when hell got too hot for even a roving correspondent I was based in Manila and then Japan. I'm not trying to make a production out of it; just explaining why it turned out that I was gone for eight months instead of eight weeks.

When I got back they gave me a leave, and some information. Not much, but just enough to send me scurrying around to Joe Elliot's apartment the first opportunity I got.

I didn't waste any time on hello-how-are-you. 'What's this I hear about you leaving the paper?' I began.

He shrugged. 'I didn't leave. I got canned.'

'Why?'

'Hitting the sauce.'

He looked it, too. The sports-jacket was back, and it was dirty. He wasn't bothering to shave once a day, either, let alone twice. He was thin, and twitchy.

'Let's have it,' I said. 'What happened to you?'

'Nothing.'

'Quit stalling. What does Partridge say?'

He gave me a grin, and to say it was twisted doesn't even begin to describe it. They could have made a cast and used it to cut pretzels with.

'Partridge,' he echoed. 'Sit down. Have a drink.'

'All right, but keep talking. I asked you a question. What does Partridge say?'

He poured for me. I was a guest; I got a glass. He gulped out of the bottle. Then he put it down. 'Partridge doesn't say anything any more,' he told me. 'Partridge is dead.'

'No.'

'Yes.'

'When did this happen?'

'Month or so back.'

'Why didn't you go to another hea—psychiatrist?'

'What? And have him jump out of the window, too?'

'What's all this about jumping out of a window?'

He picked up the bottle. 'That's what I'd like to know.' *Gulp.* 'Personally, I'm not even sure he jumped. Maybe he was pushed.'

'Are you trying to tell me—?'

'No. I'm not trying to tell you anything. Any more than I'd try to tell Doc Foster or the boys down at the office. You can't tell anyone a story like that. Just got to keep it to yourself. Yourself and the little old bottle.' *Gulp.*

'But you said—I mean, you sounded as if everything was going so well.'

'That's right. And it went fine. Up to a point.'

'What point?'

'The point where I found out why she wasn't coming back any more.' He stared out of the window, and then he went a million miles away and only his voice remained. I could hear what he said, plainly enough. Too plainly.

'She wasn't coming back to me because she was going to him. Night after night after night. Not with her arms out—not the way she'd come to me, in love. She went to him out of hate. Because she knew he was trying to drive her away. Don't you see, when he worked on me it was like—like exorcism. You know what exorcism is, don't you? Casting out demons. Ghosts. A succubus.'

'Joe, you've got to stop this. Get hold of yourself.'

He laughed. 'All I can get hold of is this.' And reached for the bottle, as he spoke. 'You're asking me to stop this? But I didn't start it. I didn't make it up. Partridge told me himself. Finally he broke down and he *had* to tell me. Do you get the picture now?—*he* came to *me* for help. And I couldn't help him. I was getting well, there's a laugh for you, I was getting over *my* delusions. I talked to him the way you're trying to talk to me, real Dutch uncle stuff.

'And I went out of his office, and the next morning I read where he jumped. Only he didn't jump—she must have pushed him—he was afraid of her, she kept getting stronger and stronger, just as I thought she would. They found him spattered all over the sidewalk—'

This time I reached for the bottle. 'So you quit your job and started drinking, just because a psychiatrist cracked up and committed suicide,' I said. 'Because one poor overworked guy went to pieces, you had to do likewise. I thought you were smarter than that, Joe.'

'So did I.' He took the bottle away from me. 'You heard what I told you. I thought I was completely well. Even when he died, I still wasn't sure about some things. Until that night, when she came back.'

I watched him drink and waited.

'Sure. She came back. And she's been coming back, every night, since then. I can't fight it off, I can't fight her off, she keeps clinging and clinging to me. But why try to explain? You don't believe me anyway. I saw the look on your face when I mentioned the part about a succubus.'

'Please,' I said. 'I want to hear the rest. I've read about those things, you know. A succubus takes the form of a woman and comes to men at night—'

He was nodding and then he cut in. 'So that explains it, don't you see? What she was whispering to me. I guess I didn't tell you, but she talks now. She talks to me, she tells me things. She says she's glad, and it won't be long now, then she'll have everything she wanted—'

His voice trailed off, and I stood up just in time to catch him as he slumped. He was out cold; his body was limp and light in my arms. Too light. He must have lost a lot of weight. I guess Joe Elliot has lost a lot of things.

I suppose I could have tried to bring him around, but I didn't make the effort. It seemed kinder to carry him over to the bed, take off his things and let him rest. I found pajamas in one of the bureau drawers, got them on him—it was like dressing a rag doll instead of a man—and covered him up. Then I left him. He'd sleep now, sleep without shadows.

And while he slept, I'd figure out something. There had to be an answer. Because Donna was my sister and I'd loved her, and because Joe Elliot was my friend, there had to be an answer.

If Partridge were only alive. If I could just talk to him and find out what he'd really learned about this delusion! He must have learned something, in eight months. Even if Elliot deliberately tried to hold back, in eight months a man like Partridge would learn—

The thought hit me then; a stinging blow. I tried to duck. But it hit harder and this time there was a numbing reaction.

'No,' I told myself. 'No.'

I kept telling myself no, but I was telling the cab-driver to take me down to the office again. I told myself no, but I told the ME I wanted all the stuff in the house on Partridge's suicide.

Then I was reading it, and then I was over at the Coroner's office, checking the report of the inquest.

I didn't ask any fancy questions, and I didn't do any fancy detective work. That's out of my line. I won't pretend to have done anything more except to jump at a wild conclusion. That's all the records showed—Partridge had jumped to a wild conclusion.

But knowing what I did, I was more inclined to agree with Joe Elliot. Partridge hadn't jumped, he'd been pushed.

There wasn't a single solitary thing I could hand on to as tangible evidence; nothing to build a case around. But I checked and rechecked, and I fitted the pieces together and then everything shattered apart when I recognized the picture.

I left the Coroner's office and went over to Smitty's Tap and drank a very late supper, not talking to anyone. I didn't know who to talk to now—surely not the Coroner, or the DA, or the cops. They couldn't help, because I had no evidence. Besides, I owed Joe Elliot a chance.

There was still the shadow of a doubt. A *shadow* named Donna, who'd come back. Maybe she'd be coming back tonight, but I wasn't going to wait.

After a while it was quite late, but I was on my way, back to Elliot's apartment. Chances were that he was still sleeping, and I hoped so in a way. Then again, I knew I had to see him now.

I went up the stairs slowly, one voice saying *let him sleep* and the other voice saying *knock*, and two of them fighting together, *let him sleep—knock—let him sleep—knock—*

It turned out that neither voice won, because when I got to the door, Joe Elliot opened it and looked out.

He was awake all right, and maybe he'd been back to the bottle again and maybe he hadn't: he looked as if he'd swallowed strychnine. And his voice was the voice of a man with a burned throat.

'Come in,' he said. 'I was just going out.'

'In your pajamas?'

'I had an errand—'

'It can wait,' I told him.

'Yes, it can wait.' He led me inside, closed the door. 'Sit down,' he murmured. 'I'm glad you're here.'

I sat down, but I kept a grip on the arms of the chair, ready to move in a hurry if necessary. And I waited very carefully until he sat down, too, before I spoke.

'Maybe you won't be so glad when I speak my piece,' I said.

'Go ahead. It doesn't matter what you say now.'

'Yes it does, Joe. I want you to listen carefully. This is important.'

'Nothing's important.'

'We'll see. After I left you this afternoon. I did a little investigating. I went to the Coroner's office, among other things. And I agree with you now. Partridge *was* pushed out of the window.'

For the first time his face showed interest. 'Then I was right, wasn't I?' he began. 'She did push him, you found some evidence—'

I shook my head. 'I didn't find any evidence. Not any *new* evidence. I just began to check the facts and see if they fitted in with a theory of my own. They did.' I spoke very slowly, very deliberately. 'I checked on one particular phase of the report, Joe. The account you gave of your own movements after leaving Partridge's office the day he jumped. The whole story about not taking the elevator down because it was crowded and you were in a hurry to get to the office. And the part about not going to the office after all because you remembered you'd forgotten your hat and went back upstairs to get it. And how you came in just as they were looking out the window where Partridge had jumped.

'I read it all, Joe. I read your account of the last meeting with Partridge, how upset he seemed. Only I was a *special* reader.'

He was more than interested now; he was alert.

'They tried pretty hard to break down your story, didn't they, Joe? Only they couldn't, because there was no evidence to the contrary, and what you said made sense. About how Partridge was fidgeting and nervous and kept looking out the window. About how jumpy he'd been the past few weeks. Good word, that *jumpy*. Good enough for the Coroner's Jury, anyway. But not good enough for me.

'Because you didn't mention anything about the shadow in your story to the Jury. You told something entirely different.'

He hit the arm of his chair hard. 'Of course I did, man! I couldn't tell them what I told you, they'd think I was crazy.'

'But you *were* crazy, Joe. Crazy enough so that your story to me makes sense. Partridge didn't jump, he was pushed—and you pushed him.'

Joe Elliot made a noise in his chest. Something came out of his mouth that sounded like, 'Why?'

'I wish I knew the answer to that. The real answer. All I can do is guess. And my guess is that there wasn't anything to this story of yours about Partridge being afraid of a shadow. My guess is that *you* were the one who was afraid—because in session after session, Partridge kept getting nearer and nearer to something you didn't want him to find. Something you tried to hide, but couldn't. Something he, as a trained analyst, found anyway. Or was on the very verge of finding. When you realized that, you panicked—and destroyed him.'

'Rave on,' he said.

'All right, I will. Joe, you're not crazy. You never was. I think this is all an act. You wouldn't murder a man except for a very important reason. Whatever Partridge found out, or was about to find out, was something vitally necessary for you to conceal.'

'Such as?'

'Such as the fact that you killed my sister.'

The words hit the wall and bounced. The words hit his face and twisted it up into the gargoyle's grin, the spasmodic twitch.

'All right. So you know.'

'Then it's true,' I said.

'Of course it's true. But what you don't know is *why*. You wouldn't know, and you're her own brother. How could I expect anyone else to understand if you never saw it? What Donna was *really* like, I mean. The way she tried to fasten her claws into me, pulling me down, trying to possess me, never letting go for an instant. Sure I loved her, she knew how to make a man love her, she had a thousand tricks to drive you mad with wanting her, holding out her arms was just the beginning. But that wasn't enough, to possess me that way. She had to have *everything*, she wanted every minute, every movement, every thought. She was making me over and trying to turn me into all the things I always hated. I could see it, I knew what lay ahead, a life of slavery to *her* house and *her* kids and *her* future.'

He stopped because he had to, and I said, 'Why didn't you get out, then? Break the engagement?'

'I tried. Don't you think I tried? But she wouldn't let go. Not her, not Donna. Even then she was a succubus. She had her claws in me and she wanted to drain me. I can't help it; there was something about her, and when she came into my arms I couldn't break free because then I didn't want to any more.

'But when I was alone again, I wanted to. You never heard about this part, but just before your party, I tried to sneak out of town. She caught me. There was a scene—or there would have been, except that Donna never made scenes. She made love. Do you understand?'

I nodded.

'And after that I was sick. Not physically sick, but worse than that. Because I knew it would always be this way; me trying to get free and she clawing me back. There'd always be succubus. Unless I got rid of her.'

Another pause, another breath, and then he rushed on. 'It wasn't difficult. I knew the spot on the road where the rail hung over the edge of the ravine. I had a wrench in the car. You remember we left late, and the road was deserted. When we got to the ravine I suggested we park and look at the moon. Donna liked that kind of suggestion. So then I— I hit her. And sent the car over. And went down myself, and finished cracking the windshield and gave myself a gash in the forehead and crawled into the car. I didn't have to do much pretending about the shock. Only it was a shock of relief, because I knew now she was really dead.'

I put my hands in my lap. 'And that's what Partridge was on the verge of finding out, isn't it?' I asked. 'All this business about the shadow was just what he told you it was—a guilt-fantasy. You felt compelled to spring it on me first because of the guilt-feeling, and you didn't want to tell Partridge anything about the possible cause of the delusion. Only he kept probing until he was too close for safety. Your safety, and his. So you killed again.'

'No.'

'Why bother to deny it? You've already confessed to one murder, so—'

'Killing Donna wasn't murder,' he said. 'It was self-defense. And that's the end of it. I didn't kill Partridge, no matter what you think. *She* did.

'I told you how she went to him night after night, torturing him, breaking him down, trying to get him to the point where he was ready to jump.

'And when he told me, that day in his office, I couldn't stand it. So I got ready to explain, I was going to tell him the truth about the shadow and what I'd done.

'I remember he was bending over me, asking me about the accident, and then he straightened up and looked surprised and I saw that *she* was there. A shadow, but not a shadow on the wall. A shadow in the room, right behind us, tugging at his arm. And he tried to scream but there was this blackness over his mouth, her hand, and she was pulling him over to the window, and his feet made little scuffing noises sliding along the carpet, and he tried to grab the window-frame but the shadow is strong and the shadow laughed so you could hear it above the scream when he went down and down and down—'

He snapped out of it suddenly. 'Too bad you weren't here earlier tonight. You'd have believed me then, because you would have seen her. She came a while before you arrived and woke me. Said she wanted me to go out there, because there was a surprise. Something to show me. At first I didn't know what she was hinting at, but I know now. You see, I counted back, but you'd only laugh. I could take you along to look, too, but you'd laugh and—'

'I'm not laughing, Joe,' I said.

'Well, you'd better not. She wouldn't like that. She wouldn't like to have anyone get in her way. And she's so strong now, stronger than anyone. She's already proved that. I'm going to do what she says. Now that she has a real claim on me, nothing can stop her.'

I stood up. 'But she can be stopped. There's a way, you know.'

'You mean you believe in exorcism now?'

'Joe,' I said, 'you're partially exorcized already. By confessing to me you've rid yourself of a portion of her power. You might have banished her forever if you'd succeeded in telling Partridge the truth, because he represented authority to you. That's the answer, Joe. You've got to tell this to an authority. Then there won't be any more guilt-feelings or guilt-fantasy, either. You'll remember what actually happened to Partridge, and once they understand the situation you can put in a plea. I'll help you all I can. There's a pretty smart lawyer downtown who—'

Now Elliot stood up. 'I get it,' he murmured. 'You're humoring me because I'm a psycho and that's what you want them all to think. Maybe you're afraid she'll be coming after you, too. Well, don't worry. She won't, unless you try to stand in her way. I'm the one she really wants, and I'm going to her. I want to see—

'Listen, Joe.' I began, but he wasn't listening.

He reached out suddenly and his hand swept across the tabletop, gripped the half-empty bottle, raised it, and smashed it down until it shattered. Then he took a quick step forward, swinging the glittering weapon.

The whole operation from start to finish was almost instantaneous, and it silenced me.

He stood there, holding the jagged length of glass that splintered down from the broken bottle-top.

'Sorry to cut you off,' he said. 'Now you'd better go. Before I really cut you off.'

I took one step forward. The gargoyle grin returned to his face, and I took two steps backward.

'I'm the one she wants,' he said. 'You can't stop me. And no sense going to the cops. They can't stop me, either. She won't let them.'

I should have jumped him then, even though he was a maniac with a broken bottle in his hand for a weapon. I often wonder what would have happened if I *had* jumped him.

But I didn't.

I turned and ran, ran out of the apartment and down the stairs and through the hall and into the street, and I kept telling myself it wasn't just because I was afraid. I had to find help, this was a job for the police.

There was a call-box two blocks down and around the corner, and I used it. I suppose it didn't take more than five minutes between the time I left the apartment and the time I got back to meet the squad car as it pulled up.

That was enough, however. Joe Elliot had disappeared. They sent out a prowl car, and they put it on the police broadcast band, and you'd think a pajama-clad man would be easy to spot on a deserted city street.

But it wasn't until I broke down and told them where I thought Joe Elliot was headed for that we got any action—and then it was because we piled into the squad car and drove all the way out to Forest Hills.

He couldn't have made the trip out there in that time on foot. He must have stolen a car, although they never found one or heard a report of a missing vehicle.

But he was there, of course, lying across her grave. And he'd been digging long enough to claw down a good six inches through the thick turf and solid soil.

That's when the stroke must have hit him. They never did agree as to the exact cause. The point is, he was dead.

And that left me to answer the questions.

I tried.

I tried to answer questions, and at the same time to leave out all the crazy stuff, the unfashionable stuff about ghosts and shadows and a succubus that kept getting stronger and stronger. *They* brought up the idea of a love reaching past the grave; it was their own idea, only of course they thought *he* was trying to reach *her*.

I tried to keep the murder part out of it too—because there was no sense opening that up now.

But they were the ones who finally got around to it, and they opened it up. The case, I mean. And then the grave.

If it had been just the case, I could have managed to hold on, I think. Hold on to my story, and to my belief, too.

But when they opened the grave, it was too much.

They dug down the rest of the way through the thick turf and solid soil; dug down to what hadn't been disturbed for ten long months.

And they found her, all right, although there were no marks or anything to prove murder. No proof at all.

And there was no explanation for what else they found, either. The tiny body of a newborn infant in Donna's intact coffin—lying there just as dead as Donna was.

Or just as alive.

I can't make up my mind which is which any more. And of course the police keep asking me questions for which there are no answers. None that they'd believe.

I can't tell them Donna wanted Joe so badly even death couldn't deny her. I can't tell them she came to him at the last and summoned him proudly, that he went out to Forest Hills to see their child.

Because there is no such thing as a succubus. And a shadow does not speak, or move, or hold out its arms.

Or *does* it?

I don't know. I just lay in bed at night, now, when the bottle is empty, and look up at the ceiling. Waiting. Maybe I'll see a shadow. Or *shadows*.

A WOMAN SELDOM FOUND

William Sansom

Once a young man was on a visit to Rome.

It was his first visit; he came from the country—but he was neither on the one hand so young nor on the other so simple as to imagine that a great and beautiful capital should hold out finer promises than anywhere else. He already knew that life was largely illusion, that though wonderful things could happen, nevertheless as many disappointments came in compensation: and he knew, too, that life could offer a quality even worse—the probability that nothing would happen at all. This was always more possible in a great city intent on its own business.

Thinking in this way, he stood on the Spanish steps and surveyed the momentous panorama stretched before him. He listened to the swelling hum of the evening traffic and watched, as the lights went up against Rome's golden dusk. Shining automobiles slunk past the fountains and turned urgently into the bright Via Condotti, neon-red signs stabbed the shadows with invitation; the yellow windows of buses were packed with faces intent on going somewhere—everyone in the city seemed intent on the evening's purpose. He alone had nothing to do.

He felt himself the only person alone of everyone in the city. But searching for adventure never brought it—rather kept it away. Such a mood promised nothing. So the young man turned back up the steps, passed the lovely church, and went on up the cobbled hill towards his hotel. Wine-bars and food-shops jostled with growing movement in those narrow streets. But out on the broad pavements of the Vittorio Veneto, under the trees mounting to the Borghese Gardens, the high world of Rome would be filling the most elegant cafés in Europe to enjoy with aperitifs the twilight. That would be the loneliest of all! So the young man kept to the quieter, older streets on his solitary errand home.

In one such street, a pavementless alley between old yellow houses, a street that in Rome might suddenly blossom into a secret piazza of fountain and baroque church, a grave secluded treasure-place—he noticed that he was alone but for the single figure of a woman walking down the hill towards him.

As she drew nearer, he saw that she was dressed with taste, that in her carriage was a soft Latin fire, that she walked for respect. Her face was veiled, but it was impossible to imagine that she would not be beautiful. Isolated thus with her, passing so near to her, and she symbolizing the adventure of which the evening was so empty—a greater melancholy gripped him. He felt wretched as the gutter, small, sunk, pitiful. So that he rounded his shoulders and lowered his eyes—but not before casting one furtive glance into hers.

He was so shocked at what he saw that he paused, he stared, shocked, into her face. He had made no mistake. She was smiling. Also—she too had hesitated. He thought instantly: 'Whore?' But no—it was not that kind of smile, though as well it was not without affection. And then amazingly she spoke:

'I—I know I shouldn't ask you . . . but it is such a beautiful evening—and perhaps you are alone, as alone as I am . . .'

She was very beautiful. He could not speak. But a growing elation gave him the power to smile. So that she continued, still hesitant, in no sense soliciting:

'I thought . . . perhaps . . . we could take a walk, an aperitif . . .'

At last the young man achieved himself:

'Nothing, *nothing* would please me more. And the Veneto is only a minute up there.'

She smiled again:

'My home is just here . . .'

They walked in silence a few paces down the street, to a turning that the young man had already passed. This she indicated. They walked to where the first humble houses ended in a kind of recess. In the recess was set the wall of a garden, and behind it stood a large and elegant mansion. The woman, about whose face shone a curious glitter— something fused of the transparent pallor of fine skin, of grey but brilliant eyes, of dark eyebrows and hair of lucent black—inserted her key in the garden gate.

They were greeted by a servant in velvet livery. In a large and exquisite salon, under chandeliers of fine glass and before a moist green courtyard where water played, they were served with a frothy wine. They talked. The wine—iced in the warm Roman night—filled them with an inner warmth of exhilaration. But from time to time the young man looked at her curiously.

With her glances, with many subtle inflections of teeth and eyes she was inducing an intimacy that suggested much. He felt he must be careful. At length he thought the best thing might be to thank her—

somehow thus to root out whatever obligation might be in store. But here she interrupted him, first with a smile, then with a look of some sadness. She begged him to spare himself any perturbation: she knew it was strange, that in such a situation he might suspect some second purpose: but the simple truth remained that she was lonely and—this with a certain deference—something perhaps in him, perhaps in that moment of dusk in the street, had proved to her inescapably attractive. She had not been able to help herself.

The possibility of a perfect encounter—a dream that years of disillusion will never quite kill—decided him. His elation rose beyond control. He believed her. And thereafter the perfections compounded. At her invitation they dined. Servants brought food of great delicacy; shellfish, fat bird-flesh, soft fruits. And afterwards they sat on a sofa near the courtyard, where it was cool. Liqueurs were brought. The servants retired. A hush fell upon the house. They embraced.

A little later, with no word, she took his arm and led him from the room. How deep a silence had fallen between them! The young man's heart beat fearfully—it might be heard, he felt, echoing in the hall whose marble they now crossed, sensed through his arm to hers. But such excitement rose now from certainty. Certainty that at such a moment, on such a charmed evening—nothing could go wrong. There was no need to speak. Together they mounted the great staircase.

In her bedroom, to the picture of her framed by the bed curtains and dimly naked in a silken shift, he poured out his love; a love that was to be eternal, to be always perfect, as fabulous as this their exquisite meeting.

Softly she spoke the return of his love. Nothing would ever go amiss, nothing would ever come between them. And very gently she drew back the bedclothes for him.

But suddenly, at the moment when at last he lay beside her, when his lips were almost upon hers—he hesitated.

Something was wrong. A flaw could be sensed. He listened, felt—and then saw the fault was his. Shaded, soft-shaded lights by the bed—but he had been so careless as to leave on the bright electric chandelier in the centre of the ceiling. He remembered the switch was by the door. For a fraction, then, he hesitated. She raised her eyelids—saw his glance at the chandelier, understood.

Her eyes glittered. She murmured:

'My beloved, don't worry—don't move . . .'

And she reached out her hand. Her hand grew larger, her arm grew longer and longer, it stretched out through the bed-curtains, across the long carpet, huge and overshadowing the whole of the long room, until at last its giant fingers were at the door. With a terminal click, she switched out the light.

THE PORTOBELLO ROAD

Muriel Spark

One day in my young youth at high summer, lolling with my lovely companions upon a haystack, I found a needle. Already and privately for some years I had been guessing that I was set apart from the common run, but this of the needle attested the fact to my whole public: George, Kathleen, and Skinny. I sucked my thumb, for when I had thrust my idle hand deep into the hay, the thumb was where the needle had stuck.

When everyone had recovered George said, 'She put in her thumb and pulled out a plum.' Then away we were into our merciless hacking-hecking laughter again.

The needle had gone fairly deep into the thumby cushion and a small red river flowed and spread from this tiny puncture. So that nothing of our joy should lag, George put in quickly,

'Mind your bloody thumb on my shirt.'

Then hac-hec-hoo, we shrieked into the hot Borderland afternoon. Really I should not care to be so young of heart again. That is my thought every time I turn over my old papers and come across the photograph. Skinny, Kathleen, and myself are in the photo atop the haystack. Skinny had just finished analysing the inwards of my find.

'It couldn't have been done by brains. You haven't much brains but you're a lucky wee thing.'

Everyone agreed that the needle betokened extraordinary luck. As it was becoming a serious conversation, George said,

'I'll take a photo.'

I wrapped my hanky round my thumb and got myself organized. George pointed up from his camera and shouted.

'Look, there's a mouse!'

Kathleen screamed and I screamed although I think we knew there was no mouse. But this gave us an extra session of squalling hee-hoo's. Finally we three composed ourselves for George's picture. We look lovely and it was a great day at the time, but I would not care for it all over again. From that day I was known as Needle.

One Saturday in recent years I was mooching down the Portobello Road, threading among the crowds of marketers on the narrow pavement when I saw a woman. She had a haggard, careworn, wealthy look, thin but for the breasts forced-up high like a pigeon's. I had not seen her for nearly five years. How changed she was! But I recognized Kathleen, my friend; her features had already begun to sink and protrude in the way that mouths and noses do in people destined always to be old for their years. When I had last seen her, nearly five years ago, Kathleen, barely thirty, had said,

'I've lost all my looks, it's in the family. All the women are handsome as girls, but we go off early, we go brown and nosey.'

I stood silently among the people, watching. As you will see, I wasn't in a position to speak to Kathleen. I saw her shoving in her avid manner from stall to stall. She was always fond of antique jewellery and of bargains. I wondered that I had not seen her before in the Portobello Road on my Saturday morning ambles. Her long stiff-crooked fingers pounced to select a jade ring from amongst the jumble of brooches and pendants, onyx, moonstone and gold, set out on the stall.

'What do you think of this?' she said.

I saw then who was with her. I had been half-conscious of the huge man following several paces behind her, and now I noticed him.

'It looks all right,' he said. 'How much is it?'

'How much is it?' Kathleen asked the vendor.

I took a good look at this man accompanying Kathleen. It was her husband. The beard was unfamiliar, but I recognized beneath it his enormous mouth, the bright sensuous lips, the large brown eyes forever brimming with pathos.

It was not for me to speak to Kathleen, but I had a sudden inspiration which caused me to say quietly,

'Hallo, George.'

The giant of a man turned round to face the direction of my face. There were so many people—but at length he saw me.

'Hallo, George,' I said again.

Kathleen had started to haggle with the stall-owner, in her old way, over the price of the jade ring. George continued to stare at me, his big mouth slightly parted so that I could see a wide slit of red lips and white teeth between the fair grassy growths of beard and moustache.

'My God!' he said.

'What's the matter?' said Kathleen.

'Hallo, George!' I said again, quite loud this time, and cheerfully.

'Look!' said George. 'Look who's there, over beside the fruit stall.'

Kathleen looked but didn't see.

'Who is it?' she said impatiently.

'It's Needle,' he said. 'She said "Hallo, George".'

'*Needle*,' said Kathleen. 'Who do you mean? You don't mean our old friend *Needle* who—'

'Yes. There she is. My God!'

He looked very ill, although when I had said 'Hallo, George' I had spoken friendly enough.

'I don't see anyone faintly resembling poor Needle,' said Kathleen looking at him. She was worried.

George pointed straight at me. 'Look *there*. I tell you that is Needle.'

'You're ill, George. Heavens, you must be seeing things. Come on home. Needle isn't there. You know as well as I do, Needle is dead.'

I must explain that I departed this life nearly five years ago. But I did not altogether depart this world. There were those odd things still to be done which one's executors can never do properly. Papers to be looked over, even after the executors have torn them up. Lots of business except, of course, on Sundays and Holidays of Obligation, plenty to take an interest in for the time being. I take my recreation on Saturday mornings. If it is a wet Saturday I wander up and down the substantial lanes of Woolworth's as I did when I was young and visible. There is a pleasurable spread of objects on the counters which I now perceive and exploit with a certain detachment, since it suits with my condition of life. Creams, toothpastes, combs and hankies, cotton gloves, flimsy flowering scarves, writing-paper and crayons, ice-cream cones and orangeade, screwdrivers, boxes of tacks, tins of paint, of glue, of marmalade; I always liked them but far more now that I have no need of any. When Saturdays are fine I go instead to the Portobello Road where formerly I would jaunt with Kathleen in our grown-up days. The barrow-loads do not change much, of apples and rayon vests in common blues and low-taste mauve, of silver plate, trays and teapots long since changed hands from the bygone citizens to dealers, from shops to the new flats and breakable homes, and then over to the barrow-stalls and the dealers again: Georgian spoons, rings, ear-rings of turquoise and opal set in the butterfly pattern of true-lovers' knot, patch-boxes with miniature paintings of ladies on ivory, snuff-boxes of silver with Scotch pebbles inset.

Sometimes as occasion arises on a Saturday morning, my friend Kathleen, who is a Catholic, has a Mass said for my soul, and then I am in attendance, as it were, at the church. But most Saturdays I take my delight among the solemn crowds with their aimless purposes, their eternal life not far away, who push past the counters and stalls, who handle, buy, steal, touch, desire, and ogle the merchandise. I hear the tinkling tills, I hear the jangle of loose change and tongues and children wanting to hold and have.

That is how I came to be in the Portobello Road that Saturday morning when I saw George and Kathleen. I would not have spoken had I not been inspired to it. Indeed it's one of the things I can't do now—to speak out, unless inspired. And most extraordinary, on that morning as I spoke, a degree of visibility set in. I suppose from poor George's point of view it was like seeing a ghost when he saw me standing by the fruit barrow repeating in so friendly a manner, 'Hallo, George!'

We were bound for the south. When our education, what we could get of it from the north, was thought to be finished, one by one we were sent or sent for to London. John Skinner, whom we called Skinny, went to study more archaeology, George to join his uncle's tobacco farm, Kathleen to stay with her rich connections and to potter intermittently in the Mayfair hat shop which one of them owned. A little later I also went to London to see life, for it was my ambition to write about life, which first I had to see.

'We four must stick together,' George said very often in that yearning way of his. He was always desperately afraid of neglect. We four looked likely to shift off in different directions and George did not trust the other three of us not to forget all about him. More and more as the time came for him to depart for his uncle's tobacco farm in Africa he said,

'We four must keep in touch.'

And before he left he told each of us anxiously,

'I'll write regularly, once a month. We must keep together for the sake of the old times.' He had three prints taken from the negative of that photo on the haystack, wrote on the back of them, 'George took this the day that Needle found the needle' and gave us a copy each. I think we all wished he could become a bit more callous.

During my lifetime I was a drifter, nothing organized. It was difficult for my friends to follow the logic of my life. By the normal reckonings I should have come to starvation and ruin, which I never did. Of course, I did not live to write about life as I wanted to do. Possibly that is why I am inspired to do so now in these peculiar circumstances.

I taught in a private school in Kensington for almost three months, very small children. I didn't know what to do with them but I was kept

fairly busy escorting incontinent little boys to the lavatory and telling
the little girls to use their handkerchiefs. After that I lived a winter
holiday in London on my small capital, and when that had run out I
found a diamond bracelet in the cinema for which I received a reward
of fifty pounds. When it was used up I got a job with a publicity man,
writing speeches for absorbed industrialists, in which the dictionary of
quotations came in very useful. So it went on. I got engaged to Skinny,
but shortly after that I was left a small legacy, enough to keep me for six
months. This somehow decided me that I didn't love Skinny so I gave
him back the ring.

But it was through Skinny that I went to Africa. He was engaged with
a party of researchers to investigate King Solomon's mines, that series of
ancient workings ranging from the ancient port of Ophir, now called
Beira, across Portuguese East Africa and Southern Rhodesia to the
mighty jungle-city of Zimbabwe whose temple walls still stand by the
approach to an ancient and sacred mountain, where the rubble of that
civilization scatters itself over the surrounding Rhodesian waste. I accompanied the party as a sort of secretary. Skinny vouched for me, he
paid my fare, he sympathized by his action with my inconsequential life
although when he spoke of it he disapproved. A life like mine annoys
most people; they go to their jobs every day, attend to things, give
orders, pummel typewriters, and get two or three weeks off every year,
and it vexes them to see someone else not bothering to do these things
and yet getting away with it, not starving, being lucky as they call it.
Skinny, when I had broken off our engagement, lectured me about this,
but still he took me to Africa knowing I should probably leave his unit
within a few months.

We were there a few weeks before we began enquiring for George,
who was farming about four hundred miles away to the north. We had
not told him of our plans.

'If we tell George to expect us in his part of the world he'll come
rushing to pester us the first week. After all, we're going on business,'
Skinny had said.

Before we left Kathleen told us, 'Give George my love and tell him
not to send frantic cables every time I don't answer his letters right
away. Tell him I'm busy in the hat shop and being presented. You
would think he hadn't another friend in the world the way he carries
on.'

We had settled first at Fort Victoria, our nearest place of access to the
Zimbabwe ruins. There we made enquiries about George. It was clear
he hadn't many friends. The older settlers were the most tolerant about

the half-caste woman he was living with, as we found, but they were furious about his methods of raising tobacco which we learned were most unprofessional and in some mysterious way disloyal to the whites. We could never discover how it was that George's style of tobacco farming gave the blacks opinions about themselves, but that's what the older settlers claimed. The newer immigrants thought he was unsociable and, of course, his living with that woman made visiting impossible.

I must say I was myself a bit off-put by this news about the brown woman. I was brought up in a university town to which came Indian, African and Asiatic students in a variety of tints and hues. I was brought up to avoid them for reasons connected with local reputation and God's ordinances. You cannot easily go against what you were brought up to do unless you are a rebel by nature.

Anyhow, we visited George eventually, taking advantage of the offer of transport from some people bound north in search of game. He had heard of our arrival in Rhodesia and though he was glad, almost relieved, to see us he pursued a policy of sullenness for the first hour.

'We wanted to give you a surprise, George.'

'How were we to know that you'd get to hear of our arrival, George? News here must travel faster than light, George.'

'We did hope to give you a surprise, George.'

At last he said, 'Well, I must say it's good to see you. All we need now is Kathleen. We four simply must stick together. You find when you're in a place like this, there's nothing like old friends.'

He showed us his drying sheds. He showed us a paddock where he was experimenting with a horse and a zebra mare, attempting to mate them. They were frolicking happily, but not together. They passed each other in their private play time and again, but without acknowledgement and without resentment.

'It's been done before,' George said. 'It makes a fine strong beast, more intelligent than a mule and sturdier than a horse. But I'm not having any success with this pair, they won't look at each other.'

After a while, he said, 'Come in for a drink and meet Matilda.'

She was dark brown, with a subservient hollow chest and round shoulders, a gawky woman, very snappy with the house-boys. We said pleasant things as we drank on the stoep before dinner, but we found George difficult. For some reason he began to rail at me for breaking off my engagement to Skinny, saying what a dirty trick it was after all those good times in the old days. I diverted attention to Matilda. I supposed, I said, she knew this part of the country well?

'No,' said she, 'I been a-shellitered my life. I not put out to working.

Me nothing to go from place to place is allowed like dirty girls does.' In her speech she gave every syllable equal stress.

George explained, 'Her father was a white magistrate in Natal. She had a sheltered upbringing, different from the other coloureds, you realize.'

'Man, me no black-eyed Susan,' said Matilda, 'no, no.'

On the whole, George treated her as a servant. She was about four months advanced in pregnancy, but he made her get up and fetch for him, many times. Soap: that was one of the things Matilda had to fetch. George made his own bath soap, showed it proudly, gave us the recipe which I did not trouble to remember; I was fond of nice soaps during my lifetime and George's smelt of brilliantine and looked likely to soil one's skin.

'D'yo brahn?' Matilda asked me.

George said, 'She is asking if you go brown in the sun.'

'No, I go freckled.'

'I got sister-in-law go freckles.'

She never spoke another word to Skinny nor to me, and we never saw her again.

Some months later I said to Skinny,

'I'm fed up with being a camp-follower.'

He was not surprised that I was leaving his unit, but he hated my way of expressing it. He gave me a Presbyterian look.

'Don't talk like that. Are you going back to England or staying?'

'Staying, for a while.'

'Well, don't wander too far off.'

I was able to live on the fee I got for writing a gossip column in a local weekly, which wasn't my idea of writing about life, of course. I made friends, more than I could cope with, after I left Skinny's exclusive little band of archaeologists. I had the attractions of being newly out from England and of wanting to see life. Of the countless young men and go-ahead families who purred me along the Rhodesian roads, hundred after hundred miles, I only kept up with one family when I returned to my native land. I think that was because they were the most representative, they stood for all the rest: people in those parts are very typical of each other, as one group of standing stones in that wilderness is like the next.

I met George once more in a hotel in Bulawayo. We drank highballs and spoke of war. Skinny's party were just then deciding whether to remain in the country or return home. They had reached an exciting part of their research, and whenever I got a chance to visit Zimbabwe he would take me for a moonlight walk in the ruined temple and try to make me see phantom Phoenicians flitting ahead of us, or along the walls. I had half a mind to marry Skinny; perhaps, I thought, when his studies were finished. The impending war was in our bones: so I remarked to George as we sat drinking highballs on the hotel stoep in the hard bright sunny July winter of that year.

George was inquisitive about my relations with Skinny. He tried to pump me for about half an hour and when at last I said, 'You are becoming aggressive, George,' he stopped. He became quite pathetic. He said, 'War or no war I'm clearing out of this.'

'It's the heat does it,' I said.

'I'm clearing out in any case. I've lost a fortune in tobacco. My uncle is making a fuss. It's the other bloody planters; once you get the wrong side of them you're finished in this wide land.'

'What about Matilda?' I asked.

He said, 'She'll be all right. She's got hundreds of relatives.'

I had already heard about the baby girl. Coal black, by repute, with George's features. And another on the way, they said.

'What about the child?'

He didn't say anything to that. He ordered more highballs and when they arrived he swizzled his for a long time with a stick. 'Why didn't you ask me to your twenty-first?' he said then.

'I didn't have anything special, no party, George. We had a quiet drink among ourselves, George, just Skinny and the old professors and two of the wives and me, George.'

'You didn't ask me to your twenty-first,' he said. 'Kathleen writes to me regularly.'

This wasn't true. Kathleen sent me letters fairly often in which she said. 'Don't tell George I wrote to you as he will be expecting word from me and I can't be bothered actually.'

'But you,' said George, 'don't seem to have any sense of old friendships, you and Skinny.'

'Oh, George!' I said.

'Remember the times we had,' George said. 'We used to have times.' His large brown eyes began to water.

'I'll have to be getting along,' I said.

'Please don't go. Don't leave me just yet. I've something to tell you.'

'Something nice?' I laid on an eager smile. All responses to George had to be overdone.

'You don't know how lucky you are,' George said.

'How?' I said. Sometimes I got tired of being called lucky by everybody. There were times when, privately practising my writings about life, I knew the bitter side of my fortune. When I failed again and again to reproduce life in some satisfactory and perfect form, I was the more imprisoned, for all my carefree living, within my craving for this satisfaction. Sometimes, in my impotence and need I secreted a venom which infected all my life for days on end and which spurted out indiscriminately on Skinny or on anyone who crossed my path.

'You aren't bound by anyone,' George said. 'You come and go as you please. Something always turns up for you. You're free, and you don't know your luck.'

'You're a damn sight more free than I am,' I said sharply. 'You've got your rich uncle.'

'He's losing interest in me,' George said. 'He's had enough.'

'Oh well, you're young yet. What was it you wanted to tell me?'

'A secret,' George said. 'Remember we used to have those secrets.'

'Oh, yes we did.'

'Did you ever tell any of mine?'

'Oh no, George.' In reality, I couldn't remember any particular secret out of the dozens we must have exchanged from our schooldays onwards.

'Well, this is a secret, mind. Promise not to tell.'

'Promise.'

'I'm married.'

'Married, George! Oh, who to?'

'Matilda.'

'How dreadful!' I spoke before I could think, but he agreed with me.

'Yes, it's awful, but what could I do?'

'You might have asked my advice,' I said pompously.

'I'm two years older than you are. I don't ask advice from you, Needle, little beast.'

'Don't ask for sympathy then.'

'A nice friend you are,' he said, 'I must say after all these years.'

'Poor George!' I said.

'There are three white men to one white woman in this country,' said George. 'An isolated planter doesn't see a white woman and if he sees one she doesn't see him. What could I do? I needed the woman.'

I was nearly sick. One, because of my Scottish upbringing. Two, because of my horror of corny phrases like 'I needed the woman', which George repeated twice again.

'And Matilda got tough,' said George, 'after you and Skinny came to visit us. She had some friends at the Mission, and she packed up and went to them.'

'You should have let her go,' I said.

'I went after her,' George said. 'She insisted on being married, so I married her.'

'That's not a proper secret, then,' I said. 'The news of a mixed marriage soon gets about.'

'I took care of that,' George said. 'Crazy as I was, I took her to the Congo and married her there. She promised to keep quiet about it.'

'Well, you can't clear off and leave her now, surely,' I said.

'I'm going to get out of this place. I can't stand the woman and I can't stand the country. I didn't realize what it would be like. Two years of the country and three months of my wife has been enough.'

'Will you get a divorce?'

'No, Matilda's Catholic. She won't divorce.'

George was fairly getting through the highballs, and I wasn't far behind him. His brown eyes floated shiny and liquid as he told me how he had written to tell his uncle of his plight, 'Except, of course, I didn't say we were married, that would have been too much for him. He's a prejudiced hardened old colonial. I only said I'd had a child by a coloured woman and was expecting another, and he perfectly understood. He came at once by plane a few weeks ago. He's made a settlement on her, providing she keeps her mouth shut about her association with me.'

'Will she do that?'

'Oh, yes, or she won't get the money.'

'But as your wife she has a claim on you, in any case.'

'If she claimed as my wife she'd get far less. Matilda knows what she's doing, greedy bitch she is. She'll keep her mouth shut.'

'Only, you won't be able to marry again, will you, George?'

'Not unless she dies,' he said. 'And she's as strong as a trek ox.'

'Well, I'm sorry, George,' I said.

'Good of you to say so,' he said. 'But I can see by your chin that you disapprove of me. Even my old uncle understood.'

'Oh, George, I quite understand. You were lonely, I suppose.'

'You didn't even ask me to your twenty-first. If you and Skinny had been nicer to me, I would never have lost my head and married the woman, never.'

'You didn't ask me to your wedding,' I said.

'You're a catty bissom, Needle, not like what you were in the old times when you used to tell us your wee stories.'

'I'll have to be getting along,' I said.

'Mind you keep the secret,' George said.

'Can't I tell Skinny? He would be very sorry for you, George.'

'You mustn't tell anyone. Keep it a secret. Promise.'

'Promise,' I said. I understood that he wished to enforce some sort of bond between us with this secret, and I thought, 'Oh well, I suppose he's lonely. Keeping his secret won't do any harm.'

I returned to England with Skinny's party just before the war.

I did not see George again till just before my death, five years ago.

After the war Skinny returned to his studies. He had two more exams, over a period of eighteen months, and I thought I might marry him when the exams were over.

'You might do worse than Skinny,' Kathleen used to say to me on our Saturday morning excursions to the antique shops and the junk stalls.

She too was getting on in years. The remainder of our families in Scotland were hinting that it was time we settled down with husbands. Kathleen was a little younger than me, but looked much older. She knew her chances were diminishing but at that time I did not think she cared very much. As for myself, the main attraction of marrying Skinny was his prospective expeditions to Mesopotamia. My desire to marry him had to be stimulated by the continual reading of books about Babylon and Assyria; perhaps Skinny felt this, because he supplied the books and even started instructing me in the art of deciphering cuneiform tables.

Kathleen was more interested in marriage than I thought. Like me, she had racketed around a good deal during the war; she had actually been engaged to an officer in the US navy, who was killed. Now she kept an antique shop near Lambeth, was doing very nicely, lived in a Chelsea square, but for all that she must have wanted to be married and have children. She would stop and look into all the prams which the mothers had left outside shops or area gates.

'The poet Swinburne used to do that,' I told her once.

'Really? Did he want children of his own?'

'I shouldn't think so. He simply liked babies.'

Before Skinny's final exam he fell ill and was sent to a sanatorium in Switzerland.

'You're fortunate after all not to be married to him,' Kathleen said. 'You might have caught TB.'

I was fortunate, I was lucky . . . so everyone kept telling me on different occasions. Although it annoyed me to hear, I knew they were right, but in a way that was different from what they meant. It took me very small effort to make a living; book reviews, odd jobs for Kathleen, a few months with the publicity man again, still getting up speeches about literature, art, and life for industrial tycoons. I was waiting to write about life and it seemed to me that the good fortune lay in this, whenever it should be. And until then I was assured of my charmed life, the necessities of existence always coming my way and I with far more leisure than anyone else. I thought of my type of luck after I became a Catholic and was being confirmed. The Bishop touches the candidate on the cheek, a symbolic reminder of the sufferings a Christian is supposed to undertake. I thought, how lucky, what a feathery symbol to stand for the hellish violence of its true meaning.

I visited Skinny twice in the two years that he was in the sanatorium. He was almost cured, and expected to be home within a few months. I told Kathleen after my last visit.

'Maybe I'll marry Skinny when he's well again.'

'Make it definite, Needle, and not so much of the maybe. You don't know when you're well off,' she said.

This was five years ago, in the last year of my life. Kathleen and I had become very close friends. We met several times each week, and after our Saturday morning excursions in the Portobello Road very often I would accompany Kathleen to her aunt's house in Kent for a long weekend.

One day in the June of that year I met Kathleen specially for lunch because she had phoned me to say she had news.

'Guess who came into the shop this afternoon,' she said.

'Who?'

'George.'

We had half imagined George was dead. We had received no letters in the past ten years. Early in the war we had heard rumours of his keeping a night-club in Durban, but nothing after that. We could have made enquiries if we had felt moved to do so.

At one time, when we discussed him, Kathleen had said,

'I ought to get in touch with poor George. But then I think he would write back. He would demand a regular correspondence again.'

'We four must stick together,' I mimicked.

'I can visualize his reproachful limpid orbs,' Kathleen said.

Skinny said, 'He's probably gone native. With his coffee concubine and a dozen mahogany kids.'

'Perhaps he's dead,' Kathleen said.

I did not speak of George's marriage, nor of any of his confidences in the hotel at Bulawayo. As the years passed we ceased to mention him except in passing, as someone more or less dead so far as we were concerned.

Kathleen was excited about George's turning up. She had forgotten
her impatience with him in former days; she said,

'It was so wonderful to see old George. He seems to need a friend,
feels neglected, out of touch with things.'

'He needs mothering, I suppose.'

Kathleen didn't notice the malice. She declared, 'That's exactly the
case with George. It always has been, I can see it now.'

She seemed ready to come to any rapid new and happy conclusion
about George. In the course of the morning he had told her of his
wartime night-club in Durban, his game-shooting expeditions since. It
was clear he had not mentioned Matilda. He had put on weight.
Kathleen told me, but he could carry it.

I was curious to see this version of George, but I was leaving for
Scotland next day and did not see him till September of that year, just
before my death.

While I was in Scotland I gathered from Kathleen's letters that she was
seeing George very frequently, finding enjoyable company in him,
looking after him. 'You'll be surprised to see how he has developed.'
Apparently he would hang round Kathleen in her shop most days, 'it
makes him feel useful' as she maternally expressed it. He had an old
relative in Kent whom he visited at weekends; this old lady lived a few
miles from Kathleen's aunt, which made it easy for them to travel down
together on Saturdays, and go for long country walks.

'You'll see such a difference in George,' Kathleen said on my return
to London in September. I was to meet him that night, a Saturday.
Kathleen's aunt was abroad, the maid on holiday, and I was to keep
Kathleen company in the empty house.

George had left London for Kent a few days earlier. 'He's actually
helping with the harvest down there!' Kathleen told me lovingly.

Kathleen and I planned to travel down together, but on that Saturday
she was unexpectedly delayed in London on some business. It was
arranged that I should go ahead of her in the early afternoon to see to
the provisions for our party; Kathleen had invited George to dinner at
her aunt's house that night.

'I should be with you by seven,' she said. 'Sure you won't mind the
empty house? I hate arriving at empty houses, myself.'

I said no, I liked an empty house.

So I did, when I got there. I had never found the house more likeable.
A large Georgian vicarage in about eight acres, most of the rooms shut
and sheeted, there being only one servant. I discovered that I wouldn't

need to go shopping, Kathleen's aunt had left many and delicate supplies with notes attached to them: 'Eat this up please do, see also fridge'
and 'A treat for three hungry people see also 2 bttles beaune for yr party
on back kn table.' It was like a treasure hunt as I followed clue after clue
through the cool silent domestic quarters. A house in which there are no
people—but with all the signs of tenancy—can be a most tranquil good
place. People take up space in a house out of proportion to their size.
On my previous visits I had seen the rooms overflowing, as it seemed,
with Kathleen, her aunt, and the little fat maidservant; they were always
on the move. As I wandered through that part of the house which was
in use, opening windows to let in the pale yellow air of September, I was
not conscious that I, Needle, was taking up any space at all, I might have
been a ghost.

The only thing to be fetched was the milk. I waited till after four
when the milking should be done, then set off for the farm which lay
across two fields at the back of the orchard. There, when the byre-man
was handing me the bottle, I saw George.

'Hallo, George,' I said.

'Needle! What are you doing here?' he said.

'Fetching milk,' I said.

'So am I. Well, it's good to see you, I must say.'

As we paid the farm-hand, George said, 'I'll walk back with you part
of the way. But I mustn't stop, my old cousin's without any milk for her
tea. How's Kathleen?'

'She was kept in London. She's coming on later, about seven, she
expects.'

We had reached the end of the first field. George's way led to the left
and on to the main road.

'We'll see you tonight, then?' I said.

'Yes, and talk about old times.'

'Grand,' I said.

But George got over the stile with me.

'Look here,' he said. 'I'd like to talk to you, Needle.'

'We'll talk tonight, George. Better not keep your cousin waiting
for the milk.' I found myself speaking to him almost as if he were a
child.

'No, I want to talk to you alone. This is a good opportunity.'

We began to cross the second field. I had been hoping to have the
house to myself for a couple more hours and I was rather petulant.

'See,' he said suddenly, 'that haystack.'

'Yes,' I said absently.

'Let's sit there and talk. I'd like to see you up on a haystack again. I still keep that photo. Remember that time when—'

'I found the needle,' I said very quickly, to get it over.

But I was glad to rest. The stack had been broken up, but we managed to find a nest in it. I buried my bottle of milk in the hay for coolness. George placed his carefully at the foot of the stack.

'My old cousin is terribly vague, poor soul. A bit hazy in her head. She hasn't the least sense of time. If I tell her I've only been gone ten minutes she'll believe it.'

I giggled, and looked at him. His face had grown much larger, his lips full, wide, and with a ripe colour that is strange in a man. His brown eyes were abounding as before with some inarticulate plea.

'So you're going to marry Skinny after all these years?'

'I really don't know, George.'

'You played him up properly.'

'It isn't for you to judge. I have my own reasons for what I do.'

'Don't get sharp,' he said, 'I was only funning.' To prove it, he lifted a tuft of hay and brushed my face with it.

'D'you know,' he said next, 'I didn't think you and Skinny treated me very decently in Rhodesia.'

'Well, we were busy, George. And we were younger then, we had a lot to do and see. After all, we could see you any other time, George.'

'A touch of selfishness,' he said.

'I'll have to be getting along, George.' I made to get down from the stack.

He pulled me back. 'Wait, I've got something to tell you.'

'O.K., George, tell me.'

'First promise not to tell Kathleen. She wants it kept a secret so that she can tell you herself.'

'All right. Promise.'

'I'm going to marry Kathleen.'

'But you're already married.'

Sometimes I heard news of Matilda from the one Rhodesian family with whom I still kept up. They referred to her as 'George's Dark Lady' and of course they did not know he was married to her. She had apparently made a good thing out of George, they said, for she minced around all tarted up, never did a stroke of work and was always unsettling the respectable coloured girls in their neighbourhood. According to accounts, she was a living example of the folly of behaving as George did.

'I married Matilda in the Congo,' George was saying.

'It would still be bigamy,' I said.

He was furious when I used that word bigamy. He lifted a handful of hay as if he would throw it in my face, but controlling himself meanwhile he fanned it at me playfully.

'I'm not sure that the Congo marriage was valid,' he continued. 'Anyway, as far as I'm concerned, it isn't.'

'You can't do a thing like that,' I said.

'I need Kathleen. She's been decent to me. I think we were always meant for each other, me and Kathleen.'

'I'll have to be going,' I said.

But he put his knee over my ankles, so that I couldn't move. I sat still and gazed into space.

He tickled my face with a wisp of hay.

'Smile up, Needle,' he said; 'let's talk like old times.'

'Well?'

'No one knows about my marriage to Matilda except you and me.'

'And Matilda,' I said.

'She'll hold her tongue so long as she gets her payments. My uncle left an annuity for the purpose, his lawyers see to it.'

'Let me go, George.'

'You promised to keep it a secret,' he said, 'you promised.'

'Yes, I promised.'

'And now that you're going to marry Skinny, we'll be properly coupled off as we should have been years ago. We should have been— but youth!—our youth got in the way, didn't it?'

'Life got in the way,' I said.

'But everything's going to be all right now. You'll keep my secret, won't you? You promised.' He had released my feet. I edged a little further from him.

I said, 'If Kathleen intends to marry you, I shall tell her that you're already married.'

'You wouldn't do a dirty trick like that, Needle? You're going to be happy with Skinny, you wouldn't stand in the way of my—'

'I must, Kathleen's my best friend,' I said swiftly.

He looked as if he would murder me and he did, he stuffed hay into my mouth until it could hold no more, kneeling on my body to keep it still, holding both my wrists tight in his huge left hand. I saw the red full lines of his mouth and the white slit of his teeth last thing on earth. Not another soul passed by as he pressed my body into the stack, as he made a deep nest for me, tearing up the hay to make a groove the length of my corpse, and finally pulling the warm dry stuff in a mound over this concealment, so natural-looking in a broken haystack. Then George climbed down, took up his bottle of milk and went his way. I suppose that was why he looked so unwell when I stood, nearly five years later, by the barrow in the Portobello Road and said in easy tones, 'Hallo, George!'

The Haystack Murder was one of the notorious crimes of that year.

My friends said, 'A girl who had everything to live for.'

After a search that lasted twenty hours, when my body was found, the evening papers said, ' "Needle" is found: in haystack!'

Kathleen, speaking from that Catholic point of view which takes some getting used to, said, 'She was at Confession only the day before she died—wasn't she lucky?'

The poor byre-hand who sold us the milk was grilled for hour after hour by the local police, and later by Scotland Yard. So was George. He admitted walking as far as the haystack with me, but he denied lingering there.

'You hadn't seen your friend for ten years?' the Inspector asked him.

'That's right,' said George.

'And you didn't stop to have a chat?'

'No. We'd arranged to meet later at dinner. My cousin was waiting for the milk, I couldn't stop.'

The old soul, his cousin, swore that he hadn't been gone more than ten minutes in all, and she believed it to the day of her death a few months later. There was the microscopic evidence of hay on George's jacket, of course, but the same evidence was on every man's jacket in the district that fine harvest year. Unfortunately, the byre-man's hands were even brawnier and mightier than George's. The marks on my wrists had been done by such hands, so the laboratory charts indicated when my post-mortem was all completed. But the wrist-marks weren't enough to pin down the crime to either man. If I hadn't been wearing my long-sleeved cardigan, it was said, the bruises might have matched up properly with someone's fingers.

Kathleen, to prove that George had absolutely no motive, told the police that she was engaged to him. George thought this a little foolish. They checked up on his life in Africa, right back to his living with Matilda. But the marriage didn't come out—who would think of looking up registers in the Congo? Not that this would have proved any motive for murder. All the same, George was relieved when the inquiries were over without the marriage to Matilda being disclosed. He was able to have his nervous breakdown at the same time as Kathleen had hers, and they recovered together and got married, long after the police had shifted their inquiries to an Air Force camp five miles from Kathleen's aunt's home. Only a lot of excitement and drinks came of those investigations. The Haystack Murder was one of the unsolved crimes that year.

Shortly afterwards the byre-hand emigrated to Canada to start afresh, with the help of Skinny who felt sorry for him.

After seeing George taken away home by Kathleen that Saturday in the Portobello Road, I thought that perhaps I might be seeing more of him in similar circumstances. The next Saturday I looked out for him, and at last there he was, without Kathleen, half-worried, half-hopeful.

I dashed his hopes. I said, 'Hallo, George!'

He looked in my direction, rooted in the midst of the flowing market-mongers in that convivial street. I thought to myself, 'He looks as if he had a mouthful of hay.' It was the new bristly maize-coloured beard and moustache surrounding his great mouth which suggested the thought, gay and lyrical as life.

'Hallo, George!' I said again.

I might have been inspired to say more on that agreeable morning, but he didn't wait. He was away down a side street and along another street and down one more, zigzag, as far and as devious as he could take himself from the Portobello Road.

Nevertheless he was back again next week. Poor Kathleen had brought him in her car. She left it at the top of the street, and got out with him, holding him tight by the arm. It grieved me to see Kathleen ignoring the spread of scintillations on the stalls. I had myself seen a charming Battersea box quite to her taste, also a pair of enamelled silver earrings. But she took no notice of these wares, clinging close to George, and, poor Kathleen—I hate to say how she looked.

And George was haggard. His eyes seemed to have got smaller as if he had been recently in pain. He advanced up the road with Kathleen on his arm, letting himself lurch from side to side with his wife bobbing beside him, as the crowds asserted their rights of way.

'Oh, George!' I said. 'You don't look at all well, George.'

'Look!' said George. 'Over there by the hardware barrow. That's Needle.'

Kathleen was crying. 'Come back home, dear,' she said.

'Oh, you don't look well, George!' I said.

They took him to a nursing home. He was fairly quiet, except on Saturday mornings when they had a hard time of it to keep him indoors and away from the Portobello Road.

But a couple of months later he did escape. It was a Monday.

They searched for him in the Portobello Road, but actually he had gone off to Kent to the village near the scene of the Haystack Murder. There he went to the police and gave himself up, but they could tell from the way he was talking that there was something wrong with the man.

'I saw Needle in the Portobello Road three Saturdays running,' he explained, 'and they put me in a private ward but I got away while the nurses were seeing to the new patient. You remember the murder of Needle—well, I did it. Now you know the truth, and that will keep bloody Needle's mouth shut.'

Dozens of poor mad fellows confess to every murder. The police obtained an ambulance to take him back to the nursing home. He wasn't there long. Kathleen gave up her shop and devoted herself to looking after him at home. But she found that the Saturday mornings were a strain. He insisted on going to see me in the Portobello Road and would come back to insist that he'd murdered Needle. Once he tried to tell her something about Matilda, but Kathleen was so kind and solicitous, I don't think he had the courage to remember what he had to say.

Skinny had always been rather reserved with George since the murder. But he was kind to Kathleen. It was he who persuaded them to emigrate to Canada so that George should be well out of reach of the Portobello Road.

George has recovered somewhat in Canada but of course he will never be the old George again, as Kathleen writes to Skinny. 'That Haystack tragedy did for George,' she writes. 'I feel sorrier for George sometimes than I am for poor Needle. But I do often have Masses said for Needle's soul.'

I doubt if George will ever see me again in the Portobello Road. He broods much over the crumpled snapshot he took of us on the haystack. Kathleen does not like the photograph, I don't wonder. For my part, I consider it quite a jolly snap, but I don't think we were any of us so lovely as we look in it, gazing blatantly over the ripe cornfields, Skinny with his humorous expression, I secure in my difference from the rest, Kathleen with her head prettily perched on her hand, each reflecting fearlessly in the face of George's camera the glory of the world, as if it would never pass.

RINGING THE CHANGES

Robert Aickman

He had never been among those many who deeply dislike church bells, but the ringing that evening at Holihaven changed his view. Bells could certainly get on one's nerves he felt, although he had only just arrived in the town.

He had been too well aware of the perils attendant upon marrying a girl twenty-four years younger than himself to add to them by a conventional honeymoon. The strange force of Phrynne's love had borne both of them away from their previous selves; in him a formerly haphazard and easy-going approach to life had been replaced by much deep planning to wall in happiness; and she, though once thought cold and choosy, would now agree to anything as long as she was with him. He had said that if they were to marry in June, it would be at the cost of not being able to honeymoon until October. Had they been courting longer, he had explained, gravely smiling, special arrangements could have been made; but, as it was, business claimed him. This, indeed, was true; because his business position was less influential than he had led Phrynne to believe. Finally, it would have been impossible for them to have courted longer, because they had courted from the day they met, which was less than six weeks before the day they married.

'"A village",' he had quoted as they entered the branch-line train at the junction (itself sufficiently remote), '"from which (it was said) persons of sufficient longevity might hope to reach Liverpool Street".' By now he was able to make jokes about age, although perhaps he did so rather too often.

'Who said that?'

'Bertrand Russell.'

She had looked at him with her big eyes in her tiny face.

'Really.' He had smiled confirmation.

'I'm not arguing.' She had still been looking at him. The romantic gaslight in the charming period compartment had left him uncertain whether she was smiling back or not. He had given himself the benefit of the doubt, and kissed her.

The guard had blown his whistle and they had rumbled out into the darkness. The branch line swung so sharply away from the main line that Phrynne had been almost toppled from her seat.

'Why do we go so slowly when it's so flat?'

'Because the engineer laid the line up and down the hills and valleys such as they are, instead of cutting through and embanking over them.' He liked being able to inform her.

'How do you know? Gerald! You said you hadn't been to Holihaven before.'

'It applies to most of the railways in East Anglia.'

'So that even though it's flatter, it's slower?'

'Time matters less.'

'I should have hated going to a place where time mattered or that you'd been to before. You'd have had nothing to remember me by.'

He hadn't been quite sure that her words exactly expressed her thoughts, but the thought had lightened his heart.

Holihaven station could hardly have been built in the days of the town's magnificence, for they were in the Middle Ages; but it still implied grander functions than came its way now. The platforms were long enough for visiting London expresses, which had since gone elsewhere; and the architecture of the waiting rooms would have been not insufficient for occasional use by foreign royalty. Oil lamps on perches like those occupied by macaws, lightened the uniformed staff, who numbered two and, together with every native of Holihaven, looked like storm-habituated mariners.

The station-master and porter, as Gerald took them to be, watched him approach down the platform with a heavy suitcase in each hand and Phrynne walking deliciously by his side. He saw one of them address a remark to the other, but neither offered to help. Gerald had to put down the cases in order to give up their tickets. The other passengers had already disappeared.

'Where's the Bell?'

Gerald had found the hotel in a reference book. It was the only one allotted to Holihaven. But as Gerald spoke, and before the ticket-collector could answer, the sudden deep note of an actual bell rang through the darkness. Phrynne caught hold of Gerald's sleeve.

Ignoring Gerald, the station-master, if such he was, turned to his colleague. 'They're starting early.'

'Every reason to be in good time,' said the other man.

The station-master nodded, and put Gerald's tickets indifferently in his jacket pocket.

'Can you please tell me how I get to the Bell Hotel?'

The station-master's attention returned to him. 'Have you a room booked?'

'Certainly.'

'Tonight?' The station-master looked inappropriately suspicious.

'Of course.'

Again the station-master looked at the other man.

'It's them Pascoes.'

'Yes,' said Gerald. 'That's the name. Pascoe.'

'We don't use the Bell,' explained the station-master. 'But you'll find it in Wrack Street.' He gesticulated vaguely and unhelpfully. 'Straight ahead. Down Station Road. Then down Wrack Street. You can't miss it.'

'Thank you.'

As soon as they entered the town, the big bell began to boom regularly.

'What narrow streets!' said Phrynne.

'They follow the lines of the medieval city. Before the river silted up, Holihaven was one of the most important seaports in Great Britain.'

'Where's everybody got to?'

Although it was only six o'clock, the place certainly seemed deserted.

'Where's the hotel got to?' rejoined Gerald.

'Poor Gerald! Let me help.' She laid her hand beside his on the handle of the suitcase nearest to her, but as she was about fifteen inches shorter than he, she could be of little assistance. They must already have gone more than a quarter of a mile. 'Do you think we're in the right street?'

'Most unlikely, I should say. But there's no one to ask.'

'Must be early closing day.'

The single deep notes of the bell were now coming more frequently.

'Why are they ringing that bell? Is it a funeral?'

'Bit late for a funeral.'

She looked at him a little anxiously.

'Anyway it's not cold.'

'Considering we're on the east coast it's quite astonishingly warm.'

'Not that I care.'

'I hope that bell isn't going to ring all night.'

She pulled on the suitcase. His arms were in any case almost parting from his body. 'Look! We've passed it.'

They stopped, and he looked back. 'How could we have done that?'

'Well, we have.'

She was right. He could see a big ornamental bell hanging from a bracket attached to a house about a hundred yards behind them.

They retraced their steps and entered the hotel. A woman dressed in a navy blue coat and skirt, with a good figure but dyed red hair and a face ridged with make-up, advanced upon them.

'Mr and Mrs Banstead? I'm Hilda Pascoe. Don, my husband, isn't very well.'

Gerald felt full of doubts. His arrangements were not going as they should. Never rely on guide-book recommendations. The trouble lay partly in Phrynne's insistence that they go somewhere he did not know. 'I'm sorry to hear that,' he said.

'You know what men are like when they're ill?' Mrs Pascoe spoke understandingly to Phrynne.

'Impossible,' said Phrynne. 'Or very difficult.'

'Talk about "Woman in our hours of ease".'

'Yes,' said Phrynne. 'What's the trouble?'

'It's always been the same trouble with Don,' said Mrs Pascoe; then checked herself. 'It's his stomach,' she said. 'Ever since he was a kid, Don's had trouble with the lining of his stomach.'

Gerald interrupted. 'I wonder if we could see our rooms?'

'So sorry,' said Mrs Pascoe. 'Will you register first?' She produced a battered volume bound in peeling imitation leather. 'Just the name and address.' She spoke as if Gerald might contribute a résumé of his life.

It was the first time he and Phrynne had ever registered in an hotel; but his confidence in the place was not increased by the long period which had passed since the registration above.

'We're always quiet in October,' remarked Mrs Pascoe, her eyes upon him. Gerald noticed that her eyes were slightly bloodshot. 'Except sometimes for the bars, of course.'

'We wanted to come out of the season,' said Phrynne soothingly.

'Quite,' said Mrs Pascoe.

'Are we alone in the house?' enquired Gerald. After all the woman was probably doing her best.

'Except for Commandant Shotcroft. You won't mind him, will you? He's a regular.'

'I'm sure we shan't,' said Phrynne.

'People say the house wouldn't be the same without Commandant Shotcroft.'

'I see.'

'What's that bell?' asked Gerald. Apart from anything else, it really was much too near.

Mrs Pascoe looked away. He thought she looked shifty under her entrenched make-up. But she only said 'Practice.'

'Do you mean there will be more of them later?'

She nodded. 'But never mind,' she said encouragingly. 'Let me show you to your room. Sorry there's no porter.'

Before they had reached the bedroom, the whole peal had commenced.

'Is this the quietest room you have?' enquired Gerald. 'What about the other side of the house?'

'This *is* the other side of the house. Saint Guthlac's is over there.' She pointed out through the bedroom door.

'Darling,' said Phrynne, her hand on Gerald's arm, 'they'll soon stop. They're only practising.'

Mrs Pascoe said nothing. Her expression indicated that she was one of those people whose friendliness has a precise and never exceeded limit.

'If *you* don't mind,' said Gerald to Phrynne, hesitating.

'They have ways of their own in Holihaven,' said Mrs Pascoe. Her undertone of militancy implied, among other things, that if Gerald and Phrynne chose to leave, they were at liberty to do so. Gerald did not care for that either: her attitude would have been different, he felt, had there been anywhere else for them to go. The bells were making him touchy and irritable.

'It's a very pretty room,' said Phrynne. 'I adore four-posters.'

'Thank you,' said Gerald to Mrs Pascoe. 'What time's dinner?'

'Seven-thirty. You've time for a drink in the bar first.'

She went.

'We certainly have,' said Gerald when the door was shut. 'It's only just six.'

'Actually,' said Phrynne, who was standing by the window looking down into the street, 'I *like* church bells.'

'All very well,' said Gerald, 'but on one's honeymoon they distract the attention.'

'Not mine,' said Phrynne simply. Then she added, 'There's still no one about.'

'I expect they're all in the bar.'

'I don't want a drink. I want to explore the town.'

'As you wish. But hadn't you better unpack?'

'I ought to, but I'm not going to. Not until after I've seen the sea.' Such small shows of independence in her enchanted Gerald.

Mrs Pascoe was not about when they passed through the lounge, nor was there any sound of activity in the establishment.

Outside, the bells seemed to be booming and bounding immediately over their heads.

'It's like warriors fighting in the sky,' shouted Phrynne. 'Do you think the sea's down there?' She indicated the direction from which they had previously retraced their steps.

'I imagine so. The street seems to end in nothing. That would be the sea.'

'Come on. Let's run.' She was off, before he could even think about it. Then there was nothing to do but run after her. He hoped there were not eyes behind blinds.

She stopped, and held wide her arms to catch him. The top of her head hardly came up to his chin. He knew she was silently indicating that his failure to keep up with her was not a matter for self-consciousness.

'Isn't it beautiful?'

'The sea?' There was no moon; and little was discernible beyond the end of the street.

'Not only.'

'Everything but the sea. The sea's invisible.'

'You can smell it.'

'I certainly can't hear it.'

She slackened her embrace and cocked her head away from him.

'The bells echo so much, it's as if there were two churches.'

'I'm sure there are more than that. There always are in old towns like this.' Suddenly he was struck by the significance of his words in relation to what she had said. He shrank into himself, tautly listening.

'Yes,' cried Phrynne delightedly. 'It *is* another church.'

'Impossible,' said Gerald. 'Two churches wouldn't have practice ringing on the same night.'

'I'm quite sure. I can hear one lot of bells with my left ear, and another lot with my right.'

They had still seen no one. The sparse gaslights fell on the furnishings of a stone quay, small but plainly in regular use.

'The whole population must be ringing the bells.' His own remark discomfited Gerald.

'Good for them,' she took his hand. 'Let's go down on the beach and look for the sea.'

They descended a flight of stone steps at which the sea had sucked and bitten. The beach was as stony as the steps, but lumpier.

'We'll just go straight on,' said Phrynne. 'Until we find it.'

Left to himself, Gerald would have been less keen. The stones were very large and very slippery, and his eyes did not seem to be becoming accustomed to the dark.

'You're right, Phrynne, about the smell.'

'Honest sea smell.'

'Just as you say.' He took it rather to be the smell of dense rotting weed; across which he supposed they must be slithering. It was not a smell he had previously encountered in such strength.

Energy could hardly be spared for thinking, and advancing hand in hand was impossible.

After various random remarks on both sides and the lapse of what seemed a very long time, Phrynne spoke again. 'Gerald, where is it? What sort of seaport is it that has no sea?'

She continued onwards, but Gerald stopped and looked back. He had thought the distance they had gone overlong, but was startled to see how great it was. The darkness was doubtless deceitful, but the few lights on the quay appeared as on a distant horizon.

The far glimmering specks still in his eyes, he turned and looked after Phrynne. He could barely see her. Perhaps she was progressing faster without him.

'Phrynne! Darling!'

Unexpectedly she gave sharp cry.

'Phrynne!'

She did not answer.

'Phrynne!'

Then she spoke more or less calmly. 'Panic over. Sorry, darling. I stood on something.'

He realized that a panic it had indeed been; at least in him.

'You're all right?'

'Think so.'

He struggled up to her. 'The smell's worse than ever.' It was overpowering.

'I think it's coming from what I stepped on. My foot went right in, and then there was the smell.'

'I've never known anything like it.'

'Sorry darling,' she said gently mocking him. 'Let's go away.'

'Let's go back. Don't you think?'

'Yes,' said Phrynne. 'But I must warn you I'm very disappointed. I think that seaside attractions should include the sea.'

He noticed that as they retreated, she was scraping the sides of one shoe against the stones, as if trying to clean it.

'I think the whole place is a disappointment,' he said. 'I really must apologize. We'll go somewhere else.'

'I like the bells,' she replied, making a careful reservation.

Gerald said nothing.

'I don't want to go somewhere where you've been before.'

The bells rang out over the desolate unattractive beach. Now the sound seemed to be coming from every point along the shore.

'I suppose all the churches practise on the same night in order to get it over with,' said Gerald.

'They do it in order to see which can ring the loudest,' said Phrynne.

'Take care you don't twist your ankle.'

The din as they reached the rough little quay was such as to suggest that Phrynne's idea was literally true.

The Coffee Room was so low that Gerald had to dip beneath a sequence of thick beams.

'Why "Coffee Room"?' asked Phrynne, looking at the words on the door. 'I saw a notice that coffee will only be served in the lounge.'

'It's the *lucus a non lucendo* principle.'

'That explains everything. I wonder where we sit.' A single electric lantern, mass produced in an antique pattern, had been turned on. The bulb was of that limited wattage which is peculiar to hotels. It did little to penetrate the shadows.

'The *lucus a non lucendo* principle is the principle of calling white black.'

'Not at all,' said a voice from the darkness. 'On the contrary. The word black comes from an ancient root which means "to bleach".'

They had thought themselves alone, but now saw a small man seated by himself at an unlighted corner table. In the darkness he looked like a monkey.

'I stand corrected,' said Gerald.

They sat at the table under the lantern.

The man in the corner spoke again. 'Why are you here at all?'

Phrynne looked fringtened, but Gerald replied quietly. 'We're on holiday. We prefer it out of the season. I presume you are Commandant Shotcroft?'

'No need to presume.' Unexpectedly the Commandant switched on the antique lantern which was nearest to him. His table was littered with a finished meal. It struck Gerald that he must have switched off the light when he heard them approach the Coffee Room. 'I'm going anyway.'

'Are we late?' asked Phrynne, always the assuager of situations.

'No, you're not late,' called the Commandant in a deep moody voice. 'My meals are prepared half an hour before the time the rest come in. I don't like eating in company.' He had risen to his feet. 'So perhaps you'll excuse me.'

Without troubling about an answer, he stepped quickly out of the Coffee Room. He had cropped white hair; tragic, heavy-lidded eyes; and a round face which was yellow and lined.

A second later his head reappeared round the door.

'Ring,' he said; and again withdrew.

'Too many other people ringing,' said Gerald. 'But I don't see what else we can do.'

The Coffee Room bell, however, made a noise like a fire alarm.

Mrs Pascoe appeared. She looked considerably the worse for drink.

'Didn't see you in the bar.'

'Must have missed us in the crowd,' said Gerald amiably.

'Crowd?' enquired Mrs Pascoe drunkenly. Then, after a difficult pause, she offered them a hand-written menu.

They ordered; and Mrs Pascoe served them throughout. Gerald was apprehensive lest her indisposition increased during the course of the meal; but her insobriety, like her affability, seemed to have an exact and definite limit.

'All things considered, the food might be worse,' remarked Gerald, towards the end. It was a relief that something was going reasonably well. 'Not much of it, but at least the dishes are hot.'

When Phrynne translated this into a compliment to the cook, Mrs Pascoe said, 'I cooked it all myself, although I shouldn't be the one to say so.'

Gerald felt really surprised that she was in a condition to have accomplished this. Possibly, he reflected with alarm, she had had much practice under similar conditions.

'Coffee is served in the lounge,' said Mrs Pascoe.

They withdrew. In a corner of the lounge was a screen decorated with winning Elizabethan ladies in ruffs and hoops. From behind it, projected a pair of small black boots. Phrynne nudged Gerald and pointed to them. Gerald nodded. They felt constrained to talk about things which bored them.

The hotel was old and its walls thick. In the empty lounge the noise of the bells would not prevent conversation being overheard, but still came from all around, as if the hotel were a fortress beleaguered by surrounding artillery.

After their second cups of coffee, Gerald suddenly said he couldn't stand it.

'Darling, it's not doing us any harm. I think it's rather cosy.' Phrynne subsided in the wooden chair with its sloping back and long mud-coloured mock-velvet cushions; and opened her pretty legs to the fire.

'Every church in the town must be ringing its bells. It's been going on for two and a half hours and they never seem to take the usual breathers.'

'We wouldn't hear. Because of all the other bells ringing. I think it's nice of them to ring the bells for us.'

Nothing further was said for several minutes. Gerald was beginning to realize that they had yet to evolve a holiday routine.

'I'll get you a drink. What shall it be ?'

'Anything you like. Whatever *you* have.' Phrynne was immersed in female enjoyment of the fire's radiance on her body.

Gerald missed this, and said 'I don't quite see why they have to keep the place like a hothouse. When I come back, we'll sit somewhere else.'

'Men wear too many clothes, darling,' said Phrynne drowsily.

Contrary to his assumption, Gerald found the lounge bar as empty as everywhere else in the hotel and the town. There was not even a person to dispense.

Somewhat irritably Gerald struck a brass bell which stood on the counter. It rang out sharply as a pistol shot.

Mrs Pascoe appeared at a door among the shelves. She had taken off her jacket, and her make-up had begun to run.

'A cognac, please. Double. And a Kummel.'

Mrs Pascoe's hands were shaking so much that she could not get the cork out of the brandy bottle.

'Allow me.' Gerald stretched his arm across the bar.

Mrs Pascoe stared at him blearily. 'OK. But I must pour it.'

Gerald extracted the cork and returned the bottle. Mrs Pascoe slopped a far from precise dose into a balloon.

Catastrophe followed. Unable to return the bottle to the high shelf where it resided. Mrs Pascoe placed it on a waist-level ledge. Reaching for the alembic of Kummel, she swept the three-quarters full brandy bottle onto the tiled floor. The stuffy air became fogged with the fumes of brandy from behind the bar.

At the door from which Mrs Pascoe had emerged appeared a man from the inner room. Though still youngish, he was puce and puffy, and in his braces, with no collar. Streaks of sandy hair laced his vast red scalp. Liquor oozed all over him, as if from a perished gourd. Gerald took it that this was Don.

The man was too drunk to articulate. He stood in the doorway, clinging with each red hand to the ledge, and savagely struggling to flay his wife with imprecations.

'How much?' said Gerald to Mrs Pascoe. It seemed useless to try for the Kummel. The hotel must have another bar.

'Three and six,' said Mrs Pascoe, quite lucidly; but Gerald saw that she was about to weep.

He had the exact sum. She turned her back on him and flicked the cash register. As she returned from it, he heard the fragmentation of glass as she stepped on a piece of the broken bottle. Gerald looked at her husband out of the corner of his eye. The sagging, loose-mouthed figure made him shudder. Something moved him.

'I'm sorry about the accident,' he said to Mrs Pascoe. He held the balloon in one hand, and was just going.

Mrs Pascoe looked at him. The slow tears of desperation were edging down her face, but she now seemed quite sober. 'Mr Banstead,' she said in a flat, hurried voice. 'May I come and sit with you and your wife in the lounge? Just for a few minutes.'

'Of course.' It was certainly not what he wanted, and he wondered what would become of the bar, but he felt unexpectedly sorry for her, and it was impossible to say no.

To reach the flap of the bar, she had to pass her husband. Gerald saw her hesitate for a second; then she advanced resolutely and steadily, and looking straight before her. If the man had let go with his hands, he would have fallen; but as she passed him, he released a great gob of spit. He was far too incapable to aim, and it fell on the side of his own trousers. Gerald lifted the flap for Mrs Pascoe and stood back to let her precede him from the bar. As he followed her, he heard her husband maundering off into unintelligible inward searchings.

'The Kummel!' said Mrs Pascoe, remembering in the doorway.

'Never mind,' said Gerald. 'Perhaps I could try one of the other bars?'

'Not tonight. They're shut. I'd better go back.'

'No. We'll think of something else.' It was not yet nine o'clock, and Gerald wondered about the Licensing Justices.

But in the lounge was another unexpected scene. Mrs Pascoe stopped as soon as they entered, and Gerald, caught between two imitation-leather armchairs, looked over her shoulder.

Phrynne had fallen asleep. Her head was slightly on one side, but her mouth was shut, and her body no more than gracefully relaxed, so that she looked most beautiful, and, Gerald thought, a trifle unearthly, like a dead girl in an early picture by Millais.

The quality of her beauty seemed also to have impressed Commandant Shotcroft; for he was standing silently behind her and looking down at her, his sad face transfigured. Gerald noticed that a leaf of the pseudo-Elizabethan screen had been folded back, revealing a small cretonne-covered chair, with an open tome face downward in its seat.

'Won't you join us?' said Gerald boldly. There was that in the Commandant's face which boded no hurt. 'Can I get you a drink?'

The Commandant did not turn his head, and for a moment seemed unable to speak. Then in a low voice he said, 'For a moment only.'

'Good,' said Gerald. 'Sit down. And you, Mrs Pascoe.' Mrs Pascoe was dabbing at her face. Gerald addressed the Commandant. 'What shall it be?'

'Nothing to drink,' said the Commandant in the same low mutter. It occurred to Gerald that if Phrynne awoke, the Commandant would go.

'What about you?' Gerald looked at Mrs Pascoe, earnestly hoping she would decline.

'No thanks.' She was glancing at the Commandant. Clearly she had not expected him to be there.

Phrynne being asleep, Gerald sat down too. He sipped his brandy. It was impossible to romanticize the action with a toast.

The events in the bar had made him forget about the bells. Now, as they sat silently round the sleeping Phrynne, the tide of sound swept over him once more.

'You mustn't think,' said Mrs Pascoe, 'that he's always like that.' They all spoke in hushed voices. All of them seemed to have reason to do so. The Commandant was again gazing sombrely at Phrynne's beauty.

'Of course not.' But it was hard to believe.

'The licensed business puts temptations in a man's way.'

'It must be very difficult.'

'We ought never to have come here. We were happy in South Norwood.'

'You must do good business during the season.'

'Two months,' said Mrs Pascoe bitterly, but still softly. 'Two and a half at the very most. The people who come during the season have no idea what goes on out of it.'

'What made you leave South Norwood?'

'Don's stomach. The doctor said the air would do him good.'

'Speaking of that, doesn't the sea go too far out? We went down on the beach before dinner, but couldn't see it anywhere.'

On the other side of the fire, the Commandant turned his eyes from Phrynne and looked at Gerald.

'I wouldn't know,' said Mrs Pascoe. 'I never have time to look from one year's end to the other.' It was a customary enough answer, but

Gerald felt that it did not disclose the whole truth. He noticed that Mrs Pascoe glanced uneasily at the Commandant, who by now was staring neither at Phrynne nor at Gerald but at the toppling citadels in the fire.

'And now I must get on with my work,' continued Mrs Pascoe, 'I only came in for a minute.' She looked Gerald in the face. 'Thank you,' she said, and rose.

'Please stay a little longer,' said Gerald, 'Wait till my wife wakes up.' As he spoke, Phrynne slightly shifted.

'Can't be done,' said Mrs Pascoe, her lips smiling. Gerald noticed that all the time she was watching the Commandant from under her lids, and she knew that were he not there, she would have stayed.

As it was, she went. 'I'll probably see you later to say goodnight. Sorry the water's not very hot. It's having no porter.'

The bells showed no sign of flagging.

When Mrs Pascoe had closed the door, the Commandant spoke.

'He was a fine man once. Don't think otherwise.'

'You mean Pascoe?'

The Commandant nodded seriously.

'Not my type,' said Gerald.

'DSO and bar. DFC and bar.'

'And now bar only. Why?'

'You heard what she said. It was a lie. They didn't leave South Norwood for the sea air.'

'So I supposed.'

'He got into trouble. He was fixed. He wasn't the kind of man to know about human nature and all its rottenness.'

'A pity,' said Gerald. 'But perhaps, even so, this isn't the best place for him?'

'It's the worst,' said the Commandant, a dark flame in his eyes. 'For him or anyone else.'

Again Phrynne shifted in her sleep: this time more convulsively, so that she nearly woke. For some reason the two men remained speechless and motionless until she was again breathing steadily. Against the silence within, the bells sounded louder than ever. It was as if the tumult were tearing holes in the roof.

'It's certainly a very noisy place,' said Gerald, still in an undertone.

'Why did you have to come tonight of all nights?' The Commandant spoke in the same undertone, but his vehemence was extreme.

'This doesn't happen often?'

'Once every year.'

'They should have told us.'

'They don't usually accept bookings. They've no right to accept them. When Pascoe was in charge they never did.'

'I expect that Mrs Pascoe felt they were in no position to turn away business.'

'It's not a matter that should be left to a woman.'

'Not much alternative surely?'

'At heart, women are creatures of darkness all the time.' The Commandant's seriousness and bitterness left Gerald without a reply.

'My wife doesn't mind the bells,' he said after a moment. 'In fact she rather likes them.' The Commandant really was converting a nuisance, though an acute one, into a melodrama.

The Commandant turned and gazed at him. It struck Gerald that what he had just said in some way, for the Commandant, placed Phrynne also in a category of the lost.

'Take her away, man,' said the Commandant, with scornful ferocity.

'In a day or two perhaps,' said Gerald, patiently polite. 'I admit that we are disappointed with Holihaven.'

'Now. While there's still time. This *instant*.'

There was an intensity of conviction about the Commandant which was alarming.

Gerald considered. Even the empty lounge, with its dreary decorations and commonplace furniture, seemed inimical. 'They can hardly go on practising all night,' he said. But it was fear that hushed his voice.

'Practising!' The Commandant's scorn flickered coldly through the overheated room.

'What else?'

'They're ringing to wake the dead.'

A tremor of wind in the flue momentarily drew on the already roaring fire. Gerald had turned very pale.

'That's a figure of speech,' he said, hardly to be heard.

'Not in Holihaven.' The Commandant's gaze had returned to the fire.

Gerald looked at Phrynne. She was breathing less heavily. His voice dropped to a whisper. 'What happens?'

The Commandant also was nearly whispering. 'No one can tell how long they have to go on ringing. It varies from year to year. I don't know why. You should be all right up to midnight. Probably for some while after. In the end the dead awake. First one or two, then all of them. Tonight even the sea draws back. You have seen that for yourself. In a place like this there are always several drowned each year. This year there've been more than several. But even so that's only a few. Most of them come not from the water but from the earth. It is not a pretty sight.'

'Where do they go?'

'I've never followed them to see. I'm not stark staring mad.' The red of the fire reflected in the Commandant's eyes. There was a long pause.

'I don't believe in the resurrection of the body,' said Gerald. As the hour grew later, the bells grew louder. 'Not of the body.'

'What other kind of resurrection is possible? Everything else is only theory. You can't even imagine it. No one can.'

Gerald had not argued such a thing for twenty years. 'So,' he said, 'you advise me to go. Where?'

'Where doesn't matter.'

'I have no car.'

'Then you'd better walk.'

'With her?' He indicated Phrynne only with his eyes.

'She's young and strong.' A forlorn tenderness lay within the Commandant's words. 'She's twenty years younger than you and therefore twenty years more important.'

'Yes,' said Gerald. 'I agree . . . What about you? What will you do?'

'I've lived here some time now. I know what to do.'

'And the Pascoes?'

'He's drunk. There is nothing in the world to fear if you're thoroughly drunk. DSO and bar. DFC and bar.'

'But you're not drinking yourself?'

'Not since I came to Holihaven. I lost the knack.'

Suddenly Phrynne sat up. 'Hallo,' she said to the Commandant; not yet fully awake. Then she said, 'What fun! The bells are still ringing.'

The Commandant rose, his eyes averted. 'I don't think there's anything more to say,' he remarked, addressing Gerald. 'You've still got time.' He nodded slightly to Phrynne, and walked out of the lounge.

'What have you still got time for?' asked Phrynne, stretching. 'Was he trying to convert you? I'm sure he's an Anabaptist.'

'Something like that,' said Gerald, trying to think.

'Shall we go to bed? Sorry, I'm so sleepy.'

'Nothing to be sorry about.'

'Or shall we go for another walk? That would wake me up. Besides the tide might have come in.'

Gerald, although he half-despised himself for it, found it impossible to explain to her that they should leave at once; without transport or a destination; walk all night if necessary. He said to himself that probably he would not go even were he alone.

'If you're sleepy, it's probably a *good* thing.'

'Darling!'

'I mean with these bells. God knows when they will stop.' Instantly he felt a new pang of fear at what he had said.

Mrs Pascoe had appeared at the door leading to the bar, and opposite to that from which the Commandant had departed. She bore two steaming glasses on a tray. She looked about, possibly to confirm that the Commandant had really gone.

'I thought you might both like a nightcap. Ovaltine, with something in it.'

'Thank you,' said Phrynne. 'I can't think of anything nicer.'

Gerald set the glasses on a wicker table, and quickly finished his cognac.

Mrs Pascoe began to move chairs and slap cushions. She looked very haggard.

'Is the Commandant an Anabaptist?' asked Phrynne over her shoulder. She was proud of her ability to outdistance Gerald in beginning to consume a hot drink.

Mrs Pascoe stopped slapping for a moment. 'I don't know what that is,' she said.

'He's left his book,' said Phrynne, on a new tack.

'I wonder what he's reading,' continued Phrynne. 'Foxe's *Lives of the Martyrs*, I expect.' A small unusual devil seemed to have entered into her.

But Mrs Pascoe knew the answer. 'It's always the same,' she said contemptuously. 'He only reads one. It's called *Fifteen Decisive Battles of the World*. He's been reading it ever since he came here. When he gets to the end, he starts again.'

'Should I take it up to him?' asked Gerald. It was neither courtesy nor inclination, but rather a fear lest the Commandant return to the lounge: a desire, after those few minutes of reflection, to cross-examine.

'Thanks very much,' said Mrs Pascoe, as if relieved of a similar apprehension. 'Room One. Next to the suit of Japanese armour.' She went on tipping and banging. To Gerald's inflamed nerves, her behaviour seemed too consciously normal.

He collected the book and made his way upstairs. The volume was bound in real leather, and the top of its pages were gilded: apparently a presentation copy. Outside the lounge, Gerald looked at the fly-leaf: in a very large hand was written 'To my dear Son, Raglan, on his being honoured by the Queen. From his proud Father, B. Shotcroft, Major-General.' Beneath the inscription a very ugly military crest had been appended by a stamper of primitive type.

The suit of Japanese armour lurked in a dark corner as the Commandant himself had done when Gerald had first encountered him. The wide brim of the helmet concealed the black eyeholes in the headpiece; the moustache bristled realistically. It was exactly as if the figure stood guard over the door behind it. On this door was no number, but, there being no other in sight, Gerald took it to be the door of Number One. A short way down the dim empty passage was a window, the ancient sashes of which shook in the din and blast of the bells. Gerald knocked sharply.

If there was a reply, the bells drowned it; and he knocked again. When to the third knocking there was still no answer, he gently opened the door. He really had to know whether all would, or could be well if Phrynne, and doubtless he also, were at all costs to remain in their room until it was dawn. He looked into the room and caught his breath.

There was no artificial light, but the curtains, if there were any, had been drawn back from the single window, and the bottom sash forced up as far as it would go. On the floor by the dusky void, a maelstrom of sound, knelt the Commandant, his cropped white hair faintly catching the moonless glimmer, as his head lay on the sill, like that of a man about to be guillotined. His face was in his hands, but slightly sideways, so that Gerald received a shadowy distorted idea of his expression. Some might have called it ecstatic, but Gerald found it agonized. It frightened him more than anything which had yet happened. Inside the room the bells were like plunging roaring lions.

He stood for some considerable time quite unable to move. He could not determine whether or not the Commandant knew he was there. The Commandant gave no direct sign of it, but more than once he writhed and shuddered in Gerald's direction, like an unquiet sleeper made more unquiet by an interloper. It was a matter of doubt whether Gerald should leave the book; and he decided to do so mainly because the thought of further contact with it displeased him. He crept into the room and softly laid it on a hardly visible wooden trunk at the foot of the plain metal bedstead. There seemed no other furniture in the room. Outside the door, the hanging mailed fingers of the Japanese figure touched his wrist.

He had not been away from the lounge for long, but it was long enough for Mrs Pascoe to have begun to drink again. She had left the tidying up half completed, or rather the room half disarranged; and was leaning against the over-mantel, drawing heavily on a dark tumbler of whisky. Phrynne had not yet finished her Ovaltine.

'How long before the bells stop?' asked Gerald as soon as he opened the lounge door. Now he was resolved that, come what might, they must go. The impossibility of sleep should serve as an excuse.

'I don't expect Mrs Pascoe can know any more than we can,' said Phrynne.

'You should have told us about this—this annual event before accepting our booking.'

Mrs Pascoe drank some more whisky. Gerald suspected that it was neat. 'It's not always the same night,' she said throatily, looking at the floor.

'We're not staying,' said Gerald wildly.

'Darling!' Phrynne caught him by the arm.

'Leave this to me, Phrynne.' He addressed Mrs Pascoe. 'We'll pay for the room, of course. Please order me a car.'

Mrs Pascoe was now regarding him stonily. When he asked for a car, she gave a very short laugh. Then her face changed, she made an effort, and she said, 'You mustn't take the Commandant so seriously, you know.'

Phrynne glanced quickly at her husband.

The whisky was finished. Mrs Pascoe placed the empty glass on the plastic over-mantel with too much of a thud. 'No one takes Commandant Shotcroft seriously,' she said. 'Not even his nearest and dearest.'

'Has he any?' asked Phrynne. 'He seemed so lonely and pathetic.'

'He's Don and I's mascot,' she said, the drink interfering with her grammar. But not even the drink could leave any doubt about her rancour.

'I thought he had personality,' said Phrynne.

'That and a lot more no doubt,' said Mrs Pascoe. 'But they pushed him out, all the same.'

'Out of what?'

'Cashiered, court-martialled, badges of rank stripped off, sword broken in half, muffled drums, the works.'

'Poor old man. I'm sure it was a miscarriage of justice.'

'That's because you don't know him.'

Mrs Pascoe looked as if she were waiting for Gerald to offer her another whisky.

'It's a thing he could never live down,' said Phrynne, brooding to herself, and tucking her legs beneath her. 'No wonder he's so queer if all the time it was a mistake.'

'I just told you it was not a mistake,' said Mrs Pascoe insolently.

'How can we possibly know?'

'*You* can't. *I* can. No one better.' She was at once aggressive and tearful.

'If you want to be paid,' cried Gerald, forcing himself in, 'make out your bill. Phrynne, come upstairs and pack.' If only he hadn't made her unpack between their walk and dinner.

Slowly Phrynne uncoiled and rose to her feet. She had no intention of either packing or departing, but nor was she going to argue, 'I shall need your help,' she said, softly. 'If I'm going to pack.'

In Mrs Pascoe there was another change. Now she looked terrified. 'Don't go. Please don't go. Not now. It's too late.'

Gerald confronted her. 'Too late for what?' he asked harshly.

Mrs Pascoe looked paler than ever. 'You said you wanted a car,' she faltered. 'You're too late.' Her voice trailed away.

Gerald took Phrynne by the arm. 'Come on up.'

Before they reached the door, Mrs Pascoe made a further attempt. 'You'll be all right if you stay. Really you will.' Her voice, normally somewhat strident, was so feeble that the bells obliterated it. Gerald observed that from somewhere she had produced the whisky bottle and was refilling her tumbler.

With Phrynne on his arm he went first to the stout front door. To his surprise it was neither locked nor bolted, but opened at a half-turn of the handle. Outside the building the whole sky was full of bells, the air an inferno of ringing.

He thought that for the first time Phrynne's face also seemed strained and crestfallen. 'They've been ringing too long,' she said, drawing close to him. 'I wish they'd stop.'

'We're packing and going. I needed to know whether we could get out this way. We must shut the door quietly.'

It creaked a bit on its hinges, and he hesitated with it half shut, uncertain whether to rush the creak or to ease it. Suddenly, something dark and shapeless, with its arm seeming to hold a black vesture over its head, flitted, all sharp angles, like a bat, down the narrow ill-lighted street, the sound of its passage audible to none. It was the first being that either of them had seen in the streets of Holihaven; and Gerald was acutely relieved that he alone had set eyes upon it. With his hand trembling, he shut the door much too sharply.

But no one could possibly have heard, although he stopped for a second outside the lounge. He could hear Mrs Pascoe now weeping hysterically; and again was glad that Phrynne was a step or two ahead of him. Upstairs the Commandant's door lay straight before them. They had to pass close beside the Japanese figure, in order to take the passage to the left of it.

But soon they were in their room, with the key turned in the big rim lock.

'Oh God,' cried Gerald, sinking on the double bed. 'It's pandemonium.' Not for the first time that evening he was instantly more frightened than ever by the unintended appositeness of his own words.

'It's pandemonium all right,' said Phrynne, almost calmly. 'And we're not going out in it.'

He was at a loss to divine how much she knew, guessed, or imagined; and any word of enlightenment from him might be inconceivably dangerous. But he was conscious of the strength of her resistance, and lacked the reserves to battle with it.

She was looking out of the window into the main street. 'We might *will* them to stop,' she suggested wearily.

Gerald was now far less frightened of the bells continuing than of their ceasing. But that they should go on ringing until day broke seemed hopelessly impossible.

Then one peal stopped. There could be no other explanation for the obvious diminution in sound.

'You see!' said Phrynne.

Gerald sat up straight on the side of the bed.

Almost at once further sections of sound subsided, quickly one after the other, until only a single peal was left, that which had begun the ringing. Then the single peal tapered off into a single bell. The single bell tolled on its own, disjointedly, five or six or seven times. Then it stopped, and there was nothing.

Gerald's head was a cave of echoes, mountingly muffled by the noisy current of his blood.

'Oh goodness,' said Phrynne, turning from the window and stretching her arms above her head. 'Let's go somewhere else tomorrow.' She began to take off her dress.

Sooner than usual they were in bed, and in one another's arms. Gerald had carefully not looked out of the window, and neither of them suggested that it should be opened, as they usually did.

'As it's a four-poster, shouldn't we draw the curtains?' asked Phrynne. 'And be really snug? After those damned bells?'

'We should suffocate.'

'They only drew the curtains when people were likely to pass through the room.'

'Darling, you're shivering. I think we *should* draw them.'

'Lie still instead, and love me.'

But all his nerves were straining out into the silence. There was no sound of any kind, beyond the hotel or within it; not a creaking floorboard or a prowling cat or a distant owl. He had been afraid to look at his watch when the bells stopped, or since; the number of the dark hours before they could leave Holihaven weighed on him. The vision of the Commandant kneeling in the dark window was clear before his eyes, as if the intervening panelled walls were made of stage gauze; and the thing he had seen in the street darted on its angular way back and forth through memory.

Then passion began to open its petals within him, layer upon slow layer; like an illusionist's red flower which, without soil or sun or sap, grows as it is watched. The languor of tenderness began to fill the musty room with its texture and perfume. The transparent walls became again opaque, the old man's vaticinations mere obsession. The street must have been empty, as it was now; the eye deceived.

But perhaps rather it was the boundless sequacity of love that deceived, and most of all in the matter of the time which had passed since the bells stopped ringing; for suddenly Phrynne drew very close to him, and he heard steps in the thoroughfare outside, and a voice calling. These were loud steps, audible from afar even through the shut window; and the voice had the possessed stridency of the street evangelist.

'The dead are awake!'

Not even the thick bucolic accent, the guttural vibrato of emotion, could twist or mask the meaning. At first Gerald lay listening with all his body, and concentrating the more as the noise grew; then he sprang from the bed and ran to the window.

A burly, long-limbed man in a seaman's jersey was running down the street, coming clearly into view for a second at each lamp, and between them lapsing into a swaying lumpy wraith. As he shouted his joyous message, he crossed from side to side and waved his arms like a negro. By flashes, Gerald could see that his weatherworn face was transfigured.

'The dead are awake!'

Already, behind him, people were coming out of their houses, and descending from the rooms above shops. There were men, women, and children. Most of them were fully dressed, and must have been waiting in silence and darkness for the call; but a few were dishevelled in night attire or the first garments which had come to hand. Some formed themselves into groups, and advanced arm in arm, as if towards the conclusion of a Blackpool beano. More came singly, ecstatic and waving their arms above their heads, as the first man had done. All cried out, again and again, with no cohesion or harmony. 'The dead are awake! The dead are awake!'

Gerald became aware that Phrynne was standing behind him.

'The Commandant warned me,' he said brokenly. 'We should have gone.'

Phrynne shook her head and took his arm. 'Nowhere to go,' she said. But her voice was soft with fear, and her eyes blank. 'I don't expect they'll trouble *us*.'

Swiftly Gerald drew the thick plush curtains, leaving them in complete darkness. 'We'll sit it out,' he said, slightly histrionic in his fear. 'No matter what happens.'

He scrambled across to the switch. But when he pressed it, light did not come. 'The current's gone. We must get back into bed.'

'Gerald! Come and help me.' He remembered that she was curiously vulnerable in the dark. He found his way to her, and guided her to the bed.

'No more love,' she said ruefully and affectionately, her teeth chattering.

He kissed her lips with what gentleness the total night made possible.

'They were going towards the sea,' she said timidly.

'We must think of something else.'

But the noise was still growing. The whole community seemed to be passing down the street, yelling the same dreadful words again and again.

'Do you think we can?'

'Yes,' said Gerald. 'It's only until tomorrow.'

'They can't be actually dangerous,' said Phrynne. 'Or it would be stopped.'

'Yes, of course.'

By now, as always happens, the crowd had amalgamated their utterances and were beginning to shout in unison. They were like agitators bawling a slogan, or massed trouble-makers at a football match. But at the same time the noise was beginning to draw away. Gerald suspected that the entire population of the place was on the march.

Soon it was apparent that a processional route was being followed. The tumult could be heard winding about from quarter to quarter; sometimes drawing near, so that Gerald and Phrynne were once more seized by the first chill of panic, then again almost fading away. It was possibly this great variability in the volume of the sound which led Gerald to believe that there were distinct pauses in the massed shouting; periods when it was superseded by far, disorderly cheering. Certainly it began also to seem that the thing shouted had changed; but he could not make out the new cry, although unwillingly he strained to do so.

'It's extraordinary how frightened one can be,' said Phrynne, 'even when one is not directly menaced. It must prove that we all belong to one another, or whatever it is, after all.'

In many similar remarks they discussed the thing at one remove. Experience showed that this was better than not discussing it at all.

In the end there could be no doubt that the shouting had stopped, and that now the crowd was singing. It was no song that Gerald had ever heard, but something about the way it was sung convinced him that it was a hymn or psalm set to an out of date popular tune. Once more the crowd was approaching; this time steadily, but with strange, interminable slowness.

'What the hell are they doing now?' asked Gerald of the blackness, his nerves wound so tight that the foolish question was forced out of them.

Palpably the crowd had completed its peregrination, and was returning up the main street from the sea. The singers seemed to gasp and fluctuate, as if worn out with gay exercise, like children at a party. There was a steady undertow of scraping and scuffling. Time passed and more time.

Phrynne spoke. 'I believe they're *dancing.*'

She moved slightly, as if she thought of going to see.

'No, no,' said Gerald, and clutched her fiercely.

There was a tremendous concussion on the ground floor below them. The front door had been violently thrown back. They could hear the hotel filling with a stamping, singing mob.

Doors banged everywhere, and furniture was overturned, as the beatic throng surged and stumbled through the involved darkness of the old building. Glasses went and china and Birmingham brass warming pans. In a moment, Gerald heard the Japanese armour crash to the boards. Phrynne screamed. Then a mighty shoulder, made strong by the sea's assault, rammed at the panelling and their door was down.

> 'The living and the dead dance together.
> Now's the time. Now's the place. Now's the weather.'

At last Gerald could make out the words

The stresses in the song were heavily beaten down by much repetition.

Hand in hand, through the dim grey gap of the doorway, the dancers lumbered and shambled in, singing frenziedly and brokenly; ecstatic but exhausted. Through the stuffy blackness they swayed and shambled, more and more of them, until the room must have been packed tight with them.

Phrynne screamed again. 'The smell. Oh, God, the smell.'

It was the smell they had encountered on the beach; in the congested room, no longer merely offensive, but obscene, unspeakable.

Phrynne was hysterical. All self-control gone, she was scratching and tearing, and screaming again and again. Gerald tried to hold her, but one of the dancers struck him so hard in the darkness that she was jolted out of his arms. Instantly it seemed that she was no longer there at all.

The dancers were thronging everywhere, their limbs whirling, their lungs bursting with the rhythm of the song. It was difficult for Gerald even to call out. He tried to struggle after Phrynne, but immediately a blow from a massive elbow knocked him to the floor, an abyss of invisible trampling feet.

But soon the dancers were going again: not only from the room, but, it seemed, from the building also. Crushed and tormented though he was, Gerald could hear the song being resumed in the street, as the various frenzied groups debouched and reunited. Within, before long there was nothing but the chaos, the darkness, and the putrescent odour. Gerald felt so sick that he had to battle with unconsciousness. He could not think or move, despite the desperate need.

Then he struggled into a sitting position, and sank his head on the torn sheets of the bed. For an uncertain period he was insensible to everything: but in the end he heard steps approaching down the dark passage. His door was pushed back, and the Commandant entered gripping a lighted candle. He seemed to disregard the flow of hot wax which had already congealed on much of his knotted hand.

'She's safe. Small thanks to you.'

The Commandant stared icily at Gerald's undignified figure. Gerald tried to stand. He was terribly bruised, and so giddy that he wondered if this could be concussion. But relief rallied him.

'Is it thanks to *you?*'

'She was caught up in it. Dancing with the rest.' The Commandant's eyes glowed in the candlelight. The singing and the dancing had almost died away.

Still Gerald could do no more than sit upon the bed. His voice was low and indistinct, as if coming from outside his body. 'Were they . . . were some of them . . .'

The Commandant replied, more scornful than ever of his weakness. 'She was between two of them. Each had one of her hands.'

Gerald could not look at him. 'What did you do?' he asked in the same remote voice.

'I did what had to be done. I hope I was in time.' After the slightest possible pause he continued. 'You'll find her downstairs.'

'I'm grateful. Such a silly thing to say, but what else is there?'

'Can you walk?'

'I think so.'

'I'll light you down.' The Commandant's tone was as uncompromising as always.

There were two more candles in the lounge, and Phrynne, wearing a woman's belted overcoat which was not hers, sat between them, drinking. Mrs Pascoe, fully dressed but with eyes averted, pottered about the wreckage. It seemed hardly more than as if she were completing the task which earlier she had left unfinished.

'Darling, look at you!' Phrynne's words were still hysterical, but her voice was as gentle as it usually was.

Gerald, bruises and thoughts of concussion forgotten, dragged her into his arms. They embraced silently for a long time; then he looked into her eyes.

'Here I am,' she said, and looked away. 'Not to worry.'

Silently and unnoticed, the Commandant had already retreated.

Without returning his gaze, Phrynne finished her drink as she stood there. Gerald supposed that it was one of Mrs Pascoe's concoctions.

It was so dark where Mrs Pascoe was working that her labours could have been achieving little; but she said nothing to her visitors, nor they to her. At the door Phrynne unexpectedly stripped off the overcoat and threw it on a chair. Her nightdress was so torn that she stood almost naked. Dark though it was, Gerald saw Mrs Pascoe regarding Phrynne's pretty body with a stare of animosity.

'May we take one of the candles?' he said, normal standards reasserting themselves in him.

But Mrs Pascoe continued to stand silently staring; and they lighted themselves through the wilderness of broken furniture to the ruins of their bedroom. The Japanese figure was still prostrate, and the Commandant's door shut. And the smell had almost gone.

Even by seven o'clock the next morning surprisingly much had been done to restore order. But no one seemed to be about, and Gerald and Phrynne departed without a word.

In Wrack Street a milkman was delivering, but Gerald noticed that his cart bore the name of another town. A minute boy whom they encountered later on an obscure purposeful errand might, however, have been indigenous; and when they reached Station Road, they saw a small plot of land on which already men were silently at work with spades in their hands. They were as thick as flies on a wound, and as black. In the darkness of the previous evening, Gerald and Phrynne had missed the place. A board named it the New Municipal Cemetery.

In the mild light of an autumn morning the sight of the black and silent toilers was horrible; but Phrynne did not seem to find it so. On the contrary, her cheeks reddened and her soft mouth became fleetingly more voluptuous still.

She seemed to have forgotten Gerald, so that he was able to examine her closely for a moment. It was the first time he had done so since the night before. Then, once more, she became herself. In those previous seconds Gerald had become aware of something dividing them which neither of them would ever mention or ever forget.

ON TERMS

Christine Brooke-Rose

The crescent street he lives in curves like a giant vampire's jaw each house a long and yellow tooth with the identical porches forming a second row. And in the last weeks of my life the street has certainly sucked my blood. I can still see and feel myself hiding behind the pillar in the last porch on the left which belongs to the rich old lady's house or after nightfall lurking among trees of the semicircular gardens that face the crescented houses. Watching him come and go. On my way to the office and again on my way home I stand behind the pillar of the last house for as long as time in my real life allows, and the rich old lady once or twice comes out and smiles at me in faint recognition of my repeated presence or of her youth perhaps unless women really did have more dignity then as if to say leave off, loneliness has its strength and beauty like unrequited love. Have you ever stood he says once when we are still on terms for hours in the cold simply to catch a glimpse of someone? We are talking about a friend of his. The man must be sick he says I could never get that worked up. Perhaps you have never loved I say or maybe merely think perhaps he has never loved. Maybe I murmur no I couldn't either. We are still on terms at that moment in time.

But as I let the street suck my blood while I still have blood to suck we are not on terms and a glimpse is better than no terms at all until I stand all drained of psychic energy from nothing not even a glimpse, glimpses being untimable in a live long day of a full irregular masculine timetable and walk away quickly as if none of it mattered to unnumb my limbs while I still have limbs to unnumb all the way to the small flat in the square block in the big lonely city.

But now there is no need. Nobody knows that my body lies there in my bed in the locked flat in the big city, its atoms all bombarded by those of the barbiturates and slowly undergoing the chemical reaction into compost that will feed no earth no worms no mulching vegetation, only the stinking air in the small room all windows closed. I die alone because I live alone. I give notice at work I have the telephone removed I stop the milk I tell the porter to forward my mail if any to Poste Restante where I call now and again, wearing the semblance of my temporal body, only to find there is no mail except the month's rent reminder and the quarter's demand for rates.

One day no doubt the rent man or the rate man or the gas man must come round and ring the bell and bang the door, and the disturbed molecules of wood will let the smell of my decay waft through and the police perhaps will scatter them with a battering ram or even with the mere brute force of uniformed bodies. I am well aware that I am acting out a fantasy since the porter has a pass-key into the smell of my decay as into all our privacies.

It is because I am acting out a fantasy that I can wear the semblance of my temporal body and move about as if I existed, which of course I do. Anyone with enough love or hate exists even when out of mind or dead. Existence is not a temporal state but an energy which does not stop merely for lack of flesh although in many dead people this energy does degrade itself for lack of love or hate so that it shrinks like a degenerate star into less than a pinpoint weighing many tons. Naturally they feel full of a heavy nothingness of which the rumour spreads apathetically sporadically through live matter like a transuranian element decaying over aeons into lead. And so this is what people in this needle of time think death is.

But I am acting out a fantasy of unrequited love or is it hate that has such driving force I can collect the semblance of my atoms and clothe myself in them and move about at will. I can also move about without the semblance of my atoms. I can do both because both exist in a potential choice which keeps me in a state of dither unable to decide which part of the fantasy I most want to act out: that of being invisibly present at my own death with all my friends aghast and shocked and sad or that of nobody knowing I have died. The first is stronger as a desire so strong it makes me take my life, suicide being a meaningless gesture which says I want to leave you today and come back tomorrow to see how you've taken it. The desire to be thus present at my own death is stronger than the desire that nobody should know I have died but the fear in it is stronger still for I know the answer can only be a slight shock a shrug a sigh of relief. I have no friends and few acquaintances. So I move along two parallel lines of existence trying to have it both ways invisible most of the time and watching my few acquaintances but also keeping up the pretence of appearing now and again at my usual haunts in the semblance of my temporal body so that nobody knows I have died. I fear their indifference more than I want their slight shock their guilt if any or their punishment.

Sooner or later however the choice will have to be made because in time the rent man or the rate man or the gas man will come round and use the pass-key into the smell of my decay.

Unless of course I choose not to act out the fantasy. Then I would find annihilation and some sort of peace perhaps. My energy too would degrade itself for lack of love or hate into less than a pinpoint weighing many tons of heavy nothingness. That would be comforting.

But the driving force of the fantasy is irresistible. I do not in fact watch my few acquaintances or my no friends who do not hold me here but him and only him. Unlike the rent man or the rate man or the gas man he won't come knocking on my door ringing the bell scattering the molecules of wood with sheer brute force into the smell of my decay. Because we're not on terms.

And the being not on terms is the driving force of the fantasy. It drains me of atoms and even of their semblance so that I still stand in the last porch of the curved street and wait for a glimpse of him as he comes and goes. And the greater watching time afforded by my death spreads like a net which must by mere totality of coverage catch all the glimpses possible in the curved space of the street and more. Even the sights of the rich old lady have increased fivefold and for her smile I wear the semblance of my atoms now and again and hide behind the pillar in the double wisdom tooth at the end of the giant vampire's jaw. Watching him come and go.

The multiplying glimpses feed me with fresh particles of psychic energy so that although the vampire's jaw drains me of semblant atoms I in turn draw strength from the glimpses it provides with which I feed the hungry monster of my fantasy which grows and grows until I can be with him at all times and places. Without the fantasy I would cease to exist, fantasy being the existence which does not stop merely for lack of flesh. Without the fantasy I would find some sort of peace perhaps.

He has another woman now reasonably since unable to accept the hurtful terms we are on I break them a married one, a little less convenient as regards consideration not his strongpoint of her timetable as well as his but more convenient in her desires that don't extend to marriage. Not that she feels happy as a quick sly convenience. I am in a privileged position divested as I can be of my temporal atoms. He also rings her after the first time with clumsy gestures and finds her sad oh what a bore he says why take it like that. I'm not a whistling cavalier to shrug it off and move away as if that was what bothered her on the contrary that would be more welcome for shrug it off and move away is what he does in emotional effect if not in physical presence because complacently he equates mere physical presence with emotional effect no generosity of conversation imagination or tenderness being required as well and my self-pity envelops her by analogy. He tells her the same blockaging things in the same words and with the same performance. It's the only way I can show you he says post-passionately as the nearest he can get to words of homage and she also doesn't say but thinks show me what that even in this he is inconsiderate? My angry self-pity envelops her by analogy but with an element of admiring envy for the way she makes more allowances. She knows and accepts as I in my real body know but do not accept that his emotions are low-powered, he has no reserves below the easy surface, his energy too would degrade itself quickly in death for lack of love into less than a pinpoint weighing innumerable tons of heavy nothingness, he would find peace he does. It is true that she is still in the gay light-hearted early phase I know so well and that in time his thoughtless words and manner will erode her gaiety. In time she must crumble from her light-hearted status as a quick sly convenience and bombard him with the atoms of a chain-reaction at which he will shrug be inarticulate move off exactly as he does when she accepts her status as a quick sly convenience. It makes no difference either way. Unless she is altogether more light-hearted through and through.

The rich old lady emerges out of the last house behind whose pillar I wear from invisibility-fatigue the semblance of my temporal body. She nods and smiles. Loneliness has its strength she says don't feed on him too long or you will lose the capacity for it. If it isn't too late she says will you come and take tea with me on Saturday? It would give me great pleasure to communicate with a young person. Madam if I am not altogether dead by then I should be delighted. Come come at your age I'll expect you at four.

He comes and goes. He walks along the double row of teeth in the curved jaw of the vampire. I do not reassume the invisibility which tires me out with vision and knowledge so that he sees me in my temporal body and crosses the road into the semicircular gardens to avoid me reasonably enough is it or cowardly. In any case the force of the fantasy drives me to move my temporal body into his path for further punishment not only from his thoughtless words and manner but from the sudden change in me the moment we are on terms, a change to my early normal vision of an affable sluggish man, a static man nobody ever gets to know any better, who has revealed no hidden dynamism despite the benefit of the doubt given over and over and I look at his thick face and unregarding eyes and think I never would but know I did how could I?

It is as if I had never known him, the last impression returning to the first hello.

—Oh. Hello.

—How are you?

—Oh, all right. Terrible cold, though, don't come near me.

He sees my eroded gaiety and crumbling inconvenience and also thinks how could he but doesn't care whether he did or not.

—I wasn't going to. Nothing could be further from my mind.

—Oh I don't know. He laughs. I wouldn't say nothing. You look well.

Behind his words and manner there is nothing but his words and manner. Love is only the intense desire to know someone and becomes unrequited or is it hate when it finds no one there to know.

—Thank you for enquiring.

The semblance of my atoms creates no semblance of communication. Even in death I say all the wrong things like why did you cross the road to avoid me when I know the answer is my behaviour too embarrassing even for courtesy which never was his strong-point me? I didn't . . . I always walk through the gardens. And things like are you happy? Now that we are on terms I endure fully the sudden change to my first normal vision of a pleasant sluggish man with hardly an atom of love in all that flesh and hardly a pinpoint of interest or curiosity except the prying kind into the weaknesses of others that make him feel so good heavens he says I never ask myself such questions. What are you doing here?

—Walking. Suffering. I don't like suffering it hurts.

—Oh? I'd got the impression you rather enjoyed it.

—So that was your reason. All the wrong things again but they get no reaction anyway. Actually I'm on my way home. I went to town to do some shopping. Window-shopping I mean, I didn't find anything. I'm er—getting married.

—What!

—Thank you. Yes. Next week. I suppose, I couldn't prevail on you, if you would I mean, if you're free, to give me away? As an old friend. I have no family. Saturday 11 o'clock at St Martin's.

—Well. I don't know. Let me see.

The pocket-diary is blank for Saturday at 11 o'clock I know because he sees his quick convenience then and doesn't write it down. Besides in my parallel invisible state I can see Saturday and the wedding-guests all made out of my psychic energy and its almost inexhaustible semblance of atoms. I can even see the white carnation in his buttonhole. Thank you, how nice, I gather the idea tickles your fancy.

—Yes, well, it is rather amusing.

—And your wife of course. I hope she'll come. Sorry it's so informal but I've only just thought of it. Asking you I mean.

—This is all very sudden. How did it, er, who's the lucky man? Are you sure you're not just rebounding?

—From the great love that was ours? Of course. So you see you owe me at least the gesture. How about you, have you found a new . . . mistress?

—I don't want a mistress. If I did, no doubt I'd fix myself up with one.

—No doubt. Well, see you Saturday then. Collect me in the hall of my block at ten to, I'll have a hired car waiting. And please, no presents, we're going abroad immediately. Bye.

So the die is cast on keeping up the pretence that I am alive, appearing here and there in the semblance of my temporal body, especially there on Saturday at 11 o'clock. Not that this way I avoid the answer to the fear inherent in the other course, the slight shock the shrug the sigh of relief if not at my death then at my removal and the resentment at even being asked for a last gesture. The parallel lines meet in the further punishment administered with his every word and manner but the driving force of the fantasy impels me along.

The matter of my rebound my present or future unhappiness and my wedding moves out of his mind as he walks towards his house, naturally since it has no existence except as the fantasy which does not stop for lack of flesh. But then the matter of his new mistress's happiness or otherwise does not dwell in his mind either. He never asks himself such questions. What do you see yourself as, I enquire in exasperation at his lack of enthusiasm for all things once when we are still on terms that drag my gaiety down into his conversational lethargy me, he says I don't see myself as anything I just drift. So that his image too must degrade itself in death for lack of love into less than a pinpoint weighing many tons of heavy nothingness which is what people in this needle of time think death is. And so it will be when I have ceased to act out the fantasy. A comforting thought. But the being not on terms is the driving force which impels me to invent new terms, for of course we are on terms even if only those of agreeing to give me away. The terms we are on feed the hungry monster of my fantasy which absorbs the hurts like immunizing poison so that the early normal vision of an affable sluggish man dissolves and the dynamic image of his absence grows.

On the morning of my marriage he emerges from his house in the vampire's jaw alone and walks along the double row of giant teeth. His wife for reasons best known to herself namely that she has caught his germ or that he has dissuaded her declines to attend. His cancellation of the quick sly convenience fills me with joy and triumph at his small preference for a tickled fancy and in my invisibility I follow him. He has so few and such small preferences I can gloat over this one. There will be time enough to fill the church with the semblance of my no friends and few acquaintances. Nobody knows that my body lies in bed in my locked flat in the square block rapidly undergoing the chemical reaction into compost that as yet feeds no earth, only the stinking air in the small room all windows closed. At the Poste Restante I collect a cheque for five guineas from him.

The area of his street is residential, dead. So dead that a big hearse waits outside the last house in the present, heading two dark and empty cars. The boot of the hearse is up as if the coffin had just been slid in or a last bouquet or wreath of flowers added to the others and all the flowers are white.

He stops. Not out of superstition or to make a gesture of homage since gestures or words of homage do not come naturally to him if at all but because the white carnations remind him of his empty buttonhole. The area of his street is residential, dead, without a flower-shop in sight.

He hesitates. I give him that, yes, I mark that up in his favour. It goes to join all the awkward short-lived tendernesses he uses when still uncertain of seduction, sham but tendernesses still and in his favour, weighing a little against the later hurts if not viewed in their light but in the light of the beginning when I so much want to count all in his favour. He looks at the house with the curtains drawn and the garlanded door half-open. The coffin underneath the mass of white flowers waits for the few mourners about to emerge and the murmuring undertaker.

He doesn't hesitate for long. His left hand quickly picks a white carnation from the end wreath on the hearse, his right hand joins the left to fix it in his buttonhole as he walks quickly on.

The rich old lady lies inside the coffin and smiles, turning her dead face towards me all surrounded with thin white hair. Death has its strength and I don't mind she says. I have seen life and willingly give a flower of my death to adorn a married man about to give away his young escaped mistress into the hands of death.

I mind however.

—My dear child, why?

—Because I created the flower for his buttonhole out of my atoms, allowing only for the semblance of a result, not for a real result with a real origin and in you of all people.

—And the origin with a free-will gesture in another human being, in two other human beings instead of in your fantasy shocks you?

—Yes.

—Dear child, don't mind so much. Come come at your age I'll see you at four.

And the real result with a real origin galvanizes me into the semblance of my atoms all in white down the stairs into the hall just as he enters. He looks astonished, white? he says. The porter looks even more astonished at my presence which waves gaily sails through the door and folds itself into the hired car, followed by all those molecules of thick flesh with hardly an atom of love beneath the white carnation.

—I thought it was informal.

—It is. But one only dies once.

—Oh come.

—I'm glad you thought of a buttonhole. And thank you for the cheque. You shouldn't have.

—You look . . . very fetching he says with surprise regret boredom impatience I feel too disembodied to care. It is the first compliment he has ever paid me apart from the privilege of being seduced by him with awkward short-lived tendernesses the only way he can show me what.

The church is fuller than I expected. All my no friends and more than my few acquaintances are there made out of more than my psychic energy on both sides of the aisle. I do not know the wedding-guests on the bridegroom's side. I know the bridegroom a little, the skilful tendernesses he uses for seduction still weighing against the brutal annihilation to come when he destroys the fantasy and its energy degenerates for lack of love or hate into less than a pinpoint of heavy nothingness. I walk the aisle on my once lover's arm to Purcell's Trumpet Voluntary. I promise to obey. I have no choice. Because one day the rent man or the rate man or the gas man will come round and ring the bell or bang the door and the disturbed molecules of wood will let the smell of my decay waft through. But I shall not be present at my own death my friends aghast and shocked and sad for the answer is a shrug a sigh of relief at my removal and my non-existence with the energy of my fantasy degenerated to less than a pinpoint of heavy nothingness. That will be comforting but you must kiss the bride yes kiss the bride.

I don't know who the best man is who kisses me, a friend of the bridegroom his façade perhaps, the skilful tendernesses he uses for seduction until the fantasy becomes destroyed. You too must kiss the bride.

He hesitates. I give him that, yes, I mark that up in his favour he has given me away made his last gesture paid his five guineas that is enough. I turn my face towards him in its veil of tulle and see him start in horror.

So the process has begun already. The fantasy loses its driving force and cannot hold the semblance of my atoms in a pretence of life. What does he see? The dead face of the rich old lady he robbed whose white carnation he stole to adorn the tickled fancy of a married man giving away his young escaped mistress into the hands of death? Or is it my dead face he sees its atoms all bombarded by those of the barbiturates, rapidly undergoing the chemical change to compost that as yet feeds no earth no worms no mulching vegetation, only the stinking air in the small room all windows closed?

He draws away. The semblances of the chief wedding-guests who are witnesses in the vestry laugh and tease him as we drink champagne a little out of place for there is no reception. I have arranged it so. No you can't get out of it you gave her away you must propose the toast you too must kiss the bride. I turn my face towards him in its veil of tulle and see him stare in horror. I search for the reflection in his eyes each one of which throws back a dead face, in the left eye very old with thin white hair and a deep regarding look, in the right eye young but crumbling with eroded gaiety, skeletal, the mouth curved like a vampire's jaw and the skull surrounded in white tulle he yells.

—All right, keep your precious carnation!

He flings it in my decomposing face. A grey aisle of silence forms through the wedding-guests who are witnesses as he bolts along it to the vestry door into the church where the remaining guests wait for the triumphal march and down the aisle of the church into the world of nice casual emotions and familiar residential streets that stand secure in parallels except for one that curves like the jaw of a giant vampire with a double row of teeth which in my day has sucked my blood.

In a month of time no doubt the gas man or the rent man will ring the bell on my door and smell the smell of my decay as it wafts through the disturbed molecules of wood. Or the police perhaps will scatter them with a battering ram or even with the brute force of uniformed bodies unless the porter uses his pass-key into the privacy of my death.

The fantasy has lost its driving force and cannot hold the semblance of my atoms in a pretence of life. My no friends and my few acquaintances dissolve, the bridegroom takes the energy of my pretence and in less than no time degrades it for lack of love or hate into less than a pinpoint of heavy nothingness. I have a tea-time date with the rich old lady at four. The process of degeneration is painful but comforting as far as I remember I have a tea-time date with understanding as far as I can tell the process is painful but comforting as far as I

THE ONLY STORY

William Trevor

I noticed the date because I was at the time reading a newspaper. It was Friday, March 26th, 1971. *A matron who danced a jig in a Nottingham nursing home was justifiably dismissed for misconduct,* I read. *Mr Justice Cummings-Bruce said that Mrs Hazel Storey danced a jig with the assistant matron, Miss Mavis Stone, after Mrs Jean Osbourne had lost her job as cook. Mr Justice Cummings-Bruce totally rejected the matron's 'unconvincing explanation' that the jig was an expression of delight at news of more patients.*

As I read, I was aware that my wife had come into the kitchen and was talking to me. I looked up from the newspaper, noticing then the day and the date printed at the top.

I had known that my wife was going to leave me because she had repeatedly said that she intended to do so. What I hadn't known was that it would happen quite like this, that she would enter the kitchen in which she and I and the children had had breakfast and where I was still drinking tea, that she would say to me that she'd taken the children to school and that at the end of the day neither she nor the children would be returning to our pleasant, semi-detached, three-storey house in Putney.

'I'll pack,' my wife said

She's fair-haired, with faded blue eyes and some freckles on the bridge of her nose and on her forehead. She's a healthy-looking girl, thirty-four last birthday, May 23rd, a Gemini like me. In letters that I've written to her I've clearly stated that she's beautiful. Other men, and women, have many times remarked to me that my wife is beautiful and seems far too young to be the mother of three schoolchildren. I somehow can't see Pamela's beauty any more, although in the interests of truth I naturally admit that once I considered her far more than pretty, a kind of goddess really. And the letters I wrote on the subject are probably still there for anyone to see.

'Now look, Pamela,' I said.

'I'll pick them up by taxi,' she said. 'We'll go straight to Belvedere Court.'

'What's Belvedere Court?'

'I told you.'

It was a block of flats where they were going to live, she and Sophie and Jemina and Jock. Her father. Wing Commander R. E. Adamson, had apparently purchased this flat in Belvedere Court for them. 'Oh, call me Reggie,' he'd said to me a long time ago now, before he formed the opinion that I was just about as suitable a husband for his daughter as a crested mynah would have been. It must have upset him terribly, poor man, that I had fathered the only three grandchildren he possessed. And yet, to be absolutely honest, I've never been able to see what he had against me.

Seeming in no hurry to pack, Pamela ground some coffee. I could read her like a book: she'd make us some and while we drank it she'd try to talk everything through yet again. She'd advanced us to the brink, me, and herself, and the children. She'd done it quite nicely, really: the flat already purchased by the Wing Commander, and arrangements made for a job she intended to take up, plus of course some kind of allowance from the Wing Commander, jolly Reggie as they used to call him in the Bayswater pubs, the Moscow Arms in particular. Everything was as neat as a new pin: after fifteen years of marriage the Wing Commander's daughter was about to walk out of the house with her clothes and her children's clothes in suitcases that were, strictly speaking, my property. In the meantime she intended to have a last crack at making me see what the Wing Commander would have called sense.

'Listen to this,' I said, reading from the newspaper. '*A matron who danced a jig in a Nottingham nursing home—*'

'Please, James.'

'*Mr Justice Cumming-Bruce—*'

'Oh, for God's sake, James!'

The trouble, as she saw it, was that I'd lost my job. Ever since we'd been married I'd worked in an advertising agency, writing about paint, wallpaper, vending machines, an airline, a steamship company, margarine, instant coffee, and repacked frozen chickens. I had written about other products as well, such as Dutch beer and electric stoves. In fact, one way or another during the course of fifteen years I'd written about almost everything. I'd described a fork-lift truck as a gentle giant and a shoe as an aristocrat. *Are You Your Husband's Status Symbol?* I'd written, an effort to interest women in a range of cosmetics. But it was with the airline account that I'd run into difficulties. I'd written a piece of prose, which an account executive had admiringly described as 'your iron hand in your velvet glove'. The advertising manager of the airline, a new man called Mr Page, didn't care for it at all. He read it and pushed the piece of paper on which it was written away from him, moving it so skilfully over the smooth teak of the agency table that it floated over the edge and fell on to the carpet. He watched me picking it up and then he said: 'Our job in the airline business is to get arses on to seats. I think we should all remember that.'

I said something to the man Page, making some joke or other, but he didn't laugh, and then I found myself saying that he appeared to have no sense of humour. I was smiling myself when I said that, to show that there wasn't anything wrong with my own sense of humour. 'I'd ask you to remember,' he said, repeating what later turned out to be his favourite phrase, 'that our job is to get arses on to seats.' Afterwards, over some gin, he said it again, looking at me in such a way as to imply that I, for one, was in no way qualified to persuade the public towards his airline. He spoke slowly; he talked a lot about the airline business and his own ascent within it; he had never forgotten, he claimed, that his job was to get arses of the public on to the seats in his DC-8s, his Tridents, and his Boeings. Suddenly, while actually nodding agreement with him, I hit him in the stomach and then across the head.

'You can take the car,' I said to Pamela. 'I don't want the car. You'll need it for the children.'

She added saccharine to her coffee and stirred it in. She hadn't expected me to say that. She'd expected me, here on the brink, to plead, to promise that that very day I'd shave and go out, that I'd look for a job, that I'd snap out of whatever it was I was in. I smiled at her and she didn't smile back. She even pretended she didn't notice my smile. She spoke, not looking at me.

'You don't mind,' she said.

In reply to that I said I thought it was much the best, for the children's sake as well as everyone else's. If Reggie was being so generous she should take advantage of it, of course she should.

'You won't even miss us,' she said, still not looking at me. She'd said it before, last night, last week, over and over again.

'No,' I said. 'No, Pamela, I won't miss you.'

That was true. I wasn't going to miss Pamela, whom I'd once believed to be beautiful, and I wasn't going to miss my three children. She was leaving me for that reason, because I couldn't love her any more and because I couldn't love them. She was leaving me because eight months ago I'd hit an unpleasant man in the stomach and then across the head, an action that should never be taken, especially when a man is holding a glass of gin and tonic in his hand. For eight months I had refused to seek other employment. In our house in Putney I'd begun a new life, reading the newspaper and the *TV Times* and the *Radio Times*, drinking tea, coffee, wine, whisky with sweet sherry in it, and eating whatever she cooked for me. I listened to the wireless and watched television, especially in the mornings, the children's programmes and the educational ones. To please her I went to see Dr Swayles because she said she thought I wasn't well, but Dr Swayles, a man who looked like an undertaker, said I was perfectly fit. 'Perfectly,' I reported to her when I returned, and then we quarrelled, like we did whenever I spoke, it seemed.

Our quarrels were all the same: she said that I had deliberately lost my job and that I now deliberately refused to seek another, that I had become a bore who'd lost all feeling for her and for the children, that I was a lump of flesh about the house. I don't remember ever saying much in our quarrels except to agree with her. I did try and explain: I tried to say that after fifteen years' involvement with paint and pre-packed chickens I felt drained, quite literally, as if tubes had been attached to me. I'd felt it when I assaulted the man Page: it was a crude, physical action, but it was all I was capable of. Some part of me was already dead. She didn't listen to a word.

'The name of the matron,' I said on the morning of March 26th, 'is Mrs Hazel Storey. She danced the jig with Mavis Stone.'

She finished her coffee and went away, leaving me to do the washing up. I removed the car keys from my key-ring and placed them on a table in the hall. I returned to the kitchen and closed and locked the door. I had no desire to see her again and certainly not to hear her voice. I ran hot water into the sink and added Sainsbury's washing-up liquid to it. I liked doing the dishes. I liked the feel of the warm soapy water.

I heard the bang of the hall door at twenty-five past one by the kitchen clock. I'd read the paper several times in the meanwhile, and I washed down the walls and mopped the floor. The day before I'd had everything off the shelves and had scrubbed them and put everything back again, more methodically than Pamela had had them arranged before, I'd cleaned the windows and the oven of the gas cooker. I'd polished the toaster with Duraglit.

I unlocked the kitchen door when I knew she'd gone and I bolted the hall door in case she tried to come back. She'd gone and she could stay gone: she didn't understand, she hadn't even tried.

I tidied the house. I was glad that at last I could do this properly. I plugged in the Electrolux and cleaned the children's two rooms and then I cleaned the room that had been mine and Pamela's. I did the landing and the stairs. I thought about mopping over the vinyl in Jock's little attic, but I decided to leave it till later.

While I worked I thought about the usual four people, Pamela, the Wing Commander, the man Page, and William. Two days ago I'd bought an exercise book in Woolworth's in Putney, and in this I intended to write down the facts. At a later time William would do what editing was necessary, William being a real writer, as you might say, not one whose services are called upon in order to get arses on to seats. William is suitable for this task in another way also because in the fullness of time, I believe, he'll become my children's stepfather.

These were the only people I thought about as I cleaned and tidied the house, because to think of other people had become an effort. I felt sorry in a way that the man Page should have become involved in this because he, in fact, was no more guilty than lots of other similar men. Faceless names come back to me: Consby, who was the managing director of the advertising firm I'd worked for, and Regan, who was one of its many fast-moving executives, and Hughes of the margarine account, Pope of wallpaper and paint, Blackledge of vending machines, who always had to eat his meals alone because of his religion, and Thomas, Edgell, Horner, Brown, Kenyon, Bottle-Travers, Cameron, Ingoldsby, Townsend, God knows who they were. But the man Page was the last, flicking the paper over the polished teak surface, watching me when I bent down to pick it up.

I wound the flex of the Electrolux carefully before putting the machine away in its usual place, a cupboard on the first-floor landing. Then I pulled down the blinds in all the rooms, starting at the top of the house. I don't know why I cleaned everywhere like that, except maybe because it gave me pleasure, although there may have been a reason that I don't know about. I know why I pulled down the blinds: because I don't like sunlight any more.

In the sitting-room, which is a long, rather narrow room on the ground floor, with the windows set in an alcove, I pulled down the blinds also. I poured myself some whisky and added sweet South African sherry to it. Then I telephoned William and told him that Pamela had gone. He said he wasn't surprised.

'Listen,' I said, about to say something further. But as I spoke the word I reached out for my drink, which was on the same table as the telephone, on the far side of some magazines. My fingers touched the glass and as I felt the coolness of it I saw that there was someone else in the room. There was someone sitting at the table in the window.

William was making a noise on the phone. I told him to be quiet and

then I put the phone down, cutting him off. In doing so I must have
taken my eyes off the figure I'd seen sitting at the table in the window.
I looked and it wasn't there any more. I dialled William's number again
and told him that everything I'd believed for the last six months was
correct: I was dead, I said again to William, and William again advised
me to seek psychiatric aid. I laughed at that. 'Who killed me, William?'
I asked.

They said I'd become a bore because I believed that the greater part
of me had suffered death. Pamela thought me a bore, and William. The
Wing Commander had told me openly, on the phone one day a month
ago, that in his opinion I was round the twist. I knew I wasn't. I knew
what had happened, and so did they except that they wouldn't admit it.
They all kept saying that I must snap out of it, a most irritating
command.

'Who killed me, William?' I asked again, and William told me for
God's sake to stop drinking and showed little interest when I said that
I'd just seen a figure at the window table. 'You do this for me, William,'
I said. 'You write down whatever I leave out.' And then I told him about
how I'd bought an exercise book in Woolworth's the day before yesterday, and how the exercise book would be here when they found the
body. The body, I explained, as I'd explained before, had no interest in
living without what had already departed.

It surprised me that people were so obtuse about this. Pamela said
I'd become obsessed with a sense of failure in my life, and kept on
saying that there was no need for it. William, who is my brother, agreed
with this view. The Wing Commander couldn't grasp what I was
talking about at all. To me it was all quite simple. 'Listen,' I'd said,
the first time I'd tried to explain to Pamela, 'when death occurs it isn't
just the body that goes. There's a person, Pamela. Did a person die,
Pamela, writing advertisements for pre-packaged fowls, earning cash
to keep you in the manner the Wing Commander accustomed you to?
Did a person give up the ghost under the strain of doing what he didn't
want to do for fifteen years, of keeping silent in the presence of men like
Page with his arses and his seats? Did a person get tired of living,
Pamela?'

I hit the man Page because I saw the figure, a shadow, really, at that
time just by the door. I hit him because the thought came into my mind
and the shadow nodded at me.

'James,' William said on the phone. 'Please, James, don't go on with
this nonsense.'

'I'm leaving the exercise book,' I said. 'I've drawn the blinds. I've
bolted the hall door.'

'But what's going to happen? What d'you expect?'

'For the shell of me to die. Today,' I said. 'March 26th.'

'James, you're terribly sick.'

I put the receiver down and saw the figure again, at the table. The head turned and looked across the room at me with my own eyes. The lips were smiling, the flesh about the eyes was crinkled in pleasant laughter lines. It was like looking at an old photograph, a brownish figure sitting there in a light-brown Donegal tweed jacket and flannel trousers.

I knew I was right. I had talked myself into it all, Pamela said in her down-to-earth way, but that wasn't so. I knew that all I enjoyed now were physical sensations, like warm soapy water on my hands. I couldn't feel for her or the children; even the Wing Commander and the man Page I couldn't dislike in a normal way. I was finished with all the important things, but no one could see it except me.

At twenty past three I sat down and proceeded to write down these facts in the exercise book I'd bought in Woolworth's. I continued to pour myself, and to drink, glasses of whisky and sweet sherry. The figure in the Donegal tweed jacket was seated near the telephone, still smiling at me. No matter what happened I did not at that time intend to kill myself.

At five o'clock I moved towards the telephone and the figure rose and went to sit where I'd been sitting, at the table in the window. I telephoned William again to say that I'd written a certain amount down in the exercise book and to tell him that I didn't intend to take my own life. He told me he'd have to come round if I went on like this. I said there was no point in that because the hall door was locked and would remain so. I'd keep in touch, I said.

After that I telephoned the airline that employed the man Page and asked the girl on the exchange for Mr Page.

'Page,' he said.

'Ah, Mr Page, I'm the man who hit you that day, about eight months ago—'

He put the receiver down, and in a way I don't blame him. I don't quite know what I'd have said to him, except to try and explain, but I doubt really that he'd have understood.

I telephoned the Wing Commander and told him that I was grateful to him for his generosity. There was life insurance, I told him, but in circumstances like these one never quite knew with life insurance companies. 'What bloody circumstances?' he snapped at me, and again I was cut off.

I wasn't afraid of either of them: there was nothing left in me to be afraid with. In the past I've always been afraid, of all the world of people outside myself. I've been afraid and pretended I haven't been because of shame of some kind: afraid of Pamela and of my children and of Pamela's father, and of William. It was fear that sat me down to write about paint and wallpapers, and fear that kept me quiet for fifteen years.

In the end it was responsible for the decease of part of me, because with all the pretending and weakness and failure that it had inspired there was nothing left of that part at all. I don't know why people have made me frightened; I don't know why it made me so ashamed that I couldn't talk about it. My son is five years old: I've looked at him and looked away, fearful because he is a human being.

I returned to the window table, and the figure returned to the chair by the telephone. I sat down and brought the facts in this exercise book up to date, up to twenty-five minutes past five, March 26th, 1971.

Near the bottom of the stairs there was a child, smiling also. Higher up, something else moved, withdrawing as I entered the hall. The child was sitting on the third step, looking at his hands, which were moving, the fingers playing some child's game. In the sitting-room the telephone was ringing, and at the table in the window the figure sat, head turned towards me. I heard noises upstairs as I picked up the receiver.

She asked me if I was all right and when I replied she said at once that I'd been drinking. William had been in touch with her, William was worried apparently, and so was she.

'Who killed me, Pamela?' I said.

'James, for God's sake, stop this now—'

'The house is full of smiling people,' I said. 'There's a child on the stairs. There's someone less than twenty feet away from me as I'm speaking to you. Others are upstairs. That's all they were waiting for, Pamela: for you and Sophie and Jemina and Jock to go.'

'It's in your mind, James. Don't you see, darling? Can't you see? Oh darling, shall I come to you?'

'I'm going to bed now,' I said, telling a lie, and then I said goodbye.

William rang as soon as I replaced the receiver. Pamela was worried, he said, and it seemed that the Wing Commander had been on to him. I told him I was going to bed. I said I thought I'd be all right, that Pamela's going off had probably caused me to snap out of it, whatever it was. As I spoke, the child came into the room. I didn't like it, seeing the two of them together. 'Thank God,' William was saying into my ear, and he told me in a typical way not to drink any more. The child was dressed in brown clothes also, with the same eyes and precisely the same smile.

I poured myself more whisky and sherry, watched by both of them. I knew what they were saying. They were saying that I'd committed a form of suicide already and I could commit another form now, after which we would rest together. I killed myself, afraid to be myself. My fear had killed the things I'd wanted to do, the books I'd wanted to write, and the people in them. 'I know a chap,' the Wing Commander's voice said again, coming at me across fifteen years, 'who runs an advertising outfit.' But I didn't want to go into an advertising outfit. 'It'll only be a year or two,' Pamela said. 'A year or two won't kill us, darling.'

The telephone rang in the sitting-room again, but I didn't answer it. It stopped after three minutes. 'I will not kill myself,' I said aloud.

There was breathing in the room, and a kind of whispering. The child was on the floor by the sofa, the other at the window table. The whispering became louder. I could see the lips of both of them slightly moving, although the smile never left them. God did not give me my small talent that I should have destroyed it over fifteen years as the servant of Mr Blackledge of the vending machine industry. What glory for God is there in that? What glory for the human state, the body and the spirit, the mind, the brain, the imagination? These thoughts did not come from me. I whispered the thoughts but the thoughts came from them. They made me whisper them and write them, as they made me assault the man Page, as they made Pamela leave this house.

I can't move now. I could not cross the room to the window table because I know that the figure at the window table will no longer change places with me. There's a kind of shaking in my body that affects this writing, but still my hand is permitted to move the pen across the paper. I can still taste the harsh, sweet mixture in my glass.

The window stretches miles away, in the narrowness of the room. Everything is blurred. the room is full of a brown mist like sepia; the smiles and the eyes come out of it.

It is silent now. The whispering is finished and I know it won't come back. I know what's going to happen in this room because I'm part of them again. My glass is empty. I cannot close my eyes.

He moves from the window and crosses to where the child is playing. He bends and touches the child. The hands move down to the child's throat, and the child does not cease to smile. The skin's drawn back from staring eyes, the tongue comes out, choking from that smiling mouth. The child's limbs jerk in convulsion. Blood trickles from the mouth, but the child still moves.

The telephone is ringing as I watch. They are dying together because they are one, and I am dying too, the rest of me, because I cannot stop the shaking in my body. My heart is thumping in a way I know to be unusual. I cannot watch them twitching and yet I cannot take my eyes away.

They'll read all this and not believe it. My mind, they'll simply say, not knowing that this room is full of death. One day I hit a man, unable any longer to pretend. I hit him, defending myself, like always I have wanted to defend myself because there was always a need for it. But when I hit him it was just too late: I was eaten away by my own internecine wars. It was only the shell I defended when I hit a man, that simple gesture of my life. I wasn't afraid to hit him because already I'd nothing to be afraid with. The spirit can die: oh yes, it can.

The telephone still rings, with desperation now. The figures jerk less as they lie ungainly on the floor. I think they fade to lighter brown as I watch, as sweat sticks my clothes to me and runs from my forehead into my eyes. I wait for an explosion inside me, watching the twitching on the floor and knowing that when it ceases the explosion will occur. I hope William will make something of this. I hope he'll understand. And Pamela. And the children some day. I hope they'll think not too badly of me, and forgive what has to be forgiven. I miss them now in these last moments, as though something has come into me again. It has, something has, and more than that's come into me: I'm frightened now. They're twitching on the floor. Their faces smile, as though they mean no harm, as though those awful throttled faces could possibly mean no harm. They know I'm frightened. They want me to be frightened. They're crawling towards me, both of them. They're going to kill me and I'm frightened now of death. My heart is shaking my whole body back and forth. My heart is pummelling me to death. They're moving slowly, oh God, I cannot move at all. I would say sorry, God, to Pamela now, and I would tell the truth at last, about being so frightened, for so long, alone. It's awful to be frightened, don't you see, all the time, of people? Oh God, make William understand. Oh God, stop them. Stop them making me lift my eyes. Stop them coming closer. Oh God, stop this sweat on me. Stop this thing going on inside me. Why cannot I cease this writing?

It is my only story, that is why. The telephone still rings; I feel a calmness now. I walk, all of a sudden, with Pamela and the children, through beech woods where we walked once, in Dorset. It was happiness of a kind. Pamela would have said it was, and the children too. And yet the shame was there, hiding away, holding back a revelation of the other. I lived alone and pretended, with that same smile they haunt me with. The shame was always the worst; I feel no shame now. I feel only that I must look on them again, my own death, my murder, my suicide. How dark the room is. Oh God, help me now. Oh God, I hope that William will underst . . .

THE LOVES OF LADY PURPLE

Angela Carter

Inside the pink-striped booth of the Asiatic Professor only the marvellous existed and there was no such thing as daylight.

The puppet master is always dusted with a little darkness. In direct relation to his skill he propagates the most bewildering enigmas for, the more lifelike his marionettes, the more godlike his manipulations and the more radical the symbiosis between inarticulate doll and articulating fingers. The puppeteer speculates in a no-man's-limbo between the real and that which, although we know very well it is not, nevertheless seems to be real. He is the intermediary between us, his audience, the living, and they, the dolls, the undead, who cannot live at all and yet who mimic the living in every detail since, though they cannot speak or weep, still they project those signals of signification we instantly recognize as language.

The master of marionettes vitalizes inert stuff with the dynamics of his self. The sticks dance, make love, pretend to speak and, finally, personate death; yet, so many Lazaruses out of their graves they spring again in time for the next performance and no worms drip from their noses nor dust clogs their eyes. All complete, they once again offer their brief imitations of men and women with an exquisite precision which is all the more disturbing because we know it to be false; and so this art, if viewed theologically, may, perhaps, be blasphemous.

Although he was only a poor travelling showman, the Asiatic Professor had become a consummate virtuoso of puppetry. He transported his collapsible theatre, the cast of his single drama, and a variety of properties in a horse-drawn cart and, after he played his play in many beautiful cities which no longer exist, such as Shanghai, Constantinople, and St Petersburg, he and his small entourage arrived at last in a country in Middle Europe where the mountains sprout jags as sharp and unnatural as those a child outlines with his crayon, a dark, superstitious Transylvania where they wreathed suicides with garlic, pierced them through the heart with stakes, and buried them at crossroads while warlocks continually practised rites of immemorial beastliness in the forests.

He had only the two assistants, a deaf boy in his teens, his nephew, to whom he taught his craft, and a foundling dumb girl no more than seven or eight they had picked up on their travels. When the Professor spoke, nobody could understand him for he knew only his native tongue, which was an incomprehensible rattle of staccato k's and t's, so he did not speak at all in the ordinary course of things and, if they had taken separate paths to silence, all, in the end, signed a perfect pact with it. But, when the Professor and his nephew sat in the sun outside their booth in the mornings before performances, they held interminable dialogues in sign language punctuated by soft, wordless grunts and whistles so that the choreographed quiet of their discourse was like the mating dance of tropic birds. And this means of communication, so delicately distanced from humanity, was peculiarly apt for the Professor, who had rather the air of a visitant from another world where the mode of being was conducted in nuances rather than affirmatives. This was due partly to his extreme age, for he was very old although he carried his years lightly even if, these days, in this climate, he always felt a little chilly and so wrapped himself always in a moulting, woollen shawl; yet, more so, it was caused by his benign indifference to everything except the simulacra of the living he himself created.

Besides, however far the entourage travelled, not one of its members had ever comprehended to any degree the foreign. They were all natives of the fairground and, after all, all fairs are the same. Perhaps every single fair is no more than a dissociated fragment of one single, great, original fair which was inexplicably scattered long ago in a diaspora of the amazing. Whatever its location, a fair maintains its invariable, self-consistent atmosphere. Hieratic as knights in chess, the painted horses on the roundabouts describe perpetual circles as immutable as those of the planets and as immune to the drab world of here and now whose inmates come to gape at such extraordinariness, such freedom from actuality. The huckster's raucous invitations are made in a language beyond language, or, perhaps, in that ur-language of grunt and bark which lies behind all language. Everywhere, the same old women hawk glutinous candies which seem devised only to make flies drunk on sugar and, though the outward form of such excessive sweets may vary from place to place, their nature, never. A universal cast of two-headed dogs, dwarfs, alligator men, bearded ladies and giants in leopard-skin loin-cloths reveal their singularities in the sideshows and, wherever they come from, they share the sullen glamour of deformity, an internationality which acknowledges no geographic boundaries. Here, the grotesque is the order of the day.

The Asiatic Professor picked up the crumbs that fell from this heaping table yet never seemed in the least at home there for his affinities did not lie with its harsh sounds and primary colouring although it was the only home he knew. He had the wistful charm of a Japanese flower which only blossoms when dropped in water for he, too, revealed his passions through a medium other than himself and this was his heroine, the puppet, Lady Purple.

She was the Queen of Night. There were glass rubies in her head for eyes and her ferocious teeth, carved out of mother o'pearl, were always on show for she had a permanent smile. Her face was as white as chalk because it was covered with the skin of supplest white leather which also clothed her torso, jointed limbs, and complication of extremities. Her beautiful hands seemed more like weapons because her nails were so long, five inches of pointed tin enamelled scarlet, and she wore a wig of black hair arranged in a chignon more heavily elaborate than any human neck could have endured. This monumental *chevelure* was stuck through with many brilliant pins tipped with pieces of broken mirror so that, every time she moved, she cast a multitude of scintillating reflections which danced about the theatre like mice of light. Her clothes were all of deep, dark, slumbrous colours—profound pinks, crimson, and the vibrating purple with which she was synonymous, a purple the colour of blood in a love suicide.

She must have been the masterpiece of a long-dead, anonymous artisan and yet she was nothing but a curious structure until the Professor touched her strings, for it was he who filled her with necromantic vigour. He transmitted to her an abundance of the life he himself seemed to possess so tenuously and, when she moved, she did not seem so much a cunningly simulated woman as a monstrous goddess, at once preposterous and magnificent, who transcended the notion she was dependent on his hands and appeared wholly real and yet entirely other. Her actions were not so much an imitation as a distillation and intensification of those of a born woman and so she could become the quintessence of eroticism, for no woman born would have dared to be so blatantly seductive.

The Professor allowed no one else to touch her. He himself looked after her costumes and jewellery. When the show was over, he placed his marionette in a specially constructed box and carried her back to the lodging house where he and his children shared a room, for she was too precious to be left in the flimsy theatre and, besides, he could not sleep unless she lay beside him.

The catchpenny title of the vehicle for this remarkable actress was:

The Notorious Amours of Lady Purple, the Shameless Oriental Venus.
Everything in the play was entirely exotic. The incantatory ritual of the
drama instantly annihilated the rational and imposed upon the audience a magic alternative in which nothing was in the least familiar. The
series of tableaux which illustrated her story were in themselves so filled
with meaning that when the Professor chanted her narrative in his
impenetrable native tongue, the compulsive strangeness of the spectacle
was enhanced rather than diminished. As he crouched above the stage
directing his heroine's movements, he recited a verbal recitative in a
voice which clanged, rasped, and swooped up and down in a weird
duet with the stringed instrument from which the dumb girl struck
peculiar intervals. But it was impossible to mistake him when the
Professor spoke in the character of Lady Purple herself for then his
voice modulated to a thick, lascivious murmur like fur soaked in honey
which sent unwilling shudders of pleasure down the spines of the
watchers. In the iconography of the melodrama, Lady Purple stood for
passion and all her movements were calculations in an angular geometry
of sexuality.

The Professor somehow always contrived to have a few handbills
printed off in the language of the country where they played. These
always gave the title of his play and then they used to read as follows:

*Come and see all that remains of Lady Purple, the famous prostitute and wonder of
the East!*

A unique sensation. See how the unappeasable appetites of Lady Purple turned
her at last into the very puppet you see before you, pulled only by the strings of
lust. Come and see the very doll, the only surviving relic of the shameless
Oriental Venus herself.

The bewildering entertainment possessed almost a religious intensity
for, since there can be no spontaneity in a puppet drama, it always tends
towards the rapt intensity of ritual, and, at its conclusion, as the audience stumbled from the darkened booth, it had almost suspended
disbelief and was more than half convinced, as the Professor assured
them so eloquently, that the bizarre figure who had dominated the stage
was indeed the petrification of a universal whore and had once been a
woman in whom too much life had negated life itself, whose kisses had
withered like acids and whose embrace blasted like lightning. But the
Professor and his assistants immediately dismantled the scenery and put
away the dolls who were, after all, only mundane wood and, next day,
the play was played again.

This is the story of Lady Purple as performed by the Professor's puppets to the delirious *obbligato* of the dumb girl's samisen and the audible click of the limbs of the actors.

*

The Notorious Amours of Lady
Purple
the Shameless Oriental
Venus

When she was only a few days old, her mother wrapped her in a tattered blanket and abandoned her on the doorstep of a prosperous merchant and his barren wife. These respectable bourgeois were to become the siren's first dupes. They lavished upon her all the attentions which love and money could devise and yet they reared a flower which, although perfumed, was carnivorous. At the age of twelve, she seduced her foster father. Utterly besotted with her, he trusted to her the key of the safe where he kept all his money and she immediately robbed it of every farthing.

Packing his treasure in a laundry basket together with the clothes and jewellery he had already given her, she then stabbed her first lover and his wife, her foster mother, in their bellies with a knife used in the kitchen to slice fish. Then she set fire to their house to cover the traces of her guilt. She annihilated her own childhood in the blaze that destroyed her first home and, springing like a corrupt phoenix from the pyre of her crime, she rose again in the pleasure quarters, where she at once hired herself out to the madame of the most imposing brothel.

In the pleasure quarters, life passed entirely in artificial day for the bustling noon of those crowded alleys came at the time of drowsing midnight for those who lived outside 'that inverted, sinister, abominable world which functioned only to gratify the whims of the senses. Every rococo desire the mind of man might, in its perverse ingenuity, devise found ample gratification here, amongst the halls of mirrors, the flagellation parlours, the cabarets of nature-defying copulations, and the ambiguous soirées held by men-women and female men. Flesh was the speciality of every house and it came piping hot, served up with all the garnishes imaginable. The Professor's puppets dryly and perfunctorily performed these tactical manœuvres like toy soldiers in a mock battle of carnality.

Along the streets, the women for sale, the mannequins of desire, were displayed in wicker cages so that potential customers could saunter past inspecting them at leisure. These exalted prostitutes sat motionless as idols. Upon their real features had been painted symbolic abstractions of the various aspects of allure and the fantastic elaboration of their dress hinted it covered a different kind of skin. The cork heels of their shoes were so high they could not walk but only totter and the sashes round their waists were of brocade so stiff the movements of the arms were cramped and scant so they presented attitudes of physical unease which, though powerfully moving, derived partly, at least, from the deaf assistant's lack of manual dexterity, for his apprenticeship had not as yet reached even the journeyman stage. Therefore the gestures of these *hetaerae* were as stylized as if they had been clockwork. Yet, however fortuitously, all worked out so well it seemed each one was as absolutely circumscribed as a figure in rhetoric, reduced by the rigorous discipline of her vocation to the nameless essence of the idea of woman, a metaphysical abstraction of the female which could, on payment of a specific fee, be instantly translated into an oblivion either sweet or terrible, depending on the nature of her talents.

Lady Purple's talents verged on the unspeakable. Booted, in leather, she became a mistress of the whip before her fifteenth birthday. Subsequently, she graduated in the mysteries of the torture chamber, where she thoroughly researched all manner of ingenious mechanical devices. She utilized a baroque apparatus of funnel, humiliation, syringe, thumbscrew, contempt, and spiritual anguish; to her lovers, such severe usage was both bread and wine and a kiss from her cruel mouth was the sacrament of suffering.

Soon she became successful enough to be able to maintain her own establishment. When she was at the height of her fame, her slightest fancy might cost a young man his patrimony and, as soon as she squeezed him dry of fortune, hope, and dreams, for she was quite remorseless, she abandoned him; or else she might, perhaps, lock him up in her closet and force him to watch her while she took for nothing to her usually incredibly expensive bed a beggar encountered by chance on the street. She was no malleable, since frigid, substance upon which desires might be executed; she was not a true prostitute for she was the object on which men prostituted themselves. She, the sole perpetrator of desire, proliferated malign fantasies all around her and used her lovers as the canvas on which she executed boudoir masterpieces of destruction. Skins melted in the electricity she generated.

Soon, either to be rid of them or, simply, for pleasure, she took to murdering her lovers. From the leg of a politician she poisoned she cut out the thighbone and took it to a craftsman who made it into a flute for her. She persuaded succeeding lovers to play tunes for her on this instrument and, with the supplest and most serpentine grace, she danced for them to its unearthly music. At this point, the dumb girl put down her samisen and took up a bamboo pipe from which issued weird cadences and, though it was by no means the climax of the play, this dance was the apex of the Professor's performance for, as she stamped, wheeled and turned to the sound of her malign chamber music, Lady Purple became entirely the image of irresistible evil.

She visited men like a plague, both bane and terrible enlightenment, and she was as contagious as the plague. The final condition of all her lovers was this: they went clothed in rags held together with the discharge of their sores, and their eyes held an awful vacancy, as if their minds had been blown out like candles. A parade of ghastly spectres, they trundled across the stage, their passage implemented by medieval horrors for, here, an arm left its socket and whisked up out of sight into the flies and, there, a nose hung in the air after a gaunt shape that went tottering noseless forward.

So foreclosed Lady Purple's pyrotechnical career, which ended as if it had been indeed a firework display, in ashes, desolation, and silence. She became more ghastly than those she had infected. Circe at last became a swine herself and, seared to the bone by her own flame, walked the pavements like a desiccated shadow. Disaster obliterated her. Cast out with stones and oaths by those who had once adulated her, she was reduced to scavenging on the seashore, where she plucked hair from the heads of the drowned to sell to wigmakers who catered to the needs of more fortunate since less diabolic courtesans.

Now her finery, her paste jewels, and her enormous superimposition of black hair hung up in the green room and she wore a drab rag of coarse hemp for the final scene of her desperate decline, when, outrageous nymphomaniac, she practised extraordinary necrophilies on the bloated corpses the sea tossed contemptuously at her feet for her dry rapacity had become entirely mechanical and still she repeated her former actions though she herself was utterly other. She abrogated her humanity. She became nothing but wood and hair. She became a marionette herself, herself her own replica, the dead yet moving image of the shameless Oriental Venus.

The Professor was at last beginning to feel the effects of age and travel. Sometimes he complained in noisy silence to his nephew of pains, aches, stiffening muscles, tautening sinews, and shortness of breath. He began to limp a little and left to the boy all the rough work of mantling and dismantling. Yet the balletic mime of Lady Purple grew all the more remarkable with the passage of the years, as though his energy, channelled for so long into a single purpose, refined itself more and more in time and was finally reduced to a single, purified, concentrated essence which was transmitted entirely to the doll; and the Professor's mind attained a condition not unlike that of the swordsman trained in Zen, whose sword is his soul, so that neither sword nor swordsman has meaning without the presence of the other. Such swordsmen, armed, move towards their victims like automata, in a state of perfect emptiness, no longer aware of any distinction between self or weapon. Master and marionette had arrived at this condition.

Age could not touch Lady Purple for, since she had never aspired to mortality, she effortlessly transcended it and, though a man who was less aware of the expertise it needed to make her so much as raise her left hand might, now and then, have grieved to see how she defied ageing, the Professor had no fancies of that kind. Her miraculous inhumanity rendered their friendship entirely free from the anthropomorphic, even on the night of the Feast of All Hallows when, the mountain-dwellers murmured, the dead held masked balls in the graveyards while the devil played the fiddle for them.

The rough audience received their copeck's worth of sensation and filed out into a fairground which still roared like a playful tiger with life. The foundling girl put away her samisen and swept out the booth while the nephew set the stage afresh for next day's matinée. Then the Professor noticed Lady Purple had ripped a seam in the drab shroud she wore in the final act. Chattering to himself with displeasure, he undressed her as she swung idly, this way and that way, from her anchored strings and then he sat down on a wooden property stool on the stage and plied his needle like a good housewife. The task was more difficult than it seemed at first for the fabric was also torn and required an embroidery of darning so he told his assistants to go home together to the lodging house and let him finish his task alone.

A small oil-lamp hanging from a nail at the side of the stage cast an insufficient but tranquil light. The white puppet glimmered fitfully through the mists which crept into the theatre from the night outside through all the chinks and gaps in the tarpaulin and now began to fold their chiffon drapes around her as if to decorously conceal her or else to render her more translucently enticing. The mist softened her painted smile a little and her head dangled to one side. In the last act, she wore a loose, black wig, the locks of which hung down as far as her softly upholstered flanks, and the ends of her hair flickered with her random movements, creating upon the white blackboard of her back one of those fluctuating optical effects which make us question the veracity of our vision. As he often did when he was alone with her, the Professor chatted to her in his native language, rattling away an intimacy of nothings, of the weather, of his rheumatism, of the unpalatability and expense of the region's coarse, black bread, while the small winds took her as their partner in a scarcely perceptible *valse triste* and the mist grew minute by minute thicker, more pallid and more viscous.

The old man finished his mending. He rose and, with a click or two of his old bones, he went to put the forlorn garment neatly on its green-room hanger beside the glowing, winy purple gown splashed with rosy peonies, sashed with carmine, that she wore for her appalling dance. He was about to lay her, naked, in her coffin-shaped case and carry her back to their chilly bedroom when he paused. He was seized with the childish desire to see her again in all her finery once more that night. He took her dress off its hanger and carried it to where she drifted, at nobody's volition but that of the wind. As he put her clothes on her, he murmured to her as if she were a little girl for the vulnerable flaccidity of her arms and legs made a six-foot baby of her.

'There, there, my pretty; this arm here, that's right! Oops a daisy, easy does it . . .'

Then he tenderly took off her penitential wig and clucked his tongue to see how defencelessly bald she was beneath it. His arms cracked under the weight of her immense chignon and he had to stretch up on tiptoe to set it in place because, since she was as large as life, she was rather taller than he. But then the ritual of apparelling was over and she was complete again.

Now she was dressed and decorated, it seemed her dry wood had all at once put out an entire springtime of blossoms for the old man alone to enjoy. She could have acted as the model for the most beautiful of women, the image of that woman whom only a man's memory and imagination can devise, for the lamplight fell too mildly to sustain her air of arrogance and so gently it made her long nails look as harmless as ten fallen petals. The Professor had a curious habit; he always used to kiss his doll good-night.

A child kisses its toy before she pretends it sleeps although, even though she is only a child, she knows its eyes are not constructed to close so it will always be a sleeping beauty no kiss will waken. One in the grip of savage loneliness might kiss the face he sees before him in the mirror for want of any other face to kiss. These are kisses of the same kind; they are the most poignant of caresses, for they are too humble and too despairing to wish or seek for any response.

Yet, in spite of the Professor's sad humility, his chapped and withered mouth opened on hot, wet, palpitating flesh.

The sleeping wood had wakened. Her pearl teeth crashed against his with the sound of cymbals and her warm, fragrant breath blew around him like an Italian gale. Across her suddenly moving face flashed a whole kaleidoscope of expression, as though she were running instantaneously through the entire repertory of human feeling, practising, in an endless moment of time, all the scales of emotion as if they were music. Crushing vines, her arms, curled about the Professor's delicate apparatus of bone and skin with the insistent pressure of an actuality by far more authentically living than that of his own, time-desiccated flesh. Her kiss emanated from the dark country where desire is objectified and lives. She gained entry into the world by a mysterious loophole in its metaphysics and, during her kiss, she sucked his breath from his lungs so that her own bosom heaved with it.

So, unaided, she began her next performance with an apparent improvisation which was, in reality, only a variation upon a theme. She sank her teeth into his throat and drained him. He did not have the time to make a sound. When he was empty, he slipped straight out of her embrace down to her feet with a dry rustle, as of a cast armful of dead leaves, and there he sprawled on the floorboards, as empty, useless and bereft of meaning as his own tumbled shawl.

She tugged impatiently at the strings which moored her and out they came in bunches from her head, her arms and her legs. She stripped them off her fingertips and stretched out her long, white hands, flexing and unflexing them again and again. For the first time for years, or, perhaps, for ever, she closed her blood-stained teeth thankfully, for her cheeks still ached from the smile her maker had carved into the stuff of her former face. She stamped her elegant feet to make the new blood flow more freely there.

Unfurling and unravelling itself, her hair leaped out of its confinements of combs, cords and lacquer to root itself back into her scalp like cut grass bounding out of the stack and back again into the ground. First, she shivered with pleasure to feel the cold, for she realized she was experiencing a physical sensation; then either she remembered or else she believed she remembered that the sensation of cold was not a pleasurable one so she knelt and, drawing off the old man's shawl, wrapped it carefully about herself. Her every motion was instinct with a wonderful, reptilian liquidity. The mist outside now seemed to rush like a tide into the booth and broke against her in white breakers so that she looked like a baroque figurehead, lone survivor of a shipwreck, thrown up on a shore by the tide.

But whether she was renewed or newly born, returning to life or becoming alive, awakening from a dream or coalescing into the form of a fantasy generated in her wooden skull by the mere repetition so many times of the same invariable actions, the brain beneath the reviving hair contained only the scantiest notion of the possibilities now open to it. All that had seeped into the wood was the notion that she might perform the forms of life not so much by the skill of another as by her own desire that she did so, and she did not possess enough equipment to comprehend the complex circularity of the logic which inspired her for she had only been a marionette. But, even if she could not perceive it, she could not escape the tautological paradox in which she was trapped; had the marionette all the time parodied the living or was she, now living, to parody her own performance as a marionette? Although she was now manifestly a woman, young and beautiful, the leprous whiteness of her face gave her the appearance of a corpse animated solely by demonic will.

Deliberately, she knocked the lamp down from its hook on the wall. A puddle of oil spread at once on the boards of the stage. A little flame leaped across the fuel and immediately began to eat the curtains. She went down the aisle between the benches to the little ticket booth. Already, the stage was an inferno and the corpse of the Professor tossed this way and that on an uneasy bed of fire. But she did not look behind her after she slipped out into the fairground although soon the theatre was burning like a paper lantern ignited by its own candle.

Now it was so late that the sideshows, gingerbread stalls, and liquor booths were locked and shuttered and only the moon, half obscured by drifting cloud, gave out a meagre, dirty light, which sullied and deformed the flimsy pasteboard façades, so the place, deserted, with curds of vomit, the refuse of revelry, underfoot, looked utterly desolate.

She walked rapidly past the silent roundabouts, accompanied only by the fluctuating mists, towards the town, making her way like a homing pigeon, out of logical necessity, to the single brothel it contained.

REVENANT AS TYPEWRITER

Penelope Lively

M uriel Rackham, reaching the penultimate page of her talk, spoke with one eye upon the public library clock. The paper ('Ghosts: an analysis of their fictional and historic function') lasted precisely fifty-one minutes, as she well knew, but the stamina of the Ilmington Literary and Philosophical Society was problematic; an elderly man in the back row had been asleep since page seven, and there was a certain amount of shuffle and fidget in the middle reaches of the thirty odd seats occupied by the society's membership. Muriel skipped two paragraphs and moved into the concluding phase; it had perhaps been rash (not to say wasteful) to use on this occasion a paper that had a considerable success at the English Studies Conference and with her colleagues at the College Senior Seminar, but she had nothing much else written up at the moment and had felt disinclined to produce a piece especially for the occasion. She paused (nothing like silence to induce attention) and went on: 'So, leaving aside for the moment its literary role as vehicle for authorial comment in characters as diverse as Hamlet's father and Peter Quint, let us in conclusion try to summarize the historic function of the ghost—define as far as we can its social purpose, try to see why people needed ghosts and what they used them for. We've already paid tribute to that great source book for the student of the folkloric ghost—Dr Katharine Briggs' *Dictionary of British Folk-Tales*—of which I think it was Bernard Levin who remarked in a review that a glance down its list of Tale-Types and Motifs disposes once and for all of the notion that the British are a phlegmatic and unfanciful people.' (She paused at this point for the ripple of appreciative amusement that should run through the audience, but the Ilmington Lit. and Phil. sat unmoved; there were two sleepers now in the back row.) '. . . We've looked already at the repetitive nature of Motifs—Ghost follows its own corpse, reading the funeral service silently; Ghost laid when treasure is unearthed; Revenant as hare; Revenant in human form; Wraith appears to person in bedroom; Ghost haunts scene of former crime; Ghost exercises power through possessions of its lifetime—and so on and so forth. The subject-matter of ghostly folklore, in fact, perfectly supports the thesis of Keith Thomas in his book *Religion and the Decline of Magic* that the historic ghost is no random or frivolous character but fulfils a particular social need—in a society where the arm of the law is short it serves to draw attention to the unpunished crime, to seek the rectification of wrongs, to act as a reminder of the past, to . . .'

She read on, the text familiar enough for the thoughts to wander: Bill Freeman, the chairman, had introduced her appallingly, neglecting to mention her publications and reducing her Senior Lectureship at Ilmington College of Education to a Lectureship—she felt again a flush of irritation, and wondered if it had been deliberate or merely obtuse. They were an undistinguished lot, the audience; surely that woman at the end of the third row was an assistant in W. H. Smith's? Muriel observed them with distaste, as she turned over to the last page; school-teachers and librarians, for the most part, one was talking right above their heads, in all probability. A somewhat wasted evening—which could have usefully been spent doing things about the house, or going through students' essays, or looking at that article Paul had given her, in order to have some well-thought-out-comments for the morning.

She concluded, and sat, with a wintry smile towards Bill Freeman at her side who, as one might have expected, rose to thank her with a sequence of remarks as inept as his introduction: '. . . our appreciation to Dr Rackham for her fascinating talk and throw the meeting open to discussion.'

Discussion could not have been said to flow. There was a man who had been to a production of *Macbeth* in which you actually saw Banquo and did the speaker think that was right or was it better if you just kind of guessed he was there . . . and a woman who thought *The Turn of the Screw* wasn't awfully good when they made it into an opera, and another who had been interested in the bit about people in historical times believing in ghosts and had the speaker ever visited Hampton Court because if you go there the guide tells you that . . .

Muriel dealt politely but briefly with the questioners. She glanced again at the clock, and then at Bill Freeman, who would do well to wind things up. There was a pause. Bill Freeman scanned the audience and said, 'Well, if no one has anything more to ask Dr Rackham I think perhaps . . .'

The small dark woman at the end of the front row leaned forward, looking at Muriel. 'I thought what you said was quite interesting and I'd like to tell you about this thing that happened to a friend of mine. She was staying in this house, you see, where apparently . . .'

It went on for several minutes. It was very tedious, a long rigmarole about inexplicable creakings in the night, objects appearing and disappearing, ghostly footsteps and sounds and so on and so forth, all classifiable according to Tale-Type and Motif if one felt so inclined and hadn't in fact lost interest in the whole subject some time ago, now that one was doing this work on the metaphysical poets with Paul . . . Muriel sat back and sighed. She eyed the woman with distaste; the face was vaguely familiar, someone local, presumably. An absurd little person with black, straight, short hair (dyed, by the look of it) fringing her face, those now unfashionable spectacles upswept at the corners and tinted a disagreeable mauve, long ear-rings of some cheap shiny stone. Ear-rings, Muriel noted, more suitable for a younger woman; this creature was her own age, at least. Her skirt was too short, also, and her shirt patterned with what looked like lotus flowers in a discordant pink.

'. . . and my friend felt that it had come back to see about something, the ghost, something that had annoyed it. I just wondered what the speaker had to say about that, if she'd ever had any experiences of that kind.' The woman stared at Muriel, almost aggressively.

Muriel gathered herself. 'Well,' she said briskly, 'of course we've really been concerned this evening with the fictional and historical persona of the ghost, haven't we? As far as I'm concerned I would subscribe to what has been called the intellectual impossibility of ghosts—and of course experiences such as your friend's, if one stops to think about it, are open to all kinds of explanation, aren't they?'—she flashed a quick, placating smile—'And now, I feel perhaps that . . .'— she half-turned towards the chairman—'if there are no more questions . . .'

Going home (after coffee and sandwiches in someone's house; the black-haired person, mercifully, had not been there) she shook off the dispiriting atmosphere of the evening with relief: the dingy room, the unresponsive audience. The paper had been far too academic for them, of course. She felt glad that Paul had not come. He had offered to, but she had insisted that he shouldn't. Turning the Mini out of the High Street and past the corner of his road, she allowed herself a glance at the lighted window of his house. The curtains were drawn; Sheila would be watching television, of course, Paul reading (the new Joyce book, probably, or maybe this week's TLS). Poor Paul. Poor, dear Paul. It was tragic, such a marriage. That dull, insensitive woman.

'Your friendship is of the greatest value to me, Muriel,' he had said, one week ago exactly. He had said it looking out of the window, rather than at her—and she had understood at once. Understood the depth of his feeling, the necessity for understatement, for the avoidance of emotional display. Their position was of extreme delicacy—Paul's position. Head of Department, Vice-Principal of the College. She had nodded and murmured something, and they had gone on to discuss a student, some problems about the syllabus . . .

At night, she had lain awake, thinking with complacency of their relationship, of its restraint and depth, in such contrast to the stridency of the times. Muriel considered herself—knew herself to be—a tolerant woman, but occasionally she observed her students with disgust; their behaviour was coarse and vulgar, not to put too fine a point upon it. They brandished what should be kept private.

Occasionally, lying there, she was visited by other feelings, which she recognized and suppressed; a mature, balanced person is able to exercise self-control. The satisfaction of love takes more than one form.

She put the car in the garage and let herself into the house, experiencing the usual pleasure. It was delightful; white walls, bare boards sanded and polished, her choice and tasteful possessions—rugs, pictures, the few antique pieces, the comfortable sofa and armchairs, the William Morris curtains. It was so unlike, now, the dirty, cluttered, scruffy place she had bought five months ago as to be almost unrecognizable. Only its early Victorian exterior remembered—and that too was now bright and trim under new paint, with a front door carefully reconstructed in keeping, to replace the appalling twenties porch some previous occupant had built on. The clearing-out process had been gruelling—Muriel blenched even now at the thought of it: cupboards stacked with junk and rubbish that nobody had bothered to remove (there had been an executors' sale, the elderly owner having died some months before), the whole place filthy and in a state of horrid disrepair. She had done the bulk of the work herself, with the help of a local decorator and carpenter for the jobs she felt were beyond her. But alone she had emptied all those cavernous cupboards, carting the stuff down to a skip hired from a local firm. It had been a disagreeable job—not just because of the dirt and physical effort, but because of the nature of the junk, which hinted at an alien and unpleasing way of life. She felt that she wanted to scour the house of its past, make it truly hers, as she heaved bundle after bundle of musty rubbish down the stairs. There had been boxes of old clothes—too old and sour to interest either the salerooms or Oxfam—brash vulgar female clothes, shrill of colour and pattern, in materials like sateen, chenille, and rayon, the feel of which made Muriel shudder. They slithered from her hands, smelling of mould and mouse droppings, their touch so repellent that she took to wearing rubber gloves. And then there were shelves of old magazines and books—not the engrossing treasure-trove that such a hoard ought to be (secondhand bookshops, after all, were an addiction of hers) but dreary and dispiriting in what they suggested of whoever had owned them: pulp romantic fiction, stacks of the cheaper, shriller women's magazines (all sex and crime, not even that limited but wholesome stuff about cooking, children, and health), some tattered booklets with pictures that made Muriel flush—she shovelled the beastly things into a supermarket carton and dumped the lot into the skip. This house had seen little or no literature that could even be called decent during its recent past, that was clear enough; with pleasure she had arranged her own books on the newly-painted shelves at either side of the fireplace. They seemed to clinch her conquest of the place.

There had been other things, too. A dressmaker's dummy that she had found prone at the back of a cupboard (its murky shape had given her a hideous shock); she had scrubbed and kept it, occasionally she made herself a dress or skirt and it might conceivably be useful, though its torso was dumpier than her own. A tangle of hairnets and curlers in a drawer of the kitchen dresser, horribly scented of violets. Bits and pieces of broken and garish jewellery—all fake—that kept appearing from under floorboards or down crevices. Even now she came across things; it was as though the house would never have done with spewing out its tawdry memories. And of course the redecorating had been a major job—stripping away those fearful wallpapers that plastered every room, every conceivable misrepresentation of nature, loud and unnatural roses, poppies and less identifiable flowers that crawled and clustered up and down the walls. Sometimes two or three different ones had fought for survival in the same room; grimly, Muriel, aided by the decorator, tore and soaked and peeled. At last, every wall was crisply white, a background to her prints and lithographs, her Georgian mirror, the Khelim rug.

Now, she felt at last that she had taken possession. There were one or two small things still that jarred—a cupboard in her bedroom from which, scrub as she might, she could not eradicate the sickly smell of some cheap perfume, a hideous art nouveau window (she gathered such things were once again in fashion—*chacun à son goût*) in the hall which she would eventually get around to replacing. Otherwise, all was hers; her quiet but distinctive taste in harmony with the house's original architectural grace.

It was just past nine; time for a look at that article before bed. Muriel went to her desk (which, by day, had a view of the small garden prettily framed in William Morris's 'Honeysuckle') and sat reading and taking notes for an hour or so. She remembered that Paul would be away all day tomorrow, at a meeting in London, and she would not be able to see him, so when she had finished reading she pulled her typewriter in front of her and made a résumé of her reflections on the article, to leave in his pigeon-hole. She read them through, satisfied with what she felt to be some neatly put points. Then she got up, locked the back and front doors, checked the windows, and went to bed.

In the night, she woke; the room felt appallingly stuffy—she could even, from her bed, smell that disagreeable cupboard—and she assumed that she must have forgotten to open the window. Getting up to do so, she found the sash raised a couple of inches as usual. She returned to bed, and was visited by unwelcome yearnings which she drove out by a stern concentration on her second-year Shakespeare option.

She had left her page of notes on the article in the typewriter, and almost forgot it in the morning, remembering at the last moment as she was about to leave the house, and going back to twitch it hastily out and put it in her handbag. The day was busy with classes and a lecture, so that it was not until the afternoon that she had time to write a short note for Paul ('I entirely agree with you about the weaknesses in his argument; however, there are one or two points we might discuss, some thoughts on which I enclose. I do hope London was not too exhausing—MCR'), and glance again at the page of typescript.

It was not as satisfactory as Muriel remembered; in fact it was not satisfactory at all. She must have been a great deal more tired than she had realized last night—only in a stupor (and not even, one would have hoped, then) could she have written such muddled sentences, such hideous syntax, such illiteracies of style and spelling. 'What I think is that he developped what he said about the character of Tess all wrong so what you ended up feeling was that . . .' she read in horror '. . . if Hardy's descriptive passages are not always relivant then personally what I don't see is why . . .' And what was this note at the bottom—apparently added in haste? 'What about meeting for a natter tomorrow—I was thinking about you last night—ssh! you aren't supposed to know that!' I must have been half-asleep, she thought, how could I write such things?

Hot with discomfort (and relief—heavens! she might not have looked again at the thing), she crumpled the paper and threw it into the wastepaper basket. She wrote a second note to Paul saying that she had read the article but unfortunately had not the time now to say more, and hoped to discuss it with him at some point; she then cancelled her late-afternoon class and went home early. I have been overdoing things, she thought—my work, the house—I need rest, a quiet evening.

She settled down to read, but could not concentrate; for almost the first time, she found herself wishing for the anodyne distraction of television. She polished and dusted the sitting-room (finding, in the process, a disgusting matted hank of hairnets and ribbon that had got, quite inexplicably, into her Worcester teapot) and cleaned the windows. Then she did some washing, which led to an inspection of her ward-robe; it seemed sparse. A new dress, perhaps, would lift her spirits. On Saturday, she would buy one, and in the meantime, there was that nice length of tweed her sister had given her and which had lain untouched for months. Perhaps with the aid of the dressmaker's dummy it could be made into a useful skirt. She fetched the dummy and spent an hour or two with scissors and pins—a soothing activity, though the results were not quite as satisfactory as she could have wished. Eventually she left the roughly-fashioned skirt pinned to the dummy and put it away in the spare-room cupboard before going to bed.

A few days later, to her pleasure, Paul accepted an invitation to call in at the house on his way home to pick up a book and have a drink. He had hesitated before accepting, and she understood his difficulties at once; such meetings were rare for them, and the reasons clear enough to her: the pressures of his busy life, Sheila . . . 'Well, yes, how kind, Muriel,' he had said, 'Yes, fine, then. I'll give Sheila a ring and tell her I'll be a little late.'

Poor Paul; the strains of such a marriage did not bear contemplation. Of course they always appeared harmonious enough in public, a further tribute to his wonderful patience and restraint. Nor did he ever hint or complain; one had to be perceptive to realize the tensions that must rise—a man of his intellectual stature fettered to someone without, so far as Muriel understood, so much as an A-level. His tolerance was amazing; Muriel had even heard him, once, join with well-simulated enthusiasm in a discussion of some trashy television series prompted by Sheila at a Staff Club party.

She was delayed at the College and only managed to arrive back at the house a few minutes before he arrived. Pouring the sherry, she heard him say, 'What's this, then, Muriel—making a study of popular culture?' and turned round to see him smiling and holding up one of those scabrous women's magazines that—she thought—she had committed to the skip. Disconcerted, she found herself flushing, embarking on a defensive explanation of the rubbish that had been in the house . . . (But she had cleared all that stuff out, every bit, how could that thing have been, apparently, lying on the little Victorian sewing-table, from which Paul had taken it?)

The incident unnerved her, spoiled what should have been an idyllic hour.

Muriel woke the next day—Saturday—discontented and twitchy. She had slept badly, disturbed by the muffled sound of a woman's shrill laugh, coming presumably from the next house in the terrace; she had not realized before that noise could penetrate the walls.

Remembering her resoluting of a few days before, she went shopping for a new dress. The facilities of Ilmington were hardly metropolitan, but adequate for a woman of her restrained tastes; she found, after some searching, a pleasant enough garment innocent of any of the nastier excesses of modern fashion, in a wholesome colour and fabric, and took it home in a rather calmer frame of mind.

In the evening, there was the Principal's sherry party (Paul would be there; with any luck there would be the opportunity for a few quiet words). She went to take the dress from the wardrobe and indeed was about to put it on before the feel of it in her hands brought her up short; surely there was something wrong? She took it to the window, staring— this was never the dress she had chosen so carefully this morning? The remembered eau-de-nil was now, looked at again, in the light from the street, a harsh and unflattering apple-green; the coarse linen, so pleasant to the touch, a slimy artificial stuff. She had made the most disastrous mistake; tears of frustration and annoyance pricked her eyes. She threw the thing back in the cupboard and put on her old Jaeger print.

Sunday was a day that, normally she enjoyed. This one got off to a bad start with the discovery of the *Sunday Mirror* sticking through the front door instead of the *Sunday Times;* after breakfast she rang the shop, knowing that they would be open till eleven, only to be told by a bewildered voice that surely that was what she had asked for, change it, you said on the phone, Thursday it was, for the *Sunday Mirror,* spicier, you said, good for a laugh. There's been some mistake,' said Muriel curtly. 'I don't know what you can be thinking of.' She slammed down the receiver and set about a massive cleaning of the house; it seemed the proper therapeutic thing to do.

After lunch she sat down at her desk to do some work; her article for *English Today* was coming along nicely. Soon it would be time to show a first draft to Paul. She took the lid off the typewriter and prepared to reread the page she had left in on Friday.

Two minutes later, her heart thumping, she was ripping out the paper, crumpling it into a ball . . . I never wrote such stuff, she thought, it's impossible, words like that, expressions like—I don't even *know* such expressions.

She sat in horror, staring into the basilisk eye of a thrush on her garden wall. There is something wrong, she thought, I am not myself, am I going mad?

She took a sleeping pill, but even so woke in the depths of the night (again, those muffled peals of laughter), too hot, the room heavy around her so that she had to get up and open the window further; the house creaked. There must be a fault in the heating system, she thought, I'll have to get the man round. She lay in discomfort, her head aching.

In the days that followed it seemed to her that she suffered from continuous headaches. Headaches, and a kind of lightheadedness that made her feel sometimes that she had only a tenuous grip on reality; in the house, after work, she heard noises, saw things. There was that laughter again, which must be from next door but when she enquired delicately of the milkman as to who her neighbours were (one didn't want actually to get involved with them) she learned that an elderly man lived there, alone, a retired doctor. And there were things that seemed hallucinatory, there was no other explanation; going to the cupboard where she had put the dummy, to have another go at that skirt, she had found the thing swathed not in her nice herring-bone tweed but a revolting purple chenille. She slammed the cupboard closed (again, the lurking shape of the dummy had startled her, although she had expected to see it), and sat down on the bed, her chest pounding. I am not well, she thought, I am doing things and then forgetting that I have done them, there is something seriously wrong.

And then there was the wallpaper. She had come into the sitting-room, one bright sunny morning   her spruce, white sitting-room— and, glancing at her Dufy prints, had seen suddenly the shadowy presence of the old, hideous wallpaper behind them, those entwined violets and roses that she and the decorator had so laboriously scraped away. Two walls, she now saw, were scarred all over, behind the new emulsion paint, with the shadowy presence of the old paper; how can we have missed them, she thought angrily—that decorator, I should have kept a sharper eye on him—but surely, I *remember*, we did this room together, every bit was stripped, surely?

Her head spun.

She went to the doctor, unwillingly, disliking her list of neurotic symptoms, envying the bronchitic coughs and bandaged legs in the waiting-room. Stiffly, she submitted to the questions, wanting to say: I am not this kind of person at all, I am balanced, well-adjusted, known for my good sense. With distaste, she listened to the diagnosis: yes, she wanted to say, impatiently, I have heard of menopausal problems but I am not the kind of woman to whom they happen, I keep things under better control than that, overwork is much more likely. She took his prescription and went away, feeling humiliated.

It was the examination season. She was faced, every evening, on returning home, with a stack of scripts and would sit up late marking, grateful for the distraction, though she was even more tired and prone to headaches. The tiredness was leading to confusion, also, she realized. On one occasion, giving a class, she had been aware of covert glances and giggles among her students, apparently prompted by her own appearance; later, in the staff cloakroom, she had looked in a mirror and been appalled to discover herself wearing a frightful low-cut pink blouse with some kind of flower-pattern. It was vaguely familiar—I've seen it before, she thought, and realized it must be a relic of the rubbish in the house, left in the back of her cupboard and put on accidentally this morning, in her bleary awakening from a disturbed night. Condemned to wear it for the rest of the day, she felt taken over by its garishness, as though compelled to behave in character; she found herself joining a group of people at lunch-time with whom she would not normally have associated, the brash set among her colleagues, sharing jokes and conversation that she found distasteful. In Paul's office, later, going over some application forms, she laid her hand on his sleeve, and felt him withdraw his arm; later, the memory of this made her shrivel. It was as though she had betrayed the delicacy of their relationship; never before had they made physical contact.

She decided to take a couple of days off from the College, and mark scripts at home.

The first day passed tranquilly enough; she worked throughout the morning and early afternoon. At around five she felt suddenly moved, against her better judgement, to telephone Paul with what she knew to be a trumped-up query about an exam problem. Talking to him, she was aware of her own voice, with a curious detachment; its tone surprised her, and the shrillness of her laugh. Do I always sound like that? she thought, have I always laughed in that way? It seemed to her that Paul was abrupt, that he deliberately ended the conversation.

She got up the next morning in a curious frame of mind. The scripts she had to mark filled her with irritation; not the irritation stemming from inadequacy in the candidates, but a petulant resentment of the whole thing. Sometimes, she did not seem able to follow the answers to questions. 'Don't get you,' she scribbled in the margin. 'What are you on about?' At the bottom of one script she scrawled a series of doodles: indeterminate flowers, a face wearing upswept spectacles, a buxom female figure. At last, with the pile of scripts barely eroded, she abandoned her desk and wandered restlessly around the house.

Somehow, it displeased her. It was too stark, too bare, an unlived-in place. I like a bit of life, she thought, a bit of colour, something to pep things up; rummaging in the scullery she found under the sink some gaily patterned curtaining that must have got overlooked when she cleared out those particular shelves. That's nice, she thought, nice and striking, I like that; as she hung it in place of the linen weave in the hall that now seemed so dowdy, it seemed to her that from somewhere in the house came a peal of laughter.

That day merged, somehow, into the next. She did not go to the College. Several times the telephone rang: mostly she ignored it. Once, answering, she heard the departmental secretary's voice, blathering on: 'Dr Rackham?' she kept saying, 'Dr Rackham? Professor Simons has been a bit worried, we wondered if . . .' Muriel laughed and hung up. The night, the intermediate night (or nights, it might have been, time was a bit confusing, not that it mattered at all) had been most extraordinary. She had had company of some kind; throughout the night, whenever she woke, she had been aware of a low murmuring. A voice. A voice of compulsive intimacy, coarse and insistent; it had repelled but at the same time fascinated her. She had lain there, silent and unresisting.

The house displeased her more and more. It's got no style, she thought, full of dreary old stuff. She took down the Dufy prints, and the Piper cathedral etchings, thinking: I don't like that kind of thing, I like a proper picture, where you can see what's what, don't know where I even picked up these. She made a brief sortie to Boots round the corner and bought a couple of really nice things, not expensive either—a Chinese girl and a lovely painting of horses galloping by the sea. As she hung them in the sitting-room, it seemed to her that someone clutched her arm, and for an instant she shuddered uncontrollably, but the sensation passed, though it left her feeling light-headed, a little hysterical.

Her own appearance dissatisfied her, too. She sat looking at herself in her bedroom mirror and thought: 'I've never made the best of myself, a woman's got to make use of what she's got, hasn't she? Where's that nice blouse I found the other day, it's flattering—a bit of décolleté, I'm not past that kind of thing yet.' She put it on, and felt pleased. Downstairs, the telephone was ringing again, but she could not be bothered to answer it. Don't want to see anyone, she thought, fed up with people, if it's Paul he can come and find me, can't he? Play hard to get, that's what you should do with men, string them along a bit.

Anyway, she was not alone. She could feel, again, that presence in the room though when she swung round suddenly—with a resurgence of that chill sensation—there was nothing but the dressmaker's dummy, standing in the corner. She must have brought it from the cupboard, and forgotten.

She wandered about the house, muttering to herself; from time to time, a person walked with her, not someone you could see, just a presence, its arm slipped through Muriel's, whispering intimacies, suggestions. All those old books of yours, it said, you don't want those, ring the newsagent, have them send round some mags, a good read, that's what we want. Muriel nodded.

Once, people hammered on the door. She could hear their voices; colleagues from the department. 'Muriel?' they called. 'Are you there, Muriel?' She went into the kitchen and shut herself in till they had gone. For a moment, sitting there, she felt clearer in her head, free of the confusion that had been dragging her down; something is happening, she thought wildly, something I cannot cope with, can't control . . .

And then there came again that presence, with its insistent voice, and this time the voice was quite real, and she knew, too, that she had heard it before, somewhere, quite recently, not long ago. Where, where?

. . . I thought what you said was quite interesting, and I'd like to tell you about this thing that happened to a friend of mine . . .

Muriel held the banisters, to steady herself (she was on her way upstairs again, in her perpetual edgy drifting up and down the house): the Lit. and Phil., I remember now, that woman.

And it came to her too, with a horrid jolt, that she knew now, remembered suddenly, why, at the time, that evening, the face had been familiar, why she'd felt she'd seen it before.

It had been the face in a yellowed photograph that had tumbled from a tatty book when she had been clearing out the house; Violet Hanson, 1934, in faded ink on the back.

Sale by auction, by order of the Executors of Mrs Violet Hanson, deceased, No. 27 Clarendon Terrace, a four-bedroomed house with scope for . . .

Someone was laughing, peals of shrill laughter that rang through the house, and as she reached the top floor, and turned into her bedroom, she knew that it was herself. She went into her bedroom and sat down at her dressing-table and looked in the mirror. The face that looked back at her was haggard. I've got to do something about myself, she thought, I'm turning into an old frump. She groped on the table and found a pair of ear-rings, long, shiny ones that she had forgotten she had. She held them up against her face; yes, that's nice, stylish, and I'll dye my hair, have it cut short and dye it black, take years off me, that would . . .

There was laughter again, but she no longer knew if it was hers or someone else's.

THE LITTLE DIRTY GIRL

Joanna Russ

Dear——,

Do you like cats? I never asked you. There are all sorts of cats: elegant, sinuous cats, clunky, heavy-breathing cats, skinny, desperate cats, meatloaf-shaped cats, waddling, dumb cats, big slobs of cats who step heavily and groan whenever they try to fit themselves (and they never do fit) under something or in between something or past something.

I'm allergic to all of them. You'd think they'd know it. But as I take my therapeutic walks around the neighborhood (still aching and effortful after ten months, though when questioned, my doctor replies, with the blank, baffled innocence of those Martian children so abstractedly brilliant they've never learned to communicate about merely human matters with anyone, *that my back will get better*) cats venture from alleyways, slip out from under parked cars, bound up cellar steps, prick up their ears and flash out of gardens, all lifting up their little faces, wreathing themselves around my feet, crying *Dependency! Dependency!* and showing their elegantly needly little teeth, which they never use save in yearning appeal to my goodness. They have perfect confidence in me. If I try to startle them by hissing, making loud noises, or clapping my hands sharply, they merely stare in interested fashion and scratch themselves with their hind legs: how nice. I've perfected a method of lifting kitties on the toe of my shoe and giving them a short ride through the air (this is supposed to be alarming); they merely come running back for more.

And the children! I don't dislike children. Yes I do. No I don't, but I feel horribly awkward with them. So of course I keep meeting them on my walks this summer: alabaster little boys with angelic fair hair and sky-colored eyes (this section of Seattle is Scandinavian and the Northwest gets very little sun) come up to me and volunteer such compelling information as:

'*I'm* going to my friend's house.'

'I'm going to the store.'

'My name is Markie.'

'I wasn't really scared of that big dog; I was just *startled*.'

'People leave a lot of broken glass around here.'

The littler ones confide; the bigger ones warn of the world's dangers: dogs, cuts, blackberry bushes that might've been sprayed. One came up to me once—what do they see in a tall, shuffling, professional, intellectual woman of forty?—and said, after a moment's thought:

'Do you like frogs?'

What could I do? I said yes, so a shirt-pocket that jumped and said *rivit* was opened to disclose Mervyn, an exquisite little being the color of wet, mottled sea-sand, all webbed feet and amber eyes, who was then transferred to my palm where he sat and blinked. Mervyn was a toad, actually; he's barely an inch long and can be found all over Seattle, usually upside down under a rock. I'm sure he (or she) is the Beloved Toad and Todkins and Todlekranz Virginia Woolf used in her letters to Emma Vaughan.

And the girls? O they don't approach tall, middle-aged women. Little girls are told not to talk to strangers. And the little girls of Seattle (at least in my neighborhood) are as obedient and feminine as any in the world; to the jeans and tee-shirts of Liberation they (or more likely their parents) add hair-ribbons, baby-sized pocketbooks, fancy pins, pink shoes, even toe polish.

The liveliest of them I ever saw was a little person of five, coasting downhill in a red wagon, her cheeks pink with excitement, one ponytail of yellow hair undone, her white tee-shirt askew, who gave a decorous little squeak of joy at the sheer speed of it. I saw and smiled; pink-cheeks saw and shrieked again, more loudly and confidently this time, then looked away, embarrassed, jumped quickly out of her wagon, and hauled it energetically up the hill.

Except for the very littlest, how neat, how clean, how carefully dressed they are! with long, straight hair that the older ones (I know this) still iron under waxed paper.

The little, dirty girl was different.

She came up to me in the supermarket. I've hired someone to do most of my shopping, as I can't carry much, but I'd gone in for some little thing, as I often do. It's a relief to get off the hard bed and away from the standing desk or the abbreviated kitchen stools I've scattered around the house (one foot up and one foot down); in fact it's simply such a relief—

Well, the little, dirty girl *was* dirty; she was the dirtiest eight-year-old I've ever seen. Her black hair was a long tangle. Her shoes were down-at-heel, the laces broken, her white (or rather grey) socks belling limply out over her ankles. Her nose was running. Her pink dress, so ancient that it showed her knees, was limp and wrinkled and the knees themselves had been recently skinned. She looked as if she had slid halfway down Volunteer Park's steepest, dirtiest hill on her panties and then rolled end-over-end the rest of the way. Besides all this, there were snot-and-tear-marks on her face (which was reddened and sallow and looked as if she'd been crying) and she looked—well, what can I say? *Neglected.* Not poor, though someone had dressed her rather eccentrically, not physically unhealthy or underfed, but messy, left alone, ignored, kicked out, bedraggled, like a cat caught in a thunderstorm.

She looked (as I said) tear-stained, and yet came up to my shopping cart with perfect composure and kept me calm company for a minute or so. Then she pointed to a box of Milky Way candy bars on a shelf above my head, saying 'I like those,' in a deep, gravelly voice that suggested a bad cold.

I ignored the hint. No, that's wrong; it wasn't a hint; it was merely a social, adult remark, self-contained and perfectly emotionless, as if she had long ago given up expecting that telling anyone she wanted something would result in getting it. Since my illness I have developed a fascination with the sheer, elastic wealth of children's bodies, the exhaustless, energetic health they don't know they have and which I so acutely and utterly miss, but I wasn't for an instant tempted to feel this way about the Little Dirty Girl. She had been through too much. She had Resources. If she showed no fear of me, it wasn't because she trusted me but because she trusted nothing. She had no expectations and no hopes. None the less she attached herself to me and my shopping cart and accompanied me down two more aisles, and there seemed to be hope in that. So I made the opening, social, adult remark:

'What's your name?'

'A. R.' Those are the initials on my handbag. I looked at her sharply but she stared levelly back, unembarrassed, self-contained, unexpressive.

'I don't believe that,' I said finally.

'I could tell you lots of things you wouldn't believe,' said the Little Dirty Girl.

She followed me up to the cashier and as I was putting out my small packages one by one by one, I saw her lay out on the counter a Milky Way bar and a nickel, the latter fetched from somewhere in that short-skirted, cap-sleeved dress. The cashier, a middle-aged woman, looked at me and I back at her; I laid out two dimes next to the nickel. She really did want it! As I was going into the logistics of How Many Short Trips

From The Cart To The Car And How Many Long Ones From The Car
To The Kitchen, the Little Dirty Girl spoke: 'I can carry that.' (Gravelly
and solemn.)

She added hoarsely, 'I bet I live near you.'

'Well, *I* bet you don't,' I said.

She didn't answer, but followed me to the parking lot, one propri-
etary hand on the cart, and when I unlocked my car door, she darted
past me and started carrying packages from the cart to the front seat. I
can't move fast enough to escape these children. She sat there calmly as
I got in. Then she said, wiping her nose on the back of her hand:

'I'll help you take your stuff out when you get home.'

Now I know that sort of needy offer and I don't like it. Here was the
Little Dirty Girl offering to help me, and smelling in close quarters as if
she hadn't changed her underwear for days: demandingness, neediness,
more annoyance. Then she said in her flat, crow's voice: 'I'll do it and
go away. I won't bother you.'

Well, what can you do? My heart misgave me. I started the car and
we drove the five minutes to my house in silence, whereupon she
grabbed all the packages at once (to be useful) and some slipped back on
the car seat; I think this embarrassed her. But she got my things up the
stairs to the porch in only two trips and put them on the unpainted
porch rocker, from where I could pick them up one by one, and there
we stood.

Why speechless? Was it honesty? I wanted to thank her, to act decent,
to make that sallow face smile. I wanted to tell her to go away, that I
wouldn't let her in, that I'd lock the door. But all I could think of to say
was, 'What's your name, really?' and the wild thing said stubbornly, 'A.
R.' and when I said, 'No, really,' she cried '*A. R.!*' and facing me with
her eyes screwed up, shouted something unintelligible, passionate, and
resentful, and was off up the street. I saw her small figure turning down
one of the cross-streets that meets mine at the top of the hill. Seattle is
grey and against the massed storm clouds to the north her pink dress
stood out vividly. She was going to get rained on. Of course.

I turned to unlock my front door and a chunky, slow, old cat, a black-
and-white Tom called Williamson who lives two houses down, came
stiffly out from behind an azalea bush, looked slit-eyed (bored) about
him, noticed me (his pupils dilated with instant interest) and bounded
across the parking strip to my feet. Williamson is a banker-cat, not really
portly or dignified but simply too lazy and unwieldy to bother about
anything much. Either something scares him and he huffs under the

nearest car or he scrounges. Like all kitties he bumbled around my ankles, making steam-engine noises. I never feed him. I don't pet him or talk to him. I even try not to look at him. I shoved him aside with one foot and opened the front door; Williamson backed off, raised his fat, jowled face and began the old cry: *Mrawr! Mrawr!* I booted him ungently off the porch before he could trot into my house with me, and as he slowly prepared to attack the steps (he never quite makes it) locked myself in. And the Little Dirty Girl's last words came suddenly clear:

I'll be back.

Another cat. There are too many in this story but I can't help it. The Little Dirty Girl was trying to coax the neighbor's superbly elegant half-Siamese out from under my car a few days later, an animal tiger-marked on paws and tail and as haughty-and-mysterious-looking as all cats are supposed to be, though it's really only the long Siamese body and small head. Ma'amselle (her name) still occasionally leaps onto my dining room windowsill and stares in (the people who lived here before me used to feed her). I was coming back from a walk, the Little Dirty Girl was on her knees, and Ma'amselle was under the car; when the Little Dirty Girl saw me she stood up, and Ma'amselle flashed Egyptianly through the laurel hedge and was gone. Someone had washed the Little Dirty Girl's pink dress (though a few days back, I'm afraid) and made a half-hearted attempt to braid her hair: there were barrettes and elastic somewhere in the tangle. Her cold seemed better. When it rains in August our summer can change very suddenly to early fall, and this was a chilly day; the Little Dirty Girl had nothing but her mud-puddle-marked dress between her thin skin and the Seattle air. Her cold seemed better, though, and her cheeks were pink with stooping. She said, in the voice of a little girl this time and not a raven, 'She had *blue* eyes.'

'She's Siamese,' I said. 'What's your name?'

'A. R.'

'Now look, I don't—'

'*It's A. R.!*' She was getting loud and stolid again. She stood there with her skinny, scabbed knees showing from under her dress and shivered in the unconscious way kids do who are used to it; I've seen children do it on the Lower East Side in New York because they had no winter coat (in January). I said, 'You come in.' She followed me up the steps—warily, I think—but when we got inside her expression changed, it changed utterly; she clasped her hands and said with radiant joy, 'Oh, they're *beautiful!*'

These were my astronomical photographs. I gave her my book of microphotographs (cells, crystals, hailstones) and went into the kitchen to put up water for tea; when I got back she'd dropped the book on my old brown-leather couch and was walking about with her hands clasped in front of her and that same look of radiant joy on her face. I live in an ordinary, shabby frame house that has four rooms and a finished attic; the only unusual thing about it is the number of books and pictures crammed in every which way among the (mostly second-hand) furniture. There are Woolworth frames for the pictures and cement-block bookcases for the books; none the less the Little Dirty Girl was as awed as if she'd found Aladdin's Cave.

She said, 'It's so . . . sophisticated!'

Well, there's no withstanding that. Even if you think: what do kids know? She followed me into the kitchen where I gave her a glass of milk and a peach (she sipped and nibbled). She thought the few straggling rose bushes she could see in the back garden were wonderful. She loved my old brown refrigerator; she said, 'It's so big! And such a color!' Then she said anxiously, 'Can I see the upstairs?' and got excited over the attic eaves which were also 'so big' (wallboard and dirty pink paint) to the point that she had to run and stand under one side and then run across the attic and stand under the other. She liked the 'view' from the bedroom (the neighbor's laurel hedge and a glimpse of someone else's roof) but my study (books, a desk, a glimpse of the water) moved her so deeply and painfully that she only stood still in the center of the room, struggling with emotion, her hands again clasped in front of her. Finally she burst out, 'It's so . . . *swanky!*' Here my kettle screamed and when I got back she had gotten bold enough to touch the electric typewriter (she jumped when it turned itself on) and then walked about slowly, touching the books with the tips of her fingers. She was brave and pushed the tabs on the desk lamp (though not hard enough to turn it on) and boldly picked up my little mailing scale. As she did so, I saw that there were buttons missing from the back of her dress; I said, 'A. R., come here.'

She dropped the scale with a crash. 'I didn't mean it!' Sulky again.

'It's not that, it's your buttons,' I said, and hauled her to the study closet where I keep a Band-Aid box full of extras; two were a reasonable match: little, flat-topped, pearlized, pink things you can hardly find anymore. I sewed them onto her, not that it helped much, and the tangles of her hair kept falling back and catching. What a forest of lost barrettes and snarls of old rubber bands! I lifted it all a little grimly, remembering the pain of combing out. She sat flatly, all adoration gone:

'You can't comb my hair against my will; you're too weak.'

'I wasn't going to,' I said.

'That's what *you* say,' the L. D. G. pointed out.

'If I try, you can stop me,' I said. After a moment she turned around, flopped down on my typing chair, and bent her head. So I fetched my old hairbrush (which I haven't used for years) and did what I could with the upper layers, managing even to smooth out some of the lower ones, though there were places near her neck nearly as matted and tangled as felt; I finally had to cut some pieces out with my nail scissors.

L. D. G. didn't shriek (as I used to, insisting my cries were far more artistic than those of the opera singers on the radio on Sundays) but finally asked for the comb herself and winced silently until she was decently braided, with rubber bands on the ends. We put the rescued barrettes in her shirt pocket. Without that cloud of hair her sallow face and pitch-ball eyes looked bigger, and oddly enough, younger; she was no more a wandering Fury with the voice of a Northwest-coast raven but a reasonably human (though draggly) little girl.

I said, 'You look nice.'

She got up, went into the bathroom, and looked at herself in the mirror. Then she said calmly, 'No, I don't. I look conventional.'

'Conventional?' said I. She came out of the bathroom, flipping back her new braids.

'Yes, I must go.'

And as I was wondering at her tact (for anything after this would have been an anti-climax):

'But I shall return.'

'That's fine,' I said, 'but I want to have grown-up manners with you, A. R. Don't ever come before ten in the morning or if my car isn't here or if you can hear my typewriter going. In fact, I think you had better call me on the telephone first, the way other people do.'

She shook her head sweetly. She was at the front door before I could follow her, peering out. It was raining again. I saw that she was about to step out into it and cried 'Wait, A. R.!' hurrying as fast as I could down the cellar steps to the garage, from where I could get easily to my car. I got from the back seat the green plastic poncho I always keep there and she didn't protest when I dumped it over her and put the hood over her head, though the poncho was much too big and even dragged on the ground in the front and back. She said only, 'Oh, it's swanky. Is it from the Army?' So I had the satisfaction of seeing her move up the hill as a small, green tent instead of a wet, pink draggle. Though with her tea-party manners she hadn't really eaten anything; the milk and peach were untouched. Was it wariness? Or did she just not like milk and peaches?

Remembering our first encounter, I wrote on the pad by the telephone, which is my shopping list:

Milky Way Bars

And then:

1 doz.

She came back. She never did telephone in advance. It was all right, though; she had the happy faculty of somehow turning up when I wasn't working and wasn't busy and was thinking of her. But how often is an invalid busy or working? We went on walks or stayed home and on these occasions the business about the Milky Ways turned out to be a brilliant guess, for never have I met a child with such a passion for junk food. A. R.'s formal, disciplined politeness in front of milk or fruit was like a cat's in front of the mass-produced stuff; faced with jam, honey, or marmalade, the very ends of her braids crisped and she attacked like a cat flinging itself on a fish; I finally had to hide my own supplies in self-defense. Then on relatively good days it was ice cream or Sara Lee cake, and on bad ones Twinkies or Mallo-bars, Hostess cupcakes, Three Musketeers bars, marshmallow cream, maraschino chocolates, Turkish taffy, saltwater taffy, or—somewhat less horribly—Doritos, reconstituted potato chips, corn chips, pretzels (fat or thin), barbecued corn chips, or onion-flavored corn chips, anything like that. She refused nuts and hated peanut butter. She also talked continuously while eating, largely in polysyllables, which made me nervous as I perpetually expected her to choke, but she never did. She got no fatter. To get her out of the house and so away from food, I took her to an old-fashioned five-and-ten nearby and bought her shoelaces. Then I took her down to watch the local ship-canal bridge open up (to let a sailboat through) and we cheered. I took her to a department store (just to look; 'I know consumerism is against your principles,' she said with priggish and mystifying accuracy) and bought her a pin shaped like a ladybug. She refused to go to the zoo ('An animal jail!') but allowed that the rose gardens ('A plant *hotel*') were both pleasant and educational. A ride on the zoo merry-go-round excited her to the point of screaming and running around dizzily in circles for half an hour afterwards, which embarrassed me—but then no one paid the slightest attention; I suppose shrieky little girls had happened there before, though the feminine youth of Seattle, in its Mary Jane shoes and pink pocketbooks, rather pointedly ignored her. The waterfall in the downtown park, on the contrary, sobered her up; this is a park built right on top of a crossing over one of the city's highways and is usually full of office-workers; a walkway leads not only up to but actually behind the waterfall. A. R. wandered among the beds of bright flowers and passed, stopping, behind the water, trying to stick her hand in the falls; she came out saying:

'It looks like an old man's beard,' (pointing to one of the ragged Skid Row men who was sleeping on the grass in the rare, Northern sunlight). Then she said, 'No, it looks like a lady's dress without any seams.'

Once, feeling we had become friends enough for it, I ran her a bath and put her clothes through the basement washer-dryer; her splashings and yellings in the bathroom were terrific and afterwards she flashed nude about the house, hanging out of windows, embellishing her strange, raucous shouts with violent jerkings and boundings-about that I think were meant for dancing. She even ran out the back door naked and had circled the house before I—voiceless with calling, 'A. R., come back here!'—had presence of mind enough to lock both the front and back doors after she had dashed in and before she could get out again to make the entire *tour de Seattle* in her jaybird suit. Then I had to get her back into that tired pink dress, which (when I ironed it) had *finally* given up completely, despite the dryer, and sagged into two sizes too big for her.

Unless A. R. was youthifying.

I got her into her too-large pink dress, her baggy underwear, her too-large shoes, her new pink socks (which I had bought for her) and said:

'A. R., where do you live?'

Crisp and shining, the Little Clean Girl replied, 'My dear, you always ask me that.'

'And you never answer,' said I.

'O yes I do,' said the Little Clean Girl. 'I live up the hill and under the hill and over the hill and behind the hill.'

'That's no answer,' said I.

'Wupf merble,' said she (through a Mars Bar) and then, more intelligibly, 'If you knew, you wouldn't want me.'

'I would so!' I said.

L. D. G.—now L. C. G.—regarded me thoughtfully. She scratched her ear, getting, I noticed, chocolate in her hair. (She was a fast worker.) She said, 'You want to know. You think you ought to know. You think you have a right. When I leave you'll wait until I'm out of sight and then you'll follow me in the car. You'll sneak by the curb way behind me so I won't notice you. You'll wait until I climb the steps of a house—like that big yellow house with the fuchsias in the yard where you think I live and you'll watch me go in. And then you'll ring the bell and when the lady comes to the door you'll say, "Your little daughter and I have become friends," but the lady will say, "I haven't got any little daughter," and then you'll know I fooled you. And you'll get scared. So don't try.'

Well, she had me dead to rights. Something very like that had been in my head. Her face was preternaturally grave. She said, 'You think I'm too small. I'm not.

'You think I'll get sick if I keep on eating like this. I won't.

'You think if you bought a whole department store for me, it would be enough. It wouldn't.'

'I won't—well, I can't get a whole department store for you,' I said. She said, 'I know.' Then she got up and tucked the box of Mars Bars under one arm, throwing over the other my green plastic poncho, which she always carried about with her now.

'I'll get you anything you want,' I said; 'No, not what you want, A. R., but anything you really, truly need.'

'You can't,' said the Little Dirty Girl.

'I'll try.'

She crossed the living room to the front door, dragging the poncho across the rug, not paying the slightest attention to the astronomical photographs that had so enchanted her before. Too young now, I suppose. I said, 'A. R., I'll try. Truly I will.' She seemed to consider it a moment, her small head to one side. Then she said briskly, 'I'll be back,' and was out the front door.

And I did not—would not—could not—did not dare to follow her.

Was this the moment I decided I was dealing with a ghost? No, long before. Little by little, I suppose. Her clothes were a dead giveaway, for one thing: always the same and the kind no child had worn since the end of the Second World War. Then there was the book I had given her on her first visit, which had somehow closed and straightened itself on the coffee table, another I had lent her later (the poems of Edna Millay) which had mysteriously been there a day afterwards, the eerie invisibility of a naked little girl hanging out of my windows and yelling; the inconspicuousness of a little twirling girl nobody noticed spinning round and shrieking outside the merry-go-round, a dozen half-conscious glimpses I'd had, every time I'd got in or out of my car, of the poncho lying on the back seat where I always keep it, folded as always, the very dust on it undisturbed. And her unchildlike cleverness in never revealing either her name or where she lived. And as surely as A. R. had been a biggish eight when we had met, weeks ago, just as

surely she was now a smallish, very unmistakable, unnaturally knowl-
edgeable five.

But she was such a *nice* little ghost. And so solid! Ghosts don't run up
your grocery bills, do they? Or trample Cheez Doodles into your carpet
or leave gum under your kitchen chair, large smears of chocolate on the
surface of the table (A. R. had) and an exceptionally dirty ring around
the inside of the bathtub? Along with three (count 'em, three) large,
dirty, sopping-wet bath towels on the bathroom floor? If A. R.'s social
and intellectual life had a tendency to become intangible when looked
at carefully, everything connected with her digestive system and her
bodily dirt stuck around amazingly; there was the state of the bathroom,
the dishes in the sink (many more than mine), and the ironing board
still up in the study for the ironing of A. R.'s dress (with the spray starch
container still set up on one end and the scorch mark where she'd
decided to play with the iron). If she was a ghost, she was a good one
and I liked her and wanted her back. Whatever help she needed from
me in resolving her ancient Seattle tragedy (ancient ever since nineteen-
forty-two) she could have. I wondered for a moment if she were connected with the house, but the people before me—the original
owners—hadn't had children. And the house itself hadn't even been
built until the mid-fifties; nothing in the neighborhood had. Unless
both they and I were being haunted by the children we hadn't had;
could I write them a psychotherapeutic letter about it? ('Dear Mrs X,
How is your inner space?') I went into the bathroom and discovered
that A. R. had relieved herself interestingly in the toilet and had then
not flushed it, hardly what I would call poetical behavior on the part of
somebody's unconscious. So *I* flushed it. I picked up the towels one by
one and dragged them to the laundry basket in the bedroom. If the
Little Dirty Girl was a ghost, she was obviously a bodily-dirt-and-needs
ghost traumatized in life by never having been given a proper bath or
allowed to eat marshmallows until she got sick. Maybe this was it and
now she could rest (scrubbed and full of Mars Bars) in peace. But I
hoped not. I was nervous; I had made a promise ('I'll give you what you
need') that few of us can make to anyone, a frightening promise to make
to anyone. Still, I hoped. And she was a businesslike little ghost. She
would come back.

For she, too, had promised.

Autumn came. I didn't see the Little Dirty Girl. School started and
I spent days trying to teach freshmen and freshwomen not to write
like Rod McKuen (neither of us really knowing why they shouldn't,

actually) while advanced students pursued me down the halls with thousand-page trilogies, demands for independent study, and other unspeakables. As a friend of ours said once, everyone will continue to pile responsibility on a woman and everything and everyone must be served except oneself; I've been a flogged horse professionally long enough to know that and meanwhile the dishes stay in the sink and the kindly wife-elves do *not* come out of the woodwork at night and do them. I was exercising two hours a day and sleeping ten; the Little Dirty Girl seemed to have vanished with the summer.

Then one day there was a freak spell of summer weather and that evening a thunderstorm. This is a very rare thing in Seattle. The storm didn't last, of course, but it seemed to bring right after it the first of the winter rains: cold, drenching, ominous. I was grading papers that evening when someone knocked at my door; I thought I'd left the garage light on and my neighbor'd come out to tell me, so I yelled 'Just a minute, please!', dropped my pen, wondered whether I should pick it up, decided the hell with it, and went (exasperated) to the door.

It was the Little Dirty Girl. She was as wet as I've ever seen a human being be and had a bad cough (my poncho must've gone heaven knows where) and water squelching in her shoes. She was shivering violently and her fingers were blue—it could not have been more than fifty degrees out—and her long, baggy dress clung to her with water running off it; there was a puddle already forming around her feet on the rug. Her teeth were chattering. She stood there shivering and glowering miserably at me, from time to time emitting that deep, painful chest cough you sometimes hear in adults who smoke too much. I thought of hot baths, towels, electric blankets, aspirin—can ghosts get pneumonia? 'For God's sake, get your clothes off!' I said, but A. R. stepped back against the door, shivering, and wrapped her starved arms in her long, wet skirt.

'No!' she said, in a deep voice more like a crow's than ever. 'Like this!'

'Like what?' said I helplessly, thinking of my back and how incapable I was of dragging a resistant five-year-old anywhere.

'You hate me!' croaked A. R. venomously; 'You starve me! You do! You won't let me eat anything!'

Then she edged past me, still coughing, her dark eyes ringed with blue, her skin mottled with bruises, and her whole body shaking with cold and anger, like a little mask of Medusa. She screamed:

'You want to clean me up because you don't like me!

'You like me clean because you don't like me dirty!

'You hate me so you won't give me what I need!

'You won't give me what I need and I'm dying!

'I'm dying! I'm dying!

'I'M DYING!'

She was interrupted by coughing. I said, 'A. R.—' and she screamed again, her whole body bending convulsively, the cords in her neck standing out. Her scream was choked by phlegm and she beat herself with her fists, then wrapping her arms in her wet skirt through another bout of coughing, she said in gasps:

'I couldn't get into your house to use the bathroom, so I had to shit in my pants.

'I had to stay out in the rain; I got cold.

'All I can get is from you and you won't give it.'

'Then tell me what you need!' I said, and A. R. raised her horrid little face to mine, a picture of venomous, uncontrolled misery, of sheer, demanding starvation.

'You,' she whispered.

So that was it. I thought of the pleading cats, whose open mouths *(Dependency! Dependency!)* reveal needle teeth which can rip off your thumb; I imagined the Little Dirty Girl sinking her teeth into my chest if I so much as touched her. Not touched for bathing or combing or putting on shoelaces, you understand, but for touching only. I saw—I don't know what; her skin ash-grey, the bones of her little skull coming through her skin worse and worse every moment—and I knew she would kill me if she didn't get what she wanted, though she was suffering far worse than I was and was more innocent—a demon child is still a child, with a child's needs, after all. I got down on one knee, so as to be nearer her size, and saying only, 'My back—be careful of my back,' held out my arms so that the terror of the ages could walk into them. She was truly grey now, her bones very prominent. She was starving to death. She was dying. She gave the cough of a cadaver breathing its last, a phlegmy wheeze with a dreadful rattle in it, and then the Little Dirty Girl walked right into my arms.

And began to cry. I felt her crying right up from her belly. She was cold and stinky and extremely dirty and afflicted with the most surprising hiccough. I rocked her back and forth and mumbled I don't know what, but what I meant was that I thought she was fine, that all of her was fine: her shit, her piss, her sweat, her tears, her scabby knees, the snot on her face, her cough, her dirty panties, her bruises, her desperation, her anger, her whims—all of her was wonderful, I loved all of her, and I would do my best to take good care of her, all of her, forever and forever and then a day.

She bawled. She howled. She pinched me hard. She yelled, 'Why did it take you so long!' She fussed violently over her panties and said she had been humiliated, though it turned out, when I got her to the bathroom, that she was making an awfully big fuss over a very little brown stain. I put the panties to soak in the kitchen sink and the Little Dirty Girl likewise in a hot tub with vast mounds of rose-scented bubble bath which turned up from somewhere, though I knew perfectly well I hadn't bought any in years. We had a shrieky, tickly, soapy, toe-grabby sort of bath, a *very* wet one during which I got soaked. (I told her about my back and she was careful.) We sang to the loofah. We threw water at the bathroom tiles. We lost the soap. We came out warm in a huge towel (I'd swear mine aren't that big) and screamed gaily again, to exercise our lungs, from which the last bit of cough had disappeared. We said, 'Oh, floof! there goes the soap.' We speculated loudly (and at length) on the possible subjective emotional life of the porcelain sink, American variety, and (rather to my surprise) sang snatches of *The Messiah* as follows:

Every malted
Shall be exalted!

and:

Behold and see
Behold and see
If there were e'er pajama
Like to this pajama!

and so on.

My last memory of the evening is of tucking the Little Dirty Girl into one side of my bed (in my pajamas, which had to be rolled up and pinned even to stay on her) and then climbing into the other side myself. The bed was wider than usual, I suppose. She said sleepily, 'Can I stay?' and I (also sleepily) 'Forever.'

But in the morning she was gone.

Her clothes lasted a little longer, which worried me, as I had visions of A. R. committing flashery around and about the neighborhood, but in a few days they too had faded into mist or the elemental particles of time or whatever ghosts and ghost-clothes are made of. The last thing I saw of hers was a shoe with a new heel (oh yes, I had gotten them fixed) which rolled out from under the couch and lasted a whole day before it became—I forget what, the shadow of one of the ornamental tea-cups on the mantel, I think.

And so there was no more five-year-old A. R. beating on the door and demanding to be let in on rainy nights. But that's not the end of the story.

As you know, I've never gotten along with my mother. I've always supposed that neither of us knew why. In my childhood she had vague, long-drawn-out symptoms which I associated with early menopause (I was a late baby); then she put me through school, which was a strain on her librarian's budget and a strain on my sense of independence and my sense of guilt, and always there was her timidity, her fears of everything under the sun, her terrified, preoccupied air of always being somewhere else, and what I can only call her furtiveness, the feeling I've always had of some secret life going on in which I could never ask about or share. Add to this my father's death somewhere in pre-history (I was two) and then that ghastly behavior psychologists call The Game of Happy Families—I mean the perpetual, absolute insistence on How Happy We All Were that even aunts, uncles, and cousins rushed to heap on my already bitter and most unhappy shoulders, and you'll have some idea of what's been going on for the last I-don't-know-how-many years.

Well, this is the woman who came to visit a few weeks later. I wanted to dodge her. I had been dodging academic committees and students and proper bedtimes; why couldn't I dodge my mother? So I decided that *this time I would be openly angry* (I'd been doing that in school, too).

Only there was nothing to be angry about, this time.

Maybe it was the weather. It was one of those clear, still times we sometimes have in October: warm, the leaves not down yet, that in-and-out sunshine coming through the clouds, and the northern sun so low that the masses of orange pyracantha berries on people's brick walls and the walls themselves, or anything that color, flame indescribably. My mother got in from the airport in a taxi (I still can't drive far) and we walked about a bit, and then I took her to Kent and Hallby's downtown, that expensive, old-fashioned place that's all mirrors and sawdust floors and old-fashioned white tablecloths and waiters (also waitresses now) with floor-length aprons. It was very self-indulgent of me. But she had been so much better—or I had been—it doesn't matter. She was seventy and if she wanted to be fussy and furtive and act like a thin, old guinea-hen with secret despatches from the CIA (I've called her worse things) I felt she had the right. Besides, that was no worse than my flogging myself through five women's work and endless depressions, beating the old plough horse day after day for weeks and months and years—no, for decades—until her back broke and she foundered and went down and all I could do was curse at her helplessly and beat her the more.

All this came to me in Kent and Hallby's. Luckily my mother squeaked as we sat down. There's a reason; if you sit at a corner table in Kent and Hallby's and see your face where the mirrored walls come together—well, it's complicated, but briefly, you can see yourself (for the only time in your life) as you look to other people. An ordinary mirror reverses the right and left sides of your face but this odd arrangement re-reflects them so they're back in place. People are shocked when they see themselves; I had planned to warn her.

She said, bewildered, 'What's that?' But rather intrigued too, I think. Picture a small, thin, white-haired, extremely prim ex-librarian, worn to her fine bones but still ready to take alarm and run away at a moment's notice; that's my mother. I explained about the mirrors and then I said:

'People don't really know what they look like. It's only an idea people have that you'd recognize yourself if you saw yourself across the room. Any more than we can hear our own voices; you know, it's because longer frequencies travel so much better through the bones of your head than they can through the air; that's why a tape recording of your voice sounds higher than—'

I stopped. Something was going to happen. A hurricane was going to smash Kent and Hallby's flat. I had spent almost a whole day with my mother, walking around my neighborhood, showing her the University, showing her my house, and nothing in particular had happened; why should anything happen now?

She said, looking me straight in the eye, 'You've changed.'

I waited.

She said, 'I'm afraid that we—like you and I were not—are not—a happy family.'

I said nothing. I would have, a year ago. It occurred to me that I might, for years, have confused my mother's primness with my mother's self-control. She went on. She said:

'When you were five, I had cancer.'

I said, '*What?* You had *what?*'

'Cancer,' said my mother calmly, in a voice still as low and decorous as if she had been discussing her new beige handbag or Kent and Hallby's long, fancy menu (which lay open on the table between us). 'I kept it from you. I didn't want to burden you.'

Burden.

'I've often wondered—' she went on, a little flustered; 'they say now—but of course no one thought that way then.' She went on, more formally, 'It takes years to know if it has spread or will come back, even now, and the doctors knew very little then. I was all right eventually, of course, but by that time you were almost grown up and had become a very capable and self-sufficient little girl. And then later on you were so successful.'

She added, 'You didn't seem to want me.'

Want her! Of course not. What would you feel about a mother who disappeared like that? Would you trust her? Would you accept anything from her? All those years of terror and secrecy; maybe she'd thought she was being punished by having cancer. Maybe she'd thought she was going to die. Too scared to give anything and everyone being loudly secretive and then being faced with a daughter who wouldn't be questioned, wouldn't be kissed, wouldn't be touched, who kept her room immaculate, who didn't want her mother and made no bones about it, and who kept her fury and betrayal and betrayal and her misery to herself, and her schoolwork excellent. I could say only the silliest thing, right out of the movies:

'Why are you telling me all this?'

She said simply, 'Why not?'

I wish I could go on to describe a scene of intense and affectionate reconciliation between my mother and myself, but that did not happen—quite. She put her hand on the table and I took it, feeling I don't know what; for a moment she squeezed my hand and smiled. I got up then and she stood too, and we embraced, not at all as I had embraced the Little Dirty Girl, though with the same pain at heart, but awkwardly and only for a moment, as such things really happen. I said to myself: *Not yet. Not so fast. Not right now,* wondering if we looked—in Kent and Hallby's mirrors—the way we really were. We were both embarrassed, I think, but that too was all right. We sat down: *Soon. Sometime. Not quite yet.*

The dinner was nice. The next day I took her for breakfast to the restaurant that goes around and gives you a view of the whole city and then to the public market and then on a ferry. We had a pleasant, affectionate quiet two days and then she went back East.

We've been writing each other lately—for the first time in years more than the obligatory birthday and holiday cards and a few remarks about the weather—and she sent me old family photographs, talked about being a widow, and being misdiagnosed for years (that's what it seems now) and about all sorts of old things: my father, my being in the school play in second grade, going to summer camp, getting moths to sit on her finger, all sorts of things.

And the Little Dirty Girl? Enclosed is her photograph. We were passing a photographer's studio near the University the other day and she was seized with a passionate fancy to have her picture taken (I suspect the Tarot cards and the live owl in the window had something to do with it), so in we went. She clamors for a lot lately and I try to provide it: flattens her nose against a bakery window and we argue about whether she'll settle for a currant bun instead of a do-nut, wants to stay up late and read and sing to herself so we do, screams for parties so we find them, and *at* parties impels me towards people I would probably not have noticed or (if I had) liked a year ago. She's a surprisingly generous and good little soul and I'd be lost without her, so it's turned out all right in the end. Besides, one ignored her at one's peril. I try not to.

Mind you, she has taken some odd, good things out of my life. Little boys seldom walk with me now. And I've perfected—though regretfully—a more emphatic method of kitty-booting which they seem to understand; at least one of them turned to me yesterday with a look of disgust that said clearer than words: 'Good Heavens, how you've degenerated! Don't you know there's nothing in life more important than taking care of Me?'

About the picture: you may think it odd. You may even think it's not her. (You're wrong.) The pitch-ball eyes and thin face are there, all right, but what about the bags under her eyes, the deep, downward lines about her mouth, the strange color of her short-cut hair (it's grey)? What about her astonishing air of being so much older, so much more intellectual, so much more professional, so much more—well, competent—than any Little Dirty Girl could possibly be?

Well, faces change when forty-odd years fall into the developing fluid.

And you have always said that you wanted, that you must have, that you commanded, that you begged, and so on and so on in your interminable, circumlocutory style, that the one thing you desired most in the world was a photograph, a photograph, your kingdom for a photograph—of me.

WATCHING ME, WATCHING YOU

Fay Weldon

The ghost liked the stairs best, where people passed quickly and occasionally, holding their feelings in suspense between the closing of one door and the opening of another. Mostly, the ghost slept. He preferred sleep. But sometimes the sense of something important happening, some crystallization of the past or omen for the future, would wake him, and he would slither off the stair and into one room or another of the house to see what was going on. Presently, he wore an easy path of transition into a particular room on the first floor—as sheep will wear an easy path in the turf by constant trotting to and fro. Here, as the seasons passed, a plane tree pressed closer and closer against the window, keeping out light and warmth. The various cats which lived out their lives in the house seldom went into this small damp back room, and seemed to feel the need to race up and down that portion of the stairs the ghost favoured, though sitting happily enough at the bottom of the stairs, or on the top landing.

Many houses contain ghosts. (It would be strange if they didn't.) Mostly they sleep, or wake so seldom their presence is not noticed, let alone minded. If a glass falls off a shelf in 1940, and a door opens by itself in 1963, and a sense of oppression is felt in 1971, and knocking sounds are heard on Christmas Day, 1980—who wants to make anything of that? Four inexplicable happenings in a week call for exorcism—the same number spread over forty years call for nothing more than a shrug and a stiff drink.

66 Aldermans Drive, Bristol. The house had stood for a hundred and thirty years, and the ghost had slept and occasionally sighed and slithered sideways, and otherwise done little else but puff out a curtain on a still day for all but ten of those. He entered the house on the shoulders of a parlour-maid. She had been to a seance in the hope of raising her dead lover, but had raised something altogether more elusive, if at least sleepier, instead. The maid had stayed in the house until she died, driving her mistress to suicide and marrying the master the while, and

the ghost had stayed too, long after all were dead, and the house empty, with paper peeling off the walls, and the banisters broken, and carpets rotting on the floors, and dust and silence everywhere.

The ghost slept, and woke again to the sound of movement, and different voices. The new people were numerous: they warmed gnarled winter hands before gas-fires, and the smell of boiled cabbage and sweat wafted up the stairs, and exhaustion and indifference prevailed. In the back room on the first floor, presently, a girl gave birth to a baby. The ghost sighed and puffed out the curtains. In this room, earlier, the maid's mistress had hanged herself, making a swinging shadow against the wall in the gas-light shining from the stairs. The ghost had a sense of justice, or at any rate balance. He slept again.

The house emptied. Rain came through broken tiles into the back room. A man with a probe came and pierced into the rotten beams of roof and floor, and shook his head and laughed. The tree thrust a branch through the window, and a sparrow flew in, and couldn't get out, and died, and after mice and insects and flies had finished with it, was nothing more than two slender white bones, placed crosswise.

It was 1965. The front door opened and a man and a woman entered, and such was their natures that the ghost was alert at once. The man's name was Maurice: he was burly and warm-skinned; his hands were thick and crude, labourer's hands, but clean and soft. His hair was pale and tightly curled; he was bearded; his eyes were large and heavily hooded. He looked at the house as if he were already its master: as if he cared nothing for its rotten beams and its leaking roof.

'We'll have it,' he said. She laughed. It was a nervous laugh, which she used when she was frightened. She had a small cross face half-lost in a mass of coarse red hair. She was tiny waisted, big-bosomed and long-legged; her limbs lean and freckly. Her fingers were long and fragile. 'But it's falling down,' said Vanessa. 'How can we afford it?'
'Look at the detail on the cornices!' was all he said. 'I'm sure they're original.'
'I expect we can make something of it,' she said.

She loved him. She would do what she could for him. The ghost sensed cruelty, somewhere: he bustled around, stirring the air.

'It's very draughty,' she complained.

They looked into the small back room on the first floor and even he shivered.

'I'll never make anything of this room,' she said.

'Vanessa,' he said. 'I trust you to do something wonderful with every-thing.'

'Then I'll make it beautiful,' she said, loud and clear, marking out her future. 'Even this, for you.'

The plane tree rubbed against the window pane.

'It's just a question of lopping a branch or two,' he said.

One night, after dark, when builders' trestles were everywhere, and the sour smell of damp lime plaster was on the stairs, Maurice spread a blanket for Vanessa in the little back room.

'Not here,' she said.

'It's the only place that isn't dusty,' he said.

He made love to her, his broad, white body covering her narrow, freckled one altogether.

'Today the divorce came through,' he said.

Other passions split the air. The ghost felt them. Outside in the alley which ran behind the house, beneath the plane tree, stood another woman. Her face was round and sweet, her hair was short and mousy, her eyes bright, bitter and wet. In the house the girl cried out and the man groaned; and the watcher's face became empty, drained of sweet-ness, left expressionless, a vacuum into which something had to flow. The ghost left with her, on her shoulders.

'I have fibrositis now,' said Anne, 'as well as everything else.' She said it to herself, into the mirror, when she was back home in the basement of the house in Upton Park, where once she and Maurice had lived and built their life. She had to say it to herself, because there was no one else to say it to, except their child Wendy, and Wendy was only four and lay asleep in a pile of blankets on the floor, her face and hands sticky and unwashed. Anne threw an ashtray at the mirror and cracked it, and Wendy woke and cried. 'Seven years bad luck,' said Anne. 'Well, who's counting!'

Sweetness had run out: sourness took its place: she too had marked out her future.

The ghost found a space against the wall between the barred windows of the room, and took up residence there, and drowsed, waking sometimes to accompany Anne on her midnight vigils to 66 Aldermans Drive. Presently he wore an easy route for himself, slipping and slithering between the two places, and no longer needed her for the journey. Sometimes he was here, sometimes there.

In Aldermans Drive he found a painted stairwell and a mended banister, but stairs which were still uncarpeted, and a cat which howled and shot upstairs. The ghost moved in to the small back room and the door pushed open in his path and shadows swung and shifted against the wall.

Vanessa was wearing jeans. She and Maurice were papering the room with bright patterned paper. They were laughing: she had glue in her hair.
'When we're rich,' she was saying, 'I'll never do this kind of thing again. We'll always have professionals in to do it.'
'When we're rich!' He yearned for it.
'Of course we'll be rich. You'll write a bestseller; you're far better than anyone else. Genius will out!'

If he felt she misunderstood the nature of genius, or was insensitive to what he knew by instinct, that popularity and art are at odds, he said nothing. He indulged her. He kissed her. He loved her.

'What are those shadows on the wall?' she asked.
'We always get those in here,' he said. 'It's the tree against the window.'
'We'll have to get it lopped,' she said.
'It seems a pity,' he said. 'Such a wonderful old tree.'

He trimmed another length of paper.

'How can the tree be casting shadows?' she asked. 'The sun isn't out.'
'Some trick of reflected light,' said Maurice. The knife in his hand slipped, and he swore.
'It doesn't matter,' said Vanessa, looking at the torn paper, 'it doesn't have to be perfect. It's only Wendy's room. And then only for weekends. It's not as if she was going to be here all the time.'
'Perhaps you and I should have this room,' said Maurice, 'and Wendy could have the one next door. It overlooks the crescent. It has a view, and a balcony. She'll love it.'

'So would I,' said Vanessa.

'I don't want Wendy to feel second-best,' said Maurice.

'Not after all we've put her through.'

'All that's happened to her,' corrected Vanessa, tight lipped.

'And don't say "only Wendy",' he rebuked her. 'She is my child, after all.'

'It isn't fair! Why couldn't you be like other people? Why do you have to have a past?'

They worked in silence for a little, and the ghost writhed palely in the anger in the air, and then Vanessa relented and smiled and said. 'Don't let's quarrel,' and he said, 'you know I love you,' and the fine front room was Wendy's and the small back room was to house their marriage bed.

'I'm sure I closed the door,' said Vanessa presently, 'but now it's open.'

'The catch is weak,' said Maurice. 'I'll mend it when I can. There's just so much to do in a home this size,' and he sighed and the sigh exhaled out of the open window into the street.

'Goodbye,' said Vanessa.

'Why did you say goodbye?' asked Maurice.

'Because the net curtains flapped and whoever came in through the door was clearly going out by the window,' said Vanessa, thinking she was joking, too young and beautiful and far from death to mind an unseen visitor or so. The ghost whirled away on the remnant of Maurice's sigh, over the roof-tops and the brow of the hill, and down into Upton Park, where it was winter, no longer summer, and little Wendy was six, and getting out of bed, bare cold toes on chilly lino.

The ghost's observations were now from outside time. So a man might stand on a station overpass and watch a train go through beneath. Such a man could see, if he chose, any point along the train—in front of him the future, behind him the past, directly beneath him, changing always from past to future, his main rumbling, noisy perception of the present. The ghost keeps his gaze steadily forward.

The clock says five to nine; Anne is asleep in bed. Wendy shakes her awake.

'My feet are cold,' says the little girl.

'Then put on your slippers,' mourns the mother, out of sleep. It has been an uneasy, unsatisfying slumber. Once she lay next to Maurice and fancied she drew her strength out of his slumbering body, hot beside her, like some spiritual water-bottle. She clings to the fancy in her mind: she refuses to sleep as she did when a child, composed and decent in solitude, providing her own warmth well enough.

'Won't I be late for school?' asks Wendy.

'No,' says Anne, in the face of all evidence to the contrary.

'It is ever so cold,' says Wendy. 'Can I light the gas-fire?'

'No you can't,' says Anne. 'We can't afford it.'

'Daddy will pay the bill,' says Wendy, hopefully. But her mother just laughs.

'I'm frightened,' says Wendy, all else having failed. 'The curtains are waving about and the window isn't even open. Can I get into your bed?'

Anne moves over and the child gets in.

An egg teeters on the edge of the table, amidst the remnants of last night's chips and tomato sauce, and falls and smashes. Anne sits up in bed, startled into reaction. 'How did that happen?' she asks, aloud. But there is no one to reply, for Wendy has fallen asleep, and the ghost is spinning and spinning, nothing but a whirl of air in the corner of the eye, and no one listens to him, anyway.

Further forward still, and there's Vanessa, sitting up in bed, bouncy brown-nippled breasts half covered by fawn lace. It is a brass bed, finely filigreed. Maurice wears black silk pyjamas. He sits on the edge of the bed, while Vanessa sips fresh orange juice, and opens his letters.

'Any cheques?' asks Vanessa.

'Not today,' he says. Maurice is a writer. Cheques bounce through the letter box with erratic energy: bills come in with a calm, steady beat. It is a tortoise and hare situation, and the tortoise always wins.

'Perhaps you should change your profession,' she suggests.

'Be an engineer or go into advertising. I hate all this worry about money.'

A mirror slips upon its string on the wall, hangs sidewise. Neither notice.

'Is that a letter from Anne?' asks Vanessa. 'What does she want now?'

'It's her electricity bill,' he says.

'She's supposed to pay that out of her monthly cheque. She only sends you these demands to make you feel unhappy and guilty. She's jealous of us. How I despise jealousy! What a bitch she is!'

'She has a child to look after,' says Maurice. 'My child.'

'If I had your child, would you treat me better?' she asks.

'I treat you perfectly well,' he says, pulling the bedclothes back, rubbing black silk against beige lace, and the mirror falls off the wall altogether, startling them, stopping them. 'This whole room will have to be stripped out,' complains Vanessa. 'The plaster is rotten. I'll get arthritis from the damp.' Vanessa notices, sometimes, as she walks up and down the stairs, that her knees ache.

Wendy is ten. Anne's room has been painted white, and there are cushions on the chairs, and dirty washing is put in the basket, not left on the floor, and times are a little better. A little. There is passion in the air.

'Vanessa says I can stay all week not just weekends, and go to school from Aldermans Drive!' says Wendy. 'Live with Dad, and not with you.'

'What did you say?' asks Anne, trying to sound casual.

'I said no thank you,' says Wendy. 'There's no peace over there. They always have the builders in. Bang, bang, bang! And Dad's always shut away in a room, writing. I prefer it here, in spite of everything. Damp and draughts and all.'

The damp on the wall between the barred windows is worse. It makes a strange shape on the wall; it seems to change from day to day. The house belongs to Maurice. He will not have the roof over their heads mended. He says he cannot afford to. In the rooms above live tenants, protected by law, who pay next to nothing in rent. How can he spare the money needed to keep the house in good order—and why, according to Vanessa, should he?

'We're just the rejects of the world,' says Anne to Wendy, and Wendy believes her, and her mouth grows tight and pouty instead of firm and generous, as it could have been, and her looks are spoiled. Anne is right, that's the trouble of it. Rejects!

'How my shoulder hurts,' say Anne. She should have stayed at home, never crossed the city to stand beneath the plane-tree in the alley behind Aldermans Drive, allowed herself her paroxysms of jealousy, grief, and solitary sexual frenzy. She has had fibrositis ever since. But she felt what she felt. You can help what you do, but not what you feel.

The ghost looks further forward to Aldermans Drive and finds the bed gone in the small back room, and a dining table in its place, and candles

lit, and guests, and smooth mushroom soup being served. The candles
throw shadows on to the wall: this way, that way. One of the guests tries
to make sense of them, but can't. She has wild blonde hair and a fair
skin and a laughing mouth, unlike Maurice's other women. Her name
is Audrey. She is an actress. Maurice's hair is falling out. His temples are
quite bare, and he has a moustache now instead of a beard, and he seems
distinguished, rather than aspiring. His hand smoothes Audrey's little
one, and Vanessa sees. Maurice defies her jealousy: he smiles blandly,
cruelly, at his wife.

He turns to Audrey's husband, who is eighteen years older than Audrey,
and says, 'Ah youth, youth!' and offers back Audrey's hand, closing the
husband's fingers over the wife's so that nobody could possibly take
offence, and Vanessa feels puzzled at her own distress, and her glass of
red wine tips over on its own account.

'Vanessa! Clumsy!' reproaches Maurice.
'But I didn't!' she says. No one believes her. Why should they? They
pour white wine on the stain to neutralize the red, and it works, and
looking at the tablecloth, presently, no one would have known anything
untoward had happened at all.

'We must have security,' Vanessa weeps from time to time.
'I can't stand the uncertainty of it all! You must stop being a writer. Or
write something different. Stop writing novels. Write for television
instead.'
'No, you must stop spending the money,' he shouts. 'Stop doing up this
house. Changing this, changing that.'
'But I want it to be nice. We must have a nursery. I can't keep the baby
in a drawer.'
Vanessa is pregnant.
'Why not? It's what Anne had to do, thanks to you.'
'Anne! Can't you ever forget Anne?' she shrieks. 'Does she have to be on
our backs for ever? She has ruined our lives.'

But their lives aren't ruined. The small back room becomes a nursery.
The baby sleeps there. He is a boy, his name is Jonathan. He sleeps
badly and cries a lot and is hard to love. His eyes follow the shadows on
the wall, this way, that way.

'There's nothing wrong with his eyes,' says the doctor, visiting, puzzled
at the mother's fears. 'But his chest is bad.'

Vanessa sits by the cot and rocks her feverish child.
'For you and I—' she sings, as she sings when she is nervous, driving away fear with melody—
'—have a guardian angel—on high with nothing to do—
—but to give to you and to give—to me—
—love for ever—true—.'

Maurice is in the room. Vanessa is crying.
'But why won't you go back to work?' he demands. 'It would take the pressure off me. I could write what I want to write, not what I have to write.'
'I want to look after my baby myself,' she weeps. 'It's a man's job to support his family. And you're not exactly William Shakespeare. Why don't you write films? That's where the money is.'

The baby coughs. The doctor says the room is too damp for its good.
'I never liked this room,' says Vanessa, as she and Maurice carry out the cot. 'And you and I always quarrel in it. The quarrelling room. I hate it. But I love you.'
'I love you,' he says, crossing his fingers.

The ghost looks forward. Aldermans Drive has become one of the most desirable streets in Bristol, all new paint and French kitchenware and Welsh dressers seen through lighted windows. The property is in Maurice's name, as seems reasonable, since he earns the money. He writes films, for Hollywood.

Anne's bed turns into a foam settee by day: she has a cooker instead of a gas ring: the window bars have gone: the panes are made of reinforced glass. She has had a telephone installed. Wendy has platform heels and puts cream on her spots.

The ghost looks further forward, and Anne has a boyfriend. A man sits opposite her in a freshly covered armchair. Broken springs have been taped flat. Sometimes she lets him into her bed, but his flesh is cool and none too firm, and she remembers Maurice's body, hot-water bottle in her bed, and won't forget. Won't. Can't.

'Is it wrong to hate people?' asks Anne. 'I hate Vanessa, and with reason. She is a thief. Why do people ask her into their houses? Is it that they don't realize, or just that they don't care? She stole my husband: she tried to steal my child. Maurice has never been happy with her. He never wanted to leave me. She seduced him. She thought he'd be famous one day; how wrong she was! He's sold out, you know! One day he'll come back to me, what's left of him, and I'll be expected to pick up the bits.'

'But he's married to her. They have a child. How can he come back to you?' He is a nice man, a salesman, thoughtful and kind.

'So was I married to him. So do I have his child.'

How stubborn she is!

'You're obsessive.' He is beginning to be angry. Well, he has been angry often enough before, and still stayed around for more. 'While you take Maurice's money,' he says, 'you will never be free of him.'

'Those few miserable pennies! What difference can they make? I live in penury, while she lives in style. He is Wendy's father; he has an obligation to support us. He was the guilty party, after all.'

'The law no longer says guilty or not guilty, in matter of divorce.'

'Well, it should!' She is passionate. 'He should pay for what he did to me and Wendy. He destroyed our lives.'

The ghost is lulled by the turning wheel of her thoughts, so steady on its axis: he drowses; responds to a spasm of despair, an act of decision on the man's part, one morning, as he leaves Anne's unsatisfactory bed. He dresses silently: he means to go: never to come back. He looks in the mirror to straighten his tie and sees Anne's face instead of his own.

He cries out and Anne wakes.

'I'm sorry,' she says. 'Don't go.'

But he does, and he doesn't come back.

The gap between what could be, and what is, defeats him.

Anne has a job as a waitress. It is a humiliation. Maurice does not know she is earning. Anne keeps it a secret, for Vanessa would surely love an excuse to reduce Anne's alimony, already whittled away by inflation.

The decorators are back in Aldermans Drive. The smell of fresh plaster has the ghost alert. Paper is being stripped from walls: doors driven through here: walls dismantled there. The cat runs before the ghost, like a leaf before wind, looking for escape; finding none, cornered in the small back room, where animals never go if they can help it, and the shadows swing to and fro, and the tiny crossed bones from a dead sparrow are lodged beneath the wainscot.

'Get out of here, cat!' cries Vanessa. 'I hate cats, don't you? Maurice loves them. But they don't like me: for ever trying to trip me on the stairs, when I had to go to the baby, in the night.'

'I expect they were jealous,' says the man with her. He is young and handsome, with shrewd, insincere eyes and a lecher's mouth. He is a decorator. He looks at the room with dislike, and at Vanessa, speculatively.

'The worst room in the house,' she laments. 'It's been bedroom, dining room, nursery. It never works! I hope it's better as a bathroom.'

He moves his hand to the back of her neck but she laughs and side-steps.
'The plaster's shockingly damp,' he says, and as if to prove his opinion the curtain rail falls off the wall altogether, making a terrible clatter and clash, and the cat yowls and Vanessa shrieks, and Maurice strides up the stairs to see what is happening, and what was in the air between Vanessa and Toby evaporates. The ghost is on Anne's side—if ghosts take sides.

How grand and boring the house is now! There is a faint scent of chlorine in the air; it comes from the swimming pool in the basement. The stair walls are mirrored: a maid polishes away at the first landing but it's always a little misty. She marvels at how long the flowers last, when placed on the little Georgian stair-table brought by Vanessa for Maurice on his fifty-second birthday. The maid is in love with Maurice, but Maurice has other fish to fry.

Further forward still: something's happening in the bathroom! The bath is deep blue and the taps are gold, and the wallpaper rose, but still the shadows swing to and fro, against the wall.

Audrey has spilt red wine upon her dress. She is more beautiful than she was. She is intelligent. She is no longer married or an actress: she is a solicitor. Maurice admires that very much. He thinks women should be useful, not like Vanessa. He is tired of girls who have young flesh and liquid eyes and love his bed but despise him in their hearts. Audrey does not despise him. Vanessa has forgotten how.

Maurice is helping Audrey sponge down her dress. His hand strays here and there. She is accustomed to it: she does not mind.

'What are those shadows on the wall?' she asks.

'Some trick of the light,' he says.

'Perhaps we should use white wine to remove the red,' she says. 'Remember that night so long ago? It was in this room, wasn't it! Vanessa had it as a dining room, then. I think I fell in love with you that night.'

'And I with you,' he says.

Is it true?—He can hardly remember.

'What a lot of time we've wasted,' he laments, and this for both of them is true enough. They love each other.

'Dear Maurice,' she says, 'I can't bear to see you so unhappy. It's all Vanessa's doing. She stopped you writing. You would be a great writer if it wasn't for her, not just a Hollywood hack! You still could be!'

He laughs, but he is moved. He thinks it might be true. If it were not for Vanessa he would not just be rich and successful, he would be rich, successful, and renowned as well.

'Vanessa says this room is haunted,' he says, seeing the shadows himself, almost defined at last, a body hanging from a noose: a woman destroyed, or self-destroyed. What's the difference? Love does it. Love and ghosts.

'What's the matter?' Audrey asks. He's pale.

'We could leave here,' he says. 'Leave this house. You and me.'

A shrewd light gleams in her intelligent, passionate eyes. How he loves her!

'A pity to waste all this,' says Audrey. 'It is your home, after all, Vanessa's never liked it. If anyone leaves, it should be her.'

The flowers on the landing are still fresh and sweet a week later. Maurice will keep the table they stand upon—a gift from Vanessa to him, after all. If you give someone something, it's theirs for ever. That is the law, says Audrey.

Vanessa moves her belongings from the bathroom shelf. She wants nothing of his, nothing. Just a few personal things—toothbrush, paste, cleansing cream. She will take her child and go. She cannot remain under the same roof, and he won't leave.

'You must see it's for the best, Vanessa,' says Maurice, awkwardly. 'We haven't really been together for years, you and I.'

'All that bed-sharing?' she enquires. 'That wasn't together? The meals, the holidays, the friends, the house? The child? Not together?'

'No,' he says. 'Not together the way I feel with Audrey.' She can hardly believe it. So far she is shocked, rather than distressed. Presently, distress will set in: but not yet.

'I'll provide for you, of course,' he says, 'you and the child. I always looked after Anne, didn't I? Anne and Wendy.' Vanessa turns to stare at him, and over his shoulder sees a dead woman hanging from a rope, but who is to say where dreams begin and reality ends? At the moment she is certainly in a nightmare. She looks back to Maurice, and sees the horror of her own life, and the swinging body fades, if indeed it was ever there. The door opens, by itself.

'You never did fix the catch,' she says.

'No,' he replies. 'I never got round to it.'

The train beneath the overpass was nearly through. The past had caught up with the present and the present was dissolving into the future, and the future was all but out of sight.

It was 1980. The two women, Anne and Vanessa, sat together in the room in Upton Park. The damp patch was back again, but hidden by one of the numerous posters which lined the walls calling on women to live, to be free, to protest, to re-claim the right, demand wages for housework, to do anything in the world but love. The personal, they proclaimed, was the political. Other women came and went in the room.

'However good the present is,' said Anne, 'the past cannot be undone. I wasted so much of my life. I look back and see scenes I would rather not remember. Little things; silly things, even. Wendy being late for school, a lover looking in a mirror. Damp on a wall. I used to think this room was haunted.'

'I used to think the same of Aldermans Drive,' said Vanessa, 'but now I realize what it was. What I sensed was myself now, looking back; me now watching me then, myself remembering me with sorrow for what I was and need never have been.'

They talked about Audrey.

'They say she's unfaithful to him,' said Anne. 'Well, he's nearly sixty and she's thirty-five. What did he expect?'

'Love,' said Vanessa, 'like the rest of us.'

THE JULY GHOST

A. S. Byatt

'I think I must move out of where I'm living,' he said. 'I have this problem with my landlady.'

He picked a long, bright hair off the back of her dress, so deftly that the act seemed simply considerate. He had been skilful at balancing glass, plate, and cutlery, too. He had a look of dignified misery, like a dejected hawk. She was interested.

'What sort of problem? Amatory, financial, or domestic?'

'None of those, really. Well, not financial.'

He turned the hair on his finger, examining it intently, not meeting her eye.

'Not financial. Can you tell me? I might know somewhere you could stay. I know a lot of people.'

'You would.' He smiled shyly. 'It's not an easy problem to describe. There's just the two of us. I occupy the attics. Mostly.'

He came to a stop. He was obviously reserved and secretive. But he was telling her something. This is usually attractive.

'Mostly?' Encouraging him.

'Oh, it's not like *that*. Well, not . . . Shall we sit down?'

They moved across the party, which was a big party, on a hot day. He stopped and found a bottle and filled her glass. He had not needed to ask what she was drinking. They sat side by side on a sofa: he admired the brilliant poppies bold on her emerald dress, and her pretty sandals. She had come to London for the summer to work in the British Museum. She could really have managed with microfilm in Tucson for what little manuscript research was needed, but there was a dragging love affair to end. There is an age at which, however desperately happy one is in stolen moments, days, or weekends with one's married professor, one either prises him loose or cuts and runs. She had had a stab at both, and now considered she had successfully cut and run. So it was nice to be immediately appreciated. Problems are capable of solution. She said as much to him, turning her soft face to his ravaged one, swinging the long bright hair. It had begun a year ago, he told her in a rush, at another party actually; he had met this woman, the landlady in question, and had made, not immediately, a kind of *faux pas*, he now saw, and she had been very decent, all things considered, and so . . .

He had said, 'I think I must move out of where I'm living.' He had been quite wild, had nearly not come to the party, but could not go on drinking alone. The woman had considered him coolly and asked, 'Why?' One could not, he said, go on in a place where one had once been blissfully happy, and was now miserable, however convenient the place. Convenient, that was, for work, and friends, and things that seemed, as he mentioned them, ashy and insubstantial compared to the memory and the hope of opening the door and finding Anne outside it, laughing and breathless, waiting to be told what he had read, or thought, or eaten, or felt that day. Someone I loved left, he told the woman. Reticent on that occasion too, he bit back the flurry of sentences about the total unexpectedness of it, the arriving back and finding only an envelope on a clean table, and spaces in the bookshelves, the record stack, the kitchen cupboard. It must have been planned for weeks, she must have been thinking it out while he rolled on her, while she poured wine for him, while . . . No, no. Vituperation is undignified and in this case what he felt was lower and worse than rage: just pure, child-like loss. 'One ought not to mind places,' he said to the woman. 'But one does,' she had said. 'I know.'

She had suggested to him that he could come and be her lodger, then; she had, she said, a lot of spare space going to waste, and her husband wasn't there much. 'We've not had a lot to say to each other, lately.' He could be quite self-contained, there was a kitchen and a bathroom in the attics; she wouldn't bother him. There was a large garden. It was possibly this that decided him: it was very hot, central London, the time of year when a man feels he would give anything to live in a room opening on to grass and trees, not a high flat in a dusty street. And if Anne came back, the door would be locked and morticelocked. He could stop thinking about Anne coming back. That was a decisive move: Anne thought he wasn't decisive. He would live without Anne.

For some weeks after he moved in he had seen very little of the woman. They met on the stairs, and once she came up, on a hot Sunday, to tell him he must feel free to use the garden. He had offered to do some weeding and mowing and she had accepted. That was the weekend her husband came back, driving furiously up to the front door, running in, and calling in the empty hall, 'Imogen, Imogen!' To which she had replied, uncharacteristically, by screaming hysterically. There was noth-ing in her husband, Noel's, appearance to warrant this reaction; their lodger, peering over the banister at the sound, had seen their upturned faces in the stairwell and watched hers settle into its usual prim and placid expression as he did so. Seeing Noel, a balding, fluffy-templed, stooping thirty-five or so, shabby corduroy suit, cotton polo neck, he realized he was now able to guess her age, as he had not been. She was a very neat woman, faded blonde, her hair in a knot on the back of her head, her legs long and slender, her eyes downcast. Mild was not quite the right word for her, though. She explained then that she had screamed because Noel had come home unexpectedly and startled her: she was sorry. It seemed a reasonable explanation. The extraordinary vehemence of the screaming was probably an echo in the stairwell. Noel seemed wholly downcast by it, all the same.

He had kept out of the way, that weekend, taking the stairs two at a time and lightly, feeling a little aggrieved, looking out of his kitchen window into the lovely, overgrown garden, that they were lurking indoors, wasting all the summer sun. At Sunday lunch-time he had heard the husband, Noel, shouting on the stairs.

'I can't go on, if you go on like that. I've done my best, I've tried to get through. Nothing will shift you, will it, you won't *try*, will you, you just go on and on. Well, I have my life to live, you can't throw a life away . . . can you?'

He had crept out again on to the dark upper landing and seen her standing, half-way down the stairs, quite still, watching Noel wave his arms and roar, or almost roar, with a look of impassive patience, as though this nuisance must pass off. Noel swallowed and gasped; he turned his face up to her and said plaintively,

'You do see I can't stand it? I'll be in touch, shall I? You must want . . . you must need . . . you must . . .'

She didn't speak.

'If you need anything, you know where to get me.'

'Yes.'

'Oh, well . . .' said Noel, and went to the door. She watched him, from the stairs, until it was shut, and then came up again, step by step, as though it was an effort, a little, and went on coming, past her bedroom, to his landing, to come in and ask him, entirely naturally, please to use the garden if he wanted to, and please not to mind marital rows. She was sure he understood . . . things were difficult . . . Noel wouldn't be back for some time. He was a journalist: his work took him away a lot. Just as well. She committed herself to that 'just as well'. She was a very economical speaker.

So he took to sitting in the garden. It was a lovely place: a huge, hidden, walled south London garden, with old fruit trees at the end, a wildly waving disorderly buddleia, curving beds full of old roses, and a lawn of overgrown, dense rye-grass. Over the wall at the foot was the Common, with a footpath running behind all the gardens. She came out to the shed and helped him to assemble and oil the lawnmower, standing on the little path under the apple branches while he cut an experimental serpentine across her hay. Over the wall came the high sound of children's voices, and the thunk and thud of a football. He asked her how to raise the blades: he was not mechanically minded.

'The children get quite noisy,' she said. 'And dogs. I hope they don't bother you. There aren't many safe places for children, round here.'

He replied truthfully that he never heard sounds that didn't concern him, when he was concentrating. When he'd got the lawn into shape, he was going to sit on it and do a lot of reading, try to get his mind in trim again, to write a paper on Hardy's poems, on their curiously archaic vocabulary.

'It isn't very far to the road on the other side, really,' she said. 'It just seems to be. The Common is an illusion of space, really. Just a spur of brambles and gorse-bushes and bits of football pitch between two fast four-laned main roads. I hate London commons.'

'There's a lovely smell, though, from the gorse and the wet grass. It's a pleasant illusion.'

'No illusions are pleasant,' she said, decisively, and went in. He wondered what she did with her time: apart from little shopping expeditions she seemed to be always in the house. He was sure that when he'd met her she'd been introduced as having some profession: vaguely literary, vaguely academic, like everyone he knew. Perhaps she wrote poetry in her north-facing living-room. He had no idea what it would be like. Women generally wrote emotional poetry, much nicer than men, as Kingsley Amis has stated, but she seemed, despite her placid stillness, too spare and too fierce—grim?—for that. He remembered the screaming. Perhaps she wrote Plath-like chants of violence. He didn't think that quite fitted the bill, either. Perhaps she was a freelance radio journalist. He didn't bother to ask anyone who might be a common acquaintance. During the whole year, he explained to the American at the party, he hadn't actually *discussed* her with anyone. Of course he wouldn't, she agreed vaguely and warmly. She knew he wouldn't. He didn't see why he shouldn't, in fact, but went on, for the time, with his narrative.

They had got to know each other a little better over the next few weeks, at least on the level of borrowing tea, or even sharing pots of it. The weather had got hotter. He had found an old-fashioned deck-chair, with faded striped canvas, in the shed, and had brushed it over and brought it out on to his mown lawn, where he sat writing a little, reading a little, getting up and pulling up a tuft of couch grass. He had been wrong about the children not bothering him: there was a succession of incursions by all sizes of children looking for all sizes of balls, which bounced to his feet, or crashed in the shrubs, or vanished in the herbaceous border, black and white footballs, beach-balls with concentric circles of primary colours, acid yellow tennis balls. The children came over the wall: black faces, brown faces, floppy long hair, shaven heads, respectable dotted sun-hats and camouflaged cotton army hats from Milletts. They came over easily, as though they were used to it, sandals, training shoes, a few bare toes, grubby sunburned legs, cotton skirts, jeans, football shorts. Sometimes, perched on the top, they saw him and gestured at the balls; one or two asked permission. Sometimes he threw a ball back, but was apt to knock down a few knobby little unripe apples or pears. There was a gate in the wall, under the fringing trees, which he once tried to open, spending time on rusty bolts only to discover that the lock was new and secure, and the key not in it.

The boy sitting in the tree did not seem to be looking for a ball. He was in a fork of the tree nearest the gate, swinging his legs, doing something to a knot in a frayed end of rope that was attached to the branch he sat on. He wore blue jeans and training shoes, and a brilliant tee shirt, striped in the colours of the spectrum, arranged in the right order, which the man on the grass found visually pleasing. He had rather long blond hair, falling over his eyes, so that his face was obscured.

'Hey, you. Do you think you ought to be up there? It might not be safe.'

The boy looked up, grinned, and vanished monkey-like over the wall. He had a nice, frank grin, friendly, not cheeky.

He was there again, the next day, leaning back in the crook of the tree, arms crossed. He had on the same shirt and jeans. The man watched him, expecting him to move again, but he sat, immobile, smiling down pleasantly, and then staring up at the sky. The man read a little, looked up, saw him still there, and said,

'Have you lost anything?'

The child did not reply: after a moment he climbed down a little, swung along the branch hand over hand, dropped to the ground, raised an arm in salute, and was up over the usual route over the wall.

Two days later he was lying on his stomach on the edge of the lawn, out of the shade, this time in a white tee shirt with a pattern of blue ships and water-lines on it, his bare feet and legs stretched in the sun. He was chewing a grass stem, and studying the earth, as though watching for insects. The man said, 'Hi, there,' and the boy looked up, met his look with intensely blue eyes under long lashes, smiled with the same complete warmth and openness, and returned his look to the earth.

He felt reluctant to inform on the boy, who seemed so harmless and considerate: but when he met him walking out of the kitchen door, spoke to him, and got no answer but the gentle smile before the boy ran off towards the wall, he wondered if he should speak to his landlady. So he asked her, did she mind the children coming in the garden. She said no, children must look for balls, that was part of being children. He persisted—they sat there, too, and he had met one coming out of the house. He hadn't seemed to be doing any harm, the boy, but you couldn't tell. He thought she should know.

He was probably a friend of her son's, she said. She looked at him kindly and explained. Her son had run off the Common with some other children, two years ago, in the summer, in July, and had been killed on the road. More or less instantly, she had added drily, as though calculating that just *enough* information would preclude the need for further questions. He said he was sorry, very sorry, feeling to blame, which was ridiculous, and a little injured, because he had not known about her son, and might inadvertently have made a fool of himself with some casual reference whose ignorance would be embarrassing.

What was the boy like, she said. The one in the house? 'I don't—talk to his friends. I find it painful. It could be Timmy, or Martin. They might have lost something, or want . . .'

He described the boy. Blond, about ten at a guess, he was not very good at children's ages, very blue eyes, slightly built, with a rainbow-striped tee shirt and blue jeans, mostly though not always—oh, and those football practice shoes, black and green. And the other tee shirt, with the ships and wavy lines. And an extraordinarily nice smile. A really *warm* smile. A nice-looking boy.

He was used to her being silent. But this silence went on and on and on. She was just staring into the garden. After a time, she said, in her precise conversational tone,

'The only thing I want, the only thing I want at all in this world, is to see that boy.'

She stared at the garden and he stared with her, until the grass began to dance with empty light, and the edges of the shrubbery wavered. For a brief moment he shared the strain of not seeing the boy. Then she gave a little sigh, sat down, neatly as always, and passed out at his feet.

After this she became, for her, voluble. He didn't move her after she fainted, but sat patiently by her, until she stirred and sat up; then he fetched her some water, and would have gone away, but she talked.

'I'm too rational to see ghosts, I'm not someone who would see anything there was to see, I don't believe in an after-life, I don't see how anyone can, I always found a kind of satisfaction for myself in the idea that one just came to an end, to a sliced-off stop. But that was myself; I didn't think *he*—not *he*—I thought ghosts were—what people *wanted* to see, or were afraid to see . . . and after he died, the best hope I had, it sounds silly, was that I would go mad enough so that instead of waiting every day for him to come home from school and rattle the letter-box I might actually have the illusion of seeing or hearing him come in. Because I can't stop my body and mind waiting, every day, every day, I can't let go. And his bedroom, sometimes at night I go in, I think I might just for a moment forget he *wasn't* in there sleeping, I think I would pay almost anything—anything at all—for a moment of seeing him like I used to. In his pyjamas, with his—his—his hair . . . ruffled, and, his . . . you said, his . . . that *smile*.

'When it happened, they got Noel, and Noel came in and shouted my name, like he did the other day, that's why I screamed, because it—seemed the same—and then they said, he is dead, and I thought coolly, *is* dead, that will go on and on and on till the end of time, it's a continuous present tense, one thinks the most ridiculous things, there I was thinking about grammar, the verb to be, when it ends to be dead . . . And then I came out into the garden, and I half saw, in my mind's eye, a kind of ghost of his face, just the eyes and hair, coming towards me—like every day waiting for him to come home, the way you think of your son, with such pleasure, when he's—not there—and I—I thought—no, I won't *see* him, because he is dead, and I won't dream about him because he is dead, I'll be rational and practical and continue to live because one must, and there was Noel . . .

'I got it wrong, you see, I was so *sensible*, and then I was so shocked because I couldn't get to want anything—I couldn't *talk* to Noel—I—I—made Noel take away, destroy, all the photos, I—didn't dream, you can will not to dream, I didn't . . . visit a grave, flowers, there isn't any point. I was so sensible. Only my body wouldn't stop waiting and all it wants is to—to see that boy. *That* boy. That boy you—saw.'

He did not say that he might have seen another boy, maybe even a boy who had been given the tee shirts and jeans afterwards. He did not say, though the idea crossed his mind, that maybe what he had seen was some kind of impression from her terrible desire to see a boy where nothing was. The boy had had nothing terrible, no aura of pain about him: he had been, his memory insisted, such a pleasant, courteous, self-contained boy, with his own purposes. And in fact the woman herself almost immediately raised the possibility that what he had seen was what she desired to see, a kind of mix-up of radio waves, like when you overheard police messages on the radio, or got BBC 1 on a switch that said ITV. She was thinking fast, and went on almost immediately to say that perhaps his sense of loss, his loss of Anne, which was what had led her to feel she could bear his presence in her house, was what had brought them—dare she say—near enough, for their wavelengths to mingle, perhaps, had made him susceptible . . . You mean, he had said, we are a kind of emotional vacuum, between us, that must be filled. Something like that, she had said, and had added, 'But I don't believe in ghosts.'

Anne, he thought, could not be a ghost, because she was elsewhere, with someone else, doing for someone else those little things she had done so gaily for him, tasty little suppers, bits of research, a sudden vase of unusual flowers, a new bold shirt, unlike his own cautious taste, but suiting him, suiting him. In a sense, Anne was worse lost because voluntarily absent, an absence that could not be loved because love was at an end, for Anne.

'I don't suppose you will, now,' the woman was saying. 'I think talking would probably stop any—mixing of messages, if that's what it is, don't you? But—if—*if* he comes again'—and here for the first time her eyes were full of tears—'if—you must promise, you will *tell* me, you must promise.'

He had promised, easily enough, because he was fairly sure she was right, the boy would not be seen again. But the next day he was on the lawn, nearer than ever, sitting on the grass beside the deck-chair, his arms clasping his bent, warm brown knees, the thick, pale hair glittering in the sun. He was wearing a football shirt, this time, Chelsea's colours. Sitting down in the deck-chair, the man could have put out a hand and touched him, but did not: it was not, it seemed, a possible gesture to make. But the boy looked up and smiled, with a pleasant complicity, as though they now understood each other very well. The man tried speech: he said, 'It's nice to see you again,' and the boy nodded acknowledgement of this remark, without speaking himself. This was the beginning of communication between them, or what the man supposed to be communication. He did not think of fetching the woman. He became aware that he was in some strange way *enjoying the boy's company*. His pleasant stillness—and he sat there all morning, occasionally lying back on the grass, occasionally staring thoughtfully at the house—was calming and comfortable. The man did quite a lot of work—wrote about three reasonable pages on Hardy's original air-blue gown—and looked up now and then to make sure the boy was still there and happy.

He went to report to the woman—as he had after all promised to do—that evening. She had obviously been waiting and hoping—her unnatural calm had given way to agitated pacing, and her eyes were dark and deeper in. At this point in the story he found in himself a necessity to bowdlerize for the sympathetic American, as he had indeed already begun to do. He had mentioned only a child who had 'seemed like' the woman's lost son, and he now ceased to mention the child at all, as an actor in the story, with the result that what the American woman heard was a tale of how he, the man, had become increasingly involved in the woman's solitary grief, how their two losses had become a kind of *folie à deux* from which he could not extricate himself. What follows is not what he told the American girl, though it may be clear at which points the bowdlerized version coincided with what he really believed to have happened. There was a sense he could not at first analyse that it was improper to talk about the boy—not because he might not be believed; that did not come into it; but because something dreadful might happen.

'He sat on the lawn all morning. In a football shirt.'
'Chelsea?'
'Chelsea.'
'What did he do? Does he look happy? Did he speak?' Her desire to know was terrible.
'He doesn't speak. He didn't move much. He seemed—very calm. He stayed a long time.'
'This is terrible. This is ludicrous. There *is no boy*.'
'No. But I saw him.'
'Why you?'

'I don't know.' A pause. 'I do *like* him.'

'He is—was—a most likeable boy.'

Some days later he saw the boy running along the landing in the evening, wearing what might have been pyjamas, in peacock towelling, or might have been a track suit. Pyjamas, the woman stated confidently, when he told her: his new pyjamas. With white ribbed cuffs, weren't they? and a white polo neck? He corroborated this, watching her cry— she cried more easily now—finding her anxiety and disturbance very hard to bear. But it never occurred to him that it was possible to break his promise to tell her when he saw the boy. That was another curious imperative from some undefined authority.

They discussed clothes. If there were ghosts, how could they appear in clothes long burned, or rotted, or worn away by other people? You could imagine, they agreed, that something of a person might linger— as the Tibetans and others believe the soul lingers near the body before setting out on its long journey. But clothes? And in this case so many clothes? I must be seeing your memories, he told her, and she nodded fiercely, compressing her lips, agreeing that this was likely, adding, 'I am too rational to go mad, so I seem to be putting it on you.'

He tried a joke. 'That isn't very kind to me, to imply that madness comes more easily to me.'

'No, sensitivity. I am insensible. I was always a bit like that, and this made it worse. I am the *last* person to see any ghost that was trying to haunt me.'

'We agreed it was your memories I saw.'

'Yes. We agreed. That's rational. As rational as we can be, considering.'

All the same, the brilliance of the boy's blue regard, his gravely smiling salutation in the garden next morning, did not seem like anyone's tortured memories of earlier happiness. The man spoke to him directly then:

'Is there anything I can *do* for you? Anything you want? Can I help you?'

The boy seemed to puzzle about this for a while, inclining his head as though hearing was difficult. Then he nodded, quickly and perhaps urgently, turned, and ran into the house, looking back to make sure he was followed. The man entered the living-room through the french windows, behind the running boy, who stopped for a moment in the centre of the room, with the man blinking behind him at the sudden transition from sunlight to comparative dark. The woman was sitting in an armchair, looking at nothing there. She often sat like that. She looked up, across the boy, at the man; and the boy, his face for the first time anxious, met the man's eyes again, asking, before he went out into the house.

'What is it? What is it? Have you seen him again? Why are you . . . ?'

'He came in here. He went—out through the door.'

'I didn't see him.'

'No.'

'Did he—oh, this is so *silly*—did he see me?'

He could not remember. He told the only truth he knew.

'He brought me in here.'

'Oh, what can I do, what can I do, what am I going to *do*? If I killed myself—I have thought of that—but the idea that I should be with him is an illusion I . . . this silly situation is the nearest I shall ever get. To him. He was *in here with me*?'

'Yes.'

And she was crying again. Out in the garden he could see the boy, swinging agile on the apple branch.

He was not quite sure, looking back, when he had thought he had realized what the boy had wanted him to do. This was also, at the party, his worst piece of what he called bowdlerization, though in some sense it was clearly the opposite of bowdlerization. He told the American girl that he had come to the conclusion that it was the woman herself who had wanted it, though there was in fact, throughout, no sign of her wanting anything except to see the boy, as she said. The boy, bolder and more frequent, had appeared several nights running on the landing, wandering in and out of bathrooms and bedrooms, restlessly, a little agitated, questing almost, until it had 'come to' the man that what he required was to be re-engendered, for him, the man, to give to his mother another child, into which he could peacefully vanish. The idea was so clear that it was like another imperative, though he did not have the courage to ask the child to confirm it. Possibly this was out of delicacy—the child was too young to be talked to about sex. Possibly there were other reasons. Possibly he was mistaken: the situation was making him hysterical, he felt action of some kind was required and must be possible. He could not spend the rest of the summer, the rest of his life, describing non-existent tee shirts and blond smiles.

THE JULY GHOST 387

He could think of no sensible way of embarking on his venture, so in the end simply walked into her bedroom one night. She was lying there, reading; when she saw him her instinctive gesture was to hide, not her bare arms and throat, but her book. She seemed, in fact, quite unsurprised to see his pyjamaed figure, and, after she had recovered her coolness, brought out the book definitely and laid it on the bedspread.

'My new taste in illegitimate literature. I keep them in a box under the bed.'

Ena Twigg, Medium. The Infinite Hive. The Spirit World. Is There Life After Death?

'Pathetic,' she proffered.

He sat down delicately on the bed.

'Please, don't grieve so. Please, let yourself be comforted. Please . . .'

He put an arm round her. She shuddered. He pulled her closer. He asked why she had had only the one son, and she seemed to understand the purport of his question, for she tried, angular and chilly, to lean on him a little, she became apparently compliant. 'No real reason,' she assured him, no material reason. Just her husband's profession and lack of inclination: that covered it.

'Perhaps,' he suggested, 'if she would be comforted a little, perhaps she could hope, perhaps . . .'

For comfort then, she said, dolefully, and lay back, pushing Ena Twigg off the bed with one fierce gesture, then lying placidly. He got in beside her, put his arms round her, kissed her cold cheek, thought of Anne, of what was never to be again. Come on, he said to the woman, you must live, you must try to live, let us hold each other for comfort.

She hissed at him 'Don't *talk*' between clenched teeth, so he stroked her lightly, over her nightdress, breasts and buttocks and long stiff legs, composed like an effigy on an Elizabethan tomb. She allowed this, trembling slightly, and then trembling violently: he took this to be a sign of some mixture of pleasure and pain, of the return of life to stone. He put a hand between her legs and she moved them heavily apart; he heaved himself over her and pushed, unsuccessfully. She was contorted and locked tight: frigid, he thought grimly, was not the word. *Rigor mortis*, his mind said to him, before she began to scream.

He was ridiculously cross about this. He jumped away and said quite rudely, 'Shut up,' and then ungraciously, 'I'm sorry.' She stopped screaming as suddenly as she had begun and made one of her painstaking economical explanations.

'Sex and death don't go. I can't afford to let go of my grip on myself. I hoped. What you hoped. It was a bad idea. I apologize.'

'Oh, never mind,' he said and rushed out again on to the landing, feeling foolish and almost in tears for warm, lovely Anne.

The child was on the landing, waiting. When the man saw him, he looked questioning, and then turned his face against the wall and leant there, rigid, his shoulders hunched, his hair hiding his expression. There was a similarity between woman and child. The man felt, for the first time, almost uncharitable towards the boy, and then felt something else.

'Look, I'm sorry. I tried. I did try. Please turn round.'

'Uncompromising, rigid, clenched back view.

'Oh well,' said the man, and went into his bedroom.

So now, he said to the American woman at the party, I feel a fool, I feel embarrassed, I feel we are hurting, not helping each other, I feel it isn't a refuge. Of course you feel that, she said, of course you're right—it was temporarily necessary, it helped both of you, but you've got to live your life. Yes, he said, I've done my best, I've tried to get through, I have my life to live. Look, she said, I want to help, I really do, I have these wonderful friends I'm renting this flat from, why don't you come, just for a few days, just for a break, why don't you? They're real sympathetic people, you'd like them, I like them, you could get your emotions kind of straightened out. She'd probably be glad to see the back of you, she must feel as bad as you do, she's got to relate to her situation in her own way in the end. We all have.

He said he would think about it. He knew he had elected to tell the sympathetic American because he had sensed she would be—would offer—a way out. He had to get out. He took her home from the party and went back to his house and landlady without seeing her into her flat. They both knew that this reticence was promising—that he hadn't come in then, because he meant to come later. Her warmth and readiness were like sunshine, she was open. He did not know what to say to the woman.

In fact, she made it easy for him: she asked, briskly, if he now found it perhaps uncomfortable to stay, and he replied that he had felt he should move on, he was of so little use . . . Very well, she had agreed, and had added crisply that it had to be better for everyone if 'all this' came to an end. He remembered the firmness with which she had told him that no illusions were pleasant. She was strong: too strong for her own good. It would take years to wear away that stony, closed, simply surviving insensibility. It was not his job. He would go. All the same, he felt bad.

He got out his suitcases and put some things in them. He went down to the garden, nervously, and put away the deck-chair. The garden was empty. There were no voices over the wall. The silence was thick and deadening. He wondered, knowing he would not see the boy again, if anyone else would do so, or if, now he was gone, no one would describe a tee shirt, a sandal, a smile, seen, remembered, or desired. He went slowly up to his room again.

The boy was sitting on his suitcase, arms crossed, face frowning and serious. He held the man's look for a long moment, and then the man went and sat on his bed. The boy continued to sit. The man found himself speaking.

'You do see I have to go? I've tried to get through. I can't get through. I'm no use to you, am I?'

The boy remained immobile, his head on one side, considering. The man stood up and walked towards him.

'Please. Let me go. What are we, in this house? A man and a woman and a child, and none of us can get through. You can't want that?'

He went as close as he dared. He had, he thought, the intention of putting his hand on or through the child. But could not bring himself to feel there was no boy. So he stood, and repeated,

'I can't get through. Do you want me to stay?'

Upon which, as he stood helplessly there, the boy turned on him again the brilliant, open, confiding, beautiful desired smile.

THE HIGHBOY

Alison Lurie

Even before I knew more about that piece of furniture I wouldn't have wanted it in my house. For a valuable antique, it wasn't particularly attractive. With that tall stack of dark mahogany drawers, and those long spindly bowed legs, it looked not only heavy but top-heavy. But then Clark and I have never cared much for Chippendale; we prefer simple lines and light woods. The carved bonnet-top of the highboy was too elaborate for my taste, and the surface had been polished till it glistened a deep blackish brown, exactly the colour of canned prunes.

Still, I could understand why the piece meant so much to Clark's sister-in-law, Buffy Stockwell. It mattered to her that she had what she called 'really good things': that her antiques were genuine and her china was Spode. She never made a point of how superior her 'things' were to most people's, but one was aware of it. And besides, the highboy was an heirloom; it had been in her family for years. I could see why she was disappointed and cross when her aunt left it to Buffy's brother.

'I don't want to sound ungrateful, Janet, honestly,' Buffy told me over lunch at the country club. 'I realize Jack's carrying on the family name and I'm not. And of course I was glad to have Aunt Betsy's Tiffany coffee service. I suppose it's worth as much as the highboy actually, but it just doesn't have any past. It's got no personality, if you know what I mean.'

Buffy giggled. My sister-in-law was given to anthropomorphizing her possessions, speaking of them as if they had human traits: 'A dear little Paul Revere sugar-spoon.' 'It's lively, even kind of aggressive, for a plant-stand—but I think it'll be really happy on the sunporch.' Whenever their washer or sit-down mower or VCR wasn't working properly she'd say it was 'ill'. I'd found the habit endearing once, but it had begun to bore me.

'I don't understand it really,' Buffy said, digging her dessert fork into the lemon cream tart that she always ordered at the club after declaring that she shouldn't. 'After all, I'm the one who was named for Aunt Betsy, and she knew how interested I was in family history. I always thought I was her favourite. Well, live and learn.' She giggled again and took another bite, leaving a fleck of whipped cream on her short, lifted upper lip.

You mustn't get me wrong. Buffy and her husband Bobby, Clark's brother, were both dears, and as affectionate and reliable and nice as anyone could possibly be. But even Clark had to admit that they'd never quite grown up. Bobby was sixty-one and a vice-president of his company, but his life still centred around golf and tennis.

Buffy, who was nearly his age, didn't play any more because of her heart. But she still favoured yellow and shocking-pink sportswear, and kept her hair in blond all-over curls and maintained her girlish manner. Then of course she had these bouts of childlike whimsicality: she attributed opinions to their pets, and named their automobiles. She insisted that their poodle Suzy disliked the mailman because he was a Democrat, and for years she'd driven a series of Plymouth Valiant wagons called Prince.

The next time the subject of the highboy came up was at a dinner-party at our house about a month later, after Buffy'd been to see her brother in Connecticut. 'It wasn't all that successful a visit,' she reported. 'You know my Aunt Betsy left Jack her Newport highboy, that I was hoping would come to me. I think I told you.'

I agreed that she had.

'Well, it's in his house in Stonington now. But it's completely out of place among all that pickled-walnut imitation French-provincial furniture that Jack's new wife chose. It looked so uncomfortable.' Buffy sighed and helped herself to roast potatoes as they went round.

'It really makes me sad,' she went on. 'I could tell right away that Jack and his wife don't appreciate Aunt Betsy's highboy, the way they've shoved it slap up into the corner behind the patio door. Jack claims it's because he can't get it to stand steady, and the drawers always stick.'

'Well, perhaps they do,' I said. 'After all, the piece must be over two hundred years old.'

But Buffy wouldn't agree. Aunt Betsy had almost never had that sort of trouble, though she admitted once to Buffy that the highboy was temperamental. Usually the drawers would slide open as smoothly as butter, but now and then they seized up.

It probably had something to do with the humidity, I suggested. But according to Buffy her Aunt Betsy, who seems to have had the same sort of imagination as her niece, used to say that the highboy was sulking;

someone had been rough with it, she would suggest, or it hadn't been polished lately.

'I'm sure Jack's wife doesn't know how to take proper care of good furniture either,' Buffy went on during the salad course. 'She's too busy with her high-powered executive job.'

'Honestly, Janet, it's true,' she added. 'When I was there last week the finish was already beginning to look dull, almost soapy. Aunt Betsy always used to polish it once a week with beeswax, to keep the patina. I mentioned that twice, but I could see Jack's wife wasn't paying any attention. Not that she ever pays any attention to me.' Buffy gave a little short nervous giggle like a hiccup. Her brother's wife wasn't the only one of the family who thought of her as a lightweight, and she wasn't too silly to know it.

'What I suspect is, Janet, I suspect she's letting her cleaning-lady spray it with that awful synthetic no-rub polish they make now,' Buffy went on, frowning across the glazed damask. 'I found a can of the stuff under her sink. Full of nasty chemicals you can't pronounce. Anyhow, I'm sure the climate in Stonington can't be good for old furniture; not with all that salt and damp in the air.'

There was a lull in the conversation then, and at the other end of the table Buffy's husband heard her and gave a kind of guffaw. 'Say, Clark,' he called to my husband. 'I wish you'd tell Buffy to forget about that old highboy.'

Well naturally Clark was not going to do anything of the sort. But he leant towards us and listened to Buffy's story, and then he suggested that she ask her brother if he'd be willing to exchange the highboy for her aunt's coffee service.

I thought this was a good idea, and so did Buffy. She wrote off to her brother, and a few days later Jack phoned to say that was fine by him. He was sick of the highboy; no matter how he tried to prop up the legs it still wobbled.

Besides, the day before he'd gone to get out some maps for a trip they were planning and the whole thing just kind of seized up. He'd stopped trying to free the top drawer with a screwdriver, and was working on one of the lower ones, when he got a hell of a crack on the head. He must have loosened something somehow, he told Buffy, so that when he pulled on the lower drawer the upper one slid out noiselessly above him. And when he stood up, bingo.

It was Saturday, and their doctor was off call, so Jack's wife had to drive him ten miles to the Westerly emergency room; he was too dizzy and confused to drive himself. There wasn't any concussion, according to the X-rays, but he had a lump on his head the size of a plum and a headache the size of a football. He'd be happy to ship that goddamned piece of furniture to her as soon as it was convenient, he told Buffy, and she could take her time about sending along the coffee service.

Two weeks later when I went over to Buffy's for tea her aunt's highboy had arrived. She was so pleased that I bore with her when she started talking about how it appreciated the care she was taking of it. 'When I rub in the beeswax I can almost feel it purring under my hand like a big cat,' she insisted. I glanced at the highboy again. I thought I'd never seen a less agreeable-looking piece of furniture. Its pretentious high-arched bonnet top resembled a clumsy mahogany Napoleon hat, and the ball-and-claw feet made the thing look as if it were up on tiptoe. If it was a big cat, it was a cat with bird's legs—a sort of gryphon.

'I know it's grateful to be here,' Buffy told me. 'The other day I couldn't find my reading-glasses anywhere; but then, when I was standing in the sitting room, at my wits' end, I heard a little creak, or maybe it was more sort of a pop. I looked round and one of the top drawers of the highboy was out about an inch. Well, I went to shut it, and there were my glasses! Now what do you make of that?'

I made nothing of it, but humoured her. 'Quite a coincidence.'

'Oh, more than that.' Buffy gave a rippling giggle. 'And it's completely steady now. Try and see.'

I put one hand on the highboy and gave the thing a little push, and she was perfectly right. It stood solid and heavy against the cream Colonial Williamsburg wallpaper, as if it had been in Buffy's house for centuries. The prune-dark mahogany was waxy to the touch and colder than I would have expected.

'And the drawers don't stick the least little bit.' Buffy slid them open and shut to demonstrate. 'I know it's going to be happy here.'

It was early spring when the highboy arrived and whether or not it was happy, it gave no trouble until that summer. Then in July we had a week of drenching thunderstorms and the drawers began to jam. I saw it happen one Sunday when Clark and I were over and Bobby tried to get out the slides of their recent trip to Quebec. He started shaking the thing and swearing, and Buffy got up and hurried over to him.

'There's nothing at all wrong with the highboy,' she whispered to me afterwards. 'Bobby just doesn't understand how to treat it. You mustn't force the drawers open like that; you have to be gentle.'

After we'd sat through the slides Bobby went to put them away.

'Careful, darling,' Buffy warned him.

'Okay, okay,' Bobby said; but it was clear he wasn't listening seriously. He yanked the drawer open without much trouble; but when he slammed it shut he let out a frightful howl: he'd shut his right thumb inside.

'Christ, will you look at that!' he shouted, holding out his broad red hand to show us a deep dented gash below the knuckle. 'I think the damn thing's broken.'

Well, Bobby's thumb wasn't broken; but it was bruised rather badly, as it turned out. His hand was swollen for over a week, so that he couldn't play in the golf tournament at the club, which meant a lot to him.

Buffy and I were sitting on the clubhouse terrace that day, and Bobby was moseying about by the first tee in a baby-blue golf shirt, with his hand still wadded up in bandages.

'Poor darling, he's so cross,' Buffy said.

'Cross?' I asked; in fact Bobby didn't look cross, only foolish and disconsolate.

'He's furious at Aunt Betsy's highboy, Janet,' she said. 'And what I've decided is, there's no point any longer in trying to persuade him to treat it right. After what happened last week, I realized it would be better to keep them apart. So I've simply moved all his things out of the drawers, and now I'm using them for my writing-paper and tapestry wools.'

This time, perhaps because it was such a sticky hot day and there were too many flies on the terrace, I felt more than usually impatient with Buffy's whimsy. 'Really, dear, you mustn't let your imagination run away with you,' I said, squeezing more lemon into my iced tea. 'Your aunt's highboy doesn't have any quarrel with Bobby. It isn't a human being, it's a piece of furniture.'

'But that's just it,' Buffy insisted. 'That's why it matters so much. I mean, you and I, and everybody else.' She waved her plump freckled hand at the other people under their pink and white umbrellas, and the golfers scattered over the rolling green plush of the course. 'We all know we've got to die sooner or later, no matter how careful we are. Isn't that so?'

'Well, yes,' I admitted.

'But furniture and things can be practically immortal, if they're lucky. An heirloom piece like Aunt Betsy's highboy—I really feel I've got an obligation to preserve it.'

'For the children and grandchildren, you mean.'

'Oh, that too, certainly. But they're just temporary themselves, you know.' Buffy exhaled a sigh of hot summer air. 'You see, from our point of view we own our things. But really, as far as they're concerned we're only looking after them for a while. We're just caretakers, like poor old Billy here at the club.'

'He's retiring this year, I heard,' I said, hoping to change the subject.

'Yes. But they'll hire someone else, you know, and if he's competent it won't make any difference to the place. Well, it's the same with our things, Janet. Naturally they want to do whatever they can to preserve themselves, and to find the best possible caretakers. They don't ask much: just to be polished regularly, and not to have their drawers wrenched open and slammed shut. And of course they don't want to get cold or wet or dirty, or have lighted cigarettes put down on them, or drinks or houseplants.'

'It sounds like quite a lot to ask,' I said.

'But Janet, it's so important for them!' Buffy cried. 'Of course it was naughty of the highboy to give Bobby such a bad pinch, but I think it was understandable. He was being awfully rough and it got frightened.'

'Now, Buffy,' I said, stirring my iced tea so that the cubes clinked impatiently. 'You can't possibly believe that we're all in danger of being injured by our possessions.'

'Oh no.' She gave another little rippling giggle. 'Most of them don't have the strength to do any serious damage. But I'm not worried anyhow. I have a lovely relationship with all my nice things: they know I have their best interests at heart.'

I didn't scold Buffy any more; it was too hot, and I realized there wasn't any point. My sister-in-law was fifty-six years old, and if she hadn't grown up by then she probably never would. Anyhow, I heard no more about the highboy until about a month later, when Buffy's grandchildren were staying with her. One hazy wet afternoon in August I drove over to the house with a basket of surplus tomatoes and zucchini. The children were building with blocks and Buffy was working on a *grospoint* cushion-cover design from the Metropolitan Museum. After a while she needed more pink wool and she asked her grandson, who was about six, to run over to the highboy and fetch it.

He got up and went at once—he's really a very nice little boy. But when he pulled on the bottom drawer it wouldn't come out and he gave the bird leg a kick. It was nothing serious, but Buffy screamed and leapt up as if she had been stung, spilling her canvas and coloured wools.

'Jamie!' Really, she was almost shrieking. 'You must never, never do that!' And she grabbed the child by the arm and dragged him away roughly.

Well naturally Jamie was shocked and upset; he cast a terrified look at Buffy and burst into tears. That brought her to her senses. She hugged him and explained that Grandma wasn't angry; but he must be very, very careful of the highboy, because it was so old and valuable.

I thought Buffy had over-reacted terribly, and when she went out to the kitchen to fix two gin-and-tonics, and milk and peanut-butter cookies for the children, 'to settle us all down', I followed her in and told her so. Surely, I said, she cared more for her grandchildren than she did for her furniture.

Buffy gave me an odd look; then she pushed the swing door shut.

'You don't understand, Janet,' she said in a low voice, as if someone might overhear. 'Jamie really mustn't annoy the highboy. It's been rather difficult lately, you see.' She tried to open a bottle of tonic, but couldn't—I had to take it from her.

'Oh, thank you,' she said distractedly. 'It's just—Well, for instance. The other day Betsy Lee was playing house under the highboy: she'd made a kind of nest for herself with the sofa pillows, and she had some of her dolls in there. I don't know what happened exactly, but one of the claw feet gave her that nasty-looking scratch you noticed on her leg.' Buffy looked over her shoulder apprehensively and spoke even lower. 'And there've been other incidents—Oh, never mind.' She sighed, then giggled. 'I know you think it's all perfect nonsense, Janet. Would you like lime or lemon?'

I was disturbed by this conversation, and that evening I told Clark so; but he made light of it. 'Darling, I wouldn't worry. It's just the way Buffy always goes on.'

'Well, but this time she was carrying the joke too far,' I said. 'She frightened those children. Even if she was fooling, I think she cares far too much about her old furniture. Really, it made me cross.'

'I think you should feel sorry for Buffy,' Clark remarked. 'You know what we've said so often: now that she's had to give up sports, she doesn't have enough to do. I expect she's just trying to add a little interest to her life.'

I said that perhaps he was right. And then I had an idea: I'd get Buffy elected secretary of the Historical Society, to fill out the term of the woman who'd just resigned. I knew it wouldn't be easy, because she had no experience and a lot of people thought she was flighty. But I was sure she could do it; she'd always run that big house perfectly, and she knew lots about local history and genealogy and antiques.

First I had to convince the Historical Society board that they wanted her, and then I had to convince Buffy of the same thing; but I managed. I was quite proud of myself. And I was even prouder as time went on and she not only did the job beautifully, she also seemed to have forgotten all that nonsense about the highboy. That whole fall and winter she didn't mention it once.

It wasn't until early the following spring that Buffy phoned one morning, in what was obviously rather a state, and asked me to come over. I found her waiting for me in the front hall, wearing her white quilted parka. Her fine blond-tinted curls were all over the place, her eyes unnaturally round and bright, and the tip of her snub nose pink; she looked like a distracted rabbit.

'Don't take off your coat yet, Janet,' she told me breathlessly. 'Come out into the garden, I must show you something.'

I was surprised, because it was a cold blowy day in March. Apart from a few snowdrops and frozen-looking white crocuses scattered over the lawn, there was nothing to see. But it wasn't the garden Buffy had on her mind.

'You know that woman from New York, that Abigail Jones, who spoke on "Decorating with Antiques" yesterday at the Society?' she asked as we stood between two beds of spaded earth and sodden compost.

'Mm.'

'Well, I was talking to her after the lecture, and I invited her to come for brunch this morning and see the house.'

'Mm? And how did that go?'

'It was awful, Janet. I don't mean—' Buffy hunched her shoulders and swallowed as if she were about to sob. 'I mean, Mrs Jones was very pleasant. She admired my Hepplewhite table and chairs; and she was very nice about the canopy bed in the blue room too, though I felt I had to tell her that one of the posts wasn't original. But what she liked best was Aunt Betsy's highboy.'

'Oh yes?'

'She thought it was a really fine piece. I told her we'd always believed it was made in Newport, but Mrs Jones thought Salem was more likely. Well that naturally made me uneasy.'

'What? I mean, why?'

'Because of the witches, you know.' Buffy gave her nervous giggle.

'Then Mrs Jones said she hoped I was taking good care of the highboy. So of course I told her I was. Mrs Jones said she could see that, but what I should realize was that my piece was unique, with the carved feathering of the legs, and what looked like all the original hardware. It really ought to be in a museum, she said. I tried to stop her, because I could tell the highboy was getting upset.'

'Upset?' I laughed, because I still assumed that it was a joke. 'Why should it be upset? I should think it would be pleased to be admired by an expert.'

'But don't you see, Janet?' Buffy almost wailed. 'It didn't know about museums before. It didn't realize that there were places where it could be well taken care of and perfectly safe for, well, almost forever. It wouldn't know about them, you see, because when pieces of furniture go to a museum they don't come back to tell the others. It's like our going to heaven, I suppose. Only now the highboy knows, that's what it will want.'

'But a piece of furniture can't force you to send it to a museum,' I protested, thinking how crazy this conversation would sound to anyone who didn't know Buffy.

'Oh, can't it.' She brushed some wispy curls out of her face. 'You don't know what it can do, Janet. None of us does. There've been things I didn't tell you about—But never mind that. Only in fairness I must say I'm beginning to have a different idea of why Aunt Betsy didn't leave the highboy to me in the first place. I don't think it was because of the family name at all. I think she was trying to protect me.' She giggled with a sound like ice cracking.

'Really, Buffy—' Wearily, warily, I played along. 'If it's as clever as you say, the highboy must know Mrs Jones was just being polite. She didn't really mean—'

'But she did, you see. She said that if I ever thought of donating the piece to a museum, where it could be really well cared for, she hoped I would let her know. I tried to change the subject, but I couldn't. She went on telling me how there was always the danger of fire or theft in a private home. She said home instead of house, that's the kind of woman she is.' Buffy giggled miserably. 'Then she started to talk about tax deductions, and said she knew of several places that would be interested. I didn't know what to do. I told her that if I did ever decide to part with the highboy I'd probably give it to our Historical Society.'

'Well, of course you could,' I suggested. 'If you felt—'

'But it doesn't matter now,' Buffy interrupted, putting a small cold hand on my wrist. 'I was weak for a moment, but I'm not going to let it push me around. I've worked out what to do to protect myself: I'm changing my will. I called Toni Stevenson already, and I'm going straight over to her office after you leave.'

'You're willing the highboy to the Historical Society?' I asked.

'Well, maybe eventually, if I have to. Not outright; heavens, no. That would be fatal. For the moment I'm going to leave it to Bobby's nephew Fred. But only in case of my accidental death.' Behind her distracted wisps of hair, Buffy gave a peculiar little smile.

'Death!' I swallowed. 'You don't really think—'

'I think that highboy is capable of absolutely anything. It has no feelings, no gratitude at all. I suppose that's because from its point of view I'm going to die so soon anyway.'

'But, Buffy—' The hard wind whisked away the rest of my words, but I doubt if she would have heard them.

'Anyhow, what I'd like you to do now, Janet, is come in with me and be a witness when I tell it what I've planned.'

I was almost sure then that Buffy had gone a bit mad; but of course I went back indoors with her.

'Oh, I wanted to tell you, Janet,' she said in an unnaturally loud, clear voice when we reached the sitting-room. 'Now that I know how valuable Aunt Betsy's highboy is, I've decided to leave it to the Historical Society. I put it in my will today. That's if I die of natural causes, of course. But if it's an accidental death, then I'm giving it to my husband's nephew, Fred Turner.' She paused and took a loud breath.

'Really,' I said, feeling as if I were in some sort of absurdist play.

'I realise the highboy may feel a little out of place in Fred's house,' Buffy went on relentlessly, 'because he and his wife have all that weird modern canvas and chrome furniture. But I don't really mind about that. And of course Fred's a little careless sometimes. Once when he was here he left a cigarette burning on the cherry pie table in the study; that's how it got that ugly scorch mark, you know. And he's rather thoughtless about wet glasses and coffee cups too.' Though Buffy was still facing me, she kept glancing over my shoulder towards the highboy.

I turned to follow her gaze, and suddenly for a moment I shared her delusion. The highboy had not moved; but now it looked heavy and sullen, and seemed to have developed a kind of vestigial face. The brass pulls of the two top drawers formed the half-shut eyes of this face, and the fluted column between them was its long thin nose; the ornamental brass keyhole of the full-length drawer below supplied a pursed, tight mouth. Under its curved mahogany tricorne hat, it had a mean, calculating expression, like some hypocritical New England Colonial merchant.

'I know exactly what you're thinking,' Buffy said, abandoning the pretence of speaking to me. 'And if you don't behave yourself, I might give you to Fred and Roo right now. They have children too. Very active children, not nice quiet ones like Jamie and Mary Lee.' Her giggle had a chilling fragmented sound now; ice shivering into shreds.

'None of that was true about Bobby's nephew, you know,' Buffy confided as she walked me to my car. 'They're not really careless, and neither of them smokes. I just wanted to frighten it.'

'You rather frightened me,' I told her.

Which was no lie, as I said to Clark that evening. It wasn't just the strength of Buffy's delusion, but the way I'd been infected by it. He laughed and said he'd never known she could be so convincing. Also he asked if I was sure she hadn't been teasing me.

Well, I had to admit I wasn't. But I was still worried. Didn't he think we should do something?

'Do what?' Clark said. And he pointed out that even if Buffy hadn't been teasing, he didn't imagine I'd have much luck trying to get her to a therapist; she thought psychologists were completely bogus. He said we should just wait and see what happened.

All the same, the next time I saw Buffy I couldn't help enquiring about the highboy. 'Oh, everything's fine now,' she said. 'Right after I saw you I signed the codicil. I put a copy in one of the drawers to remind it, and it's been as good as gold ever since.'

Several months passed, and Buffy never mentioned the subject again. When I finally asked how the highboy was, she said, 'What? Oh, fine, thanks,' in an uninterested way that suggested she'd forgotten her obsession—or tired of her joke.

The irritating thing was that now that I'd seen the unpleasant face of the highboy, it was there every time I went to the house. I would look from it to Buffy's round pink face, and wonder if she had been laughing at me all along.

Finally, though, I began to forget the whole thing. Then one day late that summer Clark and Bobby's nephew's wife, Roo, was at our house. She's a professional photographer, quite a successful one, and she'd come to take a picture of me.

Like many photographers, Roo always kept up a more or less mindless conversation with her subjects as she worked; trying to prevent them from getting stiff and self-conscious, I suppose.

'I like your house, you know, Janet,' she said. 'You have such simple, great-looking things. Could you turn slowly to the right a little? . . . Good. Hold it . . . Now over at Uncle Bobby's—Hold it . . . Their garden's great of course, but I don't care much for their furniture. Lower your chin a little, please . . . You know that big dark old chest of drawers that Buffy's left to Fred.'

'The highboy,' I said.

'Right. Let's move those roses a bit. That's better , , , It's supposed to be so valuable, but I think it's hideous. I told Fred I didn't want it around. Hold it . . . Okay.'

'And what did he say?' I asked.

'Huh? Oh, Fred feels the same as I do. He said that if he did inherit the thing he was going to give it to a museum.'

'A museum?' I have to admit that my voice rose. 'Where was Fred when he told you this?'

'Don't move, please. Okay . . . What? . . . I think we were in Buffy's sitting room—but she wasn't there, of course. You don't have to worry, Janet. Fred wouldn't say anything like that in front of his aunt; he knows it would sound awfully ungrateful.'

Well, my first impulse was to pick up the phone and warn my sister-in-law as soon as Roo left. But then I thought that would sound ridiculous. It was crazy to imagine that Buffy was in danger from a chest of drawers. Especially so long after she'd gotten over the idea herself, if she'd ever really had it in the first place.

Buffy might even laugh at me, I thought; she wasn't anywhere near as whimsical as she had been. She'd become more and more involved in the Historical Society, and it looked as if she'd be re-elected automatically next year. Besides, if by chance she hadn't been kidding and I reminded her of her old delusion and seemed to share it, the delusion might come back and it would be my fault.

So I didn't do anything. I didn't even mention the incident to Clark.

Two days later, while I was writing letters in the study, Clark burst in. I knew something awful had happened as soon as I saw his face.

Bobby had just called from the hospital, he told me. Buffy was in intensive care and the prognosis was bad. She had a broken hip and a concussion, but the real problem was the shock to her weak heart. Apparently, he said, some big piece of furniture had fallen on her.

I didn't ask what piece of furniture that was. I drove straight to the hospital with him; but by the time we got there Buffy was in a coma.

Though she was nearer plump than slim, Buffy seemed horribly small in that room, on that high flat bed—like a kind of faded child. Her head was in bandages, and there were tubes and wires all over her like mechanical snakes; her little freckled hands lay in weak fists on the white hospital sheet. You could see right away that it was all over with her, though in fact they managed to keep her alive, if you can use that word, for nearly three days more.

Fred Turner, just as he had promised, gave the highboy to a New York museum. I went to see it there recently. Behind its maroon velvet rope it looked exactly the same: tall, glossy, top-heavy, bird-legged and claw-footed.

'You wicked, selfish, ungrateful thing,' I told it. 'I hope you get termites. I hope some madman comes in here and attacks you with an axe.'

The highboy did not answer me, of course. But under its mahogany Napoleon hat it seemed to wear a little self-satisfied smile.

THE MEETING HOUSE

Jane Gardam

There should be nowhere less haunted than the Quaker meeting
house on High Greenside above Calthorpedale in the Northwest.

To get there it is best to leave the car on the byroad and walk up
through the fields, for there are six gates to open and shut before you
reach the deserted village of Calthorpe, which stands on a round lake
that is shallow and silver and clean and still. The hamlet's short street
and its empty windows and door-frames are nearly blocked with nettles,
its roofs long gone missing. A century ago, poor farming people brought
up broods of children here on tatie pies and rabbits and broth and, very
occasionally, some pork. The pigsty—one lank pig to a village—lies
above the ruined houses. Behind the pigsty you take a track up the fell
until you hit a broad grass walk nibbled to a carpet by sheep since James
I's time and before. You come to two stone buildings to the right of the
walk in the tussocky grasses. They are attached, one house bigger than
the other.

When you get near you see that the smaller building is empty. A dark
doorway gapes. There is not much roof left. But the creamy stone is
bleached and washed clean by the weather and there are wild flowers
and grasses round its feet.

The bigger building is one tall room within and is almost the oldest
Quaker meeting house in England. George Fox himself is said to have
preached here shortly after his vision of angels settling like flocks of
birds on Pendle Hill. Its floor is the blue-white flagstones of the dale and
there are three tiers of plain, dustless benches. The walls are dazzling
white limewash and on a high stone shelf is a small paraffin stove and
two now long-unused candlesticks. The Friends bring a medicine bottle
of paraffin up the fell for making tea after worship but they don't bring
candles, for the meeting house is used only on summer mornings now.
It is a secure little place and bare. If walkers look through the clear glass
in the windows they see nothing to steal.

The view from it is wonderfully beautiful and, as the Friends sit
looking out through the windows and the open door across the dale to
the purple mountains, a grassy breeze blows in; if Quakers believed in

holy places this would be one of them. They do believe, however, in a duty to be responsible about property and thus it seems odd that the building alongside the meeting house should be derelict. But it had never been the corporate property of the Friends, being part of the estate of a local farming family who had been Friends for many generations and had used the little house as a lambing shed and springtime home of a shepherd who had doubled as the meeting house caretaker.

Those days are done. The farm has passed now to a consortium at York, the sheep are brought down to low pastures and shepherds today have motorbuggies and houses below the snow line. The meeting house caretaker was now Charlie Bainbridge, who had walked up to High Greenside once a week for years, at all seasons, and he had seen the smaller building left to fall gently down. Bainbridge, a huge old man, white-bearded and white-haired, was a still fellow who walked very upright without a stick even with snow on the ground. He said the long pull up to the meeting house was what had kept him healthy.

Hawks on the ridge had watched Bainbridge for years as he moved on a weekday morning across the valley floor, passing through the six field gates, fastening each one after himself; passing through the nettle-stuffed village, passing the muck-hard pigsty and away up beyond it to the broad grass track. On the common garth wall before the two buildings he sat down each week and ate his dinner out of a paper parcel and watched the weather coming and going. Larks and lambs in season, curlews at every season. Far too many rabbits. Disgraceful multitudes, he thought, remembering hard times and good stews of old. In winter there was often a stoat turned white, a rusty fox dipping a paw in snow. In April there were rainbows, often far below him and sometimes upside down. In May, a madness of cuckoos. A preserved and empty country.

He would consider the rain as it approached, watch the storms gather, the searchlights of sun piercing purple clouds and turning the fields to strobe-light, elf-light emerald. He sat waiting for the rain to reach him and wet him, the wind to knock him about. Until it did, he sat untroubled, like a beast. Then he got up and opened the meeting house door with the seven-inch iron key that lived under a stone, and plodded about inside maybe sweeping around a bit with the broom that lay under the benches. He looked out for cobwebs, trapped butterflies, signs of damp. Accumulated silence breathed from the building, wafted out on to the fell, swam in again like tides. Silence was at the root of Charlie's life.

So that when he was walking up one day and heard canned music he was jolted. He thought it could only be picnickers or bike boys cavorting about from over the west. They'd been seen about sometimes before. But then he saw that there were two big piles of rubble in front of the smaller building and clouds of lime dust floating in its dark doorway. Banging and crashing began to drown the music and then a dirty man came through the doorway carrying more rubbish and slung it on the tip. A child appeared, and then a very thin young grubby woman. The child was whining and the man aimed a kick at it. The woman swore at the man and the man said, 'Sod you. Shit.' The woman said, 'Leave it, will yer?'

Then the three stood looking at Bainbridge.

'Good day,' he said.

They said nothing. The man lit a cigarette.

'Can I help you?'

'Ye canna. We's 'ere. We's stoppin'.'

'Are you to do with them at York, then? The farming company?'

'We's 'omeless,' said the man. 'We's Tyneside.'

'See?' said the woman, and the baby stepped out of its plastic pants and defecated beside the rubbish.

'I come here,' said Bainbridge (in time), 'to see to the meeting house. We don't use it often but it's our property. We are Quakers. The Society of Friends.'

'No friends of us,' said the man. 'Ye'll not shift us. You can't force us.'

'We wouldn't force you,' said Bainbridge, 'it's not what we do. We don't have violence. But we have a right of way into the meeting house across the garth.'

'Not now you haven't,' said the man, setting light to the rubbish.

Bainbridge left. He had never been a talker. Once or twice he had come across such people as these and had tried to understand them. Sometimes he had watched things about homelessness on somebody's television set and had always given generously to appeals for them that dropped through his door. But confronting them had been shocking, as shocking as meeting fallen angels, bewildering, frightening, disgusting and against natural order. When the Elders of the Meeting went up to High Greenside a few days later to investigate, Bainbridge stayed at home and planted onions.

The squatters at once made their position quite clear: they were not going, a point they made clearer still to the owner of the building who came over before long in a Merc from Harrogate. The owner, however, was not deeply worried. When he found that the family was not an advance party of vagrants or new-age travellers or a pop-music festival that might take root over his fields and settle there like George Fox's angels—fornicating, druggy, aggressive angels ruining pasture and stock—he said that at least the place was being used. The glass front door off a skip, the new metal windows set loose in the walls, the plastic chimneypot painted yellow and crazy tarpaulin slopped across the roof were matters for the National Park, not him. Carrying off an eighteenth-century rocking chair that the family had found in the rafters and also painted yellow, the owner said that he would of course have to tell the police.

'You do that.'

'I will. Oh, yes. Don't worry. I will,' he called and a Doberman who had been drooling and lolling with the baby in a broken chicken-wire playpen leapt at him with slippery turned-back lips, and man and chair fled down to the dead village.

'I'll give yer summat in rent when I'se in work, see? The wife's bad, see? She's had a tumour,' the man shouted after him. 'She likes it 'ere, see? Right?'

Next, a number of the Friends went up to explain to the family about the Sunday meetings and how, each week, they kept an hour of total silence at High Greenside. The music behind the glass door screamed and blared, the baby cried and it took a long time for the woman to answer their knocking. It was noon but she was in her nightdress.

'We sit in silence once a week. From ten-thirty until eleven-thirty on Sunday mornings. Only on six Sunday mornings. Only in summer. You are very welcome to join us.'

She said, 'Oh, yes. Yer comin' in?'

The flagstoned floor was still covered with lime dust and the sheep droppings of years had been heaped up with torn plastic bags of possessions—cracked shoes, rags, bottles, jars. There was a mattress with greasy coats across it and a new-looking television set and video recorded standing bewildered by the absence of electric sockets. In a little black hearth a fire of wormy sawn-up floorboards from the room above was burning, but the place was cold. The woman coughed, and behind the door that hid the stairs the Doberman boomed and clawed.

'You can't be very comfortable here.'

'It's OK.'

'We could help you. We have brought you a few groceries. And some runner beans and a stew.'

''E'd never.'

'Well, tell him we called. And about the silence on the Sundays.'

She wrapped a terrible matted cardigan more tightly around her bones. ''E'd never listen. 'E's that wild. One thing one minute, another the next.'

When they arrived the following Sunday the Friends found parts of old scrap-yard cars dragged across the garth and barbed wire fastened across their door. After negotiating all this and opening up the meeting house, they conferred, standing close together and thoughtful. The dog slavered and scraped inside the lambing-shed windows.

But seated soon on the familiar benches, their door open to a paradise morning, the dog quietened and the silence began. A different, answering silence from the house next door became almost distracting.

Or perhaps insolent; for the following Sunday the entry to the meeting house was blocked more thoroughly, this time with old roof beams, and, after they had struggled through these and silent worship had started, two transistors on different wavelengths were set outside on the party wall. An ill-tempered political argument fought with a programme of musical requests, both at full strength.

The next week it was a petrol-engine chain saw and for an hour its lilting scream, like cats in acid, seared the brain and ears and soul and a young Quaker who was a summer visitor from Leeds ran off down the hillside.

The noise was switched off the minute the hour ended and the clerk of the meeting, speaking slowly, said to the man lounging outside, 'By law, you know, you are meant to wear earmuffs when you're working one of these.'

The next week the man did wear earmuffs but the Quakers sat again in pain.

'What have you against us?' they asked as they locked up—now taking the key with them. Even Bainbridge looked shaken and drained. But the man said nothing.

The next week the saw broke down. The scream jolted and faded and died. It was a few minutes into the meeting and the man outside began to swear. He kicked and shouted, shouted and kicked, then stormed down to below the pigsty and shouted and kicked the tincan of his old pick-up van into action. Soon it could be heard exploding its way down through the fields.

The two transistors kept going when the sound of the pick-up had faded but their clack now was like balm and blessing after the saw; and a greater blessing followed, for soon they were switched off. The depth of the Quaker silence then was like hanging in clear water.

After a time, the child appeared in the open doorway quite naked—

a queer, grey, dirty, sickly thing standing in the bright air. He tottered forward and flopped down and old Bessie Calvert, a gaunt stick herself, took him up on her lap, where he seemed to have no energy to do more than fall asleep.

When, in a few minutes, his mother stood in the doorway looking for him, Bessie moved a little and touched the seat beside her and the woman, again in her nightdress, threw her cigarette in the grass and came in. She sat sideways, twisted away from people, staring sulkily out of the door, but she sat, and when the car was heard returning she did not stir. And when the man and dog stood in the doorway she did not look at them. The dog's great chain was twice round the man's wrist and the chain rattled heavily as the dog dropped down to the ground, its chin on its paws. The dog sighed.

Then the man pulled the dog away and they both stood outside in the garth, the man leaning against the meeting house wall. 'Good day,' said the Quakers passing him by at the end of the hour (there had been no tea-making this summer), holding out their hands as usual, one after another. As usual the hands were ignored but leaning against the wall the man gazed far away and said nothing. He looked very tired.

As they went off down his voice came bawling after them.

'—Next week, mind. Not an end of it. See what we do next week. Settle your silences. You'll not get rid of us. You's'll never be rid of us. We's after your place next.'

But the next week nobody was there. All were gone, the family, dog, car, television set, chain saw, the few poor sticks of furniture, the new padlock for the pathetic glass door that now stood open on the foul mattress, piles of nappy bags, flies and a mountain of sawn wood. A jam jar of harebells stood on a stone sill with a note under it saying, 'Sorry we had to go. We'd got started liking it up here.' In the paper the following Wednesday the Friends read that at about the time they had been reading the note the whole family and its dog had been killed in their wretched car on the M6 just below Tebay.

Quakers accept. Grief must be contained, translated. Friends do not as a rule extend themselves over funerals. But three of the Quakers from High Greenside did attend this one far away over in Cumbria and later on Charlie, Bessie, and the clerk cleaned out the old lambing shed, removed the rubbish—the tarpaulin, the mattress—to the tip twelve miles off. They distributed the firewood and disposed of the sagging little chicken-wire playpen. They worked thoroughly and quietly but found themselves shaken beyond all expectation.

The playpen and the now withered harebells in the jar brought them close to weeping.

It was during the following winter that stories began. Walkers were puzzled by canned music that came from the High Greenside buildings and faded as they drew near. Fishermen down by the lake at night sometimes heard the barking of a great dog. Across the dale, people saw a light shining like a low star on the fell-side from where the empty buildings stood. After Christmas the Yorkshire farmer came back with his wife to inspect but had to turn away because the wife for no reason suddenly became very much afraid. Charlie Bainbridge was thankful that the snow came early and deep that year and stopped his weekly visit—not because of ghost talk, he had no belief in ghosts, but because the place now distressed him. When the snow melted he was in bed with chronic bronchitis brought on by the long indoor months. He grew better very slowly.

So that it was almost summer again before he got up to the meeting house once more. Rather thinner but still upright, he set off soon after his dinner one day in early May. He walked steadily, opening and shutting each gate as before, circling the silver shilling of the lake, through the bad village, up beyond the pigsty to the wide grass ride. It was a balmy, dreamy day. He was happy to be back. The bank rising to the far side of him was rich with cowslips. Rabbits as usual. A lark in a frenzy, so high he could scarcely see it. As he came near the two pale buildings he said, 'Well, now then. Very good. Swallows is back.'

He stopped and for the first time in many months looked down and across the sweep of the dale, the black and silver chain mail of the walls, the flashing sunlight. 'Grand day,' he said aloud and turned to find the Doberman standing before him across the path.

Then it was gone.

He looked over at the meeting house, but did not move. He heard a thread of music, then silence. He wondered if he heard laughter.

The silence grew around him again and he waited. He tried out some remarks to himself.

'Here's some puzzle,' was the first.

'I stand here,' was the second.

'Let's see now what it's all about,' was the third.

He walked forward to the common garth, opened the gate and looked into the derelict building. Nothing. The grass was growing again in the flagstoned floor. He walked along to the meeting house and looked through the windows. Nothing. Not a shadow. The place seemed to have wintered well. A clear light flowed in over the bare benches. All quite empty.

But then he saw them, all three together, on one of the long seats. It was not a vision, not a moment of revelation. There seemed nothing ghostly in it. The man had an arm along the back of the settle and the nightdressed, bare-foot woman had the child on her knee and had folded herself in against the man's shoulder. They looked very familiar to Charlie Bainbridge, like old friends or, as it might have been, his children. And yet changed: confident, peaceful, luminous, beyond harm, they were all gazing outward from the meeting house, intent and blissful in the quiet afternoon.

NOTES AND SOURCES

'In the Dark' by E[dith] Nesbit (1858–1924). From *Fear* (Stanley Paul, 1910).

Known mainly for her children's stories, such as *The Phoenix and the Carpet* (1904) and *The Railway Children* (1906), Edith Nesbit also wrote a number of high-quality supernatural stories and tales of terror, collected in *Grim Tales* and *Something Wrong* (both 1893); *Fear*, from which the present story is taken, reprinted many of the stories from these two volumes, together with some new pieces. A late collection, *To the Adventurous*, published in 1923, contains 'The Pavilion', a weird tale about a vampiric plant. In 1880 she had married Hubert Bland, three years her senior, an incorrigible womanizer, and one of the founders of the Fabian Society, in which Edith also became actively involved. Some of her best-known ghost stories, including 'Man-Size in Marble' and 'John Charrington's Wedding', were written during the first traumatic years of her marriage to Bland. In 1917, three years after Bland's death, she married Thomas Tucker, an old friend and fellow socialist.

'Rooum' by [George] Oliver Onions later George Oliver 1873–1961). From *Widdershins* (Martin Secker, 1911).

Onions, born in Bradford, trained as an artist and worked as a designer and magazine illustrator before becoming a full-time writer. His works include *The Compleat Bachelor* (1900) and the highly accomplished historical novel *The Story of Ragged Robyn* (1945). He changed his name to George Oliver by deed poll in 1918 and was married to the romantic novelist Berta Ruck (1878–1978). His most celebrated collection of ghost stories, *Widdershins*, contains the well-known 'The Beckoning Fair One', the story of an author haunted by his own heroine. A less successful collection, *Ghosts in Daylight*, was published in 1924. *The Painted Face* (1929) contains three supernatural novellas, including the frequently anthologized 'The Rosewood Door'. His *Collected Ghost Stories* appeared in 1935.

'The Shadowy Third' by Ellen [Anderson Gholson] Glasgow (1873–1945). First published in *Scribner's Magazine* (Dec. 1916); reprinted in *The Shadowy Third and Other Stories* (Doubleday, Page & Co. Inc., 1923).

Ellen Glasgow was born in Richmond, Virginia, of a well-placed Southern family. Her first novel, *The Descendant*, was published in 1897. She went on to write a long series of novels depicting the social and political life of her home state. They include *The Battle-Ground* (1902), *The Wheel of Life* (1906), *The Romance of a Plain Man* (1909), *Virginia* (1913), and *Life and Gabriella* (1916). In 1941 she won the Pulitzer Prize for Fiction with *In This Our Life*. Glasgow's ghost stories, collected in *The Shadowy Third*, often align supernatural events with a sense of the abiding energy of human passions. Her autobiography, *The Woman Within*, was published posthumously in 1954.

'The Diary of Mr Poynter' by M[ontague] R[hodes] James (1862–1936). From *A Thin Ghost and Others* (Edward Arnold, 1919).

In 1904 the publication of *Ghost Stories of an Antiquary* immediately established M. R. James as a ghost-story writer of the first order. A prodigiously original imagination, an ability to both amuse and shock, and deft manipulation of antiquarian detail have ensured his hold over readers ever since, and his stories have probably inspired more stylistic imitators than any other writer in the genre. A scholar of international reputation in the fields of palaeography, bibliography, biblical apocrypha, and the study of medieval iconography, he was the son of an Evangelical clergyman, although he never embraced ordination himself. He remained a bachelor all his life and was successively Provost of King's College, Cambridge, and of Eton (his old school). As well as *Ghost Stories of an Antiquary* and *A Thin Ghost*, he also published *More Ghost Stories of an Antiquary* (1911) and *A Warning to the Curious* (1925). His *Collected Ghost Stories* (1931, though not in fact complete) has never been out of print.

'Miss Porter and Miss Allen' by Sir Hugh [Seymour] Walpole (1884–1941). From *The Thirteen Travellers* (Hutchinson, 1921).

Born in Auckland, New Zealand, the son of a clergyman who later became Bishop of Edinburgh, Walpole was educated in England at the King's School, Canterbury, and at Cambridge. His first novel, *The Wooden Horse*, was published in 1909 and was followed by *Maradick at Forty* (1910) and *Mr Perrin and Mr Traill* (1911), one of his best-known novels which reflected his own brief experience of schoolmastering. Amongst his other novels are *Fortitude* (1913), *The Dark Forest* (1916), *The Secret City* (1919), and *The Cathedral* (1922), the first of a series set in the imaginary Cornish town of Polchester. The first volume of the historical sequence the Herries Chronicle, *Rogue Herries*, was published in 1930 and was followed by *Judith Paris* (1931), *The Fortress* (1932), and *Vanessa* (1933). His earliest ghost stories appeared in anthologies edited in the 1920s by Lady Cynthia Asquith; these and others can be found in the collection *All Souls' Night* (1933). In 1937 he compiled the anthology *A Second Century of Creepy Stories*.

'The Nature of the Evidence' by May Sinclair (Mary Amelia St Clair Sinclair, 1865–1946). From *Uncanny Stories* (Hutchinson, 1923).

May Sinclair was the youngest daughter of a shipowner who went bankrupt. A lifelong spinster, she supported herself by writing and was a keen and serious student of psychoanlysis. She wrote over twenty novels, including *The Divine Fire* (1924), *The Three Sisters* (1914), *The Tree of Heaven* (1917), and the stream-of-consciousness narratives *Mary Oliver: A Life* (1919) and *Life and Death of Harriet Frean* (1922). Her supernatural tales, several of which treated sex with surprising candour, were collected in *Uncanny Stories* and *The Intercessor and Other Stories* (1931). In later life she became a convinced Spiritualist.

'Night-Fears' by L[eslie] P[oles] Hartley (1895–1972). From *Night-Fears and Other Stories* (G. P. Putnam's Sons, 1924).

The son of a solicitor, Hartley was educated at Harrow and at Balliol College, Oxford. He began his literary career as a short-story writer and fiction reviewer. His first full-length novel, *The Shrimp and the Anenome*, published in 1944, was followed by *The Sixth Heaven* (1946) and *Eustace and Hilda* (1947), the latter being the title by which the trilogy is known. His best-known novel, *The Go-Between*, set in Edwardian Norfolk, appeared in 1953. Hartley's elegantly written ghost stories can be mainly found in *Night-Fears* and in two other collections, *The Killing Bottle* (1932) and *The Travelling Grave* (1948). His *Collected Short Stories* were published in 1968.

'Bewitched' by Edith Wharton, *née* Newbold Jones (1862–1937). First published in the *Pictorial Review* (Mar. 1925); reprinted in *Here and Beyond* (New York: D. Appleton & Co., 1926) and in *Ghosts* (New York and London: D. Appleton-Century Company, 1937).

Edith Wharton was born in New York of wealthy parents and educated privately and in Europe. In 1907 she married Edward Robbins Wharton, but the marriage was an unhappy one and they were divorced in 1913. During the First World War she worked with a French ambulance unit and in 1924 was made an officer of the Legion of Honour. Her literary career began with the publication of poems in *Scribner's Magazine*; her first volume of stories, *The Greater Inclination*, was published in 1899. Her reputation as a novelist was established by *The House of Mirth* (1905); succeeding novels included *Ethan Frome* (1911), *The Reef* (1912), *The Custom of the Country* (1913), *The Age of Innocence* (1920), and the unfinished *The Buccaneers* (published in 1938). Amongst her short-story collections are *The Hermit and the Wild Woman* (1908), *Tales of Men and Ghosts* (1910), and *Xingu* (1916).

'A Short Trip Home by F[rancis] Scott [Key] Fitzgerald (1896–1940). First published in the *Saturday Evening Post* (17 Dec. 1927); reprinted in *Taps at Reveille* (Charles Scribner's Sons, 1935).

Born in Minnesota and educated at Princeton, Fitzgerald found instant celebrity with his first novel, *This Side of Paradise*, published in 1920. Shortly after its publication he married the glamorous Zelda Sayre and together they became the epitome of the high living, big spending, pleasure-seeking Jazz Age. Many of Fitzgerald's short stories from this period were published in fashionable magazines such as *Vanity Fair*; they were collected in *Flappers and Philosophers* (1920) and *Tales of the Jazz Age* (1922). Later collections included *All the Sad Young Men* (1926). His novel *The Beautiful and the Damned* (1922) was followed by *The Great Gatsby* (1925). *Tender is the Night* (1934) draws on the tensions of his life with Zelda, who by this time was suffering severe mental breakdown. He died of a heart attack, leaving his last novel, *The Last Tycoon*, unfinished. It was published in 1941, edited by Edmund Wilson.

'Blind Man's Buff' by H[erbert] Russell Wakefield (1888–1964). From *Old Man's Beard: Fifteen Disturbing Tales* (Geoffrey Bles, 1929).

Wakefield has been described as being one of the last major representatives of the ghost-story tradition that began in the mid-nineteenth century with J. S. Le Fanu and culminated with M. R. James in the early decades of the twentieth. Little is known of the details of his life. He was born in Kent, the son of a future Bishop of Birmingham, and was the brother of the playwright Gilbert Wakefield. Educated at Marlborough, he went on to University College, Oxford, where he read Modern History and excelled as a sportsman (he remained a passionate golfer all his life). In 1911 he became private secretary to the press magnate Lord Northcliffe and during the First World War served on the Western Front and in Macedonia (the setting for one of his best-known stories, 'Day-Dream in Macedon') with the Royal Scots Fusiliers. He married twice but had no children from either marriage. His first collection of ghost stories, *They Return at Evening*, was published in 1928 and contained his famous haunted-house story, 'The Red Lodge'. This was followed by *Old Man's Beard* (retitled *Others Who Returned* in the USA), *Imagine a Man in a Box* (1931), *The Clock Strikes Twelve* (1940, expanded 1946) and, his last collection, *Strayers from Sheol* (1961). He also wrote detective novels: *Hearken to the Evidence* (1933), *Belt of Suspicion* (1936), and *Hostess of Death* (1938). Like M. R. James, he had a penchant for malevolent ghosts and deployed his effects with great economy—a technique taken to the limit in the story selected here, one of the shortest and most unsettling of all haunted house stories.

'The Blackmailers' by Algernon Blackwood (1869–1951). Specially written for the BBC and broadcast on 11 July 1934; reprinted in *My Grimmest Nightmare*, ed. Lady Cynthia Asquith (George Allen & Unwin, 1935).

Blackwood stands amongst the half-dozen best-known writers of supernatural fiction in English. His main contribution to the genre was to transpose the conventions of the traditional ghost story into a new key, characterized by a deep personal involvement with a species of visionary pantheism—as in 'The Willows', 'Ancient Lights', 'The Glamour of the Snow', and 'The Wendigo'. But he also wrote more conventional stories, as well as a series of tales featuring the psychic detective John Silence (1908). He was born in Kent, the son of a civil servant, and grew up in a strongly Evangelical home. As a young man he became deeply interested in eastern religion and occultism (eventually this latter interest led him to the Hermetic Order of the Golden Dawn). His first collection of supernatural stories, *The Empty House*, was published in 1906; encouraged by its success he published a second collection, *The Listener*, a year later. During the First World War he worked as an undercover agent in Switzerland and with the Red Cross in France. From the mid-1930s he became widely known through his radio broadcasts as 'The Ghost Man'. He published forty-eight books in his lifetime; other story collections include *Ten Minute Stories* (1914), *The Lost Valley and Other Stories* (1914), *Ancient Sorceries and Other Tales* (1927), and *The Willows and Other Queer Tales* (1934).

'Yesterday Street' by Thomas Burke (1886–1945). From *Night-Pieces: Eighteen Tales* (Constable, 1935).

Orphaned in infancy and largely self-educated, Burke is best remembered for his vivid chronicles of life in the East End of London in such books as *Nights in Town* (1915), *Out and About* (1919), *The London Spy* (1922), *The Real East End* (1932), and *The Streets of London* (1940). For several years he worked as a bookseller's assistant and in a literary agency before achieving success as a writer. His celebrated short stories set in London's Chinatown were collected in *Limehouse Nights* (1916), *Whispering Windows* (1920), and *The Pleasanteries of Old Quong* (1931). He also published poetry, novels, and an autobiography, *The Wind and the Rain* (1924).

'Smoke Ghost' by Fritz [Reuter] Leiber Jun. (1910–92). First published in *Unknown Worlds* (Oct. 1941); reprinted in *Night's Black Agents* (Arkham House, 1947).

Leiber was one of the leading influences on contemporary horror fiction, finding universal sources of supernatural fear in the grimy urban landscapes of the twentieth century and redefining traditional themes such as the *femme fatale* in new and ambiguous contexts. He also has a considerable reputation as a writer of science fiction and fantasy, indeed is perhaps best known for his sword-and-sorcery adventures featuring Fafhrd and the Gray Mouser such as *Two Sought Adventure: Exploits of Fafhrd and the Gray Mouser* (1957). He was born, like Robert Bloch, in Chicago and educated at the university there and at the Episcopal General Theological Seminary (serving as a minister at two missionary churches in New Jersey from 1932 to 1933). His fiction includes *Conjure Wife* (1953), *Shadows with Eyes* (1962), *The Secret Songs* (1968), *You're All Alone* (1972), *Night Monsters* (1974), *Our Lady of Darkness* (1977), and *The Ghost Light* (1984). He was the recipient of many awards from the World Science Fiction Convention, the World Fantasy Convention, and other bodies.

'The Cheery Soul' by Elizabeth [Dorothea Cole] Bowen (1899–1973). First published in the *Listener* (24 Dec. 1942); reprinted in *The Demon Lover and Other Stories* (Jonathan Cape, 1945).

Born in Dublin of Anglo-Irish parents, Elizabeth Bowen spent much of her childhood at the family home, Bowen's Court, in Co. Cork, which she inherited in 1930. Her first volume of short stories, *Encounters*, was published in 1923, the year of her marriage to Alan Cameron. Her novels include *The Hotel* (1927), *The Last September* (1929), *The Death of the Heart* (1938), and *The Heat of the Day* (1949). The Second World War inspired many of her finest short stories, and she has been praised as one of the best writers of the Blitz. She often turned to the supernatural in her short fiction, handling it with her customary deftness and seeing it as inseparable from her sense of 'real' life. Collections include *The Cat Jumps* (1945) and *A Day in the Dark and Other Stories* (1965); her *Collected Stories* were published posthumously in 1981.

'All But Empty' by [Henry] Graham Greene (1904–91). First published in the
Strand Magazine (Mar. 1947); reprinted in *Nineteen Stories* (William
Heinemann, 1947) as 'A Little Place Off the Edgeware Road'.

Greene was the son of the headmaster of Berkhamsted School; he was
educated there and at Balliol College, Oxford. He became a Roman Catholic in
1926, married in 1927, and from 1926 was on the staff of *The Times*, which he
left to pursue a full-time career as a writer. His first novel, *The Man Within*, was
published in 1929. His first success was *Stamboul Train* (1932), followed by
Brighton Rock (1938), *The Confidential Agent* (1939), and *The Ministry of Fear*
(1943). These 'entertainments' showed Greene to be a skilful adaptor of popular
forms of fiction—in this case the thriller—and throughout his career he never
turned his back on the virtues of good story-telling and strong characterization,
producing novels and stories that appealed to both critics and ordinary readers.
The dissection of motive in human affairs, especially in relation to a cause or an
ideology, was one of his characteristic preoccupations. *Our Man From Havanna*
(1958), which brilliantly illustrates Greene's ability to blend accessibility with a
serious moral purpose, was followed by *The End of the Affair* (1951), *The Quiet
American* (1955), *The Comedians* (1966), *The Honorary Consul* (1973), and *The
Human Factor* (1978). His last novel, *The Captain and the Enemy*, was published
in 1988. Greene's short stories can be found in collections such as *The Basement
Room and Other Stories* (1935), *May We Borrow Your Husband?* (1967), and *The
Last Word* (1990).

'Three Miles Up' by Elizabeth Jane Howard (b. 1923). From *We Are For the
Dark: Six Ghost Stories*, co-written with Robert Aickman (Jonathan Cape,
1951).

Jane Howard was born in London and was an actress and model before
becoming a full-time writer. Her third marriage, dissolved in 1983, was to the
writer Kingsley Amis. Well crafted and strongly evocative of place and time, her
novels of English middle-class life, beginning with *The Beautiful Visit* (1950),
have continued to attract a large and loyal readership. They include *The Sea
Change* (1959), *After Julius* (1965), and *Odd Girl Out* (1975). *The Light Years*
(1990), *Marking Time* (1991), *Confusion* (1993), and *Casting Off* (1995) form the
linked saga of the Cazalet family.

'Close Behind Him' by John Wyndham (pseudonym of John Wyndham
Parkes Lucas Benyon Harris, 1903–69). First published in *Fantastic* (Feb. 1953);
reprinted in *The Man From Beyond and Other Stories* (Michael Joseph, 1975).

Wyndham was the son of a barrister and followed several different careers
before becoming a writer. He became attracted to science fiction partly through
an early admiration of H. G. Wells, describing his own work as 'logical
fantasies'. They include *The Day of the Triffids* (1951), *The Kraken Wakes* (1953),
The Chrysalids (1955), *The Midwich Cuckoos* (1957), and *The Trouble With
Lichen* (1960). His fiction typically depicts traditional English values in life-and-
death confrontation with alien forces.

'The Quincunx' by Walter de la Mare (1873–1956). From *A Beginning and Other Stories* (Faber & Faber, 1955).

De la Mare was born in Kent and attended St Paul's Choir School. For many years he worked for an oil company, but from his mid-twenties began to contribute poems and stories to magazines. In 1902, under the pseudonym Walter Ramal, he published *Songs of Childhood,* followed by several other volumes of poetry for both adults and children, including *The Listeners* (1912). Amongst his books for children are *Peacock Pie* (1913), *Tom Tiddler's Ground* (1932), and *Bells and Grass* (1941). He also wrote novels, such as *Henry Brocken* (1904) and *The Return* (1910), a story of possession. He wrote a substantial body of highly original and typically enigmatic ghost stories, including the well-known 'All Hallows', 'Crewe', 'Seaton's Aunt', and 'A Recluse', most of which can be found in collections such as *The Riddle and Other Stories* (1923) and *The Connoisseur* (1926).

'The Tower' by Marghanita Laski (1915–88). From *The Third Ghost Book* (James Barrie, 1955), ed. Lady Cynthia Asquith.

Journalist, broadcaster, critic, and author, Marghanita Laski was the daughter of a barrister and the niece of the liberal theorist Harold Laski; her grandfather was Dr Moses Gaster, Chief Rabbi of the Portuguese and Spanish Jews in England. She was educated at Somerville College, Oxford, and studied fashion design and philology before embarking on a freelance career in journalism. Her novels include *Love on the Supertax* (1944), *To Bed with Grand Music* (written as 'Sarah Russell', 1946), *Little Boy Lost* (1949), and *The Victorian Chaise-Longue* (1953), a minor classic of the macabre. Amongst her non-fiction works were *Ecstasy: A Study of Some Secular and Religious Experiences* (1961) and studies of Jane Austen and George Eliot.

'Poor Girl' by Elizabeth Taylor (1912–75). From *The Third Ghost Book* (James Barrie, 1955), ed. Lady Cynthia Asquith.

Elizabeth Taylor's first novel, *At Mrs Lippincote's*, was published in 1945 and was followed by many other similar dissections of middle-class English life, including *A Wreath of Roses* (1950), *In a Summer Season* (1961), *The Wedding Group* (1968), and *Mrs Palfrey at the Claremont* (1972). Amongst her collections of short stories are *Hester Lilly* (1954), *A Dedicated Man* (1965), and *The Devastating Boys* (1972).

'I Kiss Your Shadow—' by Robert Bloch (1917–94). First published in *Magazine of Fantasy and Science Fiction* (Mar. 1956); reprinted in *Pleasant Dreams/Nightmares* (Ronald Whiting & Wheaton, 1967).

Chicago-born Bloch was one of the most prolific horror writers of the twentieth century. An avid reader of the supernatural fiction of H. P. Lovecraft, he published his first short story at Lovecraft's instigation at the age of 17 in *Weird Tales* magazine. He later diversified into science fiction, and even crime and mystery. He is perhaps best remembered as the author of *Psycho* (1959), filmed by Alfred Hitchcock in 1960. Other novels in a similar vein include *The Scarf* (1947) and *The Will to Kill* (1954). He contributed dozens of stories to pulp magazines, as well as writing screenplay adaptations of his own work, including his novel *Night Walker* (1964). His collections include *The Opener of the Way* (1945), *Fear Today—Gone Tomorrow* (1971), and *Such Stuff as Screams Are Made Of* (1979). His autobiography, *Once Around the Bloch*, was published in 1993.

'A Woman Seldom Found' by William Sansom (1912–76). From *A Conceit of Ladies and Other Stories* (Hogarth Press, 1956).

Sansom was born in London, the son of a naval architect. He was educated at Uppingham, and for a time worked as an advertising copywriter. At the beginning of the Second World War he joined the National Fire Service, drawing on his experiences in his first published short story, 'The Wall', which appeared first in *Horizon* magazine in July 1941; it was later reprinted in *Fireman Flower and Other Stories* (1944). As well as novels, such as *The Body* (1949), he wrote five successful volumes of travel essays, beginning with *Pleasures Strange and Simple* (1953). *The Stories of William Sansom* (1963) contains an introduction by Elizabeth Bowen.

'The Portobello Road' by [Dame] Muriel [Sarah] Spark, *née* Camberg (b. 1918). From *The Go-Away Bird and Other Stories* (Macmillan, 1958).

Born and educated in Edinburgh, of Scottish-Jewish descent, Muriel Spark spent several years in Africa, which provided settings for several of her short stories, including 'The Seraph and the Zambesi'. During the Second World War she worked for the Foreign Office, beginning her literary career with the Poetry Society, whose *Poetry Review* she edited from 1947 to 1949. Her first novel, *The Comforters* (1957), was followed by many others, including *Memento Mori* (1959), *The Prime of Miss Jean Brodie* (1961), *The Girls of Slender Means* (1963), *The Mandelbaum Gate* (1965), *Loitering With Intent* (1981), and *A Far Cry From Kensington* (1988). A collected edition of her short stories was published in 1986.

'Ringing the Changes' by Robert [Fordyce] Aickman (1914–81). From *Dark Entries* (Collins, 1964).

Aickman, the grandson of the writer Richard Marsh (1857–1915), whose books included *The Beetle* (1897), has some claim to be one of the leading twentieth-century exponents of the short ghost story, although he preferred the epithet 'strange' for his subtle, often enigmatic and inconclusive stories. The son of an architect and educated at Highgate School, he was Director and Chairman of the London Opera Society from 1954 to 1969 and was also an authority on British inland waterways and author of *Know Your Waterways* (1955) and *The Story of Our Inland Waterways* (1955). Aickman's collections include *Powers of Darkness* (1966), *Sub Rosa* (1968), *Cold Hand in Mine* (1975), and *Tales of Love and Death* (1977). He was awarded the World Fantasy Award for best short fiction 1973–4 for 'Pages From a Young Girl's Diary'. Between

1964 and 1972 he edited the first eight volumes of the Fontana Book of Great Ghost Stories series.

'On Terms' by Christine Brooke-Rose (b. 1926). From *The Fourth Ghost Book* (Barrie & Rockliff, 1965), ed. James Turner.

Novelist, critic, and academic, Christine Brooke-Rose is best known for her experimental novels such as *Out* (1964), *Between* (1968), and *Thru* (1975). After nearly a decade she published *Amalgamemnon* (1984) and *Xorandor* (1986), about twins who make contact with a 4,000-year-old being through computer technology. Her non-fiction work includes *A Rhetoric of the Unreal* (1981).

'The Only Story' by William Trevor (William Trevor Cox, b. 1928). From *The Seventh Ghost Book* (Barrie & Jenkins, 1971), ed. Rosemary Timperley.

Trevor was born in Co. Cork and educated at Trinity College, Dublin. His native Ireland provides the setting for many of his novels and short stories. Amongst the former are *The Old Boys* (1964), *Elizabeth Alone* (1973), *The Silence in the Garden* (1988), and *Felicia's Journal* (1994), which won the Whitbread Award. One of the most accomplished short-story writers of his generation, his collections include *The Ballroom of Romance* (1972), *The News From Ireland* (1986), and *Family Sins* (1989).

'The Loves of Lady Purple' by Angela [Olive] Carter, *née* Stalker (1940–92). From *Fireworks* (Quartet, 1974).

Novelist, poet, and essayist, Angela Carter was often associated with the tradition of 'magic realism'. All her work was imbued with a keen sense of the macabre and frequently drew on symbolism and themes derived from traditional fairy-tales and folk myths. Her novels include *The Magic Toyshop* (1967), *The Infernal Desire Machine of Dr Hoffman* (1972), *The Sadeian Woman* (1979), and *Nights at the Circus* (1984). *The Bloody Chamber and Other Stories* (1979) contains one of her best-known reworkings of traditional material, 'The Company of Wolves' (filmed in 1984). Her last novel, *Wise Children*, was published in 1991.

'Revenant as Typewriter' by Penelope [Margaret] Lively, *née* Greer (b. 1933). From *Nothing Missing But the Samovar* (William Heinemann, 1978).

Penelope Lively was born in Cairo and educated at St Anne's College, Oxford. She married Jack Lively, a Fellow of St Peter's College, in 1957. She began her literary career by writing a number of successful novels for children, including *Astercote* (1970), *The Ghost of Thomas Kempe* (1973), and *A Stitch in Time* (1976). Her first novel for adults was *The Road to Lichfield* (1977); others include *Judgement Day* (1980), *Perfect Happiness* (1983), *According to Mark* (1984), *Moon Tiger* (1987), and *Cleopatra's Sister* (1993). A collected volume of her short stories, containing her well-known ghost story 'Black Dog', was published under the title *Pack of Cards* in 1986.

'The Little Dirty Girl' by Joanna Russ (b. 1937). From *Elsewhere* (New York: Ace Books, 1981), ed. Terri Windling and Mark Alan Arnold.

Russ was born in New York and educated at Cornell and Yale universities. She has taught English at various American universities and creative writing at the University of Washington in Seattle. She is mainly known as a science-fiction writer and won a Hugo Award from the World Science Fiction Convention in 1983 for her novella 'Souls' (contained in the collection *Extra (Ordinary) People*, 1984). She brings a strong, though never obtrusive, feminist conviction to both her supernatural and science fiction, which includes *Picnic on Paradise* (1968) and *The Female Man* (1975). *The Hidden Side of the Moon* (1987) is a further collection of stories.

'Watching Me, Watching You' by Fay Weldon, *née* Birkinshaw (b. 1933). First published in *Woman's Own* (Jan. 1981); reprinted in *Watching Me, Watching You and Other Stories* (Hodder & Stoughton, 1981).

Fay Weldon was born in Worcester and educated at the University of St Andrews. Through such novels as *The Fat Woman's Joke* (1967), *Down Among the Women* (1971), and *Female Friends* (1975) she expressed the accelerating feminist consciousness of the time. Her best-known novel, *The Life and Loves of a She-Devil*, was published in 1987 and subsequently adapted for both television and film. Other novels include *Puffball* (1980), *The Hearts and Lives of Men* (1987), *The Cloning of Joanna May* (1989), *Growing Rich* (1992), and *Affliction* (1994), as well as collections of short stories.

'The July Ghost' by A[ntonia] S[usan] Byatt (b. 1936). From *Sugar and Other Stories* (Chatto & Windus, 1987).

Born in Sheffield, the daughter of a barrister and sister of the novelist Margaret Drabble, Antonia Byatt was educated at The Mount School in York and at Newnham College, Cambridge. Her first novel, *Shadow of a Sun* (1964), was followed by *The Game* (1967) and *The Virgin in the Garden* (1978), which linked the coronation year of 1953 with the first Elizabethan age. *Possession* (1990), which won the Booker Prize for Fiction, was remarkable for its convincing re-creations of nineteenth-century literary style and was followed by *Angels and Insects* (1992), two novellas which are again set in the mid-nineteenth century. Other works include *The Matisse Stories* (1993) and *The Djinn in the Nightingale's Eye*, a collection of original fairy-tales.

'The Highboy' by Alison Lurie (b. 1926). First published in *Redbook* (Oct. 1990), as 'A Curious Haunting'; reprinted in *Women and Ghosts* (Heinemann, 1994).

Born in Chicago, Alison Lurie is Professor of American Literature at Cornell University. Her sharply satiric novels include *Love and Friendship* (1962), *The Nowhere City* (1965), *Imaginary Friends* (1967), the campus novel *The War Between the Tates* (1974), and *The Truth About Lorin Jones* (1988). She won the Pulitzer Prize for Fiction in 1985 for *Foreign Affairs* (1984). Her non-fiction includes *The Language of Clothes* (1981) and a study of children's literature, *Don't Tell the Grown-Ups* (1990).

'The Meeting House' by Jane [Mary] Gardam (b. 1928). From *Going into a Dark House* (Sinclair Stevenson, 1994).

Jane Gardam was born in Yorkshire and educated at Bedford College, London. She has written fiction with distinction for both children—e.g. *The Summer After the Funeral* (1973), *The Hollow Land* (1981), and *Kit in Boots* (1986)—and adults. The latter includes novels such as *Crusoe's Daughter* (1986) and volumes of short stories, amongst which are *Black Faces, White Faces* (1975), *The Sidmouth Letters* (1980), and *The Pangs of Love* (1983). Always inventive, Gardam's fiction, whether for children or adults, is characterized by a fluent, economic style and a keen instinct for dramatic surprise.

ACKNOWLEDGEMENTS

The editor and publishers are grateful for permission to include the following copyright stories:

ROBERT AICKMAN, 'Ringing the Changes' from *Dark Entries* (Collins, 1984), © Robert Aickman.

ALGERNON BLACKWOOD, 'The Blackmailers', reprinted by permission of A. P. Watt Ltd. on behalf of Sheila Reeves.

ROBERT BLOCH, 'I Kiss Your Shadow——' from *Pleasant Dreams/Nightmares* (Ronald Whiting & Wheaton, 1967).

ELIZABETH BOWEN, 'The Cheery Soul' from *The Demon Lover and Other Stories* (Cape, 1945), also in *Collected Stories*. Copyright © 1981 by Curtis Brown Ltd., Literary Executors of the Estate of Elizabeth Bowen. Reprinted by permission of Jonathan Cape, and of Alfred A. Knopf Inc.

CHRISTINE BROOKE-ROSE, 'On Terms' from *The Fourth Ghost Book*, ed. James Turner (Barrie & Rockliff, 1965).

A. S. BYATT, 'The July Ghost' from *Sugar and Other Stories* (Chatto & Windus, 1987). Reprinted by permission of Random House UK Ltd. and the Peters Fraser & Dunlop Group Ltd.

ANGELA CARTER, 'The Loves of Lady Purple', first published in *Fireworks*, © The Estate of Angela Carter 1995. Reproduced by permission of the Estate of Angela Carter, c/o Rogers Coleridge & White Ltd. This story is published in *Burning Your Boats: Collected Short Stories* (Chatto & Windus).

WALTER DE LA MARE, 'The Quincunx' from *A Beginning and Other Stories* (Faber, 1955). Reprinted by permission of The Literary Trustees of Walter de la Mare and The Society of Authors as their representatives.

F. SCOTT FITZGERALD, 'A Short Trip Home'. First published in the *Saturday Evening Post*, 17 December 1927. Reprinted in *Taps at Reveille* (Charles Scribners Sons, 1935).

JANE GARDAM, 'The Meeting House' from *Going Into A Dark House* (Sinclair Stevenson, 1994), © Jane Gardam. Reprinted by permission of David Higham Associates Ltd.

ELLEN GLASGOW, 'The Shadowy Third' from *The Shadowy Third and Other Stories*, copyright 1923 by Doubleday, Page & Company and renewed 1951 by First and Merchants National Bank of Richmond, Virginia, reprinted by permission of Harcourt Brace & Company.

GRAHAM GREENE, 'All But Empty' reprinted as 'A Little Place Off the Edgware Road' from *Collected Stories* (Penguin). Reprinted by permission of David Higham Associates Ltd.

L. P. HARTLEY, 'Night-Fears' from *Night-Fears and Other Stories* (1924). Reprinted by permission of the Society of Authors as the Literary representative of the Estate of L. P. Hartley.

ELIZABETH JANE HOWARD, 'Three Miles Up' from *Mr Wrong*, copyright © 1965 by Elizabeth Jane Howard. Reprinted by permission of Jonathan Clowes Ltd. on behalf of Elizabeth Jane Howard, and Jonathan Cape as publisher.

MARGHANITA LASKI, 'The Tower' from *The Third Ghost Book*, ed. Cynthia Asquith (James Barrie, 1955). Reprinted by permission of David Higham Associates Ltd.

FRITZ LIEBER JUN., 'Smoke Ghost', copyright © Fritz Lieber Jun. First published in *Unknown Worlds*, 1941, reprinted in *Night's Black Agents* (Arkham House, 1947).

PENELOPE LIVELY, 'Revenant as Typewriter' from *Nothing But the Samovar* (Heinemann, 1978), © Penelope Lively 1978. Reprinted by permission of Reed Consumer Books Ltd., and Murray Pollinger.

ALISON LURIE, 'The Highboy' from *Women and Ghosts* (William Heinemann). Reprinted by permission of Reed Consumer Books.

OLIVER ONIONS, 'Rooum'. Reprinted by permission of A. P. Watt Ltd. on behalf of the Executors of the Estate of Arthur Oliver, and W. R. Oliver.

JOANNA RUSS, 'The Little Dirty Girl' from *Elsewhere*, ed. Terri Windling and Mark Alan Arnold (New York: Ace Books, 1981), reprinted by permission of A. P. Watt Ltd. on behalf of Joanna Russ.

WILLIAM SANSOM, 'A Woman Seldom Found' first published in book form in *A Contest of Ladies* (The Hogarth Press, 1956), © 1956 by William Sansom. Reproduced by permission of Greene & Heaton Ltd.

MAY SINCLAIR, 'The Nature of the Evidence' from *Uncanny Stories* (Hutchinson, 1932), © May Sinclair. Reprinted by permission of Curtis Brown Ltd.

MURIEL SPARK, 'The Portobello Road' from *The Go-Away Bird and other Stories* (Penguin). Reprinted by permission of David Higham Associates Ltd.

ELIZABETH TAYLOR, 'Poor Girl' from *The Third Ghost Book*, ed. Cynthia Asquith (James Barrie, 1955)

WILLIAM TREVOR, 'The Only Story', reprinted in *The Seventh Ghost Book*, ed. Rosemary Timperley (Barrie & Jenkins, 1971). Reprinted by permission of the Peters Fraser & Dunlop Group Ltd.

H. RUSSELL WAKEFIELD, 'Blind Man's Buff' from *Old Man's Beard: Fifteen Disturbing Tales* (Geoffrey Bles, 1929).

FAY WELDON, 'Watching Me, Watching You' from *Watching Me, Watching You and Other Stories* (Hodder & Stoughton, 1981). Reprinted by permission of Hodder Headline PLC and Sheil Land Associates.

ELIZABETH WHARTON, 'Bewitched'. Reprinted with the permission of Scribner, an imprint of Simon & Schuster from *The Collected Short Stories of Edith Wharton*, Volume II edited by Richard W. B. Lewis. Copyright 1925 The Pictorial Review Co., copyright renewed 1953 The Hearst Corporation.

JOHN WYNDHAM, 'Close Behind Him' from *Jizzle*, copyright © John Wyndham. Reprinted by permission of David Higham Associates Ltd.

Any errors or omissions in the above list are entirely unintentional. If notified the publishers will be pleased to make any necessary corrections at the earliest opportunity.